HELLBOW RUNE

by Michael Satran

a BlackWyrm book
Louisville, Kentucky

HELLBOW RUNE

A BlackWyrm Book
BlackWyrm Publishing
10307 Chimney Ridge Ct, Louisville, KY 40299

Printed in the United States of America.

ISBN: 978-1-61318-168-3

Edited by Ian Harac
First edition: August 2014

For all the fairy tale characters
that never made it to the big time.
This one's for you.

For Mom and Dad,
who never let me quit.

Prologue

Leaving the Carnival of Monsters

"Let me tell you your fortune." Madame Zhalla said, smiling under the rubber witch mask. She was my adoptive mother, taller than me, with pale blonde hair that had been winnowed by the years.

My hair was dark, and I didn't know where I came from, so the fortune telling was a game. My mother always claimed she had the sight, and that she could see me in another place. She would tell me wonderful stories of a world of beauty, and yet she called me a wicked, dark haired thing, though everyone told me I was pretty.

My name is Symantha Markajian. I might be a gypsy or an orphan, a liar or a con artist, a stealer of wallets or a hero of stories. I lived in a carnival wagon with my adopted mother, amid the freakshow of the bearded ladies, the two headed men, the roustabouts and the archery contests. She didn't care where I come from, ran her fingers through my dark hair, and called me 'muffin.' I was fifteen years old.

My mother took my palm in her clawed rubber hands when the nights grew dark, and the lights in the fortune teller's tent grew dim. "You will grow up in a circus, and travel to places most people never see. You will meet the man you love by a pool in the forest. You will be a great hero, who will kill the King of Feathers, a wicked tyrant who rules over a wicked land. You may believe it all, or you may not believe a word of it."

I didn't believe a single thing. It all seemed stupid to me, and I had computer games to get back to. I won the computer in a card game. I was good at playing cards. We moved from circus to circus, and town to town. My mother's prophecies were notoriously inaccurate. I chalked them up to coincidence.

It was upstate New York, in the fall. My mother was working late at the fortune teller's tent, as she always did, and I crept out of our trailer, where the mist was thick and the forest was shadowed in the background. I was wearing jeans and a ratty t-shirt with a drunken fish on it. So I walked towards the forest, confident that I'd be back by morning. In the distance, the lights of the big top beckoned, and the carnival played on.

They say that's how these things always begin…

Prologue

Leaving the Carnival of Monsters

"Let me tell you your fortune." Madame Zhalla said, smiling under the rubber witch mask. She was my adoptive mother, taller than me, with pale blonde hair that had been winnowed by the years.

My hair was dark, and I didn't know where I came from, so the fortune telling was a game. My mother always claimed she had the sight, and that she could see me in another place. She would tell me wonderful stories of a world of beauty, and yet she called me a wicked, dark haired thing, though everyone told me I was pretty.

My name is Symantha Markajian. I might be a gypsy or an orphan, a liar or a con artist, a stealer of wallets or a hero of stories. I lived in a carnival wagon with my adopted mother, amid the freakshow of the bearded ladies, the two headed men, the roustabouts and the archery contests. She didn't care where I come from, ran her fingers through my dark hair, and called me 'muffin.' I was fifteen years old.

My mother took my palm in her clawed rubber hands when the nights grew dark, and the lights in the fortune teller's tent grew dim. "You will grow up in a circus, and travel to places most people never see. You will meet the man you love by a pool in the forest. You will be a great hero, who will kill the King of Feathers, a wicked tyrant who rules over a wicked land. You may believe it all, or you may not believe a word of it."

I didn't believe a single thing. It all seemed stupid to me, and I had computer games to get back to. I won the computer in a card game. I was good at playing cards. We moved from circus to circus, and town to town. My mother's prophecies were notoriously inaccurate. I chalked them up to coincidence.

It was upstate New York, in the fall. My mother was working late at the fortune teller's tent, as she always did, and I crept out of our trailer, where the mist was thick and the forest was shadowed in the background. I was wearing jeans and a ratty t-shirt with a drunken fish on it. So I walked towards the forest, confident that I'd be back by morning. In the distance, the lights of the big top beckoned, and the carnival played on.

They say that's how these things always begin…

Chapter One

Into the Woods: A Meeting with the Organ Grinder

The roustabouts were out while the music played from the big top. Even Dan, the trick archer who taught me how to shoot, was among them. I don't know a thing about guns, but I'm an excellent shot with a bow and arrow. Dan even said I might be able to go to the Olympics one day.

He called me over with a wave, and he called to me. "Hey, Sam," he said with a grin on his face. "We could go bow hunting for deer tomorrow. It's the season." Dan rubbed his beard a little bit, and stretched his muscular arms. He was brawny, but most of his strength was in his fingers.

"It's better than turkeys. They don't dodge much." My laughter was almost drowned out by the music from the Big Top.

He wrapped his calloused hands around his fingerguards and put them in his pocket. "They sure don't." He seemed pensive. "You're almost better than me."

"Horseshoes and grenades." I grinned up at him. "Didn't you say that to me first?"

Dan flexed his fingers and chuckled. "Be fast. Remember, archery wasn't always a sport." His lips grew thin. "Are you planning on wandering off into those woods?"

"Yeah," I sighed. "There's really not a lot of people my age around here. You know how it is. I just need some time."

"I'll tell your mother you're going to be out late," he chuckled. "She's going to think you're playing cards with us again."

"And taking your money," I added. "You need a different story. If I don't come home with at least a quarter of the take, she'll be surprised." I gave him a little hug. He was warm and heavy. There was beer on his breath.

We walked together for a little ways, and a few of the roustabouts waved to us. Dan ruffled my hair as if he were my mother. "Don't go too far. You know the rules. We pretty much run an archery contest and a bunch of freak shows. If you're not back in time, we'll move on without you."

I winked and gave Dan a little wave as I stepped past the edge of the furthest tent. The bearded lady waddled out behind me. "Take care!" I called, and I stepped out onto the grass at the edge of the mist. I began walking towards the forest.

***

The woods were pointed and grey in the thick fog, which clumped up around my knees in late evening. My sneakers made wet sounds in the grass, even though I could barely see it under my feet, I knew it was there.

My feet thudded, crushing the meadow beneath. The mist rose higher around my knees. It felt smooth and wet, and crawled up under my jeans. There was a little rise before the trees stood up, and they seemed thicker than before. I thought I heard one of them call my name, like music or the whisper of my mother's voice.

I moved closer, and the air seemed to giggle. The mist thickened at the forest's edge, and I walked into it. A little secret thrill trickled up my spine, and I crept into the woods, enjoying the moonlight and the shade.

The trees were tall, and they seemed a little taller as the mist slipped into my mouth and I breathed it. My lungs felt refreshed, and I stretched, leaning against a tree. The woods brightened, and the moon shone down.

That was when I saw the first creature. It wasn't much bigger than a human head, and it settled on a tree branch with its small flapping wings. It had a goat's head, and sharp wolf-teeth. Wings folded in on their cruel raven-feathers. It flexed little clawed hands, and peered at me. I couldn't do anything except stare back.

It spoke. "What are you looking at?" Its voice was hungry for something, a ragged squawk full of needs and lusts. "You're not allowed in, no, no... not allowed in." It flapped and hopped, inching along the tree. "Run, run! Run for the open lands, human! Run!" The creature clapped its little hands together, gesturing towards me with black wings. It was only a few inches from my face.

I didn't run. He was too small, and cute, in his own little monster way. "From you?" I put my hands on my hips. The taunting suddenly stopped. Dan taught me reflex exercises. I caught him, and brought him forward, squeezing tight.

It didn't really have fur so much as lumpy scales. It squawked like an angry crow. "Let go! Let go! I'll feed on your blood and eat your soul, I will! The whole thing!" His wings ruffled in my grasp.

"I'll bet I could get a lot of money for selling you." I was smiling. I was thinking of how much people would pay for it. "Do you know what Area 51 is?"

"Your soulless world is not for us," the little creature protested. It was strong for such a small monster. His teeth dug in as he bit me on the finger.

I shouted. The little creature had drawn blood. "That hurt!" I winced, but I didn't let go.

"You taste innocent," The creature hissed as it licked its lips. "My lips burn! The corrupt taste so much sweeter going down." I shuddered, releasing my grip. The creature flexed its wings and flitted up into the tree. "What's your name?" It tilted its neck and gave a slithering hiss.

"Symantha." I glared at him. "Sam for friends, which you, currently, are not."

"I'll tell them you're coming. Only the curious and innocent enter here. No one ever leaves!" The monster cackled madly as it flapped little wings, disappearing into the misty trees. I ran after the creature, my finger dripping blood onto the ground.

I never should have chased it.

***

I never saw the pit. I kicked up little clouds of dirt. My breath puffed in the cool fall air. The little monster raced through thorn bushes and thickets. It flew faster than I could ever run. I kicked up dirty leaves, and my shoes made hard splats on the rough ground.

My feet landed on air, and I tumbled into a rough, root-spattered hole. I slammed into the ground and my world spun. My fingers were dirty, and my hair was damp from the chase. Something sticky on the leaves got into my hair. I could feel dirt crawl up under my fingernails, and seep into the creature's bite. I could smell something musty.

The creature teased me with laughter, and smiled down with hungry fury. It circled, gliding with its wings, and called out with strange hooting noises. Branches rustled over the pit. A second goat head peered from behind one. I let out a gasp.

There were more of them.

They hooted and hissed and made other sounds that I couldn't describe, extending their necks and flapping their wings. I think it was how they laughed. "Ooooh, pretty girl fell in a pit," one of them cooed. I could see the sharpness of their teeth in the moonlight. From above, tiny claws scratched like daggers on the branches.

They descended on me in packs, diving and cheering, clawing at my fingers and tearing at my hair. I heard my shirt rip. I rolled onto the ground and covered my eyes, amid howls and savage cheers of "Mine!" I felt my hair grow taut, whimpering as they pulled some out. I heard thumping sounds, as if they fought amongst themselves. I could feel my blood seeping into the wet dirt.

"Tastes better." One of the creatures keened like a dog. "Angry and scared."

My eyes grew teary. The only thing I could do was die in the pit, inch by inch of skin. There were too many of them. It seemed like hundreds. "Eat you," one of them whispered. "Like all the other little girls."

That was when the music started. It wheezed and groaned, the sounds of an old accordion making its way across the forest. A high pitched yelping and chittering accompanied it.

The little winged creatures howled. "The Organ Grinder!" They began to shiver and hide. Music groaned and shuddered through the forest, along with the high pitched screeches. "It is his monkey! He comes! He comes!" There was a massive ruffle of feathers and the creatures burst up into the nearby branches. They did their best to look innocent, but there was blood on their sharp teeth. Hanging in one of their fists were a few torn strands of my dark hair. I could feel blood oozing from my scalp.

Wheezing music mingled with the sound of heavy boots, slow and dreadful. Worn, well-oiled leather boots stopped at the edge of the pit. His voice was a bitter roar. "What have you caught in your pit, little ragamoffyns?" he thundered. "Why, it is a person from the world that visits ours no more!" He laughed and scowled down into the pit. "And a pretty one at that." From under his cloak, the chittering continued.

He was an enormous tower of a man, thick in all directions. His fingers were heavy and calloused, not from bow-work, but from playing the accordion. He wore an enormous top hat. A steel monocle adorned his face, out of place amid the massive frame. His face was heavily bearded, and a brutal, jagged scar crossed his chin. Around his neck hung a leathery, beaten accordion. It swayed back and forth amidst his high backed, leather greatcoat, which had a massive collar that rose up to encircle the back of his head. He wore an old suit vest and a shirt with ruffles, and his pants were heavy and woolen. At his belt was an odd-colored pearly black stone knife.

"Get me out of here." It wasn't seemly to beg, but I knew I looked awful. There was blood in my hair, and dirt under my fingernails.

There was a horrid shrieking as something burst forth from under the greatcoat. It stood about a foot and a half tall. Patches of hair were missing from its twisted face. Its tail was wound up in a sinister little wrap, ending in a metallic knife blade. I was certain the creature knew how to use. Its hands were blighted and missing hair in patches, as if something had burned it, and its eyes were hard and cold. It reached down towards me. I shrank away. The Organ Grinder kicked it aside. His voice grew softer. "Why did you come here?"

"I wanted to see what was there," I whimpered. The ragamoffyns in the trees shuddered. The monkey hissed and waved his knife-tail at them.

"Welcome to the lands of the Otherworld." The Organ Grinder grinned. His lips opened, revealing teeth that were almost too white. "I was like you once, young and curious. But if you make a bargain with me, I shall guide you out of the forest."

"What do you mean?" I looked up into the trees again. Cold stares passed between the monkey and the ragamoffyns.

"If you give me a piece of your soul, I will lead you from here, and take you to the place where you will be safe." The Organ Grinder smiled. His mouth was wide. I thought I smelled a hint of brandy on his breath.

"Get me out of the pit first, and I'll give you a piece of my soul." I said it without even thinking, and the massive hand reached down into the pit for mine. He pulled me up easily enough, my shoes scrabbled and threw dirt into the pit. He let go of my hand. I could feel the scars on his, splitting the heavy calluses.

"The price must be paid." He smiled. I decided to try to trick him. I would walk barefoot after that.

The monkey babbled and gestured. I reached down and pulled off my shoe, handing it to the Organ Grinder. The little creature pointed with his tail-knife and stabbed into the dirt, hopping up and down. A little drool passed over its lips.

"Here," I said. "You can have half."

The Organ Grinder cackled for a moment, and burst out with a huge laugh. He took the shoe and stuffed it in his greatcoat. The monkey hid underneath the greatcoat with a rustle. The massive man grabbed his hat to keep it from falling off his head. "Well played," he said with a guffaw. "You have the wits of the Otherworld about you. I have been outsmarted." He bowed gracefully to me. "I will lead you to a clearing on the far side of the wood, where you will be safe. I did not say I would take you out of the Otherworld."

I stared into his wicked grin and cursed him in my heart. "Fine. Can you take a shower there?" I threw my other sneaker aside. I wouldn't be needing it anymore.

"You can bathe in the pool." He smirked. "But you should be careful."

We walked through the woods for a while, and he never touched me. He only stared at me occasionally as I followed, as if I were far away.

***

We walked for a while in the woods. I followed him with my bare feet on the wet earth. The Organ Grinder's boots crunched the grass, thudding against the ground.

"So what exactly is this place?" I asked him. A wry cascade of movement spread across his lips.

"It is a place of half discarded dreams and broken promises to legends." He intoned the words rather than said them. The monkey hooted. "These are the realms of the fairy tales nobody hears about, the legends of less important things and too-recent stories." He laughed. "Some of them are even true."

"What's that supposed to mean?" I muttered.

The monkey peeked out from under the Organ Grinder's cloak. Its diseased, fleshy face scowled at me.

"Modern things have legends, too," he said with a sigh. "But people do not see magic in modern things, so our stories and tales come here. The ordinary rests side by side with the legendary, and the people... deteriorate, forgotten." His white smile shone. "They don't forget me. I make sure."

"You go out into the 'real world'?" I asked the question as if the world he came from wasn't real. Maybe I should have known better.

"My time too, shall pass." He smiled cruelly as his eyes turned to red shadows. "I am, after all, only as good as my monkey. As you can see, he is a little worn around the edges." The monkey stabbed its tail at a nearby squirrel. The squirrel fled from the monkey and chittered.

"That's interesting." I let out a little whistle as the forest grew foggier. "So what's the rest of your world like?"

"It is divided into kingdoms, as most fairy realms are, though many of our Kings and Queens are Kings and Queens of unimportant things." He laughed. "There is a Duke of Mantlets, and a Queen of Chairs, a Sultan of Carpets, and a Duchess of Porters."

"They don't sound very impressive."

"You should be more careful. Sometimes ordinary things that have the most power. The things that are the most common and the most heartbreaking can destroy the greatest of creatures." A smirk crossed the Organ Grinder's face.

"Like the common cold?" I asked him.

"Yes." The Organ Grinder cackled. "Exactly."

"So who's in charge? I mean, someone has to rule over all of these people and things, right?"

"The King of Feathers rules over all of us from his castle in the sky. Although he does fly, he likes to joke that he is no greater than the King of Gold, who lives in a better fairyland. He often jests that they weigh the same, however, pound for pound."

"He sounds like a funny man. But he's actually a third heavier." It was the best joke I could come up with.

The Organ Grinder scowled again. "Make you no mistakes, child. He is indeed our king. But he is not a man at all. Black wings sprout from his back in a burst of blood when he grows angry. Although he is the most handsome of gentlemen, his demeanor is grim and terrible. He doesn't fancy little gypsy girls. If he finds out you're here, he'll kill you."

"That sounds lovely. How do I hide?"

"He finds everyone eventually." The Organ Grinder sighed, his thick hands pushing through the dark greenery. "There's your pool. I would recommend you clean yourself off, but you will have to make a bargain with its resident." His laugh seemed to make the trees rustle. "And she is not as forgiving as I."

***

The Organ Grinder turned his back and rustled off into the woods. I stepped into the clearing. "You'll see me again, lass." His voice was thick in the drape of the forest. The monkey hooted.

I shuddered as I walked away. I didn't want to see him again. I crept through the low boughs and heard something squeak in the trees above. I didn't look up. I just stared into the clearing and the misty grass near the pool.

The pool was ringed with weeds. It had a clear, supple look to it, clean despite the growth. There were a couple of rocks near it, large enough to sit on. An angry rustle filled the trees.

I moved over to a rock to sit, and see if there was anything in the pool. I was tired of monsters. The Organ Grinder was just as monstrous as the ragamoffyns. If anything, the monkey was the worst of them.

I peered into the water and stared at my reflection, and watched it shiver in the moonlight. A breeze brushed the surface. The water rippled, then spoke, laughing. "What do you want?" It sounded like my voice, only distorted, a misshapen wet bubble in the ripples.

"I want to take a bath." I probably shouldn't have said anything.

"That's all?" The voice burbled. The water rippled more violently. It quivered and slipped about, making little whorls and eddies.

"That's all."

Water shimmered and spun. Something hooded and female rose out. A tattered cloak hid strands of twisted, weed-ruined hair. "Do you want to take my place?" Her voice still mirrored my own.

"No, but I'd like to take a bath here."

She looked at my pants with confusion, and started to sob. Hands extended out from under the tattered robe, long, thin, and bluish. "Lost to the world, you are," she whispered. "In a pool of tears you bathe. I am the Weeping of Lost Children. You do not cry, child."

"And so you look like their mothers? Blue and sad?"

"You are wise, little one," she sniffled. "If you wish to bathe in the pool of tears, you may. But know that you will always be lost, no matter where you go."

I stepped into the pool while she stood and watched, and then I wrapped my arms around her wet cloak. I hugged her cold, sopping frame. "You don't have to cry today."

She let out a choked sob. The water twisted down, dragging her with it into the bottom of the pool, dark beyond dark in the reflective surface. I thought I saw her smile before the pool returned to stillness, my legs knee-deep.

I left my jeans and shirt to the side and cleaned myself off. The bath was strangely refreshing. My hair was still wet. The hooting of the ragamoffyns echoed in the distance. Dan would say I needed a weapon. It was all too easy to agree.

I broke off a curved tree branch, and wrenched some vines off a nearby tree. I tied one end of the vines to each end of the piece of wood, and made sure that it was tight, so that there was curvature. Tiny leaves hung up and down the makeshift bowstring. I had to tug them off.

While I struggled, I thought I heard a giggle through the pool, as if the water creature was laughing and crying at the same time. I popped leaves off the vine, and bent the wood tighter. It was springy enough to hold.

I broke off several sticks, leaving them jagged, and clumsily gathered feathers up. The Organ Grinder wasn't here anymore. I would probably have to hunt for food until I got to the edge of the forest. Then I'd have to steal it.

I lay down and settled in the leaves, waiting for my body to dry. A pair of smooth, beautiful hands pushed them aside. I drew back the makeshift bow and hissed. "What kind of monster are you?" I kept the point focused as the rest of him came into view.

He was the most handsome man I had ever seen. My fingers shook on the bowstring.

The man smiled to me. His teeth were as white as the moon. "You must be new." He cooed the words, as breathless as I was. "And already you're trying to kill me when you're naked." His laugh was the most beautiful sound I ever heard.

"I…sorry." I stammered while I blushed a lot.

He was slender and graceful, with an air of the aristocracy about him. His eyes were the clear green of the grass in the spring. His quivering lips were thin, his face angular. His hair was a glorious cascade of ebony. He had long fingers, and slender hips, and he was wearing a doublet made of some sort of leather, under which was a linen shirt and exceptionally fine silk pants. On his feet were riding boots. Those green eyes never left mine. "I must confess." His voice slurred a little bit, and his breath misted in the cool fog. "You are quite a beauty. Are you cold?"

He felt as I did. I knew it. I could feel it. I felt it in my heart, and my thighs shook. I let my arrow drop.

He pushed my makeshift weapon aside, gently laying the bow on one of the rocks near the pool. "You're magnificent. I must admit I've never met a woman who tried to kill me the first time she saw me." He laughed again, and my heart turned liquid. "Usually it takes three or four meetings for that." He gazed into my eyes with that moon-white smile, and he shivered, as if hypnotized. "You're different from the others." He struggled to get the words out, touching his chest for a moment, as if trying to understand the pounding in his heart.

"I want to go home..." I whimpered. "I don't know where I am."

"You don't need to know that anymore." His fingers reached out for mine. Our hands locked, and he drew me into a kiss. I felt warmer in an instant. I could feel the pulse of blood in those thin lips, and he was strong, so strong that I could feel weather change in his arms as he pulled me down. "I can't stop myself," he said huskily. "This only happens once for people like me. You're the one."

I had never done this with anyone before/ I opened my legs for him so easily. It was the only thing I ever wanted. I let out a little choke as I ran my finger across his chest. "I know." I sobbed. I was fifteen years old and I was in love. I could hear the water of the pool ripple, as if with a romantic sigh. I needed him, his heart, his touch, his flesh.

He cried too, there by the pool, as our bodies moved and cries broke the night. I clutched him desperately, and my legs grabbed his hips. I raked my fingers along his back and we struggled, beasts of lust near the edge of the clearing.

Before I collapsed against him, I thought I would never leave. Those eyes would keep me in their confidence forever. Wet grass swallowed me up against his warm body, and I huddled against him, without fire, seeking his heat. I dreamed the sweetest dreams I would ever have.

In the morning, as the warm, wicked sun beat down on my skin, I reached for my one true love. His sweet, beautiful lips and slender frame were gone. There was no one there.

The hooting and chittering drew closer. The ragamoffyns found me.

***

I rolled over and grabbed for the bow and arrows. They were cold comfort against creatures that flew. I had only bow hunted twice in my life. Both times, Dan was drunk and I was doing the firing. I pulled the first arrow back as the crowd of winged monsters burst through the tree line, their goat heads chittering and wings flapping.

Swarming, they descended. I fired the first shot. A creature doubled over, wet with red. It tumbled about like a horrid glider and smashed into the earth, making sick gurgles before dying. "True love," The ragamoffyns howled as they swirled and settled into the trees. "She has true love, and a weapon."

"Hate you," one of them hissed. "Hate all beautiful things."

They flitted about. I drew the bow back, readying another arrow. Some of them hopped up and down and made low growling noises. There were too many to shoot them all. I would run out of sticks before I killed the last one.

I walked over to the twitching monster, leaking out the last few moments of its life on the ground. I pressed my foot against its head, and stepped down hard. Something sticky oozed across my heel. There were cracking sounds. The ragamoffyns let out keening wails. They sobbed like little children. "Any of you who want the same can stay." I smiled upward.

"Hate you," a ragamoffyn hissed. "Killed one of us, you did."

"You tried to eat me," I said. "You should probably back off. I might kiss one of you disgusting little freaks or something."

There was a heated conversation in a language I didn't understand. The ragamoffyns chittered and chirped, eyes blazing with fear. They raced off through the forest, the hooting sounds departing through the woods.

I made a little grave for it. I dug a small hole with the tip of a few sticks, and scooped the creature in. I buried it in the dirt, throwing some leaves and brush on top. I didn't pray. My heart and mind were elsewhere.

True love, the creature said. I felt it in my heart, and shook. The world I came from didn't matter anymore. I had to find him when I got out of the forest. I had to ask him why he left. His 'yes' when I begged him to be with me was all that mattered.

***

I put on my clothes slowly, threw the bow over my shoulder, and wrapped the sticks in a piece of vine. I made my way over to the pool and whispered "Weeping, Weeping, come out."

"I hear your tears." The pool said. The blue skinned, watery feminine shape oozed up. "You want to go home?"

"No!" It came out of my mouth in a half-stammer. "I want to find him, the man I was with. He's perfect."

"Your journey will be long and terrible. You will be tested at every turn. The nobles will try to stop you. You must not show your heart to anyone. I can give you directions, but you are already lost." She wept blue tears into the pool.

"How do I find him?"

"You will have to go to the chapel on the edge of the woods, and ask the Stone Preacher for his help." Her voice was a murmur between sobs. "But it is dangerous. You will have to pass the Nun Who Prays for Nothing and the Vicar of Chimes to get to the one who speaks from the stones. And he may not aid you unless you pay his price." A weak smile crossed her lips. "There's an awful lot of price paying that goes on in the Otherworld."

"Why is it called the Otherworld?" I couldn't help but ask.

Weeping of Lost Children thought for a moment and started to cry. Long blue fingers grabbed me by the cheeks. Fingernails brushed against the edges of my ears Tears trickled down out of her eyes, wet and unceasing. "It is called the Otherworld because we are the myths of things that either weren't important enough for mythology, or came after the fairylands were closed." She sighed a slow sad sigh, and dried her eyes.

"That's not very reassuring." I quivered. "What other sorts of things can I find here?"

"In some places, you can find urban legends that were unimportant; in others, the mythology of the common. Many of the creatures here don't know or understand the rules, and they stay here forever."

"What are the rules?" I asked.

"You already broke the first one," she said gently. "You went into the woods after dark, and you have dark hair. That means you're doomed. All those old stories have power here, but since the true fairylands closed, we live in this place. Think of it as your home. No one ever leaves, unless they kill their one true love."

"But 1 couldn't!" I blurted. Those green eyes bored their way into my heart. I felt a little pang. I would rather live in the glade forever than live without that touch and those kisses, his hips against mine, his smile and the way he felt.

"Of course not." She grinned with a winnowing smile. For the first time, I saw thin, sharp teeth. "That's why no one ever leaves."

"What about the Organ Grinder? What happened to him?"

"Fleeing into the woods is different from coming in on your own. They say he may have lured children to their death, or burned them to keep them from becoming plague victims. They say the Organ Grinder captured his monkey and saved it from death, and turned it into a killer that danced a merry tune when he played his accordion. There are almost as many stories about the Organ Grinder as there are about the King of Feathers." Her head tilted.

"Tell me about the King of Feathers. Maybe he can help me."

"He cannot help you, child. He is wicked, and cruel. His capacity for savagery is legendary. When he puts on his black mask of ravens, and walks through the streets, everyone knows fear. He lives in a great castle in the sky, on the other side of the Mountains of Existence. Nothing has been the same since the mountains got that name, either." She sank lower in the pool.

"How did they get that name?"

"No one used to be able to climb the mountains to get to the castle, but ever since a man named Hillary climbed a mountain and said it was there, the mountains have been climbable. It's difficult to explain. It's just how things work." She shrugged and began descending. "Be careful. You will live in pain no matter what."

I turned from the pool and walked barefoot towards the chapel at the edge of the forest. I would find my one true love, and he would find me. We would be happy here, in the land beyond the world. I didn't need to go home. Everything would be perfect. I told myself over and over again, until I knew it in my heart.

***

The forest was thick and cruel in the morning. A hot sun cast shadows on the underside of the leaves. Veins of leaves turned purple, making the light seem sickly. It burned into my skin as I made my way through the thick brush.

Dew clung to the edges of my jeans. I struggled through the forests of the Otherworld, looking up at towering trees and kicking aside small rocks. My feet ached. The sun battered me all day.

As the sun set, I staggered over a rise. There were no trees left. A serpentine road overcast with gray wound across the forest.

Along its edge, a crude chapel of stones had been erected, blighting the landscape further.

As I walked towards the chapel, I could hear strange music wafting from inside. Outside the building, a few misshapen figures moved.

Chapter Two

The Kiss of My One True Love: I Meet the Stone Preacher

I stepped out to the road, and walked along the dirty path. It wasn't even paved. The sky seemed greyer than it did in the forest. Outside the chapel, a few things moved, hunched, and shuffled. They didn't seem to notice me.

I heard hoofbeats. From behind me, a weighty wagon piloted by a stooped, hooded figure, launched around a corner. Wheels of the wagon creaked in the setting sun, the horses ready to slaver, hooked up to wretched slats and battered wood. From inside the wagon, something shouted. "Halt! Halt the wagon!"

The hooded figure yanked the reins and pulled to a stop. I slid aside. "You there!" called the male voice. "Come hither, that I might see thee!" He must have been here a very long time.

I couldn't refuse. I walked over to the edge of the cart. The door slowly opened. Under the driver's hood, a serpentine tongue flicked out and hissed. Yellow eyes glared at me. The snake-thing flexed its human hands. "Don't mind him. He's just the Cowl of Serpents, huddling under his cloak." The voice seemed to echo as a handsomely manicured hand pushed the door open.

His body was lithe and handsome, but his face was wizened and old. A thick drooping mustache fell into a scraggly beard. He wore princely robes, but on his head was a battered old hat, sewn with patches. "You must be new," he cackled. "I am the Squire of Sages." His smile was missing a few teeth. No matter how he tried, he seemed unable to conceal it. "Let me guess? You were lost in the forest?" He slid his finger up to his lip, but he caught it in the space between two teeth.

The serpent creature spat out words, ruining their cleanliness with hisses. "Marked she is, Marked for us. A painful name she will have." It gave a slithering cackle, and spityellow liquid on the ground.

"You've been chewing the tree leaves again, haven't you?" He sighed. "I should beat you with my cudgel, miserable snake!" He stepped out of the wagon more fully, and drew a club out of his belt. He raised it and cracked the snake creature across the head before I could stop him.

"Don't hit him!" I shouted. "Have you no mercy for him? He's just a stupid snake creature in a hood."

"Smarter than him I once was," hissed the snake. "But he hits me over the head, and takes my mind. I must drive the cart, I must." He hacked up more yellow liquid.

"A painful name?" The Squire of Sages paused. "She is to be one of us then, one of the lost people of the Otherworld?" He paused, and began to croon a little, as if he were about to burst into song.

"Oh, God, please don't sing," I begged. "You don't have the teeth to carry a tune with."

"God has nothing to do with it, my dear," he cackled. "But I shall not sing, if you are not of the Otherworld, you will not understand it. And if you already do, well, you are one of us already. One day, you will have a name, a name like ours. Tell me, who have you met so far?"

"Other than you two, I met The Organ Grinder, and the weeping woman in the pool, and some ragamoffyns, and, uhm, him." I stammered out the words, uneven and awkward.

"Him, who?" The squire chortled a little bit. "Is that the spark of true love in your eyes, girl?" He grinned like an idiot. I could count all seven of his teeth.

"Uhh, yeah. I guess. I killed a Ragamoffyn with it. Is that bad?" It was a fantastic lie.

"Oh, heavens, no." His voice petered out. "It's about time someone chopped up a few of those nasty little things into bitter suet." His eyes blazed with a wicked fire. "What color were his eyes?"

"They were green. Green like the sea." I managed a smile. My heart jumped just at the thought, and I had to quash the urge to become giddy.

"Noble's eyes.' The squire's lips spread wider. "You'd best be sure the King of Feathers doesn't find out, dear child, until after your wedding. Or he will come with his Chain Hook Guards and his Spiked Wrath Men, and he will spit thee on a spear, and roast thee, and eat thy tender heart." He smacked his lips like a hungry dog. "He'll roast your lover alive before he burns thee!" He stepped up into the carriage, recovering every ounce of dignity he lost. "On, good snake!" he shouted. "Or you'll feel the taste of my cudgel again!"

The cart groaned under the tugging of horses. The Cowl of Serpents drove the monstrous thing forward, creaking as it lurched down the road. There was a gurgle, and the Cowl left his spittle to fester in the middle of the road. On the back of the cart, several hanging skulls clattered. They grinned at me while hanging from twisted coils of rope. I shuddered and looked towards the chapel in the distance.

It was almost dark.

***

I could hear the monsters singing as I approached the chapel. They cavorted with hunched backs in front of the church, the cadence dissonant. Sharp teeth in elongated heads were pocked with rounded domes and warts. They wore black loincloths and the top half of something that looked like old burlap sacks. The sound of their singing was like crying.

The chapel was a plain stone building, mortared together with earth, a misshapen square joined with a misshapen tower, set back a little bit from the flat, winding road. Windows adorned it at odd angles, and the only way I could get to the door was through the path of the dancing creatures. There were three of them, long fingered and yellow eyed.

I ran for the door. I didn't try to talk to them, or find out what they were. One of them leaped over me. Dirty feet crashed to earth right in front of me, lips wrought with hunger. "A girl!" he shouted excitedly, and clapped his hands together, as the other two scampered forward. "So fresh, so innocent, so full of mysteries!" He clapped his hands again. One of the things behind me hooted. I was surrounded.

"Full of mysteries," cooed one of the two behind me. "And wet, wet flesh, yes…"

"Living flesh," purred the third.

"What are you people?"

One of them stretched out a long, grey arm and squeezed my shoulder. "We are the ones who pretend to be dead, yes? The fake, fake people who fake their deaths and live with others, marry others, cavort with many and yet love no one but ourselves. When we die, we come here, but we cannot hurt others, no, no, we simply want. And want, and want."

"What do you want?"

"To finish dying," rasped the first. "But we cannot get there. We have spent our lives pretending to be dead, and now we cannot die at all." With a savage yank, he ripped his own head off. A thick grayish seepage poured forth from the wreckage of his neck. A little protrusion of bone staggered up at an angle. Thick ichor trickled down his neck and over his shoulders.

"He always does this," growled one of the two behind me.

I turned so I could see all three, and shouted "Help! They're going to eat me! I saw it in a movie! Please! Let me in!" While they stared at their friend's disconnected head, he struggled to reattach it, I ran for the door. I banged on the door of the chapel furiously.

The three of them wailed. "No, please," one sobbed. He got to his knees and groveled.

"Let us in," begged the second.

"We want to die," the third added. "Please, kill us, kill us. You can kill us!" Dirty lips and grayish skin shivered under the burlap. "It's only a little stabbing and crushing. You can do it with a crude stone knife." He licked his lips and inched forward.

The door was thrown open.

The creatures hissed unpleasantly and backed up. An arm covered in steel, with a lit candle embedded in the wrist, pulled me inside. There was a loud clang as his shoulder ground backward. The door slammed shut, loud enough to resonate.

***

The armored thing that slammed the door had candles fitted into its forearms. It was tall and powerfully built. The armor was medieval, with fluted greaves and graceful, high shoulders. The tight helmet had a tassel on it. Behind the eyeslit, cool purple eyes burned. Its voice was surprisingly jolly.

"Well, there," it thundered in masculine tones. The voice shivered among the high vaulted walls, thick with crenellations and unusual monsters carved into the stone. "You've made it past the beggars at the gate!" The candles on his forearms flickered to life. "Please allow me to introduce myself. I am the Seneschal of Votaries." It folded its arms and bowed. "While mediocre, I am strong and capable within my demesne." There was a creaking sound, like bones and flesh inside the statuary.

"Is anyone ordinary around here? Those things outside, were they really those who pretend to be dead?"

"Everyone who comes here dies in bits and pieces." He chuckled. "A little here, a little there. They don't understand how slow it is." There was a creaking sound, like he was smiling under the metal. "Still, they try to get in so that they can stop pretending."

"Why don't you just kill them?" I asked. "Don't they want to die?"

"It's terribly uncivil to kill one's guests while they're in your house," he said quietly. "And the rules of chapels are quite succinct."

"Thanks. Should I call you Sen'?" It was hard to figure out. I wasn't good at etiquette, and he seemed to be a master of it.

"I should be calling you milady," he intoned. "For your eyes are as green as trees in the summer. Come with me. I shall escort you to quarters and then you shall meet more important folk."

I stared into the reflection of his armor. New green eyes stared back. They were a dull brown before. I let out a little choke.

"Are you surprised?" We rounded a corner, and he undid the latch on an old wooden door. The wood slipped open with a creak and a thud.

Inside, the furnishings were lavish. The small room was carpeted. A thick feather bed with well fluffed pillows rested against the back wall. Squeezed into the room were an ornate desk with a high backed wooden chair, and an oil lantern, hanging on a hook. A grinding scream filled the hall as I looked inside. "What was that?"

"That is the sound of a guest who prefers more painful accommodations," the suit of armor said with a hallow sigh. "We torture them according to their wishes. Alas, for you, my noble lady, we are forbidden to do so, under the pain of the same ourselves."

"The King of Feathers said so?"

"You are quite correct," The candle on the left arm flickered out. "Oh dear, I'll have to relight that."

"Does the King have a lot of rules like that? He sounds like a really crappy person."

"The first rule of the Laird of Monasteries, dear child, is never to ask too many questions, and to spend your days in prayer." It chuckled. "With night coming on, you should sleep, and you're obviously tired from your journey. Sweet dreams."

"Who do you pray to?" I asked him. "I mean all of you, in this place." I stood inside the door and my bare feet quivered a little bit on the carpet.

"Oh…" The suit of armor clanked its hand along the top of its helmet. "We don't really think about that. We just do what we do." He reached to his other arm, pulled out the candle, transferred the flame from the lit one, and returned it. "Good night."

He slammed the door shut. I huddled in the room, slowly getting hungrier, almost too fearful to be curious. I slipped into the warm bed and slept, dreaming of my beloved. He whispered words of desire into the cleft between my legs. I woke up in a deep, hot sweat, flush with love and fear.

***

It wasn't long before I heard whispering. There was a bowl of water filled on the nightstand next to the bed. I drank a little and washed myself with the rest. I still hadn't seen a toilet, or a midden, or anything approaching it. I felt very dirty, even after the wet coolness stole my sweat and leached it.

The whispering played in my ear. I threw on a nearby robe as quickly as I could. I scuttled out of the room, praying the Seneschal wouldn't be there. The whispering grew as I slipped into the cold gothic corridor. I crept along from door to door. I could hear the sound of chanting from the church. It seemed at odds with the whispering that clawed at my ears.

My feet scraped on the flagstones as I sneaked through the hall, and followed the sound to the passageway's end. A stairway led into darkness, high and arched. The whispers grew louder. I could feel air flow up from below. Something merciless crawled into the pit of my stomach and told me I was scared. I tried not to believe it.

I walked to the first stair, and nothing happened, except that for some reason, the air seemed cooler. I crept lower into the mouth of stairs, slowly slipping downward.

***

The corridors below the church were the same as the corridors above. The air was full of a musty smell. Dark gargoyles loomed at the corners of shadowed doors. The only light came from flickering torches. There was no sign of the Seneschal. A little part of me was very grateful.

I crept along the hall. The whispering turned into a frenzied series of moans, echoing out of wooden doors barred with iron. I slipped up to one of the doors and looked inside.

A man hung from the ceiling by his legs. Hooks embedded into the backs of his calves. His hands were chained to the floor of the cell, and he wore a bone-white mask shaped like the head of an elephant. Kneeling next to his face was a small winged girl. Lustrous blonde hair and a devil's smile keened and purred into his ear. She was pretty in a buxom, cherubic sort of way, and wore a tight fitting wedding dress with a corset. She leaped into the air, fluttering toward me before I could hide. "Who are you?" Her voice was lilting and soothing.

"I'm Symantha." My lip quivered.

"True love?" She whispered as she reached out to touch my face.

I was too scared to say no. "Everyone says so." I blushed.

"I am the Wracker of Beautiful Dreams," she smiled cheerfully. "It is my job to show the vain how their dreams make others suffer, and to insert the spark of calamity into their greatest glories."

"What did he do?" I blurted.

"I don't know." She shrugged happily. "That's how it works. If I knew, I might develop sympathy or compassion for those I care for. A poor quality in a torturer, don't you think?" She licked her lips, showing sharp monster-teeth, and fluttered her wings. "Do you like his mask? I sculpt them out of the ones who don't make it through the woods." She tittered.

"It's lovely." Inside, my stomach crawled. "What do you see when you look at me?"

The creature sighed and laid her finger on the side of her nose. She tilted her head, and adjusted her corset. "I see someone who doesn't need to be here." She put her tiny head through the bars. "True love is torture enough."

"Uh, yeah?" I mangled the words as they escaped my mouth. "It's the most wonderful feeling in the world. How could it be bad?"

"You will see." A dark look covered her face. "I must return to my work." She fluttered over to the ear of the upside down man, and went back to her whispering of nothings.

"Right." My steps became shaky as I made my way down the hall. The weeping and howling continued. I had to find him, and make the empty feelings go away.

***

The whispering was replaced by a sound like two stones chipping together. The end of the long hall beckoned. I crept up to the door and settled against it, listening to see if the sound was louder. It rose only a little. I tested the door, it was locked.

The grinding became a voice filled with rage. "Bastards! My deities of earth decry your bone heresies. I hear you, sickening things! I shall grind you, I shall." I peered through the keyhole. I saw only a gray wall, and a hook that looked like the anchor for some sort of chain.

I felt a little warmth next to my head. There was a metal arm on my shoulder. I turned to see the Seneschal of Votaries, candles flickering and melting in their armsockets. "You shouldn't be down here," he said with a chuckle. "Let me guess. You're looking for the midden."

"Does it flush?" I gave him my most hopeful look.

He put his hands on his hips, armor creaking. "Of course it flushes. Water closets are common here since the Viceroy of Plumbers arrived."

He still called it a water closet. I was doomed. It was an effective lie. It got me away from the door. The seneschal guided me down the hall, and opened a door. Inside was one of the most ornate toilets I had ever seen. It had a system of gears behind it. The room smelled vaguely of lavender from real lavender plants, hanging over the doorway. "Viceroy of Plumbers, huh?"

"It is rather ostentatious, isn't it?" The Seneschal closed the door after I stepped inside. "I hope you'll be at services." I barely heard the words through the door, then clanking from down the hall.

I relieved myself while the gears clanked and whirred behind me. Surrounded by the smell of lavender, I almost forgot where I was, underground amid cold stones.

***

I crept out of the bathroom and went back to the door where the seneschal found me. I reached for the knob again to see if it was open, but thought the better of it. "Open the door!" The voice rumbled. "I shall powder your skin and mulch your wicked eyes, priests!"

"I'm not a priest," I whispered through the lock. "Are you the Stone Preacher?"

"None other, coward." The voice sounded like rock on rock. "Get me out, and I'll do you a service, as long as you let me have my revenge on these priests and their worshippers." He snarled a little bit. "I am chained apace, and cannot move."

I didn't even know what *apace* meant. "I'll try to fix your pace." The keyhole was big enough to talk through, so it was big enough to get a pen in. "I'll be back."

I crept back up the stairs, and made my way towards my room, where I opened the door and slipped inside. I rummaged through the desk, collected a few quills and crept back out. When I returned, my breathing quickened. The echoes had changed.

The chanting from the chapel grew louder. I could hear it from the bottom of the stairs. I hurried down the hall, hoping that the singing would mask my passage, and huddled near the door. I twisted the pen in the old medieval lock until I heard a pop. "The Duke of Locks must be a geezer."

The Stone Preacher was chained by his wrists and ankles, suspended in a wild gyroscope of clanking chains that moved slowly and retightened at random intervals. The chains ran into the floor and back up to the gears, catching his stone body in an endless loop of pain and release. He was made entirely of stone, from cassock to fingers to his cold marble eyes. His rocky cape of crushed gravel remained furtive and fluttering despite its rocky nature. He was well built and muscular for an animated statue, head glistening with marbled baldness. He looked down at me as chained wrists and ankles shone, attached to the chains by strange locks shaped like funnels, lined with grinding teeth.

"I do not recognize you, heretic," he intoned.

I was still staring at the gearlike locks on his wrists which ground away flesh and keys alike as he glowered. "Or the Duke of Locks could just be an asshole. That would work too."

"Spare me your talk of donkeys and crevices!" The Stone Preacher thundered. "I wish to be freed!"

"I can't pick that! It will cut my hands to pieces!" The chains moved on the gears with a grinding clank. The Stone Preacher twisted with an unnatural rumble, like stone on stone.

"Then get the key!" The monster struggled in his chains. "Do you think I am an idiot because I understand not your crude speech, heretic?" Granite eyes swiveled to glare at me.

"Actually, I think you're scared and angry. Who has the key?" I felt like a character in a video game.

"The Stone Preacher fears nothing." He growled.

"Except being tormented by a bunch of crazy priests," I told him.

The chains yanked him closer. "The Vicar of Chimes has it. He keeps it in a glass box, surrounded by razor points and wire."

"I'll be back."

The preacher shook his head and scowled with distaste. "I shall absolve you of one of your sins, heretic," he snarled. "There are rules to religion, you know."

I crept out of the room and made my way towards the chanting noises, which grew louder still. Whatever religions this place had, they would be nothing like what I expected.

**

I slipped back up the stairs and crept back to my room. A new robe had been prepared for me, hanging on a hook. I was greeted by a strange trilling sound. There was a servant of some sort in the room. Her legs were like sticks. She wore a simple cassock, and her hair, if there was hair, was in a wimple. There was a strange clicking as she walked. I felt the hairs on my forearms rise.

"Excuse me?" I asked. "I need my things."

She turned. Her face was the color of willow bark, hair slightly greenish as it trickled out from under the wimple. "Go ahead, I was just finishing up."

"What's your name?" Names were important here. I tried to learn as many as I could.

"I am the Nun Who Leaves No Stains." She whispered softly. "Once I gave myself to the flesh, as you did." She continued to clean the writing table.

"What happened?" My stomach twisted, as if it didn't want to hear.

"This and that," she said in her unearthly whisper. "My father found him, took his flesh, and cut it into pieces and hung it on hooks for me to see. I cleaned the pieces off. My father demanded that I eat them. So I fled into the woods, and here I am."

"It's been a very long time, I guess?" I looked her over. She was thin as a rail. Her mouth was a perfect rosebud in that unhappy willow face.

"It was a place called England. A man named William was King." Her lips twisted briefly. "We don't talk much about who we used to be. The Vicar will punish us if we do. I should go."

"How does he punish you?" I didn't want to ask, but I couldn't help myself.

"In the cells," she whispered. "He tortures us and makes us feel desolate, leaves us with that little beast until we are empty inside." She hurried out, and shut the door behind her as quickly as she could.

As much as I wanted to find the man I loved, I felt that I might never get out of the church. The lights in the room flickered with the sounds of chanting. I had lived in a place that we called the Carnival of Monsters. Here, I was the only one who wasn't.

***

I needed to go to services and present an aura of conversion. Stupidly, I had promised the Stone Preacher that I would help him, and free him from these strange priests. I knew what would happen if I did. He would storm through the corridors with flinty hands, and crush the life from all of them, one by one.

I had to keep my promise. I was afraid of everything.

I headed for the chapel and opened the door, moving inside as the chanting grew thunderous. There was nothing at the altar. The creature in front of it made my eyes wince.

He wore a greatcoat of shimmering material, covered in thick, sequined chime shapes. In his right hand was a long stick engraved with symbols I couldn't make out. It curled into the shape of a warped tube. His head was covered in a helmet that looked like a tall metal cylinder. The hands and feet were wrapped in metal gloves and boots. The high vaulted ceiling of the chapel echoed with his sweet musical voice. Candelabras on the walls shimmered in tune with him. He was the Vicar of Chimes, and he didn't care what people prayed for as long as they prayed in his place.

There was a nun in front of him, leading a chorus of misshapen men and women in song. Their voices shuddered in time with the music, which seemed to pour directly from the Vicar's robe. She was dressed in the robes of a traditional Catholic nun, gray and severe, all perfect curves and luxurious lines. Above her breasts, and below her perfect throat, was a shimmering void. It moved with her, wet and liquid, and affected the tone of her voice, making it more rich and desirable. Even as she sang, she motioned to me. I shifted from one foot to the other, and took my seat among the other creatures.

I opened my voice and prayed for the man I found in the woods. I prayed that he would make love to me again, touch my skin, and crush me to him. I would beg to be fucked, throw my body to his seed, and our children would be so very beautiful. I prayed for all of that.

The service ended after some time. The nun approached me, her visage smiling. "I am the Nun Who Prays for Nothing." The shimmering void whispered. It was hungry for everything. "You must be new. Welcome to our church. Did you make it past the pretenders last night?"

"I guess. Your Seneschal pulled me in." I tried to use their official titles. It wasn't easy. I didn't know a lot of the words.

"He is a dutiful soul," she said. The worshippers pushed their way out. The sounds of fighting could be heard as they beat and trampled the ones who pretend to die. The doors shut. I tried hard to stop thinking about it.

"It doesn't bother you that they crush those horrid things outside and brutalize them?" The Vicar of Chimes moved quietly out the side door, but I needed to see the whole church before I tried to rob him.

"Why should it?" she responded lightly. "It's not as if they can actually die, and it's just so much work to put them to rest."

"How does that work?" I really didn't understand the idea of it being a lot of work to say good-bye to someone. I still don't.

"The Vicar sings a song of life, and they are consumed." She lowered her voice. "I don't really understand how it works, though."

"How long does it take?" I was curious.

"A hundred and sixty-two years," She responded. "A speck of time in the Otherworld, but can you imagine singing for four hundred and eighty-six years to three creatures that smell like rotting meat and yank out their internal organs for passers-by?" She folded her hands in front of her, clasped them, and shuddered. The Vicar gave out a beautiful note from under his chime shaped helmet and exited through a side door. Somehow, I felt relieved.

"I can't really say it would be fun." I looked a little downcast. "You're not much of a nun, are you?"

"Not everything is as it appears. Not everyone goes to convents for the same reasons. Not everyone comes here for the same reasons, either. A lot of us are the people you hear about, but are just lumped into stories as the 'No one ever returned.' This is where we go, and who we are." She gave a cold smile. The void in her chest warbled.

"Great, so I don't get to go home?" I glared at her with disappointment.

"Well, you could kill your one true love, but most people, once they find their one true love, if they find him..." She stopped and rolled her eyes. She considered it impossible.

"If?" I taunted.

"Well, usually, if someone finds their one true love, they like to stay with them," she said cheerily. "Of course, most of them fall into pits, get eaten, or are burned by the King of Feathers and his army of monsters."

"So he's got an army of monsters?"

"Chain hook guards and spiked wrath men." She smiled. "He has torturers to attack your body, and demons of the mind to attack your soul. He has many weapons."

"Does he have green eyes?" I asked eagerly.

"They all have green eyes." Her eyes sparkled with dots of yellow. "It's how you can tell nobles from everyone else. You have a little touch of green in your eyes now. If you can find your one true love and marry him – but it might not be a 'him.' It could be a monster, a thing, or a bassinet. Then you will be truly happy for the rest of your days. And your eyes will turn green."

"That's not very reassuring. My lover could be a bassinet?"

"Did he touch you?" Her smile was tender.

"Yeah." I grinned. Just thinking about it made me warm and filled me with desire.

"Well, he's not a bassinet, then." She chuckled. "I should escort you to the Vicar. He's going to want to know what you're doing here."

"I love to meet priests. Lead on." I liked to meet priests because they were gullible and till boxes were easy to steal from. When you needed a few extra meals or a corn muffin, priests were the most susceptible of marks. But in this place, I needed to be sure.

***

The nun led me down a different hallway filled with spires and torches that gave off little hints of music when people passed them. Air whistled through the sconces, playing a monstrous tune at the edge of my hearing. "How do you stand it? The creepy music, I mean."

"He pays well," she said softly. "I am also lonely, and my thighs ache for companionship." She said it in a cheerful voice, as if she enjoyed her own suffering.

"Well, you chose this life."

"Yes, but no one really chooses here," she said cheerfully, knocking on the door. "Vicar? There is a young lady who wishes to speak with you!" Her voice never lost its joy.

There was a rattle of dulcet sounds as the Vicar of Chimes rose and approached the door. His voice lilted with musical notes as he opened it. It was almost like singing, but not quite. "Who is this penitent?" His warble made the thick arch of oak creak under his fingers.

"I'm not a penitent, sir. I just got here." I offered a look of false nervousness. "May I come in?" I really wanted to see the crystal box the Stone Preacher mentioned. That could be difficult. The Vicar didn't believe in anything. Fanatics were always the easiest.

He looked at me. His beautiful sing-song voice rang under his helmet as he beckoned with a gauntleted hand. "Come in. If you are new to these lands, I shall give unto thee some directions, and, if you are lucky, a map." His voice rang over the word *map*. "You are dismissed." The helmet turned to the nun. "May you find something to pray for one day."

She curtsied and departed. The Vicar shut the door. It made a booming thud that sounded like the prison doors downstairs. "I apologize for the aggressiveness of my subordinate." He almost sang. "She gets that way sometimes. You pray for your true love?" His head tilted, sensing my confusion. "It is easy to see if you know what to look for."

"So what exactly have I stumbled into? And why do you torture people in the basement?"

"Oh." The Vicar's voice was cheery. "We do it because they are violent in their religious practices. And as I have no true religion of my own, merely the pretense thereof, I am determined to deliver unto them the same cruel fates that they deliver to others, the brutal repetition of endless nonsense and being chained to things that make them suffer. They are cruel people. To them, I am crueler still."

I could tell that he was proud of his work. That didn't make me any more comfortable. "Couldn't you just leave them alone?"

"What, then, would I have, if I did not keep these penitents safe from every mad cultist, grinder of livers, and worshipper of base objects like cutting boards and wanted posters?" he cooed. "They are no better than madmen."

"What about the Stone Preacher? I heard that he might be able to help me."

"Oh, indeed, he will help you, for a sacrifice of something that you do not want. And if you are planning to stay, he has much to offer you. However, since he has declared me a heretic, I have chained him and kept him from threatening the locals. Otherwise, I would not care." His voice continued to musically lilt. It was hard not to drift off.

"Well, I would like to know a little bit more about the world." I looked around for the box, but I didn't see it. I would have to sneak in while he was at services and rob him. I didn't really want to stay in this place any longer than I had to.

"Well," he said with a wry whistle. "That's a tall order for such a little girl. To the west are the Mountains of Existence, and to the south is the Kingdom of the Dethroned. To the east is the Sovereignty of the Half-Enslaved, and to the north are the lands of the Frost Hammer Men." He chuckled. "I love that name, Frost Hammer Men. But I'd never go there."

"I'm sure you wouldn't. I don't really want to, either." I smiled, showing him the fear he knew was there. "So tell me about the Stone Preacher." I smiled. "He sounds like a really strong man. How do you keep him locked up?" For all of their humility, many priests secretly like to brag.

"I have a key to his chains." the Vicar purred. His voice sang over the words ever so slightly. "I keep it in my desk drawer. And since he is down there, and I am up here, he cannot threaten me." His voice rang with pride.

"That sounds awfully simple." I said. "May I see it?"

"It's very pretty." the Vicar said, a light ringing in his voice. "Are you sure you want to see it?" He reached into the desk drawer and pulled out a knife, and held it to my throat. Inside, I could barely see the glint of crystal. His hand moved to my wrist and squeezed. "Do you think that I am stupid?" He forced me up against a wall. His cassock was heavy. His gauntleted hand grabbed my throat.

I made a choking noise and shook my head. "No." I thought my throat was going to shatter.

"Do you think that I am easily fooled by some wicked little girl who tries to take my prisoners away?" He pressed the knife up against my throat, the blade so sharp I could feel blood trickling down my neck. I twisted my neck and whimpered as I reached for the crystal box.

"I will cut you." His voice was a ringing coo. "I will cut your wrists and your ankles, and leave you for the whispering fairy."

The thought made me sick, and the knife pricked against my throat. If I could move my fingers just a little more, I could pocket the box. "Please…" I begged. I did my best to look fearful. People who felt powerful usually didn't kill out of hand.

The singsong voice of the Vicar echoed in my ear, and he trailed the knife down along my chest, over my heart. "You are in love…" His voice was like beautiful music. His throat made a sour twang. "I could break two hearts."

"Why would you do such a cruel thing?" I couldn't bear to lose that feeling.

He leaned up against me, the thick robes warm, and his voice musical. I plucked the crystal box from the drawer, and slid it up under my back. "Because love is like music…" He whispered. "And I feel musical when I have things no one else has."

I had to dispel my doubts, and find out if he was like other men. I drove my knee upward hard, and slammed it into where his groin would be. There was a clanging sound, like metal on metal, and a musical gurgle came from under the helmet as he staggered and dropped the knife.

I ran through the door and slammed it behind me. My feet beat on the stone cobbles. I was a good runner, but I had no idea how fast the Vicar was, or even what it was.

I ran past the Seneschal of Votaries and he began to give chase, but his heavy armor slowed him down. There were a few flecks of blood on my shirt. I clattered down the stairs. I could hear the Vicar's musical voice sobbing an unearthly dirge. "Stop her!" he rang out. "She has the key!"

I thudded down the hall among the keening whispers of the little fairy creature. I popped the lock on the heavy door at the end of the hall. I slipped inside, and saw a scene of stretching and pain.

The chains had moved. The Stone Preacher was being twisted like a puppet.

***

The Stone Preacher bellowed in his chains, metal rattling with his agony. The crystal box throbbed and made a tinkling noise. I could hear the heavy thud of the Seneschal's boots coming down the hallway, and the musical voice of the Vicar in my ears.

I struggled with the box, but it was locked. Stealing the key later had become impossible. The strange monsters of the place were closing in. I hammered the crystal edge on the ground as fast as I could, beating the corner against the cold stone. "Free me!" howled the Stone Preacher. "They will pay for these indignities with crushing!"

I was so afraid of dying that I hammered on. The crystal box finally shattered. I grabbed the key and began moving for the locks, sticking the long toothed shape into the first gearlike opening. It popped open, and the Stone Preacher swayed precipitously, one of his arms free. He smiled a cruel smile. "My cold god of stone is powerful!" he thundered. "He has sent a brave girl to free me!"

The booming steps of the Seneschal grew closer. I undid the second lock. The Stone Preacher slid downward on his chains, only a few feet above the ground, still hanging by one arm and leg. He seemed to be in less pain, and the Seneschal stepped into the room. "Foolish girl! You cannot do this!"

The Seneschal reached out and put his hand on my shoulder, his arm candles lit, but the Preacher reached down with his one free hand and grabbed him by the throat.

"Stop it!" I howled. "He's just a butler!"

"I cannot!" The Preacher's voice was deep and thunderous. "He must pay the price of all who oppose my god!" He squeezed, and I screamed, as the Preacher began to crush the throat of the Seneschal of Votaries. The armor groaned and creaked, and there was a wet squishing pop, and the body of the Seneschal fell to the ground. "Die, miserable heretic!" the preacher thundered as the armor struck stone.

Leaking out from the armor was nothing but hot, melted wax.

***

I couldn't stop looking. The candles on the Seneschal's wrists sputtered and went out. The Stone Preacher roared in triumph. "Get me down!" he thundered. "There is work to do, and the suffering of the wicked to expunge!"

He was crazy, and I was scared. "You killed him!"

"As he would have killed you by destroying your purity, girl!" He thundered. "Now, get me down, and I shall aid you in your journeys for a time."

I moved over to the remaining gear locks, and undid them as quickly as I could. The preacher grabbed the chain and landed with a dull thud. "I can sense the Vicar's heresies." His voice was a muscular growl.

I could hear the Vicar's footsteps receding down the hall. I ran out of the room, trying to keep ahead of the preacher. There was a grinding behind me as the Preacher slowed, and he kicked down one of the cell doors. I could hear the voice of the Wracker of Beautiful Dreams. She begged as the cell opened, and there was a shriek of abject terror in a high pitched warble.

There was a heavy grunt and a sickening pop from inside the cell, followed by a wet bursting noise that echoed a little bit and then was gone. His hand covered with red, the Stone Preacher thudded out of the room while I stared in horror.

"Do you have to kill everyone?"

"Everyone who deserves it, in the eyes of my god." The Stone Preacher growled again. His heavy footsteps lumbered down the corridor. Somewhere upstairs, the rest of his victims awaited. It was as if I had killed them all.

I ran for my room, and stopped to quickly gather my things. The Nun Who Leaves No Stains was busy, cleaning my room. "Run!" I begged. "You have to run! He'll kill you! The Stone Preacher will kill you! I'm sorry! I didn't know! I swear! I swear!"

The Nun Who Leaves No Stains looked at me, taking the dirt and dust and neatly placing it in a bag. "I am pure." she said softly. "He cannot touch me."

There was a wrenching sound as the Stone Preacher ripped the door off its hinges, the fury of his stone muscles yanking the wood straight out of the frame. His stone head peered inside, and his teeth gritted as he saw the Nun. "Heretic! Why can I not touch you?"

"I leave no stains," the Nun smiled. "I am pure. I can kill you in an instant, thrusting my hand through your wicked stone heart, and the blood will not touch me. I will be pure even after you die. There is no stain of the body or of the soul that can do me harm. But mostly, I just like to make sure the rooms are clean. Leave, Stone Preacher, or I will feed you your wickedness and make you choke on it." Her voice was very dull, as if she didn't care about him at all.

The Stone Preacher's face twisted into a snarl. "You could make this place real and make people believe in something, and yet you are a common maid?"

"I cannot clean the whole world," the Nun responded. "One day, you too will learn that."

"Let's get out of here," I said to the Stone Preacher. "The Vicar still wants to murder me with a glass knife."

"I will handle him," the Nun said coolly. "Perhaps, for once in his murderous life, the Preacher is right."

"I will leave," the Stone Preacher said to the Nun. "But one day, I shall return."

"You are ungracious even in defeat." The Nun Who Leaves No Stains frowned. "A poor quality in a priest, sir."

"We can run now." I didn't wait for the Stone Preacher. I gathered up my things in a heap and ran down the hall. I could hear the Preacher behind me as I reached the vaulted foyer.

The Vicar of Chimes was standing there, helmeted and cruel. He was holding a heavy, massive sword, and he stood in front of me. "You are a murderer." His singsong voice echoed, and filled the room with beautiful music. The Stone Preacher arrived after me, as the Vicar finished his litany. "I will kill you for despoiling my church."

There was a sound like hobnails gliding on stone, and the Nun Who Leaves No Stains slipped into the room behind us. "Go," she said. "I am tired of living in a church where everything is for sale."

The Stone Preacher turned and crashed through the wall, shattering mortar and bending granite. "You heard her." His voice was filled with bitterness as he stared at the church. "They should have made it out of wood."

I raced through the hole and he soon followed. We hurried out towards the road as the People Who Pretend to Die ran for the hole, their emaciated, corpselike bodies passing us. As I reached the road, there was a tremulous, musical sound that rose into cacophony, like an organ that had all its pipes suddenly smashed together and twisted into knots.

Then a slim, beautiful hand tossed a chiming helmet out, and it made a few weak piping noises as it rolled across the lawn. The body followed with a sickening thud. Through the hole in the wall, I could see the Nun Who Leaves No Stains give us a sad smile. Blood rolled off her skirt like rain. She flicked red from her fingers as one would wash one's hands.

"We are going." The Stone Preacher intoned. "I could never kill such a woman."

"Where are we going?" I was afraid of the answer.

"To get you some shoes." His voice was serious. "All travelers need a good set of shoes."

We walked down the road, the heavy tread of the Stone Preacher thudding beside me. When the skies grew dark, dimly lit windows of a small village came into view.

Chapter Three

J Acquire a Pair of Boots

The village seemed built of shadows, nestled in the crooks of thick trees. I didn't realize the forest rose up around the road again. Trees towered up as high as the eye could see. Most of them were wider than houses. The Stone Preacher's rocky feet crunched behind me. In the back of my throat, I felt the desire to get away from him.

"This is the village of Woodshadow," he said with a cool tone. "There is only one inn. I do not think it has any of the running water you require."

"What do you require?" I fumbled with words. "I mean, you're made of stone and all."

"I have crushed enough bones to powder for the week." The Preacher grumbled. He seemed very serious. "These people have nothing to fear from me. They have no religion."

"Who lives here? I mean, is it families with normal people? Or more of the creepy things we met on the road."

"That's a matter of debate," the Stone Preacher said. "A lot of these people wandered into the woods, got lost, and banded together for protection. Shortly beyond this village, the road is left behind for a while. Not everyone can afford to build roads." He chuckled. "This place is couched in mysteries and ancient things, but in the days since better fairylands left it behind, many ordinary people are stuck here, unable to go home; unable to become legends."

"There's a lot of mythologizing of the ordinary?" I asked. "Is mythologizing even a word?"

"It is if you make it so, child." He seemed particularly sincere about that. "There are, of course, a few oddities here. I believe the Knight of Cobblers lives here, or he did the last time I passed this way."

"Uhh, cobblers have a knight?" I asked. "Isn't that a little weird?"

"Young lady!" the Stone Preacher rumbled. "I am made of solid, moving granite. What makes you think having a Knight of Cobblers is weird?"

"Oh..." I must have looked extremely sheepish. "Sorry about that." The biggest problem with traveling with the Stone Preacher was unless I could find a way to get away from him, stealth was impossible. He moved like granite with a slow, heavy tread. His boots practically crunched into the dirt as we made our way into town. "Do you eat?"

"I never really thought about it." The Stone Preacher clenched his fist and stared at the sky. "I suppose I did eat, once, but it has been so long since I last ate, that I don't really remember what that might be like. Furthermore, I am made of stone. I doubt that I could actually taste anything." There was a grinding crackle as he shrugged his shoulders.

We walked down dimly lit streets. Houses were built into fissures and clefts of trees, sometimes carved out from trunks. Homes had odd looking wooden doors, shaped like human faces distorted into screams of pain. "Why do all the houses look so creepy?"

"If the pain is displayed on the outside of the house, the hearth and home inside will always be safe," the Preacher muttered. "It is an old superstition, but an effective one. If fear is displayed on the outside, then it is not on the inside. Monsters cannot come in."

"Does that work?"

"It works for some creatures. Mainly the ones that feed on fear."

"Are you one of those?" I asked.

"No." The Stone Preacher said quietly. "I feed on epiphanies. It's just that most people these days seem incapable of having them unless something terrible happens." He chuckled. "You show a lot of promise."

"You want to eat my epiphany?" I asked. "Does anything happen to me?"

"How should I know?" The Stone Preacher said. "I can't even come out to get your epiphany unless you actually have one. I can leave these lands and travel to yours if you do, now that I've met you."

"Why doesn't that fill me with a great sense of joy?" I muttered sarcastically.

"Because most of the time, epiphanies don't." The Stone Preacher smiled for the first time. It sounded like walnuts cracking.

"Is that an inn?" I pointed to a building nestled in a low crook of one of the larger trees. It had a large coat of arms sign, a foaming beer mug over a haunch of meat. "It looks like it's been here a long time."

The Stone Preacher lumbered for the door. "I shall open the door for you." He said. "No one will bother us if you are with me."

***

We stepped into the inn. It was like a scene out of one of those renaissance fairs we sometimes shared field space with. The difference was more unusual creatures. There was something with the head of a clay pot talking with something troll-like, and the troll had a wooden leg. In a corner, a creature with three heads chatted with itself, while two arms fought over which mug to drink from. All of the heads were savage and ugly, with rings through their noses and ears. Next to each arm, a thick club of wood rested. There were several things with hoods talking to other things with helmets. Body-like shapes writhed on benches, hidden in the shadows.

The innkeeper was a thickly set man built like a tower, his raggedy clothes half-hidden by a leather apron. "Welcome!" His voice boomed. It highlighted his glorious beard, a mass of stringy, gray strands tucked into his leather apron. "I'm Storeo Bosquoverde. What can I do for a dirty stone man and his fine young lady?"

He trotted up to the Stone Preacher, his beard in a bit of an uproar. "Oh. The Stone Preacher! I see you are at last free of the Chapel of Indignities?" He teased and gestured in my direction. "And who is this indignity you travel with, hmm?" He looked down at my toes and tapped the sign next to the door. It boldly proclaimed the words *No Bare Feet*.

"I shall get her shoes in the morning," the Stone Preacher declared. "She had an incident within the chapel that has divested her of her footwear." His voice was a dark, thunderous grind.

The innkeeper sighed. It was as if he knew better than to challenge the Preacher. "Ohh, all right," he said, looking a little tired. "Would you like to hear a story?"

"He's very good at them," the Preacher said. "But someone stole his magic pen, and now all he has are halves of ideas, shorn off at the wits and lewdly plucked."

Bosquoverde hung his head for a moment, and sighed. "One day, I'll find it again." He looked up at the wall. "Still, being an innkeeper and having a warm fire for my unusual friends is enough for me." He gave me a clever wink. "You look like you're in love."

I'd been there for two days. Everyone seemed to know I was in love with a stranger. I was tired, and my feet were cold. I hung my head almost as low as Bosquoverde did a moment earlier. "Yeah," I said glumly. "I guess."

"I am certain that you will find him." Bosquoverde showed us over to a table. "I am certain that there will be no improprieties with your Preacher friend?" He gave a wicked smirk to us and departed, letting us take our own chairs.

I settled in and the Preacher gave a curt nod to our host. "Bosquoverde is the rarest of men," he said firmly. "He could have been a preacher or a great scribe. Instead, he lost his magic pen, and became a thing of shredded pasts. You would never know it from his joy."

"He was enthusiastic," I admitted. The Preacher was often scary. Every conversation with him filled me with a little bit of dread.

A waitress brought us food. It was so heavy and full of thick sauces that I almost passed out at the table. Once in my room, I bathed from a small bucket of cold water, and crawled to bed.

Compared to sleeping in the chapel, it was a little slice of heaven.

***

I was awakened from sleep by hooting.

I saw only darkness through the window outside. Dim lights from the hall made the room seem yellow. A low grinding noise came from the bed next to me. The Stone Preacher was sleeping. He snored like an avalanche.

The hooting came from outside my window. I rolled out of my covers and crept to stare. There was an angry owl on the branch just beyond the window. I thought about the Preacher's unholy agility. I was afraid that the Stone Preacher might kill it.

I slipped the catch on the window and opened it as quietly as I could. Cold air rushed in, as if the season was angry with me for getting out of bed. I inched my way up over the lip of the window, and closed the shutters most of the way. Still, the Stone Preacher slept.

I crept out along the ledge in my bare feet, shuddering in the cold. It didn't really register until after I had stepped away from the window that the ground was far below. My feet cracked the bark beneath them. I looked at the owl on the massive thick branch. "Go away!" I growled as quietly as I could. The creature tilted its head and made a soft hooting noise. I listened to see if the Preacher would move.

Silence greeted me from the direction of the room.

The eyes of the creature grew white. The mouth opened, and it let out a feminine purr. "I speak with the voice of the Half-bone Maiden." The owl's tone was light and cheerful. "I wish to see you, whatever you call yourself, before they give you your name." It fluttered oddly, struggling under something's influence.

"What are you?" I clutched the branch on all fours, and remembered how far down it was.

"I am the arbiter of fate that you receive, the torment of bones gone brittle, the cream and sugar in your coffee." The owl giggled through its beak. A wing covered its mouth as if teasing.

"So you want to tell my fortune?" I asked the owl. It was only a few feet away.

The owl tilted its head. "No. I wish to read your skin," The owl twittered. 'It will be soft and lovely, and tell a story of your future."

"Do I get to keep it?" I grew suspicious. "You aren't gonna cut me out of it?"

The tittering ended with a sweet little giggle. "Oh, don't be silly. You'll have to strip naked and spend some time in a mud bath and then wash off, but then I'll be able to read your skin." The owl giggled instead of hooting.

I grabbed the branch more tightly. "How do I get to where you are?"

"I'm not your fairy godmother, but I think you might journey past my home one day."

"I have a fairy godmother?"

The owl's head tilted. "I don't know the answer to that," It spread its wings. "If you will excuse me, this beast needs to fly off." The owl fluttered into the night amongst the shadows.

I shuddered and inched my way backwards along the branch. By the time I made it back to the window, I couldn't see the owl anymore.

When I crawled back into the comfort of the warm bed, I thought I was better off.

***

Lilting sounds of birds woke me from my sleep. I stretched my arms upward under the covers. I wanted to go back to a world of T-shirts, and I had only one pair of jeans. There was a thick, crisp shirt of cotton hanging next to the bed, and a pair of wooden sandals on the floor. Lumpy cotton breeches hung below the shirt. "What are these?" I mumbled in half-consciousness.

The Stone Preacher stood next to me, his arms folded. "You can't let everyone know you're from the other side. I can't spend all my time pulling you away from people who want to lure you into their homes and eat you. This is a place of legend. Monsters live here."

"Are you one of them?"

"That's a fair question." His voice rumbled, as if in thought. "Some would say yes. Others, no. That's why this is a land of failed fairy tales."

"You can always tell a fairy tale character by whether they're a failure or a success?" It was the sort of question I probably should have asked earlier.

"Not exactly," The Preacher said. "I will turn my back while you dress. A preacher should have modesty, even though my morals are impeccable and I do not lust." His feet ground as he turned away, staring at the wall.

I hurriedly threw on clothes while he was folding his arms. I decided to do the risky thing and wear the jeans anyway.

***

We went down to breakfast. The common room was almost empty. Bosquoverde served people on his own. He showed us to a quiet table. "There are some people saying that you're not from around here," he said to me as he seated the Preacher. "Are you planning on staying long?"

"No, not long." I managed a smile. "I have to find my one true love, or I'll never get out of here."

"Is he a noble?" Bosquoverde asked, with a wide grin. "Those stories always filled me with such joy, but my happy endings were all deferred into tragedies. I feared that my own conscience would keep me from enjoying them as I wrote them, so I left my world behind and came here." He let out a sigh." My songs are of this place now, as grim and tragic as what they did to me.

Nonetheless, I am still a fantastic cook. Would you like to sample my chocolate wine chicken?"

"As long as it's fresh." Chocolate and wine for breakfast. It really was a fairy tale world.

The Preacher nodded. "I do not eat, but since she wishes to see what happens, I, too, will taste it."

"A full plate, or another fork?" Bosquoverde grinned, and adjusted his beard a little bit, under his leather apron.

"A full plate. I have not eaten in many years. I do not know what it will do." The Stone Preacher smiled, revealing stone teeth.

"As you wish." Bosquoverde bowed, and turned to the kitchen. "Do you require water or coffee?"

I became excited. "There's coffee here?"

"For special guests," Bosquoverde replied. "I shall put on a pot. I grow it in some of the higher branches. I have to roast it by hand in small batches." He looked over his shoulder and gave me a wink.

The Preacher nodded. "I shall not partake," he said. "This beverage was beyond my understanding when I was mortal. Even more so now."

"Suit yourself." Bosquoverde gestured grandly. "I brew the best coffee in all this world."

"He brews the only coffee in all this world," a thin man at a nearby table muttered. "It's very good, and you're very lucky."

"Would you like some?" I would have to make some friends if I wanted to live. He was wearing a cloak and had thin black hair, his lips pursed together in a tight package. He was eating purple eggs. I didn't really want to know what sort of creature laid them. There was a glass of water next to his plate. He seemed lonely and dissolute.

"You are offering me your coffee?" The thin man's eyes brightened. His hand twirled his fork.

The Stone Preacher turned to the man. "Be off, fool. Can you not see that I am eating for the first time in over eight hundred years?" His voice thundered, and a few people in the back corner of the inn cowered as he spoke.

"I could not refuse a man such." The thin man said. "I am the Carver of Fenceposts, but, well..." He sighed. It was obvious he didn't like the name much. "Just call me Ted, okay?"

"I can call you Ted?" A little thrill ran through me. There was someone besides me with a normal name.

The Stone Preacher sighed and looked away from us as we spoke. There was a look of haughtiness and disdain on his rocky features.

"Yeah. I'm one of the last people to carve fenceposts ornamentally," he said with a gloomy shudder. "I've been here five years. Being the Carver of Fenceposts is sort of like being the King of the Ass End of Nowhere." He shrugged. "Still, it's a job."

"You never know," I said while the Preacher watched us ominously. "There might actually be a King of the Ass End of Nowhere."

"There isn't," the Stone Preacher said, a little testily. "Making obeisance to such a being would gall me. No doubt, he would have the head of a donkey, and bray unpleasant words."

"That isn't what I was thinking of," Ted muttered.

"Me, either," It made me wonder how people communicated there. "But you don't want to make him mad. He's very violent."

"The priest?" Ted asked. I couldn't call him the Carver of Fenceposts. He was still just Ted. Something about him spoke of absolute ordinariness.

"The Stone Preacher. He likes to be called by his full name." Bosquoverde brought out the pot of coffee, and set it on our table. He poured the contents into a mug.

The coffee of the Otherworld smelled Otherworldly. It was probably the only place I could get it. Its aroma smelled like smoke and candied chocolate. It wafted from the pot, prompting stares from everyone around. He poured a cup for me, and a cup for Ted. The Stone Preacher waved his hand once more, as if to indicate that it was not for him.

I drank half the pot, and Ted drank the other half. We sat in silence and savored our coffee until the dinnerlike breakfast arrived. Even the Stone Preacher seemed to enjoy it. We filled ourselves with sweet roasted meat and sauce until I could barely stand.

"The food is magnificent," The Stone Preacher said. "I am pleased that I can still taste with a tongue of stone."

"Well, I am pleased that something has entertained you that doesn't cause everyone around you to die." It was a small triumph. "Maybe you should eat more often."

"He's going to say 'It's a mere indulgence'," Ted said.

"How did you know that?" The Stone Preacher looked at Ted oddly, as if Ted were a false prophet of some kind.

"My parish priest said the same things back home. He did it to make people feel he was humble."

"Was he, actually?" The Stone Preacher asked.

"No," Ted answered. "Not really. But his wife cooked for the whole neighborhood. He was a really nice guy."

"Don't kill him. He's just Ted." I looked at the Stone Preacher and pleaded.

The Stone Preacher nodded. "He is, after all, just Ted."

Bosquoverde smiled as we finished our food. "No charge!" It was as if he were always orating rather than speaking. "It is always a pleasure to serve a man of the cloth, even if the cloth is made of stone."

We made our way out of the inn after that, and went down to the shops to try and find a pair of boots. Ted stared at us on our way out, as if he missed out on the chance to be a part of something greater than himself.

It was a look I would get used to.

***

Streets amid the thick trees were crowded. Little houses amid branches bustled with life. I had no idea how the people got up and down from some of them. I thought I could see some bridges high in the branches above.

"Are there stairs?" It was wondrous as the sun shone down through the leaves. I thought I might almost be in a real fairy tale world.

"In places." The Stone Preacher pointed out a few hidden spots where stairs were worked into the wood. "I have only been here once or twice. Even during the day, there are places where shadows lurk to eat the unfortunate."

"This place isn't very friendly, is it?"

"Bosquoverde has consented to live here, so I leave these people alone. His very presence warms the rest of the village, and brings it life with a light unlike that seen anywhere else. Even in the wicked places, there is something brilliant."

"How can one man do all that?" I asked.

"It's easy," the Stone Preacher said. "A brilliant man can inspire brilliance in others, and in so doing, all those around him benefit from his presence, as if he were a lantern in the depths of a dark world."

"And a brilliant woman?"

"It is the same, only if the woman is pretty, those around her become prettier, and if she is ugly, they all become religious." He chuckled. "Beauty, it seems, is the antithesis of my work."

It was in that moment that I decided as long as I was here, I had to be as pretty as possible. Apparently, he considered it his duty to snuff out the life of all who disagreed with him. I was safe only because I saved him.

"That's the market, isn't it?" I pointed ahead to a chaotic group of tables. People in front of them shouted, pushing at merchants. As we approached, the noise of the crowd grew. Even the usual hush that preceded the coming of the Stone Preacher dimmed. I didn't know what passed for money in this strange world. I couldn't steal in front of the Preacher. But I knew I needed shoes.

"Indeed." The Stone Preacher's voice was a gravelly rumble. "I am certain that my contacts here can provide us with shoes for one of your stature."

"I have stature?" I asked. "Look, no offense, but I'm not exactly a titan among women."

"Have you looked in the mirror these past few morns?" the Stone Preacher said quietly as we walked. "Nobility is inherent here, whether you like it or not."

***

The market was a mix of old and new, tossed together in a weird form of chaos that struggled against itself. Well-dressed people in Victorian garb mixed with the quasi-medieval, and a few sets of jeans and T-shirts could be spotted among them. It was like watching the history of the world crushed together: howling and furious.

"This is how we live. We haggle over scraps of value, and try to give meaning to absences in each other's lives. As a preacher, it is my job to show them wisdom." The Stone Preacher gestured broadly towards the madness, and we stepped into it.

"Does that include killing them?" I asked as we passed the first few stalls.

"If necessary." The Preacher's lips crackled with granite joy.

A dirty woman in a shawl, fat and misshapen, held out a hand to me, holding a crisp apple. "Apples for sale, my lady?" She cackled, looking at my eyes as if she could see something I couldn't. A horrible feeling spawned in my stomach that the Preacher may have been right.

"No thanks," I said quietly. "I've heard stories, and I don't want an evil stepmother."

"Grulka is not a stepmother." She chortled. "But Grulka might be evil."

"Away, hag!" The Stone Preacher ground forward, rumbling like rocks rolling on the ground, and the crowd parted from him. "She has no name yet, and is not royalty! You cannot have her!" He gave the hag a light shove, and she tumbled to the ground. The wizened face turned purplish black. The rag covered woman turned thin and spindly, a mouth of sharp teeth and bulging eyes peering out from behind a hooked nose. Under her skin, warts burst forth.

"Grulka hates you! Hates all you pretty folk!" She scowled and ran off into the crowd, clutching the apple.

"She's going to be trouble." I watched her run off through the crowd. "I get the feeling that I just avoided something unpleasant."

"The hag switches bodies," The Preacher said. "You eat the apple, she takes your body, you get her old one. The problem is, she has to eat you to look like you. She stalks you for days, begging you for just a little piece of your flesh, and all the while, the pain gets worse."

"Why didn't you kill her?" This worried me. "If ever there was a creature that deserved it, it would be that one."

"It takes a virgin princess to undo the curse of the hag." He said, staring wistfully. Armed watchmen descended upon the creature. "Clearly, from the color of your eyes, that's not you." He offered a rocky grin.

I didn't answer, I just pressed on through the market with him. In the distance, I heard the screaming of the hag as watchmen surrounded her, beating her with clubs. I heard a horrible gurgling sound and some spitting, and then mewling sounds as the wood crashed down. "It looks like most other people don't like hags either."

"Once the hag is named for what it is, they can be subdued and chained up." The Preacher's teeth sounded like chains running over gears. "You can even cut their limbs off, and as long as you don't sew them back on, the creature is helpless. No more apples for that one, in the name of my stony god."

"That sounds lovely." There was a little part of me that enjoyed what happened to the hag. I wondered if it was me, or if it was this Otherworld, sucking away my compassion and replacing it with pleasurable mercilessness. "Let's go get some shoes."

I heard shouts of "Cut deep!" as we made our way towards the cobblers. I heard swords rise and fall while I imagined them cutting apart Grulka's warty flesh.

***

Grulka's screams gurgled to silence as we pressed our way through the crowd. "Why do I feel more comfortable with that than I should?" We stepped around a young couple, cooing over each other in linens and medieval garb.

"She is a hag." The Preacher tapped his chin, as if he had to think about it. "It could be that you are deriving pleasure from the wickedness and twistedness of this place, as many others do. On the other hand, it could simply be relief that you are no longer threatened by it." His shoulders ground in a shrug. "I choose not to dwell on it."

We wandered past a couple more vendors, and worry crossed my face. "Isn't that what leads to jadedness and wickedness in the first place?"

The Preacher didn't answer as we made our way through the crowd.

When we got to the cobblers, the smell of drying leather was fierce in the air. It made me gag. "You're really not used to how it's made, are you?" The Preacher smirked, the corner of his lip making a stony cracking noise.

"Well, I didn't think there would be such an awful smell." I choked back a gagging sound. The shoemaker's shop smelled like something died. There was no fresh air to be had, even as the Stone Preacher led me inside. He was amused. His nose was made of stone. He probably didn't need to breathe. All I could smell was urine from tanning leather.

"You buy all your shoes in those markets," The Stone Preacher said, his voice vicious. "Now you'll learn. A pair of shoes is made for a person. It defines them, the way that a journey does. You need the right pair of shoes for the right kind of journey."

The cobbler's shop was built into the crook of a tree, as all the other houses and buildings were. Its windows were shaded. The reeking stench from the back of the tree forced me desperately inside. I bravely pushed the door open. The scent of strong perfumes designed to counter the wretched odor hit my nostrils. The Stone Preacher rumbled his way in behind me.

There was a man in the most disturbingly thin plate armor seated at a table, hammering nails into the sole of a leather shoe. His helmet was up. Sweat burdened his face, a laughing visage flicking upward to stare at us. He rose, the oiled joints of the armor making no noise. "Milady." He bowed and deferred, thin lips spreading to reveal narrow, amused teeth.

His gaze flicked to the Stone Preacher behind me and his eyes grew cold. "Another of your transgressors?" He glowered. "What wickedness is this that you have brought another here for me to shoe like a horse before you crush them into meat?"

"At ease, good Knight of Cobblers. She has saved my life. I cannot take hers. It is the rules of this world that we live in." The Stone Preacher bowed. "The right journey, as you have told me so many times, requires the right pair of shoes, and as you are the finest shoemaker in the lands of the Otherworld for over fifteen days ride, I believe we should not let our noblewoman to go barefoot." His throat ratcheted.

The Knight of Cobblers stepped from around the table. He stared as though I were his new toy. "Off, off, wretched sandals." He smiled. "What kind of shoes would one who is to be a blessed bride like?"

"I'm not really much for slippers." I quivered as I kicked the sandals off. "I'd really like a nice pair of boots, if it's all the same to you."

"Boots indeed!" the Knight's voice was a cheerful chuckle. "Your new savior is wise, Stone Preacher. Only an idiot would journey some of these lands in dainty footwear. I have a little magic that may sometimes help thee in such boots." He laid out two wooden boxes filled with wet clay, as if he had been waiting for me. "Stand you in these, and then I'll bake it, and by tomorrow's end, you shall have a pair of boots that is like no other." He smiled. "If you are truly royalty, the boots will take to you like no other."

"What if I'm not?" I mumbled to the Stone Preacher. "What if this is all a wicked illusion, or if Grulka cast a hex on me?"

"Oh." The Stone Preacher yawned, his mouth hollow. "You'll die. But it will look spectacular."

The Knight of Cobblers shrugged. "He speaks truth." He motioned to the wooden boxes, and I stepped into them, my feet sinking in. He motioned. "Now step out. You will have boots as lovely as that of any other noblewoman." He gave me a supple bow.

I stepped out of the clay and the Stone Preacher provided a bowl for me to wash my feet. I did so as quickly as possible. "I'm going to die?" I put my hands on my hips. "This is a really stupid idea! He makes a set of boots for me, and if they don't fit right, I die?"

The Stone Preacher shrugged. "Your eyes are turning green. They should fit. In this world, if the shoe fits, then one is truly among royalty. You're not in your world, with its unimaginative rules anymore. You're in this one."

"So what exactly does happen if the shoe doesn't fit?" I scowled as I walked for the door of the shop.

"Fare you well!" The Knight of Cobblers seemed very enthusiastic, as if he had a great deal of faith in his work.

"Well," The Stone Preacher said as we walked for the door. "Your feet and legs will be afflicted by horrid, searing pains. Then, the boots will burn the flesh right off your body, and you will walk on your bones all the way to your grave."

I slammed the door in the Stone Preacher's face and stormed off down the street. I wanted nothing more at that moment than to go home, though my heart shook for the touch of the man I met in the forest.

***

The Stone Preacher threw the door open with a loud crash. I had made my way halfway back to the inn when he caught up with me. I could still hear the crash. I was afraid of what those hands could do to me. "You must wait," The Stone Preacher said. "You are unschooled in the ways of this world. I already prepared a grave for you in case the boots failed thee."

"Excuse me? You dug a grave for me?" I shook my head. "This is unbelievable!"

"I am only being practical," the Stone Preacher protested grimly. "I will say honorable last rites for you. You have saved my life. I will honor that bargain."

"When did you dig a grave for me?" I wanted to hit him, but he was made of rock.

"Oh, I dug it this morning, while you were sleeping. Bosquoverde had a little patch of garden that he wasn't using. I persuaded him to part with it." The Stone Preacher grinned a sinister granite smile.

"You were going to bury me in his garden?" I scowled. "What would my mother say? Here lies Symantha, buried in the garden of some coffee-brewing tree house freak!"

"It seemed the perfect place for a princess that is not a princess. A bower that is not a bower. I made certain that all of the proper accoutrements were acquired."

"You got me a coffin!" I shouted. "You bought a coffin!" People were beginning to stare. The eyes of the whole crowd were upon us. "And now I'm supposed to be a princess?" I scowled. "This is complete bullshit."

"Well..." The Stone Preacher said quietly. "If I had known you would be so miserable about receiving last rites, I might have waited until after lunch. Your eyes are turning greener than any of the others I have seen."

Tears rolled down my face. I shook a little bit as the Stone Preacher led me back to the inn. When we opened the door, Bosquoverde saw my tears. He handed me a handkerchief from somewhere in the depths of his apron. Ted stared at me as though I were about to break into a million pieces.

I clutched the handkerchief and stormed up the stairs. The more I held it, the more I wanted to throw it away. It was an anchor to something I didn't want anymore.

***

The Stone Preacher left me alone in the room. After a few hours, I finally gathered the courage to look out the window. There it was. My grave settled open and shallow, deep, perfect and rectangular, as if shaped by the earth itself. There was a beautiful headstone, but even from the far distance, I could see there was no writing on it. I would die nameless.

I got up and went downstairs, settling into a seat at a table away from the Preacher. Bosquoverde chuckled to me as he walked over. The Stone Preacher remained impassive. "I take it you saw the gravestone?" Bosquoverde grinned, pouring me a cup of coffee.

"I can't afford that." I quietly stared at the cup.

"The rich and those who are about to die always can." Bosquoverde chortled. "And if your eyes are as green as I see, then you could be one or both of those, so who am I to refuse one of your station?" He gave me a wink as if he were a dirty old man.

I thought about that and drank half the cup while it was hot. I managed a murmur and a little gasp. It was hotter than I expected.

"I honestly believe that you are not going to die." His smile was clever. "The Preacher is only testing you, as he usually is. It is part of his ethos, to resist the cold grasp of the grave even as he struggles towards it."

"So he's dead, yet not?"

"More set in rigidity." Bosquoverde chuckled. "He is a creature of absolutes. He does not waver from them. Hence, the Stone Preacher. If you want to find out how he was turned to stone, you'll have to ask him. He's very bitter about it."

The Stone Preacher looked at me impassively. "Maybe I had better not ask," I said quietly. "But he bought me a coffin! Do you know what it's like to find out that you're probably gonna die, and your grave is outside in the yard?"

"No." Bosquoverde said wryly. "Most of us aren't so fortunate as to actually be able to have someone else dig a grave for us here. A lot of people are hacked apart, and left to hang. Others are wrapped in rusty wire and left to rot. In this world, the things you do in life determine your punishment or reward in death. I believe one day, I shall become a tree, if I am lucky, and continue to live my life so."

"You want to spend the rest of eternity as a tree?" The thought had not occurred to me that he might enjoy this idea.

"It is better than having your ideas stolen and hung out to rot while the wicked turn your soul to bitter poison." He laughed. "Here, have some more coffee."

For some reason, I found it very difficult to refuse. Even Ted, watching me from his table, seemed a little intrigued. "So I'm lucky." I drank the cup one sip at a time.

"Yes. Lucky and noble." We laughed. For a while, I almost forgot that my grave was right outside, waiting for me to come in and grow cold.

***

As the Stone Preacher rejoined us, the hooting of a diseased monkey came from outside. "He can't bring it in!" Bosquoverde thundered. "I'll split that stupid top hat of his if he tries to bring that putrescent, rotting beast in here!" He stormed off towards the door and threw it open. The Organ Grinder pushed past him.

"Sir!" Bosquoverde's voice was furious. "Keep your disgusting little beast outside!" The monkey peered out from under the Organ Grinder's greatcoat, and gave a wicked hiss, stabbing at Bosquoverde with its knife-tail.

Bosquoverde was faster. He reared back with a heavy boot, and kicked the monkey out the open door. There was a howling screech. Bosquoverde slammed the door hard as the Organ Grinder punched his kidneys.

"Stop them!" I snapped to the Stone Preacher. "I haven't eaten dinner yet!"

The Stone Preacher sighed, and rose from his chair. Bosquoverde jabbed his boot down hard on the boot of the Organ Grinder, and turned. The Organ Grinder began to throttle him with a guttural growl. "Vile animal hater!" Bosquoverde's throat began to redden. The two men struggled against the door as the keening screech of the monkey continued. Knife-thumps hacked at the wooden door while the ominous grind of the Stone Preacher approached them, gliding across the wooden floor.

Bosquoverde lashed out with a punch to the stomach, but the Organ Grinder did not double over. "You dare to bring a plague into my restaurant?" He choked out the words as the Stone Preacher grabbed the two men and slammed them up against the door.

The Stone Preacher's voice was cold. "She has asked both of you to stop fighting. If you do not, I will handle this my way, and the inn will be hers. It would be terribly unfortunate, Organ Grinder, to see what she would do to your monkey." His granite fingers tightened on their throats.

The Organ Grinder winced and relented, and as he did, Bosquoverde stepped back from his belligerent stance. The Stone Preacher, purring in a gravelly echo, releasing them. "I hope it is to your liking that they are still alive."

"Uhh, yeah." The hooting of the monkey was louder now. "It stays outside." I scowled at the Organ Grinder and drew myself up to my unimpressive full height. "How dare you bring that thing in here? It's disgusting!"

If I was going to be a princess, I might as well use the power. Bosquoverde slipped behind me for a moment and smiled. "That's the way, lass," he murmured.

The Organ Grinder recovered from his momentary silence. Ted stared, open mouthed as eyes of everyone in the room turned in our direction. The Organ Grinder swallowed hard, adjusting his monocle, and picked his hat up off the ground where it had fallen. "My apologies," He rumbled. "If it is your wish, young lady, that I not challenge this innkeeper over the presence of the monkey, then it shall stay outside." He glared at Bosquoverde while the monkey hooted and scratched at the window.

As the evening went on and it grew colder, the monkey hooted less frequently. The bitter silence continued during dinner and after. All night I dreamed of the wretched monkey, lying dead in the street after being hurled under wagons and carts by passers-by.

***

I wasn't so lucky. I awoke to burning sunshine in my eyes, and the hooting, diseased monkey peering at me through the window. A wicked blot on my morning, it rubbed its pustule covered face against the window glass. The Stone Preacher glared at it from his bed, and rose in a granite rumble. "Do you wish me to kill it?"

I stopped and looked out the window, but the little monster was gone. The glass was scratched by the knife sewn to its tail. "Not yet." The ease with which I said it frightened me. I would have to show more compassion, or I would never find him. I was becoming wrapped in the world around me.

"You are learning a little of power and position," the Stone Preacher said. "I find the Organ Grinder a disgusting creature, but you have outsmarted him, and he is therefore at your mercy. Use it wisely, for he is a powerful ally when you may require one, but a deadly enemy if you should betray him. The monkey is a piece of his soul, and like it or not, it follows him like a plague, murdering and poisoning all who come too close to him. Even so, he is jolly when his monkey is not threatened. If you can avoid being sickened, you may come, in time, to like him." The Stone Preacher's granite lips grimaced. "The disgusting freak has been between the legs of many a noblewoman. Don't avail yourself of his pleasures. His music is most seductive when he is near his cart."

"Right. His cart." I twitched. I felt violated just talking about the Organ Grinder. "Let's go down to breakfast, shall we?" I tried to sound more noble, and felt better immediately. When the Stone Preacher turned his back and I bathed from the basin of cold water, I felt something cruel twitch at the nape of my neck. No matter how hard I tried to wash it off, it wouldn't go away.

***

Breakfast was a crude affair of biscuits and gravy, washed down with last night's overheated coffee. Bosquoverde couldn't save it when he flavored it with mint leaves. The Stone Preacher sat across from me, while the Organ Grinder sat next to me with a grin, carefully combing his mustache and fingering his monocle. It was a testament to everyone's fortitude that no one was discomfited by breakfast. The Organ Grinder seemed to enjoy it, his wicked smile savoring the grease and gravy as he cleaned his mouth after every bite. With every disgusted gaze from the Stone Preacher, he seemed to enjoy it more.

"Magnificent," the Organ Grinder chortled. "It is just like they used to make for me back in the orphanage."

"This breakfast may make orphans out of all of us." Ted laughed from his nearby table. I laughed with him. The most ordinary man in the room was suddenly the most comfortable.

"You were an orphan?" I turned to face him. "I'm an orphan, too."

Bosquoverde walked by the table and smiled. "Everyone here is, in some way. Often those who are most exiled become the greatest among us. You should be careful that you are not too much of one."

"Why is that? Will I become like the King of Feathers?"

"I see that you are smart as well as noble, young lady!" The Organ Grinder said. He slid a leathery hand across my leg. It felt like desire and rutting in the dirt.

"Unhand me!" I snapped. "Or Holy Lad here rips out your throat and feeds it to your monkey!" I turned my gaze cold.

The Stone Preacher eagerly prepared to rise from his seat, but I held up a hand. Being in the nobility business was getting more appealing. The Organ Grinder removed his hand.

Bosquoverde chuckled. "She learns fast." His rumbling laugh echoed through the inn. "Let me see if I have something to settle your stomachs, good people."

"My stomach is settled." The Organ Grinder smiled. "And this coffee is perfect."

"It's swill," Ted said from his table.

I didn't add in that the Organ Grinder's preferences reflected his social station among the underclass. "Yeah. And the Stone Preacher doesn't eat."

"I ate once in the past eight hundred years," The Stone Preacher said calmly. "I'll be fine. My stomach is made of stone, but that doesn't mean I'll put swill into it."

"You're outvoted." Bosquoverde said. "I apologize for the awful meal, but a few people saw your grave and decided not to sell me fresh food this morning." He scowled at the Stone Preacher. "You should know better than to frighten the nobility with your beliefs, sir."

"It's all right." I said. Then I got up and ran for the door. My stomach was making sickening gurgles. I desperately needed to throw up.

***

I flung open the door and raced for anything that was not the roots of the tree. My stomach was heaving. I could hear the hooting of the monkey, so I leaned against the nearest thing I could find. I could feel wood and old paint. My fingernails scratched against creaking boards. I clutched the corner of it, there was a hooting screech as I threw up all over the wheel of a tired old wagon. There was a loud bellow from the monkey, followed by an irritating whisk of knife-tail as I dry-heaved.

The wagon was covered with a low, slatted roof with a small box window built into one side. The boards creaked, and the cracks in the wood were caulked. A door rested in the back of the wagon. Two steps led up to it. Wooden wheels groaned under my weight, as if the whole thing were about to collapse. It was hitched up to a horse that looked ready to sag into a pile of meat and bones.

The Organ Grinder was standing behind me. His breath was as heavy as my vomit. Bosquoverde and The Stone Preacher were right behind him. "If you're going to throw up on my cart, lass, you should let me have a kiss afterwards." His face twisted in a lewd grin.

I answered him with a gagging cough. There was nothing that he could say that didn't make me feel violated, now that I understood what he was. He seemed so nice in the forest. Bosquoverde patted me on the shoulder. "You're not used to greasy biscuits for breakfast. I believe your temperament is becoming more refined, at a pace with your station."

"You mean that I can only eat sweet things and properly prepared foods or something?" I gagged and coughed, trying to inhale the leafy air of the trees.

"Something like that," Bosquoverde said. "The rules of the Otherworld and nobility are strange."

"Who rules this land? I mean, not the whole thing. He's got to have subordinates, right? Dukes and Chancellors and all that other stuff?"

"We were wondering when you'd get around to that," Bosquoverde said with a sigh. "His name is the Duke of Bells."

"Bells? That's as corny as the King of Feathers." I covered my mouth. I was outside. It was a foolish thing to say. A pair of passersby took a few steps away, as if to shun me.

"Well, there's more to it than that," Bosquoverde continued. "He is the greatest authority on bells in all the land. He even wears a bell-shaped helmet on his head."

"So he looks like a guy in an upside-down tuba?" I asked.

"Hush!" The Organ Grinder said. "The watch approaches. We must now explain ourselves to them. Fortunately, we have a priest with us." He let out a lurid smile. "Absolve us of our sins, O Granite One."

The Stone Preacher lifted up a hand, and I stepped in front. "Please, sir, don't kill him!" I clasped my hands together. "I have only just met him, and I feel unclean!" It probably wouldn't have been so wonderful a lie, except it felt true on the inside.

I never really noticed the tabards of the watchmen, but there was a coat of arms with a picture of a bell in the upper right-hand corner. Even their helmets looked vaguely bell-shaped when looked at the right way. "What's going on?" The Watch Captain paused. He was a sallow-faced man of vengeful demeanor. His hand was already on his sword belt, and he looked suspiciously at my jeans.

The Organ Grinder moved to speak, as the monkey huddled under his cloak. The Stone Preacher stepped forward and interrupted him. "Good Captain, I was merely adjudicating a dispute." The gravelly voice washed over the ears of the Captain. He seemed unfazed by talking to a priest in a cassock made of stone.

"Oh," the Captain said coldly. "It's you." His gaze flicked up and down over the Stone Preacher with disdain. "Do not kill anyone in town, or I will hire the Viscount of Miners to dig holes in your rocky body until you give up your crude diamond soul, and carve it into a ring for my wife to wear."

"That was civil," Bosquoverde muttered.

"Your threats do not offend one of the priesthood," the Stone Preacher rumbled. "I am a peaceful preacher, engaged only in corrections of heretical morality."

If I had something left to do so, I might have vomited again. The Captain smiled and said "See that you do not correct too many heresies. I know of your methods. You create much work for those who dig graves. The Bey of Gravediggers is most displeased with you."

"Does everyone have a title around here?" I complained. "There's nothing noble about being a gravedigger, really."

The Captain turned, adjusting his bell like helmet. "My lady." He bowed, as if he hadn't noticed something. "You must be new." He backed up a little bit. "I shall inform the Duke of your presence at once!" Then he ran, beckoning for his men to follow.

"Now you've gone and done it," Bosquoverde said. "This will turn into a gigantic mess. This land is the ultimate expression of 'Ignorance of the Law is no excuse.'"

"What's that supposed to mean?"

"It means that the Duke of Bells will likely be insulted that you have come unannounced, and use his political influence to demand favors of you," he said serenely.

The Organ Grinder smiled. "His wife is a rare flower that I have yet to possess."

"You're all crazy," I said. "Bosquoverde, could I have some water, please?"

"At once, my lady." Bosquoverde said. "Shall we go inside?"

We headed inside back to the table, and I washed my mouth out with water. I despised my flesh for feeling anything at the touch of the Organ Grinder, and went upstairs to rest. I left everyone else at the table. I didn't need them to feel uncomfortable.

***

I rested on my bed briefly, recovering from the awful breakfast. The fact that the Organ Grinder enjoyed it so much made me resolve to stay sick. I drank water for a good part of the morning, and rested in a weary haze. Most of the time, I stayed in the bed, clutched at my sheets, and wished I were both somewhere and somebody else.

By the time the sun was high in the sky, my stomach subsided. The feeling in my mouth was left behind. I rose from the bed and washed my face. I felt the grey sun was a threat, glowering at me from behind the window. I almost craved darkness, as if it would protect me from the slimy touch of the Organ Grinder.

There was a knock on the door as I finished washing my face. I walked over to the door and opened it. Ted was standing in the doorway. He was holding an ornately carved fencepost. "I worked on this all night for you," he said sweetly. "May I come in?"

"Uh," I managed. "Sure... You do prefer Ted to 'Carver of Fenceposts,' right?" Something in my stomach gurgled. I didn't like that feeling. I thought the biscuits were gone.

"Yeah," he said and sat down on the Stone Preacher's bed. "So, tell me, Symantha, since you haven't been given your name. What are fence posts for?" He seemed curious. An odd light shone in his eyes.

"They make boundaries." I said. My voice quivered a little bit. I really didn't think Ted was so creepy. I hadn't really thought about how he had made it up here. "They keep people from getting in."

"I guess that's one way to look at it," Ted smiled. "Or you could look at them as markers that denote people who aren't capable of protecting themselves." His lips split into a wide grin, and he leaped for my throat. From under his coat, a massive thick piece of wood lifted out. His hand wrapped around my neck, squeezing. I began to choke.

I kicked him hard, struggling against his hands. He began pressing the wooden spike into my stomach. It was dull, and it was beginning to cut. I didn't have enough wind to breathe. I gagged as he drove the dull point in hard, and my eyes opened wide. "Why?" I wanted to throw up again.

He had carved my face into the hilt of the pos. It was smiling. It moved and giggled, mirroring my lips in the thick pine. Even its eyes had a little bit of brightness. "When I put it in the ground with your soul," he whispered eagerly "Your body walks away." He licked his lips and pressed up against me, trying to break my stomach open. He punched me, and I fell back against the window.

"Everyone wants a title," Ted said eagerly. "I'm not just the Carver of Fenceposts. I'm also a builder of graveyards. You'll smell so much better dead."

I rolled to one side. Ted, whatever he really was, smashed the post through the window, shattering the thick glass. I could feel the fencepost pushing at my throat and my neck. It was consuming me. I looked at the fencepost for just a second. It giggled at me as I crawled out through the glass. I could feel my face becoming less expressive and more wooden.

"I'd thank you again for the coffee, milady," Ted whispered, "but I don't want to be the Carver of Fenceposts forever." I backed up along the branch, hearing thumps along the stairs. People were coming, attracted by the sounds of breaking glass.

The bruise where Ted punched me throbbed on my face. "You will speak forever, my lady," he whispered. "Cold and in the ground as your fencepost talks in your voice…"

"That's pretty sick." I felt wooden. Everything about me was crawling into the fencepost as I backed further away. "Did you convince the Stone Preacher to dig my grave, too?"

"No, no," Ted's tongue slithered out and he licked his lips again, inching forward. He was bigger and heavier. It was the only advantage I had. "He did that all on his own. It's just something he does."

He lunged at me with the fencepost and I screamed in a monotonous whimper. The fencepost was taking my voice along with everything else. I tried to call for help, but made only a soft keening noise. There was something thumping on the door.

Ted turned briefly to look. "There are no repercussions if I put you in your grave. Just another noble bride, out to meet her wicked harlot's end." He thrust the fencepost forward and I slid around it, and kicked him as hard as I could. The carnival had hardened me. This wasn't my first street fight. The threat of dying stopped me from being scared.

There was a hammering on the door of my room.

Ted doubled up as the cruelty in my heart soared. He clutched the fencepost weakly in his hands. I wrenched it away from him. He whined like a hurt animal. Tears began to fall from his eyes. I spun the fencepost around and drove it hard at him. I had the anger of a hundred victims, consumed by a cold emptiness.

There was no nobility in this place. I could feel it. "I want my soul back!" I shrieked, and thrust the fencepost forward. I didn't see Ted jumping too. My anger, fueled by his jump, fixed the fencepost squarely in his guts. Momentum carried him off the tree branch. Ted scrabbled at the post, sobbing toward the ground below.

The Stone Preacher kicked the door down, followed by the Organ Grinder and Bosquoverde. Even as the Organ Grinder burst into the room, he knelt as a gentleman might. "Milady, we had no idea."

The Stone Preacher glided out onto the branch, mysteriously supporting his granite weight. Bosquoverde looked around to make sure there were no other dangers. "I didn't know." His gravelly voice was somewhat comforting. "He seemed so ordinary."

Together, we looked down into the grave that the Stone Preacher dug the previous day. Ted's corpse lay there, thin, and broken, impaled on the wood of the fence post. His face had turned to solid wood. Blood leaked out around the edges of the post in an uneven red mass. Babbling incoherently from the top of the post, Ted's voice whispered "So beautiful. I'm sorry."

"I'm glad he's dead." I stared vengefully into the hole in the earth.

"So am I," the Stone Preacher said thoughtfully. "It means I didn't dig a grave for nothing."

***

By the time we got out to Bosquoverde's garden, the Organ Grinder was already talking to the Fence Post. He was covering its mouth while it blubbered. I heard Ted's muffled cries through the Organ Grinder's thick, meaty hand.

Bosquoverde and the Stone Preacher just glared at the Organ Grinder and he stepped aside.

"Stop torturing him," I said. "That's really a little cruel to do to someone after they're dead."

"Please," Ted wept. "I'm going to be like this forever." His little wooden head cavorted on top of the post. Wooden lips dripped sap and blood.

"The bleeding will stop soon." The Stone Preacher said. "Then he'll be dead. But the fencepost won't stop talking."

"Can we fix him?" I asked.

"Don't be ridiculous, milady," Bosquoverde rumbled. "He's dead. His last fencepost contains his soul. It's just how things work around here."

"So we can talk to him?"

Ted's wooden head filled with cheerful smiles. "I shall talk to you, my lady, if you stick your finger in my mouth."

"Do you really think I'm going to let you bite my finger?" I shook my head. "I'm not some innocent little girl found by the wayside!" I slapped the post hard. The wooden head made a thudding sound.

Ted's voice whimpered. "No, please," he whispered. "I saw your eyes, those beautiful green eyes. If I could stop you," The wooden head stopped, trying to find words. "I could stop you from finding your true love, and being with them forever. I would be rich. I could gain my own noble title." The head sneezed out bile and blood.

"What?" I stared at the others, confused. "Do any of you believe this idiot? He tried to stab me with a fencepost and fell off a tree!" The Stone Preacher grabbed the fencepost and choked the wooden head violently. "Is it true?" He demanded. The slim, granite fingers squeezed on the head, and it made a weeping choke. When the Stone Preacher removed his hand, the wooden face had a broken nose, and his stone hand was stained with blood and bile.

"Yes. Five million half-lunas, and a place at court." Ted the Fence Post wept through the mangled face. "It doesn't matter. I'm dead now."

"Congratulations, Lass!" The Organ Grinder clapped me on the back. "You're worth five million half-lunas. Too bad I can't claim it, seeing as how you outsmarted me and those are the rules."

Bosquoverde looked over at Ted, then grumpily at the Stone Preacher. "I assume you'll want to take care of this?"

"I need three witnesses," the Stone Preacher said. "You know the rules of these sorts of things. One for the mother, one for the father, and one for the nobility." He smiled at me. "That would be you, my child with no name."

The Organ Grinder stuffed Ted's body into the grave, cracking the knees and neck of the corpse so that the body would fit into a space meant for me. He began filling it in while the Stone Preacher recited a litany of forgiveness.

When the Stone Preacher was done, we all gathered around the fencepost, and Bosquoverde gave me a fiery brand from the kitchen to burn the fence post. Ted's screams echoed through the fire as the broken face was consumed. We all watched in silence.

Somehow, when it was all over, I felt as if I had lost a friend.

***

It was hard to sleep that night. I shuddered in bed while the Stone Preacher slept, heavy with fingers latched into each other. He was granite in a deathlike state. It only made me feel more uncomfortable.

I woke up early, and bathed while the Stone Preacher slept, or seemed to. It was impossible to determine whether he was *actually* asleep. His chest didn't rise and fall, and his peaceful gaze focused on something or somewhere else.

I got dressed and skulked down to breakfast. Bosquoverde was waiting. "Where's the Organ Grinder?" The thing that bothered me most was that I didn't know where he was.

"He's in his cart," Bosquoverde said thoughtfully, "mourning the loss of five million half-lunas because of your shoe."

"He's not mourning with anyone, is he? I've never met such a disgusting creature." As if in answer, there was a faint hooting. The knife-tailed monkey crawled across the window.

"I don't know." Bosquoverde said. "I'd rather not find out." He shuddered, looking through the window at the monkey. "I am sorry that such a creature is one of your protectors."

"Oh, believe me, I'm sorry too."

"No need to be, it is the way of things. I have acquired fresh beef, and shall grill it, serving it to you over eggs, accompanied by a delicious leek cream." Fresh food and Bosquoverde were apparently important to each other.

"Thank you," I managed. "Is this one of those noble lady meals I'm supposed to eat?"

"Indeed." Bosquoverde rose, and tucked his beard into his apron. "I shall serve thee in but a moment." He laughed and headed for the kitchen. Already, I felt hungry.

The Organ Grinder stepped into the inn, a broad smile on his face as he toyed with the strap of his accordion. I wasn't hungry anymore.

***

The Organ Grinder lumbered over to me, smiling lewdly. He settled into a chair and set the accordion to one side. His smile grew wider. "Destiny, it seems, has made me your protector." He chortled.

I crossed my legs and put my sandaled feet up on the table. "As long as the monkey stays away." I scowled. "Don't think of trying to get into my pants, you disgusting freak."

"There was a local girl named Kayla." He yawned. "She sufficed nicely. Now she weeps that there will never be another but her precious Organ Grinder."

There was a thudding glide as the Stone Preacher came down the steps. "You should forgive him." The cassock rustled a little bit. "He is a beast and cannot help his true nature."

Bosquoverde emerged with my sumptuous breakfast and slid it down in front of me. "You, sir, need no food." His smile was harsh as he turned to the Organ Grinder. "And you, sir, shall have the last of the greasy biscuits and gravy from yesterday."

"Ahh, most fortunate." The Organ Grinder chortled. "It seems I am well beloved after all, and the honor of my beloved mother is sustained." He gave a gruesome laugh.

I ate quickly, not wanting to be there when the Organ Grinder ate the things that had made me vomit only yesterday, and were now a day older and greasier. It didn't matter whether it was made for me or not. All I wanted was to be away from the Organ Grinder during meals.

The food was rich and succulent. I felt as though it could sustain me for days. I was in a magical world of smiles when Bosquoverde brought the Organ Grinder's disgusting breakfast. I barely noticed it.

"The food is to your liking?" Bosquoverde asked, a smile on his face. "You look better than you've looked in days."

"Yeah, I think I got all my energy back from the first bite." I laughed. I didn't even feel bad about the Organ Grinder, eating his greasy biscuits in front of me.

"You have revitalized her indeed." The Stone Preacher grinned. "Today she is fit to try on her first true pair of boots."

"You bought her boots?" Bosquoverde raised an eyebrow.

"It is the way of the priesthood to prevail upon servants of the crown for noblewomen," he said in gravel tones. "As long as the crown dares not touch my cassock, I do as I wish."

"That's useful." I sipped my drink. "Is this the last of the coffee?" It actually hurt to think that this might be the last cup of coffee I might have for weeks, even months.

"Yes," Bosquoverde said. "There won't be any more until spring. I am sorry." He gave me a disappointed look. "I know how much you like it."

"I'll be back." I stared back brightly. "Let's go try on some boots." I said to the Preacher, and got up out of my chair.

"The energy of youth," the Stone Preacher rumbled. "You will be here when we return?" He glowered to the Organ Grinder. "Despoil her in any way, and I shall rip out your head from your body with your spine still attached." He followed this statement with a low grin.

"Of course." The Organ Grinder gave a slight bow from where he was sitting. "These biscuits are delicious. I shall savor them."

We headed out the door, away from the Organ Grinder's meal, into a world of shopping for shoes. It was a place I had rarely ventured. As we moved away from the inn, I could feel the eyes of the Organ Grinder's monkey savoring my flesh from behind the cart.

***

The Knight of Cobblers' shop was just as fragrant as it was the previous day, but the crowds were less. That just made the smell stronger. We made our way through the door as quickly as possible. The Stone Preacher showed no signs of discomfort.

The Knight smiled as he placed the boots on the counter. I knew in an instant that they were mine. The leather called to me, as if always there, waiting for me. They were tooled with runes and symbols, intricately carved into heavy, solid hide. The soles were thick and hard, built for traveling. I knew that I would wear the boots forever.

"These are boots of fire," he said sternly. "They are risky to wear, but for one of noble blood, they are the height of grace and social importance. When you wear them, you can run across the sky, leaving a trail of burning footprints behind you. They will always keep you warm, even on the coldest days. They are as comfortable as if you had bought them in the finest shop of the greatest city." He smiled to me. "The magic is truly in you, child, and not in the boots at all, but only one of your blood can use them, so I have crafted them with you in mind." He pursed his thin lips.

"Should I try them on?" I asked the Preacher. He knew much more about the Otherworld than I did, and having my feet on fire all the time was a little scary.

"You should indeed," the Preacher said. "Like every other pair of shoes, they still have to fit." His teeth ground into another stony smile.

I took off the sandals and slipped into the boots. They were the most comfortable things I had ever worn. "I made molds of your feet and constructed the boots around them," the Knight said firmly. "No one else could really wear them and enjoy them as much as you."

"I'll keep that in mind." I was very nervous. "So how do I fly?"

"You think about running into the air, and your very will commands the boots to work." The Knight of Cobblers chuckled. "But I would suggest that you try to do this outside. If you do it in here, my shop might burn down."

I raced outside without another thought. I had completely forgotten about landing.

***

The Stone Preacher followed me out as I raced forward and shouted "Fly!" I leaped into the air and nothing happened. Instead, I fell on my face. Learning how to fall was part of being raised in a circus. It wasn't as painful as it would be for some.

It still hurt. Grass stains on my face reminded me that it would probably take a few tries. I didn't even hear the Stone Preacher laughing until I started getting up. "That didn't work." I muttered.

"That's because there isn't a command word." The Preacher said with a sardonic growl. "Everyone thinks there's a magic word." He shook his head as I struggled to stand. I was embarrassed, and my ribs hurt.

"So I was too enthusiastic..." I sighed. "How do they work?"

"Concentrate..." The Stone Preacher said. "If you concentrate on running with the boots, you'll be taking off in no time. You'll have to learn, though."

I ran forward and tried to imagine running in the boots, taking off into the air. My feet warmed a little bit, as if I would never grow cold. There was a crackling pop, as if they were suddenly on fire. My feet didn't burn. I ran forward, leaving a few flickering footsteps on the grass. I thought *up* and I rose, leaving flaming footprints in the air as I ran forward. "I'm flying!" I shouted. "I'm flying!"

I threw my arms wide as if I were running on a racetrack. In seconds, I was embracing a tree with my face. People stopped to laugh. There were splinters in my nose. All I could breathe was wood. I crawled down the tree, about eight feet above the ground, and shook my head. "Learn," I muttered. "This is going to take a while, isn't it?"

"A few days," The Stone Preacher said. "You should consider yourself lucky. Most people don't get off the ground on their first try." He let out a grinding chuckle. "I think you should go upstairs and clean off before trying again." He added, almost conspiratorially. "And next time, you might want to try it in a place with no giant trees around."

The thought that I was better than most beginners consoled me. My second bath was quick. The next day, my journey would begin. It filled me with a secret thrill, as if there were magic in the world and all I needed was to be magical, too.

Chapter Four

The Knave of Carpenters and His Town of Wood

I walked down to dinner with new boots and a smile on my face, settling into a table by the fire. I should have felt hotter. There was a smooth, silky warmth all over my body. Bosquoverde was quick to attend to me. The Stone Preacher got up from a table where he was talking to something with two heads. His approach was solemn and fast.

"Where's the Organ Grinder?" I asked. "I don't see him."

"The Organ Grinder is out feeding his monkey," the Stone Preacher said sullenly. "The little beast, whom I would love to crush, craves his favorite little aperitifs. Since you have forbidden the monster to enter this establishment, he's outside. Do not let the filthy cur touch you."

"The monkey?"

"No, the Organ Grinder."

I laughed. "It was an honest question."

Bosquoverde interrupted me with a plate of steaming vegetables and unusual looking meat cubes. "Should I be scared?" The meat glared back at me with its purple, berrylike color. It smelled rich and musky, as though it had just been butchered.

"Not really. Every so often, a fantastic beast of some sort is slain, and its flesh is available at the market for a good price."

"What kind of fantastic beast was it?" I asked. "I usually like to know what I'm eating before I taste it."

"I believe it's manticore." The Stone Preacher said in his voice of gravel. "It smells awful raw, but if the right amount of heat is applied, it becomes most delicious."

I nervously poked the meat cube with a fork. The fork sank in. "A lot of people react this way when they are new," Bosquoverde chuckled. "It's often challenging to discover what can be eaten and what can't."

"Some of us would rather not discover what can't," I said coldly. "Around here, it really looks like that means that whatever it is, it's about to eat you."

"I shall not argue your point, since I am an unarmed innkeeper." Bosquoverde let out a subtle chuckle. "Already you prove that the most important part of a noblewoman is not her weapons or her magical boots, but rather, her wit. And your wit, though unrefined, is refreshing." He slipped away to perform the duties of innkeeper.

The Stone Preacher grinned. "You do learn quickly. A fine noble you will make, if we can keep you alive long enough to claim your prize."

"True love is a prize? There are times when I think it's like being kicked in the shins."

"It's a prize for us," the Stone Preacher said with a chuckle. "To have a patron whom you once protected, and who is now elevated above you in the world, such that favors of hospitality or necessity may be freely called upon is terribly important."

"So that's why you and the Organ Grinder keep spending so much time around me? You think I'll be able to do something for you when this romantic quest comes to an end?" I focused my gaze solely on the Stone Preacher, as if the Organ Grinder wasn't there.

"I think the Organ Grinder just wants to be between your legs, the way he is with every other woman, half woman, and monster he comes across. However, I loathe the sounds of his accordion music. You should endeavor to hate it, too."

My stomach turned. Thinking about the Organ Grinder rutting with all sorts of creatures on the dirty bed inside his cart made me lose a portion of my appetite. I had to stare at the manticore cubes for a little while and think it over before eating another.

"You shouldn't stare at your food," Bosquoverde said as he passed by.

"He mentioned the Organ Grinder," I responded. "It slows my appetite."

Bosquoverde glowered at the Stone Preacher. "If you did not spend time making the lady sick, perhaps she would have more energy."

"If I did not spend time making the lady sick, perhaps she would learn to feign sickness, as other noble ladies do."

"Why should I pretend to be sick when every time someone mentions the Organ Grinder, I get sick anyway?" I scowled. "It's bad enough he follows us around."

"To everything in the realm of my cruel gods of stone, there is a purpose," the Preacher said. "Perhaps there is a reason for him to be here. One that will arise, no doubt, when you least expect it."

"Do things really work like that here?" I demanded. "I refuse to bow to the will of some idiot's fairy tale plot!"

"That depends on whose story it is." Bosquoverde chuckled as the Organ Grinder thudded in through the door. "We should all pray that it isn't his." He looked to the Organ Grinder with a subtle glance. I looked up with a feigned pleasant smile.

***

"Ahh, my nameless lady," The Organ Grinder chuckled as he settled into a seat with a thud. "Do your pleasures need refreshing?"

"Not with you." I turned my face into a scowl.

"That is good." The Organ Grinder smiled. "Many resist my charms for centuries. I have a little book in which I keep their names, in case I need assistance."

"Truly, you're a disgusting man."

"I have no complaints." The Organ Grinder smirked unpleasantly. "I prefer to think of myself as prudent. There is, by the way, a gentleman outside who wishes to speak to you."

"Well, he should come in here," I said. "It's cold out there, and it's warm in here. What makes him think I should just go out there?"

"He calls himself the Knave of Carpenters. He says you should go outside and see him, or he'll cut down the whole town," The Organ Grinder sighed. "There is a price on your head, you know. You should take it far more seriously."

"Why didn't you send him in here?" I asked.

"Because, quite frankly, any one of these knavish bastards could be my knavish bastard, and as loathsome as you find me, I have certain scruples, and killing members of my own family is against my rules," He chuckled. "I wish there weren't so many of them."

"Well, perhaps you should control your urges, then." The Stone Preacher grimaced.

"He has twenty men," the Organ Grinder said to the Preacher. "You're only a match for six or seven of them, with perhaps five for me, and four for Bosquoverde." He glowered. "And the girl can't fight. Or at least, she's shown no ability to."

"And the town guard?" Bosquoverde's face turned curious.

"I haven't seen them, so they're either frightened or dead, or, the Duke of Bells wants to see what happens." The Organ Grinder smiled. "His lovely wife, so buxom and with a ruby smile," He sighed wistfully.

"I can fire a bow," I said. "I've just never fired one at a person."

"Ahh, fifteen and still unblooded." The Organ Grinder chuckled. "Do you have anything from your hunting days that the girl might use?" There was a bitter moment that longed for a reconciliation that would never come.

"And arrows, too." Bosquoverde said. "I'll go get them. Preacher, take her outside and see what the Knave wants. She'll have to negotiate this herself. It's not our place."

"You guys are serious. We're just going to kill twenty one people?" I looked at the little group of men as if they were insane.

"No one else is going to do it for us," Bosquoverde grumbled. "Besides, lass, he's threatened to cut down my inn, and that means there will be no coffee for you ever again."

The thought saddened me. "Wait a minute. Not your place?" I snapped. "You mean I have to actually negotiate with this freak myself?"

"We don't even know if he's a freak," Bosquoverde chortled.

"Yes we do," the Organ Grinder said. "He has a working lathe for a hand."

***

The Stone Preacher and I walked out of the door of Bosquoverde's inn and looked at the little group of men. They were fat, thin, and otherwise misshapen. They wore dirty leather aprons and had dirty faces. A collection of weapons that the cheapest of union bosses couldn't be proud of were in their hands. Even their shoes were old.

"May I ask to whom I have the pleasure of speaking?" A screeching voice from the back made its presence known with an edge to it like the chipping of wood.

"I am the Stone Preacher!"

I don't know where I summoned the courage, but I stepped in front and put my hands on the belt loops of my jeans. "Shush!" I glared out at the crowd of miscreants. "I'm Symantha, but that's Lady Symantha to you! Go home! Or I'll let him kill you!"

The screeching voice grew closer, rasping in the dark. A slender-shouldered figure with a barrel like gut oozed out of the shadows. He had male pattern-baldness, fringes of dark hair, and a long, beaky nose. A few of his teeth were missing, and he wore a vest that smelled of glue and wood. "Lady?" He squinted as he came into the light. A miniature lathe was built into the stump of his left hand. It gave a chilling grind as it whirred. "Well," He licked his lips. "Not yet. You'll bring us all titles and the pleasure of killing you, besides." His breath quivered on his lips, screeching as he spoke. "I am the Knave of Carpenters. The Duke of Bells would like to see you, but I do not believe that you should reach him alive. The Duke did not mention you being alive."

"Did he make fun of your hand?" I asked sweetly. "It's always a subtle pleasure to meet a man who only plays with his wood."

"A noble in the eyes, but not in speech, I see," The Knave of Carpenters chuckled. "I believe that you are worth your price. I shall wash your mouth with soap before you die."

The Stone Preacher remained silent, but let out a slight rumble.

"There are more than enough of us with picks and shovels to hack you apart." The Knave smirked. He licked his lips like someone about to eat. In the half darkness, I could see the lathe turn on his wrist. It made a little grinding sound, as if warming up. There were no members of the Watch anywhere. We were on our own.

"That may be, but I demand a day's courtesy to decide what to do," I smiled. "Or are you afraid to fight a little girl in a fair battle?"

"You?" The Knave of Carpenters sneered. "Battle me?" His lower lip twitched a little bit. "I'll tune your head as if it were wood, and leach and shape the skin from your skull if that's what you want!"

"Don't encourage him," the Stone Preacher rumbled.

"Well?" I raised my voice. "Hear ye! Oh, hear ye!" My voice thundered around the trees. "This fat, overweening, brazen coward believes that I, a poor, helpless innocent maid, am incapable of besting him in fair combat!" Several lights came on in the treelike windows. "If he really is serious, let's clear a space tomorrow, and sell some tickets, make an event of it, and have some money change hands! You all like money, right?"

The Stone Preacher made a rumbling noise that sounded as though he was choking. "You did not."

"Yes!" I grinned proudly. "Yes, I did." The Knave of Carpenters stared at me viciously as I turned my back on him, and he looked around, howling at the people staring out of their windows. "See you tomorrow, tradesman." I taunted him with the last word.

"Keening bitch!" the Knave snarled, his lips twisting up. "Tomorrow I'll sculpt your head into a bowl!"

The Stone Preacher stared in disbelief as I walked back towards the door of the inn. Even the Knave's men tried to hold him back from cutting me down. "That was very impressive." The Stone Preacher gave a gravelly smile as we stepped through the door. "You don't really intend to fight him, do you?" "Yeah," I smiled evilly. "I kinda do."

***

We gathered in my room, huddling there while the Knave of Carpenters was busy establishing temporary authority with the local townsfolk. Every so often, we heard the sounds of blubbering as someone else was brutally beaten. "So," I said as I flopped onto the bed, "Does anyone think I should actually fight this guy? We have a day to escape."

"Don't be ridiculous," the Stone Preacher said. "You called him out. If you run away now, you'll forever be a laughingstock. Legends build upon themselves, you know. Do you really want to be the Squire of Cowards, or the Whimpering Maiden?"

"I agree!" The Organ Grinder chortled. "You have to fight him now."

"Can't I just shoot him in the throat with arrows?" I asked. "It's not as if he's actually a noble or something."

"You could," Bosquoverde said. "It would give you a reputation as an unpleasant person, but I see no reason why not. He did threaten my inn, and possibly all hope of ever seeing a decent cup of coffee again."

"Well, then." I smiled. "You should endeavor to provide them with all the food and wine they want." I laughed a little bit. "Stuff them like geese, and cook your richest foods for them."

"They're swine!" Bosquoverde scowled at me. "Their culinary palates are no better than that of the Organ Grinder!"

The Organ Grinder laughed. "And they'll be the better for it!" He chortled. "Then they will realize the true value of biscuits and gravy!"

"Bosquoverde, think of it this way. They will be pleased in their last moments, and you will not have sent the wicked to their graves starving." I gave him a pleasant smile. "Now go, cook. It is what you do best, and I am eager to smell the results, if not to taste them."

"You aren't going to poison their food, are you?" the Stone Preacher asked. "I will not be a part of such a monstrous act."

"Why would I need to do that?" I was beginning to enjoy myself. "Bosquoverde, make sure they eat as much as possible." I let out a little sigh.

"What now?" The Organ Grinder asked. He had a luminous grin on his face as Bosquoverde made his way downstairs, heading for the kitchen.

"Now we wait." I chuckled a little bit. I was enjoying myself too much. "People who overeat and overdrink are not very good at putting up resistance." I settled back into the bed and closed my eyes. It was time to get some rest before the slaughter began.

***

The moon rose in the sky as we crept along the backs of trees. The little group of bandits had settled into a laughing circle. We stole out the back door of the inn, in search of their drunken laughter and wild, furious belching. The disgusting sounds they made could be heard all over town.

They had captured a few of the local beauties. Their screams and whimpers were louder than the laughter.

I was the smallest, so I peered around the corner of a tree. The group of bloated men was drinking ale and carousing with helpless women. Among the ladies was a very uncomfortable man in a dress, his wig starting to shift. Some people would sacrifice anything for their families, even their manliness. But in this world, spending eternity as the Man Who Wore Dresses was probably not the way I would want to be remembered. When everything is legend, sometimes it's better not to be noticed at all.

Several of them were sleeping on the ground, their bellies full. I looked about for the Knave of Carpenters in the darkness. I couldn't see him.

"Where is he?" the Stone Preacher hissed. "I yearn to crush these heretics."

"What exactly makes them heretics?" It really was a poor time to ask the question, just before killing them all in their sleep.

"They serve only their desires." The Stone Preacher said in a cold voice.

"So why haven't you killed the Organ Grinder?"

"The Organ Grinder is a part of the world, much as I am. As much as it would please me to kill him, he would have to commit graver sins."

"Let's go," Bosquoverde said. "We're wasting time."

***

They leaped out around the corner of the large tree, and one of the laughing men made an exhausted, wicked grunt. The Stone Preacher grabbed his throat and crushed it. I barely even saw him move. The fat body kicked and struggled in the granite grip, and blood began to leak out from under the edge of his mouth. There was no mercy here for anyone.

Bosquoverde brought a large kitchen knife out from under his apron, and charged a skinny, drunken man who was getting to his feet. He stabbed the thin man's chest over and over again. The kitchen apron grew wet with red.

I drew back Bosquoverde's hunting bow, and began firing arrows into the crowd of drunkards. Chests heaved with woozy terror below lips stained with vomit. On their chests, red circles blossomed around wooden points. Everything was screaming chaos and struggling bodies.

Into that chaos, the Organ Grinder sauntered, playing his accordion. The killing had only just started. He gave the two men who charged him a ruthless grin, dancing a few heavy steps as their weapons flashed in the darkness. Then he drew a blunderbuss out from under his leather greatcoat and fired the old gun with a wretched roar. It filled the air with powder and smoke. One of the men fell as the other closed in on him.

I fired another arrow into a man rising to his feet. He slammed downward, whimpering something. I didn't care what it was. I just wanted to survive. The Stone Preacher finished strangling his heavy burden. He charged a group of men who were getting to their picks and shovels, swinging the dead body like a weapon.

Bosquoverde leaped upon a man who had an arrow in his leg and slit his throat, yanking greasy hair back as more blood spattered over his apron. "For the lass!" he thundered. "We shall kill these carpenter boys and send them to their dirty mothers in shame!"

There was a gurgling screech. The knife-tailed monkey jumped from underneath the Organ Grinder's coat toward a hatchet wielding man. The diseased beast landed on the face of his attacker, stabbing at the man's throat with the tail knife. There was a thin red rain of droplets. The monkey hooted in triumph, licking the blood from its knife as the Organ Grinder tamped his blunderbuss down with powder. "Good work, my little pet!" The Organ Grinder smiled.

I fired more arrows into the clearing as the Stone Preacher began beating other men with the corpse of their friend. Wet thuds drummed through the clearing as the fat weight rose and fell in granite hands. Several of the men blubbered as the Stone Preacher beat them to death, his granite face locked in a merciless smile. The sobbing didn't stop from a thin body until long after it died.

Bosquoverde closed with a man who held an axe in one hand. An arrow already made one of his target's arms limp. The wounded man grabbed Bosquoverde by the beard, pulling it out from under his apron. Bosquoverde slashed with the knife and cut off his own beard, driving the knife into the man's chest. He staggered backward, bleeding. Bosquoverde drew out another crude implement, a frying pan shaped into the face of a hungry pig. "As pigs you are, with pigs you shall die!" he shouted. He brandished the iron pan, swinging it brutally into the face of another attacker, a man barely more than a boy. There was a wet crack as the pan connected. The youthful face spat out teeth.

I grinned and fired more arrows into the howling mass of people. They were starting to wake from sleep with cries of pain. I pinned one to the ground through his arm. He flopped while the Stone Preacher crushed him to death with the fat sack of flesh in his hand, now soft and bloody. A few braver men charged him with picks and shovels.

Bosquoverde's back was to a tree while two of the thugs thrust at him with crude farm implements. There was a gurgling howl as he bashed the frying pan against one of their hands. "Go home, lads! Go home! For I'll have more mercy for thee than the Organ Grinder or this granite priest!" His voice was thunder in the night. The lights of some tree houses flickered on. The dim glow of candlelight marked the passage of bandits into the next world.

Some of them ran. The Organ Grinder would have none of it. He and his monkey chased the fleeing men into darkness. I heard wailing, hard thumping sounds, and a vicious snap. The Organ

Grinder, shadowed in the roots of a massive tree, hurled a dead body into the clearing. The monkey twisted its fingers in a dead man's hair near the root of a tree. The tail-knife stabbed into the throat, head, and face. It beat and punched the dead man, licking blood from its tail knife.

"I think that's most of them," The Stone Preacher chuckled. "Did any of you see the Knave of Carpenters?"

We stepped into the clearing to search for the man with a lathe for a hand, our clothes covered in blood and the smell of death. We turned the bodies over one by one, searching the dead there in the light of the sun, which was coming up over the horizon. "Ahh, Tuggins!" a middle aged woman wailed from her tree house as the first few rays of the sun battered their way through the leaves. "It's me Tuggins! No! No! He promised me a new table, he did!" Her sobs rent the morning air. As I saw the wounds on the men, I staggered away from the carnage and bent over a large root.

I put the bow down and vomited up bile. My nose filled with the scent of blood and wood. My chest heaved for a few seconds.

"He's not here," Bosquoverde said, patting me gently on the shoulder. "The rat has fled, leaving his men to die. We shall see him again, I'm sure. Hopefully, lass, he won't be so brave as to try and take you on himself."

The wailing for Tuggins continued as we made our way back to Bosquoverde's.

Standing in front of the door, the Watch Captain was waiting for us with a squad of men. His arms folded as he looked us over in bloody garb. He smiled like a hyena.

***

"It seems that in your zeal to prove your nobility at court, you have slain a certain Mr. Tuggins!" The Watch Captain smiled again. It was more like a snake this time. "I despise you and all your visiting breed." He scowled. "Arrest them!"

The men did not move. One of them spoke. "Sir, we do not think that we can handle the innkeeper by himself, never mind that he's with that trenchcoated Organ Grinder and the Preacher of Stone." It was refreshing to see some cowardice.

Bosquoverde scowled at the Watch Captain/ I put my hand out. "Good Captain, Mr. Tuggins threw in his lot with a group of despicable bandits intent on procuring my head for display. I had no intention of giving it up to him and his band of cutthroats, so as far as my entourage is concerned, this was entirely self-defense. You should look no further than that."

The Watch Captain's face wrinkled unpleasantly. "The Duke of Bells shall hear of this." He gathered his men with a wave of his hand. "Come, then." They marched off toward wherever the guard post in town was.

"Yes!" The Stone Preacher ratcheted. "Run, heretics, lest I crush your bones and feed your meat to other corpses!"

The Organ Grinder began to creep off, a smirk on his face as the monkey hopped behind him. He idly fingered the keys of his accordion. "Where are you going?" I demanded.

The Organ Grinder's smirk grew wider. "If the Watch Captain is gathering his forces to report to the Duke of Bells, then his wife is unattended, and my cart is empty." He gave a little romantic sigh, and the monkey cooed.

"So what's going to happen to us because we killed Tuggins? Couldn't this Duke of Bells take it badly?"

"He might try to use it to his advantage," Bosquoverde said. "He's not particularly interested in harming you himself because that could cause him trouble. On the other hand, if one of his lackeys were to accidentally dispose of you, then he could wash his hands of the affair."

The Stone Preacher nodded. "He might try to have you killed in secret. The Knave of Carpenters might be his agent, albeit not a very smart one. You should not sleep alone."

The Organ Grinder grinned. "Leave that to me!" Bosquoverde clenched his fists and I turned to the Organ Grinder. "I would rather sleep with a pickaxe and a dead body."

The Stone Preacher shuddered.

"It should be you," Bosquoverde looked at the Stone Preacher. "I have an inn to run, and the Duke will not dare to move against me, lest his wife be deprived of my cooking on her special days. Besides, you have been doing this for a while now. She is still alive, so I know that she is safe."

"What do any of us really know about the Duke?" I asked. "Are we going to arrange to meet him? These people have a desire to do everything in a mannerly way, even when they're being murderous and nasty."

"We need to prepare you to be announced," Bosquoverde said. "The Organ Grinder and the Stone Preacher will teach you what you need to know. I'm just a humble innkeeper."

"So you say, anyway." I leaned the bow against the table. "What's for breakfast?"

***

Breakfast was raisin-flavored cornmeal cakes and a delicious potato soup. Although there was no coffee, there was spicy mulled cider that made it a wonder to behold. Even the Stone Preacher was forced to admit these were worth having.

Bosquoverde had just come back from the kitchen, and I had just finished my fifth cornmeal cake, when the door flew open. The Knave of Carpenters stood there, his leathers covered in dirt and grime. His teeth were gritted in anger. A little blood leaked out from under his lip. His voice was thunderous and wailing, like a large animal being tortured. "Bitch!" His shriek echoed across the tavern while patrons began ran for cover. "You and your cadre murdered my men in the dark! Like cowards!"

"A coward only deserves a coward's death. You proved your colors by running, and now your color is very dirty indeed."

Bosquoverde clapped. His smile broke out under the wide, thick beard. "Spoken like a true noblewoman." He let out a little chuckle. "We'll break you of your social class yet."

The Organ Grinder's monkey hooted, and leaped up on the table. It chittered furiously and slavered.

The Knave cocked his head in surprise. "What is that thing? It killed three of my best."

"It's my monkey!" the Organ Grinder proclaimed. "And he dances, too."

"I would encourage you to sit down and negotiate with us." I said as politely as I could. "I am prepared to compensate you for the death of your men, in exchange for your disappearance from this area and a promise not to be a bandit anymore."

The Knave laughed, and pulled a chair up close. The monkey hissed right in front of him, and the Organ Grinder shouted "Heel!" The monkey shrank back, the knave still within easy reach of its tail.

"What sort of deal were you thinking of cutting?" He leaned closer, his smile spreading as he put his hand on the chair. "I require food. I could be of great use to you, if you wished it."

Something in my stomach crawled. I could feel that he was lying. I broadened my smile. "That sounds like an interesting arrangement." I leaned towards him. "Tell me more."

I took my chance as his lathe hand rested quietly on the edge of the chair. I grabbed the Organ Grinder's monkey by its tail. While it screamed, I plunged the knife end deep into the eye of the Knave of Carpenters. He howled and clutched at his face as the monkey screeched, kicking and wailing. It tried to bite me.

Everything was happening too fast. I forced the lathe back towards the Knave's face and stabbed again, deep into the bloody eyesocket. The lathe whirred to life, ripping flesh and tearing the owner's skull. The Organ Grinder reached down for the hooting monkey. Blood streamed out all over the floor.

The Organ Grinder cooed and stroked the monkey, offering it the knife on the end of its tail to lick, I stared in horror as blood leaked out of the Knave of Carpenters head. Bosquoverde grimaced. The Stone Preacher clapped politely, the thunderous grind of stone on stone.

The Knave of Carpenters died as he had lived, all failed guile and malicious intent.

***

The few patrons in the room grew quiet. The monkey hissed from the hands of the Organ Grinder. "Impressive." There was a sardonic smirk on the Stone Preacher's lips. "I didn't think you had that in you. You may have noble blood in you after all. It took you less than four minutes to betray him. Hasty, to be sure, but I hardly think your impetuousness could be punished socially." He idly dabbed a napkin into a pitcher of water. "You should wash your hands. There's blood all over them."

Bosquoverde passed the napkin and handed it to me. I wiped and cleaned myself while I stared at the Knave's corpse. No one was touching the body. "It's all right, lass," he said quietly. "You're learning." He glared at the Organ Grinder. "The next time you bring that monkey in here, I will kill you myself and you will be carried out along with the leftovers."

"Don't," the Stone Preacher rumbled. "Someone might eat him."

"Someone clean this thing up!" I shouted. It was one thing to kill someone from far away with arrows. It was another to do it with a knife up close while a crowd stared, like it was a show under the big top.

Two peasants leaped up from a table and carried the body off. The lathe hand thudded against the floor. I grimaced and sat back down, staring and shaking. The lathe hand ripped off when the door closed, lying on the floor of the inn, wet and bloody.

Bosquoverde got up from the table, and shouted to his servers. "You, there, wenches! Clean this place, and let no trace of blood contaminate this place of dining! And someone get that machine hand out the door."

I raced for the back door, hurtling through the kitchen without so much as a word, and grabbed a thick root of the tree. I dry heaved for half an hour. No one came outside. It was as if everyone was already over the whole wicked business, and my feelings didn't matter.

***

When I came back in, the place was empty, except for Bosquoverde, the Organ Grinder, and the Stone Preacher. "Did the watch come?" I was a little nervous.

"I told them the lady was out in back, but that her health was in question," Bosquoverde said. "Everyone is saying how brave you were."

"I was scared. There was nothing brave about it. My life is worth more than some pile of gold half-lunas." I protested. "I'm sorry about the monkey." The monkey hissed at me. I wasn't sorry. The little beast knew.

The Organ Grinder gave me a wicked smile and patted the stone knife at his belt. "All things come around in time." He gave a throaty chuckle. Bosquoverde clenched his fist.

"You should be more careful," the Stone Preacher said to the Organ Grinder. "It's a poor thing to threaten someone who is both a murderer and a hero, except to Goodwife Tuggins, who no doubt has it in her mind to butcher this poor young thing."

"Is murder on everyone's mind here?" I asked. "We killed a lot of people. We had to, or they were going to kill us, but is this really the way of the world around here?"

"In moments of tension, sometimes, yes." The Organ Grinder grinned. "That is why I am careful to acquire favors from every noble lady who spends the night in my cart, for there is none better at the bedding of noblewomen than myself." He chuckled. "Of course, the magical accordion helps."

"You enchant them?" I scowled. "You're just a rapist! That's all!"

"Actually," the Organ Grinder said, "not all of them are pretty. Sometimes I have to use it on me."

I shuddered. There was something equally disgusting about seducing oneself with accordion music to sleep with ugly women. Every time I saw the Organ Grinder, I really thought I might be looking at the most disgusting creature alive. I had already met monsters, half-insane fencepost carvers, and creatures that tried to kill me. "That's not very reassuring."

The Stone Preacher raised his glass as the blood was wiped from the floor. "I consider it a great reassurance that this carpenter's knave has passed on. It was inevitable that you were going to kill someone face to face," he said in reverent tones. "It might as well have been him."

Bosquoverde shook his head. "How can you say such things? Can't you see she's bothered by the taking of lives?"

"That only makes her killings all the more precious in this world." The Organ Grinder's face brightened. "As the progress of loss continues, the more profoundly she will be affected."

"Why are you helping me then, except to savor my misery?" I asked the Organ Grinder.

"That's a fair question." The Organ Grinder thought about it. The monkey gave a gurgling screech from under his coat. "Perhaps I simply wish to be the first to bed you after you grow tired of your husband." He cackled madly and shouted "Bosquoverde, ale! I shall have you at arm's length the day after!"

Bosquoverde plunked a large mug down in front of the Organ Grinder. "The sooner you are in a drunken stupor, the sooner the rest of us will be rid of your warped philosophy."

The Organ Grinder simply laughed again. "The sooner I am in a drunken stupor, the sooner I shall care less about who my accordion seduces." He stroked the monkey underneath his greatcoat. It made a satisfied hooting noise.

"Whatever reservations the young lady may have about voicing her opinions," The Stone Preacher rumbled. "I assure you that I have no compunction, Organ Grinder, about telling you how disgusting you are. If you were not needed, I would snap your neck and hang you from a gibbet with your corrupting phallus pickled in a jar."

"Could you not be so medieval about your punishments?" I asked the Stone Preacher. "No offense, but that's really gross."

"You shouldn't blame him," Bosquoverde said. "Almost everyone's medieval here. I'm almost as medieval, but I have a touch of the modern about me. After all, coffee doesn't come from nowhere." He winked surreptitiously.

"I think we need to visit the Duke of Bells," I said seriously. "None of this is going to end until we see him. I'm tired of people trying to kill me."

"Are we abandoning our quest for the source of the joy in your heart?" The Organ Grinder asked. "It would be my pleasure to give you a reason." He took a massive gulp of ale and belched savagely.

The Stone Preacher grabbed the Organ Grinder by the shoulder and squeezed. A grimace broke out under the thick beard and mustache. "Stop," the Preacher said. "Now! Or your arm comes off at the shoulder."

The Organ Grinder nodded. The monkey climbed out of his coat. It jumped up and down on the wounded shoulder with a nasty smile.

"It's just a detour. I don't want to have to go on this journey with some mad, bell-shaped noble making loud clanging noises and chasing me with his army."

"Practical." Bosquoverde chuckled. "I shall endeavor to clean up after your terrible mess, and to tell the story of your adventures here. I will not come with you."

"Why not? You're the only one I trust out of the three of you." I was desperate for Bosquoverde's company.

"There is a dressmaker fifty miles from here, whom you must see if you wish to make an appropriate appearance at the court of the Duke of Bells," Bosquoverde said. "But I cannot leave my inn behind. You are not the only one I make supper for."

"I could command it, and you would have to go," I tapped my eye gently.

"And I could refuse, and you would have to punish me." Bosquoverde grinned.

"But who will feed me?" I gave him my best piteous look. I knew I wasn't going to have very good food for a while.

"I will pack you a basket filled with all manner of smoked meats and sandwiches. It will be as if I had made them myself." He grinned. "I have a smoker in the basement. It is simply not the season for using it."

"Thank you," I grumbled. "I guess we'll travel in your cart." I said to the Organ Grinder. "Don't get any ideas, or I'll have the Stone Preacher kill you."

"Very well." The Organ Grinder sighed. "As pretty as you would look with your eyes rolled back into your skull and your lips stained with my desire."

I slapped the Organ Grinder in the face. He broke into a smile. "That's how it always starts." He chuckled. The monkey licked its lips, as if it had drawn some pleasure out of the slap.

The Stone Preacher sighed and looked at me. "You still have a lot to learn, young lady."

We spent the rest of the day in quiet contemplation of Bosquoverde's many fine foods, and, stuffed to the gills, we all staggered to sleep, preparing to leave early in the morning.

***

I awoke before the sun came up, dreaming of leeks, lentils, and the meat of some creature I didn't recognize in a burgundy wine sauce. After washing and drying my feet, I put on my new boots. I was looking forward to practicing outside of town, where I couldn't set anything on fire or burn anything down.

The Stone Preacher rumbled up, still sitting in the other bed. "Are you ready to go?" he said in his usual grind of rock on rock.

"Not quite." I heard some weird animal's coughing sounds from outside. "What's that?"

"It's probably the Organ Grinder, hooking up his horses to the cart. You must understand that even though his beasts breathe acid and look a little rancorous, they are never in the best of health, and he treats the poor creatures terribly." The Stone Preacher shrugged. "It is his nature, much like the wind or the sun."

"Is everyone and everything around here weird?"

"This is a world of legends about ordinary things." The Stone Preacher sighed. "It is complicated, and never fully understood. You should finish bathing."

It was the first time I had ever seen the Stone Preacher bothered about anything He turned his back while I bathed.

I didn't ask him any more questions then. I should have.

***

We came down to breakfast. Our table was filled with various foods. Bosquoverde had prepared a meal that would take two hours to eat. There was another roast, similar to the roast from the previous night, but in a lighter sauce filled with spicy capers.

Bosquoverde folded his arms over his apron in the kitchen doorway. My smile was as wide as the moon. "Do you like it? I worked all night on it."

I didn't even answer him. I ran to the table and began eating. "Thank you!" I managed between bites. "Thank you so much." I was as dainty as possible. Overwhelmed by the sheer amount of food, it was difficult to decide what to eat.

The Stone Preacher sat down next to me. "I think she is pleased." He nodded with a little satisfaction. "And I must say, I believe I shall eat a portion of that roast."

Bosquoverde walked over. "It is the least I could do for one who brings such joy to my life. Much like my own dear daughter, who wandered into the eastlands and never returned."

"You may still see her again." The Organ Grinder chuckled. "You should probably find her before I do." He stood in the doorway with a wicked leer, the diseased, knife-tailed monkey hopping up and down near his thick boot. He clumped over to the table, pausing to sweep the monkey out through the door. It rolled about in the dirt, screeching as the door slammed.

Bosquoverde's face changed to a glower. "You should eat, sir." I was filling myself so full that I only half heard the conversation. My goal was to preserve his picnic basket for later, and savor the sandwiches and meats inside as much as possible.

The Organ Grinder looked at the huge, heaping plates of food, and settled in. His plate was shortly piled with various things. Like me, he was looking to eat two or three meals in one sitting. "I should, indeed," he said with a wry grin. "Oh, you don't have to worry about your Tuggins problem anymore."

I almost spit up my roast. "I didn't need to know that." I said between bites. "Could you stop doing that while you travel with us? I think I feel a little queasy."

The Organ Grinder smiled. "It is not my fault that so many ladies desire my touch, or the music of my accordion."

Bosquoverde sighed and went back into the kitchen. He came out with a large picnic basket and placed it next to my table. "I have also prepared for you a second roast, which is wrapped in wax paper at the bottom of the basket. You should eat it within the first two days. You should also be wary, for the basket itself has a touch of magic about it, and it is not always friendly."

"An evil picnic basket?" I said between bites of cornmeal pudding. "Thanks. I see you're glad to be rid of us. What does it do?"

"I don't really know," Bosquoverde said. "I know that I received it from a man who told me that one day, I should send a girl on a journey with it." He winked. "My guess is, that would be you."

"Do those things happen all the time around here?" I shook my head. I was far too into my face-stuffing to really care about the picnic basket one way or the other.

"As a matter of fact, yes, they do." Bosquoverde smiled.

The rest of the meal was mostly the sounds of eating. I stayed behind briefly to give Bosquoverde a hug while the Organ Grinder unhitched the cart. The Stone Preacher kept a watchful eye on him.

"Take care, lass," Bosquoverde said. "I trust that your journey to the dressmaker should not be eventful."

"That sounded almost like you were saying it with your fingers crossed." I grinned. "Can I keep the bow? Just in case?"

"I have no use for it," he said with a grin. "After all, even the most foolish of adventuresses should not go unarmed." He walked back into the kitchen and returned with the bow, along with a fresh quiver of arrows.

"I'll see your cooking again, right?" I asked as I made for the door. I shouldered the picnic basket. It was too full of good food not to take.

"At least until the basket is empty." Bosquoverde returned to the work of taking care of his other patrons.

When I got outside, the bloated, heaving form of Goodwife Tuggins exited the cart. As we got up on it and the Organ Grinder cracked the reins, she gave him the most romantic of hideous, gap-toothed smiles. The Stone Preacher walked alongside, the withered, almost skeletal horses lumbering their way through town.

As we rode out, I thought I heard the monkey chitter from under the Organ Grinder's coat, but it turned out to be only the creaking of the wheels.

The road stretched out before us, a sinuous monster, and the rising sun troubled me with its angry light.

Chapter Five

The Priest of Gears and His Clockwork Temple

Our cart wound along the road, and it was almost noon when the Organ Grinder called a halt, pulling the cart to the side of the road. He rested the horses. "I was informed that I was not to mistreat the horses in your presence." He grinned at me, his smile wide. "Bosquoverde insisted, or he would feed my kidneys to the pets of his patrons."

"What exactly went on between you and him? It must be pretty bad for you to gloat all the time and for him to be angry all the time."

"It was his wife and his daughter." The Organ Grinder sighed. "Such lovely lasses, so pretty and ripe. And at the same time too." He gave a pleasant little sigh. "His wife, alas, moved to a church, I know not which one, and his daughter ran off into the eastern wilderness to do as I do with the barbarians and the Sword Hounds."

"What's a Sword Hound?" I asked.

"They're five foot dog people who use swords and are proud of it," he said. "Let us open your basket, and see what is for lunch."

"Right," I said. "Are they as vicious and evil as everything else around here?"

"I don't know," the Organ Grinder said while the Stone Preacher opened the picnic basket. "I'm not attracted to Sword Hound women."

I shuddered. I didn't want to think about Bosquoverde's daughter hacking about with some dog people in the wilderness. I settled down by the side of the road and opened up the picnic basket. Inside was a blanket, a heap of sandwiches wrapped in paper, smoked meats, and a big bowl filled with chutney. I spread out the blanket and removed items from the basket. The Stone Preacher studied the sandwiches. "They do not amuse me." His voice was hollow. He turned to stand guard while the Organ Grinder and I ate.

From under the Organ Grinder's cloak, the monkey crept towards the basket. I thought I might be able to stop it, but the thought of being stabbed by the knife-tail kept me from reaching out. "How now?" the Organ Grinder said. "You are a fast learner, my dear. You would learn faster if you spent some time in the back of my cart with me, however, we all have different tastes."

While I was distracted, the monkey reached into the picnic basket and fumbled inside it. There was a sudden snap. With a wicked screech, the monkey withdrew his hand. There was a wet ring of blood around its wrist. The picnic basket chomped a little bit, as if satisfied. Clutching its wrist, the monkey ran back under the Organ Grinder's cloak.

"That didn't look particularly friendly." The Stone Preacher seemed amused, yet satisfied. "Although I do not eat, I believe it was definitely worth stopping for lunch."

The Organ Grinder scowled and pulled some bandages out of his greatcoat pocket. H spoke soothing words to the monkey while he cleaned and dressed the wound. I couldn't help myself. I ate four sandwiches, oblivious to the monkey's pain. "You don't seem pained at all by the injury to my monkey, even though the presence of his tail, however illicit, saved your life." He adjusted his monocle.

"I'll be honest. He's disgusting," I said. "I thought I'd have to wash my hands for a month after I touched it."

"You are not alone in your assertion," the Organ Grinder said with a wry chuckle. "But many come to love my monkey as an ordinary pet after a night in my cart. No doubt, you too will one day see such wisdom."

"I'd rather sleep with a chainsaw." I looked over to the Stone Preacher, who nodded grimly. The look on his face told me that he had no idea what a chainsaw was.

The Organ Grinder sighed. "You will not console me, even though my monkey is wounded?" Under the greatcoat, I heard an animalistic whine. It was the only animal I'd never felt pity for when hurt.

That was when the picnic basket growled. An odd hiss, like the whispering of wind came from inside it. "Do you want to know?" I asked the Stone Preacher, eyeing the basket.

"There are some things that even my cold stone god cannot answer," the Stone Preacher whispered, his voice making chiseling sounds. "As long as you are capable of reaching into the basket without getting hurt, I do not particularly care to know what goes on inside it, wounded monkey or no wounded monkey."

The Organ Grinder moved back from the basket, eating his sandwich as if his monkey hadn't been harmed in the slightest. "I'm going to practice with my boots now." I walked further off the road. "I can't afford to get fat."

"There aren't many fat nobles," the Organ Grinder said. "But I don't have to use my accordion on myself all that often."

I launched myself into the air as the boots flamed to life.

It was almost like running. I climbed upward, leaving burning footprints, and circled around a little copse of trees. I was careful not to touch the leaves with the boots. I didn't want to accidentally burn the forest down. This was a vengeful world. I didn't want vengeful things coming to kill me.

I raced back in a burning sprint. I could smell smoke as my footsteps hit air. It was the most wonderful feeling; gracefulness and smooth warm heat rolled into one. I landed in a rush of burning footprints, and scarred the landscape. My landing was wobbly. I staggered and limped back to the picnic site. The Stone Preacher was waiting next to the basket. The Organ Grinder was already seated on his cart.

"Are you all right?" The Stone Preacher asked. I staggered to pick up the basket. "You look a little hurt." From under the Organ Grinder's cloak, the monkey stuck its diseased face out.

"No problem." I grinned. "I'm fine. I'm getting the hang of the flying boots and all. Why didn't you put the picnic basket in the cart?"

"Absolutely not," the Stone Preacher said. "The Organ Grinder refuses to touch it, and so do I. I don't know what it does, or what it can bite." He looked grimly down at the picnic basket on my arm. "Be careful that it does not eat you."

As we got into the cart and made our way down the road, clopping sounds of the horses battered dirt. When we reached a bend in the road, there was a slight lurch in the wagon.

I thought I heard the picnic basket coo.

***

We drove the cart for a while longer. The cold began to batter the Organ Grinder slightly as he drove the horses on. He wrapped his greatcoat around himself. The wind whipped up. "It might rain, or snow." The monkey made an angry squeak under the coat.

"What does it rain or snow around here?" I asked him, since the Stone Preacher was walking alongside the cart, his gaze staring out at the world, untroubled by the weather.

"Usually, water." the Organ Grinder said. "Sometimes blood, if the Duke of Chirurgeons is in a particularly bad mood, or poison, if the Countess of Apothecaries is having a tantrum."

"When was the last time it rained poison?" I asked. "No offense, you understand, I just want to be prepared. How did people survive?"

"We're not in her lands, but most of her people poison themselves regularly. If she has a tantrum, visitors tend to die, and their goods are distributed amongst her people. She's really terribly nice. She has the most beautiful almond eyes."

"Is everything all about your disgusting conquests?"

"Don't be silly." The Organ Grinder chuckled. "If nothing else, at least my conquests mean that I am well-traveled," He gave me a nasty wink. "Perhaps one day you, too, will spend time with your legs spread for the Organ Grinder."

The Stone Preacher drew alongside and scowled at the Organ Grinder. "It seems I always hear you when you are at your most vile." The Organ Grinder once again focused on the road.

"Thanks." I waved to the Preacher. "What's that?"

Up ahead was a massive building built of thick black basalt. Crude towers stretched skyward above a thick blocky shape. Smoke and steam poured from a couple of windows. There was an unusual hissing, the sound of hot metal and grinding machines. "That is the temple of the Priest of Gears," he said with a sigh. "He actually worships the concept of Deus Ex Machina, and is constantly trying to build him."

"He worships a god who he's trying to build? Everyone needs a hobby, I guess." I stared at the black building. "We don't have to stay outside. It'll be warm in there. Let's visit."

The Stone Preacher looked at me with a grinding smirk. "I was actually rather hoping you would say that. We will reach your dressmaker tomorrow, I suppose."

"Don't kill him!" There was fury in my voice. "We killed so many people yesterday, my head spins to think of it." The nobility act was becoming a little less of an act. It worried me in the pit of my stomach that, somehow, this place was becoming a part of me.

The Organ Grinder gave a deep chuckle, drove the cancerous horses towards the massive building, and tethered them at a small metal post in its shadow.

***

We left the cart behind and made our way towards the massive basalt doors. They opened with a dull mechanical noise, without any of us knocking or asking to be let in. Standing in the doorway were two men, covered in sweat and dressed in heavy leather aprons. They wore thick leather boots and gloves. Hairy faces and pockmarked skin spoke of long hours of hard work around high heat. "I bid you greetings. I am Brother Click, and this is Brother Clack."

"Should I be concerned? These guys are the doormen, right?"

"We shall participate in the great building. When our god comes to life, he will be magnificent." Clack said.

The Organ Grinder turned to the Stone Preacher. "Heretics?"

"How can they be heretics?" the Stone Preacher said. "They haven't built their god yet."

"I am Symantha, and this is my entourage," I said gently. "We would request lodging for the evening, if you would be so kind."

The two portly men chuckled and bowed. "We shall inform the Sisterhood of Symmetry of your coming," Clack said. "They will take your request to the Vicar of Interconnection, and he will inform the Priest of Gears."

"Couldn't you just use a phone?" I asked.

"A phone?" Click asked.

"Never heard of it," Clack responded. "You must be new."

The Stone Preacher turned to me. "Many of the tools of your modernization are anathema to the residents here. To hear a noble speak of it so has probably shocked them."

"Indeed," Click and Clack responded. The looks on their faces were bitterly malevolent.

"Come in." Click said. He mopped some sweat from his forehead. Clack ran off to inform the Sisterhood of Symmetry, whatever they were. I had learned not to assume that anything here was entirely human.

The three of us went inside. The doors ground shut behind us. "An engineering marvel." Brother Click chuckled. "The vibrations of your footsteps trigger a reaction, which opens the door if it's closed, and closes it if it's open."

"They're building a god of engineering? Won't that bring technology and all the other things that you said people thought were bad?" I directed my question to the Stone Preacher, away from Brother Click's ears. It was difficult to be heard over the noise of the temple.

"I am not sure," the Stone Preacher said. "You can never be sure how things will turn out. It could have a glorious ending, but more than likely something bittersweet will happen."

"You mean like 'cars are cool, but there's pollution?'"

"I don't really know what you're talking about. But if that is a way for you to understand what happened, I am certain that there is a reason for it."

The Organ Grinder laughed out loud. "Everyone has their own means of understanding."

"Ahh, the famous Organ Grinder." Brother Click bowed. "If it would not be too much, sir, perhaps you could breathe a little life into our Sisterhood?"

"He's not breathing anything on anyone," I said sternly to Brother Click. "I'm not indulging his greasy whims while he travels with me."

"A true lady," Brother Click bowed again. "At least until he gets his hands on you." He smiled a little bit under his breath as Brother Clack returned.

Brother Clack bowed, beginning to move off. "This way. I will take you to a waiting room while the Sisterhood informs the Priest of Gears."

Brother Click sighed. "So I get to watch the door again?"

None of us responded. Brother Clack motioned as he guided us through a massive hallway. Basalt resonated with the noise of heavy, primitive machines. The noises alternately damped and boomed like thunder.

A heavy stone door shaped like a circle rumbled open. We stepped inside.

The room was dull and bland. Heavy metal books bound with iron rings settled on a stone slab, along with a stone pitcher. Several wooden chairs were haphazardly arranged around the table.

Brother Clack stepped back and the door closed automatically, with a slow, rolling thud. Then the sounds were muffled enough that we could speak. "Are we trapped here?" I asked.

"I don't think so," the Organ Grinder said. "I've never been here before, but this looks like a waiting room."

The Stone Preacher rumbled. "This Priest of Gears has always been reputed to be something of a bureaucrat. Now I find he is also something of a dull host. Let us see what books he has."

The Organ Grinder gave a lewd smile while I sat in a chair and folded my arms. It was becoming amusing to see the verbal duels between the two of them. "I hope it is erotica," He said. "That would be a priest after my own taste."

"Your own tastelessness, you mean," the Stone Preacher countered.

The Organ Grinder picked up one of the two books and opened it. "Dreadful." He said. "It is nothing but numbers."

The Stone Preacher glided about the room before settling on the other book. "They are the same. An incomprehensible religion is the same as one which is fully understandable, to be sure, but to what end does this Priest of Gears think we will be served by numbers and formulae?"

I walked over to the book the Organ Grinder put down and flipped it open. I stared at the formulae and numbers and settled back in my chair. "I don't know. It's like a big math project, or their prayer book, or something."

"If this is a prayer book, I am the King of Trees," the Stone Preacher grumbled.

The stone door ground open, and Brother Clack returned. He was a little cleaner, as if he had taken some time to wash his face. "The Sisters of Symmetry will see you now," he said. "Have you read our prayer books?" He indicated the two books lying on the stone table.

"I see the King of Trees is among us," I teased the Stone Preacher. "Perhaps if the Organ Grinder made obeisances to you, you would have a kingdom sooner than you think."

"Your wit is amusing." The Stone Preacher growled. "But do not test me, or you shall find accordion music between your ears soon enough and the Organ Grinder between your legs soon after."

"This way." Brother Clack turned and headed from the room. I shuddered as the door closed behind us. The booming noise echoed through the massive temple. Somewhere above us, voices rose in eerie, mechanical song.

***

We passed several worshippers along the way to the Sisterhood's chambers. Their feet were covered in heavy boots and leather aprons. Some of them carried metal basins filled with molten glass, copper, or other metals. Tongs in their hands, which they used to hold the basins, were red with heat.

We made our way into a huge room. Heavy, grinding chimes moved automatically on gears overhead. Gargantuan black basalt pillars supported the vaulted ceiling. They were probably carved from the same massive piece of rock. The room was walled with stone bas-reliefs of primitive wheels, pulleys, and other machines. On the back wall there were two large depictions of interconnected gears, connected to a massive, engraved construct of a vaguely humanoid shape in the center. A few hallways led off into darkness. I didn't want to know where they went.

"What's that?" I whispered. Two female figures stepped around a pillar, their bodies covered in reddish purple robes, their faces hooded.

"That's their god," the Stone Preacher murmured. The female figures glided forward, a kind of unearthly, mechanical beauty in their stride. "I would suggest avoiding blasphemy. These ladies are not door servants."

The two women spoke as one, as if they had been trained. Their grace and etherealness told me they might not be women at all. "We are the Sisterhood of Symmetry. We greet you in the name of the Priest of Gears." They gave wicked little bows, almost too full at the waist. Their arms gracefully extended, as if it were impossible to curtsy.

"This is the Stone Preacher, and this is the, uhm, legendary Organ Grinder, and I'm Symantha, who might be nobility if I live." I tried to return the bow. I almost threw out my back.

"We are not unaware of your station to be," the women intoned. They deliberately inserted clicks and clacks into their speech, as if it were part of their daily behavior, an affectation trained to the point where it had become habit. "The Priest of Gears wishes you to pass a test if you are to see him, if you wish to be deemed worthy of gazing upon the great machine god."

"Great. He's building a giant calculator and wants us to worship it," I grumbled. "Pocket protectors be praised."

The Stone Preacher nudged me. It felt as if I had been punched by an elephant. The Organ Grinder just kept his smile turned to the faces of the two women, his fingers idly drifting towards the keys of his accordion.

"We do not understand your strange comment. But we understand it may be blasphemy. Blaspheme not the machine god." Hoods turned in perfect unison. My skin crawled.

"What kind of test is this?" I asked. "Is it something the nobility have to endure?"

"Numbers do not distinguish between noble and common. Our purpose is so great that tax collectors and kings alike obey our power. The Priest of Gears serves this holy cause."

The Stone Preacher's face twisted in confusion, as if he didn't know what to do.

"You shall travel the Clockwork Maze. If you live, we shall greet you at its height, and take you to see the Priest of Gears."

"Why is everyone always trying to kill us around here?" I asked the Organ Grinder.

"You won't let me sleep with them," the Organ Grinder said with a sarcastic smirk. "This is your fault."

The two unusual nuns glided over to one of the hallways and gestured politely with another of their elegant bows. I didn't return it this time. We made our way toward the long dark hall. I heard the sound of clockworks hammering away. It felt as though all the steel and rock in the world battered at my ears, threatening to crush me.

***

The corridor was dark and cruel. The loud noises grew as we walked. There was a rush of air above our heads. It trickled through my hair, making my neck shiver. The hallway was lit by strange greenish lamps that made the Organ Grinder seem paler and slightly more vicious. The lights made the Stone Preacher look ominous and cruel. They kept me in between them, the Organ Grinder in the front and the Stone Preacher in the back.

The two nuns followed us with their unusual gliding walk. "It seems you are determined to keep the Organ Grinder away from the girl," they said in their lilting unison.

The Stone Preacher turned his granite head. "It suits my purposes to do so," he said with thick tones.

The two nuns giggled, and cast a cryptic glance at the Organ Grinder. "And him?"

"I will not stop you from sullying your faith with the Organ Grinder." There was a grim cadence in the Preachers voice. "But it pleases me to know that even the Organ Grinder may have reached his limit with the two of you."

The Sisterhood giggled, a high pitched titter that seemed to make the greenish light waver. We emerged into the light of a high, vaulted room filled with clockwork madness. "We will stay outside." They said it in unison, though one of them tilted their head.

Gears moved and ratcheted, extending outward and moving in synergies that I could only begin to figure out. Up near the top of the arch was a small corridor-like exit, mirrored with light that shone down over the massive array of clockworks, and swinging platforms. "And we have to go up there?" I asked. "You know, we don't have to meet him."

"What makes you think we have a choice?" the Stone Preacher asked. "It is expected for one of your station to make the journey. Fear not. We will go first. As your guides, we are bound to precede you through the deadly maze." He bowed with a grinding crunch, and his cassock shuddered.

"What do you mean, 'we'?" The Organ Grinder asked. "Should it not be you alone, Preacher? I can avail myself of these two fine—"

I cut him off. "Nay, Sir Organ Grinder." I scowled, letting my lips drip with sarcasm. "If we go, you go."

"Oh, so it's Sir Organ Grinder now, is it?" he teased me, as if he found it amusing. "Will you make me your knight of rutting?"

"Just go." My stomach turned again. "And go first. I'm certain the Preacher can make it up." I put my hands on my hips and waited for the Organ Grinder to move to the first gear. It slithered about and ratcheted in fury, leading off into empty space. I had a plan, but it could kill me.

The Organ Grinder blew me a slurping kiss as he stepped onto the gear. The mass of clockworks began to turn. The Sisterhood of Symmetry giggled between leaps as he vaulted and ran over the gears. A sliding platform swung by him and he jumped for it, bouncing off it to cascade to another gear, which carried him upward, graceful and smooth. He was far more physically capable than he let on. From under his coat, the loathsome cries of the monkey resonated between the grinding clockworks.

"He is good," the Stone Preacher chuckled. "It's easy to see how so many women would wish to spend the night in his cart, even if he is loathsome."

"Why are you laughing?" I asked. "It's like you don't care about any of the things he does, and only protect me because you want something."

"All things come to me in the end," the Stone Preacher rumbled. "Either by my hand or by the hand of another."

The Organ Grinder barely dodged a too-low platform. His teeth gritted as he was knocked down by a clanking piece of machinery. The monkey wiggled under the greatcoat. The powerful legs of his master vaulted up, catching a rope that seemed to lead nowhere, and swung to another rotating gear, which carried him easily toward the exit. He bowed, refined in victory, and slipped through the opening.

"It's your turn," the Stone Preacher said to me, his gravelly smile making a slow crackle.

"I must insist that you go first," I said coyly. "I am a lady, after all." The Stone Preacher bowed and turned towards the abyssal opening of clockworks without another word. He leaped onto the first gear, and it clanged with his massive weight. His rocky body rippled, as if momentarily finding its balance, moving up with a savage noise that sounded like an avalanche.

He thudded onto the first gear and rotated around, vaulting upward with a great rumble. He grabbed the platform and swung, leaping upward as he stretched his legs. His cassock groaned, and he tumbled through the air, landing on one of the rotating cogs. He dodged a pendulum that must have been sharp-edged. I couldn't tell whether the Stone Preacher could feel pain.

There was a clacking sound. The Stone Preacher glided up the metal edge of the gear, and leaped through the air to land on another one, which rotated downward. He struggled up to the top of the cog, and jumped to the next, which spun beneath another whirring, sharp pendulum. "Can those things cut him?" I asked the two nuns behind me.

"I do not know," one of the nuns said. "But he is not nearly as attractive as the Organ Grinder." They gave twin romantic sighs.

I felt sick. There was no sign of the Organ Grinder from the hole near the ceiling. The Stone Preacher stretched his granite legs from the top of one of the gears and leaped, passing through the hole. The booming crash echoed through the entire chamber as he landed.

The Sisterhood of Symmetry turned to me. "It is your turn, Lady Symantha." The two of them giggled. Their laughter was drowned in the whirr and grind of the gears, but I simply smiled, ran forward, and my boots licked to life with roaring flame.

There was a shrieking gasp from the two nuns as I raced upward through the gears, dodging one of the swinging, razored, pendulums. I left hot, flickering footprints in the air, trailing dissipated wisps of smoke. My breath grew ragged as a grinding mass of cogs passed by me. I ran for the hole, the fierce clatter of machines in my ears whirring and dimming knowledge of my surroundings.

I dove upwards, passing over a pendulum as it swung back towards me. The scything blade rushed beneath me as I hurtled into the opening. I staggered towards the lip and fell short, grabbing the edge as I smashed into it. The Stone Preacher reached out for my hand and pulled me up. Behind me, a gear stained with red blood, a little matted hair and skin ground against the wall as my boots slid past the edge.

"That wasn't so bad, was it?" the Organ Grinder said. "See? My twin escorts come to me even now." A wicked smile crossed his features, as the Sisterhood leaped onto the gears, moving like mantises. Their habits billowed out, cloaking them in their own grace.

They vaulted and hopped across the gears like insects, sensing each motion and movement of the cogs as though they did this every day, completely in tune with their surroundings. They danced together and apart, graceful and sinuous, until they joined us at the exit.

"You have passed the test of the maze." Their voices were pleasant. Their lips clicked with music. "Now, we will offer you refreshment." They glided past us and down a narrow hall, from which strange chiming music emanated.

***

The two nuns led us down a hall to another sitting room, and they graciously poured us water in cool wooden cups. There were a few chairs haphazardly strewn about the room, and a table upon which the pitcher rested. "Please relax." Their dual voices were soothing, and one of them glided about the room, passing us our cups.

I moved to sit. The Organ Grinder did, too. The Stone Preacher remained standing, out of respect for the chair. I sipped my water, leaning back as I kept my eyes on the two nuns. I was nervous about drinking. It could have come from any number of pools, or been part of a magical enchantment or potion. "So tell me," I smiled to the Sisterhood as the Organ Grinder ogled his potential conquests. "Why does this Priest of Gears hide above a deathtrap?"

"Our Priest of Gears has many enemies," The nuns of the sisterhood intoned. "Not all enjoy or are pleased by the body-altering methods of our gearworks."

The Organ Grinder raised an eyebrow in skepticism, and the Stone Preacher studied their forms closely. "Did you choose this change?" The Preacher's granite voice purred with a vicious sort of concern.

"We did indeed." The Sisterhood smiled. They seemed largely excited to talk with a priest of another faith, but still cast sly glances at the Organ Grinder. I did my best to hide my discomfort. I wasn't sure if it was working.

"What sort of body alterations are we talking about?" It was an honest question. After everything I had already seen, I wasn't expecting a comfortable answer. I already wished that I hadn't taken that sip of water.

The Sisterhood smiled. "You have survived the test. We may show you." They removed their cassocks, revealing their sculpted, narrow bodies wrenched tight into vicious mechanical corsets. Their legs were sinuous and smooth, perfect clockwork tools of brass and silver at the joints and legs, the perfectly curved hips as elegant as flesh. Their arms were formed likewise, hammered gold and steel, with smooth metallic digits that looked like they could crush anything. They were perfect mirror images of each other under the habit. We couldn't see their hair color. The Organ Grinder coughed. "Our Priest of Gears is very generous, don't you think?"

I stared. "How did this happen?" I looked to the Stone Preacher. There was a slow grinding creak of his jaw opening wide. He didn't understand what happened either. It was the first time I had seen him unable to say anything.

The Organ Grinder began to stammer. "Wha—how—no…" He appeared frightened. Those brass and silver legs looked as though they might crush him if he used his powers of seduction on them. Unfortunately, he already had. It should have brought me pleasure, but there was none.

"Those corsets? Are they attached?" I asked.

"We remove our arms and legs periodically to clean them and polish them," they said with a cheerful smile. "Do you not like them?" They smiled cheerfully to the Organ Grinder. "They say you are the greatest lover in the world. Is it true?"

The Organ Grinder's face was covered with fear. The two nuns would probably kill him if they went to bed with him. He would die a bloody mess in his cart. "Indeed it is," he managed.

"We volunteered to have our arms and legs removed and replaced with these wondrous constructs," they said together. "It gives us power and strength. The Priest of Gears is most brilliant, and one day, his god shall change the world." They put their cassocks back on, seeming very proud of themselves.

The Stone Preacher turned to me. "Fascinating. Self-mutilation is not heresy. They volunteered for this. Their religion is true."

"What if their master's isn't?" I asked. "That's a good question, right?"

The Stone Preacher thought about that for a moment. "All religions need martyrs." His smile spread. "This sisterhood will spread his religion long after he dies." His gravel voice paused for a moment in thought. "As long as they only take volunteers."

I thought I was going to be sick, but the cool water calmed me. I drank the rest of the glass without even thinking about it. "What happens to your arms and legs? I mean, where do they go?"

"We don't know" I shuddered at the Sisterhood's answer. "We suspect that they are burned to fuel the forges or that they are added to the clockworks that turn the gears somehow. Our very bodies are a part of this place." They gave the daintiest of happy smiles.

There was a series of thumps. The Sisterhood turned to an empty section of wall, which opened with a heavy thud, sliding into the floor. Shadowed in the doorway was a half-mechanical man, his fingers and legs all gold and steel.

***

"Good day." His voice was hollow and brassy. Powerful arms and legs were made of steel and gold. His chin jutted out as his massive body clanked into the room. He was gigantic, wide and taller than the Organ Grinder or the Stone Preacher. His epaulets were gears. The ornate steel and brass breastplate he wore seemed to be a part of him, much like the Sisterhood's corsets. There was a large symbol of interlocking clockworks hammered into his breastplate.

The giant bowed to the Stone Preacher "Ahh, the Stone Preacher, a legendary man of the cloth – or granite, as it were." His teeth were human, as was his face. Unlike the Sisterhood under their robes, there was no hint of visible flesh.

The Stone Preacher gave the Priest of Gears a nod. "I see your faith is true, for you do not do anything to your subordinates that you have not already done to yourself. You are no heretic." I felt a great sense of relief. The Stone Preacher was not going to kill anyone else right now.

I rose and bowed. I had no skirt to curtsey with. "A pleasure to see you, great Priest of Gears. I am the Lady Symantha, in search of my one true love."

The Priest of Gears flexed his hands. Spikes popped out from under his epaulets as his gaze flicked over me. "Green eyes, indeed. And with such a powerful entourage, you are no doubt going to stir up the usual assassins, plots, and intrigues." He smiled and his breastplate clacked. His whole frame was sculpted into muscle. A little steam hissed from under the armor from time to time. "You are a creature of destiny, or you are dead."

"That doesn't sound very positive, but I thank you for your compliment nonetheless." I offered a subtle smile. If they wanted pompousness and formality, I would give it to them. My people were all things to all people. "Do you approve of my entourage?"

"You have brought the famous Organ Grinder to my demesne." He thought for a moment while he looked at the Sisterhood of Symmetry. They giggled and watched the Organ Grinder the whole time. "If you could convince him not to play his accordion within our temple, it would be appreciated."

I turned to the Organ Grinder, keeping the same formality of tone. "Good sir, if you could not play your music within these walls, the pastor of this place would appreciate your kindness." I hoped that he would try anyway. I was certain that the Priest of Gears could tear the Organ Grinder apart without weapons.

The Organ Grinder looked up at the Priest of Gears, his eyes flicking over the mountain of mingled flesh and metal. "It shall be no trouble, sir." He maintained his decorum. It was the first time I'd seen the Organ Grinder scared of anything.

"See that it is so." His voice rumbled from deep in his chest. "We value our sisterhood greatly." The Sisterhood of Symmetry gave him a pained stare, followed by a pout.

"We apologize for wasting your time with such triviality, but we were wondering if you might be able to put us up for the evening," I said gently. "We have come a long way. I do not wish to spend the night in the Organ Grinder's cart."

The massive hands of the Priest of Gears clasped together with a scraping noise. "I see that you are tired. I have tested you unfairly. You shall be quartered here, in separate rooms." He turned to the Sisterhood, who stopped giggling and cooing at the Organ Grinder. Their faces turned slack and serene at once. "You shall spend all night in prayer to our god which is to come. Neglect not your duties to it." He gazed ominously at the Organ Grinder. "I would hate to have to grind your organ."

The Organ Grinder shuddered. His monkey stuck his knife tail out from under the coat and made a fearsome hiss.

I smirked. "Well put. I believe that our friend the Organ Grinder shall be sleeping alone this eve."

"I require no room," The Stone Preacher smiled with a gravelly grind of his lips. "I shall protect the young lady from the lascivious clasp of the Organ Grinder."

"So be it." The Priest of Gears eyes twinkled. "I cannot refuse a man any less than I would do myself, were the opportunity offered."

The Sisterhood escorted us to our quarters, through another path that involved only stairs and elevators, no rooms of grinding winches and sharp edges. The rooms were spartan and cruel. Simple stone beds owned pillows filled with straw. There was a stone bedpan on a small carved rock table in the center of the room.

Our luggage had been brought in and piled up. Bosquoverde's longbow was placed neatly on my bed, along with a fine set of unusual looking clockwork arrows in a long wooden box. It was marked with the symbol of the Priest of Gears. There was a well-written note in blocky script that read *For the Lady's Personal Use.* I didn't know what to think of them.

***

I moved to the Stone Preacher's door first, then the Organ Grinder's, and gathered us in my room to study the strange container. "Do either of you have any idea what these are?" I asked. I looked down at the arrows. Several gears balanced on each side.

"I think once the arrow hits its target, the gears drive it in deeper," the Stone Preacher said. "Fascinating devices, these. I would be careful with them. They may obey the very words from his lips."

The Organ Grinder stared. "Perhaps he is attracted to you. They are most exquisite. He did more than likely discover that you had archery skills. It could be a sweet gift of romance, followed by a delicious night of furious rutting."

I turned to the Organ Grinder and scowled. His monkey screeched under the coat, as if it hungered for blood when the Organ Grinder was through with my flesh. "Why is it always about rutting? What about lovemaking, or hand holding, and romantic things?"

The Organ Grinder smiled. "All ladies shall love the Organ Grinder." He chuckled lightly to himself, and the Stone Preacher grumbled.

"Unfortunately for you, I hate the accordion." I scowled.

"You will learn," he said with a dry tone in his voice.

The Stone Preacher interrupted. "I will stay in this room with the girl. You will return to yours." His voice was firm and commanding. "I do not wish assassins to visit us again. It would do good to cut them off so that they cannot leave. Plus, it will give that wretched monkey something to do."

"What would that be?" the Organ Grinder asked. The monkey slavered and hissed under his leather greatcoat, anticipating bloodshed to come.

"That would be stabbing people in the kidneys from behind." The Stone Preacher glowered, and his voice was an ominous rumble. "It seems a great number of people have a vested interest in killing her. Fortunately, they appear to be suicidal enough not to care about us. I propose we take advantage of it."

"I don't know about the two of you, but I'm sleeping next to the longbow and using these weird arrows. If they shoot me and I die, then it was nice knowing you." I settled onto the bed. "Out, Organ Grinder. Your monkey makes me sick." I don't know how I got the strength to say it, but it filled me with magnificent pleasure.

The Organ Grinder bowed and departed, the monkey's knife tail scraping along the floor under his coat. The creature's head peered out from underneath, growled, and spit on the floor. The heavy basalt door slammed shut.

The Stone Preacher turned to me. "Must you despise him openly?" He gave me a gravelly smirk. "I would save my distaste for him as a private affair. It is a technique you must learn if you wish to survive here."

"I think the technique I need to learn to survive the Organ Grinder is how to kill the monkey. That thing is a pestilence."

The Stone Preacher chuckled. "You must restrain yourself from slaughtering the monkey, and the man. He saved you from the pit. It was only to serve his own lecherous purposes, no doubt, but we must find out why he left you at the pool and departed."

"He had someplace to be." I said. "And then I met the most magnificent man, and he—" I stopped and breathed in deeply. Just thinking of my nameless lover brought a fire into my heart and made my throat jump.

"True love, indeed," the Stone Preacher said. "Remember that the Organ Grinder can be trusted, but only to a point. Sleep now, but with one eye open." His body glided in a circle on the basalt, and he turned his back, his head tilting down into a resting, yet watchful position. If I had known what would happen during the rest of the night, I might have wished to die.

***

I slept on my bed as if it was made of steel, tossing and turning on the harsh bunk. My eyes flicked open as I took a look and fumbled around. Something had brushed against my hand. It was wicker, slippery and well-tuned. My fingers brushed against the picnic basket. I realized that I hadn't eaten, and reached out to light a strange lamp that rested next to the wall. The room was suddenly illuminated with odd, hazy light.

I could see enough to get a sandwich, so I opened the picnic basket. My eyes widened. The Stone Preacher was struggling with a man in a corner. There was a sack of some kind over his granite head. There was no sound in the room; the usual grinding noises of the Stone Preacher were absent. I reached down to the side of the bed and swung the bow over my leg, stringing it as quickly as I could.

The Stone Preacher kicked and struggled. His arms were going slack in the creature's grip. I didn't want to know what could make the Stone Preacher die as if he were a normal man. My lips quivered for a moment, and I drew back one of the strange clockwork arrows and fired. There was a thrumming noise as the arrow left the string, and it slammed into the assassin. The arrow wound up, compressed itself, and it drove deep into flesh. The thing's hands momentarily let go. There was a flash of metal in darkness. The Stone Preacher fell to the ground, struggling with the bag on his head.

The Organ Grinder flew backwards into the room and slammed against the wall. He didn't make any noise, either. Something was eating all the sound. There was a second thing. Out in the hall, something humanoid flailed while it clutched its face. I couldn't hear the monkey's usual screeching, but I knew it was there.

The assassin fled and raced down the hall, and the silence lifted. I could hear the monkey screeching again.

"…must have fled together." The Organ Grinder said, clutching his throat. He was wearing a brown nightgown covered with sweat, human blood, and machine oil.

"Was it the Sisterhood?" I asked the Organ Grinder.

"No, I would know if such lovely women were trying to kill me. They were far too taken with me to try, even if they were willing to kill you."

"How can you be sure?" the Stone Preacher managed to say, rumbling to his feet.

"If you have to ask that, I don't know how smart you really are," I retorted. "Are we going to chase those guys in our pajamas? I have nineteen arrows left."

"Why not?" the Organ Grinder said. "They headed towards the gear maze. They won't get far."

"You've been memorizing the layout," the Stone Preacher rumbled. "An admirable quality in a seducer, Organ Grinder."

"I tried the elevator we came down in." The Organ Grinder's leer returned. "But the door was locked. And the Sisterhood look particularly willing."

I moved out into the hall and covered it with the bow. "Come on, you two, I don't want to keep those guys waiting."

"You should stay here," The Stone Preacher warned. "If they can crush me, they'll mash you to a pulp."

"Even though the two of you are my guides, I'd like to point out that it's my true love we're looking for, and these arrows hurt them a lot more than you two do." I began stalking down the hall in my nightgown. "Let's fight."

"That's more like it." The Stone Preacher gave a rocky smile, his lips forming into something vaguely resembling a satisfied stare. "An aura of command."

"Fantastic," the Organ Grinder murmured. "It means it will be all the sweeter when I finally possess you."

"Don't enraged husbands ever catch up with you and try to kill you?" I asked the Organ Grinder as we made our way down the hall.

"Certainly." The Organ Grinder smiled. "Usually, the lovely ladies beg for mercy on my behalf." He looked down at his accordion. "Of course, some of the husbands aren't immune to the accordion, either."

"Why are you still alive? Hundreds of years of this must have made you enemies."

"Power is more important to the nobility. I am not afraid to be the means by which blackmail is carried out." He let out a little romantic sigh and wiped away a tear from under his monocle. "No one wants to admit that they were seduced by a dirty organ grinder in a cart with his monkey, and no one wants anyone else to know, either."

The Stone Preacher grumbled. "If the Lady Symantha did not have some smattering of twisted affection for you, and if you did not fight for her, I would crush you to a pulp." His fists clenched. "Fortunately there are nearby miscreants upon whom I can expiate my anger."

"What kind of religion has such obscenely violent priests?" I asked.

"Mine." The Stone Preacher said, and glided down the hall ahead of us. "We'll try to keep them off you long enough to shoot them. Don't miss."

***

The grinding of the cogs hid the sound of pursuit as we hurried towards the maze of gears. As we got closer, the grinding sound thundered. The noise seemed to move with an eerie warble down the hall. "That's not the same sound we heard before." I peered down the corridor. I could see a figure darting about in the gears. It was too hard to aim between the moving parts.

"I know," the Stone Preacher said. "Does it worry you?"

"A lot." I raised my voice. As we walked down the hall, we came closer to shouting.

The Organ Grinder grinned. "It's not too late for you to return to your quarters, milady." He idly fingered the edge of his beard.

"I'm not returning so you can 'claim your reward' for saving me." I scowled. "Is there no despicable tactic that you won't use?"

"I've never needed to kidnap anyone, though some of my adventures did involve rope." A sly wink oozed across his features.

I didn't want to respond to, or even think about, that. We emerged into the entryway, the massive roaring of gears and clockwork unspeakably loud. There was a strange warble, as if voices were carrying over the machines. "Hello, new lady," one of the voices keened. "We see you have brought your protectors with you. Are you afraid?"

The Organ Grinder elbowed me as I stared. "Answer them, but stay hidden. If we can hear them, they can hear us."

The Stone Preacher nodded, his rocky eyes scanning the clockwork madness for our attackers.

"I am not afraid of you!" I called back. "I can shoot you from here!"

There was twittering laughter that echoed through the gearworks, and a rough grinding noise behind us. A large stone block moved to cut us off, and pushed us forward.

"Come to us!" the voice called. It was a cross between a hiss and a singsong, with a weird clatter to it. "Then you can try up close."

The Stone Preacher and the Organ Grinder leaped onto the gears. I stepped into the space left behind. The stone block moved down the hall towards me. I raced for the rolling first gear and activated the boots. My feet roared to life with flame. Everything felt warm. The Stone Preacher and the Organ Grinder hopped from gear to gear, looking for adversaries.

The first gear hurtled out of the darkness, spikes popping out from the edges of its teeth. The Stone Preacher vaulted towards the hurler, still shaded amid whirring, clanking motion. I barely dodged it while it came back around for another pass. "It's hunting me!" I shouted as the Organ Grinder held his position.

"Dodge, then, girl!" he thundered.

The stone block in the doorway ground to a stop, leaving no ledge behind. We were trapped with the assassins. The door at the top of the room, barely visible, was locked.

The gear was still returning when the second assassin struck. He was short and portly under his robes, but he moved with grace across the gears. A weird howling sound crept from his lips. His fingers popped as he dug something out from his robes. A birdlike, razor sharp clockwork falcon flew. I drew a clockwork arrow and fired at him, then ducked down. The hurled falcon blazed past me. My arrow jammed into the assassin's arm with a dull click. The arrowhead turned, jamming itself deep into flesh. From under the robe came a dark, wailing scream that seemed to pour from his entire body.

The Stone Preacher had made it to some of the upper levels, where there was a slight spatter of blood on the walls. I must have wounded the gear thrower earlier.

The falcon thrower grinned as he recovered his composure, and pulled twin sharp gears out of his robes. He twisted them, and spikes erupted. "I have something for you," he said energetically. Masked features shifted under his hood. The mask was lined with stitches, and wrought with little flecks of bone.

Then the Organ Grinder was upon him. He grabbed the falcon thrower by the throat and they fell onto a gear. They rolled about, struggling for purchase as the Organ Grinder drove a knee into the assassin's crotch.

He hit only metal. The assassin head-butted him. Up in the rafters, the Stone Preacher closed on the other assassin. The flying, spiked gear hurtled back toward him, while the clockwork falcon focused on me. I nocked a second clockwork arrow and launched it towards the thing, which rolled almost completely out of the way. The arrow punched through a wing and carried it off, and it tumbled into the gears below. I heard metal splinter and glass shatter.

The Stone Preacher dodged. The spiked gear flew back into the hand of the hooded assassin, who leaped over the Stone Preacher and rode the rotating gear up to the next one. A sharp, bladelike protrusion rotated past the assassin. The Stone Preacher followed after him, grim and merciless as his granite skin.

The Organ Grinder struggled on the gear as it approached another. He drove a knee into the gut of his opponent, who didn't even grunt. The monkey howled, and leaped under the hood of the assassin with a screech. The Organ Grinder rolled away. The assassin rolled in the other direction while the gears wound. I drew the bow and fired. The monkey, sensing where the arrow headed, jumped back out from under the cloak. The clockwork arrow slammed into the chest of the assassin as he sat up. There was a wicked, grinding clunk, followed by a thud.

The assassin tumbled off the gear, down into the clockworks. His hood fell aside. Click shrieked in pain. Hard, grinding metal swallowed him up, wrenching his face into blood and shards. His body followed. Hungry for movement, crushing gears pounded and pulled at his dirty frame.

I raced upward, chasing the Stone Preacher. The other assassin hurled the spiraling gearknife at him. It wound past him with a vicious bounce, rebounding off some sort of ball in a line of tracked, rolling spheres. It headed straight for me. I turned and ran, trying to outrun spinning death as Clack hissed vengefully.

The Organ Grinder took off his thick leather coat, and hurled it at the spinning wheel of blades. There was a thump as the whole mess fell onto a large metal disc below.

With an overwhelming shuddering noise, the whole room stopped. The Organ Grinder grabbed for his coat, and planted his foot on top of it. "I'd gut you like a fish if that had been destroyed!" He shook his fist upward just as the Stone Preacher reached him.

Clack pulled a pick attachment from just under his cloak and jammed it into the metallic glove on the edge of his wrist. I fired another arrow at him. The Stone Preacher pulled back and dodged. The shot went wide. I was still compensating for the movement of gears, but they weren't moving anymore.

"Who sent you?" I shouted. "You're nothing but a pigeon hunt now, and I still have seventeen of these left!"

"The Duke of Bells obeys the wishes of the King!" he thundered. "Your romantic heresy in this land will end in blood! There can be no other outcome!" He slashed at the Stone Preacher again. The pick drove hard into my protector's arm.

I fired the next arrow. The hard, driving thunder of the clockwork arrow drilled through Clack's arm and pinned it to stone. "Really?" I asked as the Stone Preacher closed in. My boots flickered less. The Stone Preacher moved like liquid oil across the metal. "Don't kill him!"

Clack quavered and mewled like a desperate puppy. "No, don't kill me! Listen to her! Listen to her birthright."

Silent and furious, the Stone Preacher pulled away.

I had been concentrating too much on getting information, and not enough on the others. There was a thunderous roar. Clack's head erupted in a spray of blood, bone and metal. I turned to look at the Organ Grinder. He was smiling. In his hand was a heavy, old revolver. On his shoulder, the monkey made a soft hoot in bloodthirsty pleasure. "I don't have to," The Organ Grinder said. "I'm hardly noble, and I have a gun. What I don't have is a lot of bullets." He jingled a small bag from the trenchcoat he had recently redonned.

"You idiot! You killed him!" I shouted. "What the hell were you thinking?"

"I was thinking, perhaps, that he already told me everything I needed to know." The Organ Grinder chuckled. "Perhaps one day you will be kind enough to allow me to claim what might, perhaps, be my due?"

"Shove it up your accordion," I said. "I'd rather sleep with a frog."

"That happened to some other girl," the Organ Grinder smirked. "But she wasn't bad in bed, either."

The door to the chambers above flew open, as if forced by a powerful foot. Looming above us, their slender waists tilted to allow us a view of their faces, was the Sisterhood of Symmetry. "Oh." They said it together, as if collectively surprised. "This might take a bit of cleaning up!" They giggled to the Organ Grinder, as if he were their hero all over again.

The Stone Preacher looked up at the Sisterhood and bowed, as if he had known they would arrive later rather than sooner. They didn't return his gaze at all.

***

We all gathered near the door as cleaning crews arrived. Heavy grinding sounds of the Priest of Gears began to lumber down the hall. "What is all that noise?" His voice was filled with fury. His armor and mechanical attachments were louder now that the maze below us stopped moving.

I ran up to the door in my boots of fire. It was a comfort to stand on ground again. The Stone Preacher and the Organ Grinder hauled themselves up. The Sisterhood giggled and chatted with the Organ Grinder as the Priest of Gears strode forward. His gaze fixed on the Sisterhood with ominous intent. "Organ Grinder!" He thundered. The Sisterhood moved in front of him to protest their innocence.

The Stone Preacher smiled. Suddenly he was having a good time.

The Priest of Gears pushed the Sisterhood apart. They let out a little gasp as the massive man clanked towards the Organ Grinder, his ominous face wrenched in a metallic grimace. Clockworks ground under his arms. Legs thudded towards his target. The monkey keened in terror under the Organ Grinder's coat. He still smelled of blood and gunpowder.

"Good Priest of Gears." I bowed gracefully to him in my boots and my nightgown. My hair was a mess. I could smell the reeking of the dead from the broken gearworks below. "Your doormen tried to murder me this evening. Their bodies are in your test of fitness." I saw the Organ Grinder breathe a sigh of relief as the massive man turned towards me.

"Your story should be confirmed by my Sisterhood," he intoned. He walked to the edge, and peered over it.

I saw the Stone Preacher's head turn, and hold up a hand. His liquid motion stopped before he could push the Priest of Gears into the abyss that he made.

"I believe that those are the bodies of my doormen, yes." His body whirred as it turned. He glared at the Stone Preacher, and locked eyes with me. "And my gift to you, dear lady, is embedded in one of them." He gave a cold nod.

"It was hard to care about his well-being when he was trying to murder me, my good lord." I gave him my best deferential curtsey, even though I was only wearing a nightgown. I think I saw the Organ Grinder trying to stare at my not-too-impressive cleavage.

The Priest of Gears turned to the Organ Grinder. "I will trust that these words are true, as long as you lay your hands not upon the Sisterhood." He sounded like an angry wind-up doll.

The Organ Grinder bowed, leering wickedly at the Sisterhood. They returned his gaze with playful smiles. "I swear that these words are true, and that I shall not lay a hand upon your Sisterhood, in all their radiant beauty and glory." He returned to his feet with a rustle of leather. The monkey hooted under the greatcoat. The Organ Grinder kicked him.

The Stone Preacher stepped in front of me. "I must insist that you return the lady to her quarters."

The Sisterhood turned to the Priest of Gears. "It does not matter. She will be gone in the morning." They offered subservient bows. "We are certain that they will not make any more trouble."

"You may begin repairs." The Priest of Gears glowered at us and motioned with a heavy steel hand, little clacking sounds echoing from his gauntlet. "I shall return these guests to their rooms. When you dig what is left of Click and Clack out of our maze, dear sisters, I shall allow you each to select a new arm." He turned and began walking down the hallway. We followed.

"Did he say 'select a new arm?'" the Organ Grinder asked, wincing. "How does that work?" The Sisterhood gave the Organ Grinder a playful wave and giggled, covering their mouths with delicate brass fingers. He returned it with a curt nod.

Filled with petulance and disappointment, the Sisterhood lowered themselves into the maze of gears to dig out the bodies. The Priest of Gears guided us to the elevator, and opened it. By the time we returned to our rooms, the faint grinding sounds returned.

When I closed my door, I was warmed by the thought that there would be no more assassins for me in this grim mechanical place.

***

When I awoke early in the morning, the Stone Preacher was shaking me gently. "It is early," he whispered, "but we should leave."

I jumped out of bed and threw on my clothes, gathering up my bow and my remaining arrows. I shoved my feet into my boots as quickly as I could. "Is something wrong?"

"It would be rude to overstay our welcome. I do not wish to discover the Organ Grinder in bed with those two women," he said as we quickly packed.

"How so? You almost sound jealous!" I teased as I shouldered the picnic basket. I thought it gave off a little twitter. I was in too much of a hurry to care.

"I am actually worried for his safety," the Preacher said. "If they are the Sisterhood of Symmetry, then they will each want a whole one, and as there is only one—"

"They can only have half. Let's get him and get out of here." As much as the Organ Grinder deserved to die, and being ripped in half by selfish women was probably the most appropriate death he could ever deserve, I would have to look at it. We raced to the room next door and banged on it.

The Organ Grinder yanked the door open, pointing his revolver at us. He was wearing silk pajama bottoms. There was no one in the room with him. He looked bleary-eyed and tired as he reached for his washbasin to bathe his fat, hairy body. "You can come in now." He said with a disgruntled tone. "Are we leaving so soon?"

"Actually, the Stone Preacher was worried about you. He thought they were going to rip you in half, and so did I."

The Organ Grinder let out a loud roar of laughter that echoed down the hall. "Rip me in half?" He said with a smirk. "I haven't slept all night. I've been dreaming of those two wicked minxes forcing me to choose one." He winced. Blood trickled down his lip. "Oh, curses!"

The Stone Preacher grabbed the Organ Grinder's things, and the monkey crawled out from under the bed, bleeding from under its fingernails. I picked it up and we ran together, hurrying for the door. "He's only surviving because half his soul is trapped in the monkey!" The Stone Preacher said. "He'll die if he stays here much longer."

"How does that work?" I ran as fast as I could for the door.

"I'm not sure." The Stone Preacher glided ahead of us, forcing open basalt doors with gestures. A few surprised penitents got out of our way.

"They are powerful entities in a place of power who desire me!" The Organ Grinder wiped his lips with a dirty handkerchief as he ran, throwing on clothing awkwardly. "We need to be more careful."

We raced for the exit, the dull, heavy doors barred as the night crew turned them for us. The monkey hooted and screeched as we threw ourselves out the door and raced for the cart. The Organ Grinder began strapping in the horses. I threw his greatcoat over his shoulders. He bounded up into the driver's seat of the wagon, and we hurried away from that place in the dark.

I thought I could feel the Priest of Gears gaze at us from the top of his basalt tower while the Sisterhood of Symmetry giggled next to him. As the road stretched out before us, I forgot about the eyes of the Sisterhood, and dreamed of a man with green eyes. The days would be so magnificent I would never need my boots to keep warm.

Chapter Six

A Beautiful Meeting with the Knight of Lies

The road wound through hazy pastures tainted with frost. We passed small houses shuttered in the cold. No one came out of their homes to look. It was as if the rumor of the Organ Grinder's presence had slammed doors shut and made people lock up their wives. I sat next to the Organ Grinder as he drove the cart, fearful of what the inside might smell like. The Stone Preacher walked alongside.

The smell of cooking food came to our nostrils, overwhelming even the odor of the horses in the cold. Their breath puffed out in the chill. The Organ Grinder bid the horses move towards the smell.

All at once, the road ended. We were in a small, haphazardly arranged village nestled in the hills. The Organ Grinder pulled the cart up towards a large building with some horses tied out front. "Is this an inn?" I asked. "Not as cheerful as Bosquoverde's."

The horses tied to the stabling post looked ill watered and malnourished. The wood of the building sounded rickety in the wind. "The dress maker lives here, in this village." The Stone Preacher said. "Most of the village, however, is not such a wonderful place."

"You brought me here anyway? That was kind of you."

"If you want the best dress, this is where it can be found." The Organ Grinder smiled to me as he got down from the cart. "It will be a pleasure to peel it off you after you wear it."

"Shut up!" I interrupted. "No rutting if you're going to follow me around."

"I beg to differ." The Organ Grinder smiled. "May I remind you of whose cart this is?" He gave me a wicked leer.

"Fine. No rutting with me, then!" I scowled as the Stone Preacher helped me down from the cart. "I have somebody, and we're going to find him, and that's that."

"He could be a monster from the blackest pit, a serpent in disguise, or something of that nature. The sooner you disabuse yourself of your true love, the better." The Organ Grinder reached under his coat to pet the monkey.

"Is corrupting relationships all he does?" I asked the Stone Preacher.

"When he uses his accordion in a nonsorcerous manner, it's actually somewhat pleasant." The Stone Preacher responded. "It's just that he's the sort of man who takes advantage of opportunity, including things other people might not consider opportunities."

"You slept with the monster and the serpent, didn't you?" I asked the Organ Grinder as we walked up the steps of the inn.

"I'm not going to lie to you." The Organ Grinder rubbed his chin. "The monster was a little difficult, but the serpent in disguise was very generous. She still comes by every now and again."

There was an unusual grinding sound. The Stone Preacher was rolling his eyes. "Now you've got him started," he said. "He's going to talk about his conquests all evening."

"Well, after two or three attempts on my life, I think it would be nice to hear about people who aren't after me, even though the subject is uncomfortable." I sighed and we opened the door to the inn.

***

It was nothing like Bosquoverde's. The dimly lit tavern creaked and groaned under our feet. It felt as if we were standing on the skeleton of some long dead beast. Sconces for torches, most of them empty, adorned the walls. The crowded, crammed-together patrons looked as though poverty had befallen all of them. There was a sickening grunt of pleasure from a staircase to our right. A man and a woman rutted on the edge of the stairs. It looked like something out of a homeless shelter gone wrong.

The innkeeper, in wretched clothing, shambled forward out of the crowd. He stared at the three of us through skinny, wrinkled features. "Greetings, travelers." His voice was choked with mucus.

There was an unpleasant fierceness to him. He limped towards us in sandals wrapped with dirty linen. Thin arms and legs supported a face covered with grease and charcoal, as if he had spent a great deal of time near a hot fire. His voice was a grinding wheeze. Unpleasant lips licked as he looked me over, staring at my eyes. "Good day," he cackled. "Good day to you, my lady. I am Runhundimont, also known as the Knave of Innkeepers."

"Ah." The Organ Grinder bowed as he let out a little chuckle. "The famed Runhundimont makes his presence known. How long have you been here?"

The Knave of Innkeepers scratched his head for a moment. Little flecks of skin fell off his balding scalp. I tried my best to conceal my disgust. "Four years, perhaps five. My work is almost done." He licked his lips and stared at me maliciously.

The heavy, granite arm of the Stone Preacher reached out for the Knave of Innkeepers, and the malicious smile retreated. "If you touch the girl, I will yank your head out and mount you on your spine, and you will become the Knave of Talking Skulls, speaking your sins for all eternity." He flexed his hand. There was a slight, unearthly rumble.

From under the Organ Grinder's coat, a knife-tail stuck out and waved in the direction of the innkeeper. I didn't know whether to be pleased or sickened that the Organ Grinder's monkey was intelligent enough to like me.

The Knave of Innkeepers gave a little quiver. "Of course, milady." He said. "Do you require rooms for the night?"

"I think we do." I smiled. "Your room, I think, will do nicely."

The Knave of Innkeepers protested "My lady, where am I to sleep?"

"Well," I idly tapped my nose. "There's always the stable or the outhouse, that might be appropriate for one such as you." I scowled. "Plus, yours is the only clean room in the house, isn't it?"

The Stone Preacher looked at the Organ Grinder. The Organ Grinder looked back. They both burst into laughter and folded their arms as if I had discovered the man's only weakness. The Knave of Innkeepers nodded once. "I will prepare it." He scowled and slunk off into the crowd.

"That was well played," the Stone Preacher said with an admiring look on his face. "How did you know? You've never even heard of him."

"I must agree." The Organ Grinder said with a sly smile. "How did you figure that out? He is the Knave of Innkeepers. He ruins inns and drives them into the ground, while looting towns of all their money. This place must be suffering and starving. I like it already."

"We should help the townspeople," I said. "Not because he is wicked, cruel, and is draining their every penny, but because nothing should ever be allowed to be this dirty. Even the back of the Organ Grinder's cart isn't this disgusting."

The Organ Grinder shot me a dirty look, but nodded. "Don't eat anything," he said. "The only food he serves will be of no value, and may contain poison, worms, or some magic potion to consume you."

I idly patted the picnic basket. "That's all right. We have this to keep us safe, I think." I smiled. The Stone Preacher looked over at it. "Well, there was some sort of magic on it. We should be careful with it."

The tightly packed crowd of customers once again gave way to the passage of the Knave of Innkeepers. "This way," he said, leading us back towards the kitchen, through the dense mob. I thought I felt someone put his hand on my behind and give me a sharp pinch. I couldn't see who it was in the darkness. I gave the Organ Grinder a mean look anyway.

***

We pushed through the crowd and into the kitchen. The Knave led us through some unpleasant looking men in greasy aprons cooking. The food had seen better days before it started. Any odor that came off it was so loaded with grease and gristle that it made my stomach turn. My romantic experience was refining my palate. I hugged the picnic basket closer, hoping no one would try to take it.

The Knave of Innkeepers opened a door near the back of the kitchen, and it led down into a brightly lit room that flickered with light. From the top of the stairs, I could see a thick carpet and the hint of a beautiful wooden table. "This is my sanctum," he said with a pause in his breath. "I hope everything is to your satisfaction."

"If such is the case, I would like the key to the room," I said firmly. It looked like the room was too deep for windows. I didn't want to be trapped inside.

The innkeeper dug the key out of his misshapen pocket, and placed it in my hand. "Fare you well," he said with a sly grin on his face.

"Clever indeed," the Stone Preacher said. "I am certain that he did mean to lock us in and hold us in some manner."

"Absolutely not," the Organ Grinder said with a sigh. "He is far too disgusting to contemplate taking hostages with us here. After all, we are notable individuals schooled in the art of violence, and he is a wretched coward."

We walked down the stairs into the room, and stood in the doorway amid the bright light. It was a scene of horribly mismatched opulence. There was a king-sized bed, with mammoth posts holding it up, a couch and several chairs, all leather and strange designs, strewn about the room. There was a low flat table of glass with a jewel box on top of it. Paintings signed by artists I didn't know adorned the walls.

All of the art was terrifying. It was as if someone had consumed all the pleasantries of beauty and art and crammed it into a distorted mirror. They were filled with scenes of tragedies and horrible acts, things that made me avoid looking at them.

"My goodness!" The Organ Grinder thoughtfully stared at one of the lewder pictures. "I think that's me!" Suddenly, it was a lot easier not to look.

I was reassured by the Stone Preacher, who wasn't looking either. He began taking the pictures down and turning them around. "I'm certain that it is," the Preacher said. "However, I need to sleep tonight. This room is worth a fortune. He must have purchased all of it with his exploitation of their lives." His face screwed up into a rocky grimace.

"We should steal it," I said. "We should distribute all these things to those people and let them sell what they can."

"An altruist," the Organ Grinder said with a smirk. "If such truly is the case, you won't last long here."

"I'm being materialistic. I didn't say we wouldn't take anything for ourselves."

The Stone Preacher scowled at me while he was taking down the paintings. The Organ Grinder gave me a sly wink. "That's my girl," he said. "We'll make a noble of you yet."

"Won't the Duke of Bells be angry that we're poaching his right to law enforcement?" I asked. "Isn't this innkeeper hiding things from the Lord With a Hundred Pounds of Brass on His Head?"

"That depends on whether or not he gets his tithe," the Stone Preacher said. "The Duke would be obliged to reward you if he didn't know of the situation. However, if he condoned it, we might have to fight him and his men."

"Why would we have to fight? Couldn't we just apologize?"

"Unless you want to face him in a duel personally, my dear girl, we'll probably have to fight," the Organ Grinder said. There was a sinister chitter from under his greatcoat. "It's not so bad. We have a bloodthirsty monkey on our side. That's four against two hundred."

"Two hundred?" I yelped. "Why didn't you say something about that earlier?"

"You did not ask," The Stone Preacher said. "We have a dressmaker to see in the morning, and some lovely sandwiches and roasted meats in your basket. You and the Organ Grinder should enjoy them. I find myself incapable of eating at the moment."

"You're incapable of eating most of the time. That just means you're bitter and angry about something."

The Stone Preacher looked at me with grim and sinister eyes, and his fingers locked behind his back with a hard, rocky grind. "No one ever paints me." His voice was serene. "They can't. I'm set in stone."

***

There was a momentary silence while I considered the Stone Preacher's words. "You can't be painted?" I shouldn't have been curious.

"Not at all," the Stone Preacher said. "I have been sculpted, as such, my curse prevents me from ever taking form on canvas." He chuckled. "When you get your name, you get your power and your curse. It is the rules."

The Organ Grinder gave me a sly smirk. "Some of us got different curses than others."

"I'll cut off your curse and feed it to your monkey," I said. "You can keep the bed. I'll stay on the couch because two people have trouble fitting."

I walked over to the picnic basket and pulled out a sandwich and a bottle of wine. "This looks and smells like heaven compared to what's upstairs," I sighed, admiring the food and bottle.

The Organ Grinder grinned at me while the Stone Preacher took up a guarding position near the door. He reached into the picnic basket and took a sandwich. Then he sat down and ate while I was eating. "Are you going to keep all the wine for yourself?" he asked. "It is your right."

"It's also my right not to be stupid drunk," I said with a grin. "Borrow your corkscrew?"

The Organ Grinder offered his hand and I passed him the bottle. He grabbed the monkey's tail from under his coat and there was a horrid screech. He drove the knife into the cork of the bottle and yanked it out. I wondered if Bosquoverde would feel violated at what was happening to his food.

I searched around for glasses while the Stone Preacher stared at the door, and returned with a couple of opulent goblets I found stashed under a small nightstand. I found a handkerchief in an oblong dresser drawer and cleaned the glasses with it. I handed one to the Organ Grinder. "There you go," I said.

"Romance the lady at your peril," the Stone Preacher said to the Organ Grinder. "As if you were capable of romancing anything."

The Organ Grinder chuckled between bites of his sandwich. "I think I'll simply have some wine." He sipped a little bit from his goblet. "This is very good." He chuckled. "I must thank Bosquoverde when next I see him."

"If he doesn't throw you out of the inn along with the monkey." My voice turned sour even between sandwich bites. "Just what is it between you two anyway?"

"The more you ask, the less I'll tell." The Organ Grinder responded. "Though I find his sandwiches most delicious." He savored every bite as if he were the world's finest gourmet. It made me wonder what was in the sandwiches that could appeal to such a crass man.

The rest of our dinner was wrapped in quiet. We went to sleep full of wine and sandwiches. I dreamed of the man with the slender build and green eyes and clutched the couch in terror when the Organ Grinder's monkey crawled out from behind him, licking its lips as though I were its next conquest.

***

I slept poorly. There were rustling sounds and thumps at the edge of my ear after we put the lights out. In the dark, after hazy dreams of monsters, I opened my eyes. The rustling and thumping continued, and there were screeches from somewhere in the room.

Like a statue, the Stone Preacher stood with his head bowed in sleep, and the Organ Grinder snored roughly. The bumping continued, along with the hissing, and I blinked my eyes to adjust to the darkness.

The monkey was struggling with his arm in the picnic basket. The picnic basket was pulling back. In the dim light, the monkey's tail stabbed at the picnic basket, and the basket struggled with a creaking of wicker. I moved quickly to one of the torches and lit it. The sight was unbelievable.

The picnic basket had four short, stubby wicker legs. One of the flaps was curved into a toothy, savage mouth as it bit down on the monkey. The wicker frame rippled a little bit and stretched. There was a dire rustle to its movements as its brown framework rattled. It had hands on stumpy arms that extended out of the center of the basket. They were too short to be of much use.

The Organ Grinder began to mumble his way awake, and the Stone Preacher's eyes snapped to life as the struggle between the monkey and the basket bounced around the room. I chased the basket. It cooed and began dragging the monkey over to me. A little blood trickled down the monkey's wrist. The Organ Grinder sat up and drew his revolver.

"Let go!" I shouted at the picnic basket and yanked hard on the toothy flap. The monkey gave a little whimper and crawled back towards the Organ Grinder, scowling and chittering at the basket. A few drops of blood fell to the floor from the monkey's paw.

"Stand away, girl!" the Organ Grinder shouted. "It's alive!" I shielded the picnic basket from the Organ Grinder, and it rustled behind me, seeking shelter. He drew back the gun and pointed it at me. "It hurt my monkey. It must be destroyed."

The picnic basket rustled some more, and quivered behind me as the Stone Preacher walked up and grabbed it by the handle. "It seems to like her." the Stone Preacher said. "We'll have to reserve judgment."

"Thanks," I said to the Stone Preacher. "Besides, it's got all our food. The monkey was trying to steal it."

The Stone Preacher glowered at the Organ Grinder. "You should keep your monkey in your greatcoat more often." A quiet crackle of small rocks sounded in the air. "A living picnic basket, unusual." His voice turned to gravelly amusement. He was probably taking secret pleasure in the Organ Grinder's wounded monkey.

"It's safe for now." The Organ Grinder said as the monkey hid under the nearby greatcoat. The whimpering sounds of the wounded animal faded to silence. The picnic basket sat there in the Stone Preacher's fist.

"Go back to bed." I took the picnic basket from the Stone Preacher, and held it close as I made my way back over to the couch. The Organ Grinder scowled as he pulled the covers back over him, and gave a faint chuckle.

With the picnic basket next to me, I lay down on the couch. Even the faint drone of the Organ Grinder's accordion in the back of my head faded. The basket settled next to me and purred with an odd, reedy, rustle. I slept much more comfortably after that.

***

I awoke to movements of wicker against my leg, and a slight rush of air passing through the basement. The Stone Preacher had opened the door to wake me, while the Organ Grinder snored quietly in the bed. "Awake," the Stone Preacher whispered. "If we arrive at the dressmaker early, she may have time for you."

"Is she busy?"

"No, she has a bath, and this inn most assuredly does not." His voice remained a whisper.

I gathered my things, slid off the couch, and hurried for the door. We slipped up the stairs as the Organ Grinder rolled over in the bed. I thought I heard a little creak. The picnic basket sprang to life and followed us, as if it had a hungry life of its own.

"It looks like you made a friend," the Stone Preacher said as the basket slipped through the closing door.

"How do you know it's a friend?" We crept through the cold kitchen in the early morning.

The Stone Preacher let out a little gravelly rumble in his throat. "It hasn't tried to eat you."

Three of us rushed across town in the first rays of the sun.

***

We arrived at the house, which was nestled into the side of a hill. A heavily armored man settled on a horse, waiting outside. His armor was smooth and polished, hazy purplish in color. He was even more handsome than the man I knew I loved, his features perfect, his nose flawless, and his jaw square. His beauty didn't do anything for me. There were stains of blood on his spurs. He held a long black lance that rested idly on the ground while he held it near the point. When he spoke, it was with venom and distaste. "Bad day to you," he said viciously. "I am not the Knight of Lies."

"You're lying now?" I asked.

The Stone Preacher turned to me. "Are you sure you wish to handle this yourself?"

"I think I can handle him." I smiled and curtsied to him as best I could. "I am Lady Symantha, Sir Knave who claims to be a Knight, and I wish to see the dressmaker."

"I, too, am here to see the dressmaker." The Knight of Lies frowned. His gaze passed over me with severe distaste. The picnic basket opened its lid and hissed at the Knight's horse from behind us. It didn't seem to like the two of them.

"Of course." I smiled. "And you have no message at all for me?"

"None." The Knight of Lies frowned deeper. At least he was easy to understand.

"Can you give it to me now?" I asked. "It is my prerogative, one would hope."

"Yes. I shall make preparations to deliver the message at once."

"We'll see you later, then," I said, and walked past him to the door of the dressmaker. The Stone Preacher raised a rocky eyebrow. The Knight rode off without another word.

"How did you know he wasn't going to kill you?" The Stone Preacher asked.

"I thought you might be faster than anything, as long as they're also standing on the ground." I said. "That…is how it works, isn't it? You have trouble dealing with things in the air?"

"You're learning. Perhaps too fast for your own good. You should not have told me that."

"Why not?" I asked. The picnic basket settled down by the tethering bar, drawing its legs up beneath itself. It looked innocuous, as if trying to lure other animals closer so that it could eat them. It made me wonder about Bosquoverde, and how honest he really was.

The Stone Preacher pushed on the door to the dressmaker's shop. It creaked open. "You might have to kill me one day. Always count your friends among your enemies, and you will live a long life."

"Right," I said. "A life without friends you can trust isn't worth living."

We stepped into the dressmaker's shop, and the Stone Preacher closed the door behind us. "That's the only life anyone has around here. Perhaps you aren't learning as fast as you'd like."

***

There was a creaking shudder as the door closed. We stepped into a scene of weaving madness. There was a large tub of bubbling water off in one corner, with a changing screen next to it. Six looms shuttled, clattering through the building. Light footsteps approached through bolts of fabric, heaped in massive piles, to meet us.

She was tiny and almost fairylike, spindly and slender. Her face was young. Grayish-white hair and long fingers spoke of age. She was wrapped in a copious gown of ochre silk that billowed around wide hips. "You must be new." She gave a dainty curtsey to me and then bowed her top half. "I am the Duchess of Weavers." She gave me a green-eyed stare.

"And you live in this unpleasant town?" My voice dripped with curiosity. "Can I know why you don't live in a fine castle with servants and the like?"

"Oh, all that rubbish. Almost everyone has a title here, it's all about politics and who is controlling, manipulating, and using whom. As for your friend the Stone Preacher, he is welcome to stand but not to sit. I do not have a chair capable of holding his weight, I'm afraid."

"He's not exactly my friend."

"Then he's been teaching you." Her smile brightened. "There's always an obligation to newcomers to explain the rules and help people live by them. We could just feed off the newcomers and exploit them, but then there would be a set of different rules, and we'd all have to learn them all over again." She gave a little giggle. "I assume you've come to me for a dress, and perhaps a cloak to keep the cold off?" She gestured to the bath. "I don't fit the dirty, so into the bath with you."

I slipped behind the screen and hurried in. I bathed as quickly as I could. "Should I be wearing anything when you're fitting me?" I asked.

"I would prefer you not," she said coolly. I could hear the slight rumble of the Stone Preacher turning his back. "I shall come behind the screen and take your measurements."

"That's fine," I said as I waited for her. She slipped behind the screen and took out a length of white silk. She measured me everywhere, and made little humming noises. All the while, the looms clacked in the background.

"Is there anything in particular you would like? I am obliged to provide you with something you enjoy. It is your first serious dress, after all," Her lips opened, then twitched, almost like a smirking cobra. "Who is the husband?"

"I don't know," I told her. "We're looking for him, and many of the local nobles don't like me."

She yawned. "Pish-tosh." A sarcastic, bored look crossed her face. "That's always how it goes. How many attempts on your life have there been?"

"Three," I said with a sigh.

"Well, there's always going to be more." She gave a petulant little sigh. "Until you're actually married, the attempts won't stop, and whoever it is will marry you if you look upon his naked face. You'll be terribly happy, of course, and wicked to everyone who isn't your one true love, but I know that look." She gave me a light laugh. "I've seen it before."

"How many times?" I asked, a little scared.

"Seven hundred and sixty two." She said with a lilt in her voice.

"How many did you make dresses for?" I was warm and comfortable despite my nakedness. Her fingers daintily made marks on a piece of paper while she chatted with me.

"Five hundred and forty-seven," she said quietly. "Including you, that is."

"And how many lived?" I asked as she scuttled away from the screen to bend over a desk.

"Oh," she paused and touched the side of her nose. "Eight. You can get dressed now."

"Just eight?" My chances just shrunk. "What happened to the others?"

"Jealous lovers killed them; assassins murdered them; some got eaten by monsters." She gave me another smile while I struggled back into my clothes. "True love doesn't always win out, you know. You have to fight for it. Most of them weren't willing to kill for it. But I can already see that you are. You've been blooded a few times."

"Well," I managed softly. "It doesn't mean I like killing people or anything."

"You had better start. This isn't a forgiving fairyland, by any stretch of your imagination. This is where dark legends go to smile." She patted me gently on the head.

"Thanks, I'll keep that in mind. So how do I pay you?"

"You don't have to," she said idly. "You find him and you survive. But a little money is nice."

"And your husband was the Duke of Weavers?" I asked.

"Yes. I counted myself in the five hundred and forty seven," she sighed sadly. "What a fool I was."

"What happened?" I asked.

"I fell in love with him, found him, and then I changed." She smiled a little sadly. "I bound him up in silk and drank his blood and he died." She rustled away from me, and the dress slipped aside. She scuttled up the wall on her eight spider legs, neatly tucked under her hairy abdomen. "Your dress will be ready in the evening." Her voice was cool as she settled on the ceiling. Her legs moved the looms through the near invisible threads tied to her eight feet. "He tried to have me killed the whole time."

I was so paralyzed with shock that when the Stone Preacher came up to me and guided me out, I didn't even know how much time had passed. I was still shaking when the picnic basket rubbed against me with a little clatter of wicker and shook me out of it.

***

"She's a spider!" I gave out a quiet sputter as the basket walked along behind us. The Stone Preacher's neck rumbled a little as he shook his head.

The picnic basket let out a surly growl as we walked back towards the inn under the dim morning sun. The Stone Preacher didn't say a word.

"She's a spider!" I said again. "I can't even begin to understand how that could happen."

"When she received her name, it happened," the Stone Preacher said. "She became the thing that she was supposed to become. It depends, sometimes, on who or what gives you your name. You should be safe, however, with the Organ Grinder and me."

"Define safe? She's a spider! She's got eight legs, and a hairy abdomen, and probably sharp teeth."

"Well, yes." The Stone Preacher grew morose. "I very much liked the Duke of Weavers. He was a cheery fellow until she ate him."

"You knew him?" I tried not to sound surprised, even though I was. "And she ate him? And you didn't do anything?"

"Oh, yes, just because he was cheery doesn't mean he wasn't evil."

"Is everyone evil around here?" I asked. "What if I don't want a name anymore?" I asked as the picnic basket hopped up to the back door of the inn and settled itself there, waiting for us as the rays of light beat down on us in the cold.

"It's not a question of want," The Stone Preacher cautioned. "You are in love. You have only to think of him and he fills your whole mind, doesn't he?"

"Yes," I was almost back by the pool in an instant, his breath eager for mine, his fingers pinning down my wrists. I wanted everything.

The Stone Preacher opened the door and sighed. The lights of the kitchen were already on. Several unpleasant-looking fat men were making equally unpleasant breakfasts. "Then you don't have a choice. You will find him and you will live, or you will die along the way."

"Have you done this sort of thing before? Escorted a young girl and become their mentor?"

"Of course not. The Organ Grinder has, but I'm sure you know what happened to them. People of no consequence, the lot of them. Several of them committed suicide. I'm sure I'll have to take that up with him one day."

We walked down the stairs and opened the door to the basement, where the Organ Grinder was dressing the monkey's wounded wrist. He was fully dressed in his top hat and leather greatcoat. Oddly enough, he smelled as if he had bathed. "You're clean?" I stared in surprise.

"Of course I am." The Organ Grinder smiled. "There's no town in all the land where a lady won't give me a bath. Ah, the magic of a well-played accordion." He took a moment to grin at the monkey, and then carefully adjusted his pants.

"I'm pretty sure that wasn't all you were playing, was it?"

"Her husband was out at the market." The Organ Grinder smiled wickedly. "He never saw a thing." He licked his lips. "She was a little chunky, with strawberry blonde hair and a few freckles, but she'll never forget me, like all the others."

The Stone Preacher shook his hand and began moving towards the Organ Grinder with his stony fingers extended, as if to crush his throat, but there was a keening scream from the door. We all turned to look. The Knave of Innkeepers was standing in the doorway, with his hand missing. Blood from his wrist stump fountained onto the stairs. There was a horrid crunching and chewing sound coming from the picnic basket. The Knave was in too much shock to do anything else as his blood dripped on the growling wicker below.

***

The Organ Grinder rolled away from the Stone Preacher and fired bullets at the picnic basket as it began to flee up the stairs, and the Knave of Innkeepers began to babble and sob. "My hand!" he shrieked. "It ate my hand!"

I couldn't help but stare at the basket as it fled. The Organ Grinder rolled to his feet, beginning to give chase. The Stone Preacher turned and gave chase while the Knave of Innkeepers crumpled to the ground, his blood leaking out over the stairs.

"Help him!" I snapped to the Stone Preacher as the Organ Grinder hurried up the stairs after the fleeing picnic basket, which stopped at the top to give a loud belch in between its chewing sounds.

The Stone Preacher shouted "Don't shoot!" as the hammer of the Organ Grinder's revolver clicked on an empty round. The empty clicking continued as he fanned the trigger.

The Organ Grinder shook his fist at the picnic basket as it growled at him from the top of the stairs. It chewed on its prize while the Stone Preacher bandaged the Knave's hand.

"Don't shoot the basket!" I shouted at the Organ Grinder. "It's still got all our food!"

The Organ Grinder turned to me as he flipped open the cylinder on the revolver, and dumped the shells into his hand. "It has to die," he said grimly. "That could have been my monkey's hand."

"It's my basket!" I said angrily. "And you owe me! Those are the rules! Obey them or I'll find a way to have you quartered." I gathered myself up to my full height and gave the Organ Grinder my most commanding look.

The Stone Preacher raised a rocky eyebrow that sounded like a fingernail scratching across rock. "Now," he murmured, "you're beginning to understand, girl."

The Knave shook his head and swallowed, continuing to whimper about his hand. "Keep it away," he wheezed. "Keep that thing away."

"Why?" the Stone Preacher said. "You tried to steal a sandwich, didn't you?"

The Knave nodded through twitching lips. He was breaking out in a sweat.

"Right," I said. "Don't mess with the picnic basket. Bosquoverde gave it to me. It likes me. It only attacks people who threaten it."

The Stone Preacher nodded. He turned to the Organ Grinder. "Apparently, everything in the world is yours to control except, it seems, this girl and her basket." A wide, creaking grin split his lips.

"Come here!" I beckoned to the picnic basket. I was a little afraid to do it at first. The basket popped out its stubby legs and came over. It rubbed and creaked against my leg, much as a cat might.

The Organ Grinder had finally finished reloading, and covered the basket with the barrel of the gun. "I'm shooting it if it tries to bite you," he said firmly. "Besides, I could use a little more aiming practice."

The basket shied away from the Organ Grinder and cuddled up against me. It made weird rustling noises, as if wind blew through it. The rumbling growl echoed up and down the stairs. "Put the innkeeper in his bed," I said firmly. "For trying to steal my sandwich, I think we should liberate his other things and pay for my dress."

"I think that's a wonderful idea," the Organ Grinder said as he carried the Knave over and dropped him unceremoniously into the bed that he had just vacated. "We could take just about everything. You are a noble, after all."

"Well, yes," I said. "But I'm really not interested in his drafty old inn, and we've already had to pay him and eat our own food. Speaking of which, I haven't had any breakfast."

I opened the picnic basket and looked inside while it purred with its wickerlike rattle. There was no sign of the Knave's hand at all, and there wasn't any blood on the inside of the basket. Several of the sandwiches had been replaced, and there was a new bottle of wine in there, as well. The sandwiches smelled like fresh baked bread, and the wine bottle seemed very old. The picnic basket hiccupped.

***

"It ate his hand?" The Organ Grinder's voice filled with surprise. "And now it's full of sandwiches and wine! Are those wrapped pickles I smell?" He made his way over to the basket to take a look. It shifted lazily and growled at him.

"It smells like the sandwiches are made on fresh-baked bread," My voice quavered. The basket had eaten the Knave's hand and now it was full. "So what does it mean?"

"I think it means it needs to be fed to keep it full of food," the Organ Grinder mused. "Interesting. No wonder it was trying to eat the innkeeper. It was down to the last sandwich. You make terribly interesting friends." His smile widened, enjoying the whole incident.

The Stone Preacher looked at me. "You've acquired an unusual companion. It's up to you to take care of it and give it what it needs."

"It eats people!" I said. "That's what it needs! How are we going to get rid of it?" My voice frayed a little bit with worry. The Basket, in response, rubbed against my leg with a crackle of wicker, and made a happy little growling noise.

"Don't let it eat unless you need it to," the Stone Preacher said firmly. "Overuse of a powerful enchantment like this can have dire penalties."

"Powerful enchantment?" I snapped. "It bit off his hand and swallowed it like he was a chew toy! What could it do to us?"

"I don't know. I've never been a particularly appetizing meal for creatures of that sort."

"Did you ever stand in a pot while people threw vegetables, water, and meat into it, and heated it up?" I asked. "That's probably as close as it gets for you."

"That old story?" the Stone Preacher frowned, giving me a dire look. "That was someone else, I'm sure."

"Did anyone ever try to eat you?" I said. "If I don't keep a tight rein on whatever the hell this thing is, we're all going to be run out of town. And if anyone really doesn't like us, well, it will just leap at them and start eating! We have to get rid of it!"

"You can't get rid of it!" the Organ Grinder scowled, defeated. "Bosquoverde gave it to you, and only you can control it. That's how these things are. If you let it go, it will follow you wherever you go and eat what it wants, including all the people in this town you're oh-so-interested in helping! You've got a basket, and it eats people! It is not the end of your life!" The monkey peeked out from under the Organ Grinder's greatcoat and hooted furiously.

"It turns them into delicious food?" I raised my voice to the Organ Grinder. "Isn't that cannibalism? I mean, really! Isn't it?"

"Not exactly," the Stone Preacher said. "It's a just punishment for stealing food, as far as these sorts of rules are concerned."

I looked down at the basket, which was still rubbing against my leg like a pet. "All right," I said grumpily to it. "You can stay." The picnic basket gave a happy rumble in response, and settled onto wicker feet. I was never going to be comfortable eating sandwiches again.

"Now that's all settled." The Organ Grinder smiled a little bit and reached for the basket. The lid opened gingerly, as it turned to growl at the monkey. "I think I'll have a pickle." He took a pickle, unwrapped it, and began chewing. "This is delectable."

I glowered at the Organ Grinder and began piling the Knave's things up into a set of neat and organized piles. 'We should take everything that's lootable. I don't have any fantasies of stealing from the rich and giving to the poor, but no one ever pays the Duchess, and this town is suffering. Everyone is dirty here. They can use the money to buy soap."

"Spoken like a true member of the nobility," the Stone Preacher said. "Redistributing wealth by force after you've brutally dismembered the ruling power."

"It was the basket," I snapped. "I was only taking advantage of the situation." The basket made a chirping noise of satisfaction.

"False humility." The Organ Grinder laughed. "I think you're finally beginning to understand how people behave around here."

"I'll keep that in mind when I shove your accordion down your throat," I grumbled. "Now help me loot this idiot's room while he's incoherent and in shock."

***

We arranged everything into several neat piles, and took all of the most valuable, sorting them into bags. We assembled them and left the basement, leaving only the most worthless things in a mound for the Knave of Innkeepers to have. I took more pleasure in it than I should have, but he tried to eat my sandwich, and the picnic basket didn't like him very much.

We walked through town, leaving a small bag of goodies in front of each door. I didn't know who they belonged to, and I didn't particularly care. It just brought me pleasure to take away the Knave's hard-stolen things. There was no way I could fit them all into the Organ Grinder's cart.

We kept a larger portion for the Duchess of Weavers, and travelled back towards her hut as the sun lowered on the horizon. It took some time to convince the people that I wasn't going to kill them or have them flayed. The picnic basket followed us the whole time, flouncing about like a hyperactive dog. Every so often, it would open its top and offer one of us a sandwich.

The Knight of Lies gave us a cold shake of his head as we passed him on the street. There was a little celebrating going on as we dropped off packages of things, and more than a few fistfights. "Oh, my, order has been restored!' He thundered pleasantly as we passed him, and headed for the Duchess's home. The rioting continued in his wake.

"It's utter chaos," the Stone Preacher said. "He's the Knight of Lies. He's going to lie about everything."

"Yes, and it's refreshing to see that a liar approves of you." The Organ Grinder smirked. "No doubt his chastisement will be forthcoming in the back of my cart."

"I really did not need to know that part," I scowled. "So you sleep with men, too?"

"I prefer women, but I have been known to enjoy a little sodomy now and again." The Organ Grinder leered at me and tipped his top hat. "It has its entertainments."

The Organ Grinder smiled. "Sometimes, I even take my time with priests," he leered at the Stone Preacher. "One day, you too, shall bow to the will—"

"Shush!" I snapped. "If you keep talking like that, I'll have your entrails hung from a pole."

The hand of the Stone Preacher was already half-raised to the Organ Grinder's throat.

"Oh, that's very fetching!" the Organ Grinder said. "She learns fast. She might not need our help soon. Shall we slow down our lessons?"

"No," the Stone Preacher said. His grin rattled with gravelly teeth. "Why would I want to do that if it frees her from the state of your wanton lusts? You are a beast, and that monkey is only the emblem of your beastliness. One day, if you are lucky, I will be the one who crushes your throat. There are millions of more gruesome deaths in this world."

The monkey hissed at the Stone Preacher from underneath the coat, and the picnic basket growled back.

I opened the door to the Dressmaker's shop, and the rattling and shivering of looms crashed against my ears. "Just a moment!" I heard the Duchess of Weavers voice echoing over the clack and bustle of multiple looms. "I'm almost done with it!"

***

Her monstrous lower body twisted a few strands of thread from behind a loom, and the Stone Preacher looked at me, as if making sure I wasn't going to have another episode of shock.

"I cannot wait to see how you look in it," the Organ Grinder said. At my feet, the picnic basket made a whirring rattle. It peered under the Organ Grinder's coat, as if it were hungry for the blood of the monkey.

"I can't wait to see how I look in it, either," I said sullenly. All it took was the Organ Grinder opening his mouth, and all the fun was taken out of the enterprise of getting a new dress. Outside, there were shouts and the sounds of fighting.

The Duchess popped her head up over a loom and smiled. "Oh, you'll be ravishing," she said with a smile. "Good enough to eat." Her face twisted into a petulant pose. "I didn't mean that."

"Oh, here's your payment." I held up a small bag filled with various gems and jewelry. I didn't even bother to figure out how much they were worth. I was a noble now. Not caring about throwing money around was part of it.

"Goodness," her tone filled with slight surprise. "Is that what all the rioting and looting is all about?" She gave me a winsome smile. "And if there isn't rioting and looting now, there will be soon." She took the bag and slipped it into her dress.

"I suppose I should try it on, just to make sure it's perfect," I said with a little grin. "And no blood drinking."

The Duchess of Weavers gave a bitter sigh. "You take all the fun out of trying on dresses, my dear."

"Ask the Organ Grinder," I said. "He ruins people's fun every day." I scampered for one of the dressing screens in the back of the heap of looms, and began slipping out of my jeans and shirt. The Picnic basket followed, looking for people to eat.

"Will you play your accordion for me?" The Duchess of Weavers smiled. "I always thirst for a little companionship, and you might do nicely."

The Organ Grinder's wicked leer turned into a bitter frown as I slipped behind the dressing screen. Victory was sweet.

There was a rustle from behind the screen, and the Duchess stuck her head around the corner, her hands holding a beautiful gown in silver and white. It had a thick bodice which would push up my meager cleavage and a heavy cinch at the waist. It had a beautiful light blue sash at the hips. It felt like spider silk. It probably was. The most sensational part of it was the way it shivered against my body, almost as if it were making love to me. But it wasn't him. It wasn't the man with the green eyes. I felt nothing at all.

"It's…" It was the only word I could get out of my mouth. I had never had a dress like this, ever. I had worn jeans and patchwork things all my life. The piece of a fairy tale world drifted over my shoulders and settled on my hips, fitting just right. I let out a little squeal.

"Perfect?" the Duchess of Weavers said with a grin. "I knew you'd like it. After all, so many other girls come in and want black, or purple, or midnight blue." She laughed. "I made your cloak purple and sewed it up with runes of protection so that you might survive a few assassination attempts."

"A cloak of runes?" I said. She held it out to me. It swirled with limpid hues of purple and black, and the very fabric of it was rich and thick and smooth. "Did you make this in a single day as well as the dress?"

"Actually, no." the Duchess said with a casual smile. "This was the cloak I wore in the days before I grew rounder in the hips, and thirsty for other things than water and wine." She leaned lazily against the dressing screen. "It simply doesn't fit me anymore, and you're the first person to cause rioting and looting here, so I supposed you might need it." The smile spread so wide I could see the sharpness of her teeth.

"How did you get it?" I asked thoughtfully.

"Oh, I got it from a smooth-talking raccoon man who told me it would protect me. But it protects me from everything." She scowled at the Organ Grinder. "Even this man's filthy bullets."

The Stone Preacher looked angrily at the Organ Grinder, who looked defeated. "I wouldn't sleep with her." He frowned. "She's nice, but she's not worth becoming lunch for."

"It sounds like someone can't live up to their principles." I peered around the corner of the screen. "If you can call what you do principles."

The Stone Preacher smiled. "We need to be going." He said. "I'm certain, if we hurry, that we can make the Duke of Bells' castle by noon tomorrow and announce you to the world. Besides, I would hate to leave the Organ Grinder prey to the romantic advances of such a lovely lady while he still has one to escort."

I quickly changed, folding the dress into a large bag as neatly as I could, then sauntered towards the door and smiled at the Duchess, who curtsied politely to me in the wide, heavy dress she wore. "Thank you for everything." I returned the curtsey as though it mattered. Then I turned to the Organ Grinder. "Put a bullet in the dressmaker, and I'll feed your monkey to the picnic basket."

The Organ Grinder grumbled. "As you wish." He sighed. "I only have two bullets left. I mustn't waste them." The basket scuttled out from behind the dressing screen and flounced after us. I held the door open for it and it followed my bodyguards. The sudden rush of terror at surviving the dressmaking spider woman washed over me again. The picnic basket rattled its wicker frame against me to snap me out of it.

***

There was fighting in the streets. The Town Watch was trying to pacify looters. The Stone Preacher looked at me with a wry smirk. The picnic basket made slavering noises at the mob.

The Organ Grinder chuckled. "So much for a bath," he said with a sigh. "The streets will run red with blood, no doubt."

Under the Organ Grinder's coat, the monkey peered out, hooting at the violence. The Organ Grinder and the Stone Preacher took up positions on either side of me. The picnic basket growled angrily at anyone who came too close as it trotted behind. We escaped back to the inn room as the Watch struggled to subdue the rioting population. I had to grab the handle of the picnic basket to keep it from gnawing on the wounded.

The Knight of Lies was standing outside the entrance to the inn, amid a crowd of garishly heaped dead bodies. Nearby, lay several weapons. Next to him, his horse was a wretched, bloody heap "Count the living among them!" he said with a cheery smile. I supposed that meant that he was sad. From under the Organ Grinder's coat, there was a satisfied chittering.

"How did you kill all those people?" I said.

"I told them to continue looting, and that they didn't want my horse." The Knight said with a smile. He cried through the whole statement, as if he couldn't help but lie. I wanted to know his story, but no matter what, he couldn't tell. He would have to make something up.

"You couldn't tell them who you were?" I asked him as I turned to the Stone Preacher and the Organ Grinder. "Go get our things.

I'll stay out here and ask him a few questions." The picnic basket growled and looked at the dead bodies hungrily while the Stone Preacher and the Organ Grinder went down to collect our luggage. Nearby, the Organ Grinder's cart remained untouched. The sounds of violence were beginning to die down.

"I didn't." He sniffled. "I told them that I was the Knight of Lies." He hung his head a little bit. "They believed me." He shook his head. "Now I have a horse." He bent down and stroked its bleeding, wounded neck. He drew his sword and thrust it into the beast's heart. "Hello, old enemy."

I stared in shock. The picnic basket looked about furtively, making a slight wickerish shuffle. I knew what it wanted. "Good sir. May I have your old friend?" I asked the knight.

"He is of great use to me now," the Knight of Lies said. "Of course not."

I nodded to the basket. "You can have the horse." The wicker rattled, and the mouth on the basket opened, and it leaped forward to chew at the fresh killed flesh of the horse. As the horse's bones cracked and the basket stripped the rapidly bleeding flesh, the Organ Grinder emerged from the inn with the first of the bags. The Stone Preacher followed him with the rest. The Knave of Innkeepers limped to the door, staring as they packed up our goods.

"My things!" he shrieked. "They're mine! They belong to me!" He staggered about as the Watch came over, pointing with his bloody stump. "These thieves looted my home, and robbed me! And that pretender there is playing at being a noble! Look, her eyes have a touch of falseness! Look there!" His finger pointed at me as if it were an unerring arrow.

There was a dull belch from the picnic basket as it waddled over to me, leaving the half-eaten horse behind.

I laughed at the innkeeper. It felt sweet. "He lies. He has lied to these people, extorted them, forced them to live like dogs, and makes sure almost no one takes a bath here."

"Harlot!" He locked eyes with me. "I know what you do in the back of that cart with that disgusting Organ Grinder! He shall pleasure thee like a cheap beast, and you shall savor it like wine!"

The Knight of Lies studied the scene. "I shall arrive now." He bowed to me in the most deceptive manner I have ever seen. "I shall make my way through the air itself." He tromped off along the village path, shouldering his lance as if it were a trinket. "We shall not meet again."

I didn't care what the basket had done to the innkeeper. "See how he speaks to me?" I said to the nearest guard. "See that he is whipped at once."

The guards moved forward with brutal leers and grabbed the Knave of Innkeepers by his shoulders. The Stone Preacher was already walking away. I settled into the cart next to the Organ Grinder, with the mouth of the picnic basket hanging open, quite near to him and his disgusting monkey.

As we drove away, the sound of whips thrashing against the back of the Knave of Innkeepers was like music. I savored the noise of splitting flesh under the lash, and enjoyed the sound of his screaming. It brought me more pleasure than it should have.

***

The road before us crackled in wintry dust. We trotted out of town on the creaking cart. My breath puffed into the cold air, and I wrapped the cloak of runes around myself to stave it off. The boots could keep me warmer, but I couldn't ignite them. The old wood of the Organ Grinder's cart would burn. As much pleasure as it would bring me, I didn't want the monkey to slit my throat in the middle of the night, or my new pet to eat me.

In the distance, a troop of fifteen armed riders waited. They wore silvery leather armor. There was a faint jangling in the air as their commander raised his arm. They stood at the ready in the center of the road, with crossbows loaded. The commander's voice was firm and demanding. He shouted as the Organ Grinder yanked the reins. The tired, skin and bones horses ground to a weary stop. "Do not move!" The captain tilted his head as the crossbows raised, and stared at the Organ Grinder savagely.

"I am the Sergeant of Obedience! We are here to escort you to the castle of the Duke of Bells at once!" He continued to shout. The troops advanced forward slowly, their crossbows still on us. "Fail to comply with the orders of the lord of these lands shall result in your death!" He suddenly gained enthusiasm. It was turning out not to be my day.

Chapter Seven

The Witching Hour in the Court of the Duke of Bells

"Very well!" I adopted a pompous tone. "You may escort us. Please guard our front and our rear."

"I obey!" He took up a position in front of our cart while the Organ Grinder and the Stone Preacher remained somewhat wary.

"Are you sure you wish to let them surround us?" A dim rumble came from the back of the Stone Preachers' throat.

"It does seem like an ambush, and a lot like a team of assassins," the Organ Grinder said. The monkey chittered, as if it agreed. The picnic basket growled at the nearest soldier, showing teeth from under its wooden lid. The soldier shuddered. The coat of arms studded with bells on his horse rustled in the cold air.

"If they were assassins, not only would we be dead, but they wouldn't allow us to maneuver to where they greeted us," I said. The men rode horses around us, taking up defensive positions. "They would have been hiding behind one of those hills, and we would have been full of arrows."

"They're called bolts," a soldier laughed. "It seems the noble lady is not from around here." He cackled and his fat belly shook.

The Organ Grinder shook his head. "I am not from around here either. Guard your wives, good gentlemen, for you travel with the legend that is the Organ Grinder. Now that you have insulted me, I shall spare none of them the visit they waited all their lives for."

Several crossbows turned towards the Organ Grinder. I held up a hand. "Don't shoot him!" I snapped. The monkey hissed from under the coat, as if sensing the crossbows rising towards it. "Or I'll have all your heads!" The picnic basket uttered a low growl as if it needed to be fed. I reached in, pulled out a sandwich, and chewed thoughtfully. It was turkey and cheddar, with little bits of bacon and a deliciously spiced cranberry sauce. If only it hadn't been one of the Knave of Innkeepers hands, it might have tasted better.

The crossbows lowered. One of the men stammered. "Yes, milady."

The Stone Preacher's face was a mask of grim satisfaction. His feet rumbled slightly, walking next to the cart. I didn't know what he was thinking. His silences were always the most frightening thing about him.

***

The Sergeant and his men led us to a turnoff in the road amid cold hills and leafless trees. They laughed, talking about their drinking habits and their card games, and stared ominously at the Organ Grinder whenever anyone mentioned their wives.

I was worried that they might kill us all, but the Stone Preacher maintained a vast sense of satisfaction throughout the entire journey, even when the night grew dark and the air grew bitter cold. I wrapped myself in the magical cloak and shuddered, though the boots kept me warm. The moon was high enough in the sky for me to see it for the first time.

It was as monstrous as the world I was in. It shone with an ugly reddish-purple light, a mean, sickly eye of vengeance that struggled to spit venom upon the world. I could not hide from it, even in the daytime. When its light struggled through the trees, it made everything appear about to drip with blood. I could feel it clawing at my stomach.

Everyone else felt the same way. No one else was looking up. I saw the monsters first, flying towards us on dirty feathered wings, with bat-like folds. Elongated spines protruded off the wings' edges.

There were three of them. They hunched and shuffled in the air like old cavemen, towering over the biggest guards by at least two feet. Hunchbacked brown bodies were covered with warts and filth. There was a sickening wave of stench that assailed my nostrils as they drew closer. Wide, squared-off jaws jutted from their mouths. Low, flat heads were covered in thin strands of greasy hair. They carried a single huge club in both hands.

They spoke in voices both guttural and sophisticated. "I do perceive a need for meat and keening flesh!" their leader thundered as he flew in, smashing one of the guards to a sticky pulp. His horse went with it. A dying whinny followed body parts spraying about. The smell of blood and urine wafted to my nostrils.

"Their souls are but as offal to our noble cause!" the second one declared as it flew by.

I drew my first arrow while the guards began to react. The Organ Grinder ducked low to avoid the swishing club of the third.

"Curses!" it bellowed. "A terrible miss, worthy of agony and being tied to a retching post while one's innards are tormented by hot pokers!"

"What are they?" I shouted as the guards drew their crossbows, and the Organ Grinder drew his revolver, hurriedly loading the last of his bullets into it.

"Gluttonous Orators!" The Organ Grinder shouted. "They feed not only on the meat of the dead but on their very creativity, and use it to write speeches about the deaths of their victims! They're hard to kill!"

The Stone Preacher leaped onto the cart, and it groaned under his weight as the creatures came around for a second pass.

The Sergeant readied his men. "Fire!" He shouted as the guards closed up in a line. Crossbows thudded and twanged, rocketing towards the lead beast as it let out a howl. It tumbled a little bit lower from pain.

In that moment, the Stone Preacher jumped. The roof of the Organ Grinder's cart cracked. "Thrice cursed preacher!" His bellow was so loud even the monsters took notice. "You owe me a caulking!"

As the lead monster fell, The Stone Preacher's hand rose up to meet it, and grabbed it by the throat. They tumbled towards the ground and crashed into the dirt, rolling down a dark embankment to rest in a small, muddy pool.

I drew my bow and fired at the second creature. The clockwork arrow roared forth, slamming into dark brown flesh. There was a clicking, wet, sucking sound. Blood spurted from its stomach in wet, greenish gouts.

It turned to notice me, howling hungrily. "I cannot express my distaste that my meal has superlative archery skills!" it declared. "How am I supposed to swallow food if there is a hole in my stomach?" The wound didn't seem to slow it as much as I had hoped.

"Impressive!" the Sergeant thundered! "The girl can shoot indeed! We might not all die here, after all!"

I thought of the boots and began to run, trying to buy the crossbowmen enough time to set up for another volley.

The third creature blazed for the Organ Grinder, club outstretched as it readied its swing, and let out a muscular howl. Like a gunfighter, the Organ Grinder laughed, and fanned the trigger, firing off his last two rounds into the creature's chest as it drew close. It doubled up as its massive frame bubbled with green blood from the bullet holes, and crashed to the earth, rolling and gurgling as it spit up reddish-black foam.

The picnic basket leaped off the cart. The Organ Grinder's monkey leaped with it. They descended on the broken creature while it spasmed and tried to get up. There was an agonizing howl as the monkey jabbed its knife-tail at the monster's eyes. The picnic basket chewed on the floundering beast's hand. There was a wet, disgusting pop as the creature sat up. The hand came away, vanishing into the mouth of the basket. Blood gushed from the stump as the picnic basket chewed happily.

The monster bellowed at the loss of its hand and the bullet wounds. It staggered to its feet. "Incompetent am I, laid low by forces weaker than myself! Unworthy am I to feast upon the raw flesh of the unimportant, and to my death I go, while my beastly body lies here, undone by common creatures!" Then its jaw grew slack and its wrist bled profusely. Only his desire to give the dying speech sustained him. He crashed to the ground.

From above, I could see the Stone Preacher and the lead monster trading punches as they wrestled on the ground. Greenish blood and stone chips flew. The creatures could hit hard enough to damage him. I was grateful that they did not have giant picks instead.

I ran like the wind in the boots, and dove in low, low enough that the guardsmen could fire another volley at the creature. "Shoot!" I screamed as I blazed overhead. "Shoot him now!"

The reloading had already commenced. The Sergeant gave the command, boldly raising his hand to shout "Fire!" as the crossbow bolts were loosed.

It was the end of him. The creature's club smashed down, crushing him in his armor, the metal screeching from the impact as the flesh inside was pulped and twisted. "Vile slayers of my brother!" The creature's bellow was as brutal as it was persuasive. "How dare you send him to the afterlife of tongue-tied men, to live out his days in incoherent babble? Now he is unable to teach speeches of meat and blood to his little ones, and to feed upon the flesh of your selfish kind!" The horse's back snapped amid the monsters words. The shrieking whinny melded with oratory as hooves flopped and spasmed on the ground. Wet froth poured from between its teeth.

The creature was too weak from the wounds the Preacher inflicted to fly. I savored the moment. I drew back an arrow and fired. The creature smashed about amidst the guardsmen, knocking another off his horse. The arrow punched deep into the creature's flesh. It must have struck something vital. "I, too..." it began, struggling with words, "am slain, losing the virtues of my life in mere vagaries, to sp—" He clutched at his chest as something greenish and vile leeched out of his mouth. "to spit up blood, and die – at the hands of a mere human whore – aspiring to be..."

He crashed to one knee and staggered. The remaining guardsmen moved to the edge of the embankment, where they began to reload. I fired another arrow, and it slammed into his back, bursting out through his chest, spraying his blood across the ground. "...more than..." He managed before his last breath gave out.

"At least you have a friend to join you in the afterlife." I muttered as the crossbowmen finished reloading.

It wasn't needed. The Stone Preacher grasped the thing by the neck, pulling hard and tugging. There was a horrible wrenching crack. In a moment of horror, illuminated by the purple moon, it did not manage to speak a single word. The head and spine were ripped from its body. "Heretic!" the Stone Preacher shouted. "You will live eternally in the coldest of places!" Its terrified eyes died open while its mouth struggled to speak.

I began running down in fiery footsteps, taking pleasure in the fact that my enemies were in the deepest of their hells. As I landed, one of the soldiers walked over to a twitching horse, and thrust his sword deep into it, ending its pain.

***

The Sergeant of Obedience was dead. Crushed bodies of men and horses had to be pulled out of the way. The Organ Grinder tied his cart to the dead horses, and began dragging them off the road one at a time. The Stone Preacher hurled the dead body of the creature down the embankment, while horrified soldiers stared.

"Does one of you know where we're going?" It was more of a demand than a question. The picnic basket growled viciously.

"Stop that! Just because I won't let you eat anymore!" The basket settled back and gave a low, greedy whine. I had no idea what to do with it, but it was cute, in a monstrous way.

The soldiers turned to look at me. One gathered the courage to speak. "The Duke has bid us escort you, and so we shall. We have no time to bury the bodies, but we will retrieve them later. I am now in temporary command. The rest of you, take up your positions!"

I waited for the Organ Grinder to drag the cart back up the embankment. His horses looked like they had baleful hate in their eyes. Their shabby coats were laced with sweat and more than a little pain. "Hop up!" he thundered to me. "It is a great day when a new lady is introduced. All the world should see you in that lovely dress of yours."

My boots still burned, so I ran across the air, and plopped into the seat. As I flew, the picnic basket gave a panicked yowl. It settled into my lap when I sat, giving little wicker shivers.

The Stone Preacher glided up to the cart, and he gave a crackling smile of rock. His fingers were stained with blood, and his cassock shrouded in gore. "I fear I shall need a new cassock. I am quite unpresentable."

I smiled to him. "Then we shall request one of our host and postpone his event, whatever it might be, until the afternoon of the next day." It was all too easy to be in charge. Giving orders was starting to become more natural. There was still a queasy part of me that didn't like it. Most of it felt very good.

The Stone Preacher chuckled. "An excellent means of providing for one's entourage when one has limited funds."

"That depends on what you consider limited." I smiled and showed him my little bag of loot from the Knave of Innkeepers. "I thought I should have some jewelry to go along with my dress, and it wasn't as if the Knave needed all those rings with only one hand, and those bracelets wouldn't stay on." I gave him a wink that was more merciless than it should have been. I was just trying to survive.

The cart began to creak forward, and the Organ Grinder leered at the corpses in the embankment. "No doubt, there will be some lonely wives in need of consolation, and I, The Organ Grinder, am an expert at such things." His satisfaction at the nature of the situation made him tug the reins a little harder. "A lady wedded to the Sergeant of Obedience would be very pliant indeed."

"Have you no mercy, even for the grieving?" I said as the entourage made way through the dark hills.

"I offer no more than a pleasant diversion that shall help her pass her grief." The Organ Grinder smiled. "Besides, it doesn't break your rule. I'm not interfering in any relationship. She can't have a relationship with the dead."

"Don't be too sure about that," I muttered. "A lot of things don't seem to work the way they usually do."

"Wise," the Organ Grinder said. "If she is some sort of horrible monster, I shall cry for help at once. However, I believe that she is merely plump and repressed, as most women married to military men are. I shall stretch her out." He gave me an amused look.

"Just drive the cart." I rolled my eyes and gathered my cloak about me, savoring the warmth it brought. Every so often, the Organ Grinder's leg would bump against mine in the seat. My skin crawled until I dreamed of my green-eyed lover by the pool.

***

We were escorted for minutes that seemed like weeks, the gloating eyes of the Organ Grinder musing over thoughts of the Lady of Obedience, and what orders he might give. The hills were bleak; the air was thick and uncomfortable, with angry wisps of fog trying to chill us.

When we crested a low rise, we could finally see it. The castle was settled on an oval hill, twisted like a weeping eye. It looked like a series of misshapen towers built around a heavy, distended lump in the shape of a crude bell. Highlighted by the dark, the home of the Duke of Bells looked like a monstrous cyst, bloating out from the hill as if the land itself were trying to excise it.

There was a tinkling noise that wafted through dry air. The wind died suddenly, as if afraid of the castle. Our escort raised their swords. One of them reached to his saddle for a trumpet. He raised his hand to call a halt. "All hail the Duke of Bells!" he thundered. The rest of the men echoed him "All despise the weakness of the Sergeant of Obedience, dead in a ditch!" The men echoed this too, with only slightly less enthusiasm.

"That was an indictment." I muttered under my breath, looking to the Organ Grinder.

"Indeed," he replied. "The Duke of Bells must be in a fouler mood than usual." Under the greatcoat, the monkey gave off an odd trilling noise. The tinkling sound grew louder as we drew closer. We wended our way around the hill to a large, bell-shaped gate.

It looked like an angry mouth, studded with spikes. A drawbridge lolled like a tongue over a dry, unpleasant moat. Guards wearing the Duke's heraldry loomed at the entry and in towers. They looked as vicious as the men we killed in the town where I met Bosquoverde. The picnic basket growled. I slapped it on the handle. "Quiet. Or is that, heel?" The basket turned its attention to the Organ Grinder's leg. "No!"

The Stone Preacher turned to the Organ Grinder. "You have been here before?" He said with a gravelly shudder. "Does that increase or decrease our chances of survival?"

"I believe it increases our chances, as the Duke was out visiting the Count of Locks when I did visit, and the Duchess received me in a warm and friendly manner." An all-too familiar smile spread across the face of the Organ Grinder. The men shook their heads.

As we made our way across the drawbridge, I could see large, warty toads hopping about the moat, their mouths filled with unpleasant teeth and scraps of flesh. "What are those?" I asked. "Carnivorous toads aren't exactly common where I'm from."

"They are the pets of the Duke of Bells, and one of the reasons he has his name," the Organ Grinder responded. "The ringing sounds you hear come from the toads. They make them at mealtimes, and when they feast on the unfortunate or the unwary. I probably should have told you."

"He feeds people to carnivorous toads?" I snapped. "Yes, I think it might have been nice to know that. So why are we here again?"

The basket looked over the edge of the moat. I heard an odd lip smacking sound from it. I did my best to ignore it.

"To acquire his support for your presentation to the King of Feathers," he said. "If two nobles support you, the King must accept. It is one of those boring courtly rules."

The Stone Preacher nodded as we made our way into the courtyard, where people stabled horses and ran madly about, performing tasks and tending to chores.

"Leave your cart here!" one of the men snapped at us. "I shall report in, and let my commander know you have arrived. Servants shall be with you shortly."

The Organ Grinder brought the cart to a halt. The men dispersed while the trumpet holder ran off to make his report. A thin, reedy man approached us, his impeccable clothes ruffled and full of arranged haughtiness. His narrow visage glowered at the dirty cart.

His eyes were fierce and slitted, wrapped in slenderness and wrinkles. The rest of his body was as narrow. He wore a thick burgundy doublet designed to protect him from the cold. Rich purple pants made him seem even more pompous and bitter. He carried a pocket watch and wore thin rounded glasses, but his shoes were garish – black savage shoes that curled a little at the tips. They were affixed with unpleasant spurs that he seemed to view every so often with an oily smile on his face. "I am the Knight of Attendants." He bowed. "The Duke of Bells wishes to know your business here."

"They gave a title to a gofer?" I rolled my eyes. I didn't even try to hide the disgust I felt. Everyone here had a title. I couldn't wait to see the King of Dungsweepers, then get as far away as possible before the stench overwhelmed me.

The Knight looked at me disdainfully, and gained a sheepish smile that made him look like a creative miscreant about to torture animals. "And who might you be?"

I decided to be as arrogant as he was. "My name is Symantha, but that's Lady Symantha to you, you unspeakable little toad." The picnic basket growled at him. "Hush."

The Knight did not budge. "Of course." He looked askance at the moat. "I may have been one of those things once, but now, I fear, those days are behind me."

"Was he really a toad?" the Organ Grinder asked the Stone Preacher.

"I do not know," the Stone Preacher said. "Frog transformations are not uncommon, but at the same time, they don't usually come from creatures like this."

"We should be quartered. I wish to see the Duke of Bells in the morning." I tried to remain as commanding as possible.

"I shall escort you to quarters befitting your high station," he said. "Do you wish quarters provided for your servants, or will they be staying with you?" He glanced at the picnic basket, and his eyes opened wide. Drool ran down the edge of its wicker lip.

"That answers that," the Organ Grinder said. "He used to be a toad, indeed."

"Used to be?" the Stone Preacher murmured in a gravelly rumble. "Some things only change what they look like."

The Knight of Attendants turned on his heel and walked out of the courtyard toward a bulky looking wooden door, thrust open by wary guards on the other side. It groaned like an angry beast. Our footsteps carried us through, the guards watching us and staring.

Behind us, the door slammed shut. We could hear the front gate begin clanking down, as if we were being swallowed by a hungry mouth, to be digested by something huge and terrible.

***

The Knight of Attendants guided us down a wide hallway, towards an elegant set of double doors. Torches flickered on the walls. There was a musty, smoky smell. Inside, the croaking of the toads echoed in our ears.

"It is my duty to inform the Duke of your arrival." His voice was grim and perfunctory. Under it, I thought heard a muscular croak. He neatly squeezed through the door after opening it and left us in the hallway.

"This could be a trap to murder us," the Organ Grinder said with a dull smile. The monkey chittered and looked out of the coat.

The Stone Preacher's voice rumbled a little bit. "I do not think so. Perhaps you, if the Duchess likes to talk about the music you play too much, but we have not been slaughtered like beasts already. I suppose we might be actual guests, as opposed to toad fodder."

At the mention of the toads, the picnic basket perked up. It ran a slithering tongue out of its lid.

"Stop it," I said harshly. "You'll get to eat something soon. Do you have a sandwich?"

The basket gave as contrite a shuffle as it could, and opened. Inside was a beautiful array of sweetmeats and the few remaining sandwiches, along with the bottle of wine. "How does this work?" I asked the Stone Preacher. I pulled the sandwich out and began to quickly eat it.

"I don't know. I think it likes to eat the toads, though. That could be useful."

"As unpleasant as this sounds, I'm worried that the toads might want to eat it." I offered a sandwich to the Organ Grinder. "This is really starting to look like one of those 'don't eat anything he serves you' things, so I'm just going to make sure I've had a little something to eat before we go in there."

"I thought we were waiting until morning," the Organ Grinder said with a wry chuckle.

"If I heard someone wanted to wait to see me until morning, and I were the Duke of Bells, I would demand to see that person immediately before anything untoward or unpleasant happened." I smiled. "Of course, he might try to have us murdered in our sleep, but that seems to happen a lot around here."

The Stone Preacher chuckled slightly as I passed a sandwich to the Organ Grinder. He took it to eat, demolishing it in just a few seconds. "Clever girl," the Stone Preacher said while the Organ Grinder's mouth was full. "You are a fast learner after all."

The door opened, and the Knight of Attendants bowed to us. "The Duke and his Duchess will see you now." He smiled as if he had a mouth full of sharp teeth.

"Good sir, please tell them that I am not presentable, and as such, wish to present myself to them in a manner more befitting their station. I have no wish to offend such a noble lord." I curtsied as I talked. Laying it on as thick as possible was the way of these people.

The Knight of Attendants nodded once. "You are rather dusty from the road. There appears to be some greasy ichor on your strange pants."

I looked down at my jeans. They were covered with the blood of the winged, speechmaking giants. I hadn't even noticed in the dark.

"If I could but have an hour to freshen up, good sir, I shall be with them presently." The Organ Grinder and the Stone Preacher stood at my side like statues, waiting for me to finish.

"Of course, milady." The Knight of Attendants didn't stop smiling. "You are right. It would not do to appear before the Duke in such a bloody and disheveled state. It may even heighten the offense you have given him by arriving without any proper heralding of your coming."

"Tell the Duke that I apologize for such an offense, but as we were beset by monsters on the road, creatures which slew the Sergeant of Obedience and two of his men, we had little choice in this matter. I had no time to write a letter of introduction." The lies became easier as I spoke. It was becoming fun.

The Knight gestured and escorted us down the hall, next to a heavy wooden door. "You two gentlemen should wait outside. Inside is a changing room, where the lady may bathe." He unlocked and opened it for me. Inside was a simple wooden tub filled with water, and a dressing screen. The Organ Grinder dragged in my luggage and returned to the outside. The picnic basket rushed inside, and made unusual sniffing noises, as if looking for trouble, or hidden toads.

The Stone Preacher glared at the Knight of Attendants, as if sizing him up, and turned to me. "Be as quick as you can." His voice was gravelly and grim. "I would hate to kill anyone before I really got to know them in such a lovely castle."

I slipped inside and bathed in a hurry, eager to get the stench of the road off me. Then I took my time getting dressed while the picnic basket guarded me. No one came near. When I was finally in my dress, the basket gave a little contented coo, and opened, offering me a bottle of something delicious and minty.

***

I drank enough from the bottle to cleanse my breath and placed it back in the basket, which eagerly followed me to the door. I had done my hair up in a single, looping braid and wound it around my head, pinning it up with a small clasp.

With the dress on, I felt as if I could conquer the world. It was sinuous and smooth. I felt as if I was in a different place. I thought of the man with the green eyes by the pool, opened the door. I was unafraid.

The Organ Grinder's eyes opened and his face drew into a magnificent leer. It was the reaction I needed, but not the reaction I was hoping for. "Good lady," he said. "It would be an honor to play my accordion for you." He bowed as though my anger was enough to cut his head off.

I scowled at him and turned to the Stone Preacher. "It is acceptable?"

"With no servant to do your hair, and the picnic basket having short arms, it will have to do." His gravelly voice was dry, and echoed in the corridor.

The Knight of Attendants came around the corner. He gave a magnificent bow. His shoes had been recently polished. "This way, milady." His voice had attained a slight quaver, as if the absence of jeans and blood had somehow ennobled me on its own.

We walked down the hall, our footsteps echoing off grim, torch-lit stone, to arrive in front of the same magnificent door we passed the night before. The Knight of Attendants opened the door, standing to one side. "The Lady Symantha, as yet unnamed." I felt the wicker of the picnic basket peering out from behind my leg.

The Knight gave a waving gesture with his hand. We stepped into a room of delicate precision and infinite madness.

***

The room seemed cobbled together out of tinkling chimes and half-assembled clappers, with walls made out of resonating metal. I stepped into the chamber with a series of soft, smooth taps, gliding on the slow burning of my boots. The silver and white dress quivered in silky wisps, billowing as smoke left my heels.

There were no attendants and no sycophants. It was already too late in the evening. There was only the Duke and Duchess of Bells, seated in inverted bell-shaped thrones, laughing slightly as a pony-sized carnivorous toad chewed on raw meat in front of them. I didn't know what kind of meat it was. The Duke looked up at me, admiring me in my sheath of silver.

His high, slender form was ensconced in a thick bronze-colored doublet with solid black metal boots. Narrow eyes and subtly curved ears seemed to show sympathy for ringing objects. His skin was a pale metallic shade, with hair almost fused to his head. He wore thick pants made of some unusual lizard hide, tooled with the coat of arms that hung above the twin thrones. "I am the Duke of Bells." His voice was as beautiful as the ringing of chimes. "You are a magnificent one. I assume you are here to receive a notice of affirmation, that I might report your nobility to the King of Feathers?" He gave me a skeptical stare. The toad at his feet croaked. "May I introduce the Duchess of Bells, my lovely and clever wife?"

She was full figured and attractive, with meandering blonde hair that trickled about her face, touched with a little hint of green to match her eyes. Full lips gave a solemn smirk as her lips flicked open. She gave the Organ Grinder a bitter, subtle glance. She was wearing a beautiful gown of something silvery that rustled against her large chest. She tilted her head to me, her lips opening to speak. I had never been so jealous of a body that I did not have. She was shaped elegance and deliberately cultured poise, but her words cut me and my desire for perfect love. "My husband," she cooed delicately, "I do not approve."

The Duke looked down at his fat toad as it finished swallowing the piece of meat, and idly crossed his legs in his chair. "That is unfortunate," he said, as the Organ Grinder returned the Duchess's glance. "Do you feel your usual jealousy, my flower?"

The Duchess's voice rang in the chamber of cast iron bell pieces. Her legs crossed daintily under the massive gown. "Oh, no, such a waif could not possibly compare with my beauty." She idly brushed a finger against one of her elegant curls. It was as if the world were nothing more than an audience for her voice.

I curtsied before them and made obeisance to the Duke, whose hand idly caressed the warty back of the carnivorous toad. From under my dress, the picnic basket made a little rustling noise, and peered out as best it could to look at the toad. I knew it hungered.

"It seems you, too, have an unusual pet." The Duke's voice was solemn, the echoing of bells in his voice swimming in the tones of the toad.

My throat tightened. The Organ Grinder and the Stone Preacher waited behind me. The picnic basket slavered at the massive toad while I daintily curtsied. "I do indeed, my lord." I gave him a fond smile, that the Duchess of Bells did not receive nearly as warmly.

"My wife does not approve of you," he said sternly. "This represents a problem to me. Although I am the master of this palace and the master of these toads, this fine lady does represent *my* master in many things. As such, until you can present yourself to me at a time when she is not here, and such a time shall not come again for seasons, I fear that you are quite my guest, and prisoner." He yawned idly. The toad gave a wretched croak.

The Organ Grinder reached into his coat. The monkey flicked its head out of the massive leather shroud, giving a vicious screech. I raised my hand to halt the Organ Grinder.

"My lord, how long might this take?"

A pout framed the Duchess of Bells face. She seemed far less attractive as the Duke responded. "Oh, five score years and ten. I fear you shall be elderly when you reach him." He let out a low chuckle. "Guards, escort them to fine quarters. I am amused by this latest gambit."

The walls ground open, shell-like hidden doors clanking aside. Over forty heavily armored men surrounded us. "Gambit? What does that mean?" I said. "We aren't playing cards, are we?"

"He's testing you." the Stone Preacher said as the guards escorted us out of the presence of the Duke. "It is his right as your first petition. Almost no one exercises it anymore. Someone must be blackmailing him, or he has a vested interest in your failure. Doing so during the first petition is almost unthinkable." He gave a grim smile that wracked his lips, as if he were about to spit up gravel. "You have powerful enemies, my dear. You will be a magnificent creature indeed, when you receive your title."

I bore that thought with more than a little pleasure as we made our way up flights of stairs both sinuous and misbegotten.

***

The armored men clanked their way up the stairs in slow, ominous progression. Their footsteps were so hollow that I thought that they might not be men at all. We reached the top of the stairs after passing a few doors. Air slithered across our ears, as if there were few windows so high up.

The guardsmen opened the door. We stepped into a large, circular room that had two open windows. A fire crackled in a fireplace in between the two windows. There was a large bed that had been made and fluffed up, done every day regardless of the promise of guests. The quilt was patched in places. Gray light shone in the windows from an angry moon. There was a small case of books with no titles on their spines resting against a wall.

I walked in along with the Organ Grinder, hearing a little chittering from under his coat. The picnic basket crawled up the stairs after the guards, and gave a little whiffling noise as it slipped through the door.

"I shall remain outside," the Stone Preacher said coolly. "You gentlemen may go."

"You should listen to him." I said firmly. "He'll kill you as soon as look at you. You're all godless cretins and heretics in his eyes."

The guards nodded, turned, and clanked down the stairs, keeping a careful eye on the Stone Preacher until the last of their metal-sheathed forms turned the corner of the stair.

The Organ Grinder clapped behind me while the door was still open. "That was highly diplomatic," he said. The monkey cooed with excitement, as if the Stone Preacher were already ripping the men apart.

There was a hiccup from the basket as I closed the door, and it spit out some toad bones, letting out a little belch. "Oh, God!" I rolled my eyes. "You can't just eat the toads! They don't belong to you!"

The picnic basket shuffled a little bit and opened its lid. Inside was a magnificent set of plates and well-carved roast beef, dripping with just the right amount of blood. It rustled with warm heat. I took out the portions carefully, placing them on the nightstand next to the bed. There was a pot of mashed potatoes with a succulent gravy and candied carrots, balanced underneath the platters. "I can't believe it made roast beef out of a carnivorous toad." I rolled my eyes. "It's evil, but it makes such good food."

"It's like a chef and a murderer all in one!" The Organ Grinder's eyes lit up with a wicked light, and headed for the plate of roast beef. "You do realize that the Duke has just imprisoned you here? You don't seem to care about that." He began eating his roast beef, so I took the other plate and began to eat it too.

The picnic basket flopped over next to the bed. It must have been tired from making the roast beef. "The windows are open. I can fly down. The question is, how I can pass the Duke's ridiculous test? I mean, there's a way, but it means that I have to risk your life."

"As long as it is not taken." The Organ Grinder smiled. "I cannot refuse you, milady. Perhaps one day, I shall play my accordion for you."

I lowered my voice to a cold whisper. "You won't be. You're going to play the accordion for the Duchess. And I will save your life from the Duke."

The Organ Grinder raised an eyebrow. "I thought you said I wasn't allowed to do anything like that." He chortled. "It is a fine evening in the castle of the Duke of Bells."

"Why not?" I sighed. "It's not her first time, and I don't want to spend a year or more in this creepy place. We'll just climb or fly down the wall, you can play the accordion for her outside. I'll hide under the bed. While she's busy, I'll take her keys and get into the Duke's bedchamber. Then I'll have a talk with him. Hopefully, he won't want physical revenge."

"I thought you were a noblewoman. But it seems you have the mind of a thief."

"I'm a lucky gypsy girl. I think we're going to need to dismantle this bed. After all, you'll be using another one soon." Then I stopped myself. "Tie yourself up in the sheet. Quickly. We can jump out the window, and I can lower you, as long as I can keep the boots away from it." I gave him a little grin.

"It is a risk worth taking for the flesh of a duchess!" the Organ Grinder purred excitedly. He tied the sheet around his waist while he extended the remaining length of cloth to me.

I took the sheet and stepped to the window, willing the boots to life as the Organ Grinder followed me out, and we stepped into the air of the courtyard, flush with the window in the dark. It was like lifting an anvil. He was heavy, wide, and full of bones. His weight pulled me down toward the ground below. I struggled to hold on, pressed as near to the side of the building as I could without touching it.

We lowered ourselves to the ground, with only a quiet thump against the cobbles of the courtyard, slipping towards the cart as if it was our only chance of life. We dodged a few toads. The Organ Grinder slipped a hand into his greatcoat pocket, covering the monkey's mouth.

As I slipped away with the Organ Grinder, I thought I could hear strange hooves beat the air, as if a monstrous animal of some kind were being driven towards the castle on the wind.

***

We arrived at the Organ Grinder's cart amid the shadows, skulking along the wall. Our fingers pressed against the moss between the stones. The shadow of the cart shielded us from prying eyes while we crept inside.

"You could always take the place of the Duchess." The Organ Grinder leered. "It would be an acceptable substitute." He gave me a knowing wink. "You didn't even tell the Stone Preacher you left the room."

"I'm certain that if he hasn't figured it out by now, he is choosing to remain ignorant to make certain we survive."

The Organ Grinder pulled a key out of one of his many leather pockets, and opened the door. "Your temporary home, milady." He grinned wickedly. "Under the bed with you."

I looked inside, and my stomach crawled. The wood was rickety and slightly splintered. A crude fold-out writing desk had a book left open on it, locked into place by metal bars. It was covered with images of crude eroticism. The door to a rickety wardrobe bolted to the wall contained two formal outfits that looked slightly repaired.

The center of the cart was a massive, dilapidated bed. It smelled of old sex, unclean sheets, and was marked with deep tears from fingernails. The monument to its occupant was framed by a thick oaken headboard that teetered a little bit on loosened tacks, and had a thick railing top that was easy for hands to grab. At the foot of the bed was a thick, heavy trunk. From behind me, the monkey leapt forward and opened it, revealing a bed far cleaner than the massive one that filled most of the cart. The monkey crept in and pulled the door down quietly, giving a hoot to me before the trunk closed. I felt safer already.

I turned to the Organ Grinder, my eyes narrow. "You didn't say it would be inside."

"I didn't say it wouldn't be. You should have asked." He gave me a merry smirk. "Remember that this is your plan." He reached for his accordion, hung around his neck like a garish monster, and lifted it up in his massive fingers. "Don't worry. Only women can hear its magic. It's one of the rules." The smirk transformed into the smile that people have when they're about to ruin someone's life.

The accordion's gnashing tones filled my ears, and I crawled beneath the bed as the Organ Grinder began to play the most evil and seductive of songs, murmuring the name of the Duchess of Bells with softness and passion. I shuddered at the thought that it could be me. The Organ Grinder slowly capered from left to right outside the cart, while I watched with a taste of bile rising in my throat. The men guarding the ramparts went about their duties, looking for monsters on the far side of the walls.

As the Organ Grinder danced, I slipped under the bed, pressing myself against the floor so I could see the Duchess when the Organ Grinder brought her inside. I moved my head to the edge of the trunk at the foot of the bed, and peered out the open door, as a pair of footsteps approached, subtle and quiet.

"Ahh, my dear, you have arrived." The Organ Grinder licked his lips and extended his hands, taking the hands of the Duchess and leading her up the rickety stairs.

"My husband will never know I'm here." She smiled, as if she had initiated the incident, her lip quirking as she undid her magnificent silk gown and pressed herself against him. Her breath quickened, and then she opened her beautiful lips, and sucked on his mouth like a beast.

The Organ Grinder turned her to face the headboard and flipped up her skirt, and then pushed her onto the bed, pinning her head down so that she could not see, then crawled up after her. I heard the sound of unbuttoning pants, and a wicked slap that sounded like spanking. Still on the floor, I could hear the Duchess grunting, and I inched my way to the door as her breathing grew heavier and the Organ Grinder chuckled. From inside the trunk, the monkey began to hoot and screech as it savored the victory of its master.

As I crawled out through the door, there was a wet, pumping suck of flesh on flesh, and hungry moaning from the Duchess of Bells as if she were receiving the gift of true love itself. As the air freshened, I rose on my boots of fire back to the window. In the absence of the Organ Grinder, I felt cleaner already.

The feeling lasted only a few moments as I saw the wooden cart buck and roll, rattling a little in the darkness. The guards turned to look at it, and shook their heads, as if the noise came only from the wind.

***

I slipped to the door and opened it to make sure the Stone Preacher was still guarding the door. He was staring right at me, his eyes narrow and ominous as he put his hands on his hips, grinding against the stony cassock. "Was it really necessary to do that?" His voice was low. "You could simply have snuck in."

"I need to blackmail him," I said firmly. "That's how he works. That's how this whole place works. You already taught me that. Honestly, if we want to live, we need to start thinking about ways to manipulate their rules."

The Stone Preacher's lips flicked a gravelly smile to me. "Will you be taking the stairs?" He turned his back.

"I think I'll sneak back out the window," I said calmly.

"Then as far as I am concerned, you are still inside." He reached back and closed the door with a soft click.

I made my way towards the window and crept out, sticking to the edges of the tower that were shrouded in shadow. I hoped that flame and smoke from my boots did not betray me. Night air clutched at my skin. I scuttled along the edges of the stone, letting my fingers touch mortar and the moss. It was cold out. I huddled in my cloak, praying that it would protect me from the guardsmen if they should look my way and shoot.

I held in little breaths in the cold, quickly skirting from tower to tower in search of the Duke's bedroom. I peered through windows but found empty spaces. In one of the tower windows, I saw a chamber filled with torture implements. There were holes pushed into the walls to make it colder in the cell where prisoners were kept. I saw a wracked and mangled body that had been stretched beyond recognition. I slipped past the window and scuttled along the lip of the roof to the next tower. I didn't know how many more sickening sights or noises I could stand. The sounds of the Organ Grinder's cart creaking still carried through the air.

I floated next to the window and saw the Duke of Bells, wrapped in covers with his wife's side of the bed open next to him. He slept peacefully, unable to hear the creaking of the cart and the lustful moaning of his wife. I didn't even pity him. Perhaps I should have. I crawled in through the window, and scuttled across the room to the edge of his bed. I slipped my finger up to his lips and pressed sharply against them. "Shh," I hissed. "Do you know where your wife is?"

The Duke of Bells mumbled in his sleep, and there was a low croaking growl from behind me. I had forgotten about his massive toad. I should have brought the basket. He rolled over. "Go back to sleep, Mondie," he mumbled, idly gesturing towards the toad. The toad growled again, louder.

I kept my finger over his lips and pinched his nose. He gave a coughing sneeze and awakened. "How dare—" His voice was almost drowned out by the chiming howl of the toad.

I repeated myself, glaring into his eyes. "Shh. Do you know where your wife is?"

His reptilian eyes flicked to the empty space next to him. "No, milady, I do not." He scowled at me.

"I do. I have, of course, conditions that you must meet before I agree to tell you." I gave him a sly wink.

The chiming growl of the toad turned into a low hiss, and it hopped to the door and guarded it. The toad made a ringing, slavering noise, a little drool dripping from its mouth. Its tongue hung out, long and wet. It glared at me as if I were nothing but meat.

"That is not surprising. May I sit up, or is there to be a knife at my spleen?" He said it very matter-of-factly, in a bored, polite manner.

"I didn't bring one. I'll have to stand on your bed and burn you and that disgusting toad to death." I gave him a little smile of meanness.

"Very well. You spoke of concessions that I must make?"

"I shall require you to spare the lives of my associates no matter how offended you may be," I said icily. "If you do not, I shall publicize the stain on your relationship and embarrass you greatly."

"The stain on my relationship, eh?" He flicked his gaze to his wife's empty space in the bed, and he glared at me. "The Organ Grinder!" He clenched his fist. "I shall have him at a—"

I ignited the boots. "I'll stand on your bed, good sir, and set it all aflame, but I do not really wish to do this, as you do not know where they are, and I do. I really do not wish to hear the sounds of the Organ Grinder rutting with your widow every night." I gave him another smile as the boots gave a little crackling roar. Near the door, the toad chimed and recoiled.

"Oh, very well, I'll spare the disgusting creature. He might prove useful against my enemies in the future. But you must publicly beg for his life, as if it was you that truly desired him." He gave me a lascivious smirk of victory.

"What woman does not desire the Organ Grinder? Although none of us would truly love to hear the fleeting sounds of his accordion, in the end, we are bound, powerless to resist." I gave a false sigh. I would kill the Organ Grinder before I let him touch me.

"Then we are agreed. And you have passed your presentation test to me." He gave a leering chuckle. "I almost find it pleasing. Where is my full-breasted, sweet-lipped harlot?" He gave a malicious smile.

I looked toward the window, and imagined that I could hear the creaking of the Organ Grinder's cart, and the low greedy moans of the Duchess of Bells as the Organ Grinder pulled her hair and used her. "I beg your pardon, my lord, but I am certain that your wife can have no objections, for even now, she spreads her legs for my despicable associate, the Organ Grinder, whose life I now beg you to spare in exchange for this information." I curtsied as daintily as I could. "Listen well. You should hear her moaning from the cart like a common whore."

"I hear nothing. But nonetheless, I shall call for guards to search the Organ Grinder's cart, and you shall wait here, guarded by my noble beast." The toad gave a whining croak and slobbered on the floor.

I smiled. "Are you sure the toad will be enough?"

The Duke of Bells chuckled in his bed, and moved over behind a screen to quickly bathe in cold water and dress. "You are right. I have four guards hiding in secret panels here. They are all female, and hideously ugly." He smirked.

"Of course." The Duke of Bells left the room, dressed in his magnificent finery, and I made my way over to the window. It wasn't long before I heard the banging of weapons on the door of the cart, and a wicked crack as the Duke and his men forced their way inside. The savage moans of pleasure from the Duke's wife, echoing through the courtyard, gave way to the pleasurable sighs of sweet release. I watched as the Duke yanked the Duchess and the Organ Grinder from the cart, and his men beat them savagely with the butts of their weapons, until all was suddenly still.

"Take them both to the dungeon." the Duke thundered, his voice ringing. I could hear him all the way at the top of the tower. "We'll decide their punishment in the morning!"

***

The morning came with icy sunlight and a wicker rustle from the picnic basket. It must have hopped up on my bed while I was sleeping. I hadn't seen the Organ Grinder all night. The Stone Preacher chuckled outside my door when I passed. The lid on the basket opened, and the warm smell of Bosquoverde's coffee wafted across my nostrils. "You really can make anything, can't you?" I asked it.

It didn't respond. I reached inside, pulled out the coffee, and took a sip. It was perfectly prepared. At the edge of the bed was a sickly looking, bloody toad leg. Somehow, it must have gotten in. The picnic basket hiccupped.

I dressed slowly after my coffee and wobbled to the Duke's audience chamber, woozy and wearing the dress from the previous night. Somehow, it had been cleaned and hung over the dressing screen. The Stone Preacher followed me down the stairs, remaining carefully behind me as his creaking walk echoed in the torch-lit halls. Behind him, newly energized by my departure, flounced the picnic basket. It swiftly overtook him.

The doors opened with a creaking sigh. Twelve armed guards surrounded the Duke of Bells with massive polearms. The Duchess of Bells was naked, chained to one of the heavy weapons. It rested savagely at her throat, the large blade quivering against her neck, the guardsman a little too eager.

The Organ Grinder was dressed in only breeches and a shirt. The monkey was nowhere to be seen. I thought he might still be trapped inside the Organ Grinder's cart, locked inside the wooden chest at the foot of the bed. The thought brought me more pleasure than I ever thought possible. "Ahh!" the Organ Grinder said as he turned to view me. "My savior has arrived!"

"Oh, aye, your savior, wretched seducer and poisoner of my heart." I gave a mocking sob and looked pleadingly to the Duke of Bells. "Is he to die?" I stared at the Organ Grinder. "He is of much value to me. I have not yet been pleasured by his manliness, for I have not the courage to do so."

The Stone Preacher didn't seem to find it funny. His fingers locked tightly behind his back.

The Duke of Bells glowered at his wife. "Is this what you favor then, my sweet? The lascivious poundings of a stupid, meat-driven peasant with no knowledge of caresses or true pleasures of love? Or simply the filthy rutting of flesh against flesh, and the wet stink of stained sheets with some hairy, foul seducer?" His slit eyes stared down at the Duchess.

The Duchess wept, her lips sobbing. "It was not my fault! His wicked music captured me, and took me to his side! I could not resist. It was as if I was a puppet to the stains of his ignoble, hairy body!" She shook her head. The polearm chain rattled in the hands of its guard.

"She was quite exquisite!" The Organ Grinder smiled. "It is clear you've never given her such pleasure. Why, you should perhaps hire me to do what you never could yourself!" He chuckled and was clubbed on the back of his head by one of the guards. The Stone Preacher's lips cracked into a rocky grin. Now he was enjoying himself.

"Charlatan!" I mock-sobbed. "You promised me what you gave to her, you vengeful top-hatted swine!" I moved up and slapped him right on his most recent bruise. The Organ Grinder gritted his teeth.

"I shall spare this unworthy beast." The Duke of Bells walked up to the Organ Grinder, kicking him in the throat with a metal boot. The Organ Grinder gagged and wheezed as he rolled on the ground. Whatever was inside the armor of the Duke's guards tittered. "As you have not begged for the life of my wife, I am afraid she will be tortured in place of your acquaintance." The Duke chuckled and kicked the Organ Grinder in the crotch, and he doubled over, clutching himself. "Take this fool away and give him back his things. See that he is forced to remain in the company of Lady Symantha until she is ready to depart."

I offered a curtsey. "My good Duke, if I might prevail upon you for a moment, I would like to witness what is to be done to your wife. She is, after all, your wife, and if you are intent on keeping her, I would like to see how this is done." The Organ Grinder was dragged off. The Stone Preacher grinned until the doors slammed.

The Duchess looked up, all traces of fear and terror gone from her eyes as she defiantly rose. The guardsman yanked on her chain as she struggled up. "Filthy amphibian!" she shrieked. "I kissed you and gave you everything! You never touched me! You never touched me!" She gave a gagging choke, dragged back down to the ground, her beautiful skin touching the dirty floor.

Several of the carnivorous toads hopped about the chamber. From behind me, I thought I heard a little gulp as the picnic basket ate one.

"Ahh, but I need you," the Duke of Bells said solemnly. "Your ceremony shall be tomorrow, my lovely guest. My wife shall be in attendance, with her new scars, of course. I trust that your associate shall properly comport himself in my presence." He stared at me with toad eyes. In that instant, I knew what he was. I felt very sick. "You may watch the torture of my wife. I trust that you will not feel too much shame at watching tadpoles inserted into her flesh. The little beasts do need to be fed, or I will have no more toads."

I stared in horror. Even the Stone Preacher appeared completely revolted. The picnic basket rubbed against my leg and made a rustling clack, as if it were about to slurp soup. "Fetch my tailor! Have him make my wife a dress through which her injuries may be seen!" He smiled cheerfully – almost too cheerfully – a wide, toad-like smile.

The guardsmen opened the door and dragged the Duchess out, yanking her by her iron chain as the Duke gestured to the exit. "Good lady, you must depart. I need to be alone with my shame and my grief." The Duke grinned like a madman while the cursing of the Duchess faded in the corridor.

As we left, I dared to look behind us at the Duke, brooding on his throne. For a moment, I thought I saw a long, bulbous tongue flicker out from between his lips. I led the picnic basket and the Stone Preacher upstairs, praying that it was only a trick of the light.

***

"Does that Toad Prince stuff really work?" I asked the Organ Grinder when all of us were finally back in the room.

"Did you really mean what you said about allowing me to pleasure you?" He grinned as if being beaten to a pulp and seducing the Duchess was all in a day's work for him.

"No. I lied, but it was an agreed-upon lie. I chose to spare you over his wife, as much as it pains me to do this. I think being tortured by toadlings is really disgusting. You should, too."

The Stone Preacher shook his head with a little grinding noise. "You really have outdone yourself," he said grimly to the Organ Grinder. "Your monkey is still bitter and starving in the cart, is it not?"

The Organ Grinder hung his head as if he had forgotten all about it. "Aye. The poor little beast will be starving when we get out of here. And the poor Duchess, to pay so for being married to a toad."

"He really is a toad, isn't he?" I rolled my eyes. "She kissed him and he became a human, sort of."

"These things happen," the Stone Preacher rumbled thoughtfully. "But she's no more his one true love than the Organ Grinder can love only one woman."

"I thought you said these people always find each other."

"It's not always people," the Stone Preacher said. "You were lucky. Your one true love happens to be male and reasonably human. Didn't you listen to the Duchess of Weavers?"

"You mean...the toad at his feet?" I made my way to the window to heave up dinner.

"Well, he is a toad himself." The Organ Grinder said calmly as I inhaled the air.

As I opened the window, I heard a keening wail, a mournful howl that sounded like doomed sadness wrapped in bitter feelings. Something flipped down over the lip of the tower, shrouded in shadow. A chain lashed out for my face. The Stone Preacher yanked me backward, shielding me with his armored body. Spikes on the metal links clanked off his rocky cassock.

The Organ Grinder had just looked up when the thing clacked through the window. He stared in horror and dived for the fireplace, grabbing a poker as his leather greatcoat rustled on the ground.

It was armored and heavy. It seemed as if a thing of its mass couldn't possibly be athletic. Somehow, though, it still moved with liquid grace. The chain swirled back over its head as it whirled it like a small toy. It came for me again.

I dived behind the bed. Fearsome, gold-lit eyes rested behind a twisted metal mask, the thick mail grinding against itself as it let out a gruesome, keening sob. From the window, there was the sound of creaking metal, and a second one crawled into the room.

"Chain Hook Guards," the Stone Preacher said coldly. "The King of Feathers knows where you are."

"What does that mean?" I said from behind the bed, as I scrambled behind the bed and grabbed my last few clockwork arrows. The chain of the first one slithered underneath the bed and pulled it forward, while the second one leaped at me, the echoing of sad songs and tearful encounters in my ears.

"It means the Weeper in Shadows has come!" The Organ Grinder charged one of the two chain-wielding things, and wrapped the poker around its chain as it lumbered for him. A nasty- looking hook popped out of some strange metal arm sheath, and it advanced.

"What's a Weeper in Shadows?" I said. "That doesn't sound like it has a title."

"Royal assassins don't have titles!" the Stone Preacher said as he tackled the second one. "Stay down!" I flattened behind the bed, but behind me there was a dire, crackling rustle. The wind itself had had died and gone to hell, and behind me, something stood.

She was a woman wrapped in the trappings of midnight blue leather and murder. Her tight, fitted corset kept her skinnier than anything I had ever seen. Her face was hidden behind a wrathful, face-mirroring mask of bolted iron. Her fingers were long and slender, and her body was possessed of a monstrous grace. She twisted her hand and withdrew a knife of ice from her belt. It glistened, and she slashed downward at me as I rolled away.

"Fast," she whispered. "You are fast like the sunset. So beautiful you are, to die so young." The bolted iron mask twisted into a playful grin. The ice knife slammed into the bed, cracking the mattress as the sheet froze and shivered.

I kicked out, but she vaulted up and over me onto the bed. The Organ Grinder slammed the poker hard against the hook, and pulled the guard aside, kicking the armored creature in the stomach. It doubled over and keened like a bird, armored head twisting.

The Stone Preacher got a firm grip on the other guard, and hurled it up against the ceiling. The throw was so hard it powdered stone. The creature crashed to the floor as the Stone Preacher rolled aside.

"So beautiful," the Weeper in Shadows purred above me. I scrabbled for my bow, and she drove the knife down, flipping off the bed to slam it between my fingers. She was faster than anything I had ever encountered. I could barely see her. I withdrew my hand and she kicked me hard in the face. My head slammed back against the icy bed. "But you will not die pretty."

In that instant, the picnic basket leaped, and gave a savage roar as the Weeper began to stand. It barreled into her and chewed at the hand holding the knife. She went down in a heap and rolled to her feet, punching the basket against the wall. It was all I could do to keep my head, and the wicker basket shuddered a little bit and dropped off with a dull hiccup. "Stupid creature!" she hissed. "Making a new knife will take weeks! I will cut out your love with your heart, and make it cold."

The Stone Preacher rolled to his feet as the basket fell. The lid closed on the knife with a clapping sound. The Organ Grinder beat the poker hard against the head of the chain hook guard. The other guard was struggling to get up. I finally cleared the haze from my mind, and grabbed the chilled bedpost, struggling to stand up. "You're losing." I forced the words out as the Weeper in Shadows crawled backwards from the door, clutching her bloody hand.

"I have not lost yet." She blew me an affectionate kiss as the Stone Preacher drove a rocky foot into the fallen guard. I could feel the sting of her sadness on my cheek. "I still live forever, and you are still mortal." The metal mask quirked into the faintest of smiles and dived out the window. Something whinnied, flying towards her as she vaulted downward. I heard a leathery thump. She gave a saucy wave as a creature floated up above the lip of the window. "May the best woman win!"

It was a massive, hairy-winged, horse-headed snake, more than fifteen feet long. Its scales were purplish russet. The tail was adorned with a massive stinger that glimmered with strange, reddish liquid. Its back was fitted with a black saddle, which had two leather loops along the sides. These held a quiver of arrows, and a massive, serrated sword that looked as though it was made to make people suffer as they died. The tail lashed down through the window. I rolled under the bed, the heavy tailspike turning the bed-ice to a rose color. Frozen chunks exploded across the room. The tail withdrew, and the massive mount flew upward, out of sight through the window.

When I turned to look, the Stone Preacher was tossing the second guard out the window. It gave a series of chirping screams before it crashed to earth. Then he bent down and helped the Organ Grinder up with a rocky hand. "I hope you wanted an adventure," he said with a rocky chuckle.

"I must confess that this is far too much adventure for me," the Organ Grinder said with gritted teeth. "The Duchess is one thing, but I do not know if I can survive another attack like that without the monkey."

I shook my head. "You can take your monkey and stuff it. Who is that crazy woman?" I rolled my eyes. "You knew about the guards, but it might have been nice to tell me he has a personal assassin!"

"It comes with the territory," the Stone Preacher said. "Only it seems she's already in love with your paramour herself. I don't think you want to die of a broken heart, do you?"

"That can happen? That might have been nice to know too."

The Organ Grinder shrugged. I thought I could hear the creature flying away. I was too hurt to chase her. "We didn't want to worry you. Don't worry. It only happens sometimes." He smiled a little bit. "At least if you don't die, there are options." He straightened his coat and brushed his mustache and goatee.

"That thought never leaves your mind, does it?" I sighed.

"Of course it doesn't," the Organ Grinder chuckled. "You have an appointment to keep."

The picnic basket wiggled. There was a creak as the basket opened, a fresh-baked smell coming from within. Where the knife had been was a delicious quartet of muffins. "You're okay!" I ran to the picnic basket and gave it a hug. It gave a strange rustling noise that might have been a purr. I took out a muffin and nibbled on it. It was like a little taste of heaven. It almost made me forget that the bruise on my face might take a few days to heal.

The Stone Preacher turned to look out the window and gave a gravelly rumble, as if he were breathing. "I shall guard the window instead of the door." His voice sounded like rock on rock. "This was unexpected."

***

The Duke's men arrived early in the morning to escort us to the torture chamber. I was already awake and dressed, in my jeans, t-shirt, cloak, and boots. I shook the Organ Grinder. "Get up!" I shook his arm while he snored. "You're going, too."

The Organ Grinder whuffled in his chair, and finally stopped making deep honking noises. "I don't know how any woman can stand you." I rolled my eyes. "But you don't stay afterwards, do you?"

"Of course not," the Organ Grinder said. "I believe that I should bathe before our trip to the chamber, don't you?" He gave me a look of relief that it was the Duchess instead of him.

I moved to the door and rapped sharply on it while the Organ Grinder bathed behind the screen. Excited by what passed for commotion, the picnic basket ran over and began bumping against my leg. Inside, I could smell something like toast. The Stone Preacher opened the door and looked down at the basket. "All right," he said. "I will eat something." The basket creaked open, revealing a plate of buttered toast. The Stone Preacher nibbled on it.

I took one, too. "Let's get out of here." The picnic basket gave a rustle, insisting. "Oh, all right. I'll eat some toast. I know you're hungry for tadpoles." I looked over at the Stone Preacher. "We'll be lucky if we survive this."

We made our way down the stairs. A heavily armored guard brought us further down, into the castle dungeons. Howls of lawbreakers and the wailing of victims carried through the halls. The Organ Grinder took a deep breath. "Ahh... the smell of suffering." He chuckled. "This Duke of Bells has quite a hospitality program for his guests: blood, broken bones, tears, and urine, all aching for ventilation!"

"Could you stop that?" I snapped. "We just ate."

The Stone Preacher nodded grimly to the guard. "It is as if the two of them are married." He chuckled in gravelly tones. "Fortunately for the young lady, she is in love with another." The guard snickered. The Organ Grinder's face went sour.

The guard marched us down the bleak hall to a barred door and opened it. He gestured to walk inside. Determined to lead, I moved through the door first. The Stone Preacher and Organ Grinder took up positions on either side. The picnic basket huddled under my cloak, savoring the scent of fresh tadpoles.

My eyes were greeted by a scene of savage nightmares in dim torchlight. An oily fat man, with blubbery lips and strange horns, stood over and behind the body of the Duchess; chained to a set of metal bars arranged in awkward positions. Her body showed signs of a night of punishment and wrath. Her dress was ripped and torn in places, yet her flesh had not known the taste of the lash. I took in the scene and somehow kept my breakfast down.

Next to the apparatus was a squirming, writhing bucket filled with hungry tadpoles, propped up on a metal stand. The bucket was adorned with paintings of frogs. It bubbled, like a cruel piece of swamp brought to life.

"Good morning," the Duchess said with a cold tone in her voice, even though it made the bars move and wracked her face with pain. "It's so kind of you to make it. Do you like what you see?"

The fat man stepped out from behind the thick metal bars, recurved legs bent like a cat's, covered with some sort of ugly grayish fur with patches of white. His oily, scarred chest rested above a bloated belly, which hung over a dirty loincloth. His tongue slavered as he shifted in the torchlight. Fat, bluish-white fingers caressed the swampy water in the bucket. The picnic basket rustled, as if it were about to have a meal. I nudged it, urging it not to feed. "I am the Ravager of Skins." The fat man bowed low, more courteous and elegant than the Duke of Bells.

"A pleasure to meet you," I said icily. "Is there no way I could prevail upon you to end this before it starts? She has been exceptionally civil about the whole thing."

The Duchess looked to the Organ Grinder bitterly. "You knew this would happen?' She shrieked and flew into a terrible rage, pain wracking her voice as she struggled with her bonds. "That was my first sex in a hundred and seventy years, you bastards! You filthy toad-mating beasts! I'll kill you! I'll kill you!" The Ravager slapped her.

The Stone Preacher walked up to the Ravager of Skins, grabbed his hand, then squeezed. "Get on with it. If you follow with unauthorized punishments, I will kill everyone in this castle but the Duchess, and break you into pieces small enough for my lady's pet to eat."

The Ravager winced in pain and glared at the Stone Preacher. "As you wish..." Words came through a gritted scowl.

From the smirks on the face of the Organ Grinder and the Duchess of Bells, I got the impression it was a minor victory. The Stone Preacher let go, returning to his position near the door, while the Ravager winced, rubbing his wrist.

"My thanks," I chuckled. "You may begin now." The Stone Preacher returned to his position near the door.

"I demand a moment of time with my fellow lady," the Duchess wheezed. "Come you closer, unnamed one." A little smile spread across her lips. "I would have words with thee."

"Go on," the Ravager said coolly. "She is still my Duchess. I cannot refuse."

I walked forward, and she drew me into a grab, though the metal bars wracked her with agonizing pain. "There is no escape," she whispered. "Unless you kill him, there is no escape. Choose wisely." A little blood trickled from her lip. As her bosom pressed against mine in the desperate embrace, I could see needles pricking her beautiful back.

I nodded. "I'll try." I thought I was going to cry, but she brushed her hair against my eyelids so that no one could see. There was a little quirk of a smile as her lip brushed against mine.

"Your victories will be small. But they are all you can expect. Greatness is a punishment of its own." She let go, and sagged, half overcome by pain.

The Ravager smiled, and stepped up to her. He cut slits in her wrists and her legs, and dug out the tadpoles from the bucket. I held tight to the handle of the picnic basket while the Organ Grinder and the Stone Preacher remained cold and impassive. "Always defiant." He smiled as he pressed a tadpole into each slit.

Her lips parted with bitter shrieks as the tadpoles were pressed into the open wounds. "I'm not afraid! You makers of harlots! You beasts! I'll throttle you and feed on your blood, you subordinate bastards! You wish you could have me! You wish for it!" Her eyes filled with tears of pain, and her back dripped with little droplets of blood.

I could not stop crying, even when the Ravager of Skins took out a hot poker and pressed it against the tadpoles, killing them one by one. The Duchess shivered on the rack in the remains of her dress, glassy eyed with pain. I ran to her, and cradled her lazy, exhausted head in my hands. The picnic basket ran forward. It chewed up the toad babies, and gave a satisfied little burp.

The Ravager reached out a hand to stop me, but the gravelly movements of the Stone Preacher's arm made him reconsider. "She'll live." He smiled a little bit. "One day I shall be the King of Skins, and I shall wear yours, Stone Preacher. An impervious soul in an impervious body." He gave the Organ Grinder a lewd smile.

"Then we shall see, Organ Grinder, if there is no flesh you cannot enjoy."

I barely heard the words. As the door guard stepped in to return us to our rooms, I knew I would not sleep all night. For the first time, wrapped in my sheets, I could see my companions weren't sleeping either. Only the picnic basket seemed to get any rest at all.

***

Bleary eyed, we staggered from our room the next morning. The picnic basket had produced an entire pot of steaming, black coffee. Even the Stone Preacher drank a cup. He seemed desperate to be wakeful, to purge from his mind the image we saw. We hadn't left the room all day. It seemed as though the only purpose of the Dukes treatment of his wife was to make us desolate.

We were wearing our traveling clothes. The picnic basket followed us down the stairs, searching the floor for wayward toads as we descended. I drew up my hood around my head, hoping it would shield me from the vileness. The guards at the massive doors looked at me with vicious dispassion.

We made our way into the Duke's throne room. The tinkling of chimes was more somber. The Duke was wearing a massive, bell-shaped military helmet on his head, but slit toad eyes could easily be seen through it, a reminder of his venality. "Ah, my lovely unnamed lady, how nice it is to see you again!" The bell helmet creaked, as if he were smiling widely. At his feet, the massive toad croaked and throbbed, making sagging hoots.

Sitting next to him was the Duchess, resplendent in a new gown. It was backless and deeply cut, with smooth slits in the legs. Her legs had been scarred from the red-hot poker. Burned welts shone in the bright light. High shoulders accentuated the backlessness. Her lips were twisted in a grimace of pain. If she turned around, I knew I would see her ravaged back, smooth skin laced with wretched dots of dried blood. Her arms were as marked with scars as her legs. She clutched at her throne with desperation, as if movement were difficult for her.

The Duke gave us a polite nod. "After much consideration," he purred through the helmet, his words muffled. "I have decided to accept the consequences of vouching for you. Your skills of manipulation are impressive, and I shall speak for you at court. However, you will need another noble to vouch for you, will you not, my dear?" He smiled coolly to his wife, and stroked one of her scars. She glared at him viciously and winced. "Does it hurt? You should be grateful I did not have them damage your face, my dear. But that would not have the effect of keeping up appearances." He gave the Organ Grinder a pleasant smile. "Would it now?"

The Organ Grinder said nothing. "My associate is too wise to be unprovoked by such obvious baiting," I said with a dainty curtsy. "My lord Duke, if you could but recommend another to whom I might petition, I would be pleased indeed."

"I do indeed have a friend." The Duke of Bells voice was idle. "He is the Count of Locks, and he will, no doubt, be very pleased to see you."

The Duchess struggled to speak. "My lord, are you sure that this is wise?" Her voice halted with pain. Her face struggled with the desire to recover.

"My dear, how many times have I requested that you not gainsay me in front of our noble guests?" The Duke's eyes bulged. His guards rustled forth from their chambers.

"Most noble lord, may I have that in writing?"

The Duke tilted his helmet. "You mean so that you can kill me, and take the voucher to court?" A slitted eyebrow widened. "Most droll, but no."

The Organ Grinder said nothing, and tried to avoid the Duchess's gaze. The Stone Preacher's teeth ground. I looked from left to right. "My lord, if we wanted to kill you, we would do so and get a voucher from your sadly bereaved widow." I gave him the politest of smiles.

The Duke of Bells tilted his head and tapped his fingers. "What do you think, my lovely wife?" He said with a cheerful grin. He gently brushed his wife's hand, and the guards moved closer, around the four of us. The picnic basket let out a growling rustle. Polearms were leveled at it.

"I think you should not grant such a foolish request." Her teeth were tight. The long, beautiful fingers twisted with pain. The Duke's drawing his hand over the scars worsened it.

The Duke gave a slimy grin. "I shall craft you a brief letter that shall supply you with a voucher." His helmet shifted a little bit on his head, and he reached to a side table next to the throne for a pen and parchment, as if he had been expecting this. He idly wrote a note on a piece of paper, and stamped it with a seal of wax, his bell shaped helmet humming as he whistled. He took a few moments to leer at his wife's scars while he wrote.

"My thanks, noble lord." I curtsied to the Duchess of Bells. "I look forward to my next visit, my lady." The Organ Grinder gave me a subtle leer. "And you, sir, will not be coming with me when I do."

The Stone Preacher bowed, his rocky form making a smooth crackling noise. Then, as if it was nothing, he drove his foot into the blade of the polearm closest to the throne, and smashed it into metal shards. In an instant, the picnic basket leaped forward, and charged the massive toad, hissing and roaring. A tongue slithered out of its mouth, and it bounded forward to leap on the fat, monstrous heap of greenish warts, chewing as the basket and the creature rolled about.

The Organ Grinder moved, grabbing the broken polearm and shoving it into the gut of one of the guards, snapping it off in his stomach and kicking him hard with his steel-toed boot. The guard crumpled while the Duke of Bells stared at the basket and his toad.

I reached for the sword of the fallen guard. I barely knew how to use one, but it was long and sharp. I didn't think I really needed to figure out the part about where the point end went. As I reached for the weapon, I saw the Duchess smile.

The Stone Preacher grabbed two of the men by their throats and squeezed. Gorgets cracked. The wet smell of crushed toad flesh spewed into the room, the ringing noise echoing as their voices turned from sweet music to damp, horrid croaking. They died wheezing.

The Duke drew his weapon, and charged me with a massive leap. His voice was a horrid croak that still echoed with musical beauty. "Lying witch," his voice throbbed. "I'll end your romance now."

He thrust at me with the sword. It was all I could do to get out of the way. I didn't know how to use the sword, and he had had hundreds of years of practice. The Stone Preacher and the Organ Grinder were in the midst of the guards. More were coming. Wet thuds and horrid gurgles of music came from the press of battle. I focused all of my attention on staying alive.

On the ground, the toad had its tongue wrapped around the picnic basket, which had stuffed its leg into the creature and bit down hard. Wails came from the creature. The picnic basket hissed as the wicker began to crack.

I backed up, throwing a torch sconce in the way. It deflected the Duke's blade. His voice rang with bitter anger. "Harlot!' He shouted. "I'll feed you to my children!" He swung again. The torch sconce developed a large dent, its top flickering with fire.

Furtively, as though all of her future smiles depended on it, I could see the Duchess slipping forward to pick up one of the massive polearms. In her hands, it looked almost overbearing, but she seemed to have a small idea of how to use it. I looked at the Duke and began to laugh. "I think you just lost."

As the picnic basket struggled and chewed, the Duchess stalked forward, her eyes narrow with the hate of ages, and placed the blade of the polearm squarely against the back of the toad. "Stop them now!" She purred. Her fingers tightened on the blade. The toad gave a ringing, bitter sigh. There was a wet crunch as the picnic basket chewed through the toad's leg, and the Duke of Bells head turned.

"Mondie?" His voice cracked, and he began to run, heading back with massive, heavy bounds. The toad gave a sickening croak. I wasn't as fast, but I didn't have to be.

The Duchess turned to look at the Duke. "Call them off." She said angrily. "Or your mate dies. I don't want to sleep next to a toad anymore."

In the press of men, the Organ Grinder and the Stone Preacher were surrounded. The Duke raised his hand. "Put up your weapons!" he said in deep, musical tones. "This battle must end." He ran to the toad and hugged it, and I pulled the picnic basket away. It was slavering and licking its chops. It was too late for the creature's leg.

"Excellent!" The Organ Grinder smiled. "Perhaps I shall be welcome here after all."

The Duke of Bells scowled at the Organ Grinder, staring in horror at the wounded toad. He hugged it, and it made sad noises that we couldn't understand. Then the Duchess gave a wicked grin. While the Duke was kneeling, she moved the blade to his throat. "I have the Duke. And as I am Duchess, I believe that you men serve me?" She gave a pleasant coo.

The Duke looked up, eyes wide and round in his bell shaped helmet. "Amalinda! You promised! These are the rules! You'll be a vagabond with no lands! An outcast! A swine!"

"And you're a toad. Seize him!" she said coldly. The guards moved forward while the Duke held up his sword. I tackled him and held onto his arm. Two of the large, heavy guards shambled forward to grab him as I was tossed aside. "I want him to see this."

The Duchess of Bells smiled, and the Stone Preacher grinned with a crackle of rock. Ever so politely, more gentlemanly than I thought he could be, the Organ Grinder turned away with a dainty set of half steps. Then he folded his arms and cocked his head, as if listening. The Duke struggled in the grip of his guards, and the Duchess spoke in a voice of ice. "I've wanted to do this for four hundred years." She raised the polearm above her head, and brought it down savagely on the massive toad, which gave a sobbing sigh and crawled broken on the ground. In that instant, the picnic basket pounced, and began ripping out the throat of the lumpy creature.

The Duke of Bells screamed the name of his true love aloud as the Duchess brought the polearm down again. The basket began to eat in earnest, savoring the pieces of toad flesh. It belched and slobbered as the Duchess turned to her weeping husband. I took his sword away and handed it to her while the Stone Preacher watched. "I believe this is yours?"

"No," she said gently. "He wronged you greatly. His life is yours, if you wish it." Her face twitched with pain. The Organ Grinder's back was still turned.

I handed her the sword anyway. I knew what was going to happen, even as the sobbing Duke of Bells lost the strength to resist his own guards. The massive creatures pushed him to the floor. "You must watch, then," the Duchess said. "Be strong, always. The slightest sign of weakness could mean your life." She turned to the guards, her voice hallow. "Make sure he can see the basket eating it." Then she raised the sword, a happy smile on her lips. With sickening hacks, she cut the Duke of Bells apart, limb by limb, his spurting blood pooling on the floor. Her dress stained red and brown. The Duke of Bells died staring at his toad lover, a drooling gaze of brokenness on his lips. Even after he was dead, she chopped for a very long time.

***

We made ready to leave as soon as it was over. The Duchess limped with us to the drawbridge, riding on a beautiful horse that seemed oddly out of place, now that we knew what lived there. She kept the polearm and the sword, and somehow managed to seem beautiful, even though she left her life behind. We were in the

Organ Grinder's cart. The monkey hooted from under the greatcoat once more, angry that it missed all the bloodshed.

The Duchess shivered in the cold. "You have a long journey ahead of you."

"We do, I guess." I smiled. "So do you."

The Organ Grinder gave the Duchess a pleasant leer. "Until we meet again, my lady." He tipped his hat.

The Duchess rammed the butt of the polearm into his stomach. "Shut up," she said. "Obviously, you're no more romantic than my former husband."

The Organ Grinder winced and doubled over. The Duchess smirked as she put the polearm back into its hanger on the side of her saddle.

The lips of the Stone Preacher cracked into a rocky smile, and the picnic basket shuddered. It was stretched to the gills. I opened the lid and looked inside. There was a beautiful wrapped string bag loaded with sweetmeats, cheeses, and food that smelled so delicious that I could barely manage to stop looking at it. It nudged at the edge of the cart. "I think that my basket wants you to have this." I reached in and handed her the string bag. "You could travel with us, you know."

"I do not think that it would be appropriate to visit my former husband's best friend in this horridly bloodstained dress." She offered a wink. "I'll figure out how to survive. You are but a child." She leaned in and kissed me on the mouth, gently. "Don't worry. It only works on animals." She gave a light little laugh, and rode off into the mist and fog. The horse's hooves thundered as her bloodstained dress whipped in the cold wind.

"Do you think she'll make it?" I asked the Stone Preacher as the hoof beats vanished, and our cart began to creak and thunder along the road.

"She is an incredible woman," the Stone Preacher said. "I suppose it would do to have a little bit of hope, for once."

The Organ Grinder smiled. "I, too, hope she survives. She is a fantastic lover. I especially like it when she—"

"Shut up!" the Stone Preacher and I said together.

We rode then, for a while, in the angry mist, hoping that the Duchess was as safe and relieved as we were. Behind every tree and hill, I feared that the Weeper in Shadows waited.

Chapter Eight

The Count of Locks Grows Desperate

After several miles, the sky overhead grew dimmer. The fog was no thinner than before. The cart creaked on the wet road in the sunless afternoon. We could barely see twenty feet in front of us. The Organ Grinder held the reins while the monkey made keening sounds.

In my lap, every so often, the picnic basket shuddered. It produced four smoked hams, six bottles of wine, and two mint chocolate pies since we left. I figured the thing overate. It leaned against me with a lazy creak of wicker while the Stone Preacher glided alongside the cart.

As night fell, we pulled over to the side of the road, and opened the basket. It was bursting at the seams. We stored the smoked hams in the storage trunk inside, and packed away the jars of jam and fresh baked breads that the basket had made. Inside, there was a fresh, delicious roast that dripped onto a beautiful wooden tray, complete with a carving knife and holding fork. Next to it was a bottle of wine that wafted lazily from an open jug, and a simmering tray of fresh vegetables in some sort of broth. It was like a little slice of heaven in the cold and damp. "What do you think?" The Organ Grinder grinned as he held back the monkey from attacking the food.

"I think the food is scary." We walked over to the nearest rock and spread everything out.

Even the Stone Preacher was unable to resist the lure of the roast. "We should allow the basket to eat more toads." His body gave an unusual shudder that crackled through the wind. "It seems to make the best food so far."

"We really shouldn't have let it eat as much as it has." I watched the basket closely. It did seem larger, as if stretched by everything it ate. "That makes you nervous, doesn't it?"

The basket rustled lazily next to me. The Stone Preacher nodded. The Organ Grinder chuckled, and the monkey hooted from under his greatcoat. "You should cheer up." His voice was jovial. "I cannot wait to see what kinds of casseroles it makes."

"In case you haven't figured this part out yet, Mr. Grinder, since you will not give me your real name, this state of affairs only lasts until it decides to eat us!" I shaved off a little piece of the roast. I didn't want to know or understand where the food came from.

The Organ Grinder laughed. "We are larger," he said firmly. "I'm sure we can wrestle it down."

"Tell that to the Knave of Innkeepers, or... uh... Mondie." I winced, remembering the Duchess of Bells hacking the toad and the Duke apart. My appetite couldn't be spoiled. The picnic basket rubbed a little bit against me, making rustling wicker noises. Shortly thereafter, it creaked open. Inside was a large strawberry shortcake.

"You can stop now." I said to the basket. It had already rustled into what passed for sleep. "I guess we're having dessert."

"It looks delicious." The Organ Grinder smiled, neatly wiping his mouth with a handkerchief from inside the greatcoat.

"It's fattening you up for the kill," the Stone Preacher responded. He took a little of the cake anyway. While we ate and discussed how far we were to travel, the weary horses grazed on marsh grass under the cold grey sky.

***

We were awakened by bitter cold. I had to turn my boots on and glide about just to stay warm. The Organ Grinder huddled in his greatcoat. From inside the coat, I could hear the screeches of an uncomfortable monkey and rejoiced. As disturbing as the picnic basket could be, the monkey was still the most horrid creature.

The Stone Preacher stood there with his arms folded. "It occurs to me that I didn't really fight those guards for any particular reason other than the fact that the Toad Prince turned your stomach." He gave a grinding smile.

"That's it? That's what sparked it?" I sighed and nibbled on the warm, fresh toast that the picnic basket made. It scampered around the rock, finally free of lethargy. "And no more toads for you, for a while!" The basket opened its lid, teeth and all, and made a little whimpering howl, looking contrite. Then it looked at the Organ Grinder's coat and slavered.

"I must confess, the pleasure of watching the basket eat the Duke's favorite toad did fill me with a certain amount of joy," the Stone Preacher said. "Why, it was almost a divine experience."

The Organ Grinder was nibbling on some sausages, remaining silent while the Basket slavered. "Thank you for not killing the Duchess," he said. "I really rather liked her."

"That makes me wonder what you do to the ones you hate." I scowled. "You are the most disgusting man in all of creation, more than likely with the most disgusting monkey!"

The monkey peered out from underneath the coat and hissed at me. The basket growled. I idly stroked the lid of the basket. "No, the Organ Grinder needs his monkey. Besides, who will play the accordion for you when you're gone?"

The picnic basket looked at me as best it could, and little eyes peered out from under the lid. Then it growled again and rubbed against my leg. The Organ Grinder chuckled. "It's a pet and a kitchen at the same time." His smirk widened. "I wonder where Bosquoverde found it."

"Probably the same place that the monkey lost its tail and had a knife attached to it." I snapped. In the background, there was an odd whistling. "Do you hear that?"

The Stone Preacher was already running forward, into the fog, as I finished.

"No!" The Organ Grinder said fiercely. "I did that! It was an essential part of my circus act." He seemed unconcerned with the Stone Preacher's urgency.

There was a heavy thud and a shrieking yelp from the fog as the Stone Preacher subdued something. Then we heard the sound of something heavy being dragged.

"You were in the circus?" It explained so much. "Animal cruelty was part of your act?"

"Why yes!" The Organ Grinder grinned savagely. "I've lived a long time. We used to regularly maim animals in the circus. It was part of the job!" He turned towards the fog where we could hear the Stone Preacher approaching. "Hopefully, the Preacher has caught something edible. I would really like to supplement eggs and sausage, although the basket does a marvelous job." The basket's lid flicked open to flash the Organ Grinder a toothy smile.

From the fog came the howling noise of an old woman. "Let go of me, false priest! I'll bleed your rocky knees and shatter you to flinders with curses!"

The Stone Preacher emerged from the fog, chuckling. "Silence, old wretch! Or I'll strangle you for calling me false! Know you who I am? I am the Stone Preacher. Only the wishes of that girl to not have so much blood on my hands keep your warty throat intact!"

Her nose was sharp and hooked, and her features wrinkled. Her skin had a light purplish tone to it, with pinched, sunken cheeks. She was clad in a ragged cassock and carried a heavy string bag on her back. Her thin, skinny frame was wiry down to the dirty old boots on her feet. The Stone Preacher had his hand firmly clamped around her bony wrist. His eyes were savage and narrow.

"I am but a seller of cheese!" she shrieked. "I'll place a curse on you, man of granite!" Her voice was a despicable cackle.

"A seller of cheese?" The Organ Grinder flicked his gaze to her. "Out here? More than likely you're a witch in disguise, or some hag looking to be pregnant with a noble's son. Sadly, even I don't have the fortitude to sleep with you. If you're very good, I won't let my monkey kill you. Even then, my lady here, for whom we are responsible, might feed you to her picnic basket."

"You had better not be offering me anything besides cheese." I pulled the bow off my back and leveled an arrow at the old woman, the memories of the hag from the tree village leaping to mind. The monkey hooted, hopping out from the Organ Grinder's coat and cavorting on the rock. The picnic basket slurped.

"No, I swear, it is good cheese!" She struggled for her bag, and dragged out a round sphere of grey, cold rind. "It is marinated in wine for a year or more! Please!" She struggled and kicked in the Stone Preacher's grip.

"You'll take a ham for it, I suppose?" I sighed. "Get her one of the hams out of the cart. And stop strangling her." I looked over to the Stone Preacher with a mild fury. "Now, if you please."

The Stone Preacher sighed and let go of the woman, who clutched her throat and choked a little bit. "I suppose you're going to institute some regime of equality and harmony?" he said, in a gravelly voice tinged with sarcasm.

"No, but we can't just kill everyone we meet. We've already killed a lot of people." I watched as the hag stood.

She clutched the cheese sphere for a moment and pressed it into my hands. "Take it. It will help you. It has the power of silence."

"What?" I shook my head. "All cheeses have that power. Just shove them in your ears."

The Hag shook her head. "No, no, it makes you silent. Chew a little bit and move quietly, like the wind." She looked a little sheepish.

I put the arrow away. "That's worth two hams. Promise it's not a deadly poison that will put you to sleep for a hundred years or something like that?"

"She is a liar," the Stone Preacher said coldly as he stuffed the first ham into the hands of the witchlike, warty faced old woman, and went back for a second.

"I shall curse you, man of rock!" She hissed. "It is no lie. That's the other cheese."

"No cursing." I turned my gaze back to her. "Or I'll feed you the whole thing."

The Stone Preacher ground up into the cart, which creaked under his weight, and returned with the second ham, which the old woman struggled to hold up. "There you are," he said. "Now you have ham and poisoned cheese. Enjoy the rest of your miserable heathen life."

"A plague of slow erosion upon you, man of rock! I'll have ham for supper and breakfast, thanks to your nameless worm!" She cackled furiously and staggered off into the fog under the weight of several pounds of meat.

"You're not going to gain converts like that," I said as I made my way over to the cart.

The Organ Grinder smirked. "Who would want to convert that? It isn't as if she'll turn into a beautiful princess. Everyone knows that story, but no one has ever seen it."

"I find it likely," the Stone Preacher muttered in his gravelly tones, "that she is still just an ugly hag. Even if she turns into a beautiful woman, it doesn't change the fact that she knows how to make poisonous, deadly cheeses. I assume you had some reason for giving her two hams? Do you really wish that thing to show up at court and thank you?"

"It's better than watching you die with your rock parts flaking off because she cursed you. My dress was made by a spider, an innkeeper gave me an evil picnic basket, and my bodyguards are disturbingly lustful and violent. It's not as if I've won the lottery for fairy-tale princesses here."

The Organ Grinder smirked, and climbed back up into the cart. "If there was a drawing, I would love to spend it rutting with you all the way to the home of your true love."

"Who we are going to try and find at the home of the King of Feathers, who lives in a castle in the sky. I'd like to point out that these mangy old nags can't fly. So unless you're thinking of not coming with me, we'll have to find someone who does."

"Indeed." The Organ Grinder smiled. "But first, your second voucher, then a journey to a place where such a man can be found. There is a city where flying vessels can be had. Just not here."

"There's a place with boats that fly?" I asked. "What's the price of flying on one?"

The Organ Grinder chuckled. "Perhaps you should leave that to the two of us." The monkey hooted. The picnic basket bounced up into the seat next to him as I climbed up into the cart.

"I could," I deliberately paused. "But that wouldn't be nearly as much fun."

We shaved off pieces of ham and ate. The cart clattered down the foggy road. I stuffed the supposedly magical cheese into the picnic basket. The basket didn't seem to have any desire to eat. It rustled against my leg and creaked, as though the weight of the cheese had made it happier. After hours of travel, the basket began to wheeze. I could see a village, outlined in the distance through the swampy mist.

***

The wagon creaked on the musty trail as we approached the village. The Organ Grinder laughed as we reached more solid ground. "It appears at least one good thing has happened." He grinned as the mangy horses picked up speed. "We're not in the swamp anymore." The monkey, all too eager to agree with his owner, let a little bit of the knife flick out from between the greatcoat buttons.

"For once, I am inclined to agree with him." The Stone Preacher rumbled. His gray feet were covered with muck. As he reached dry ground, he brushed them against the dirt, making sounds of grinding gravel. .

The basket rustled as we made our way into town. Handsome buildings were sealed with heavy locks of steel. Every door was locked tight. Lights shadowed in windows spoke of a town that was not welcoming of strangers. On a hill above the village, a massive stone building stood, square, unpleasant, and ringed with guard towers. It didn't look like a castle so much as a massive stone block. Dim lights flickered in several of the tower windows.

There was only one inn. Several horses were tied to posts in front of it. None were so mangy as the Organ Grinder's. He guided the cart over and tied up his horses, and I finally slipped down from the cart. The inn had a long, flat porch and a single wooden door in the center, framing a number of unevenly shaped windows. The smell of roasting food wafted from the chimney on top. The most frightening thing was that no one walked around town at all, not even guards or watchmen.

"Why are there no guards?" I asked. "Every other town has had them."

"Perhaps it is because there are no people," the Organ Grinder offered. The monkey peered out of the greatcoat, making an unpleasant whiffling sound before slipping back in.

The Stone Preacher surveyed the town in unpleasant quiet. He breathed deeply, tasting the air. It sounded like the rasping of wind over stone in a canyon. "Something is amiss," he said fiercely. "Do we want to find out what it is?"

"It will only make trouble if we do," the Organ Grinder said. "I opt for a quick voucher and a doughty escape from this Count of Locks, if we can at all achieve it."

"It will make more trouble for us if we don't," I said grumpily. "How much trouble could we have avoided by not dealing with the Duke of Bells, or by you, Sir Organ Grinder, telling us that he was a toad?"

"So I am to be knighted, then?" The Organ Grinder chuckled. "What shall I be the Knight of? Lechery? Rutting? I love it. Sir Organ Grinder."

"Maybe the Knight of Dirty Old Carts Who Takes Advantage of People, or the Knight of Accordions," I sneered. "I wouldn't want you to lose any of your old world charm."

"I do believe I prefer to be the Organ Grinder." The monkey hooted in assent from under the greatcoat, as if it was doing all the talking and had thought of the idea itself.

The basket echoed my assessment by rattling around, as if it produced something small and unpleasant. I would have to find out what it was later. It probably tasted good. I dropped the basket to the ground. It ran around the Stone Preacher's legs before coming back, seeming to exercise.

"How adorable," the Stone Preacher muttered. "It's sizing me up as a food source."

The basket shrugged itself, and settled next to me.

"Well, it knows what's bad to eat, at least." I headed for the door of the inn with the basket following me. It gently pushed against my leg, then bounded up the steps after me, like a hunting dog.

The Organ Grinder and the Stone Preacher came up behind me. I turned and slapped the Organ Grinder in the face.

"I must say!" The Organ Grinder glowered at me. "What was that for?"

"For staring at my rear when the cloak flutters just so," I said firmly. "Now back off, for my one true love awaits. Since you're not him, if you do that again, I will feed your monkey to the picnic basket."

Consumed with radiant thoughts of slim beauty and magnificent green eyes, I stormed through the door of the inn into rage and chaos.

***

I walked in to find the fury of a bar fight, already in progress. In a corner, something that looked like a man-beaver was punching furiously at a squat, hairy man. Two other men, both fat and bearded, smashed chairs against each other, sending splinters flying. On the bar, one man was beating another senseless. A barmaid in a tight corset, a sharp knife in her hand, stabbed at a fierce-looking man. When her target moved too slowly, she kicked him in the knee.

The host of the inn crawled up to me. "Rooms for how many?" He asked the question through bleeding lips. There was a knife wound on his leg that had probably come from the barmaid. One of his teeth sagged, hanging by a thread.

"That will be one room. One of my bodyguards doesn't really sleep, and the other is a despicable letch." I sighed. "Do the rooms have more than one bed?" I did my best to ignore the whirl of the battle around me.

The Stone Preacher stepped through the door.

"Yes, milady. Shall I send a messenger to inform the Count of Locks of your arrival, or do you wish to drop in unann—" His voice was cut off. Just as he was about to rise to his feet, one of the two large chair-swinging men tripped over him.

"Unannounced it is." I glared at the fat man, still getting to his feet. "Cease and desist. This is unseemly." I was beginning to enjoy the perks of being noble. "I require my room key."

The fat man struggled to his feet while the Innkeeper crawled to his desk. "I am the Squire of Mauled Innkeepers," he wheezed. He fumbled under the desk and pulled out a massive key. "You're in room seven." He breathed very hard, as if the massive man had broken something inside him. He was slender and not very strong. His fine-looking doublet was rumpled, as if he had tried to escape from the core of the bar fight and not made it very far. He was mostly bald, with a narrow mustache that made it through the carnage.

The fat man finally managed to stand. "I'm sorry, milady." He managed, and sheepishly made his way to the door. His opponent followed him, lumbering past the desk.

"There isn't much order here, is there?" I asked the innkeeper as the Organ Grinder dodged the two enormous men and stepped in. "So is there also a Knight of Mauled Innkeepers?"

"None whatsoever... To both of your questions. There may have been one once, but it's likely that he was beaten to death. I took this title upon myself to save others from having more lofty ones, and thus enduring more significant beatings." He bowed, wincing in obvious pain.

The Organ Grinder chuckled a little bit. "Self-sacrifice is rare in these places." He bowed to the innkeeper. "In deference to the fine lady who I escort, I am the notorious Organ Grinder. I am obliged to warn you to hide your daughters."

The Squire sighed. "Alas, I have no daughters, and no wife to warm my bed, however, there is a certain Countess of Locks who might entertain you, should you be able to unfasten her extremely complicated chastity belt."

"They still have those?" I turned to the Stone Preacher. "You mean I could be stuck wearing such a thing?"

"It is highly unlikely that the object of your desire is as possessive as the Count of Locks." The Stone Preacher rumbled. The bar fight swirled, not far from us. "It is likely that you are safe. However, I would caution you against being unprepared for such things. Carry a set of lock picks with you, if you are capable of using them."

"A lady never tells, and hedges the truth when she must." I gave him a knowing wink. Unfortunately, I didn't have any lock picks available when they were most useful.

"The bar fight should be over shortly." The innkeeper grinned. "If you wait but a few hours, the place should be clean enough for you to be served a proper meal."

We made our way to the stairs, edging carefully against the wall. Screams of pain and heavy thumps of fists echoed in our ears. The stairwell was spartan, and the hallway dull and unadorned. When we opened the door to room seven, it was anything but plain.

***

The floor to our room was covered in a dense carpet of lustrous burgundy. The walls seemed made of wood so thick that no sound could pass through them. There was an ornate mirror above the dresser. Two massive four-poster beds settled on the carpet as though trying to crush it. The dresser and nightstands were all padlocked with hooped slabs of metal. It didn't seem as if my key would fit them.

"Well," the Stone Preacher muttered. He tamped the carpet down with his weight. "It seems as though this Count of Locks is very thorough."

"I guess everyone here really tries to live up to their name," I sighed. "I guess we'll leave what baggage we have hanging about."

"At least the room looks neat and organized." The Organ Grinder smirked. The monkey hooted. The picnic basket ran about the room, spinning in a circle. It gave a wilted flop and lay at the foot of one of the beds.

"I guess that one's mine." I moved over to the bed, patting it for the basket to hop up. Even though it was doglike, I worried that it might eat me in my sleep. Still, it had been rather well-fed lately, so it was probably safe. The basket hopped up and went inert.

"We should probably go down to dinner in a while, though not until the chaos dies down." I settled onto the bed and stretched.

"Do you think there will be tables left?" The Organ Grinder said. "My monkey aches to perform." The picnic basket wiggled and slurped, as if dreaming of eating the monkey. The Organ Grinder gave the basket a nervous glance. "It still disturbs me."

"Well it disturbs me, because it's both cute and violent." I rolled my eyes.

"Good," the Stone Preacher murmured. "At least that means we're all aware of how dangerous it is. Bosquoverde either had no idea what it was, or he is far more devious and malicious than I ever suspected."

On the bed, the basket made a rattling sound that was vaguely like snoring. I looked over at it. "He has been making an awful lot of food lately."

"Only because it's a vicious friend in battle," the Organ Grinder mused. "Have you tried bonding with it?"

"It's a basket. I hugged it once. I don't know if it's pettable. It doesn't exactly have fur or feathers. And it eats people. You never know when it might grab a hand."

"You're doomed," the Stone Preacher said quietly.

"How do you know that?" the Organ Grinder asked. "It's not as if it's anything other than a basket with some sort of ensorcellment on it. She should be fine."

"I should think it should be obvious," the Stone Preacher said. I leaned over the basket and idly petted the lid as if it were an animal. "She's petting it. And she called it 'he.'"

"Great," I sighed. "Other fairy princesses get cute little animals. I get a carnivorous basket." The basket growled contentedly. "It's okay. Don't let them get to you. It really is kind of like a pet, isn't it?"

"That depends on what you consider a pet." The Organ Grinder chuckled and reached underneath his greatcoat to pet the monkey. It made little chittering sounds. My stomach churned. "You're not making a happy face."

I scowled. "I'm sorry. I find your monkey repulsive."

"We are a team," He smiled. "He was a handsome monkey. A miserable skeptic captured him and tortured him after I bedded his wife. It took me four months to find him, and another to teach the monkey to kill him with the knife on his tail. Shortly thereafter, I wandered through the fog, much as you did, and here I am." He chortled a little bit. "Surely his story is no worse than your own?"

"I suppose not. What about you?" I looked over at the Stone Preacher, and his eyes turned narrow.

"That is not something that you truly wish to hear. Suffice to say that I am very old, and when I do slip up and tell you, as I am sure I will, I can guarantee you that you will never have a compassionate word for me again." He gave me a cracked, granite smile. "We should wait for dinner in silence. It would seem the Organ Grinder is a bit of a storyteller."

"I don't think I need to hear any more of his story." I laughed.

"That's good." The Organ Grinder smiled. "I would only tell the rest of it to someone I knew better."

We waited a while, made small talk that didn't go anywhere, until enough time had passed that we felt safe walking into the taproom for dinner.

***

We left the picnic basket sleeping on the bed while the rest of us went downstairs. The Organ Grinder kept the monkey concealed in his greatcoat, fearful of what the basket might do to it in his absence. When we arrived, the dining room was still fractured. Broken bottles were swept into a corner. A shattered mirror hung messily on a twisted nail. Several small groups of people sat at irregularly arranged tables among the mess.

There were bloodstains on the floor. The reeking smell of suds from bad beer filled the air. A wide blonde barmaid came over to us, dressed in a heavy coarse skirt of grey and a cheap linen blouse. There was a bandage around her head, and it was stained with more than a little red. Her shoes were thick, plain, and wooden.

"I am to wait on you." Her grin was infectious. Her lips were puffy when she smiled. She had been in the middle of things. "What can I get you?"

"Food that's safe, and beer that doesn't taste like the floor." The contradiction of the place was distressing. The excessively comfortable room and the sleazy tavern recovering from a brawl didn't add up.

The barmaid led us to a table from which much of the chaos had been cleared. There were still a few coins on it. She scooped them into her dress as she pulled out the chairs. The Organ Grinder gave an appreciative look to the barmaid. She returned it with a grin that was almost as lewd as his own.

We settled into the wooden chairs while the barmaid went to get our food. The innkeeper was nowhere to be seen. "I suppose somewhere else in town is an Inn with horrible rooms and fantastic food." I said.

"No doubt," the Stone Preacher droned. "Truly, this place is somewhat terrifying."

"You're afraid of something after all." The Organ Grinder chuckled through his lips. The monkey echoed his laughter. "Would you care to honor us with what it is?"

"It is the sense of discord," the Stone Preacher murmured. "It is as if the town itself resists the influence of the Count of Locks."

"What does it mean?" My eyes flicked around the room. People were staring at us from what few tables had survived the onslaught of brawlers. We were strangers here.

"I'm not sure," the Stone Preacher said. "We could be walking into a secret war of sorts, or we could be walking into a situation where the Count is hated by his people. Remember who his friend is, even if his friend is currently a little cut apart."

"Dead is dead." The Organ Grinder smirked. "Most things don't come back around here." The monkey chittered satisfied assent from under his greatcoat.

"That's only most," the Stone Preacher responded. "And sometimes one is enough."

I let them bicker amongst themselves and allowed my mind to drift away from the conversation. Someone was watching us from one of the tables. He was thin and hooded, as many were in the inn. Eyes peered out from under his hood with an unpleasant glare. "I think we might have another assassin," I said.

"Really?" The Organ Grinder chuckled. "I see you're starting to become adept at spotting them. Thankfully that doesn't seem to have taken too long."

The Stone Preacher's rocky neck turned in his granite cassock, and he eyed the hooded figure. "He is trouble of some sort, but of what sort, I am not certain."

"Oh, thank you so much for explaining." I sighed. "Are all your explanations so ambiguous?"

"It keeps me from getting into trouble with noblewomen who have sharp tongues and like to say 'Why didn't you tell me?'" A creaking grin accompanied a slight rustle of gravel. I couldn't tell if he was chuckling under his breath.

"Assassin or no," The Organ Grinder observed. "He's a quick one."

When I turned to look back at the hooded man through the small crowd of revelers, the seat at the table was empty. "What do you think?" I asked the Stone Preacher.

"We'll see him again. After dinner we'll pay a visit to the Count."

"We're not staying there," I said calmly. "He sounds like the sort of man who runs a giant prison."

"You do learn fast," the Organ Grinder chuckled. "What a treat it will be when you hear my accordion music."

"Keep dreaming!" I snapped. "It's the rules. You can't. Or you already would have." I stepped on his foot to accentuate the point.

"Caught again." He idly petted the monkey under his cloak. "What if he makes us stay?"

"Then we escape." I grinned. "Never lock up a girl from the circus."

When the food arrived, it was despicably thick and greasy, yet somehow flavorful and rich. My stomach thought about rejecting it, but once it settled, it was magnificent. I thought about the room, and the food, and only became more worried. I didn't like this town.

***

After dinner was over, we composed ourselves amid the ruins of the messy brawl, and went back upstairs to gather our things. The picnic basket was happy to see us, as much as I thought it could be. It hopped down off the bed and rubbed against my leg, making little wicker creaking noises. Even though the thought made me uncomfortable, I was beginning to think of it like a pet. I was worried the others were too.

We gathered our things and went downstairs, out through the messy foyer into the street. The Squire of Mauled Innkeepers was cleaning more of the mess. Our barmaid waved to us as we slipped out the door.

The Organ Grinder looked up at the squat angry castle on the hill. "We are resolved to sleep here?"

"I would rather sleep in the comfortable inn than something that looks like a haunted castle on angry pills." It sounded less funny than it should have.

"Do we wish to take the cart?" The Stone Preacher gave the Organ Grinder an eye-creaking look.

"The answer is no," I said. "I'd rather get out of this one without having to deal with a scene of wife-torture, thank you. Does this happen often around here?"

"Only when they get caught." The Stone Preacher looked over at the Organ Grinder. "You didn't suffer too much in the cell, did you?"

"I was perfectly fine." The Organ Grinder grinned. "After all, the Duchess of Bells is quite an achievement in seduction."

"Achievement in seduction?" I rolled my eyes as we walked up the dirty trail. "Playing the accordion and calling someone's name until they wander out ensorcelled and act like a cheap prostitute in your presence is not seduction."

"You should have seen me in all my glory. Once, I was a famous lothario."

"And now you're an infamous beast." I scowled. "I'd say you should be more like the Stone Preacher, but he kills too many people."

The Stone Preacher gave a crackling guffaw that sounded like the clatter of bricks. The picnic basket drew close to my leg and hid from him. "It isn't as if you've never killed anyone." He smirked. "You're just like us now. Morally bankrupt and destined for twisted greatness."

"That really doesn't thrill me," I said. "Finding the love of my life thrills me. It just means going through the Count on the hill and his massive prison. Is there really a Countess of Locks?"

"To be sure." The Stone Preacher muttered. "If that fortress is any indication, he's probably already locked her up."

"I hope he's not as disgusting as the Duke of Bells."

"That would be difficult," the Organ Grinder said. "After all, the Duchess was so lovely, her skin so soft and creamy, her moaning lips so—" He was cut off by the growl of the basket. Apparently the Stone Preacher and I weren't the only ones disgusted.

The castle of the Count of Locks came into clearer view as we crested the hill. It was as ugly and horrible as I first thought. Squat, angry bars covered small windows. The towers were covered with arrow slits and spikes, slick with bloodstains and moss. Guards in heavy armor patrolled the walls with dull, metallic clanking sounds. From where we stood in the sunset, we could see massive pots that reeked of tar atop brutal towers.

"Oh, that's magnificent!" The Organ Grinder chortled. "Hot, burning tar for guests. Truly, this Count is more than the sum of his parts. I suspect that getting the key to his wife's chastity belt will be nigh impossible. A worthy challenge."

"Don't think of it as a challenge. Think of it as a no-no. We're not here to sleep with his wife."

"Correction: *You* are not."

The Stone Preacher shook his head as we approached the massive block of stone. The thick, squared-off teeth of the raised drawbridge beckoned, like steel tusks. "Hail the gate!" he shouted. "An unnamed noble approaches!"

With a clanking that sounded like the rage of a thousand doors never meant to open, the drawbridge slowly descended.

***

The stones of the castle beyond the drawbridge were black and gritty. A darkened hall was lined with sputtering torches. We made our way forward into the massive heap of rock. My eyes grew accustomed to the half-dark. "There's no courtyard," I said, looking at the dim lights and the guards spaced every so often in their grim armor. Their eyes were filled with a dark, hallow stare.

"You were right," the Organ Grinder said coldly. "The place is a prison." The monkey hooted from under his coat as the drawbridge slammed into place behind us.

We moved down the corridor warding ourselves from what was in it. Sound changed when we passed guards, as though their armor was designed to amplify the wails of prisoners.

"And the question that follows from that—" the Stone Preacher murmured "is why should there be?"

"I think that the most telling sign of this place's discomfort is that no one has actually bothered to greet us," I said icily.

"Why should they?" The Stone Preacher answered. "It is not as if most people ever leave here. The villagers are far too afraid of the Count to actually oppose him."

"As am I," the Organ Grinder said. "The Countess of Locks is completely off limits."

"You should be more afraid of me than him," I said. "Unlike him, I know how to use that revolver in your coat."

"How are you going to get it away from me, my pretty little thing?" he chuckled.

We stepped up to a large set of double doors. The monkey hooted with a dry cackle. The picnic basket, flush against my leg, peered out from under my cloak.

The doors were made of a strange reddish wood I couldn't identify. Settled into the murky bricks, they were covered with thick metal bands that had savage-looking spikes. In the center of the doors, a mammoth lock looked as though it would require a key the size of a man's head. The lock looked hungry, as if ready to eat us alive.

"That's easy," I said dryly. "You have to sleep sometime, and I won't be shooting at your head." The picnic basket cooed. A rustling smirk crossed face of the Stone Preacher. Victory in a duel of barbs was sweet.

The Organ Grinder inhaled sharply. "Well, I am certain that after a single night of pleasure, you could not bear to part with such a magnificent beast," he murmured. "Shall we?"

"I'm sure that after a single night, your magnificent beast will be a dirty old nag, never to rise again and destined for the glue factory." The doors opened with a slow, booming creak. The grim audience chamber of the Count of Locks opened.

***

The Count of Locks sat in the middle of a group of armored prison guards. Every shield had the symbol of a lock on it. Their eyes were as cold and hollow as the men in the corridors. They seemed larger, as though he had selected the largest men available for the task of protecting him. The Count of Locks was afraid.

The Count was dressed in a thick suit of armor that looked as though it could turn aside anvils, his head trapped in a massive helmet that he could flip down at the first sign of battle. A huge ring of keys formed his belt. The creaking plates shifted as he turned. There was an empty throne next to his seat, and no sign of his Countess.

The Count's pupilless eyes shone with a whitish light, though the rest of his face appeared quite human, with a coppery skin tone. Mailed fists rested idly on the edges of his seat. His voice was a serene declaration of power, rather than the oily tones of the Duke of Bells. "May I know to whom I have the pleasure of speaking?" He inclined his head slightly. The armor shivered as if tuned perfectly to his shape. It was only at those moments that I could see how big a man he really was, and how little protection in a fight he must need.

"The lady prefers to have her escorts speak for her." I curtsied politely to the Count of Locks, and indicated the Stone Preacher. The Organ Grinder shot me an unpleasant look.

"What is that?" The Count of Locks focused on the picnic basket. It cowered under my robe, rustling against the heels of my boots.

"It is a pet," the Stone Preacher responded. "Truth be told, it eats all kinds of creatures, and produces food." The Count raised a single eyebrow, and his lip quirked.

"Your pet may stay." The Count idly wiggled his fingers, as though he were thinking about something. His voice sounded like the dull thud of locking things away. "It is fortunate that you are to come at this time."

"The lady is tired, and has journeyed for a long while," The Stone Preacher intoned. The Organ Grinder merely leered at the chair where the Countess of Locks should be sitting. I raised a finger and signaled the Stone Preacher, and deferentially nodded to the Count.

"May I inquire as to the location of your wife?" I asked congenially.

"I heard that the legendary Organ Grinder might be in town." He gave the Organ Grinder a wicked smirk. "So I forced my wife into a chastity belt and locked her in the dungeons." He gave a hollow chuckle. "Do you think me a fool?"

The Organ Grinder bowed respectfully. "No, my lord. You are no fool."

I scowled at the Organ Grinder. "He did not give you leave to speak." I folded my hands and looked as dainty as possible. "Forgive my impertinence, my lord, but I must beg your indulgence and speak in person." I felt like I was robbing a candy store. The observation of formalities was the most important thing to the nobles of this world.

The Count of Locks nodded once, a clicking sound like a lock echoed from the back of his neck. "Of course." He gestured with his hand, the noise sounding like tumblers. I had picked more than a few locks. He sounded well oiled, without a hint of scraping.

"If it is fortunate that we are here, then something must be troubling you." I gave him a deferential glance. "I shall require your voucher at court, if I am to aid you. Your friend the Duke of Bells mentioned that I should come and see you."

"Ahh, the Duke of Bells." The Count of Locks steepled his gauntleted fingers, and settled back in his chair. He slammed the helmet down. "How is my old friend, despicable toad though he may be?"

"The Duchess is sharp in her manner." I gave him a winning smile. "He's going all to pieces." I curtsied. There was a creaking clack from under the helmet. I wasn't sure whether he was smiling or frowning.

"Then you should not mind my sharp-tongued wife in her cell of straw and brackish water." His voice was bland and dull, as if he had expected something to happen, and been disappointed.

"Of course not." My stomach crawled. "What must I do to gain your vouchership?" I kept my face a formal mask, trying to hide my distaste.

"It is very simple. You are new, and there is a secret group that plots against me and my strategies of imprisonment. They call themselves the Brotherhood of Doors, and they mean to end my life." He gave a clicking sigh.

"And what do they want?" I wondered if this question had a meaningful answer.

"They want me to unlock everything." The Count of Locks gestured in fury. "It is preposterous. Doors without locks of any sort! Everything is to be invaded, with no privacy, and criminals free to roam as they will, with no ability to prevent entry. They are madmen."

"So there is no possibility of compromise?"

"It would not be the first attempt on my life." He let out a clattering sigh. The Stone Preacher raised an eyebrow, making a brief scraping noise.

"And we are now your guests?" I asked. "So they will likely try to dispose of us as well?"

"They will try to liberate you. Whether or not they believe your freedom can be discovered through your deaths is uncertain." His voice took on robustness, as though he were more sure of himself.

"That doesn't sound particularly pleasant," the Stone Preacher rumbled. "Liberation at the hands of the armed is often a prelude to a different kind of tyranny."

"Indeed." The Organ Grinder murmured. "I much prefer liberation of a different kind."

I turned to the two of them. The picnic basket shivered against me under my cloak. "If you would not interrupt—" I changed the tone of my voice to seem more pleasant, turning back to the Count of Locks. "If solving this problem appears to vex you, I shall try."

The Count lifted his helmet with a dull click. The sound of something unlocking popped through the large chamber. "So be it, then. I shall have my guards show you to your quarters. Fear not. There are locks on the window and the door, and all the windows are barred. You are most safe."

"I thank you for your security, my lord," I daintily curtsied again. The basket shivered against the back of my leg.

The guards gathered about us to escort us. I could not help but wonder how much of a prison the castle really was for guests. The doors to the audience chamber opened with a powerful thud. Surrounded by swords and pikes, we made our way through corridors and the sounds of wailing men.

***

The chamber our escorts left us in was wide and handsome. A thick burnished brown carpet made even the most hardened feet feel comfortable. A massive four poster bed was in the main room, with two side rooms for servants. Each had a bed that was comfortable, if not as large. There was a reasonably sized dresser and a small closet, with a large trunk at the foot of the bed. A large screen hid a huge wooden tub, which was currently empty. I hoped by morning it would fill with water. A single window, barred with iron and shuttered, looked out on the landscape and gave me a view of the village below. It was a comfortable prison.

I made my way inside and patted the four-poster bed, hoping that the picnic basket would hop up on it. It shuffled over and rubbed against my leg. "Something bothers it," I said. "It doesn't like it in here."

"Maybe it can't chew through the bars," the Stone Preacher suggested. "Of course, there isn't a lot it can't bite, so maybe that bothers it."

"It hasn't tried," the Organ Grinder said. "Maybe it's just unnerved. Or hungry."

"I hope it's not hungry," I said. "It ate enough toads to last a year."

The basket wiggled a little bit and opened, producing a warm plate of crepes and some candied fruit and syrups. "You've been holding that in all day, haven't you?"

"That explains a lot," the Organ Grinder said, reaching in and taking out the plate. He then spread some candied fruit and syrup on a crepe and ate it. "These are very good. You should try one."

"I suppose I can't refuse it." I ruffled the lid and it made a little wicker creaking sound. Then I folded some fruit into a crepe and poured some syrup on it. I nibbled thoughtfully. "I hope it can make more of these. They're terrific."

The Organ Grinder was already on his third after the basket produced another plate. The Stone Preacher turned his back and watched the door. He didn't seem afraid of the window.

"Is there some reason you're looking that way?" the Organ Grinder asked between bites, getting out a greasy handkerchief. He wiped his lips and goatee.

"They're the Brotherhood of Doors," I said. "What are the chances that if they show up here, they'll come through a window?"

The Stone Preacher chuckled, a low gravelly laugh that vibrated through the cold steel bars on the window. "You certainly have the right of that." He mused. "I would not entirely trust our host, but this Brotherhood concerns me."

The door creaked, and the Stone Preacher moved, his hand swift and grinding as it opened into nothingness, with no hallway beyond. A hooded man stepped through it, his features concealed. By the time he made it through the door, the Stone Preacher's hand was already around his throat. The door closed of its own volition.

"Interesting," the Organ Grinder murmured. "Now that's a way to get in and out of the Countess's bedroom."

"She's in the dungeon." I snapped. "You're destined to be lonely in bed again."

The man made choking noises as he struggled. The Stone Preacher turned, holding him high with a single arm. "Do you want me to kill him?"

"What part of 'No killing unless I say so' gets past my say-so?" I demanded. "Maybe we should question him before we crush his throat?"

The man made a choking noise under his mask. He wiggled in the Stone Preacher's grip. "You can start by letting go of him."

The Stone Preacher released the man, and he fell to the ground with a thud. He made some choking and gasping noises while the Organ Grinder gloated quietly at the gagging man's misery. He finally stood. "I am the Eighth Doorman," he said. "Tonight the Count dies. We give you this warning because you are not of his house. As you are nameless, our Brotherhood does not wish you harm. If you stay, we will be forced to end your lives." He wheezed. "My message is delivered."

"Let's tell our host," I said firmly. All I could think about was being far from those green eyes, empty and lost forever.

"This is how you repay hospitality?" the hooded man managed. He turned, and began to run for the door. There was a shriek and a hooting noise, and he fell to the floor. His leg leaked blood. Cackling and jumping up and down, the monkey slithered out from beneath the Organ Grinder's greatcoat, its tail raised to stab the Eighth Doorman again.

"It is when you say 'leave or die.'" I smiled.

The Stone Preacher reached down for him, and grabbed him by the throat once more. When I opened the door. We all walked through it. There was an odd clicking sound, and a slamming noise. Somehow, the hooded man had vanished. Even when the

Stone Preacher squeezed to crush the man's throat, his hand closed on empty air.

"The Count!" I urged. "We need to hurry." We ran down the stairs, past armored figures guarding locked rooms and the screams of the tortured in cells. I thought I saw one man with a lock driven straight through his arm and bolted to the wall. By the time we reached the doors of the audience chamber, I wondered why I was trying to save him, not his prisoners.

***

The massive doors to the audience chamber were off their hinges. Inside, savage shadows of men slashed and whirled at each other. We stepped in over the bodies of the dead. In an instant, there were weapons and combatants all about us.

There was almost no light at all, save from flickering torches outside. Metal weapons clanged off each other. Shouts of confusion reached our ears. I blinked my eyes and tried to adjust them to the light. Already, the Stone Preacher leaped upon the nearest man in a battle-frenzy. There was a rough crunch, and something that sounded like a snap. Then there was wheezing and the feeling of something dead under my boot.

In the darkness, the picnic basket growled. There was a brief flash of metal. There was some screaming and a disgruntled rattle of wicker from it. "What happened?" I shouted. "I can't see!"

The Organ Grinder yanked a torch from a nearby sconce, and lit it with a puff of gunpowder. There was a sharp cracking noise. Slowly things became visible. The Count of Locks was up on his throne, beating away two men with long key-shaped weapons. There were twelve hooded doormen. When they saw us, they began to advance.

"Should we shoot them?" I asked. "We might have to negotiate. It is three to one."

The Count of Locks shouted "Kill them! You'll be their enemy forever for accepting my hospitality!"

One of the hooded men tackled him. The pair bounced off the throne in a struggling heap of arms and legs. The Count seemed to have trouble getting up. The armor looked very heavy. The hooded man on top of him reached out to raise his faceplate.

I drew my bow and fired an arrow. It slammed into the back of the Doorman, making him howl in pain. "That sounds like a yes."

"Look at that, lass." The Organ Grinder chuckled. "Didn't you say you were out of arrows? It seems you have a magic all your own." He leaped into the mass of hooded men and struggled to get the key-shaped weapon. As they closed in, I heard a hooting shriek. The monkey leaped out from his greatcoat, stabbing with its tail beneath the strange hoods.

I really had fired without thinking about it. When I reached back for the next arrow, there was nothing there. I had no weapon. The doormen were closing in. The Stone Preacher hurled the sack of dead flesh he held into the midst of the advancing men. Others struggled to yank down the Organ Grinder. There was a howl of pain from under someone's hood. The monkey gave chittered with victorious glee as red spurted. The hooded man collapsed as the monkey leaped to save its master. Prone men beneath a corpse dug their way out from under the heap of their crushed friend.

I reached for the sword of the Stone Preacher's victim, and pulled it out while the struggle continued. The Stone Preacher advanced forward, kicking one of the men into a savage bend. I heard bones crack. The man flew back into the depths of the room. The Organ Grinder rammed his torch into the face of one of his grapplers. There was a horrible shriek. The monkey hopped on the burned man's face, slashing at blistered flesh.

Knives and swords flashed at the Stone Preacher, but clanked off his rocky cloak. Dust showered as the Count of Locks punched one of the doormen in the face. His hand slipped under the cloak and back out again.

I rushed to aid the Organ Grinder. The basket leaped forward with me. In the torchlight, I could hear something rattle. The basket vaulted forward, and dug its teeth into the hand of one of the Brotherhood. There was a crunch, a gulping sound, some blood, and an odd wickerish pop. I saw the basket heal after a few apples rolled across the floor. I let out the first battle cry of my life and thrust at the wounded man, driving my sword into his stomach. He flopped on the ground and let go of the Organ Grinder, who turned and kneed one of his captors in the groin.

The Count of Locks drove a knee into the stomach of the man he fought and hurled him across the room with a savage roar. "Vile usurpers! Villains of insecurity! I'll hurl you all into dark chambers with no windows and rip out your miserable eyesockets!" Bone cracked against the wall. The Doorman slumped to the ground.

"Colorful sort, isn't he?" The Organ Grinder chuckled.

The monkey hacked and stabbed at blisters of the man with the burned face. Then the basket leaped. It gave a brutal, rattling growl and latched itself onto the leg of one of the Doormen. There was a horrified scream, and dull snapping noises, as if the bones of his leg broke in several places. I reversed the sword and slammed it down onto his hood. I was rewarded with a thud. The crunching sounds continued. I watched in shock as the picnic basket devoured the leg of my attacker. He spastically toppled.

While the basket chewed, the Stone Preacher raged. He picked up two opponents by the throat and slammed them together like sacks. They wheezed under his fingers. He slammed again, kicking one of them hard enough to make bones crumple and flesh sag. Attackers who could still move ran for the doorway.

They vanished with a heavy thud. The entry to the hallway was a door to somewhere else. I stared after them.

"Good lady!" The Count of Locks approached while still-living doormen moaned and writhed. I recognized one of them from before. He was the one who warned us. "You, along with your unusual cohorts, have saved my life, and for that, I believe my voucher is yours." He gave a few clicking noises as he clattered to us, offering a smooth and honorable bow.

"Of course." I curtsied politely, and glared at the picnic basket. "Excuse me, good sir. I need to restrain my pet. You might need to interrogate some of them."

"It is useless." The Count's shoulders clattered with the sound of closing thuds. "They go to and from here as they please, even though this is the first time they've attempted to kill me."

"Perhaps it is not you they were after?" I asked. "Perhaps your wife or guests?"

The hand of the Count of Locks moved to his armored chin, and the well-crafted fingers creaked against the metallic helmet. "I shall dwell on that. Guards! Come take these despicable doormen away! Reveal their faces and chain them! I shall enjoy their suffering in rooms they cannot escape!" He chuckled to himself. "You should return to your quarters, milady. In the morning, I shall have your voucher. You may depart these safe premises for other shores until I make them even safer." His smile was wider than it should have been.

I journeyed up the stairs with the Organ Grinder and the Stone Preacher, the monkey and basket following. I couldn't help but feel discomfort at what was going to happen to the Count's prisoners. If it was half as bad as how the Duke of Bells treated his wife, it wasn't going to be much of a life for them. I didn't want to know.

But I had to.

***

I huddled under the covers and pretended to sleep. All I heard was the snoring of the Organ Grinder. The picnic basket rustled at my feet. I threw aside my quilt and hurried into my cloak and boots. In the pit of my stomach, the desire to know clawed. I reached into the basket and dug out a knife, just in case I needed one. The basket slept on.

I slipped through castle hallways, blending into corners as guards passed by. Wherever the most guards were, that was where the entrance to the deepest dungeons would be. I couldn't find any of the Brotherhood in the dungeons above. They were too close to the exit. The Count of Locks would place them somewhere so dark they couldn't see doorways.

The stairs to the lower dungeons were blocked by a thick, iron-bound door at the bottom of a flight of stairs. Beyond, the hollow whistle of air beckoned. A heavy thud of feet clattered, faint against the wood. My hearing was becoming clearer.

The door was guarded by a massive statue of metal, with a huge lock built into the center of its chest. It was vaguely humanoid, with a head that had two tiny jeweled eyes and a massive, wide-jawed mouth filled with clockworks and sharpness. It had barrel-like fists, and a heavy chest on crude two toed feet. Carved into its waist was the shape of a loincloth. The creature had no visible anatomy.

I crept up to the statue, and prayed that it wouldn't move, come to life, or do any of the awful things that I had seen in movies or read in books. It didn't. It sat there impassively, its massive, squat body over the stairwell door. I slipped up to it and listened. Dull footsteps of guards came from the other side of the door, their voices a muffled throb.

I crawled up into the shoulders of the statue and shimmied behind the neck, trying to get into a position where I could slip behind the guards and hide, making my way into the prison below. The question was whether it was any different from the prison above. I gathered my cloak about myself and huddled. The runes shimmered as I scuttled into the darkness. The Duchess of Weavers said it was supposed to protect me. I didn't know whether

I was invisible or there was a trick of the light, and I was just good at hiding.

I waited there in the dark while cold air collected. I shivered against my cloak. Finally, the low clatter of footsteps thudded along the hall. Two men shuffled into view. I pressed against the statue. The two guardsmen clanked forward, talking as they hammered on the massive door.

"Open it!" the first one thundered. "I ache to be with the suffering bastards!"

The second chuckled in a low tone of voice. Laughing, tired men on the other side forced the thing open. In a hurry, I crawled, praying they did not look up. I scuttled above their heads as they spoke to each other, stared down into the depths of agony.

It was a massive, yawning pit laden with guards and screams of the tortured. The circle of stairs seemed to go on and on. The few tortured faces I could see whimpered and begged. It wasn't so much a prison as an abattoir for victims, living out their lives as meat without purpose. A thick lip of stone marked the spiral of descending cells.

I moved quickly, leaping to the edge of the stone lip, and crawled along it, looking up and down. My boots of fire crackled lightly. I moved slowly to try and hide the smoke, keeping them on so I would not fall. I inched along the lip of the circle, staring into the rings of stone, looking at the doomed and the sullen. It was always light. Many of them tossed and turned, struggling to force themselves to sleep. As the guards kept their eyes on the prisoners, I hid in shadowy torchlight, listening to the screams of pain.

I didn't see any of the Count's prisoners from the battle, so I kept my eyes open. It was difficult to see at times. The torchlight quivered in between the shadows of the moving guards. I didn't even know what the Brotherhood looked like under their masks. I didn't even know how I was going to get out.

There was a whisper from nearby. I froze. "Your fingers are not from here." Someone had seen me.

***

I crawled up over the lip and stared into the eyes of a skinny man in black brocade, held behind cold bars that had almost rusted shut. His lips were bruised; his nose broken in more than one place. I couldn't see any guards about. I flitted over the edge and pressed myself against the rock wall next to his cell, hunkered down below the lip. "Who are you?" I asked. "Are you of the Brotherhood?"

"As surely as you are not." His smile cracked open wide. Several of his teeth had horrid cracks in them. His jaw was twisted, as if he had been punched there. His eyes were laden with cold anger, as if he promised revenge against the Count of Locks from his cell.

"Then we should get out of here." I pulled the knife that I dug out of the picnic basket before I left. I picked the crude lock with it. It opened with a quiet click.

"Grab my hand," he said. "Where we are going, they cannot stop us." He pushed open the door. I reached out for his hand, as a guard came around the corner, saw us, and began to shout.

"Escape!" The guard's voice was thunder, and he began to beat his sword against his armor. "Sever his fingers! Kill the woman!"

I grabbed the brocaded man's hand. He stepped forward, the horrible sound of wind on air whistling through my ears as we vanished and reappeared elsewhere. "Welcome to the Palace of Archways." He smiled at me with a savage grin. "They have been trying to find this place for ages." The room was thickly carpeted. Pillars ran from floor to ceiling. Archways surrounded it. A massive table sat in the center, wrapped in fur, as were accompanying chairs. The floor was of solid marble, but everything creaked and shuddered under our feet.

"Now what?" I asked him. Hooded men slipped out from around corners and behind pillars, their faces calm. On one or two of them, I could see injuries from the battle in the Count's audience chamber.

They drew swords and spears. One pulled out a modern looking automatic pistol. They all pointed them at me as the crack-toothed man grinned. Cold, bitter air whistled through his teeth. "Now you are my hostage. Did you really think I couldn't see your eyes, if I could see your fingers?"

I thought, just for a brief moment, I might have been better off in the prison, being killed by the Count's guards.

Chapter Nine

A Sinister Meeting with the Brotherhood of Doors

I put up my hands, surrounded by hooded, armed men in the cold. I didn't fear the ones with spears. The gun bothered me. I didn't know if the cloak would protect me against a bullet. "Gather her up," the brocaded man said. "We of the Brotherhood believe in freedom above all else, and demand entry into all things and places."

"There are places you're not getting into." I scowled as I kept my hands above my head.

"We don't need to get into that place," the man with the split teeth chuckled. "I am certain that your friend the Organ Grinder has been there far too many times already. I shall grace you with an introduction. I am the Hoodless Master of the Brotherhood of Doors. You could, perhaps, call me by my title, rather than my real name, which is a secret."

"It's probably something like Herbert or Fitzpercy." I sneered. Two of the hooded men forced my arms down behind my back and bound my hands and wrists with rope. One of them kicked me in the back of the knee. Another shoved my face into the marble, twisting my hair. "All right! Hoodless Master! I get it! I get it!" I wasn't going to let them see me cry.

"I am gratified that you understand. You and your kind's pretensions towards nobility have soured this world long enough." He scowled. "Who or what did you go to bed with, little witch?" He leaned in and teased my chin line. "Fortunately for you, you're still a nameless wretch who isn't fully ennobled, or I'd have some friends of mine disembowel you."

"Looks like you grew up in the middle ages." I scowled as two of doormen brought me to my feet.

"Actually, it was the French Revolution." The man smiled down at me. "I took this Brotherhood and made them real, bloody revolutionaries. Before that, they were common criminals. But who made them that way? It is the nobles of this land who are the real criminals, and I will ensure that you never become one of them." He smiled as two men dragged me off. Only then did I begin to hear faint traces of his accent.

"How are you going to accomplish that?" I snapped. "Is it really as simple as just killing me? Stuffing me with hundred-year sleep potions or something equally farcical and stupid?"

"Don't be ridiculous. I can't afford to have you martyred. The Count of Locks and your ridiculous-looking friends will come for you." He chuckled as I was yanked through an arch. "Traps are so wonderful, and kicking, struggling, cow-eyed nobles make the most wonderful bait for the socially obligated."

They pulled me into a dark corridor, dragged me through hallways and down stairs while I kicked and struggled. I bit one of them on the hand. He punched me hard in the mouth. I could taste blood on my tongue, but swallowed it instead of spitting on them. This was a magical world. Having someone's blood could give someone a hold over you.

They threw me in a cell with a small bucket of water and a plain straw pallet. "Down with the nobility." One of them chuckled. "You'll eat the rats or starve. The food's terrible." One of them punched me in the face hard. The other used the opportunity to chain my arm to the wall. The other arm soon followed. The two men laughed. One of them idly rubbed his battered knuckles before heading off, leaving me alone with bruises and thoughts of escape. My toes barely touched the ground. Silence from other cells told me they didn't take a lot of prisoners. It wasn't very reassuring.

***

I was still twisting and struggling in my chains when a man with a thick, crude piece of wood arrived. He beat the bars of my cell with a lurid smile on bloated features. I could see marks of black and yellow on his teeth. His eyes were a feral, thuggish blue, and he wore a fur loincloth half-hidden by his burgeoning gut. His hood and cloak were stained with old lard and grease. Dirty, cracked boots clacked roughly on the ground. "So you're her." He salivated, then smashed the slab of wood against the bars. "If I'm lucky, they'll let me despoil you, give you a bastard child." I could smell his breath from where I was standing.

"If you're lucky, I won't feed you to my picnic basket." I said defiantly. I had never wanted to see the thing eat someone so much, or so desired to hear someone scream as the basket chewed through flesh and bone.

He laughed, a disgusting series of noises that ended when he gurgled phlegm in his throat. "You're lucky I'm just your jailer, and not your torturer." He smirked. "You've got true love, and it's all pretty-pretty, but I love breaking girls like you and making them useless to the loves of their lives." He stuck a thumb at himself, chortled proudly, then spit his mucus onto the floor. "One day, there won't be any nobility, or true love to make it work. Then men like me will have a chance with noble beauties like yourself." He made a sniggering noise.

"You'll have a chance with pretty girls when you lose weight and bathe. I think your smell frightens prostitutes," I snapped. "Who's fattening you up, anyway? Your master must be a cannibal."

"Full of bile." He chuckled and slammed the club against the door again. "I think it's time for your first beating." He leered as he unlocked the door, and wiggled his bloated way into the cell. That was when I decided to make him work for it.

My legs were still free and fairly long, so I made a soft whimpering sound before cowering back against the wall. I hoped by stepping into the kick, it would get past all the fat and grease to something important.

"Oh, now that I'm about to beat you, you're afraid." He gave a hacking wheeze and drew back the large club.

I stepped in and kicked him between the legs as hard as I could, igniting my boots as I drove forward.

There was a ringing sound of steel on steel as my boot caught metal underneath. A hissing sound was followed by the smell of burning hair as the fat man dropped to the ground, scrabbling for the club with one hand and unhooking the burning loincloth with the other. He floundered as he got the thing off, and began reaching for the slab of wood.

I did the only thing I could. I kicked him again with the flickering boot, leaving burns on his fat. He howled in pain. Footsteps pounded down the hall. Two other members of the Brotherhood burst in, their hooded faces marked with rage. One kneeled next to his friend, the second picking up the club and smashing me in the face with it. There was a moment of half-awareness as the club smashed into my stomach. I wasn't aware of anything for a while after that.

***

When I woke up, I was half-naked and tied over a set of three metal bars. My breasts pressed against one while my stomach was folded over the highest. My ankles were tied to the lowest bar. I could feel my skin cold against the metal. My boots were thrown with my other clothes nearby, and my fat, burned jailer gloated. He was wearing a new loincloth of red silk. His black teeth were displayed in a vicious smile. "It is the duty of every prisoner to escape." He smirked. "You could have been well treated, but now I shall make your stay here envied by the dead." He cackled and grabbed his club, splintering it against a heavy wooden table.

"You really get off on this, don't you?" I snapped.

He brought the splintered side of the club down hard on my back, and I could feel the skin opening as the slivers of wood dug in. "I enjoy making nobles suffer. One day, I will have your pretty flesh, and your noble blooded bastards will be born from me – fat, lazy, and lecherous." He chuckled and came around to tilt up my chin. "If you are lucky, you will come to enjoy my touch."

"If you're lucky, my picnic basket will be full before it's finished with you." I gave him a cracked smile. I knew if I ever saw him again, I was going to feed him to it. I didn't care about the consequences. The satisfaction of seeing him eaten would be enough.

He beat me slowly, keeping me just on the edge of wakefulness, alternating the club with punches and slaps from fat fists. When I finally lost consciousness through my tears, I regretted that it didn't come sooner.

***

I awoke, hanging in my cell, with the boots displayed across the room, on the other side of the bars. Splinters in my back burned. I ached from the bruises and punches. I struggled to regain consciousness as I hung in sullen agony. I was dressed in my shirt again, but it was filthy; stained with sweat and blood.

I looked left and right, peering to make sure there was no guard. My fat torturer was nowhere to be seen. I could feel splinters in my back, pressed against cold stone, and gritted my teeth rather than scream. He wanted me to try to escape, so that he could torture me again. I wanted to escape, so I could avoid being tortured. It was all a big game of suffering.

I wiggled to make sure nothing was broken, and was rewarded with only dull throbs. Everything that had been hit felt like agony. The torturer was good at his work. I didn't know how much time had passed. I had to get out of the cell. I didn't know how many more beatings I could endure. Concentrating through pain was hard. I pinched my hands and hoped that they were small enough to squeeze through the shackles. I tugged as hard as I could. I felt my skin scraping, adding to the pain of my bruises, but I pulled anyway.

I was rewarded with a skinned, bleeding hand free of restraint. It felt like victory all by itself, but there was another manacle. I would have to do it again. I twisted and rubbed the blood onto my other hand, wetting it, then gritted my teeth and pulled. This manacle was tighter than the other one. I managed to slip my hand through. I wrapped the more-injured hand inside my blouse, already wet and stained, to staunch the flow.

There was no way I could reach the boots from the cell door, and the light was dim. I took a deep breath, tilted my head, and tried the door. It was open. I raced for the boots and threw them on. I would need them to get out of here, but couldn't fly through narrow, dark corridors.

Perhaps too eagerly, I pressed myself against the wall, and hurried forward, trying to leave one prison and return to another.

***

I slipped past the wall of cells, peering into them to see skeletons and half-rotted bodies cooling in lime, chained to the wall. Every single door was open. At least the Brotherhood practiced what they preached. From down the hall, noises came, so I dived into a cell, hiding amidst mulch and musty smells. My bloated jailer sauntered down the hall, chuckling to himself and singing a crass song about rape and young girls.

I waited for him to pass, and he moved to the door of the cell. "Escape!" he thundered. I burst from my hiding place and ran. I threw open the door to the cell block and turned, hoping that what I expected would be true. The door had a lock on it; it just wasn't applied. I laughed as the Jailer raced down the hall, and held the door open for as long as I could. I wanted to see his look of misery.

Just before he reached the doorframe, I slammed the door and locked it. Then I gave him a cruel little giggle and ran off, through the corridors. There was a heavy pounding on the locked door, and howls of discontent. I flattened into an alcove, knowing that help would come for him.

I loved every minute of it.

Two hooded men of the Brotherhood passed me. One of them sniffed the air for a moment, as if he could smell my bloody blouse, and detect the splinters in my back. They raced for the noise of the fat, howling monster.

I moved in the opposite direction, up a set of stairs and toward a large door. A little light flickered from it. I wasn't really looking at my surroundings, but I knew I would have to get a look at what was on the other side before slipping through it.

I peeled back the door the slightest bit, and looked out upon the conference table and the wind-whipped Palace of Archways. I didn't see anyone. There was a dull click, and the Hoodless Master was pointing a single-shot eighteenth-century pistol at the side of my head. "You are fast," he smiled. "But not as fast as a musket ball."

***

They tied me to a chair in the Palace of Archways. Apparently, a building full of unlocked doors didn't have any rules about tying people up. My wrists were bound to the arms of the chair, and my boots were bound to the massive, ornate legs. At least the cushions on it were comfortable. It was better than the prison cell.

The ropes dug into my legs, cutting at my wrists while the blood dried on my fingers. I could feel the Hoodless Master's pistol pressing against my head. The two men with him smirked a little bit as the cold wood pressed against my skin. "Her shirt's covered with blood," the first one said.

"What's your name?" I didn't expect an answer.

"Calvort of the Fifth Door." He sighed. "I don't suppose you'd settle for a humble woodsman?" He gave me a sheepish smile.

"I can't." Those green eyes called to me and made everything clear, taking away the pain and making me think of the need between my legs, lying in the grass next to the pool. "My love is spoken for."

The second of the two thugs gave a laugh. "We'll be doing the speaking soon. When the sounds of freedom ring throughout this land, all doors shall be open to us. The Count will unlock his dungeon, and all those trapped inside will pour out and sing songs of liberation."

"What if some deserve to be locked up? There could be monsters or other strange creatures that inhabit those dungeons." I looked over the pudgy man's face. There wasn't any doubt at all.

"It does not matter," the Hoodless Master said. "The point of liberating things is not just freedom, but also its representation." He admired my bloody hands and shivering form. "You were certainly willing to bleed for your freedom, as temporary as it was."

"Does Calvort of the Fifth Door ever get a promotion, or does he just sit there next to the fifth door forever?" I wiggled a little bit in the chair. The first step was getting one of them to trust me.

"He does, when his merits overflow to the next rank." The Hoodless Master whistled through cracked teeth. "Why do you think we do this? It probably didn't start the way you think it did."

"Let me guess. Either you're the old Count of Locks, and he deposed you, or you're really just a dirty old man who enjoys watching young girls suffer." I pretended to think about it as I talked. People who like to talk sometimes leave openings in their conversation.

"Sadly it is neither of those things." He let out a little sigh, the yellow of his teeth shining as the moon rose higher. He glared at me, and then he squeezed my bloody hand, twisting it. I screamed as my wrist bucked and my bones ached to snap. "The Countess used to be my wife. True love. Ha! If she had loved me half as much as she loved him, she would have stayed. You dare to contaminate my soul with another relationship of stains and mold?" He punched me in the nose. I could feel the blood run down over my lip. "There's your love! All gore and corpses."

"It's not like that!" I screamed back at him. "I love him more than anything! I don't even know his name! He's just the green-eyed man! He's just the green-eyed man." My eyes added tears to the dribble of blood that poured out of my nostril and ran across my lip.

"There, there." The Hoodless Master petted my head and tilted it back, and rammed a dirty handkerchief into my nostril to soak up the blood. "I'm sure it will all be fine. There's no such thing as a true love that death can't cure. When I have the Count of Locks, I'll have you quartered. Make no mistake. I'll find some method of keeping your head alive. You'll sit and stare at an open door every day, wishing that you could be free." He let out a low chuckle. "It will be interesting to see how much you scream then. Keep your head back. If only you were a commoner."

"Yes, if only I was a dirty thug with cracked teeth who beats up women tied to chairs." I scowled. "Your real hooded master is missing. Obviously it was burned off and replaced with the caresses of the fat, lonely jailer."

Calvort stood up, and the other thug moved away. The master reached back his fist, and yanked out the handkerchief. It was wet and filled with red, congealing blood. He laughed and hit me in the stomach so hard my eyes slammed shut with pain. When I opened them again, the Hooded Master and his two assistants were gone.

I dreamed of green eyes again in the cold and clung to that thought. My lips and bloody hands were stung by wind. I loved him more than ever, and prayed that I was not in a land of make-believe.

***

I hung my head as the wind whipped around me, and struggled with my bonds. Everything hurt. My head throbbed. I couldn't tell whether anything was broken, but I hoped that it wasn't. Whatever doctors were like around here, I didn't want to meet one.

Cold clutched at me in my chair. The blood in my nostril was drying. I had to think of a way out on my own. There wasn't a Stone Preacher to murder all my enemies or an Organ Grinder to seduce and rape them. I breathed in through my mouth and thought hard about the boots, even though I wasn't running.

They ignited. With a roaring crackle, the flaming boots burned to life, and the chair began to smolder. Heat roared against my feet, and made my bruises feel better. I had only a few minutes before fire broke through the chair.

I struggled against the ropes as hard as I could. The smell of burning velvet and feathers hit my nostrils. I could feel the blood drying in my nose as I struggled to stand.

I struggled and writhed against the ropes, leaning forward on the conference table. Someone shouted "Fire!" I couldn't see him. I thought it might have been Calvort, but already I could hear footsteps. I kicked and struggled with the burning strands. I turned and settled back against the table, inhaling the smell of burning wood, and kicked forward.

The front legs of the chair gave way. My legs shot ahead as I saw hooded men closing in on me from all directions. They drew spears and axes. There was no sign of the Hooded Master. I thought I could see Calvort among them. The torturer burst forth from the stairwell, carrying a large bucket of water. The conference table crackled with flame.

"Hi," I said with a pained grin on my face. I ran to stand on the table, leaving flaming footprints on it as the remains of the chair blazed on my back. I yanked on the ropes with bloody hands and wiggled. In a series of crackles and pops, the chair finally gave way. The sounds of burning wood flew to my ears.

The Torturer howled in rage. "She's burning the table!" He ran forward with the bucket of water. The others stabbed and slashed at my feet, batting at the fire with their weapons to put it out. Cold wind whipped up smoke around the burning table.

I ran up amid the clouds of smoke, and raced for one of the archways. My feet pounded with whiplike cracks as my heels thumped. The air burned, leaving a smoky trail of footprints behind. "Open, please open!" I begged. I leaped through it, my feet clattering on stone on the other side of the arch. There was a rough, rocky hill there. Little stones clattered as I landed. I could see the Brotherhood chasing me while the fat, bloated Torturer hurled water on the table behind them.

My lungs ached. My hands convulsed as I stepped forward and ran down the embankment. Whipping winds sapped the air from my lungs. I could feel the pain of beatings and tortures shoot through me. My legs were too weak to run through the air anymore.

I stared down into thick gray clouds that coalesced and writhed with thunderous growls. I turned back to look. Hooded men raced forward, their Master close behind them. "Get her!" he shouted. "She's a mere slip of a thing! She can't escape! She's too weak to fly!"

I decided there was somewhere to go. It was better than letting the torturer touch me.

With cries of fury in my ears and the clattering of weapons behind, I leaped off into the grey mist, my boots of fire burning. The feeling of descent knotted my stomach as I burst through overcast clouds.

**

I was blind and had nowhere to go but down. If kept the boots alight, I didn't have to fly so much as summon the strength to land. Even if I didn't make it in one piece, I would be on the ground. The Brotherhood didn't seem to have any way to follow me.

I plummeted through the cloud. Booming noises shook smoke from my hobnails. The sounds of thunder rattled my bones and wracked my skin. I felt the scabbing on my fingers crack from the wind. My feet struggled to pedal through the grey mist as boot-flames roared beneath me. I gathered my cloak around myself, trying to keep from dying or hitting the ground too hard.

When I broke free of the mist, lightning crackled above me. Rain sheeted down as my boots gave off hisses of heat and steam. My stomach jumped. I struggled to control the descent as I fell toward bleakness and solid ground. I tried to breathe in the thin air, savoring the scent of my path down. Beneath me, the few lights looked like dots. I thought I could see the Count's prison-fortress on the horizon.

I turned toward it, letting the wind carry me. I struggled to stand, the rain battering me as I began to tumble. It was almost like flying, but more like an awkward crawl. My fingers scrabbling for purchase on air as I made my way lower.

As the ground approached, I could see farmhouses and barns outlined in darkness. The Count's castle on the hill was the only brightly lit thing for miles. I had to run now. There was no choice. I struggled and willed my legs to move.

I battled against the wind, my legs pumping, trying to judge the distance to the ground. My eyes were blurry, and my feet flickered with rearing flame. It was hard to see as I willed myself to move.

I couldn't move far or fast enough. My legs lost their strength. I tumbled downward into the chaos of barnyards and farmland. I struggled to pump my legs as I floundered, righting myself as I came in low. I smashed through the thatched roof of a barn, and crashed in a cloud of fire into a mound of hay. My legs feebly moved as straw and floor ignited around me, and I stared into the face of a horse, which made a loud noise. I heard a dim crackle as the boots went out.

My pounding heart finally rested for a time. I welcomed the darkness that came with clutching at the dirt and dung. The last thing I saw before unconsciousness was something that looked like a woman. My eyes closed before I could be sure. I felt the boots cool as the rain poured down from the hole above. Then sleep crushed me.

***

The sun hammered my eyes awake. I woke up in a bed defiled with the scent of someone else's lovemaking. Staring down at me past a thick, heavy quilt was a matronly woman with a small smile on her face. Her hair was tied back under a scarf. Her clothes were plain along with her visage. "Who might you be?" She passed me a bowl with some hot liquid in it.

"I'm just trying to get back to the castle." I gave her a bright and cheerful smile. "Just Symantha. And as long as you're not the Hoodless Master of the Brotherhood of Doors, you're my new best friend. May I know your name, since you saved me, and at some point, I'm obliged to give you something for it?" I spooned a little soup into my mouth.

"I'm a little round to be that wicked old frograper." Her mouth lit into a scowl. "Comes into my house sometimes and demands we join his revolution. I'm a madam, not some high and mighty soldier of fortune aiming to make a name for herself." She cackled a little bit. "My husband's a few years younger n' me, but he likes his women a little jiggly, and I'm fine with it. I'm the Unrepentant Goodwife of Harlotry."

"Does he really rape frogs?" I asked. "No offense, I've had a few problems with amphibians since I got here. This is good soup." I lied to her easily. As long as the soup was soup, after the night I had just had, it would have been heavenly. I focused on eating instead of her name.

"And why did I wake up in a prostitute's bed?" I asked, tapping my eyes as if they meant something to her.

"Oh, that's all there is, milady," she cackled. "Are you one of those folk that would care for a sample now?" She lewdly unbuttoned the top of her blouse.

"I think I'll pass," I responded coldly. "Might I have directions and a bath? I've got to get back to the castle before anyone else dies today."

"Is there something wrong with dying?" she asked me. I noticed that my hands had been washed, and my shirt cleaned.

"There is when you need a vouchsafe at court." I said. "I think my arrival has provided an opportunity for the Brotherhood to kill the Count."

"Gods, not again." Her face took on an exasperated look. "It happens every time that disgusting Duke of Bells in the next county sends someone this way."

"Well, this is the last time that will happen, then." I smiled. "He is dead. Don't tell too many people." I sat up in bed and began getting dressed as quickly as I could. Privately, I wished the Duchess of Bells had killed the toad prince sooner.

***

When I opened the door of the room, I discovered that there was a staircase leading down and the smell of pancakes wafting up. My body ached with bruises and the savagery of the cold. I made my way downstairs, gathered in my cloak as I limped past a group of prostitutes eating. There was still a large pile of flapjacks in the center of the table. The sixteen women sat, pretty and posturing as they munched on their pancakes and butter. The Goodwife was serving them as she fussed around the table. "You're off already?" She asked. "You're not even going to ask me for breakfast?"

"No." I made my way for the door. "But I was thinking of asking you which way the castle was from here." I hoped the picnic basket would have something for me when I arrived. I had to make sure that I got back before the Brotherhood made a new attempt on the Count's life.

"You can't miss it." She said with a laugh. "You'll be able to see it as soon as you get outside."

I stepped outside and raced forward in my boots, limping a little bit as I couldn't get my thoughts together. I was in too much pain to fly. I would have to walk.

I summoned all my strength, and limped down the road towards the castle, my aches giving me strength and anger. Rage boiled in my fingers and I shook the edges of my cloak. I knew I shouldn't be walking, and as my eyes focused on the castle, the only thought that passed through my mind was that no one could be trusted in this place.

It stayed with me with every hobnailed boot step.

***

As the day wore on and I got closer to the castle, I didn't get any warmer. My legs hurt and my teeth clenched. I wrapped my cloak around myself. The wind grew stronger as my feet crunched along the frozen road. I hoped that the Organ Grinder and the

Stone Preacher hadn't simply abandoned me. I prayed that the picnic basket wasn't gone. I wanted to make sure I fed the torturer to him one day.

The sun burned brightly as it rose in the sky, but the air was still cold around my ears. The guards, ever wary, gazed towards the outside, and the drawbridge was raised. I could see points of their spears shining in the bright sun. I struggled up the rocky hillside trail. I hadn't noticed how difficult it was before. I had been sitting in the cart the whole time.

When I finally reached the drawbridge, I cupped my hands and shouted out. "Lady Symantha the Yet To Be Named demands that you lower the drawbridge! I am tired, angry, in a great deal of pain, and I've been tortured by people wearing ugly green hoods!" My voice echoed against the wall of the castle. There was no response.

I let out a sickening little croak. I had dried my throat out with the first shout. I wet my lips, and made my second attempt. "Please! Lower the drawbridge! Look at my eyes, you clowns!" One of the guards finally turned and pointed. The drawbridge rumbled down.

"Thank you!" I looked at the guards as they marched out of the citadel, and they all lowered pikes around me. "It's so nice to see you all."

Their leader looked at me with an impassive gaze inside his locked-up helmet. "It's a pleasure to see you too."

He drew back a heavy mailed fist and knocked me out in a single blow.

***

I woke up on cold, moss-covered stones, the stinging punch somehow managing to hurt me more than all of the brutality I had previously been through. My jaw throbbed.

"Good to see you're coming around." The Organ Grinder laughed a little bit. "I'm afraid we've all been arrested."

"No kidding," I muttered.

"I am bereft of my beloved accordion, and he has taken my monkey." The Organ Grinder sighed. "Where did you go, young lady?" He scowled down at me. From a nearby cell, I could hear some frenzied hooting.

"I followed a member of the Brotherhood back to their, uh, castle." I winced. "It's pretty far up." I rolled over and inched my way over to the side of the cell, crawling upward until I could sit on the crude wooden bed.

"Far up?"

"It's a big chunk of rock, filled with archways, floating in the sky. All that overcast stuff you see up there? It's just the big chunk of rock and the clouds that surround it." It took almost all my strength to talk.

The Organ Grinder crossed his arms and leaned back on the wooden bench. "How are you?" he said, showing unusual concern.

"Well enough to know that the Brotherhood will try to kill the Count again now that I've gotten back here." My voice was ragged and my throat dry. "I found out what it's all about, though. Where's the Stone Preacher?"

"A few cells down. He says he's going to give them a few days before he crushes their ribcages and breaks their spines. If you and he are not given your freedom, he says he will kill everyone in this house, save only the Countess, a prisoner like himself." The Organ Grinder smiled. "Such a lovely individual, really. Why is he with us, again?"

"I did notice that he didn't include you – or your monkey – or the basket." I sighed. "Where is the basket?"

"The basket, I believe, is upstairs in your quarters. I believe it is sleeping." The Organ Grinder chuckled. "Do not ask me how a basket sleeps. I do not know."

"It is an unusual thing, isn't it?" I was worried about a picnic basket that ate people? The thought didn't comfort me at all.

"Indeed. Do you have a plan for getting out of here?" He smiled through his broad white teeth.

"Yeah." I sighed. "Perhaps being a noble prisoner has certain advantages. Let's try this the easy way first, before we try to get out of here." I began to rattle the bars of my cell as best I could. I could feel the torture wounds begin to crack open. Blood trickled down across my back. "Guard! I require a guard!" My voice carried up and down the massive cell block. Dim torches flickered everywhere in the spiral of cells and darkness.

The low clanking of armor brought an impassive, helmeted face to the door. "Although I am a prisoner, I would request of you the cheese that is in my pack. Could you have it brought to me?" I bowed to the guard as respectfully as I could. Then I winced for a moment and collapsed against the bars.

"At once, my lady!" The guard clanked off, and I collapsed to the ground in a false half-faint.

"Hurry!" the Organ Grinder shouted. "She will die without her cheese!" Either he was fooled, or he had been to prison before. In this place, there was almost no way to tell what was and wasn't a lie.

The torches flickered and the light burned at my eyes. I bled onto my ruined blouse and clutched my cloak of runes around me. Apparently magical protections weren't of any use in the cell.

It wasn't the magical protections I was interested in.

***

It seemed like hours before the guard returned with the unusual globe of cheese. "Your cheese, milady." He laughed and clanked off. "Perhaps later, you would like some wine?"

"Water will be fine." I called after him. "It can even be the nasty sort you like to torment prisoners with." I grinned to the Organ Grinder. "See? I do think of you. Just not in that way."

The Organ Grinder smiled. "What exactly do you intend to do with this cheese?"

"Well, if it works, then we'll be as quiet as the wind." I said, breaking off a piece and handing it to him. "If it doesn't, I'll be poisoned, and the Count of Locks, being the dreadful militant that he is, will scour the countryside for the old hag, and you'll get out until they fix me." I winked. "There's more than one way out of jail."

"I wouldn't want them to fix you," the Organ Grinder quipped. "I like to leave bastards behind." He shoved a little cheese into his mouth.

"Let me guess." I cut myself off a slice and nibbled on it. I was so hungry I could have eaten the whole thing, but I didn't know how long the effect lasted. "That's your idea of a joke?"

"It is a joke," the Organ Grinder chuckled. "Let's see how quiet this cheese supposedly makes us, shall—" His voice suddenly cut off.

I tried to respond, but I couldn't say anything. I tried taking a few steps. I couldn't hear them. The cheese was magical after all, but didn't bring me very much comfort.

I hand-signaled to the Organ Grinder, and began rattling the bars. He was larger than me. The slight clinking of my frame didn't make very much noise. I was worried that I wouldn't be able to hear anything either.

The bars whispered too. When he and I touched them, there wasn't the slightest hint of sound. I cursed bitterly. No noise came out of my mouth. I untied my cloak from around my neck and waited. I still couldn't hear anything.

The Organ Grinder rattled the bars harder. Still there was no sound. His massive frame pushed and pulled on the steel rods, digging his fingers in until his hands reddened and he had to let go for shortness of breath. I shook my head. I didn't even know how long it lasted.

As our silent rattling finished, a guard passed and his head turned oddly. The usual clanking of his armor was absent. I was completely silent. The guard moved over to us, and his voice rang across the cell. "What's this about?" he bellowed in his metal faceplate. "Are you taunting me?"

I shook my head as the guard stepped forward, and the Organ Grinder shook his head also. Then the guard grabbed me by the throat and yanked me up against the bars. I threw the cloak around his neck and tied it to one of the bars, pulling hard against it as the magical fabric of the cloak strained. I could feel my face purpling as the guard squeezed.

The Organ Grinder leaped for the guard through the bars and grabbed his throat. We struggled for a moment there as my face was pulled against the grate and the Organ Grinder rammed the guard's head against the bars. I broke off a piece of the cheese and shoved it into his mouth. The Organ Grinder the metal gauntlet away from my throat. As I fell, the guard smashed against the bars. He didn't make any noise either and slumped silently to the ground, the cloak still tied around his neck.

It took us a few minutes to right him and get the keys. The next rotation hadn't passed. Neither had the silence. After we opened the door, we struggled to get the man's armor off. I pointed to the Organ Grinder as we tugged and pulled at it.

Underneath the armor was the palest man I had ever seen. His skin was chalky, almost ghostly white, as if he never saw the sun. His lips were a pallid, sickly bluish shade.

It took four tries with the guard's key-ring to get him out of the armor. When we did, his whole body was the same whitish shade. Next to the lock on the back of his armor was a time and date stamp that I didn't recognize.

"Three hundred years?" The Organ Grinder gasped. The cheese had worn off.

"He's been in his armor for three hundred years?" I blinked. "That's insane." I whispered. I realized I was talking again. I turned the key in the slot again, and the man's boots clacked off. "He's locked in."

The guard's speech began to slur as I unlocked the chest plate, and he began to gurgle and rattle with horrible, wet choking sounds. The armor clattered off around him. The guard sagged in a wet, bloody mess.

In the center of his back, there was a wide, massive hole that had been cut by a sharp, serrated weapon. The locking mechanism of the armor had been forced into hole in his chest cavity, right where his heart would be. I watched the guard die, without knowing who he was, the wet, red well filling up in the center of his broken spine.

It took some time to remove the locking mechanism from the back of the armor and leave the front lock piece intact.

***

I threw my cloak back on. We slipped out of the cell toward the Stone Preacher's, leaving the dead guard behind. Each of us held a piece of the cheese in our fingers, in case we needed to be silent again. "You are my prisoner." The Organ Grinder, wearing the guard's armor grinned.

"A position, I'm sure, that your many rape victims have suffered already." I scowled. "You must promise me that your accordion will never be used to ensnare me when we're trying to survive. Or so help me, I'll have you executed in my new lands when all this is over."

"Feisty, indeed." The Organ Grinder chuckled. "We should go up and get out of here."

"We should find the Countess and get her out of here." I snapped. "The Count is completely insane."

"And the Duke of Bells was not?" The Organ Grinder smirked. "This world does not have the laws of the world we came from."

"We should also find the Stone Preacher." I said, as I slipped up to the door of the Stone Preacher's cell. He was settled quietly on the granite floor, meditating and praying in deep hollow tones.

"I was waiting for you," the Stone Preacher whispered. "I could have left this cell at any time."

"Where's the Countess?" I asked. "If you have so much control over rock and stone, can you find her from here?"

The Stone Preacher's eyebrow rose with a heavy, granite creak, and his face split into a wide, opalescent smile. For the first time, I saw how shiny his stone teeth were. "I was wondering when you would ask that question," he said. "Allow me to unleash my power, and I will find her."

"The subtle way, if you don't mind. There's no sense in killing everyone else in this massive jail."

The Stone Preacher nodded. There was a dull, heavy rumble like the sound of a gathering avalanche. His body shook, and the stone yawned up around him beneath his feet, swallowing him up. As the Stone Preacher descended, the rock reformed around him, as if the hunger of the earth consuming him had been satisfied.

"What was that?" I looked to the Organ Grinder, stuck in the armored trap.

"He is a legend of stone," the Organ Grinder said. "Some people say he can do anything with it."

The creaking of armor alerted me to the coming of another guard, and I tapped the Organ Grinder on the shoulder and motioned in his general direction as the heavy footsteps came up the deep, spiraling walkway.

"We should move back." The Organ Grinder rumbled a little bit inside the armor.

"We're going to have to fight our way out now." I said. "I hope you have a lot of protection in that stuff."

"We don't have to fight all the way out," the Organ Grinder said. "As long as we have the Countess hostage. May I remind you that in feudal societies, hostages are exchanged like prisoners?" He gave an unpleasant grin.

"Touch her in the way you like to touch women and I'll break your knees." It suddenly occurred to me that I was having fun. Queasy and fearful as it made me, this was an adventure again.

The guard made his way up around the corner of the spiral. The Organ Grinder walked up to him. "Excuse me," he said in a dull, boring voice. "The Stone Preacher has left his cell."

The other guard's hands moved slowly upward for a moment, reaching for a sword at his waist. The Organ Grinder punched him with a mailed fist. The guard staggered, and I raced forward, bumping him back against the railing. I grabbed the sword. It was the only thing available.

"Oh, dear," the Organ Grinder said. "A terrible accident has occurred." He bent over in the massive armor, and yanked the man's leg up, flipping him over the edge. There was a dull, moaning that carried all the way down the center of the spiraling pit, and a faint, wet, thud.

"They'll be coming soon," the Organ Grinder said. "I hope you're a little better with that thing than last time."

"Well, I'll stay on the cell side, then." There was a dull clang and a popping sound from a few levels down, and we heard horrified screams. I took a moment to peer over the side. The Stone Preacher was hurling guardsmen down the center of the hole. I could see shadowy shapes floundering and dying in a bloody heap, and I thought I could see the edges of some blackish pools that might be blood under their bodies.

"I hope he has the Countess." Four guards came around the edge of the spiral. "Drop your weapons! Our friend has the Countess. What kind of weasel sends his own wife to jail because a dirty pervert is coming, anyway?"

They drew their swords anyway and lumbered forward. They didn't have any intention of putting us back in our cells.

***

The Organ Grinder rushed toward the men as one of them raised his sword, and smashed against him. The two armored figures crashed together, and wrestled against the wall, four armored hands locked on each other, struggling over the weapon.

The other three shambled at me, so I ran. I hoped the heavy armor would slow them down until I found the Stone Preacher. Unfortunately, there was only one path. Other guards were starting to shout and point from other places in the spiral. I stayed low and ran. The guards clanked after me while the Organ Grinder and the last guard struggled over the sword.

As I rounded the corner, I heard a loud clang ringing sounds of metal. A scream echoed through the central pit. I turned my head to look. A dark shape plummeted below, the thud louder than the last time. I hoped it wasn't the Organ Grinder.

The clattering of armored feet approached behind me. I brandished the weapon, putting my back to the cell window. I held the sword as far in front of me as I could. The first of them lurched forward and swung. I ducked under his weapon, slashing at his knee. The blade cut slightly, and the massive figure buckled. I turned as the other two surrounded me.

They were well trained. One swung high, and another low. I jumped between the blades and rolled flat on the ground. The hard clank of approaching footsteps grew nearer. I rolled and kicked the wounded guardsman in the knee. He screamed and fell, dropping his sword and clutching the wound.

The two guards recovered from their swings and turned to face me, chuckling behind their grim, masked helmets. "It won't be long now," one said.

"That lucky dive won't save her," the other laughed. Then they charged, their metal boots furious and loud, swords raised above their heads.

I struggled to my feet and put up my sword as the two men clanked forward. One swung down while the other swung across. I parried the downward swing, my arms shaking, stepping forward into his guard to try and push him back. The other swing came in like a blur and then stopped with a weird metallic clanking noise.

The Organ Grinder, taller than the guard, his fingers thick and bereft of his gauntlets, was grabbing the other guard by his gorget, choking him. "I'm so sorry to be late." He smirked. "I had to slash the throat of your other friend, and my monkey was nowhere about to do the dirty work." His mustache twitched along with his wicked leer.

The sounds of fighting had broken out all along the spiral. I could see hooded figures grappling with the armored men. There were keening shouts and horrible groans, and the sounds of keys being turned in men's backs. In the distance, I thought I could see the Hooded Master ripping the lock out of someone's spine.

The guard brought his sword down again/ I parried as best I could while the Organ Grinder hurled his opponent over the edge, laughing the whole time. I thought I heard the victim's neck snap as he crested the rail from the force of the throw. The noise of the crack was enough. I heard a sobbing wail as the body vanished from sight. I shoved the sword into an eyeslit, twisting it sharply as the body fell to the ground, pulling the heavy weapon's weight with it.

"Such magnificent carnage!" the Organ Grinder chuckled as a clatter of weapons and metal hit the ground behind us. The Stone Preacher was dragging a very attractive, dark-haired woman, wearing only a cassock, chains on her wrists and ankles, and a beautiful obsidian tiara. The outline of some sort of metal sheath was visible that trapped her waist and loins.

"My goodness. That really is a chastity belt!" The Organ Grinder smiled. "It shall be my pleasure to open it for you, milady!"

"And it shall be my pleasure to let you, my dear Organ Grinder." She was lovely, with slender angelic features in a pleasant, smooth face. Her eyes sparkled with desire and ambition. Her lovely frame could not be hidden, no matter how hard the cassock tried. Long dark hair clustered in a beautiful, smooth pompadour belied the fact that her prison experience couldn't be anything other than suffering. It was almost as if she had spent extra time in her cell, primping and fussing as much as she could. Her smile matched her demeanor, even as she was dragged along in the Stone Preacher's grip. "I suppose this isn't really a rescue from prison after all?"

The Stone Preacher's face twisted into a scowl. Alerted by the clanking of metal, he turned, punching a guard hard in the face. The guard fell backward and thudded into a heap, the imprint of the Stone Preacher's fist embedded in the metal. Blood leaked out from under the lip of the helmet. "Think of it as an exercise in the education of virtues," he muttered, his voice dour.

"No, it isn't." I held the sword to her throat as the Brotherhood of Doors began surrounding us. "You're going to get us out of here. If the Hoodless Master wants you so badly, I'm keeping this sword right here until you get them to back off."

Her eyes widened and her lips crinkled into a devilish, amused smile. "The Hoodless Master? Ha! He offers only chaos and delusionary power. I shall prefer the Count of Locks to him." I pressed the sword a little closer against her throat as we began leading her up the spiral. "But I will say this for you. If my husband does not vouch for you after such cleverness in the face of his assassins, I shall surely write you a letter in secret." She gave me a wink, and the Organ Grinder a smile of lust that would melt steel.

The Hoodless Master shouted from across the spiral with a wicked cackle, turned to a prisoner in a cell, and drove the sword into his belly. There was a wretched scream, and he dived forward, vanishing fingertips first into the dying prisoner's mouth. "The Count! Slay him!" He shouted. "Hold off those people, and save my bride from the Organ Grinder!" His words echoed as the Brotherhood of Doors closed in on us, stepping out of nearby cells and bursting forth from the bodies of dying guards.

This wasn't turning out anything like the way I had hoped.

***

"No!" the Countess of Locks shouted. "Leave me to the Organ Grinder! I shall suffer his dirty caresses!"

"You see?" The Organ Grinder chuckled. "They can never go back." His face twisted with a smirk.

"We're going to have to fight them all to get your accordion and your monkey." I sighed. "Along with the basket."

The Stone Preacher simply raced forward into the small crowd of Doormen, and grabbed two of them, his mouth closed. He hurled one aside, tossing him, yowling, over the edge with a single hand, and punched his fist right through the chest of the second. Blood and organs erupted out the back. He paused for a moment to flex his fist before letting the dying man fall off.

"Bring me my monkey! Where is my accordion?" The Organ Grinder's voice was a furious roar. He clanked his way to one of the doormen and punched him with a mailed fist, making him double over. Then he drove a knee into the man's chest, and shoved him over the rail. I heard crashing sounds as the guard spiraled down into blackness.

The Countess of Locks looked on with delight as the Stone Preacher and the Organ Grinder waded through the horde of men. I kept the sword firmly pressed against her throat. "You're disgusting, allowing these people to kill people for your amusement like that."

"You have a sword at my throat," she said haughtily. "What makes you think I'll deny it under those conditions?" I turned to look at the battle as two of the Brotherhood of Doors burst through the raging press on the narrow walkway.

"They tortured me," I said firmly. "I have a sword now." I charged the first Doorman with it and swung as though I needed to cut the world in half. My anger fueled the swing, and there was a wet, horrid crack as I embedded the weapon in his ribcage. His blade flew away and clattered against the wall. The other Doorman leaped past and wrapped his hands around my throat.

I stared into Calvort's face, and he pressed his hands around my fingers, pinning me to the ground as his fat-faced grin stared down at me. "You'll die a noble's death, as far as I'm concerned." He grinned and punched me, and I could feel my bruises ache while I struggled to grab a weapon. He was so heavy I thought I might lose consciousness.

The Countess of Locks ran forward, tugging at the sword in her chains while he bashed my head against the stone. I could feel a little bloody wetness at the back of my head, and hear screams of pain and breaking bone from the remaining Doormen. There was the sound of something that sounded like talking cut off by a throat being ripped out. Calvort's eye erupted with a blade, and his body fell on top of me.

"Get up," the Countess of Locks said fiercely. "You need blade practice, and this one's lodged in his skull." She sighed and let go of the hilt.

I struggled to get the dead man off me, and the Countess pulled hard, helping me up with a sparkle in her green eyes. When we got to our feet, the bodies of the Brotherhood were spread around like discarded meat, ripped and torn apart. "We need to get upstairs." I said to the Stone Preacher. "The Count's probably in danger."

"Do we really have to save him?" the Countess asked.

"If you want to get out of that chastity belt, we do. I'm pretty sure that if we don't, the Brotherhood will wind up with the key, and with the Organ Grinder's eyes all over you, I don't know that the Hooded Master will let you out."

The Organ Grinder laughed a little bit. "She does have a point. I assure you, my dear, that our second time together shall be as delicious as our first."

"You stay out of this!"

The Stone Preacher grabbed the Organ Grinder's wrist, squeezing hard. He gave me a cold nod without saying anything.

We raced up the stairs. The Stone Preacher gestured with his hand, and the stony frame bent around the iron door to the prison. It fell inward with a dull crash. From the Count's throne room, we could hear the sounds of fighting.

***

The hallways were strewn with the dead and the dying. Wherever there was a member of the Brotherhood of Doors, the Stone Preacher stepped forward onto their heads and crushed them to pulp. By the time we reached the open doors of the throne room, his feet were covered with blood and bits of bone.

The screams and clatter of more violence came from within. The room was brightly lit. The last few guards, clad in their armored shells, battered against the shields and swords of the Brotherhood. A few feet from the throne, the Hoodless Master was swinging at the Count of Locks with a massive, bladed hammer, smashing against the armor as the Count shielded his once-smiling face from the blows.

The Hooded Master raised his hammer to swing, and the Countess of Locks stepped into the room, her eyes fierce. 'Will someone get this miserable belt off of me?" Her voice was mixed with fury and disgust.

I covered the Organ Grinder's mouth. The Stone Preacher turned to me with a cracking, rocky grin. "Your reflexes are improving." He moved inexorably in a smooth glide towards the members of the Brotherhood, and punched his fist right into the spine of the nearest one. When I turned to look, the Organ Grinder was gone. I could hear footsteps from down the corridor.

There was a shuffle, and the rustle of thick, dirty flesh. From the corridor behind me, the torturer sprang, his fingers holding a thick spear that had knobs and spikes along its length. I slipped inside the door and screamed.

"Unbelievable," the Countess of Locks murmured. "Husband, a heap of suet is attacking!"

The Stone Preacher began wading through the Brotherhood, tossing them about like ragdolls. He reveled in the sound of cracking bones. His thin smile stretched across his face. It made a sound like the cracking of slate.

I backed away from the torturer and waited for him to thrust the spear again. "You will enjoy the caresses of my flesh." His voice was filled with lust and drool. Then he lunged.

I spun forward, and his thick, beastly arms swung the spear sideways, trying to pin me on its spikes as I backed up through the throne room. I heard a horrible clang as the Count of Locks' armor bent inward. The Hooded Master drew out a knife and began to hack and stab at the chest plate, trying to peel it open.

The Stone Preacher reached for the last member of the Brotherhood, and hurled him bodily onto the spear in the torturer's hands. The sudden addition of weight staggered the bloated giant. The massive weapon clattered to the floor. "That's more like it." The Countess of Locks purred. "Now, wherever is the Organ Grinder?"

From the doorway came an unholy chittering. The monkey pounced, ruthless and savage, jumping on the head of the torturer, stabbing at his skin and eyes with the knifelike tail. The knife was too short to penetrate the folds of fat. The Torturer screamed as his reached up to rip the creature off.

"I am right here." The Organ Grinder smiled, and lifted a powerful hand to squeeze the Torturer's wrist, his smile wide. "Fear not, my lady." He looked over at the Hoodless Master. I ran toward the Master, sword outstretched.

The Hoodless Master yanked the breastplate open, and ran his tongue across his lips while the Count's face gurgled, thick and waxy. I drew the sword back and swung with all my might, but the Hooded Master was faster and bigger. He slammed the hammer into my sword and shouted "There! Do you see? This is the charlatan that took her from me!"

Inside the chest of the construct, the Count of Locks was a bitter-faced, twisted dwarf, his face stained with wet, red blood. His back hunched in a terrible hump. One of his legs was far shorter than the other. The gears and pulleys he used to control his impressive armor compressed him into a sickly, bloated shape. His voice, still deep and resonant, bellowed his fury at me. "My honor is not yours to take! Unhand me, and speak not of this!" His one good eye blinked at me, while the glassy orb of the other bulged from his eyesocket, making his whole face seem deformed. Gnarled fingers twitched on one of the knobs, and he kicked and struggled as the Hooded Master fished him out. "Do you like that your smooth, silky skinned wife chose me over you, miscreant?" He chuckled and clenched his small fists, struggling to free himself.

"I despise liars." The Stone Preacher said, and grabbed him by the wrist.

I was almost so overcome by horror that I barely escaped the Hoodless Master's backswing. "Don't kill him!" I shouted. "I need him!" I pushed forward and slid the sword down along the hammer towards the Hooded Master's fingers. He reached back for another swing while guards surrounded the Torturer with pikes and swords.

The Organ Grinder smiled. He seemed more gentlemanly than usual. "Good sirs, if I might have a kerchief to cleanse my hands of this bloated thing?" He smiled evilly to the Torturer as his monkey leaped back to his shoulder, chittering angrily at the fat man.

I brought my sword forward, hearing a momentary wicker rustle. As I brought the weapon down on the haft of the massive hammer, there was a sharp, pained howl from the Hooded Master. The picnic basket had sunk its teeth deep into the man's leg. It was chewing. It ripped away great chunks of flesh and meat. As the teeth grew bloody, I could see bones just above the boot line.

He screamed in pain, and raised the hammer high above his head to crush the picnic basket.

With rage and fury, I drove my sword forward. "Don't touch it!" I hissed, and drove the sword desperately into his chest, hearing the clank of armor. "You starved me and I haven't eaten in days!"

He brought the hammer back, and tried to swing again, but the basket lunged under his guard and tugged at his leg. As he turned, I stepped in and swung with everything I had. This time the blade cut cleanly. The Hoodless Master's head rolled across the floor. His body toppled to the floor, lying there as the head disappeared. "Did he escape?" I asked the Count.

"I'm not sure," the Count wheezed in the Stone Preacher's grip.

The Countess of Locks ran to the Stone Preacher and dropped to her knees. "Please!" she begged. "Kill him! I wish only to stay with the Organ Grinder!" She clutched at his arm desperately.

The Stone Preacher gently pushed her away and deposited the Count of Locks into his armor. "No," he said firmly. "You are as disgusting as your husband. You deserve each other." He folded his arms and waited for me to give him an order.

The Countess of Locks looked disappointed, and moved over to her throne with a dreary looking sulk. "I simply despise this belt, it itches. Husband, despite you arresting this young lady, she, along with her unusual companions, has somehow managed to save your life. Vouchsafe her at court, at the very least. This young lady deserves a name, and all the privileges that go with it."

The picnic basket made a weary rustle and flopped against my leg. It opened, and the warm smell of a cinnamon custard pie wafted through the room. I looked to the Organ Grinder. "Where did you find them?" I asked. "That was what you meant to do, right?"

"They were just down the hall. One of the Brotherhood must have freed them. I found a couple of his fingers." He gave a pleasant wink.

The Count of Locks propped himself up inside the shattered armor, his massive ocular bulging. "You may demand three things of me," he said. "That is the rule of my household."

"Very well, my lord." I curtsied to him, as he dripped a little blood out of his mouth. "I wish for you to vouch for me at court." I smiled. "You will take your wife out of that stupid chastity belt, for the second." The Countess of Locks grinned, as if I had played the game correctly. I pointed to the Torturer. "And I want to feed that miserable bloated heap of suet to the picnic basket." The basket wiggled a little bit. I sighed and took the pie out.

The Count of Locks stared at me with his ocular. "So be it!" He thundered, his deep bass voice never wavering. "Do you wish to stand on ceremony?"

"No thank you, my lord. It can eat him now."

The fat torturer howled, his bloated gut hanging down over his naked loins, as the prison guards held him in place with a ring of thick metal pikes. He looked at me with a pitiable glance, and tears formed in his eyes. Behind me, the Picnic basket rustled, and I could hear the low slavering from its lid, and the slithering of tongue over teeth. "Please," he whimpered, "don't."

"All right," I said with a cheerful smile. I looked down at the basket and stepped aside from it. "You can have the whole thing." I made a little gesture of allowance to the basket.

The Count of Locks, struggling in the ruins of his armor, seemed amused.

The torturer screamed as the basket charged forward, and bit him fiercely on the hand, chewing mercilessly through the fat, skin, and bone. His screams and sobbing continued, blood pooling on the ground as the basket devoured him, savoring the massive heaps of lard. After the hands were chewed off, the rolling, flopping sack gave a shuddering sob as the basket dived between his legs and chewed slowly. The red pool sloppily grew wider as the basket feasted, the screams descending into gurgles, and then quiet. It finally ate the head. The sickening crack of the skull popped through the audience chamber. A little purplish blood trickled out of the basket. The long tongue slithered out and lapped it up. The rest of the feasting lasted for a very long time.

I watched the whole affair in silence, imagining everyone else's horror. It wasn't until afterwards that I realized they were all gazing on me with approval. All I could think about was bruises, my splinters, and the pain in my breasts where they tortured me. I could barely hear the polite clapping of my own bodyguards, and the pleasurable wheezing of the Count of Locks.

"Well done!" the Count of Locks said, finally struggling to stand, hunchbacked and twisted. "I believe even my wife approves of it. Don't you?"

The Countess was red faced and holding back bile. She swallowed hard. "Yes, my lord." She focused her gaze on the Organ Grinder, who stood next to the Stone Preacher and watched.

"I shall allow you to stay in my castle this evening, to heal and rest a little bit, but then you must journey on. Keeping things under control is a difficult business, you know." He smiled. "May I have a piece of custard pie?"

"You are the lord of the castle." I said with a light laugh. "You may have it all."

The Count smiled. "You are free to return to your quarters." He said. "I shall have a servant come and clean them."

We collected ourselves and walked out through the damaged door, and made our way back to our room. The picnic basket began to smell of a wonderful roasted chicken. A full meal, I knew, awaited us once we opened it.

When I slept that night, I was tormented by a horrible vision of the Count of Locks, hanging in chains from the wall of his own bedroom, while the Organ Grinder and the Countess rutted with heavy, meaty grunts in his bed, leaving the sheets sticky while she taunted her twisted husband. The Count of Locks screamed, wept, and cursed the name of his wife, while sweat ran down her forehead and she begged the Organ Grinder to give her his children.

I awoke a little early. The Organ Grinder was in his chair. I heard only the sounds of snoring while the monkey slept.

***

We drove out of the castle before the sun fully rose, and the wretched creaking of the cart echoed, reminding me of my dreams the previous night. "Did you?" I said to the Organ Grinder as the Stone Preacher rumbled a little bit alongside the horses. "Did you chain up the count and bed his wife in their marriage bed?"

"Why, no!" The Organ Grinder chuckled. "But I wish that I had thought of it."

We rode through the hills into the hazy morning. For three days after that, the basket produced some of the most succulent meals imaginable. Halfway through the next day, a massive city appeared on the horizon, its walls stony and guardsmen numerous.

Chapter Ten

The Petitioning of the Queen of Castles

As we drew closer, I could see guards moving back and forth on the walls. A long line of carts formed at the gate. We passed through a few towns, but none at an appropriate time to stop. The rudely creaking wagon of the Organ Grinder lumbered up to the massive stone barbican.

It was several stories high, with a thick, rocky tollbooth built into the wall. There was an occasional scream of pain that vibrated off the rock walls and echoed back to us. "You will not like this." The Organ Grinder smiled. "The Queen of Castles takes a toll in blood for all who pass through the walls of her city."

The picnic basket let out a low growl, and gave a wickerish rustle to indicate displeasure. There was an unpleasant chittering from under the Organ Grinder's greatcoat.

"Well, that's okay," I said winningly. "Does she do something unpleasant with it?"

"I am not sure." The Stone Preacher said coldly. "I do not have any blood to give."

"You took someone else's, didn't you?"

"I shall not lie." The Stone Preacher rattled a little bit. "I grabbed a man's fingers and squeezed, and scraped it into a bottle for them.

Even the Organ Grinder winced. A contented coo came from the picnic basket as the line moved forward. I opened the basket and took out a smoking pastry loaf that smelled of cheese inside. I didn't know what it was, but I needed to stifle my conversation, so I took a bite. It was filled with a rich, creamy cheese that had been baked around a caramel core, and frosted with a light coating of sugar. My mood brightened.

"At least your basket's been more stable after eating the torturer than it was after all the toads." The Organ Grinder smirked as the line inched forward.

"It's cooking with fat instead of cooking with something else, I guess." I said. "I don't understand how it does what it does, and I don't care." I scratched the top of the basket with my fingers. It made low growling noises of contentment. "Thanks for this, by the way. Whatever it is." Over the past few days I learned that the picnic basket would occasionally make foods none of us recognized. It was still full of torturer, and occasionally hiccupped.

We wended our way along the slow, creaking line of carts, horses, and disaffected men. When it was our turn to reach the toll station, the sky was almost completely gray.

***

We ground our way up to the booth at the edge of the castle, parked in the center of the plains as if meant to oppose all passage. The old wooden cart creaked. Bony horses heaved as though the Organ Grinder were about to choke them to death with the reins. I sat next to the Organ Grinder, his smirk crossing his features, while my fingers stroked the wicker of the basket. It made little growling sounds. Two guards stepped up, one on each side of the gate. A metal tollbooth, covered with bars, loomed impassively in the stone.

One of the guards looked up at the Organ Grinder and smiled. "Your blood, sir. It is good to see you again, Organ Grinder." He chuckled, and the monkey hooted viciously under his coat. "I listened to what you told me. His wife will never know." He guffawed and pulled out a knife. The Organ Grinder held out his hand. There was a quick slash, and with a swift movement, the guard let a little of the blood from the Organ Grinder's hand dribble into a cup. The second toll-taker stepped up and swiftly bound it. A red stain spread across clean linen.

"Now, milady, it is your turn." The toll-taker said. He approached me, holding out the knife, with his linen-binder behind him.

I reluctantly held out my hand, and stared at him. "Cut anything important and I'll kick you in the head." The basket growled in assent, its tongue crept out.

The toll taker chuckled. "Milady's pet is unusual." Then he drew out the knife and slashed, holding the cup. My blood dribbled into it. The linen binder stepped forward, and wrapped my hand tight. It hurt more than it should have. "And I see that you are new here. Have you come to the Queen of Castles for succor before you journey on?"

"I suppose you could call it that." I gave him a wincing smile. It was as if I could still feel the knife, cutting and bleeding me. "What do you do with all the blood?"

"We feed the stones with it," the toll taker said. "It is the wish of the Queen of Castles that we pour the blood of all who come into the foundations. But she is far older than us, and I no longer care why." He gave me a cheery laugh. "So is there anyone else in your party?"

The Stone Preacher came around the side of the wagon, a rumbling glide in the air as his stony, cassocked form stepped forward. "Oh, yes." The Stone Preacher chuckled. "I have no blood to give, as I am stone. Are the two of you new?" His rocky eyebrow flicked up. "Nonetheless, I have blood to give." He grabbed the linen-binder, and squeezed the man's finger, so hard that the man buckled and screamed. There was a wet, sickening pop from the Preacher's fist. A stream of blood trailed into the cup. "Bind yourself up, worm." He sneered as the toll taker laughed. "I cannot stand sycophants."

"We'll take it." The keeper's voice was low. "Thanks for breaking him in. I was beginning to think no one ever would." The face of the linen binder was white. He gritted his teeth and whimpered as he tied off his own wound. The toll taker took the cup with the collected blood, walked to the tollbooth, and stepped inside. I saw him make a pouring motion. There was a faint trickling sound as blood traveled downward into the foundations of the citadel.

The toll taker raised a hand. There was a thick rumbling of stone and metal. The gate rose, loud and steely. With a crack of the reins and creaking from rickety wood, we made our way forward. Spires beckoned with promises of decadence, tightly fitted streets, and narrow, defensible walkways.

I didn't start to feel cold and trapped until metal crosshatches slammed down behind us.

***

The massive castle's streets were narrow and tight. We wended our cart through the squeezes of granite and miserable alleyways as people jumped out of the way. The Organ Grinder's horses' hooves clattered on the cobbles, making the wagon creak as though it were about to fall apart. Some women in the road would occasionally point and stare, some at the Organ Grinder, others at me, cackling and smirking. Their appearances ranged from beautiful to unpleasant. Those who were with their husbands gave looks of being caught or discovered. I thought I saw one man grab his wife and punch her in the mouth.

The Stone Preacher waded behind the wagon. It amused him to keep his eye on the mocking ladies.

They quickly went silent.

"We need to find an inn," the Organ Grinder said calmly. "I would not stay out on these streets for long. I appear to be famous."

"In the same way that plagues are famous," I said. "Did it ever occur to you that maybe if you only slept with half the number of women, the population might actually increase due to lack of the violence that you leave in your wake?"

The Organ Grinder laughed wickedly. The monkey made weird noises under his greatcoat that tried to join him. "I do not know if you are being witty or serious, however, you entertain me." He reached into a pocket for a dirty handkerchief and blew his nose.

The picnic basket hissed. I moved a hand to quiet it. "Find us an inn. I hesitate to stay in any place that our friend the Preacher would find comfortable."

"At once, my lady." He shook the reins violently. One of the horses spat up phlegm on a passer-by.

We rode down the street, passing alehouses and shops, with the sun shining down on our heads and glinting off the Stone Preacher's teeth.

We finally stopped at a place with several carriages tethered outside. It was opulent in appearance. But appearances could be deceiving. The Organ Grinder pulled the rickety cart up to the tether poles, and dismounted, swiftly tying the horses off with a brutal grunt. "Let's see you beasts free yourselves from that!" He scowled, and slapped one of the horses roughly on the face.

"There's no sign!" I said. "What kind of place is this? Not some sort of brothel, I hope."

"It is the Inn of the Duke of Servants." The Stone Preacher rumbled. "He has chosen well, if the Duke is for you. But, he has chosen poorly if the Duke is against you."

"What's that supposed to mean? We don't even know what this place is," I said and began getting down. I shouldered the basket. I didn't want it to eat anyone important.

"His servants are all invisible except when you want to see them." The Organ Grinder smiled. "It is like every other inn, only better."

It wasn't until I stepped through the doorway that I realized that in winter here, even the sun was cold.

***

We walked into the inn when the concierge, wearing an elegant uniform and smiling the blandest of possible smiles, appeared before us. He was blond, thin and shifty eyed, but his elegance protected him as a sheath might. His sudden manifestation startled the monkey, and it shrieked. The picnic basket made no move on my arm.

"Ahh, my goodness. A true lady and her companions. Questing for our true love, are we?" He gave me a sinister wink. "Fall prey not to the Organ— oh." His face fell as he noticed the massive frame of the Organ Grinder in his ruffled vest behind me. "I suppose you're at least somewhat safe from that."

The Stone Preacher ground his way in through the door, his eyes narrow and diamond-like. "I suppose that members of the clergy get to stay for free?"

The concierge thought that over for a moment, and wrung his hands so hard I thought his fingers would snap. "I suppose." I saw a bead of sweat trickle down his forehead.

"It would be kind of you if you did not charge an additional fee from my manservants." I smiled. "Do you have a separate policy for animals?" It occurred to me that this place might be more pleasant than others I had stayed at.

The monkey chittered under the Organ Grinder's coat, and the man bowed gracefully. "For you, my lady, we shall make certain that the monkey's needs are taken care of."

"It needs to kill things. You might want to skip that," I responded, and turned to the Organ Grinder. "It serves you right."

The Stone Preacher let out a grim chuckle as the Concierge checked our baggage. "Is there a chapel where I might pray?" he asked.

"We do not have such things," the concierge said coolly. "Come, I'll take your luggage." We handed over our small bags and boxes to him, and he gathered them all up in his arms. Then he suddenly faded from view.

"I hope we still have heat," I muttered.

"Very few places outside the Church of Gears have heat here," The Organ Grinder responded. "It does take some getting used to, and it does eliminate a place for my favorite activities." He gave a lewd smirk.

"No doubt, the Duke of Servants will come to greet you personally," the Stone Preacher added. "I'm certain, Organ Grinder, that his servants are all yours."

"You can't see them," I said calmly. "There's no point."

"On the contrary." The Stone Preacher's lip cracked into a wicked, unfathomable grin, with a sound that reminded me of a slab of slate cracking underfoot. "That is precisely what I was trying to say."

I couldn't withhold a snicker at that, even as I marched up the stairway with the basket on my arm. We went up the stairs and into the room, where the door, already opened by our invisible man, revealed the splendor beyond.

I didn't even hear the rustle of footsteps when the concierge left. Somehow, I knew he was gone.

***

The room was opulent, without any trace of dirt. There was a massive bed that had to be less comfortable than it appeared. Several large chairs for lounging in were covered in smooth, well-tanned leather. Dressers were carved from a type of wood I didn't recognize. Faint reliefs of human faces shone under the stain. The bed had the faces as well, worked into the wood as though they were effigies of living persons. There was a window across the way, from which I could see a massive, spired palace that shone with light.

"What kind of wood is this?" My fingers ran across it. The faces were uncomfortably real.

"The kind that comes from a tree that eats people," the Stone Preacher rumbled. "I haven't seen one of those trees for many years. When people sit under its attractive boughs, they fall asleep. And then it eats them. They are peaceful, as if still sleeping, but it preserves their faces for reasons no one understands."

"That's not very reassuring." I said as I put some things into the dresser. "It is dead, right?"

"One might hope that the people could have been freed, but obviously, this tree was enough of a danger to have it cut down."

The Organ Grinder chuckled. "And when I freed the ladies, oh, to enjoy the glorious reward!"

The Stone Preacher gave a rattling shake of his head. I just scowled. "Well, we're going to sleep here, so I hope it wakes up and eats you." I said fiercely.

"Well wishes, indeed." The Organ Grinder chuckled.

We were still unpacking our things when the Duke of Servants arrived. He was clad in a simple black doublet, his excessively ornate hat, jeweled and studded, denoting his station. It seemed he came alone, but there could have been invisible people in the room with him.

He was a powerfully built, severe-faced man, with a wide square jaw. The scars of swordwork covered his knuckles. The black doublet barely reined in his powerful arms, and he looked out of place in the hose and simple black shoes of a butler. He belonged on a battlefield, and his cold eyes knew it. "Ahh, Lady. Are you named or unnamed?" He gave the most deferential bow I had yet received.

"I am, as yet, unnamed." I smiled a little bit. I realized that as my journey had continued, I was becoming more formal and pompous. I curtsied as gently as I could.

"Oh, shove off with that. I'm only a Duke of Servants, it is not as if I hold much sway at court, either here or at the Castle in the Sky."

"You've been to the Castle in the Sky?" I thought of my lover, those green eyes burning, his breath in my mouth.

"A few times, milady." He said with a smile. "You'll get there too, one day, if you're lucky. If not, of course, you'll probably die alone and with your eyes removed in some strange manner or with your heart frozen to ice by the Weeper in Shadows." He shrugged.

"You've met her?" I asked.

"I have been fortunate enough not to."

"How did you become the Duke of Servants?" It was an impertinent question. I asked anyway.

The Duke of Servants explained. "I had an honorary dukedom when I arrived, and so, mockingly, they allowed me to keep it. And then, as I was a Duke of Servants, my servants were suddenly invisible when people thought it necessary. I have no idea how it works." He gave me a cheerful smile.

"May I see them?" I asked, almost excited. I wanted to see it in action.

A crisp looking maid shimmered into view. She was portly and cheerful and worked at cleaning the mirror above the bureau with a smile on her face. It was like she hadn't been there before. "As you can see," she said. "We are here to meet your every need."

The Organ Grinder turned and leered at the maid, eyeing frowzy hair and joyful features.

"Every need but that one." I snapped. "No more, Sir Organ Grinder, unless it is necessary." He gave me a look of steadfast disappointment.

"I see you know the Organ Grinder well. Do you know him personally, without even having a name yet?" The Duke chuckled. "I would assume not, by the way you speak to him."

"I am trying to get her to change her mind." The Organ Grinder smiled.

The picnic basket let out a low growl and rustled from its place on my arm. I tugged, but it growled louder, and then I was half-dragged across the room. "Down!" I snapped to the basket. "Not in front of our host!" The basket quieted, but slavered as it saw the monkey's tail peek out of the Organ Grinder's coat cuff.

The Duke frowned. "I see you have acquired yourself a pet."

"I would not call it a pet," I said. "The basket was a gift from a friend."

"An innkeeper named Bosquoverde gave it to her," the Stone Preacher said. "I've been trying to part them ever since, but she seems to like it, and it seems to like her."

"It saved me from the Duke of Bells." I petted it, and the basket quieted.

The Duke of Servants eyed it curiously. "I've seen a basket like that somewhere before. No matter. It's not important, I'm sure. If it likes you, you, at least, will be safe." He gave a graceful bow to us. "If you would settle in, dinner will be served precisely at four."

"An early dinner would be lovely," I said. The maid slipped out, red-faced.

I left the picnic basket on the bed. It had been making food for a while, and it was overly hungry. Lately, I had been feeding it too often. I was worried that it was still full of torturer.

The Duke bowed and smiled, departing in a stiff, formal display of grace that I had thought possible only for professional dancers. In the course of the conversation, I had forgotten to keep an eye on the Organ Grinder's hands.

***

We went down to dinner at the appointed time, and took seats in the dining room, where several other groups gathered. It was a beautiful room, with a thick, plush carpet, and separate booths, each situated at the point of a twelve pointed star. There was a central buffet, with roasted meats, salads, and a few elegant-looking desserts. Servants politely served people on a short line. The booths were all richly paneled in deep black wood, and the chairs were of the same construction – deep, high backed, and comfortable. A massive chandelier dominated the space above the buffet, threatening to rip its way out of the ceiling, collapsing on food and servants.

Everyone else was rich, or looked it, and were settled around tables in elegant clothes. As I walked in with the Stone Preacher and the Organ Grinder, there were a few looks of shock and some glares of disdain. The Organ Grinder paused, and gave each one of them a solemn and perfect bow. He even kept his eye on the more attractive wives as he settled in his chair.

"Friends of yours?" I snapped as I slipped into my seat, which had just been pulled out for me.

"I wouldn't call them friends." The Organ Grinder smiled as the vicious scowls of husbands followed him.

When the Stone Preacher sat in his chair, it creaked, but managed to hold his granite mass. "I suppose it's not as sturdy as it seems," he murmured.

"Nothing elegant is." I idly pulled out my napkin and settled it into my lap. "The Organ Grinder is proof of that."

The Organ Grinder chuckled. "You have a way with words, my dear. Your name shall be well known by all one day."

"That might not be the most wonderful thing." I smoothed the napkin in my lap. "Look at some of the people we've met. Everyone famous is infamous."

The Organ Grinder undid his greatcoat and settled it over the back of the chair. The monkey peered out of a pocket. He gently shoved it down. A servant appeared next to him. "Good sir.' He said to the well-dressed servant. "May I have some raw meat for my monkey?"

"Of course, sir." The servant took a few steps and vanished.

"You feed it raw meat?" I stared. "No wonder it's so bloodthirsty."

"Well," the Organ Grinder smiled. "It does prefer eating things while they're still alive." There was a brief rocky crackle, then the Organ Grinder let out a painful grunt.

"What was that?" I didn't really want to ask, but I had to.

"I'm standing on his foot," the Stone Preacher responded. "Our charge has to eat, Organ Grinder. You are not helping." With a slight shift, his granite robes rustled. The Organ Grinder's face returned to a more ruddy shade.

"I'll keep that in mind." I said. "Don't stand on mine, please?"

The Stone Preacher's rocky eyebrow creaked wide. "I was rather hoping that you would not make that request of me in the event that I needed to kill you before this was over."

"Excuse me?"

"There are rare cases where people need to be maimed or crippled in order to find their true love, and so, since I cannot hobble you, I fear I shall have to ask the Organ Grinder to do it." The Stone Preacher smiled as if he had won a great victory.

"Don't think I'll allow him to do it either." I snarled as a selection of juices was wheeled by on a cart, served to us by intermittent servants.

The staff winked in and out as needed. I presumed it worked for everyone differently based on what he or she wanted. The air was full of laughter and enjoyment. A graceful looking servant, wearing a red doublet with a coat of arms I didn't recognize walked down the stairs towards our table. A hat that looked like a cross between a biscuit and a creampuff perched on his head. He carried himself with more dignity than a typical waiter. "Ahh," the Organ Grinder said with a smile. "The Queen of Castles has noticed you."

"Is that good or bad?" I said. "I've learned that most of the places we visit have a tendency to be bad."

"Well, she's a very nice woman, but I've never been able to get into her skirts, so I would say that it makes her good for you and bad for me." The Organ Grinder chortled.

"Someone is actually immune to your accordion?" I didn't believe it. "I think I need a blood transfusion."

The Stone Preacher rumbled. "The Queen of Castles is safe." He gave a rocky smile. "As long as she stays within these walls, nothing can harm her. Most of the time, however, she is too afraid to leave her palace." He chuckled. "She can't wall in the world, fortunately for the rest of us."

"What's that supposed to mean? Does she just hate the outdoors?"

The servant bowed very low, and smiled to us. "My Lady, the Queen of Castles, would like you to join her for a meal tomorrow evening, in one of her most secure dining rooms." He produced an invitation from under his shirt.

"Why, thank you." I gave him an elegant smile. "I believe this is yours?" I pulled a coin out of my pocket and thrust it into his fingers as he passed me the invitation. "I am flattered. Such flattery deserves a reward."

"Did you unconsciously manage all that, or were you deliberately trying to be pompous?" The Organ Grinder leered.

The servant dashed off, not even waiting for a reply. "Actually, I learned it all from you." I said. A wicked crack of rock told me that the Stone Preacher was trying not to laugh. "Except for the rutting part. That I don't need to learn from you."

"Oh, managing it all on your own?" The Organ Grinder laughed. "Care to show me?"

The Stone Preacher interjected. "You have no respect for anything, do you? I beg of you to find some sacrilege that you are guilty of so I may crush you as the heretic you are."

I gently put my hand on the Stone Preacher's wrist. "Easy, now. He did get us out of the Duke of Bells situation in a roundabout way."

"Don't remind me," the Stone Preacher growled. "Having to be a bodyguard along with the Organ Grinder is the worst ennobling experience I've ever had."

"There have been others?" I asked. "What happened to them?"

"One of them is now the Princess of Halberds, a truly violent one, to be sure, and the other seven died." He sighed. "Two butchered by swamp creatures, one slaughtered and eaten by carnivorous bedding, and four killed by the Weeper in Shadows."

"Four!" I shouted in a high pitched voice. "You mean this woman who showed up and tried to kill us has killed other would-be princesses? Why didn't you tell me any of this?"

The Organ Grinder snickered. "Perhaps he didn't want to worry you. Perhaps he feels he's obligated to a heretic? Or perhaps, there is a stirring in those miserable stone loins after all and he wishes to feel his rock hard member pierce your pliant—"

I shoved my hand over his mouth, muffling his voice. "There are people watching us." I hissed. "Could you please not be so graphic?"

The Stone Preacher merely chuckled. "I like her. I am forced to admit that saving one's life encourages one to be rather a more efficient protector, praise the cold granite from which I spring." He stopped, tilted his head, and his neck made a sound like splitting ice, cracking off a ledge. "Besides, other than the fact that she owes you her life, she can't stand you."

"I can't wear the same dress that I got from the Duchess of Weavers." I changed the subject. "I need something new. She's a Queen. I have to be classy, but not as classy as she is. We need to go shopping."

"Oh, bother a woman and her clothes," the Organ Grinder snapped.

"That's because you don't see women with them on very often," I retorted. "At least I can trust the Stone Preacher to keep his hands off me."

The Stone Preacher chuckled. "I'm sure in a city this large, there will be a tailor or seamstress you may find."

We finished dinner as swiftly as we could, and headed for the door. Around us, servants seemed to vanish into thin air. We didn't need them at the moment.

***

The streets were brightly lit, even without people. The cold night wrapped around us in the cramped stone. "I can't believe we're looking for a tailor at this hour," I said. "Do you think we'll be able to wake one?"

"Wake one?" the Organ Grinder chuckled. "I'll strangle the man with his own intestines if he does not provide you with the correct clothing." The monkey hooted its vicious assent.

"Threatening shopkeepers is poor form," the Stone Preacher murmured. "You see why I yearn to yank out his spine and feed it to him?"

"I think everyone wants to yank out his spine and feed it to him." I smirked. "What makes you so special?"

"I think I've been outwitted." The Stone Preacher chuckled as the Organ Grinder stalked through the streets, eyeing shops as if he was trying to remember the way.

"I hope he hasn't slept with the tailor." I muttered.

"It would certainly be expected." The Stone Preacher's lips thinned with a grim cracking noise.

"How did you hear me?" I reacted with more surprise than I should have. He had done this before. "I wasn't trying to be heard."

"You are touching the ground," the Stone Preacher said. "If you touch any piece of earth or rock, I will always be able to hear you and know where you are, until our journeys together are complete. Perhaps, even after that." He folded his hands in front of himself and there was a grinding thump as he interlocked his fingers.

"I suppose that's useful for timely rescues. They don't have to be nick of timely, though, I'd hate to wind up missing an arm." I grinned as the Organ Grinder pushed open the door to a shop of some sort, and bellowed at those within.

The picnic basket chased after the Organ Grinder, and I had to run a little bit to catch up as he held the door open for me. I ducked under his arm and stared as I heard the Organ Grinder grunt in pain. The Stone Preacher was grabbing his wrist fiercely, and when I turned, his hand was a few inches from my behind. "You never stop, do you?"

"I can't help it," the Organ Grinder leered. "It's my nature."

The tailor shop was magnificent. There were bolts of cloth neatly organized in rows, and a perfectly cushioned podium upon which to stand. There was a large wooden counter with a smirking short man behind it. He was mostly bald, and he was covered in a fairly modern looking business suit. The suit had thin blue pinstripes and was largely grayish. His shirt was pink and his collar was white. He wore a tie in pink and white with some narrow blue lines that ran through it. He was the first person I had seen with cufflinks. "Ah, young lady," he murmured. "I understand that someday, you will be able to repay me for my services?"

"That depends on what you mean by repay. I am traveling with the notorious Organ Grinder." The basket rustled, rubbing against my leg, making wicker creaking noises.

"I am the Tailor of Tailors." The little man smiled. "I am the tailor that other tailors employ above all others, which is better than being the tailor that people laud above all others. They are not the same thing, you know."

"That sounds good. I need a dress, quickly, that is good enough to attend a queen in, but not enough to overshadow her." I said desperately. "I came in and got summoned. I was trying to stay under the radar."

"What's radar?" the tailor asked. "I've been here since what you would call 1928." He gave a little grin. "If you're special, like me or so many others here, you don't really age."

"Radar is a way that they, umm, use radio waves to find stuff." I managed. "It's not important."

"You are right." The Tailor of Tailors examined the Organ Grinder and the Stone Preacher, and sighed. "Will they be requiring clothes as well? I don't know that I can do anything for the priest."

"You'll have to ask them."

The Stone Preacher gave a rocky bow. "I fear my raiment is a part of me. Your craft in motion is pleasure enough."

The Organ Grinder smirked. "Ever the valiant defender." He chuckled. "I shall require a new vest, and pants, I believe."

"What do you take as payment?"

"I feed on the joy of my clients." The Tailor of Tailors chuckled. "It is an easy lifestyle. I also take foodstuffs. What is in the basket?"

A part of me inwardly shuddered. I should tell him what the food came from, but I couldn't bring myself to. I looked inside, and the wonderful smell of cinnamon and raisins rose up from the basket. "It's chicken, stewed prunes and raisins, and rice. The basket is magical, but you can't keep it." I pulled out the plate and pressed it across the counter. "It's all yours."

The Tailor looked over the food. "That smells lovely. First I will eat, and then I will fit you. I think I have some things in the back here that we can simply adjust." He settled onto his chair to eat. "Make yourselves at home."

***

We relaxed while the Tailor ate his meal. After dinner, the basket wiggled, giving him a beautiful chocolate cupcake drenched in custard for dessert. I felt a moment of greed. If feeding the tailor would get me to the Queen's castle, it was worth losing the cupcake.

The Tailor slipped into the back, and we heard the sound of him washing his hands. He walked out with a simple red vest with ruffles for the Organ Grinder, and a pair of grey pants. "I think these should do for you. But my lady here, I still can't get used to saying that, is of the nobility, and will require something a little special." He gave me a sly smile, as if to make me feel more important.

"That's nice of you to say." I said with a laugh. "Do you have something you can adjust?"

The Tailor of Tailors laughed. "I have a dress. But it is made of living silk, and it has to like you." He winked.

"How do you get a dress to like you?" My gaze turned to the Stone Preacher. "This isn't like the one who got eaten by the carnivorous bedding, is it?"

The Stone Preacher shook his head. "There was a fight. She got kicked into it. And she wasn't capable like you. The bed ate her."

The Organ Grinder gave a mock solemn glance at the Stone Preacher, and stepped to the fitting podium. "I'll risk it." I said. "What's the worst that could happen?"

"It could eat you like the picnic basket eats its victims," the Stone Preacher said solemnly. The Tailor of Tailors covered his mouth and gave a violated shudder.

"It shouldn't be so bad." The Tailor hurried into the back, bringing out something that was hanging on a thick wooden hanger.

It was black and burgundy with vast sweeping folds at the hips that made it look like a cross between a dress and a military uniform. The colors blended into each other in a rich, magnificent swirl. Shoulder straps adorned with strange lace seemed to writhe slightly in the bright light. I reached out to touch it. The dress felt almost as beautiful as it looked.

"It feels..." I managed.

"Like beauty itself, doesn't it?" The Tailor of Tailors gave a proud smile.

"It does have a radiance to it," the Stone Preacher declared. "But you should still be careful, I think." His rocky hand settled onto my shoulder.

"I don't see anything different," the Organ Grinder murmured. "How very odd."

"That's because there's nothing for you to see until the dress comes off," I taunted.

The tailor made his way to the podium, deftly fitting the Organ Grinder in but a few minutes, as I studied the dress, watching the light shimmer and be consumed by it. "Does it talk?" I asked, as the Organ Grinder remained where he was.

"I don't think so." The Tailor smiled, his eyes skimming over it. "I made it out of the flickering that silk makes when it rustles in the spring, and the moonbeams of the red moon when it rises, thick and angry, above the autumn sky."

"You can make fabric out of light?"

"I could just be telling a story," he said. "But if so, it is a really good one." He motioned to the Organ Grinder to step down from the cassock. "It's your turn, young lady."

"I'm not undressing in front of the Organ Grinder," I said firmly. "Do you have a screen?"

The Stone Preacher raised a rocky eyebrow. The Tailor of Tailors chuckled, motioning to a screen that was half-hidden behind a rack of clothes. "Over there."

I ran behind it, eager to try the dress on. I had privately hoped for something a little less ostentatious, but he was offering me something magical. I prayed that it wouldn't eat me, and slipped out of my clothes, changing into the burgundy and black fabric. I felt as if I were wearing the sweetest perfume. The dress seemed to whisper on the air as I stepped out from behind the screen. I didn't need to be fitted at all.

The Tailor stared for a moment. "Almost as if it was meant for you." He said with a wide smile. "I think we are done here." The Organ Grinder reached into a pocket and handed him a few coins. "Your things will be done tomorrow morning, sir. As for you, young lady, I believe the dress is yours. In fact, it was never mine, more or less, to begin with." He winked and moved to the door of the shop.

The Organ Grinder raised an eyebrow. "Impressive, but I still think you'd look better without it."

The Stone Preacher glided for the door, and the picnic basket glowered at me, growling at my leg. It didn't like the dress. That didn't seem to be as much of a surprise as I thought it would be. I slipped it onto its hanger, and when I brought it out, the Tailor of Tailors wrapped it in a bag of woven mesh. The others were outside, except the picnic basket, which growled and looked impatient as I made my way out. "Thank you." I said, and curtsied daintily. I needed the practice.

"You're welcome, my dear." The Tailor of Tailors chuckled. "At least you appreciate my skills." He gently opened the door to the shop, and I slipped out, radiant with my new dress, and walked down the street with the Organ Grinder and Stone Preacher on either side of me. The picnic basket skittered after us with a dry rustle of wicker. The Organ Grinder's monkey was strangely silent in the streets of the grey fortress.

"I don't think that went too badly." I grinned. "This dress is going to be wonderful."

"I'm sure it will be for you," the Stone Preacher rumbled, his voice appreciative of something. I wasn't sure what it was.

The Organ Grinder turned to look at me, and he was saying something. I couldn't hear him. My head grew light as I could feel the burning of rope at my neck. My feet weren't on the ground. A powerful tug dragged me higher, up and over the edge of the building. I grabbed at the rope and tried to free myself as I panicked. The dress fell from my hands and hit stone, trapped in its mesh prison. I kicked, pushing against the wall of the nearest building as cords drew me up. My fingers tried to release my throat while I lost breath. I stared into the iron mask of the Weeper in Shadows, peering over a building lip.

***

I struggled in the grip of the rope, and tried to swing back and forth, but her feet were planted firmly against the lip of the building. I wanted to beg.

The iron mask turned up into a curious, wicked smirk. She wrenched the rope, and I slammed into the building with a choking gasp. I could hear her laughing. There was a dim, grinding rumble of something coming up from below. She gave a sharp tug on the rope, pulling me higher as something covered in spiked armor peered over the edge.

The Stone Preacher rose up to meet him. His hand came out and grabbed the rope. The Weeper's perfectly sculpted iron eyes flicked sharply, her hands letting go. "Cheating already," she purred. "Good girl."

There was a thunderous crash of stone on metal, and a clanging noise as I was yanked upward. I slammed into the building wall, and was dragged roughly onto the rooftop. The Weeper drew her knife of ice and brought it down. I lifted the rope up, twisting to one side as the ice knife slashed it and a portion of rope froze.

To my left, the Stone Preacher was engaged with two armored things with vicious spikes jutting from their mail. They might have been human, but I couldn't quite tell. I didn't have time to think about it. The Weeper in Shadows was leaping for me, the knife leaving frozen mist in the air. I grabbed the frozen piece of the rope and tried to bat away her arm. She reversed the angle of the knife and thrust it right for my heart. I ignited my boots and rolled up, placing them in the way. There was a noise of ice on fire, and a small puff of steam.

The Organ Grinder's monkey crested the lip of the building, and let out a howling shriek of bloody violence. It landed on her arm and the sudden weight threw off her aim as it screeched and stabbed.

The Weeper in Shadows yanked the monkey's tail and brutally flung it away. It slammed into the edge of the building and lay still, stunned. "A dirty monkey to do your fighting for you?" She hissed. "Your stupid basket can't get to me up here, all wicker and lies of preparation."

I leaped for her and tried to hold her down, but she was wiry, strong, and taller. She brought the knife up butt first, and kicked me in the stomach. I spit up a little blood and punched her as hard as I could, flexing my fist before impact, as the roustabouts had taught me. She toppled back a little bit, and rolled into a fighting stance. She was beautiful, graceful, and faster than any acrobat I had ever seen. She spun the ice knife in her hand and came at me, and I backed away towards what was left of the rope, keeping the frozen piece in my hand. Flight was no advantage here.

There was another loud clang and a crackle. One of the Spiked Wrath Men hammered his fist into the Stone Preacher's robe, and there was a cracking sound.

"Did you really think I wouldn't change my choice of soldiers when I realized who your bodyguards were?" She leaped at me with the frozen blade. "They'll spike him to rubble."

I brought the piece of rope up in time to block it.

"Someone taught you a little bit, smooth like the wind and fast like wild horses."

The picnic basket came sailing over the edge of the roof, and I heard the Organ Grinder's voice. "I believe, my lady, that you are missing something!" His voice was thunderous, and I heard a door slam. He must have gone into the building and looked for stairs.

The basket growled and the Weeper in Shadows cursed. "You!" She shouted to one of the armored men in spikes. "Squash it!"

The picnic basket ran forward and jumped at the Weeper, but she lashed out with a sweeping kick and booted the basket towards the armored figure, who turned away from the Stone Preacher to let out a howl and clench a fist.

The picnic basket leaped at the Spiked Wrath Man, and bit hard into his leg. I heard some strange metal clanking sounds. When the smell of blueberry pie drifted through the air, I knew who was winning. The armored fist slammed down on the wicker front. The basket flexed and wobbled a little bit, impaled momentarily on the points as the man toppled, legless. Strange orange blood and a burgundy fluid that smelled like rusted metal leaked out from below.

I tackled the Weeper in Shadows as hard as I could. We went down in a tumble of arms and legs while she was off balance. She drove a knee into my stomach a second time, and I coughed hard as I punched her with everything I had left. It wasn't enough. She planted her legs in my gut and thrust me off. The Stone Preacher gripped his remaining opponent and slammed him through the roof. There was a loud crash, and the sound of splintering stone.

"You will lose a fifth girl to me." The Weeper in Shadows chuckled to herself. "It doesn't matter that you finally found one who can fight." She gave me a coy wink, and darted away across the rooftop, her advantage of surprise lost.

The Stone Preacher reached down, still holding the other spiked man, and grabbed his head, twisting his neck so hard that it came off with a wet pop. More burgundy fluid spurted skyward. The rest of the body crashed into the room below.

I didn't see the Organ Grinder. The Stone Preacher was wounded. I did what I felt like doing instead of what I should have done. I chased after the Weeper in Shadows, who leaped from building to building.

***

The Weeper was barely visible as a black dot in the distance, so I ran as fast as I could across the castle's night air, leaving a burning trail of smoke behind. There was a bitter feeling in my stomach. I wanted to hurt her. I wanted to ask her why. I wanted to kill her. But my bow was back in the room, and she had a knife.

I chased her anyway. The leaping dart of her graceful form sprung between rooftops. I left a roaring trail of smoke and flame, running as fast as I could. She darted between two buildings and I dived to follow, but she was quick, like liquid, and one with the shadows she was named after.

As I dived between the buildings a chain lashed out, catching me in the chest, and a hook jammed into the wall. The Chain Hook Guard spun its weapon at me. I watched helplessly as the sudden impact shook the rope from my hand. It was waiting where the Weeper in Shadows had been only seconds before. She had planned the whole thing.

I grabbed the chain and pulled, flipping up to stand on it, causing the guard to buckle under the new weight and plummet to the ground. From above me, I heard the Weeper's laughter. With grace and fury, she dived at me from above as the chain circled around my leg, the boots so hot that it began to melt.

I tried to run upward, but the guard was too heavy, and he crashed into the ground while I slammed into a nearby window. I crashed through wood and glass, while splinters rained about me. The air filled with the scent of molten metal and burning wood.

I was in a bedroom of some kind, cheap and tawdry. The broken shards of the window nestled against a dusty wardrobe. A dirty bed dominated the room, and a single, closed door led out. There was a bedpan and a wooden bowl sitting on the nightstand next to the bed.

The Weeper in Shadows blazed by the window while I struggled to stand up. I was dragged forward. I had to plant my feet against the wall as I heard the dull thump of her weight bump outside. She pulled hard/ I felt my leg strain. It was all I could do to pull back. I could see her leather-clad fingers at the windowsill when the melting chain gave way.

The Weeper in Shadows crawled over the edge. I drew the remaining chain into my hand. One end still hot, I spun the heavy weight around my head. She drew the ice knife with a smile on her iron-masked face.

"You are special, beautiful like the sunset." She murmured. "It's almost a shame I have to do this." Her legs tensed and she came at me, crossing the knife over her body in a smooth, swift series of motions before she leaped.

I swung the chain at her as she came in. She rolled to the left, landing on the bed as sparks flew along the ground and ignited the dry floor.

"Fire?" She scowled at me. "You really know how to hurt my feelings, don't you?" The blaze began to spread as I brought the hot, sparking chain down on the bed. The dry bedding roared to life as she flipped over the chain, planting her boot in my stomach.

She kicked me so hard I flew out through the window. The length of chain slid across the burning room. It was all I could do to run upward, out of the range of the Weeper's leap.

I landed, panting on the roof. The Weeper in Shadows vaulted out of the window, grabbed the lip of a window across the street, and swung herself up to the stony slats of the building across from me. "Who are you? Why are you doing this?" I called out to her from where I hid, desperate for an answer.

"You'll know when you see me." She called out. "Just before I freeze your heart and break it, pieces shimmering as you whimper and die." Her tone hardened. She began running up the slats, liquid in her movements. "You're different from the others! I have to try harder." She vaulted over the rooftops with a sinuous leap. I couldn't see her anymore.

The refreshing thought that my enemy was not unstoppable was replaced by a sense of exhaustion. I crumpled to the rooftop and exhaled hard, staring up at the bleak sky. Warm heat bubbled up from below as the room we had fought in burned. It was all I could do just to survive here.

***

I dragged myself to the inn, my clothes ruined and my face smeared with ash. My hair was burned in places. I limped through the door, looking gaunt and haggard. The concierge appeared before me. "Milady, are you all right?" He put his hand on my shoulder.

"Yes, if you consider suffering from smoke inhalation and having all my clothes ruined all right," I said. "Have you seen either of my associates?" It was hard to be formal when standing in ragged clothes and a still-magnificent set of boots.

"I believe they are waiting for you in the drawing room." The concierge bowed with wave of his hand. "I shall escort you." He turned and stiffly made his way toward a set of doors, which he lightly spread open. "In here." His voice never lost its blandness.

The Stone Preacher was on his knees, clutching his hands in prayer, and he rose with an odd relief in his grim eyes. "You should not have chased her," he said calmly. "I prayed to my cold stone god to protect you, and it seems that he has."

"It really is rude to run away from your bodyguards," the Organ Grinder said, turning from his position near the window. The monkey chittered angrily at me.

I put my hands on my hips and kicked the door shut. "What right do you have?" I snapped at the Stone Preacher. "Seven other people just like me have died under your care! Four of them to that woman! At least I lived through the first couple tries! And you, you great towering pervert in your leather coat! Where were you?" I fixed my gaze on the Organ Grinder with bitter anger.

"We were chasing you," the Organ Grinder said firmly. "We put the picnic basket in the room. I had to pull it off the poor armored fellow before he was completely consumed. Then he writhed around for a few minutes and died."

"You just let him die?" I stared. "What was the point of pulling the basket off then?"

"It's difficult for him to sneak around and seduce women when he smells of puff pastries and savory meats every few minutes," The Stone Preacher said. "Please don't get too far away from us again, Symantha who has no name. I would really love to complete this task, for once."

"Do you get something out of it if you succeed?" I asked.

"I don't really get very much. But, the satisfaction of success in the face of such difficult odds means that I have served my god well."

"That's it?" I asked. "Are you really serious about that? I think there's also a little bit of guilt. All those girls dying to the Weeper in Shadows and all the other failures? It doesn't bother you at all? Maybe the Organ Grinder's right and you do want to screw me!" I didn't even realize how loud I was.

The Stone Preacher solemnly shook his head. "You hold no attraction for me, child. We are all here for different reasons, and yet there is no Hell except to have no stone beneath you." He smiled. "You do not understand this world yet. Few of us completely do."

The Organ Grinder yawned. "He means that we are here to guide you because it is our duty as inhabitants of this place, and as you have seen, many of us are strange, powerful, or have unusual pets." He smiled and took the monkey out of his coat. It cooed on his hand and swished its knife-tail about looking for something to stab.

"Well, I have an unusual pet, at least." I sighed. "I should go and see it. It's probably putting out a spread right now." I headed for the door. "And I beg forgiveness for being angry."

The Stone Preacher nodded once and followed, while the Organ Grinder added, "True forgiveness comes from spreading your legs for me, and allowing me to sample the delicious pleasures of your flesh."

"It's good to see you haven't changed," I muttered. We went upstairs to the room.

When we arrived, the picnic basket had set out a five course meal on the bed, and leaped to greet me, running on its strange little legs. The long tongue slipped out of the lid and licked at me for a moment, and then it rubbed its wicker frame against me. I looked at the meal: Whole roast turkey, gravy, cranberry sauce, sweet potatoes, green beans, and a pumpkin pie. "What the hell?" I muttered. "I need to sleep. Did you guys manage to keep my dress?"

"The new one?" The Organ Grinder smirked. "I dream of seeing you taking it off in front of me, so I kept it. But I believe we should eat, before your basket eats us."

I laughed and carved the turkey for the Organ Grinder. The monkey pounced on his plate and started to eat. Everything was delicious. In the morning, I was going to meet my first queen. I felt better than almost anyone who had been in a fight.

"Sleep well," the Stone Preacher said. I crawled into the bed after cleaning up the dishes and placing them neatly on the salver that had been left by the door. "And you, dear Organ Grinder, will be sleeping on the floor."

The Organ Grinder sighed. "And just when I thought you were going to miss that part." He took one of the cushions from the couch, falling asleep in his greatcoat.

I turned to the Stone Preacher, who vigilantly stood at the window in case the Weeper in Shadows returned. I decided not to challenge him.

Just before I went to sleep, I drew out a knife from my clothing and stabbed the bed fiercely in the center two or three times, just to make sure the bedding wasn't carnivorous. I thought I heard the rocky lips of the Stone Preacher crack the slightest of smiles.

***

I awoke to the jingling sound of music in the streets below, and the thwacking of a tambourine. The smell of cinnamon and butter wafted through the air. The basket was open on the bed next to me. I reached in and pulled out a plate, covered with cinnamon raisin toast and butter. There was a clatter and a pop from inside the basket. I could smell eggs. I reached in and pulled out the plate. Without even thinking about it, I leaned to one side to devour them with the fork and knife resting on the edge.

The Organ Grinder was singing in the bath. The Stone Preacher stood next to the bathroom door, blocking it. I couldn't tell what the Organ Grinder was singing. "You're awake." The Preacher's voice was solemn.

"Is that his singing voice?" I said between bites, eating as quickly as I could. "Leave it to the Organ Grinder to keep the first bath away from a lady." His voice sounded horribly off-key. The Picnic basket made a growling rustle, as if it was unhappy with the noises.

"Yes, it is, and I'm certain they'll draw another bath for you," the Stone Preacher rumbled.

"If we live," I said, my voice dripping venom. "His singing might kill us."

"Just because someone has musical talent – with an accordion, of all instruments – does not mean that they can sing." The Stone Preacher almost intoned the words, and rapped sharply on the door while I ate. "Organ Grinder, clean yourself off! The Lady requires the bath, and it will need to be redrawn!"

There was some rustling and rumbling, and an unearthly screech from inside. "He's bathing the monkey?" I asked.

"We're visiting a Queen. What do you think his motivation is?"

"He had better not. Keep an eye on him. Throttle him if he plays a single note of accordion music."

The Organ Grinder slipped out of the bathroom wearing his new vest. I heard a gurgle as water drained. "We had best get some servants." He chuckled as the monkey, reeking of too much perfume, peeked out from under the vest. "I fear the lady is no longer asleep."

"Who could sleep with you bathing a knife-wielding monkey?" I shook my head. "Breakfast was delicious. I hope the basket makes you stale bread and dirty water."

"I hope it does too." The Organ Grinder added. "You seem to have forgotten the pleasure I take in the eating of unpleasant foods."

In response to his statement, the picnic basket growled, and gave another low rustle.

"I did," I said. "I admit it. You're vile and disgusting, and nothing will ever change you."

The Stone Preacher opened the door. I heard footsteps, but saw no one. There was the sound of a bath filling, and steam poured out of the room.

The hiss of steam covered the Organ Grinder for a moment, who was about to settle into a chair. "That's why you keep me around." His voice was low and sinister. "Because you hope I'll change."

"I hope you change into a carnivorous toad," I snapped. "Then the picnic basket will eat you and the monkey, both."

"Truly, a noble wit brought on by the fires of survival." The Organ Grinder sighed. "I should find a town crier and see if he has any news-sheets."

"They have printing presses?" I asked. 'With real newspapers?"

"Primitive ones." The Organ Grinder said coldly. "The Stone Preacher doesn't like them. He doesn't like the education of the masses. He says they lose religion over it."

"How do you know that?" I asked.

"He is a legend in some of the lands I've been through." The Organ Grinder smiled, and the monkey rustled around under his new vest.

"I will translate," the Stone Preacher said icily. "He means that he slept with some of the ones I introduced here who survived." His voice sounded like sharp nails on a chalkboard.

"Oh, that's reassuring," I said as I made my way into the bathroom along with my dress. "It gives me such faith that the notion of an underclass is deserved." I slammed the door behind me.

Even though I slipped into the bath and relaxed, I thought I heard the Organ Grinder swear that my flesh would be his in the end no matter what.

***

I came out of the bath and toweled myself off quickly, only to feel a rustle at my neck. Like a serpent, the dress slithered out of the mesh bag and over my body, settling into the perfect fit for my frame. I slipped out the door. "I assume we're keeping our weapons here?" I asked the Stone Preacher.

"That would be safe. You look magnificent. I am unsurprised."

The dress slithered and adjusted itself a little on my body. It was like being caressed by the world.

"But I would recommend you take your bow," the Preacher said with caution, "in case you are asked to perform a contest of skill. Every lady should know how to do something, even if it is a military talent like archery."

"Well, apparently being presentable is everything here, so we should appear with all our allies." I smiled and scooped up the picnic basket, petting it. "Thank you for breakfast." It gave a little wicker rustle, rubbing contentedly against my wrist as I petted it. "Let's put our things in the cart."

"You want to pack up?" the Organ Grinder asked. "Surely you realize this is the most secure castle in the entire world. The Queen of Castles is very thorough."

"That just means it's hard to get in." I winked to the Organ Grinder. "I am much more concerned about getting out, and I have recently been imprisoned by a bunch of lunatics who can come through any door. They must have hated her."

"As you are responsible for their demise, it might be a good idea to present it," the Stone Preacher rumbled. "There is nothing like a little camaraderie between people who hate the same things." He cracked his knuckles. It sounded like a little earthquake.

"I'll remember that." I gathered my luggage and headed for the door. The Organ Grinder idly tossed his old vest into the waste bin.

***

When we arrived outside the inn, the Knight of Lies was sitting on his horse next to our cart. I curtsied as politely as I could while the Organ Grinder and the Stone Preacher loaded our baggage.

"I have come to tell you everything is safe in your travels." He smiled and bowed resolutely, his square, handsome jaw grinning under his armored helm. "It will be my greatest pleasure to see the end of your life. Stay in the castle of the Queen forever once you have seen her."

"My thanks, sir knight." I gave him a coy wink. "Your contrary advice, as always, is appreciated. You should have a lady to defend from time to time." I gave him a knowing wink. I slipped my finger into the quiver on my back, and handed him a clockwork arrow. I didn't know I had any left.

"I do, indeed, have a lady." The Knight smiled. "Such military virtues are the height of social standing." He bowed on his horse, the shiny armor creaking a little bit, and he kicked the horse hard, making it rise up on its hindquarters. "I must stay, for the day is long, and my time can be wasted!" He hurried the horse onward, the arrow affixed nimbly to the pommel of his saddle as he rode off.

"Why would you want a secret affair with a man who lies all the time?" The Organ Grinder laughed. "You could have the Organ Grinder or your rocky friend here."

"Why would you think that?" I said. "It's obvious he likes me enough to fight for me, and if I do have to have a secret affair with someone, it might as well be with a known liar, for then I can have him be honest, and no one will know whether it's a lie or not." I winked and closed the doors to the cart. "We should park it a few streets away from the castle in case we need to get out of there."

The Stone Preacher raised a rocky eyebrow, and the Organ Grinder turned to face me. The Stone Preacher put a granite finger to the Organ Grinder's lips. It meant that he had something important to say, so I listened. "You have a fine mind." A slight smile formed on his rocky lips. "Whoever your true love is, you may well find them and have a destiny worth achieving, regardless of your pedigree. Unfortunately, that is highly insulting, and we can't do it."

"Oh, would you please stop flattering her?" The Organ Grinder sighed. "She is as susceptible to the accordion as all the rest of them."

"Go ahead," I snapped. "Play it." I drew another clockwork arrow from the quiver, instinctual and smooth. The bow appeared in my hand as if I had strung it. "In the second that you play your accordion, I will remove your desire for it."

The Organ Grinder stared. The Stone Preacher's jaw dropped open. The picnic basket growled. It had taken me that long to realize what I did. "Did I just... That's cool."

"It's impressive." The Organ Grinder smiled. "You may yet be one of us, if you can master the crafting of those arrows and figure out what magics they associate with."

"I'm not sure I want to be one of you." I climbed up onto the cart.

The Stone Preacher moved over and gently took my hand, while the Organ Grinder untied the horses. His lips moved, calling words from deep in his stony throat. "You don't have a choice anymore."

As he got into the driver's seat of the cart, the Organ Grinder took the reins and chuckled at the Stone Preacher's comment. He found it much funnier than I did.

The picnic basket settled into my lap against the smooth fabric of the dress. The cloth wiggled, adjusting its silk in the perfect manner. As the cart pulled away, the castle seemed larger and more threatening. The Organ Grinder's fierce look somehow made me think I could take on the world.

***

The castle towered before us as the horses pulled the cart through the streets. We were in line behind two carriages that were far more opulent. I thought I could feel the eyes of people in the carts in front of us staring as we drove forward.

The castle was a massive fortress with thick battlements and shored up walls. Mortar between the stones was covered in rich, red moss. Spires rose high into the sky, shining with reflective burgundy gloss in the morning sun. It was larger than I feared it would be. There were three to five times as many heavily armored men and women patrolling as there had been at other castles. A huge drawbridge, covered with spikes and sharp metal protrusions, hung closed over a yawning moat. From the moat, I heard wet splashing, as if something swam in it.

When we arrived, the two carts in front of us drew to a stop. The drawbridge creaked open slowly and winched down. As it reached the halfway mark, there was a clacking, as if a hundred thousand metal spiders had all started walking. The guards on the walls pointed crossbows at us.

"I guess she's not fond of visitors." I said calmly.

"You should be inside the cart, my dear." the Organ Grinder said.

"I would rather eat hard leather straps and dirt gravy for a week than spend another second in your dirty rutbox." I scowled. "Now stop trying to get me into bed."

The drawbridge descended with a massive thud. Carriages shook as the weight hit the ground. The monkey hooted under the Organ Grinder's greatcoat. The picnic basket huddled up against me. The lid opened to offer a muffin. I hoped it wasn't running out of food.

The Stone Preacher walked along with us, focused on the men with crossbows. His rocky eyes stared up as the cart lurched forward.

I took the muffin before it got cold, and nibbled as we creaked across the drawbridge, to the contemptuous looks of men above. The muffin was rich, delicious and buttery, with a hint of cranberries and a fruit I couldn't identify. It never occurred to me until that moment that the world I was in might have different fruits and vegetables than the "real" word.

I thought about that all the way into the courtyard. The Organ Grinder drew our rickety cart to a stop amid clacking of wooden wheels. The two other nobles and their ladies were getting out of their carriages, resplendent in rich cloaks and fine clothing. The dress jerked a little bit and yanked at my chest, as if hiking up my bosom. I felt the fabric tighten.

"It's jealous of other dresses," I said with a smirk. "It figures."

There was a seneschal waiting at the back of the cart, patiently standing near the wooden door with chipped paint. His clothes were suitably formal. He wore a rich pair of black boots that had been polished to a mirror shine, and a short half-cape that seemed to float a little bit across his shoulders. The man appeared bald under his tricornered hat. His opulent silk garments shone in the morning sun. I hopped off the cart and walked over to him. The Stone Preacher and the Organ Grinder took up positions on either side of me. The picnic basket followed in my wake, the lid closed.

"May I have your name, milady?" the seneschal asked.

"I am as yet unnamed." I smiled. "However, may I know yours?"

"I am the Squire of Cloaks," he said congenially. "I shall endeavor to make you welcome here, and as you are unnamed, to follow you through these lands until you leave them." He bowed deeply. "It is my duty to my fellow citizens of the Otherworld."

"My thanks, but I fear there is no room in the Organ Grinder's cart for you," I said.

"Oh, I don't know." The Organ Grinder chuckled. "I might be able to do something with him."

"You have not leave to speak," I said to the Organ Grinder, who silenced himself at once.

"If you could take us to the Queen of Castles?" It was almost a rhetorical question as the other nobles were led off through a large gateway on the other side of the courtyard. It had a portcullis thick with bars and sharp points. Just looking at the gate made me afraid.

"I shall." The Squire of Cloaks gestured with his hand, and led us along the side wall, opening a door that seemed nearly invisible, built into the rock. "The others are here for the blood toll. Nobles are considered different once they're named." He smiled. "We'll go through here."

The heavy hidden door slid open. Once we were inside, there was a series of dark corridors that twisted and turned through the depths of the castle. "You aren't taking us the back way to kill us, are you?" I asked. "Because if you are, the Stone Preacher will crush you, the Organ Grinder will grind you, and the picnic basket will eat you." I gave him a pleasant smile as we began ascending a dull gray stair.

The Squire of Cloaks gave no response.

At the top of the stair was a thick iron lever, next to a solid stone wall. "And now, you will see the truth of this palace." He smiled, yanking the lever down.

As the light shone from the room beyond, what little I could see was both magnificent and impressive in decadence.

***

We came in from the long side of a rectangular room. Gold and silver tiles shone on the floor and reflected off a shimmering ceiling. Our footsteps clattered along as the Squire of Cloaks guided us forward through marble pillars. At one end of the room was a set of double doors. Somewhere in the shimmering walls it seemed as though there were exits.

To our right, the Queen of Castles beckoned with a silver-gloved hand. She was slender and thin, with pinched tight lips. Wide blue eyes gazed out at the world as if it would throttle her. She wore a magnificent blue dress whose opulent brocade made it seem as though her pale skin shone with sunlight. The crown of jeweled platinum atop her head, seemed inconsequential in comparison. She held a thick scepter in her other hand, peering at me with the eyes of an old woman sizing up a younger rival.

She sat in a high-backed golden chair, the arms of stone curved slightly inward. Metal plates, ornate and thick, hung from the arms of the chair. Wide legs sat on a circle of stone that almost made me believe that it could swivel. Strange heraldic devices and runes covered the entire chair. It reflected in the light of the shimmering ceiling, making the Queen of Castles seem to glow.

I walked forward, the Squire of Cloaks nimbly stepping to one side as the Organ Grinder and the Stone Preacher flanked me. She offered me a soft smile. I curtsied daintily as the picnic basket rustled up under my skirts. I thought that I could hear the Organ Grinder's monkey emitting a quiet growl from under his coat. When I curtsied, the Organ Grinder and the Stone Preacher knelt. I knew the Organ Grinder was trying to look up the Queen's skirt.

"You may rise," she said gently. "I understand that you require those who may be willing to vouch for you in name, instead of a letter?" She spoke in a low, soft whisper, and leaned forward on her throne. "I understand I no longer have that dreadful Duke of Bells to entertain?" She gave me a cheerful smile.

There was a contented coo from under my skirt.

"Whatever is that?" She stared down at me from her throne.

"It's my picnic basket. It's more of a pet, though." I gave her a sheepish look. "It eats people and makes food out of them. It's really not too complicated."

"I trust that it will not eat me?" she said firmly.

The picnic basket peeked out from under the hem of my dress, and quickly slunk back beneath its many folds. The dress moved a little bit, as if conspiring to cover it up. "Oh wait. The toads. Of course." She gave me a subtle grin. "Your bodyguards are wise, though I must admit, the reputation of the Organ Grinder precedes him." She gave him a coy wink.

The Organ Grinder and the Stone Preacher remained kneeling.

"As long as you don't proceed with him, I really don't care, great Queen." I winked.

"Oh, I assure you, as long as I am within this castle, I am quite safe, even from his accordion." She chuckled as she looked to it, hanging from around the Organ Grinder's neck.

"How?" I asked. "I thought no one the Organ Grinder desired could resist it?"

"My castle protects me." She laughed gently, and her wide eyes relaxed. "It is who I am."

"Oh," I said with a half-grin. "You truly have a lovely throne room. It is to be admired. What are the plates on the chair arms for?"

"I have many throne rooms. It is too easy to be caught and killed if one meets people in only a single location." She smiled as if she were clever. "The plates protect me from missiles. I twist the arm of the chair, and the plates fly forward to protect me. I am dumped below this throne room, arriving elsewhere. I don't like to leave my castle. It is my home."

"It really is very impressive." I added. "It must have taken hundreds of years to build."

Her lips pursed. I could see slight wrinkles at the edges of her eyes, hidden by a touch of well-applied makeup. "The strength of a castle is the strength of all of those who bled and died to build it. Thus we take a toll of blood and pour it into the foundations, to make the castle strong. The blood of the people is strong in defending them, and the castle defends us in return. Do you not wish to be safe?" The Queen of Castles' lip quivered a little bit. "I only wish to be safe, and well-defended."

"What happened to the King of Castles?" I asked quietly. "You must have loved him very much."

"He was a special man. But he went outside one day, and never returned." She hung her head, as if she were responsible. "I am not sure he loved me, though." She gave a sheepish little smile, and clutched her scepter tightly, as if it were her anchor.

"I would beg of you your support," I said. "I'm sure that you can't be persuaded to leave, but if you could write some sort of letter, I would appreciate it and, promise to look for your King of Castles whenever I can."

"I like you," she said, her voice warm. "Though your bodyguards are like night and day, and without any sort of order. I shall endeavor to do better than that. I shall send you to the Enchanter of Devils, a printer of some renown, and he shall have your visage proclaimed as noble throughout my city. He will heed my missive."

"Thank you, great Queen." It was all I could do to not stammer. She was everything a queen should be.

"The Squire of Cloaks will accompany you on your journey to see the Enchanter. But be wary, for although he is a man of great honor, he is also a man of many tricks, and on the few times he has come to see me, I feared that there was more to his motives." Her visage glared coolly at the Squire of Cloaks. "Take you this note." Her hand reached for a compartment in the throne for a pen. She reached into a sleeve, took out a scroll and dashed off some words. She rolled it up again, imprinting it with a burning signet ring on one of her fingers. It was so bland compared to the rest of her majesty that I barely even noticed it.

"You should stay for dinner this evening," she said with a pleasant grin. "It would honor me if you would participate. I'm sure you would appreciate eating food that is not from your basket." The picnic basket let out a little sigh, as if it were relieved. It must have been tired.

"I would love to. Thank you." I murmured, and I looked to the Organ Grinder and the Stone Preacher. They had not spoken the whole time. "May my bodyguards have leave to speak?"

"Of course, my dear." Her eyes darted to the Squire of Cloaks with a bitter look on her face.

The Organ Grinder purred. "I would love to spend the night in your lovely castle." I gritted my teeth. He couldn't stop being dirty. It was his nature.

The Stone Preacher rose a little bit, the rocky movements grinding up as he stood. "Good Queen, I would appreciate it if there was a place where I could pray to my cold stone god." His lip quivered a little bit, and there was a sound like gravel scattering.

"I shall escort you to rooms myself," she said. "I would have the Squire do it, but he is now assigned to your party." She stood, regal and brilliant, and marched us toward the door. I turned and followed. The Squire of Cloaks fell into step with the rest of us. I noticed him pull a flask of wine when the Queen no longer looked at him. He drank swiftly as we made our way towards the exit, shoving it back into his pocket as if nothing had happened.

As we stepped out into the wide, three-way hallway with the Queen of Castles, there was an ominous metallic clatter; the sound of metal on stone. Chain Hook Guards were on every side of us. Behind them, pressed into a corner of the ceiling, her icy knife drawn, the Weeper in Shadows giggled behind her expressive iron mask.

***

"What is the meaning of this?" The Queen of Castles' voice turned shrill in the corridor. It carried around the armored soldiers while the Weeper in Shadows remained poised above with her knife.

The Weeper in Shadows smiled, her iron mask creaking. The Stone Preacher glowered upwards at her. "I suppose I must do you the honor of requesting the girl, even though, good Queen of Castles, you are harboring a fugitive." Somehow, the iron-masked assassin managed to bow gracefully, even while she was squeezed into the upper corner of the ceiling.

"A fugitive from what?" the Queen of Castles snapped. "She is a guest in this place!"

"The King of Feathers wishes her dead. I execute his will." She idly folded her fingers and swished the ice knife through the air. "He wishes no new appointments, though she is soft like a whisper and as beautiful as the sun." Her iron lip quivered as she spoke. Her metal mask raised its eyebrows.

The Stone Preacher glowered up at her. "It is not his to decide. The laws of this land are as stony as my god, and so I will grant her that chance. Besides, I actually like this one."

The Organ Grinder chuckled, and the monkey screeched, while the picnic basket rustled under my robes. There must have been twenty or more Chain Hook Guards.

The Weeper in Shadows launched herself towards me, knife outstretched as her guardsmen lashed out with their chains.

The Stone Preacher stepped into their midst as the Squire of Cloaks pushed me to the side. The Weeper in Shadows drove her knee into his stomach as I rolled sideways and called my bow to me, reaching into the quiver for the arrow I knew was there.

Chains whipped towards the Stone Preacher. He raised his arm so that several of them wrapped around it, then flexed his inward and pulled sharply towards him, yanking so hard that two guards flew forward.

"Run!" The Organ Grinder raced to one side through whirling chains, grabbing the Queen of Castles by the wrist. The monkey exited from under his greatcoat while the picnic basket and I gave chase. I fired the arrow behind me as the Squire of Cloaks rose to his feet. It slammed into the Weeper's shoulder, and she let out a shriek.

The Stone Preacher spun the two guards in a circle, smashing them against their fellows. The Weeper in Shadows rolled out of the way, her shoulder leaking blood as the armored monsters smashed together in the vast hallway. The Preacher released the chains to dire moans and shudders, and came after us with the fury of an avalanche.

"The walls!" I shouted to the Queen of Castles. "Get us upstairs where your guards can protect us!" I followed after the Organ Grinder as the picnic basket chased my legs.

With a thunderous, quaking rumble, the stones of the castle cracked under the Stone Preacher's footsteps. He gained on us with every second.

The Squire of Cloaks struggled away from the Weeper in Shadows. He gracefully swirled his cape around the slashing hand holding her frozen knife. Icy shards glistened as he pulled her arm out of position. Her teeth gritted as blood leaked from her shoulder.

The Weeper in Shadows winced as the trapped knife made her vulnerable. "Get up! Kill them! Don't spare anyone!" She vaulted upward, splitting her legs wide, and turned to the side, kicking forward at the Squire as we turned a corner. We heard a dry thud followed by racing footsteps.

The Stone Preacher passed us both, and stood fiercely at the corner, waiting for me to pass.

"There's more than one stairwell! Find them! Cut them off!" Her voice was a furious shriek, tinged with signs frustration. "You will bleed your love in red, red sobs." Her voice dropped to a low murmur.

Just beyond the corner was an arch with a rising stairwell. The Organ Grinder reached it first, dragging the Queen of Castles. Her panting breath in ornate brocade left little puffs of smoke in the cold air of the tower. I raced around the corner with the picnic basket, which growled like an angry animal as it chased the Organ Grinder up the stairs. I barely saw the Stone Preacher grab the Squire's wrist and hurl him upward through the opening.

Breaking the fall by spreading his cloak out, the Squire spun around as the Stone Preacher glided through the arch. The clattering army of Chain Hook Guards lumbered down the hall. As I climbed, the Squire gracefully fell in step behind me. In the distance, I thought I heard a snap of metal.

The Stone Preacher raised his hands and brought them together. The archway slammed shut, stone merging with stone. He raced up the stairs after us, his glide swiftly carrying him past everyone, even the Queen of Castles.

We burst out onto the high battlements. The clanking of the Weeper's soldiers echoed through the other stairwells. The Queen's guards moved to block them, forming shield walls and carrying spears.

"They won't last long," I muttered. "I guess we're going to have to jump."

"That's the spirit!" The Stone Preacher thundered. "Truly, you have a great destiny that awaits you!"

"Jump?" The Queen of Castles stared at me as if I had cursed her home. "No! I won't! I'm not leaving! I'll die here!" She shrieked and struggled in the Organ Grinder's grip, but he held her fast.

"You'll die if you don't leave." I looked down over the edge of the battlements. It was a much longer fall than I expected. I had been up to the top of the big top more than a few times, but that was easily a fourth of the distance.

"Hang on. Let's get out of here." I grabbed the Organ Grinder by his other hand, and scooped up the picnic basket and handed it to the Queen. It cooed as if it belonged there, and settled onto her arm.

I let the boots roar to life and jumped furiously outward, running as fast as I could, leaving the Squire of Cloaks and the Stone Preacher behind. It was too much weight. The monkey shrieked, and the Queen of Castles screamed. I could barely hear them over my own screams and the Organ Grinder's mad laughter. In a mix of arms, legs, and opulent clothes, we plummeted towards the ground, wreathed in fire.

***

We crashed to earth in a tangle of arms and legs and rolled around in a messy, dirty heap as guards began to move toward us. The Organ Grinder moaned, letting go of the Queen's wrist, and the monkey whined. There was a dull rustling sound from the picnic basket as the Queen of Castles stood. It wiggled as if to dust itself off. Then the basket nudged me, trying to clear the cobwebs.

"It's not the best landing I've ever had," the Organ Grinder chuckled. "But I'm alive and the lovely Queen of Castles is still within arm's reach." He gave her a lewd leer.

"Touch me again and I will have you executed," she said grimly, wiping the dirt from her brocade gown as best she could.

From the wall, there was a heavy rumbling. I turned to look. The Stone Preacher simply ran straight down the bricks. He raced towards us in a relentless glide, and came to a smooth, graceful stop. "Has anyone seen the Squire of Cloaks?" His voice was a little crackle of rock.

Looking up, I saw the Weeper in Shadows leaning over the edge of the castle. I imagined the trickle of red rolling down her shoulder, but I could feel her smile of admiration from the battlements above.

As we watched, the Squire of Cloaks circled around, already descending, mantle outstretched. He glided to the cobbles in front of us.

The Organ Grinder was already running for his cart, yanking the reins and leaping into the driver's seat. "Get on!" he thundered. "Lower the drawbridge, you yellow-livered half-dogs! Your Queen's life is in danger! I'll spit you all on spears and bugger your wives if you do not! I am the Organ Grinder! Do you hear me?"

From within the castle's gate house, there was a creaking sound. Winches turned as the massive drawbridge slowly lowered. I leaped into the seat next to the Organ Grinder, and the Stone Preacher moved over to the back of the Organ Grinder's cart, opening the doors. "In here," he rumbled to the Queen. "You and the Squire should be safe inside." The picnic basket bounded up beside me, an open lid dispensing a wrapped cheese that rolled across the cobbles.

The Queen of Castles glanced around, a look of nervousness on her face. The Squire of Cloaks dragged her into the cart. The Squire slammed the door shut as the Organ Grinder drove the emaciated horses towards the sinking drawbridge. The thunder of hoofbeats mingled with shouts and cries of pain, and sounds of fighting from the battlements.

I drew out my bow and covered the guards at the barbican as the drawbridge continued to lower, and the Organ Grinder sped the horses on. "We're gonna die!" I shouted. "Slow down!"

"Slow down so your friend up there can kill us?" The Organ Grinder shook his head. "On, gaunt horses, ha!" His voice was mirthful, yet full of fury as the Stone Preacher ran alongside, cloak crackling with the movement of rockslides. "The Queen of Castles shall share my bed, and the world will hear her moans!"

"Just drive the cart!" I shouted and wished the bow away, hanging on to the seat and the picnic basket with all my strength.

The Organ Grinder spurred the horses forward as the weight of the Stone Preacher alongside the cart pushed the drawbridge down. The picnic basket pressed against me with a terrified rustle. We left the edge of the drawbridge and vaulted over the moat. A greenish tentacle, covered with suckers, flicked up out of the water as horses and cart slammed onto the street. We bounced about as the Organ Grinder let out a wild laugh.

The Stone Preacher kept pace with us, leaping boldly across the divide. He crashed to the ground on the other side of the moat. He landed on his knees, planting his fist. The street cracked out around him, hurling bricks and mortar into the sky. Then he took off after the careening wagon, leaving a wake of cracking footprints behind.

We skittered down the street, knocking over a few merchant stalls as the wagon evened out. We could hear pained screams coming from inside the cart.

"We have to get out of the city," I said to the Organ Grinder. "Just keep heading towards the mountains!"

The Organ Grinder drove the horses forward amidst the shops and stalls, and turned the cart to the left at a large intersection. "Out is out!" he thundered, and looked to the Stone Preacher. "We need a plan!"

"The Queen can get us out if she chooses it."

The Organ Grinder scowled at me, as if he were reluctant to let the Queen out of the back of the cart, and lashed the horses forward. "You ruin all my fun," he said playfully. "No matter. I love my skin more than I love bedding royals."

***

The Organ Grinder drove for the gates of the city, the cart bouncing uncomfortably. I looked over our shoulders for pursuit. There were only screaming people shaking their fists, those who had leaped aside, and some crushed fruits and vegetables. The unpleasant smell of something I didn't recognize wafted towards my nostrils as we thundered towards the gate.

"We need to let her out!" I said firmly. "She can pass it off as a kidnapping or something!"

The cart ground to a stop in front of the gate, as the Organ Grinder sighed. "Will you take all my pleasure from me?" he said bitterly as the Stone Preacher rumbled to a stop next to us. "Good Preacher, if you would open the back?"

The picnic basket flipped open and coughed up a large steamed turnip, which rolled about on the ground until the Preacher accidentally crushed it with a rocky foot.

"Good Queen, it is time for you to leave."

"No," she said in haughty tones. "I'm not coming out." This spurred a dry chuckle from the Organ Grinder as he began guiding the horses towards the exit.

From inside the cart, I could hear the soothing words of the Squire of Cloaks, and then the Queen shrieked. "Unhand me!" I heard a sound of flesh being slapped.

"Stay on the line." I said to the Organ Grinder, as the Stone Preacher reached into the cart. The Squire of Cloaks screamed in pain.

I moved as quickly as I could, but I wasn't fast enough. By the time I got there, the Stone Preacher dragged the Squire of Cloaks out and tossed him into the mud, while the Queen cowered in the back of the cart. "Miserable wretch!" he thundered. "To lay your hand upon a Queen so when her life is not in immediate danger!" He raised his fist as the Squire struggled on the dirty cobbles.

"Don't!" I said to the Stone Preacher, stepping in front of him. "You promised. What would the Nun Who Leaves No Stains say? She'd have to come all the way here and clean up the mess."

The Squire of Cloaks grabbed the hem of my cloak and kissed it desperately as the Queen watched him, her eyes narrowed with disdain. "Thank you, my lady, for saving me!" He kneeled before me.

The Stone Preacher's lips cracked in a rocky scowl. "He is a despicable miscreant who knows not his place. He has done something wicked, I am sure of it!"

"*No* means *no*." I said and slipped into the wagon. "My queen, if you would signal us through?" I knelt and curtsied.

"I can do it from in here." She said fiercely. "Send someone."

"You really do not want to spend the night in here, in the Organ Grinder's dirty cart, my queen." I said coolly. "You know what he'll do to you."

"I don't care!" She cowered on the bed. "Don't leave me outside!"

"You are the Queen of Castles!" I said fiercely, and stepped in and grabbed her wrist, but she grabbed the headboard. "Squire, assist me! She assigned you to my needs! Do it or she'll have you flogged!"

The Queen of Castles screeched in horror as the Squire came in and helped me pull her out, her eyes glazed with terror as the Stone Preacher slammed the doors to the wagon shut. "How could you?" she shrieked. "There is no roof! The sky is open! A torrent of blood could consume me! Birds could carry me off! I could be kidnapped by peasants!"

"Oh, Queen," I dropped to my knees at once. "I beg of you to let us pass from your city without complaint, and to seek shelter then!"

"Let them through!" She shrieked in terror.

The double gate began winding up for us, and the Organ Grinder pulled the cart out of the line. I raced for the back and grabbed on, yanking the Squire of Cloaks up against the wood while the Stone Preacher moved alongside it.

"Let them through! I command it! Get me indoors! Get me indoors! Please!"

The cart raced under the barbican. Creaking wheels shuddered and picked up speed. With the hollow sound of tombs being sealed, the portcullis thudded shut nearby her. "Why? She seemed so very nice."

"You need her permission to leave," the Squire of Cloaks said. "Unless you're a merchant or a farmer, or paying the blood tax, no one except you has been allowed to leave the city in four hundred years. This is the only revenge they can take. There will be no summer festival this year, to be sure. It is just jealousy – nothing to worry yourself about."

The Queen of Castles started to weep, trapped in the dirty streets of her own city while the cart creaked under the portcullis, the wooden wheels straining quickly.

"No, please!" The Queen of Castles sobbed. "I'm not safe! I'm not safe out here!"

I stared at her through the bars of the portcullis as we began driving out. She cried like a small child. "Please, don't leave me outside. Don't, please don't." Tears streaked her face. She drew up her hands, raising her dirty gown to wipe her eyes.

Just before we drove out of sight, I heard the Queen begging, and the hard hammering of desperate fists against a door. "Please, I beg of you! Let me in! I am your Queen! I am your Queen, damn you!"

The portcullis slammed down. The Organ Grinder forced the horses forward, into the murderous world beyond.

Chapter Eleven

The Enchanter of Devils Prints a Message

We traveled along the road for hours, well into the dark, until we pulled over to the side of the road to make camp. The Squire of Cloaks was sullen and silent. He wrapped himself in his dirtied cape as he huddled by the fire we made. The Organ Grinder, on the other hand, was smirking and feeling particularly full of himself.

"Did you see them?" He laughed uproariously. "The old nags can still leap a drawbridge!" The monkey hooted assent, and he settled against a rock while the Stone Preacher watched.

I found myself petting the picnic basket as he said it, unconsciously bringing it from the realm of "monster" into the realm of "pet." "I was pretty scared." I unconsciously called the bow to me and began rubbing the wood down with a cloth. "There was something in that moat."

"Moats, dear girl, are a halfpenny a baker's dozen." The Squire of Cloaks stared listlessly. "I shall travel with you for a while, I think, after we reach the Enchanter of Devils."

The Stone Preacher turned to the Squire. "Your Enchanter has truck with the wicked?"

"Fool," the Organ Grinder snapped. "Not that kind of devil. A printer's devil! An assistant who carries out the boring tasks of setting type and arranging letters! I suppose it could be considered wicked, but only by people who hate to read. I do dearly love to read. After all, where would the world be without erotic stories?" He gave a low chuckle and looked me over as the picnic basket flipped open to reveal some sandwiches.

The Squire of Cloaks laughed. "You really are the Organ Grinder." He chuckled lowly to himself. "If the Queen were still in the back of your cart, she would be screaming, indeed." He cocked his head and thought for a moment.

"It's a good thing she isn't here," the Stone Preacher said coldly. "I don't like you. You are manipulative and sly. You have a manner about you that seems to convey a hidden meaning." He rolled his neck in his stony cassock, and we heard rocky cracks, like sticks slapping a surface. "I believe you covet the Queen of Castles for yourself."

"Who would not?" The Organ Grinder laughed. "It seems I have competition! I could teach you to play the accordion!" He clapped the Squire of Cloaks on the back in the manner cultivated by rough men who drink together.

"Teach another your craft while you're with me on this journey, and I'll punch you in the nose," I said. "I almost think you do it to bait me."

The Squire of Cloaks grinned from ear to ear, but said nothing.

The Organ Grinder also said nothing. The monkey gave a playful shriek, as if acknowledging my wisdom. Then the Organ Grinder focused his monocle at the Squire of Cloaks and leered while I reached into the picnic basket, and pulled out a large sandwich. "I guess it's sandwiches again." I rolled out the blanket that the basket produced thereafter.

The basket gave a little whine, and rattled, and I opened it again. Inside was a group of sliced vegetables and some condiments. The Stone Preacher raised an eyebrow. "Perhaps your one true love is the picnic basket?" It was a joke. For some reason, it shook me to my core.

Everyone else laughed all the way through dinner. All I did for the rest of the meal was chew halfheartedly and stare down the road, in the direction of the Castle in the Sky.

***

The unearthly sounds of the accordion ground through my sleep, beating on my ears as I tossed and turned. I thought I heard the monkey screeching. I could feel the picnic basket growling lowly. I tried to sleep through most of it, refusing to open my eyes. All I heard from the cart were creaking sounds. I huddled under my cloak and let my boots smoke a little bit to warm me. Meaty grunts echoed from within the cart. Finally, the shuddering of wood ended. I balled up my fists and struggled to dream of pleasant things until morning.

When I awoke, the cart was creaking again, the wooden slats shuddering and squeaking, and I winced a little bit, as I stared at the Stone Preacher. "Oh, good morning." I shook my head and reached for the basket, as the wonderful smell of cinnamon and raisins wafted out, along with the odor of meat wrapped in pastry.

"I think it's French toast," the Stone Preacher said firmly.

"I wonder if the Squire of Cloaks will want..." I turned to look at the Stone Preacher, and then my eyes fell on the cart. "Oh, my God!"

"The Organ Grinder did warn you that he was not very discriminating. There is one good thing to come of this." His rocky features cracked with a dull grind into a smile.

"What's that?" I was rapidly losing my appetite.

"You can have all the French toast yourself." The Stone Preacher chuckled. Noises of gravel rustling underfoot came from his lips.

There was nothing to do but finish breakfast. The cinnamon-raisin French toast was so delicious I was almost able to forget the creaking of wooden wheels. Every so often, between bites, I thought I could hear the hooting shrieks of the monkey and vicious grunts from the Organ Grinder and the Squire of Cloaks. Eventually the noises stopped. I reached into the basket for a meat pastry.

The door to the cart opened shortly thereafter, and the Organ Grinder stepped out in his new vest, stinking of rutting. He gave a pleasant leer to me, adjusting his hat as he shoved the vest crudely into his breeches. "Ah, my good lady. Would you like a turn now that I am done with your new squire?" He gave a lewd chuckle. "I fear the old man shall miss breakfast, though I am far too taken with the wicked products of your basket to not partake."

I tossed the Organ Grinder one of the wrapped beef pastries. As he took it, I rose to my feet, balled up my fist and punched him in the nose. "I told you. Don't do that again. I barely got any sleep!"

The Organ Grinder rubbed his nose, still in shock for a moment. A little blood trickled from one of his nostrils. "You magnificent witch!" He bowed gracefully to me, out of respect. "You should have said you wanted to sleep more clearly. As you desire your lover so badly, I cannot be blamed for bedding someone else if you say nothing." He took a bite of the pastry with a smirk. "You are forgiven and should be rewarded. Would you like a reward?" The leer returned.

The Stone Preacher rumbled up behind the Organ Grinder and grabbed him by the shoulder. He scowled as he squeezed. The Organ Grinder winced. "Eat. Your new lover can sleep it off in the cart."

I hurried behind some bushes to change out of my dress, which dress neatly folded itself and slithered into my pack while I got my clothes on. I wished that all clothes would be so compliant.

The Organ Grinder gulped the pastry down in two bites and hurried to the driver's seat with a laugh. "He may not be able to walk for a while! Up, fair damsel! I shall have you in the end yet!"

I sprinted for the cart from around the bushes, still pulling my shirt on as my boots thudded along the ground. They roared to life with fire as I sailed upward, pausing to bend down and grab the picnic basket. It growled in discomfort as I leaped onto the cart, settling into my seat. "If you had but an ounce of courtesy in your body—" I snapped.

"Ahh, but it is good that I do not." The Organ Grinder leered and squeezed my leg a little bit. The picnic basket growled. "Who else is there to show you how not to behave?" He laughed madly and spurred his emaciated horses forward, whipping their mistreated bodies fiercely. Their scarred coats shuddered to life. The picnic basket wriggled for a few minutes in my lap while it tried to get at the Organ Grinder. I pulled to hold it back from him.

The horses thundered forward, dragging us along. As the Stone Preacher ran alongside the cart, I gazed fitfully from time to time at him, hoping that he would protect me.

***

The winding road soon grew thick with trees and snow. Flakes swirled around us angrily as the grey sky clouded. The wagon struggled through the snow as cold wrapped around us. My boots ignited involuntarily. I had to shut them off to keep myself from burning the cart.

"Sorry about that," I murmured. "I guess the boots don't like the cold either."

"If you burn my cart, I shall have to enslave noblewomen and make them build me a new one." The Organ Grinder licked his lips. "That is the magnificence of my magic. While I rut with one of them, the rest are but common laborers, until I choose one to be my harlot." He laughed uproariously in the cold as I stroked the picnic basket. It huddled under my cloak and made a discomfited noise.

"You really are a prince among men," I snapped sarcastically. "Even dirt has more scruples than you."

"You have so few yourself these days," the Organ Grinder sneered. "Why, I believe you are only moments from spreading your legs for me with your lover nowhere in sight!"

The snow swirled around us as the wagon creaked on. The dull rustle of the Stone Preacher's feet crushing the snow grew louder as the snow piled up. The horizon drew closer and the sky darkened, while the horses made fearful noises as they struggled down the snow-covered path. That was when the moaning began.

It was desperate and beautiful at the same time, and the noise filled me with prickly nervousness as the horses slowed to a stop. "Damn you!" The Organ Grinder's voice was loud. "Move, you worthless beasts!" He reached under the seat, opening a hidden box. He pulled out a whip, flaying the horses. They only shuddered under the lash.

"What is it?" I asked the Stone Preacher. "Is it something about this section of road?"

"I am not sure. I am only certain that it has nothing to do with faith or faithlessness. Those things, I can sense."

"That's not helpful." The snow fell as I hopped off the wagon. The horses' mouths opened, dull and slobbering. I activated the boots as soon as I hit the snow. Warmth shuddered through my bones, replacing the greasy body heat of the Organ Grinder. The picnic basket leaped off and followed, eager to be close to me and far from the monkey.

I rammed my fingers hard against the door of the cart. "Squire! Open the doors!" I shouted. "Is not my safety and ennoblement your concern?" There was more thumping and creaking as the snow grew fierce. The moaning turned into a singing noise, rich and beautiful. The Organ Grinder hadn't stopped whipping his horses.

The Squire burst out of the cart with a ragged gasp, his eyes filled with terror. "I know that voice." He grabbed my shoulder as if he were going to break it off. "He's coming for us."

"Who's coming for us? If you had a problem with coming out here, you should have told us! Now we're all going to die, screaming in terror while the Organ Grinder beats his horses to death!" I slapped the Squire of Cloaks in the face.

"It is the King of Castles!" he responded, his face contorted in sheer, stark terror.

"Why would the King of Castles oppose the will of his Queen?" I stared at the Squire of Cloaks in utter shock.

The Squire of Cloaks hung his head, broken like a child that had its favorite toy taken away. "The King is not the Queen's one true love. He is my own. We fought, as is often the way of such things, and I slipped my knife between his ribs, and he died." He sobbed and shook in the cold snow, dropping to his knees as the wind whipped up. "I want to be with him, but I can't. I'm too weak, and too old."

In response, the picnic basket howled ominously, and the snow fell thicker and faster.

***

"He wants to kill himself to be with his true love? Pathetic." The Organ Grinder taunted the Squire, fixing his monocled gaze upon him. "Were not your howls of pleasure and the creaking of that bed an indicator of your true nature?"

The Squire of Cloaks whimpered in the snow, his knees making a deep *V* shape in the white powder, which grew thicker in the cloud of flakes.

"This is your fault," I said to the Organ Grinder. "I'd punch you again, but you're expecting it now." I put my hands on my hips and glared up at him. "You seduced him with your stupid hand organ or accordion, or whatever it is that you call it, and now his cold, dead, lover wants to kill us!"

The Stone Preacher leaped for the Organ Grinder and they went down in a heap in the snow, the massive, stone hands reaching around the bullish neck to pin his large body to the ground. "Wretch of wretches!" the Stone Preacher thundered, slamming his weight down hard as the monkey inside the Organ Grinder's coat writhed and squealed. "You have cost this girl her life! The King of Castles was a legend among legends! And now you despoil his love with your... your accordion!" The Stone Preacher's throat rattled, like the first rumblings of an avalanche.

The Organ Grinder pushed up against the Stone Preacher, but the granite weight was too much for him.

I leaned down and shook the Stone Preacher. "Stop! We need every warm body! This isn't solving anything! Look!" The picnic basket turned, making a low growl in the direction of the wagon.

The Stone Preacher's head turned as the Squire of Cloaks sobbed wretchedly in the snow, punching his fists into the white mounds. His hands came away bloody from the crude rocks on the trail underneath. "I'm sorry!"

"We need a plan." I shook the Stone Preacher again as the rocky fingers released the Organ Grinder's throat. "Now get up and stop killing him. I don't want to die because of him."

The Stone Preacher ground his way to his feet, rocks cracking as he righted himself. "One day, Organ Grinder," he gave a thoughtful grin to me, and his lips cracked open, a little shiver of rocky lips sounding like a heavy wind against stone. "One day I shall give you everything that you deserve."

The Organ Grinder struggled to his feet, rubbing his throat. "I shall look forward to seeing you in my cart." The monkey gave a horrid yowling under the greatcoat.

"That was uncalled for," I said. "Organ Grinder? Can you drive the wagon in this snow?"

"No." The Organ Grinder recovered his breath. "Can you not see that my horses are but withered nags that cannot pull the cart in such frigid weather?"

"I could pull it," the Stone Preacher offered. "But it would be slow."

The picnic basket settled a little bit on the ground, as if disappointed. I picked it up and became as cheerful as possible. "Are you hungry?" I asked it. "You can eat as many of our enemies as you want if we survive this."

"No!" the Squire of Cloaks cried. "Don't give my lover to that thing! Murderous woman! You deserve not the Queen's praise!" He began to sniffle, the tears freezing on his face. It was getting colder.

"You were the one who didn't tell us that he might try to kill us!" I hissed. "Be grateful that I don't have him eat you!"

"Oh, so it's 'him' now, is it?" The Organ Grinder let out a belly laugh. "One might say that the basket is no different from my friend the monkey." He reached in and petted the monkey. It let out a wicked little trill that I had never heard before.

"Yes! It is!" I said fiercely.

The Squire of Cloaks stood and shook my shoulder, pointing into the storm that piled snow on top of the Organ Grinder's cart.

Hard crunches of footprints in the snow echoed at the edge of my ears. Humanoid shapes at the edge of my vision slowly lurched through impenetrable weather.

"We can no longer run." The Stone Preacher rumbled. "They touch the ground. There are forty one of them."

"Then we fight." I reached back for an arrow, as the bow appeared in my hand. I think I smiled then. All I did was look out at the thick, swirling snow, eagerly waiting for barely visible forms in the thatch of flakes to come closer.

***

The Squire of Cloaks shuddered against the door as I drew my first arrow and fired. The clockwork dart slammed through the body with a deep grind, as if rammed through brick. The creature crumpled with a heavy thud, hurling up a puff of smoke as the shadowy shapes grew closer.

The Stone Preacher thundered out to meet them while the Organ Grinder chuckled, and stepped into the cart, laughing for a moment as I heard the trunk inside the cart open with a jingling of keys. The Stone Preacher crashed into the advancing humanlike shapes with a horrible booming of rock on rock.

I heard the heavy thumps of something shattering in the snow, as I fired my bow. Oncoming footsteps grew faster and heavier. Snow kicked up around the feet of our attackers as the mass of forms and shapes slowly came into view, surrounding us.

They were made of rocky bricks, glued together with mortar. Thick blocky heads and powerful, four fingered fists stood out amid falling white. The monsters were largely featureless, but somehow, I knew they could see. In most weather we could outrun them, but the snow made things difficult. I was afraid to fly up. I didn't know what I would find.

The creatures shambled forward. Bricklike faces were marked by shallow, rocklike depressions for eyes. One of them swung at me before I could move. The fist crashed into the snow, hurling white in all directions. The ground made a deep cracking sound as I jumped aside. I tried to draw another arrow as I leapt. I made the boots flare, pulling the arrow back against the string, firing into the massive heap of bricks. It launched forward and crashed into the monster, throwing up rocky powder and sinking into it with a loud crack.

As the creature tumbled to the ground, I turned my head. I could see at least twelve more. We were surrounded. They moved forward, slow and heavy. The Organ Grinder burst forth from the cart, emerging with a large stone hammer, the thick rocky head attached to a long wooden haft. "Here's a scepter for your King to swallow!" He leaped at the nearest man of brick, slamming the rocky head forward. The hammer crashed into its chest, sending stone shards everywhere. The brick man fell backward, a thick gout of blood spewing out of the center of its chest. The castle-creature thudded to the ground. From inside the shattered shell, I heard a dull clattering sound as the coppery smell reached my nostrils.

Inside the cracked chest of the creature was a corpse drowned in blood. Steam from the rapidly cooling liquid puffed out into the snow, melting the flakes as they fell.

***

Snow dripped into the chest casing and began to freeze the blood, making it run and pool into strange shapes as the Organ Grinder shouted in my ear. "Gather courage, girl!" He shouted, swinging the massive hammer at the nearest brick man, shoving it away as I reached for another arrow, snapping out of my shock.

In the distance, I heard the cracking sounds of brick men breaking apart as the Stone Preacher disappeared into their midst. There were wet pops and red stains, bursts of blood spattered white as the strange castle men came on. The Stone Preacher's command over rock crushed them to flinders as they surrounded him.

I fired the arrow into the chest of another one, slipping as I did so. I released the string too soon. There wasn't enough force to drive the arrow in as the stony men lumbered towards us.

"Duck!" the Organ Grinder thundered. I obeyed as his hammer swung, punching the clockwork arrow fully into the rocky man's chest, splitting mortar and spraying long ago bled blood.

The creature toppled. I rolled behind the Organ Grinder, snow sticking to my hair and face. Everything was wet and red. There were still more of them. Some flopped on the ground, making odd wailing noises as shattered housings oozed and left wet stains in the snow. I fired again, the arrow flying into the midst of the advancing creatures.

In the distance, there was a strange, whistling howl, a powerful set of cracking noises, and a massive booming sound, as if a pair of rocks hit the ground. There was a horrible roar and the sound of rocks displacing snow. Then there was only the silent glide of a single figure walking back toward the wagon as the creatures whirled in the haze of flakes.

A keening noise came from under the cart. The low legs of the picnic basket struggled, unable to see and unable to help me. I walked over and dug it out, feeling a little sense of shame that I hadn't even looked for it. It huddled in my arms and cooed piteously, wind whipping through chilled slats.

The Stone Preacher returned though the snow, wet and covered in blood, the frozen red blotches of his footprints filling the air with the taint of extinguished life. As he came closer, the sounds of the creatures fleeing receded. Then we only heard whimpering sounds from the Squire of Cloaks, begging for his lost love.

***

"Pull yourself together!" the Organ Grinder snapped, crunching his way through the snow towards the Squire. He grabbed the Squire by the shoulder and punched him in the mouth. "Snap out of it! One night with the Organ Grinder does not make you unfaithful." He laughed wickedly under his mustache. "But we'll have a few more from you and then we'll see!"

I grabbed the Organ Grinder by the coat and the basket growled. "Stop it! Can't you see he needs you now, like all the others?"

The monkey chittered fiercely as it waved its knife tail at me from under the coat.

The Squire winced as he bit down on his lip, cleaning and licking it. "I'm sorry, my love. It was the Organ Grinder, it was all him, our nights will…" His voice choked before he finished the sentence. "…never be the same." He broke into soft whimpering noises.

I leaned down and took his hand. "Do not worry." I whispered softly, as the Stone Preacher began roaming around the campsite, crushing the heads of the bricklike creatures. My fingers were still wet and red. "You are not alone, I, too, feel the desperate need for the touch of my Organ Grinder."

The picnic basket growled, the dim wicker rustle blocked every few seconds by the Stone Preacher smashing brick faces into bloody rubble.

The Squire nodded and clutched my hands.

The Organ Grinder gave me a lewd smile. "Not now…" I scowled. "We'll all freeze to death."

"Oh, bother that." The Organ Grinder smirked. "There's nothing wrong with a little cuddling when the horses can't move."

The Stone Preacher's head creaked up. Finished with the gruesome task he gave a rocky smile. "Now all of you must rub yourselves down with snow." He smiled. "We wouldn't want any of this rotting blood to infect your bodies, would we?"

I had never been so grateful to be frozen and miserable. The Stone Preacher grabbed the Organ Grinder and turned him around so that he couldn't see me. I removed all my clothes and wrapped them in a pile, rubbing myself down as the Organ Grinder leered at me. "It'll be your turn soon. It's a good thing I still have the dress." I shivered as the bloody garments shone a little bit, beginning to freeze. I scooped more snow all over the parts of my skin that were stained with red, then slipped back into my boots, warming myself as I slipped inside the cart and shut the door.

I whistled for the dress and it slithered across the floor out of my bag, wrapping around me and gathering its silken folds. I inhaled a little bit in my boots. It was nice to be warm again. I heard stomping sounds from outside and peered out.

As I levitated up so that I wouldn't set the cart on fire, I turned my head to look as the Squire of Cloaks desperately washed his hands in the snow. The Organ Grinder jumped up and down as he rubbed snow over his flesh, cleaning the blood from himself as he covered his flaccid genitals, gritting his teeth.

"It looks like someone's lost his mood." I chuckled.

"My mood never dampens." The Organ Grinder let out a laugh. "Would you care for some proof?"

"I don't need any." I laughed and floated over to his clothes, the dress rustling and flicking its way up from the burning boots. I settled onto the heap of the Organ Grinder's clothing, and let the roaring of the flames char up his pants and his shirt. The smell of burning cloth and sweat rose into the sky. "All you need to prove is that fire is an incredibly useful tool." I floated over to my own clothes and settled onto them, the burning launching another plume of smoke into the air.

"Are you trying to let them know we're coming?" The Organ Grinder scowled. "I need my spare clothes, and you'll have to drag that hammer in after me." He gave me a dirty look as he slunk inside the cart, followed by the Squire of Cloaks. His eyes tainted with bitterness and lust, he scowled at me as he closed the door.

The Stone Preacher glided over to the small fires and applied his massive weight to them, crushing them out. The smoky flames vanished under the rocky cassock. "He is right." the Stone Preacher said to me. "Now they will know where we are, and might come back."

"I hope not. As fun as it is to inflict casualties on the King of Castles, he might not remember us fondly if we kill too many of his followers."

The Stone Preacher turned to me, his eyes ablaze with fervor. "Wise beyond your age, too." He murmured as he placed a heavy granite hand on my shoulder. "You will make a fine noblewoman, if you survive to the end of your journey."

"I'll go melt the cart out." I smiled and walked back toward the wagon and the horses. "Don't worry, I'll be careful."

With deadly scrutiny, the Stone Preacher's eyes followed me with every step around the trapped wheels. The flames never came close enough to the rickety, dry wood to burn it. Steam flew upward from near my boots. Wheel by wheel, the cart came free.

***

The snow stopped after a little while. I moved far enough away from the cart to talk to the Stone Preacher, my boots warming me while I watched the cart tilt and shake, little creaking noises moving on the wind. I turned my back to it.

"You look desolate," the Stone Preacher said, looking at the shivering basket on my arm.

"I almost let it die," I said, as I petted the thing. It made weird rustling noises and huddled against me, letting out little growls. "I'm sorry you couldn't eat any of them." A low and strange hiccup came from it.

"Perhaps you should have let it die." The picnic basket growled at him. "Sometimes it is better for a noble to not have such attachments. You aren't the lady of dogs, though you might become the Duchess of Picnic Baskets." The noise of rocky laughter drowned out the moans from the cart.

"Something like that." I stroked the basket gently. "But, you know, we all develop attachments to things we shouldn't. That's how people fall in love in the first place." I kept my back to the cart so I wouldn't have to think about what was going on inside too much.

"Are you cold?"

"I have my boots to keep me warm. How does the bow trick work?"

"No one really knows. It's just something powerful nobles can do with practice, and you're obviously well-placed among the upper classes. It's a talent many would kill to possess, even for a short time. If you are not confirmed by their acclamation, which, at the court of the King of Feathers, no one may refuse, then they have the right to kill you until you get there. Rules are tricky thing. Even the most complicated of them can be gotten around. Thus do I find solace in my grim faith and those who have any faith at all."

"So you find comfort in rigidity?" I raised an eyebrow. "Doesn't that make you more like the Organ Grinder than you want to admit?"

"Not in any way I would like to admit," the Stone Preacher grumbled. "And certainly not in the way he practices his rigidity." He made a brief sound like rock shearing off a cliff.

"Was that a dirty joke?" I laughed and huddled a little bit in my dress, suddenly feeling colder.

"I will never tell. I am, after all, made of stone, and don't truly have a sense of humor as you understand it."

"You have other emotions." I said. "It's just a matter of what you find funny."

"I don't find anything funny. How do you think I got here, anyway?"

"I would love to hear it." I shuddered. "But I'm sure your story is long, and as cruel as my own."

"Your story is not cruel yet," the Stone Preacher rumbled. "Merely violent and with some bumps. The cruelty always comes when you review it later, and you look into the mirror to discover that much of your time would be so different had you not walked in the woods. Everything here is about the one mistake that cannot be undone."

"Walking into the woods?"

"No." The Stone Preacher said. "Did anyone tell you what was going to happen?"

"My adopted mother." I said sheepishly. "She said I'd meet the man I love and kill the King of Feathers, a wicked tyrant who rules over a wicked land."

"That must be why he's trying to kill you." The Stone Preacher said firmly. "After all, it isn't as if you did anything else unusual. He must know the prophecy, too, and, anxious not to be killed, he is sending his assassin after you, along with anyone else he can. This might be harder than I thought. Why didn't you tell us about the prophecy?" There was anger there, the dim rumble of rock in his voice shuddering. At least it blocked out the sounds of the cart.

"I thought telling you might make you just snap my neck and walk away." I sighed. "It would be fair, that's for certain. I did, well, lie."

"You only withheld the truth," the Stone Preacher nodded, "and the Organ Grinder and I are obligated. He was the first to find you, and I am one whom you rescued. We cannot refuse our duty. It is part of the laws of this world."

"This world has laws?"

"Metaphysical laws, as well as those codified by men, yes. But he who has the gold makes the rules. Unfortunately, the King of Feathers has the most gold."

"So he's rich as well as evil? He sounds friendly."

"He wears black leather, and you cannot see his face. His power lies in his anonymity, but when he spreads his wings, they burst out of his back in a shower of blood, and he is radiant in his cruelty, a magnificent killer. I have no idea how a mere slip of a girl like you is supposed to kill someone like that. They say he is so fast his wings can cut you from across his throne room."

"Why haven't you killed him? Are you afraid of him?"

"I am a priest," the Stone Preacher said coldly. "I still have some conscience. Regicide is the worst crime one can imagine. In my time, it was like killing God. I cannot do it."

I thought on that as the snow melted. When the creaking did not stop, I motioned to the Stone Preacher and got up in the driver's seat. We drove on then, with the basket huddling against me for warmth, the dress clinging to me with a smooth rustle. The faint hooting of the monkey came from within as the Stone Preacher pushed snow aside with his earthy walk.

***

After the creaking finally stopped, the gaunt horses pulled us weakly into a small cluster of buildings. There was a makeshift town center with a general store, an inn, and a well, crudely angled into the ground as if something had upset it. Brown grass poked out of the snow. Behind the buildings, the smell of glue and heat wafted in the winter air, a massive towering block of a structure looming over the rest of the town.

I dismounted, spreading my arms for the picnic basket, which vaulted from the seat to land in my hands. It made a happy whistling noise, as if the wind passed through it.

The Stone Preacher shook his rocky head. "It is your pet, as surely as if Bosquoverde knew it."

"Maybe." I lowered it to the ground. "We can tie the horses here and go see this Enchanter of Devils. Hopefully, he enchants his assistants and not us."

The Stone Preacher chuckled. "Do you wish to wake them?" He sneered at the cart. "All warm and pleasant in their cuckold's bed?"

I gave him a sarcastic smirk. "Of course I do. Am I allowed to be unladylike?"

"Of course you are." The Stone Preacher chuckled. "He is the Organ Grinder, after all. It might do him some good."

I pounded on the door with my fist, shaking the rickety cart and making the wheels creak. "Organ Grinder! Quit fooling around, you dirty bastard! We've got a message to print and a true love to find! Not just the one you found this week!"

The Organ Grinder threw open the door in his nightgown, while the Squire of Cloaks shuddered in the bed, the smell of male fleshly pleasures reeking out of the room. "You dare to offend my parentage?" He scowled down at me. "Oh, it's you."

As he spoke those words, the Squire of Cloaks began to whimper and sob, rubbing his buttocks under the dirty sheets. He crept over to his soiled clothing, full of shame. His cape seemed unrumpled. "Yes," he managed through choked sobs. "We should help her."

"Get dressed." I snapped. "If you're afraid of smelling like that first, we can all get an inn room and you can clean off. I'm going to see the Enchanter."

"Finally, some spine in you, girl." The Stone Preacher murmured. "You're becoming more like us every day."

"Really?" The Organ Grinder laughed, leering as the Squire of Cloaks slipped under his arm and out of the cart, looking around furtively as if he thought he might be noticed. "She'll not be like me until her legs are open, and those pert little breasts jiggling as she moans."

"Say anything like that again, and I'll cut out your tongue." I watched the Squire of Cloaks gaze at me, a jealous scowl on his face.

The Squire shook his head. "There is no need, milady. You know my shame, and I am content."

We headed up the steps to the inn. I dreaded what I was going to find inside. Mounted into the door was a carved woman's head, laughing under its long hair. It opened its lips as we approached. "Good day." Its voice was a musical lilt. "Welcome to the Inn of Unrepentant Arrangements." It ran a wooden tongue across lacquered lips. The door clicked open into bustle and skullduggery.

***

We stepped into a room with little light and booths where occupants were barely visible. The podium was occupied by a quiet-looking lady wearing a plain gray dress and a white hat with a feather. Lovely features and curled dark hair were gorgeous in a suit of leather, armored with small studs. There was a sword on her hip and a smirk on her features. "Ah, travelers." Her smile spread open. "I am the Lady of Masks. How may I assist you this fine eve?"

"What is this?" The Organ Grinder scowled. "You don't have a mask on."

Her features lit up with a wry giggle. "If I was wearing one, Organ Grinder, I would not let you know. And you do not know if it is my name, so you cannot call me to your bed. A relief, to be sure, as you stink of rutting." She gave the Squire of Cloaks a winning smile. "I'm sure he'll tire of you sooner or later."

The Stone Preacher nodded to her once, with a rocky creak in his neck.

"And you, my lady?" she said with an elegant laugh. "Do you have your name yet, or is this one of those journeys only a few survive?"

"The second." I curtsied to her. "If you could show us to a table and get us rooms, I'm sure that we'll find a way to pay you."

"Oh, I am certain you shall." She chuckled throatily, and led us through the maze of darkened tables to a booth. "Safe food will be served to you." She gave me a knowing wink. "We endeavor to make sure no one dies here."

"In that case, I shall watch my back when I leave." I sat down, watching the Squire of Cloaks look around nervously. The monkey under the Organ Grinder's jacket gave a hoot, and the picnic basket settled into the booth, curling up next to me with an eerie rustle.

She laughed and departed as the Stone Preacher took the chair that gave us access to the outside world. "This place is unexpected," he rumbled. "We are surrounded by unsavory folk. The Organ Grinder should be right at home." He glowered at the Organ Grinder, who looked about without really looking up.

"Don't worry. I know all about unsavory folk. I was raised in a circus, remember?" I looked over the crowd.

The Squire of Cloaks spoke softly. "These people are not interested in anything except your money, and your blood if you cannot pay them. The Lady of Masks is a sinister woman indeed. Behind her cheer lies something much more unpleasant. But if we are to stay here, we must pay her with something."

"With what?" My curiosity rose, as dangerous as that was. "The only money here is half-lunas, and we don't have any. Exchanges seem to be made on the promise of later favors."

The Squire raised an eyebrow. "Indeed, the concept of debt is high, but your allies are impressive. Everyone is afraid to offend someone who could be the bride of someone rich and powerful. Or," he shuddered, "something that destroys you in a way so gruesome that you wish you had been nicer to them."

The Organ Grinder chuckled and ran his hand along my leg. "That is why there are those like us, myself and the Stone Preacher, who obey our obligations and initiate people into this world. I could initiate you further."

I scowled. "Hands off." I heard the sound of the picnic basket's jaws snapping shut just as the Stone Preacher moved. The Stone Preacher grabbed the Organ Grinder's wrist and gave him a look as the groping hand was brought out from under the table. The Organ Grinder's face was a deep purple shade.

"And you, hands off *him*! What am I, some kind of babysitter?"

The Squire of Cloaks sighed, rubbing his forehead as though he had been relieved for a moment that the Organ Grinder's attention had turned to me. "He was saving your fellow bodyguard from losing a hand. The basket eats people, doesn't it?"

"Yes." A guilty thrill mounted in my throat. "I've lost my temper a couple times and fed people to it."

"Why didn't you have it fight?" The Squire asked. "You might have made a better showing." He bit his lip and looked at the Organ Grinder's crotch.

"It was scared. Something about your King of Castles frightens him." I wondered what a dead man who bricked up dead people and made bloodbags out of their corpses was like.

"It frightens you, too." The Organ Grinder chuckled. "Look at you, twitching like a half-spent beast after its first terrifying orgasm."

"Sex isn't fear. Sex is about sharing. Maybe if you knew that, you wouldn't be so vile." It was really one of the few words I could use to describe the Organ Grinder.

"It is his nature." The Stone Preacher rumbled. "You can no more change the Organ Grinder than you can change your toes. Well, the Priest of Gears might be able to help you with that, but I'm certain you wouldn't like the result."

The Lady of Masks returned with our food herself, and leaned in to whisper to me. "You will have to pay with something." She let her breath run across my ear. "A promise."

"If I pay you with promises, what debts do I collect?" The others watched me, silent. The monkey chittered under the Organ Grinder's coat, and the picnic basket let out a little hiss from under the lid.

"Be careful," the Stone Preacher said. "Giving your word can be as dangerous as keeping it."

The Lady of Masks murmured softly, her fingers stroking along my leg. She leaned in and whispered in my ear. "Many debts," she murmured. "One favor, to be named later, and if you cannot do what it is that I request, I promise you it will be dire."

"Are you making a pass at me? I'm not attracted to women." She gave me a blank look.

"Oh, you are so terribly clever," she teased. "But if I wanted that from you, I'd just drug your food and you'd wake up next to me. You would become…" Her head tilted as if she was thinking of the right word to use. "Pliant."

The Organ Grinder cried out "Ah, a kindred spirit!" He smiled at the Lady of Masks, but she just scowled at him. The Stone Preacher raised an amused eyebrow, and the Squire of Cloaks remained silent, as if it was not his place to speak.

"I'll accept your favor. But if you abuse me or my new rank upon the completion of my journey, I will put an arrow through your eye." I gave her a cheerful smile. "And I know I'm good at that even if I die on the way."

"You promise to kill me even after you die?" The Lady of Masks laughed lightly. "A promise is a promise, and that is a daring one indeed." She gave me a sparkling laugh. "Perhaps one day you'll change your mind about women. Until that day, however…" She clapped her hands, and waiters brought us food and water, fine roasted birds and a large jug of water, with a plate piled high with fruit that somehow seemed fresh and appetizing.

"I will see you later…" She smiled and walked off through the crowd as the meal began with the Organ Grinder ripping off a turkey leg and biting into it. He slipped a finger up and rubbed the edge of his monocle, flicking his gaze to the sumptuous walk as she glided away.

"I don't think I'll be making friends with her on a personal level," I said.

"How would you know?" the Stone Preacher rumbled, his eyes locked on her swaying form. "She's probably the only person in the whole Otherworld who could be your one true love and you would never know it unless you took her mask off."

We went to sleep shortly after dinner. My dreams were bland, without a hint of all the nervousness I should have had.

***

I woke early, and crept out of my room while the Organ Grinder snored and the Stone Preacher remained silent. The picnic basket followed me to the door, hurrying away from the Squire of Cloaks, who whimpered and cried in his sleep, his fists clenched and his breath shallow. "Oh, all right," I whispered. "You can come, too."

I loped down the hall of rooms to the stairs. The whispering rustle of the basket followed as I made my way to the main room. The Lady of Masks was seated at a table while her servants bustled about. The aroma of baking bread wafted from the kitchen. "So, I suppose you haven't decided to indulge me?"

"Sorry." I grinned and slid into a chair across from her. "The Organ Grinder snores." The Picnic basket gave a rustling coo.

"As good a reason as any," She purred and drummed her fingers on the table. "Would you like some breakfast?"

"I would love some." I smiled. "But I'd like to talk with you a little bit about masks, if I could."

"Well," The Lady of Masks leaned forward and signaled a waiter into the kitchen with her hand. "I do like to talk about it. It's what I'm all about, after all." She gave a pleasant laugh.

"I was interested in one in particular. It's made of iron, and a blonde woman with a knife made of ice uses it."

The Lady of Masks smirked. "I shall mourn your death in days to come. I trust that you will try to fulfill your promise from beyond the grave?"

The picnic basket made a sad little whine. "Oh, hush. We'll make it, you and I." The basket rubbed against me, making a little creaking sound.

"And you have confidence." She chuckled. "Never a bad thing, I suppose. What I can tell you is that the Weeper in Shadows has always had the confidence of the King of Feathers, but never his eye. It is said she roams the land for those who find true love, and murders them in bloody revenge for the thing she cannot have."

"What can't she have?"

"Her one true love. Not all true love works the same way, after all, as you have no doubt discovered from your travels here. Apparently, she fell in love but he did not reciprocate. Something about a one-way mirror or a waterfall. I'm not terribly sure, all of this is rumor."

"I thought that was impossible. I mean, once you find your one true love, aren't you supposed to be happy forever?"

"Well, you know what they say. Not everything happens the way you think it's going to." She smiled at me, her features smooth and graceful, tilting her white hat with its white feather. "One might say she resolved to break the hearts of any and all who sought the same. The mask of iron represents her heartlessness, and her devotion to coldness, as does her knife of ice that shatters the hearts of all it pierces."

"She sounds even more awful when you haven't met her for a few seconds." I winced. "She sounds like a lost cause."

A wry grin crossed her perfect features. "We are all lost causes in one way or another, Lady Symantha without a name." She leaned toward me. "I am sure that you will find something that makes your heart flutter and survive. Even the Weeper in Shadows fails from time to time."

"And that's supposed to make me comfortable?" I asked. "How many times has she failed?"

"Once." The Lady of Masks laughed. "I meant to give you more hope than that, but you are a clever girl. She met a man once, and the King of Feathers commanded that she marry him."

"That sounds unfortunate. What happened?"

"He died." The Lady of Masks smiled cruelly. "She broke his heart with her knife of ice and stabbed him in fury until her eyes glossed with hate. She hasn't taken off her mask since."

"What's since?"

"Time passes oddly here. But when you meet the eyes of your true love, you won't care about that anymore. You'll want to stay here forever. That is, if you live and he doesn't kill you."

"You mean that really happens? People murdering their loved ones like that?" The picnic basket huddled against me, and let out a little moan.

"Why not?" The Lady of Masks purred. "It happens in the world you come from." She leaned back in her chair as the waiter brought me two sausages, a thick crust of bread, and an egg. "I have to be off. I have to put on a new face. It will be a few hours." She winced for a moment, and something waxy and brittle broke away from her cheek, revealing three long scars in the open space. "But you'll have left by then." She got up and slipped towards the kitchen, disappearing through the doors with an elegant glide that left dire shudders in my imagination.

I ate breakfast in silence, wondering what lay underneath the rest of the perfect façade. When the others came down to breakfast, there wasn't a conversation at all.

***

We made our way to the printer's after breakfast, the warm feeling of fullness bolstering our wills against the cold. Even the cloak of runes and the boots of fire didn't protect me from the chill. The long wooden house smelled of pulp and glue.

As we made our way up to the door, two heavyset men loomed, one on either side of a plain wooden door. "Back off!" one of them snapped, drawing a thick metal ball covered with flanges, studs, and spikes. "You're not welcome here, Organ Grinder!"

The other moved in front of the door. I shouted back, "He is my bodyguard! He stays with me! The Queen of Castles has given us license to print a missive."

The Organ Grinder peered at the two men. "Do I know you?" I elbowed him.

"It doesn't matter whether or not you know them," the Stone Preacher said with a dry rumble and a cracking sound. "What matters is that they do not like you."

The Squire of Cloaks nervously put his arm into the elbow of the Organ Grinder, quivering a little bit in terror. "Stand aside! This man is my prisoner!" His voice cracked as he spoke. The two men laughed at him raucously.

"I'm afraid it's true. The Organ Grinder is his prisoner. I have had to endure his sniveling the whole time." I walked forward. "Look at my eyes. I haven't the time for your threats! And if you don't stand aside, I'll turn the Organ Grinder loose on your women!"

The guards looked at each other and stepped back into their guardian positions as we walked forward.

"That's it!" The Organ Grinder snapped his fingers as we made our way through the door, the Stone Preacher grinding in as it shut behind us. "I fear I've already had the wife of the man who spoke first! That's where I remember him from. A little pale in the face and long in the tooth, but still, her delicious howls—"

The Squire of Cloaks covered the Organ Grinder's mouth with a gentle hand before the Stone Preacher could break a limb. Inside the coat, the monkey chittered with violent glee.

The first thing we heard when we walked in was the noise. The room filled with the clatter and grind of printing presses. Thudding noises and rickety clacks filled the air. Bright lights shone down, reflecting off dull metal. People ran about, most of them human. Several were horribly misshapen, and walked with a limp. Others were hunchbacked with strange faces, somewhat lizard-like, or more like wounded beavers.

"Well…this looks like a perfect place to send a message," I said, looking around for someone who had more authority. I heard the heavy sound of hard workshoes. A well-dressed man in a Victorian waistcoat and bright plaid pants scurried across the floor, out from between the presses. His fingers stank of glue. Yellow nails glistened with the roughness of years of work. There was a long poker on his waist, with a thick brass handle and a sharp, unpleasant-looking tip.

He bowed to us, his old, bald head shining in the bright light. Thick, round-rimmed glasses reflected the light and the dust. He gave us a gap-toothed smile. "Good day to you, my boy. I am the Enchanter of Devils. What missive may I print for you, perhaps, if I am lucky, a new book?" He reached into his pocket and pulled out a mangled pocket-watch. "Oh, dear, this thing will never work again."

"A new book would be lovely!" the Organ Grinder boomed. "Why, I do believe I have read all the erotica that currently exists!"

"Be silent!" I snapped. "You are my bodyguard, and the Squire's prisoner!" I glared at the Organ Grinder, and the monkey hissed vengefully under the greatcoat.

The Stone Preacher chuckled. "For a newcomer who is unnamed, she is a quick study." His voice was all gravel and amusement. He glared at the Enchanter of Devils as if he were about to vengefully crush every bone in his body.

The Squire of Cloaks wrenched the Organ Grinder's wrist, and he mock grunted. "You'll pay for this, Squire." The Squire looked away from him, his face twisted in real rage.

The Enchanter of Devils bowed. "If you are here, Squire, what is the missive of your Queen?" His gaze was piercing, even behind the thick glass knobs that enabled him to see.

The Squire idly passed the Organ Grinder off to the Stone Preacher with a smirk. The Preacher forced the Organ Grinder's hand into a hammerlock. "Stop!" the Organ Grinder bellowed. "You're hurting me!"

"Good," the Stone Preacher retorted. "Perhaps I shall spare your life after you apologize for your base godlessness."

The Squire bowed low. "The Queen of Castles demands that you proclaim the nobility of the lady." He flourished with his cloak.

The Enchanter chuckled, drawing out his poker and tapping it on the ground. "I suppose I could be persuaded to print something up." He peered at me. "You're not cutting a very impressive figure, young lady. I would suggest a simple proclamation, no more than a page." He smiled. The gaps in his teeth showed.

"Well, do you have someone who can do it? I would hate to waste your time."

"You shall pay me back in time, dear girl." The old man cackled, idly tapping the poker handle. "I suspect that you will one day have something I will need." His voice raised to a shout, his dry lips thundering words over the clatter. "Bazelgard! I demand a task of you!"

From around the corner of one of the presses, something skittered on lizard legs. One eye was larger than the other. Odd little horns poked out of its face with sharp teeth ensconced in a long snout. Its legs were like those of a kangaroo. A slithering, forked tongue popped in and out of its mouth as it stared up at us.

"Hew-manzzz," it mewled, and flicked its eyes over us. It wore suspenders that held up knickers, and an odd little button up vest. It couldn't have been more than two feet tall.

"Bazelgard is one of those things that wandered in without anyone really knowing what he is or how he got here," the Enchanter said. "He'll take you to my office. I'll be along shortly." He cackled merrily and resheathed the poker on his belt, as Bazelgard hopped forward. The picnic basket ran its tongue out of the lid. I had to shove it back in on the way.

***

We sat in the office of The Enchanter of Devils. It looked like a nightmare for bureaucrats. Vast piles of paper covered his massive oak desk. A series of overstuffed wooden file cabinets bulged. Paper was piled high on the chair behind the desk. Our seats were covered with worn leather and fur.

The Organ Grinder chortled. "Why, he is almost as messy as myself!" he marveled. "I have never been lucky enough to be in his office."

All I did while I sat in my chair was gag. Bazelgard seated himself on the desk staring at us. "Uv...course...!" Bazelgard said, reaching into his pocket for a handkerchief and blowing his nose. There was a dull sizzle as the fabric slowly dissolved.

The Stone Preacher grumbled. "It is the messes you leave behind that make you who you are, Organ Grinder," he rumbled. "Were I not as obligated to the girl as you, I would crush every bone in your body and feed them to this creature."

The pop-eyed lizard leaned forward. "You mean me?"

I idly petted the Picnic basket as it hung on my arm. "No. He means this." The lid opened, and it slavered in Bazelgard's general direction.

The larger eye widened in fright. "Uv...course..." The words came as a struggle. Angled legs twitched a little bit at the edge of the table.

"Do you agree to everything?" the Stone Preacher demanded. "Some little homunculus that does whatever this Enchanter of Devils says?"

"Pleez," the creature whined, trying to answer the Stone Preacher. "Me am homunculus!" He thumbed his chest proudly as the Squire of Cloaks and the Organ Grinder stared. The monkey hooted from under the Organ Grinder's cloak.

The Enchanter of Devils threw open the door, staring at Bazelgard. "Oh," he muttered. "You've been talking to Bazelgard, haven't you?" He shook his head and peered at us. "Has he been agreeing to everything again?"

"Yes, sir. He's agreed to everything since we came in here."

The Enchanter sighed. "Forgive the more formal introduction, but I am the Enchanter of Devils." He closed the door and bowed to us. The heavy thud of the door resonated behind him. "Since the Queen of Castles is paying for your proclamation, I am certain that I will be paid in turn."

The Organ Grinder leered at the Squire of Cloaks, who looked at him nervously. "It is so." The Squire of Cloaks fumbled with his cape and looked away from the Organ Grinder.

"Then let us discuss particulars." The Enchanter scooped up Bazelgard as he made his way over to the other side of the desk. He picked up the heap of paper on it. He looked around for a space to put it and dumped it on the floor "There." He looked at us with a gaze of relief. Thick glasses magnified his own eyes.

"That sounds lovely. I think we should keep it as simple as possible." I settled back in my worn chair. "There's no need to be flowery. The Queen's acceptance of my nobility is enough."

"I like simple," the Organ Grinder chuckled. "It has so many additional uses."

"Then perhaps something a little more complicated." The Stone Preacher offered words with a dry, mossy rumble. He clenched his rocky fist. I could hear stone split.

"You'll excuse me." I looked over the old man carefully. "My bodyguards have some very different ideas about what I should be like."

The Enchanter of Devils chuckled. "Such is the way of the nobility. That is why I am merely a legend who gives voice to their proclamations. As such, they all need me, and don't bother me," He cackled. "Do you want a 'Hear ye, Hear ye' at the start?"

"That might be useful. Just put it into the words of the Queen of Castles, as if she had spoken it. But you might want to leave out any fear of the outdoors."

"Noticed that, have you? The poor woman's been locked out again?"

"Well, they say she always gets back in eventually," I sighed. "She's still their Queen."

"Eventually, someone always takes pity on her. She is a good ruler, she just has a few odd idiosyncrasies is all," the Enchanter cackled. "Keeping the blood tax from her King, before he died." He glared at the Squire of Cloaks. "There are those who say that her adjutant here had something to do with it, but surely that is just a rumor." He grinned maliciously at the Organ Grinder, who returned the grin with one of his own.

Bazelgard wheezed on the desk. "I... agree." Taking a sheet of paper from a pile, he dug a piece of charcoal out of a pocket. The little monster began to scribble and draw, cooing as his long, lizardlike tongue slithered out of his mouth to lick his enlarged eyeball.

"No matter what you might think, you're not a homunculus," the Enchanter said. "But a respectable printer's devil you are indeed."

"Are all of the little monsters here like him?"

"It's no matter. As their minds are fairly empty," the Enchanter of Devils let out a wheezing cough, "it is easy enough to ensorcel them to proclaim things. It's not enough to simply write a proclamation. One has to actually *proclaim* it." He got out a handkerchief and wiped his lips, then cleaned the thick lenses on his face with the other side of it. "Many here cannot read." He smirked. "In fact, it's to my advantage to keep portions of the population illiterate."

The Organ Grinder cackled. "Thank you then, sir, for keeping me in foolish peasants when the more noble folk are unavailable." He gave the Squire of Cloaks a nasty smile.

"You are my prisoner for now." The Squire of Cloaks blushed a little bit as he spoke to the Organ Grinder, but the Enchanter of Devils didn't seem to pay attention. The Stone Preacher just gave a rocky scowl.

"So, what do you want it to say?" The Enchanter of Devils put his hand back on the poker. "It can say just about anything."

"How about 'The Queen of Castles has accepted the nobility of Symantha, who has yet to achieve her name among her peers?' That's pompous and short. It fits on a sheet of paper."

"I like it." The Organ Grinder smiled. "Of course, I would like anything that might allow me a chance at lying between the legs of one I rescued. An appropriate reward, to be sure."

"You have no shame." The Stone Preacher clenched his fist. "Nonetheless, I am tempted to accept the words of the one we defend."

"Your opinion, Squire?" The Enchanter of Devils chuckled as Bazelgard scribbled furiously, and he turned, bringing the poker down hard next to the creature's leg. "Not so fast, Devil! You'll ruin it and have to start again! Already I have offended the King of Trees twice this year. I should turn him into a book by pulping him! Hah!" He snarled for a moment and gazed at the wall, as if his mind were somewhere far away. Bazelgard shuddered, but continued drawing, the bulging eye staring at his master in terror.

"It is adequate, Enchanter. Most adequate." The Squire nodded, as the Organ Grinder pulled him closer.

"Adequate?" The Enchanter's face twisted in rage as he drove the poker hard onto the ground. "There can be no adequacy in this!" He grabbed the sheet away from Bazelgard as he held it out.

As one, our faces fell, our eyes open wide. In the picture, I was more beautiful than anything I could possibly have imagined, but the other half of my face was still missing. There was only an empty blackness there. Where my features were, there was only a starry, drawn outline of the night sky.

"I agree," Bazelgard chirped.

***

"This is who you are," the Enchanter said coolly. "There can be no doubt of it. Noble, indeed. I have never seen such a likeness."

"What does it mean?" I asked. "It's got to mean something. Everything means something around here, no matter how strange or unusual."

"I do not know. Bazelgard only draws what he sees on the inside." The Organ Grinder and the Stone Preacher looked at each other, and the Stone Preacher looked at the knife on the Organ Grinder's belt, the one I had never seen him use.

"It's beautiful, but it's also kind of like a monster," I managed.

"Why, there is nothing monstrous about it!" the Organ Grinder boomed. "Do you see anything unusual or monstrous about me?" He reached into a pocket, dug out a thick flask that smelled like brandy, and took a swig.

I saw the Stone Preacher in his granite cloak grit his teeth. I thought I heard a faint sound of earth grinding against earth.

"Look around you!" The Enchanter of Devils raised his poker and jammed it up against the ceiling, where it made a dull thud. "Many of us are monsters here! Some more so than others! Be grateful you didn't change into a writhing mass of frogs! I hear that's happened!"

"Uh, right." I said. That wasn't a comforting thought. The idea that the Duke of Bells could still be alive slithered through my mind and made my stomach shudder.

For the first time since I had arrived, I clutched my fingers and stared at the Enchanter's poker. Everything had seemed like a strange dream until right then. All I could think of was how desperately I was to go home.

The Enchanter laughed, and raised his hand. "As payment is from the Queen of Castles, Bazelgard, I do make thee a proclaimer!" He waved the poker about and brought it down savagely on the creature's head. A sparkling trail of light burned out of the edge of the poker and writhed around Bazelgard.

Bazelgard clutched his head and howled, eyes bulging, his new voice thunderous. "Hear ye! Hear ye!" His voice roared through the office as he grew wings of thick, rusty metal. "The Queen of Castles has accepted the nobility of Symantha, who has yet to find a name among her peers!" He held the scroll with my likeness in his hand, and fluttered off, bellowing his proclamation into the press room, hurrying for the door with metallic clanks.

He forced the door open with a firm shove, and read the proclamation again. I turned and stared at the Enchanter of Devils. "How does it work? He can talk eloquently now, but he was so stupid before! How is he supposed to deliver messages with bruises all over his head?"

"I enchant them for resilience and strength, that they might carry their messages far and wide!" The Enchanter of Devils laughed a little bit. "He will return when his message is fully proclaimed."

"And when is that going to be?" The Stone Preacher scowled, his voice making a dull, shuddering rattle.

"I do not know," the Enchanter responded, his gaze flicking over us. "He could have a safe journey. He could have an unpleasant one. He could get lost. It is rare but it happens. The enchantment rarely fails. Oh, and he could be eaten by one of the many threats that attack people on the road when they're alone. They rarely bother the messengers, though. I don't understand that at all."

"So, your form of magic is very limited." I looked him over as the poker sparked. "Do you at least know when he dies?"

"An unusual question to ask." The Enchanter raised his finger high as the Organ Grinder peered at him. "But yes, I do, indeed!" His eyes lit up with cheerful mirth, visible even behind the thick glasses. "I can see what happens to my Printer's Devils clearly, even though my normal vision is clouded behind these lenses."

"Did you consider taking the glasses off?" the Squire of Cloaks asked.

"No," the Enchanter responded coldly. "It does not make a difference."

"That's odd. It must be some sort of curse." The Stone Preacher offered, a little tinkle of rocks bouncing off each other creeping into his voice.

"Indeed. I am cursed, but I know not how or why. Perhaps a message that was delivered in the real world somehow has come here to punish me." The Enchanter of Devils shrugged his sloped shoulders. "Even then, I am terribly old, so what of it? It is not as if I expect the same eyesight I had as a youth of five and twenty. Everything ages, though the nobles with the most power age the most slowly." He grinned. "You could live forever, girl!" His eyes burned into mine, as if only partially focusing on me.

"I'm not sure I want to. Wouldn't I get bored?"

"That's usually what happens." The Enchanter of Devils smirked. "Then the betrayals and games start, couched in blood, manipulation and warfare. Lucky things are mostly peaceful. Many who come here come to a war already in progress. They don't live long."

"Why does this not reassure me?"

"Because it shouldn't." The Organ Grinder smiled. "Have some brandy. It makes one more relaxed, less nervous, and susceptible to the sounds of my accordion." He grinned. "However, as I am obliged to not use the accordion on you, I regret to inform you that you will merely get drunk."

"Sure, why not? I could use a little pick me up." I took the flask and sipped from it, handing it back to the Organ Grinder as I let the brandy burn down the back of my throat.

"That's better." The Organ Grinder said. I could feel my face flush red. I did feel better, and I wasn't thinking about whatever was happening to Bazelgard anymore. "We should go. There's no need to dawdle. I can't let the Enchanter be attacked by the Weeper in Shadows. I suggest you have some answers ready, Enchanter." I gave him a coy smile. I didn't realize how much I meant what I said. "She will be ready for answers when she gets here."

The Enchanter cackled as he looked me over. "There is a hint of poetry in your voice at times. Perhaps you are more like her than you think."

***

We walked back to the wagon in silence, making our way through cobbles and streets until we returned to the Organ Grinder's cart. The Squire of Cloaks sighed, got into the back, and slammed the door with a thud. I watched the Organ Grinder untie the horses, The Stone Preacher stood patiently by the side of the cart as I climbed into the driver's seat.

The Organ Grinder laughed and climbed up next to me, his grinning leer growing wider under his goatee as he lashed the horses. "Hah! A beautiful journey awaits us, with more rutting at the end of it to be sure!" The wagon jerked forward, and the horses picked up speed. Brutal hooves thudded along the rocky trail.

I turned to the Organ Grinder with a shake of my head. "Can't you understand he's in love with the dead? What you're doing is creepy!"

"Because it's a man?" The Organ Grinder fearlessly sneered.

"No. Because of the way that you do it."

"Dear child." The Organ Grinder ran his finger across my legs as I tried to wiggle away from him. "Your body was built for this. You should enjoy it. Perhaps you could even enjoy a little accordion music."

"Keep your hands on the reins. I'd hate to have to apologize for making you drag the cart while I feast on the roasted flesh of your horses. Don't think I won't do it, either."

"At least you are learning how to threaten people. And very creatively! I particularly like the idea of the smell of roasting horseflesh after a fine seduction, grinning as I watch a noble's face after having taken his wife, with the poor bastard laughing as I roast his horse, even as his wife begs me for more."

"My ears tire of this." I scowled.

The Stone Preacher glided alongside the cart as wheels clacked and popped. Rolling wood bumped and shook me as we creaked along the trail. Woods rose up around us as we thundered forward. I thought I heard the sounds of the Squire of Cloaks inside the cart, sobbing his shame into a pillow.

Chapter Twelve

The Jack of Forests Gives a Gift

The Organ Grinder drew us into a clearing as night fell. The moon shone on us, as if to make us feel colder. I dropped off of the cart with the basket over one arm, and moved to let the Squire of Cloaks out. The Organ Grinder got down as the Stone Preacher approached me.

I heard more painful whinnying as the Organ Grinder whipped the horses with a quirt. "You like the Organ Grinder too much." The Stone Preacher's voice ground in his throat. "You are giving him too much leeway. You must teach him a lesson, or you will rut with him in the dirt."

"Punch him. Don't break anything, because we need him, but I really can't stand the sounds of animals in pain."

"Then I shouldn't punch him," the Stone Preacher chuckled. "Unless you want to hear the monkey."

I pulled open the door to the cart. Inside, the Squire of Cloaks made little whimpering moans as he sat on the bed, his head buried in his hands. "Get up. It's time for dinner. The basket will make us something."

The squire gave me a broken look and shambled for the door, face pale and uncertain as his feet touched ground in the cold forest. The Organ Grinder moved over to a space near a rock and began to clean it off as the picnic basket dropped down off my arm. It made little cooing noises and hopped up on the rock, opening the lid as the Stone Preacher's gaze fell on it.

"I wonder what it will make?" the Stone Preacher rumbled. "It could murder you all at any moment. Clearly the creature is some form of unpleasant monster."

In response, the picnic basket spat out a roast turkey with all the trimmings and a large bowl of cranberry sauce. Then it hid behind me, growling.

The Squire of Cloaks chuckled as he sat down to eat. His face brightened as he tried to eat without looking at the Organ Grinder. He pulled out a knife from his belt and cut off some turkey, while the picnic basket rustled next to my leg.

"I'll wait." I petted the basket while warm smells rose into the winter air.

The monkey made odd chittering noises as it slipped out of the greatcoat and sliced off a piece of turkey with the knife on its tail, taking it and eating. Its eyes sparkled with glee as it chewed savagely, and hopped away from the rest of us.

I looked over at the picnic basket and sighed. "Do you have a knife and fork?"

The Picnic basket wiggled from left to right. The lid didn't open. "I think that's 'no.'" The Organ Grinder chuckled. Sinister eyes lurking under the lid glared hungrily in the direction of the monkey.

The basket settled next to my leg protectively. I turned to the Squire, who had been silent while eating slowly and methodically. "May I borrow your knife?"

The Squire looked up, as if to answer. Whizzing sounds and dull thumps throughout the camp stopped him. Arrows slammed into the fire and the Organ Grinder's cart. An arrow thudded into the turkey and knocked it from its rocky perch onto the monkey. A dry, hooting screech escaped into the evening.

The Organ Grinder reached for the turkey to rescue the piece of his soul. An arrow slammed into his hand. His face twisted in pain. His mouth opened in a bellow of rage.

I called my bow, turning to look at the Stone Preacher as he began running for the mad shapes of trees in the dark. I looked at my hand, but there was nothing there. I had drawn an arrow out. There was nothing to nock it to.

Laughter echoed in the trees as the Stone Preacher reached the edge of the forest. The Organ Grinder roared in tune with monkey-screeches. "Stone Preacher! Stay your wrath, or your fellow travelers, who are softer, will die!"

The Stone Preacher's rumbling legs ground to a halt. A slim man stepped out of the forest. His face was covered with rough stubble, and he wore an ugly cloak of green and brown. His handsome features were obscured by a thick scar that drove down over green, beautiful eyes. He was wearing a set of worn, well-oiled leather armor. A brownish hood covered his eyes, and he carried a thick bow over his back, black as the trees of the forest. He leaned against one of the towering spires of wood, and smiled, fingers resting against his sword arm.

I gazed into his eyes and saw nothing special. He was not the one. The picnic basket inched up against me and climbed up onto my arm, even as the man stared at it curiously.

"I am the Jack of Forests." He motioned with his hand to the rest of us. "Come forward slowly. For now, you are my prisoners."

***

They blindfolded us and marched us through the forest. Sounds of raucous laughter filled our ears as we were pushed over crunchy snow and hard ground. The air seemed cold, even in my boots. The picnic basket huddled on my arm, letting out low growls as I walked through the woods, making unhappy little noises from time to time.

I thought I heard the Squire of Cloaks whimper occasionally as we stumbled through the forest. From time to time, the Organ Grinder's monkey made little screeches. After what seemed like a few hours of marching, everything merged into dull thuds of the Stone Preacher's earthy glide.

We were guided over to a log and seated our feet shuffled against the wood for a second while our hands were tied behind us. The Stone Preacher's weight tilted the log slightly up. I could feel the warm heat from a fire nearby. I sweated as the boots shivered against the log.

The blindfolds were yanked off. The Jack of Forests stood in front of us, laughing with a cruel amusement. "I'd rob you all and butcher you, but quite frankly, I'm a little more interested in what some noble is doing in my forest with her entourage, hm?" He chuckled and idly fingered his bow. "Do you have a name, girl?"

"Not yet, I'm working on it. Can you get me out of these stupid ropes? I'm feeling a little tight, here."

"Perhaps you wouldn't be if you would let me loosen you up," the Organ Grinder leered.

One of the Jack of Forests' men punched the Organ Grinder in the back of the head.

"You must be the Organ Grinder." The Jack of Forests smirked. "You'll be having a lonely night. I have your accordion and your monkey. Just a precaution, you understand." He grinned, gesturing to a cage above in which the monkey was hanging, shrieking and howling. Several reddish burns where the hot turkey had fallen on it marked its flesh. The knife tied to its tail had been removed. The accordion was piled up with the rest of our weapons, even the Organ Grinder's stone knife. The Jack of Forests gave me a sly smirk. "You travel with a man of fell reputation and a murderous priest, who seems to like you enough to let you live."

The Stone Preacher rumbled as his rocky head turned to the Jack of Forests. "It is my obligation and my duty."

"Oh, you mean like your obligation and your duty to my love?" He sneered. "She is dead and I am not, so it would seem that you are about to fail again." The Stone Preacher hung his head with a rocky glower.

"You're going to kill me?" I said. "Listen, maybe if you told me what this is all about..." I clutched the picnic basket. "You're an archer – and a really good one, if you can pull that thing." I looked over the black bow for a moment. It was engraved with thick runes, worked into the teakwood in silver. It would take more than me to pull it, and he knew it.

"I'm thinking about it." A grin crossed the Jacks face. "I keep your bow from you because I can. I used to be the Prince of Archers, but I ran into a couple of bad turns."

The Squire of Cloaks made a haughty noise. "You rebelled against the King of Feathers. You are a traitor and a thief."

The Jack of Forests kneed the Squire of Cloaks in the stomach, and then drove his fist hard into the face of the older man. "I gave up my title because I don't want to live in a world where everything is based around how many people you can exploit." He scowled. "I just want to live out here in the forest with my little crew of miscreants, and steal enough to eat and pay for cheap prostitutes."

"Well, that's a lofty goal," I muttered under my breath. "Looks like Robin Hood really got the shaft."

"Oh, so it's Robin Hood, now, is it?" The Jack of Forests sneered. "I'm tired of being compared to some mealy-mouthed Englishman who was as much of a bandit as I. He wasn't even real! Or even worse, Scottish with an unpronounceable name!"

The Organ Grinder finally recovered from the blow to the head. "Perhaps, lass, you should threaten him with the picnic basket?" His eyes gave a merry grin.

"Shut up, or I'll feed you to it." I gave the Organ Grinder a scathing look.

"I love dissent among companions." The Jack of Forests laughed. He kicked the Squire of Cloaks in the groin. The older man doubled over in his cape with a gasping wheeze, spitting up blood. "It makes robbing them so much easier. You have a picnic basket that eats people, hmm? I see something new every day. How much do you want for it? Give me the basket and I'll let you go."

The picnic basket growled furiously, a wiggling wicker rustle struggling against my arm. "How did you stop me from calling my bow?"

"Oh, that." He chuckled. "I'm the Prince of Archers. I invented that trick. But I much prefer the Jack of Forests. If you like, I'll let you have an archery contest for your life, but it would be unfair to kill you when you know you'll lose."

"Don't take the deal," the Stone Preacher rumbled. "He'll just shoot you the first chance he gets."

"Tell you what." I risked it anyway. "Five shots, we both use your bow, winner walks away with it. And if, by some misbegotten chance I should win, I get to keep it, and you teach me how to shoot as well as you. If I lose, you get the basket and kill me."

The Jack of Forests chuckled and kneed me in the stomach. "Very well." I clutched my guts and doubled over, falling off the log. "In the morning."

I lay there in the snow, clutching my stomach and gasping for breath next to the Squire of Cloaks

"You're an idiot," the Organ Grinder glared down at me. "We're all going to die."

"I agree," the Stone Preacher rumbled. "However, you have survived longer than most."

I didn't know whether it was worth it to die just to get the two of them to agree. All I knew was that I had to figure out a way to trick him by morning.

***

I heard some rustling behind me, and someone untied my hands. "I'm the Warden of Staves. A shame the Jack is going to wipe you out." He was big and hairy, and smelled like dirty wheat. Fat thick lips and a burgeoning gut pushed away from his body. The Warden of Staves reached for his quarterstaff, a black thing covered with knobs and protrusions that made a dull thudding noise as he slammed the butt of it into the ground. Heavy leather armor, with black metal knobs all over it protected him from swords, and hid fat legs.

I got to my feet. "Untie them," I said. "If they're going to watch me die, they'll do so with circulation in their hands."

The Jack of Forests looked at me, then over at the Warden of Staves. "Promise me they won't attack?" He gave a coy smirk.

"Don't be ridiculous," I snapped. "The Organ Grinder's head is ringing, you've kidnapped his accordion and his monkey, and the Squire there can't seem to do anything but whine. The only reason you haven't confined the Stone Preacher is that he's a prisoner of the fact that the rest of us are soft and squishy."

The Stone Preacher scowled at me, his lips opening in a rocky crack. "I failed to protect his lady. It is a minor sore spot between us."

"Well, you could have warned me that you had these sorts of enemies!" I glared at the Jack of Forests. "How did all of this come about anyway?"

"It's really simple," the Jack of Forests said. "The Stone Preacher swore to protect the one I cared about most. I had an enemy trapped. Rather than face me in an archery contest my enemy knew he could not win, he agreed. During the contest, with his first arrow, he turned, fired, and put an arrow in her heart, then laughed maniacally while the Stone Preacher crushed him to pulp." He gave me a savage glance. "That's why I don't want to be the Prince of Archers anymore."

I sighed. "Well, at least his grievance is legitimate."

"You see?" the Jack of Forests snapped. "I'm not a malcontent. I'm just bitter!" He laughed raucously. "Of course, because they've protected you and coddled you, you have to protect them if you wish to find your true love because those are the rules." He smirked. "I'm really sorry I have to kill you. You know you have no chance, don't you?" He reached for a flask at his hip and downed everything inside as the others were untied.

"I could just have the Stone Preacher smash you into pulp," I said.

"He won't. He owes me a debt. His guilt is written in granite all over his face."

The Stone Preacher sighed, his voice a dim rumble. "I cannot, anyway. You agreed. It's the rules."

The Organ Grinder chuckled. "This is probably the end for you. You certainly can't rely on any of us for help, and the Squire is no help anyway." He reached down to run his fingers over the Squire's male pattern baldness, grinning as the man coughed on the ground. "Well, no help with that."

I thought about my handsome man's green eyes, and stared at the Jack of Forests for a moment, locking eyes with him. "Why wait until morning? Let's do it in the dark. Besides, at least if I'm shooting arrows with you, we'll see how good you really are, hmm?" I gave him a coy, seductive smirk. If I was going to die, I was going to die with my true love in my heart and an arrow nocked. It was better than anything else I could come up with. I had a plan. It wasn't very good, but it was better than no plan at all.

The Jack of Forests laughed a little bit. "I see you know how to even the odds." He chuckled. "It doesn't matter. I'll still kill you when I win."

"I'll spare you if I win." I said. "You'll make another bow, but I need all the allies I can get."

The Jack of Forests laughed. "Spoken like one of the nobility already." His voice became a wicked cackle. "Warden! Prepare the target!"

***

The Warden of Staves chuckled as he ushered the group forward, waddling a little while supported by the thick chunk of wood. We were surrounded by dirty men and women, a miserable group of bandits huddling in the snow. They gazed at me as the Warden waded forward, his feet crunching on snow.

"You're sure about this, now?" The Jack of Forests grinned. "It will be a shame to take your picnic basket and feed your corpse to it."

The picnic basket whined, and looked up at me, opening its lid. It slavered piteously, as if unable to stop itself.

I looked down at it and sighed, ruffling the handle for a moment. "Don't worry." I smiled to it. "I promise I'll have lots of flavor." A little whimper slipped out from under the lid. It sounded like crying.

"I have to admire the fact that you are so willing to die for your subordinates." He chuckled as the Organ Grinder looked upward, towards the screeching monkey in the distance, hanging in the wood cage. "In some ways, you remind me of my Elyse, before the Stone

Preacher failed to protect her." He glared at the Stone Preacher, whose hands were clenched into angry fists of cracking rock.

"Thanks for the backhanded compliment." I grinned.

The Organ Grinder grumbled. "We could kill at least fifteen.' He smiled up at the monkey in the cage. "They are rabble."

The Warden of Staves waddled forward, pulling out a large target made of straw and wood from behind a tree, and rolled it into position. "Here you go!" he thundered, whacking it with his staff. It made a dull noise, its painted circles indistinct in the dark.

"We should back up," I said. "This shot is too easy."

The Squire of Cloaks threw himself to his knees. "Please, good Prince of Archers! Spare me! I'm not with them! I serve the Queen of Castles! It was all the Organ Grinder, he made me do it! He made me! Please!"

The Jack of Forests looked down, laughing cruelly as he drove a steel-toed boot into the stomach of the groveling squire, who rolled back a little bit and heaved. "Right. Everyone back up. No one's going to be able to say the girl didn't die bravely." He chuckled. "I'll shoot first. I hate suspense."

The little group of bandits ushered us backward, with the Squire of Cloaks staggering to his feet and crawling towards the mob in the back, his face concealed.

The Organ Grinder laughed as I shook my head. "What's so funny?" I snapped.

He turned to me and sneered. "I thought he might have kicked *me*. I fear that without my accordion, I am merely a thug with a sap and a knife, and some superior ability to strangle people and punch them."

I shook my head. "Forgive me, Jack of Forests, but I must honor the laws of hospitality. One for one." The Jack of Forests stared at me as I turned, brought up my knee and drove it into the Organ Grinder's groin. The Organ Grinder's face purpled and he gritted his teeth.

"You bitch!" The Organ Grinder wheezed. "Abusing my obligations..." From the back of the mob, I thought I heard the Squire of Cloaks giggle.

The Jack of Forests let out a little cough as his men went for their weapons, and the Organ Grinder doubled over. "Don't shoot!" He shouted. "That was unexpected. It's all fine."

"Behave, Organ Grinder." I snapped. "I want some sleep when we camp at night, damn you!"

The Warden of Staves chuckled, and several of the bandits burst out laughing.

The Jack of Forests waved his hand, and everyone went silent. He called the black bow to his hand, and fired a casual shot into the center of the target. He wasn't even trying hard. "There!" He shouted. "Best of five! You cannot win, girl!" he smiled. "You had better prepare to be clubbed to death."

I laughed, and I ignited one of the boots. "You had better prepare to teach me some tricks." The men laughed as I lifted up my foot and brushed the arrow with it until it was aflame. "Give me that." I took the bow from the Jack of Forests. It was hard to draw. My teeth gritted as I pulled back the string. I sucked in half my breath and let the rest out as I fired. The arrow loosed from the string and slammed into the target, a flaming arc that thudded into the straw and wood.

The straw ignited as the Jack of Forests stared in disbelief. "You, you..." He sputtered. "You cheated!" There was a little trill of triumph from the picnic basket near my feet.

The little group of bandits all began laughing, as though a massive joke had been played. The Warden of Staves chuckled. "I think she won. Destroying the whole target! I could marry a girl who fights dirty."

"Fine." The Jack of Forests scowled. "I am defeated. I bow to your superior cunning."

"I'm spoken for," I said fiercely. I looked at the Stone Preacher, who was spending most of his moments trying to conceal a half-cracked smirk. The Squire of Cloaks was visibly mopping his brow.

"Bring down my monkey!" the Organ Grinder thundered. "Bring me my accordion! I shall have pleasure for all this eve!"

I glared at him. "Just music." I said coldly. "All is forgiven for the knee, since you're still among the living?"

"Oh, yes." The Organ Grinder scowled as if remembering how much pain he was supposed to be in. "I shall forgive this incident on account of the fact that we are all still alive. Do not try my patience again, or I'll pin you down and make you a slave to my accordion, as I have so many others." He twirled his mustache with a wicked grin.

We headed back to the campsite, led by the Jack of Forests. It looked as though we were going to be spending a few days there.

***

We settled in around a campfire, and the Jack of Forests knelt next to me with a wry smirk on his features. "You'll have to come inside my tent. Do not worry, nothing will happen. I know where your heart lies and I did lose."

I sighed and left the Organ Grinder and the Stone Preacher chatting with the bandits around the fire, and made my way towards the darkened tent with the Jack of Forests, carefully hidden between two trees. "No killing!" I said to the Stone Preacher over my shoulder.

"Is he really that murderous?" the Jack of Forests asked as I slipped through the flap of the tent. "I really had no idea."

"Only when you touch me."

The Jack of Forests followed, ducking into the tent and igniting a lantern with a match. He settled into a wooden chair, brought to life in the shadows. "Do you like the chair? I stole that one. I suppose it amuses you to see a prince stealing things."

"That depends on what you're a prince of around here." I smirked. "Since I'm sort of a gypsy, I really don't see anything wrong with stealing, if you can get away with it."

"You'll fit in fine." The Jack of Forests crossed his legs. "So you want to learn to be a better archer? Make no mistake: You're very good but the best archers have a little something extra." He took the black bow off his back and placed it into my hands.

"You drew it. It was hard for you, wasn't it?"

I nodded. "I thought because it was made for you. You're taller and probably a little stronger."

"Yes and no." He smirked. "It's because the bow is engraved with runes, including a rune of attunement. I painted it black so that no one would be able to see them. An archer's power is always in his bow. Or in your case, her bow. It's a good thing your breasts aren't terribly large. An archer can't afford to have those things get in the way."

"Thank you so much for complimenting me on something I'm a little disappointed about." I sighed. "I saw the runes. They were silver to me."

"You're welcome. Now, this bow is yours, so you will have to trace the runes while I turn them over to you. Make sure you see them all, and make you note of what they mean. If you are not careful, you will become a slave to the wood. A bow like this is made to hunt and kill." He smiled and petted it. "Quite frankly, the prospect of making a new one, now that I am older, thrills me. Perhaps you shall be lucky, and be a Princess of Archers indeed." He took the black bow and placed it in my hands, unstrung.

"Thanks." I lowered my voice to a whisper. "Do you realize that you're now a traitor whose head is worth somewhat less than five million half-lunas?"

"Five million." The Jack of Forests chuckled. "Oh, it is a great day to be considered a traitor! Perhaps this will raise the price on my head too! If one is going to be a bandit, one should be a *despicable* bandit, and part of that means getting a high bounty on one's head." His eyes sparkled with excitement. "Let us begin the teaching of passage, and trace these runes, that I might pass on your gift."

His hand took mine, and we traced the images and glyphs one at a time. Even though he spoke in a language I did not understand, I felt as if I understood anyway. Whatever magic the language held, it echoed inside my body and told me the bow was mine.

When it was over, I dripped with sweat, and so did he. We never did more than hold hands. The ritual was taxing. My clothes stuck to me. "Draw it." His voice was a whisper.

I reached for the bow and strung it, wrapping it around my leg, then drawing it up into a firing position. The bow was supple and almost weightless, yet I could feel every inch of strength running through its curves. "Wow." The runes of the bow crackled with bluish energy. I could see them in the light of the tent.

"You can dim that light if you want," the Jack of Forests said. "Don't worry. I won't return to being the Prince of Archers or take my bow back. I'm the Jack of Forests now."

"I have a stupid question." My throat quivered.

"What is it?" The Jack of Forests snickered. "You're very good at learning these things. Most people take twice as long for a ritual of possession."

"Where does the bow go when someone like you or I sends it away?"

The Jack's face grew somber, and he rubbed his chin. "I don't know. It was just a trick I developed. The runes of possession are things anyone can use."

"I should get some breakfast." Sunlight peeked through the doorway of the tent.

"Yes," the Jack of Forests nodded. "And then get some sleep."

I wandered out of the tent and found a place to sleep near the campfire. Others were sprawled around the logs in the early morning. The Organ Grinder snored there under his leather greatcoat. The monkey slept on top of his hat, flicking the knife-tail idly in its sleep. Some of the bandits had moved off to their tents, eager to avoid the Stone Preacher, who rested standing up in the shadow of one of the grimmer trees.

I huddled up against one of the logs and let my gaze flick over the granite features of the Stone Preacher. He seemed a little more distinct for a moment. Then the exhaustion of the day before claimed me. I sunk into a black, hot sleep. Just before I passed out, I felt the familiar rustle of the picnic basket settle up against me.

***

The Jack of Forests foot kicked me awake, and I could hear the boisterous laughter of the Organ Grinder echoing in my foggy head. The smell of cheap alcohol assailed my nostrils. The nudging of the boot in my stomach didn't help as my guts swirled. "What's that smell? It doesn't smell like breakfast."

"It is for them." The Jack of Forests grinned at me, as I opened my eyes to the Organ Grinder laughing and sharing drinks with some of the bandits. "It seems your bodyguard has endeared himself to several of my men."

"Let's hope he didn't endear himself too much," I muttered. "Is there anything to eat that isn't booze?"

The Jack of Forests thought for a moment. "I have some smoked meat and some moldy cheese. And there's a pitcher of beer in my tent that's a little better than the swill outside."

With a slight, rumbling glide, the Stone Preacher slipped up behind us. "There are days when I am fortunate that I do not need to eat." He gave a rattling chuckle.

I turned to the Stone Preacher and grinned. "We'll scrape the mold off the cheese and eat that, I guess."

"I have to take you into the forest today," the Jack of Forests said. "I assume that the Organ Grinder will be fine with my men."

"He's fine with any man, woman, or monster. Have them guard their body openings, and keep his accordion away from him until this is over."

"I will accompany you," the Stone Preacher said grimly.

Hearing that, the Jack of Forests turned to me. "You do not trust me?" The look on his face fell and his lip quivered savagely.

"It doesn't matter whether I trust you or not. The fact is, even if the Stone Preacher didn't feel he owed me something, I really wouldn't be able to stop him from doing anything anyway. It isn't that I don't trust you. It's that he doesn't trust anyone."

The Jack of Forests let out a dry chuckle. "Very well." He fingered the sword on his hip. "Let us off into the woods, then, and I will teach you the secrets of rune carving. Perhaps your friend the Stone Preacher could use some ornamentation?"

I shook my head as the three of us glided out of the camp, followed by the picnic basket. It hopped along behind us like a dog. I heard a little squeak as we made our way out of camp. I saw the tail of a squirrel disappearing under the lid. It didn't bother me anymore.

We made our way through the trees until we came to a small clearing. The green of the leaves was so dark that it was almost black, and the sun reflected off the dull brown branches with an eerie shine. "Here," the Jack of Forests said. "We'll sit here. These look old enough."

"Does that matter?" I looked around, imagining the small mouths of hungry monsters hiding in the foliage.

"The Jack of Forests nodded. "It does. The ancient places have more power. Together, we will carve a single rune, and then I will leave you to perform the basic invocations. Tomorrow, you will learn how to put them into arrows."

"Put them into arrows? You mean make magic arrows?"

"Be grateful that I did not shoot you with one." The Jack of Forests grinned. "The runes are potent. It is said to give up one's Runebow is to bring a horrible curse upon oneself."

"And you don't believe in that?" I raised an eyebrow. "Here?"

The picnic basket settled on a thick root, and howled at the Stone Preacher with a low growl. The Stone Preacher shook his head, and thinking we did not see him, leaned down to ruffle the lid of the picnic basket. A low rustling noise came from the basket. I would have said something, but I was learning that secrets were good to keep.

The Jack of Forests walked over to a tree. "What do we want it to do?"

"We could make it talk, but it's a tree. It would probably talk slowly." I grinned. "And making it sing and dance is right out. That thing's five hundred feet tall. It would probably crush us."

The Jack of Forests laughed. "You are fairly experienced for one who is not of the Otherworld. A lot of the stupid tricks from other fairylands don't really work too well here."

"Have you ever been to one of them?" I asked. "It seems there's a lot of bitterness among the locals about it."

The Jack of Forests shook his head. "Believe it or not, despite being a traitor, an outlaw, and all that other nonsense, I actually like it here. It keeps me alert." He took out a thick, stubby knife from his belt, and began carving something into a tree. "We're going to craft a rune of blue light. You're going to take this and carve it into the tree. The bow you now own also has this rune, but you need to be able to understand how it works."

"Why blue light?"

"When I was the Prince of Archers, I was less rough. But since you seem to be going in that direction, I figured it was a fair bet if you could cheat enough to win." He reached out for my hand and took it, and together, we traced some lines in the tree: a strange and unusual shape that was part *V*, part *X*, and part circle.

"That is the first rune," he said. "All others come from it. You will be on your own from here, as other runemakers are." He grinned. "When you make one of these, you put a little of yourself into it. It's not permanent, but it vests it with a personal touch."

"So it's like a dog marking its territory?" I asked.

"This is powerful magic," the Stone Preacher rumbled. "You should be grateful he is teaching you this. You will have to figure out what to do with it once he finishes."

"Nothing is simple," I muttered petulantly.

"Now for the invocation." The Jack of Forests tilted his head back, and the picnic basket gave a whistling noise and opened its lid. He let out a low murmur in a deep, strange tongue. I felt compelled to join him, our voices joining in the dark trees. The noise seemed to merge with something in the tree. I felt a low humming noise. From behind me, I could hear a low growl rumbling from inside the basket.

The tree crackled and shivered with a strange, bluish light, which sizzled and popped with tiny bursts of lightning. It illuminated the bark and the shape of the symbol, and hissed there, burning itself into the wood. "Is it supposed to do that?" I asked, blinking.

The Stone Preacher stared for a moment, and I could hear the crack of his jaw as he ground his teeth into a grimace. "No," he said. "I don't understand this at all."

The Jack of Forests face was silent as the sizzling light burned down, leaving the symbol to mark the face of the tree. Then he turned to me and said "This is very different. I don't know what it means either."

The picnic basket rustled forward and rubbed against my leg, and gave a weird trilling noise, as if trying to console me.

***

We made our way back to camp, the trees dark and angry as they glowered over us. As we made our way back, we could hear the sounds of boisterous laughter from the Organ Grinder and the Jack of Forests' men. "Someone's been making friends." I muttered.

"I shudder to think at what sort of thing they might be laughing about." The Stone Preacher rumbled as he glided behind us.

The picnic basket gave a low hiss, and a hungry growl. "Don't eat him." I said. "He's still useful." The basket let out a whining rustle.

The Jack of Forests strode into the clearing in front of us, raising his fist as he glared wrathfully at the Warden of Staves. "What's all this about?" His voice was rage and fury.

The Squire of Cloaks was tied to a tree, his cape being used to bind his wrists, while the men laughed and the Organ Grinder chuckled thunderously. The squire's pants were down around his ankles. Mugs of some steaming, alcoholic beverage were passed around. The bellow of the men's laughter echoed through the clearing. "They don't like the Queen of Castles very much!" the Organ Grinder bellowed, his face red from too much alcohol. "I tried to stop them! They were many and I was but one!"

Next to him, on the ground, came the drooling hiccups of a drunken monkey, the knife tied to its tail seeming to hold it to the earth.

I called for the bow and it came to my hand. Blue sparks of lightning crackling from the silver engraved symbol. I pointed it at the crowd. "Stop drinking." I nocked an arrow. "Or I'll shoot you all."

There was a moment of silence and fear. The only sound anyone heard was the whimpering of the Squire of Cloaks, his voice tinged with sadness and humiliation.

"She will," the Stone Preacher scowled, and clenched his fist. The ground wrenched under several of the men, and a number of them were hurled backward, the steaming liquid splashing skyward.

The Organ Grinder glowered. "This is how you treat your bodyguards?"

"And this is how you treat our honored associate?" I indicated the Squire of Cloaks, who whimpered a little bit, caught in the knotted trap of his own cape.

"Ahh, it's just a little subdual." The Organ Grinder's eyes lit up with a merciless fire. "He'll come to love it even more, sooner or later."

"Untie him," the Jack of Forests said with a yawn. "Or I'll let her shoot you. It's not my fault if her fingers slip." He grinned and slid an arm around me casually, as if testing the quality of my aim. I didn't falter.

The Organ Grinder stood and reached down for his monkey, scooping up the creature and opening his greatcoat. "Fine." He wobbled over to the Squire of Cloaks, and gently undid the cape and wrapped it around him. "Are you feeling better, sir?"

The Squire of Cloaks nodded with a pathetic whimper, adjusting his cape. "I am," he managed. He wiped a few tears away from his eyes, his ruined dignity apparent in the rumple of his clothes.

The Organ Grinder chuckled. "And thus we are all friends again, sharing our bounty and our rotgut!" He came over to me and thundered. "So how did your training go?"

The point of the arrow never wavered from his eye. "It went fine. I know a little bit about runecarving and invoking and getting magic to do what I want it to do. I also know that tomorrow, I'm training right here, out in the open, so this had better not happen again."

"The drinking?" The Organ Grinder laughed. There was a sickening belch and a hiccup from inside the leather greatcoat.

"No," the Jack of Forests said. "The buggering. As for the rest of you men, it would seem that you are violating some of my rules. If I catch anyone holding down this good squire, I'll apprentice you to a few arrows and hang you from a tree while you bleed out."

I put the bow away, laughing a little bit myself. "All's fair, then." I said. "What will you do for a bow while I have yours, and you make a new one?"

"That's easy." The Jack of Forests laughed. "One of my men will loan me something." He looked over to the Warden of Staves, whose belt buckle was conspicuously hanging open. "We should get some women here. I'm tired of hearing the grunting."

"Why doesn't that make me feel reassured?" Out of the corner of my eye, I saw the Squire of Cloaks slip into the forest to weep.

"You have his bow," the Stone Preacher rumbled. "And he is still the Prince of Archers. That makes you very impressive to them."

"Thanks. Let's get some rest and possibly some dinner."

***

Dinner was some sort of game animal, in a stew. The Jack of Forests dug it out of clay pots that the bandits buried in the earth. I didn't know what it was, but anything was better than starving. Greasy meat and sauce settled in my stomach. With the Stone Preacher watching over me, I lapsed into a hazy sleep.

The boisterous laughter of the Organ Grinder and the shouting of the men penetrated my sleep, along with the chittering of the Organ Grinder's monkey. I shuddered on the ground. There was a whispering rustle and an odd whine. My eyes snapped open, pained with dawn's light. The mouth of the picnic basket was right in my face. A long tongue slithered out and fiercely lapped at me.

"It's waking you up." The Stone Preacher rattled, staring down me with the Jack of Forests next to him. "That really put you to sleep."

I rubbed my forehead. "More like it made me sleep funny." The picnic basket nudged me up. "You're not hungry, are you?"

The Picnic basket shut its lid, as if to indicate that everything was fine.

The Jack of Forests smiled. "Today you're going to learn to craft a proper arrow." He held out a hand to pull me up.

"I've never really done that before. It involves hunting birds, doesn't it?" I got up and dusted myself off, and the picnic basket hopped up and down. It seemed very excited.

The Jack of Forests laughed. "Only when you're desperate. Come on."

I followed the Jack of Forests and looked over to the Stone Preacher. "Is there another picnic basket around?" I asked. "It's awfully excited this morning."

"There's a bucket. It doesn't move, so the basket hasn't shown any interest in it."

The Jack of Forests chuckled a little bit. "Oh, you've been working on him." He slapped his thigh. "The legendary Stone Preacher, cracking a joke."

"I didn't do anything." I said. "It's in his nature to be sarcastic."
My head throbbed from wooziness.

The Jack of Forests tilted his head, as if he had to think about
that. As I turned to look, I could hear faint sounds of the Organ
Grinder snoring, and the flopping thud of the monkey's knife tail
banging against the ground. The Squire of Cloaks huddled in
sleep, hands against his knees, making little whimpering sounds.

We walked over to the Jack of Forests tent, and he sat down
against the base of the nearest tree. "All right," he said, crossing
his legs. He drew an arrow out of his quiver. "You should come
here, and have a seat." The picnic basket raced over at once and
settled down. "Not you." The basket wiggled and gave an odd
rustle.

The Stone Preacher's neck made a rocky quiver. He scanned
the foliage above, but there was no sound or motion there.

"The Runes you carve on arrows will be much smaller," the
Jack said, taking one from his quiver. He reached down and took a
small knife out of his pocket. "It's very sharp. It will have to be to
cut steel or iron and mark it. Be careful. You will never get back
an arrow that you fire like this."

"Why not?" I asked.

"May I borrow your bow?" It was more of a command than a
question.

The Stone Preacher looked at the Jack of Forests, his eyes
narrowing with a small crick of rock echoing. "If this is a trick, it
will be the last arrow that you fire."

"Do you really think I would be so stupid as to try anything
with you standing three feet away?" The Jack of Forests laughed.
He took the knife and etched the rune into the arrow, his lip
quirking in a deliberate grimace. "You have archer's eyes. I can see
them. Remember what you see. I can only do this once, and I am
certain that you will take a long time to perfect this."

"What can I do with it?" I asked.

"You will learn." He said. "The same way I did. By trying and
understanding the nature of your mythology. My enchantments
never miss, but there is clearly more to yours than that.
Observe!" He launched the arrow skyward into the foliage, and
there was a horrible ripping sound of plants and branches, and
then silence.

"That's funny." I said. "Shouldn't it have stuck in something?"

Too late, the Stone Preacher's head turned.

The treetops rustled. A whistling dart of ice that slammed into the ground next to the Preacher. Mud and mulch thickened around his feet as I stared up into the blonde hair and iron mask of the Weeper in Shadows. "Amazing in life, in death your heart of steel shall rust away," she whispered. "Graceful as liquid you are, yet bound by your passion, you waver. Your love is nothing compared to my own. I shall break your heart into frozen shards." She twirled the arrow and hurled it into the tree next to the Jack of Forests, diving through the air.

The clank of chains and the rustle of spiked armor filled the forest. As the Stone Preacher struggled to move, I knew we were surrounded.

***

"Run!" the Stone Preacher thundered. "I cannot reach you." Rocky legs struggled in the frozen muck.

I turned to run as the Weeper dove. The picnic basket leaped into the air. My feet pounded as the clatter and clank of armor made their way toward the camp. There was a scream and horrid gurgle from the nearby woods. Something sounded like chains shattering bone.

The Weeper in Shadows tumbled to the arrowhead she hurled into the tree, spinning and kicking the picnic basket away. It made a rustling yelp and followed me, making pained whistling noises as we raced for the other side of camp.

The Jack of Forests reached out for the Weeper's leg, catching it and trying to hurl her toward the ground. As she fell forward, she moved into a cartwheel, grabbing his arm and chest with her legs and slamming into the ground. "Just like old times, most handsome of princes whom I do not desire."

The Jack of Forests rolled and tried to drive his elbow down, but she crossed her forearms and spun away, tumbling to her feet with the force of the block.

I shook the Organ Grinder, stinking of alcohol, to wakefulness. "Get up! She's here! She's here, damn it!" I drew back my hand and slapped him across the face. Under the coat, I heard the monkey screech. The Organ Grinder gave a lurching moan as bandits began drawing weapons and struggling awake. I couldn't see the Squire of Cloaks anywhere.

The Jack of Forests drew my bow and fired at her. The Weeper let out a low chuckle as she deflected the arrow of crackling lightning with her knife of ice. It sailed off into the trees and exploded, a dull roar that shattered branches and shrieked through the woods. "Call it!" he shouted. "It's not mine anymore!"

"A teacher always, so gracious in your ultimate loss." The Weeper's smile spread as she spun the ice knife around. "A gift as precious as you give should be shared with no one. You have shown me your weaknesses." Her tongue slipped out of her lips and ran across them.

I called the bow and fired, the arrow blasting towards her as I planted my foot on the chest of the Organ Grinder. The Weeper was as quick as a turn of her head. She hurled her knife towards it. There was a sparkling, powerful explosion. I was blown backward. I tumbled to the ground with a dull thud. I could feel my ears ring. My head spun.

Armored monsters were everywhere. Small groups of bandits struggled against single guards. The lash of chains and the ring of swords echoed through the clearing. The Jack of Forests struggled to his feet as the frozen knife returned to the Weeper's hand. He drew a sword, plain and unornamented, swinging it as he tried to disarm her. "Unfaithful wife!" he thundered. "You will give up everything for me? I hold you to your promise!"

"A promise forced is a promise undeserved," the Weeper responded coolly, and nimbly stepped aside. "You are nothing without your bow, and you have given it to her." She drew back the knife and tumbled forward, pinning the sword to the ground as ice grew along the blade. She spun forward with a brutal kick at the Jack of Forests, trying to drive a heavy boot into his midsection.

The Organ Grinder struggled to his feet. "Monkey!" he thundered. "There are soldiers everywhere! Kill some! As for me, I spy a lady who requires my attention." Grinning devilishly, the Organ Grinder reached for his accordion, rolling and scooping it up as a long, spiked chain slashed into the ground. The monkey leaped forward towards the Chain Hook Guard and drew back its tail, driving it through an eyeslit in the helmet and stabbing. There was a howl of pain from inside the armor, and a shriek of pleasure from the knife-tailed creature.

From the shadows, the Squire of Cloaks darted forward, leaping with his cape as the Weeper's kick snapped forward. It wrapped around her leg and threw off her aim. She tumbled with it, flipping forward and driving her other knee into the Squire's face. The force of the blow broke the Squire's nose and stained the

Weeper's greaves with blood. "So complicated in your broken heart, that I have no right to kill thee." she whispered as the Squire crumpled.

A Chain Hook Guard lashed out and grabbed me. Metal barbs dug into my wrist and pulled as I scrabbled for the bow. I called it to my hand. The guard yanked me away as I floundered, flopping along the ground towards it. I struggled to draw an arrow out of my quiver, and nocked something. I wasn't sure whether it was a stick or a rod or an arrow. I fired anyway. The shot rocketed towards the Chain Hook Guard and exploded in a bluish blast of lightning, knocking him away from me. It did not rise. My head spun, struggling to take things in. There was suddenly a growling picnic basket in its face, ripping and tearing. There was a weird metallic pop and a gout of blood. The guard's head disappeared into the basket. The basket made a hiccupping noise, and made its way to me, nudging me towards consciousness.

The Jack of Forests raced for the Weeper in Shadows while the Organ Grinder fitted his fingers to the grips of his accordion. The Weeper blocked her husband with a rolling leap, turning over and using the momentum to hurl the knife of ice at the Organ Grinder. There was a funny sound and a hiss as the air froze. The accordion ripped, letting out a frozen moan as the knife sought the Weeper's hand. The Organ Grinder cursed. "Witch!" he thundered. "Accordions are expensive to repair!"

The Jack of Forest's counterattack drove a fist into the mask of iron. She rolled away, catching the knife as she went. "Did you really think I'd allow myself to suffer at the hands of the Organ Grinder, sobbing for the rest of my life yet begging for his filthy touch?" Her iron mask scowled. She brought up the knife.

I began forcing myself to my feet, my ears ringing. There were screams as Spiked Wrath Men cut down the bandits of the Jack of Forests. Strange noises rang as a chain lashed by with a bandit attached, his intestines hanging out as he was dragged.

"Run! We have to run. There's too many of them!" The picnic basket fled at once, dodging slashes of the guards as it made for the edge of the woods, pausing only to snap up someone's missing leg and gulp it down.

The Jack of Forests leaped at the Weeper in Shadows. Even though the reach of the sword was longer, she parried every stroke, using the length of her leather-clad legs to deliver a kick to his midsection as one of the thrusts came down.

The Stone Preacher struggled in the icy ground. He balled his fists, bringing them down hard on the frozen ground to reach soft earth. Loud, splitting cracks of ice and dirt followed his punches. "Witch! Your bloody terrors will end! I will spit your intestines on a spike and curse your wicked King!"

The noise caught the ear of the Weeper, who shouted to her guards, "Kill as many as you can! The Preacher is freeing himself, in resonance and in thunder!" She let out a low, sinister trilling. I could hear muscular wings flapping from across the trees. From above, the massive, horse headed snake dived down, stinger lashing towards me as the Weeper flipped onto its back.

The Jack of Forests cursed, and staggered forward towards the rising animal. A Chain Hook Guard found him, and he batted the chain away. "Run!" he shouted. "Run now! There are too many! Men! We must retreat! There are too many of them!"

In the distance, the Warden of Staves screamed, lashing about him and battering his way towards the edge of the clearing. Wooden thuds caused howls of pain and strange moans from the Weeper's spiked soldiers.

I tried to roll away from the stinger. The hook dragged across my arm, seeping into my open wound, and withdrew, the powerful mount rising up as the Weeper chuckled. "Poison leaks into your veins, my sweet child. With it, all your beautiful dreams shall turn to empty sighs. I shall cut out your heart when you have nothing, and mount its frozen beauty in my collection." The iron mask gave me a jaunty smile as the rustling sounds of the beast flew up, into the sky and out of sight.

The Organ Grinder burst into a run, heading for the edge of the forest, pausing only to grab his monkey from where it stabbed into the eyes of a dead soldier. It waved its knifelike tail as he stuffed it into a leather pocket, and it began licking the blood from the knife, savoring it as I followed.

"The Squire!" I shouted. "Grab the Squire!" The Stone Preacher sank into the ground, and rose next to the Squire of Cloaks, a single stony hand picking him up as we ran for the edge of the forest and the cart. As we made our way through the woods, the lines of green and brown shivered with the faint whispers of the Stone Preacher's glide. I kept my eyes on the coattails of the Organ Grinder, leading us back to the cart and the speed of his ruined horses.

***

The Squire of Cloaks stopped bleeding when we reached the cart. The emaciated horses grazing comfortably by the side of the road. Everyone was breathing hard except the Stone Preacher. There was no sign of the Jack of Forests or the Warden of Staves. "Do you think they made it out?"

"I do not know." The Organ Grinder raced to the cart and grabbed the reins of the horses. "Everyone get in! We flee like cowards, but we survive to flee again!"

The Stone Preacher glided forward toward the cart and unceremoniously hurled the unconscious Squire of Cloaks onto the bed in the back, slamming the door. He began gliding down the road as the Organ Grinder lashed the reins. I grabbed for the cart, pulling myself up into the seat. The picnic basket settled into my lap. The tongue lolled out of the lid with a dry wheezing sound.

"That was tiring." I was short of breath. I pushed a layer of sweat aside from my forehead, and stared at the wound on my arm. It was bruised. Purple liquid gathered around the edges of the wound. I gripped the side of the cart. It shouldn't have been that hot. The cold gray sun provided almost no heat. The wind whipped at my face as the cart raced down the road.

The Organ Grinder lashed the horses faster, his teeth gritted. "Onward, miserable beasts! You shall have no feast tonight, only a taste of the lash!" He whipped the animals as the wagon sped up. My breath was beginning to catch. Things were turning blurry.

"I don't feel so good." It was hard to get the words out. My tongue was thick and my skin felt wet. The picnic basket pressed against me, keeping me in my seat as the forest blurred with my vision.

The Organ Grinder turned to look at me, staring at the wound on my arm, and he let out a guttural laugh. "You've been poisoned, lass!' He bellowed, slowing the cart as we came around a curve in the road. "Preacher! We need a plan! A good one! Wake the Squire! Perhaps he knows someone!"

The Stone Preacher stopped as he heard the wagon slow, his rocky tread crashing back towards us as the sound of his footsteps hammered against my ears. His voice was a dull mumble. I wobbled, and heard the picnic basket whine and growl against me.

I toppled from the cart and fell into the ruts of the trail. The world swirled around me as my fingers scrabbled in the ground, scrabbling against the wooden wheel. Then I coughed up something. My vision faded in and out as I sank into a burning haze.

Chapter Thirteen

The Death of the Squire of Cloaks

Something picked me up, and cradled me/ I heard the whinny of the horses. I couldn't move my fingers. In my throat, something caught. I heard the rumble of the Stone Preacher. "You've been poisoned." His voice faded in and out as I heard the Organ Grinder's boots strike the road. Each footstep and word was a mountain crashing around my ears.

I remember gasping a few times, and hearing the Organ Grinder shout something that sounded like "healer" and "alchemist" into the door of the cart.

By the time the Squire responded, all I could hear were mumbles and moans. A cold feeling grew in the center of my chest. I clutched the Stone Preacher's rocky arm, and made little choking noises. Then I spit up something else and things were dark for a while.

***

When I woke up, I was lying on a bed under multiple blankets. The picnic basket was settled at my feet, trilling. It slithered up the bedclothes to lick my face. The room was small and cramped/ I could hear the Organ Grinder and the Stone Preacher arguing with someone. It was a voice I didn't recognize. The Squire of Cloaks sat next to me, shaking his head and mopping my brow with a handkerchief. His nose looked much better.

"Oh." He withdrew.

"...take her now that will wake her swiftly!" The Organ Grinder's voice roared through the door. "Just slip her legs right over my head and take her! She'll wake in an instant, and her smile will last the rest of her life!"

The picnic basket growled lowly as the Stone Preacher spoke. "You will do nothing of the kind. You know the rules."

"Fie on the rules!" The Organ Grinder scowled. "This is the most dangerous thing I have ever done! I shall expect some compensation when it is all over!" I could hear the muffled screeching of the monkey through the door.

"Gentlemen, your friend has been tending to her." The voice was old and wheezing, as if buried in a hundred coffins before being let out to breathe air. "Let us see if she is awake, before your treatment gets you bitten by the basket. The creature disturbs me."

The door to the room opened. An emaciated man peered in. He was bald, with a strange tattoo on his forehead. He dressed in thick fur robes that hung loosely on a gaunt frame. Savage green eyes glared at me while I settled in the bed. He bowed graciously from the doorway. A necklace slipped out of the heap of furs, and drew my attention down to thick iron boots on his feet. The boots were bolted with odd clasps around his calves. "Ah, the lady is awake!" He raised a hand. "You see, Organ Grinder? There is no need for your crude methods!" A disturbing leer punctured his graceful bow and he rose.

"It does not matter," the Organ Grinder sneered. "I always get what I want in the end."

The Squire knelt before the man. "Good sir, I fear the lady needs more rest."

I propped myself up on my elbows. "The lady wants out of bed!" The picnic basket leaped forward to lick my face again, and the long tongue slithered over me. I struggled out from under the blankets. "How long have I been unconscious?"

"Two weeks." The man smiled. "I am the Count of Alchemists, and I do believe you are cured. Would you like some muffins? Alchemy has many uses, after all!" His eyes twinkled. "Caution, good Squire, caution!" He wheezed, flicking his head back and forth.

"You need to let him stand. That's what you've forgotten."

The Count cackled, "Oh, yes! That's it! You have leave to rise, Squire of Cloaks."

The Squire of Cloaks rose. "Thank you, my lord. It was getting uncomfortable bending."

"Well, what you do with the Organ Grinder in his cart is your own business, my lad!" He thumped the Squire of Cloaks cheerfully on the back. "And you shouldn't thank me. You should thank the lady!"

"Could I get a shirt?" The Organ Grinder and the Stone Preacher peered into the room. I yanked the cover up over my breasts and scowled at the Organ Grinder. "Don't even try it!"

The Stone Preacher let out a gravelly chuckle. "I think you just, as she might say, got compensated." Then he slammed the door and waited for me to get dressed.

***

The Stone Preacher opened the door, holding a loose-fitting peasant shirt, and daintily placed it on the bed. "If you wish to retain your modesty, the Squire and I should depart."

"Of course." The Squire dipped into a smooth bow and stood up. "We should not tarry here, for our journey is long."

"She may require bed rest," the Stone Preacher rumbled. "She might not even be able to stand up."

I threw the shirt on under the covers and staggered out of bed. My knees buckled. I clawed my way up against the quilts, looking at the two of them. "That's one for not standing up. Can I get a crutch or something?"

"Wait here." The Squire slipped out of the room while the Stone Preacher guarded the door.

There was a heavy thump and a yelp from the Squire of Cloaks. I saw the Organ Grinder's hand spank him on the rear. "Good sir! We need a cane!" The Squire of Cloaks called out to the Count.

"All the better to spank you with!" The Organ Grinder laughed at the Squire, a lewd look on his face. I managed to pull myself up onto the bed to sit.

"You be silent!" The Count of Alchemists staggered forward under heavy robes. "I have this crutch here that should do. The restoratives should work soon, within a day. Until then, I'm afraid you'll have to limp about on this." He winced. "I have never been so disgusted with a visitor as I have with this Organ Grinder. Squire, how much longer must I endure him?"

The Squire of Cloaks hung his head, as if searching for an answer. "I do not know, my lord." He took the cane from the Count of Alchemists and walked it over to me, shaking his head. "My lady, please. I can bear his touch no longer."

"I'll speak to him." I said. "If you could leave the room?" I paused briefly. "Stone Preacher, if you could bring the Organ Grinder in here at once?" I folded my arms and settled on the bed. "Preferably in a hammerlock?"

The Stone Preacher glided forward, ahead of the Squire of Cloaks, and grabbed the Organ Grinder by the throat. There was a choking screech from the monkey. The Stone Preacher dragged him in, putting the big man into the requested hammerlock with thin granite arms. "Our lady has need of you… in no manner that you will enjoy."

"This is your last warning." I said coldly to the Organ Grinder. "You should unhand the Squire of Cloaks and free him from your wicked spell, or I'll cut off your magic wand and feed it to the picnic basket." I gave him my most sincere grin. The picnic basket opened its mouth, wide with teeth. I yanked on the handle. "No eating. You've eaten enough."

The picnic basket let out a low whine.

The Organ Grinder's face winced. "It shall be as you wish." He grimaced as the Stone Preacher squeezed hard on the arm, the bearded face red with pain. "My lady, my lady, please! Make him stop!"

"It really is no worse than what you inflict upon others, but it shall be as you wish." I assumed a haughty. "Release him!" I let tones of arrogance creep into my voice. The Stone Preacher let go of the Organ Grinder and stood up.

The Squire of Cloaks passed me the cane with more than a little glee on his face.

"Thank you," I said. "Really, I just want some sleep. I can't stand the noises of you rutting with everything within five miles of us, and we're already fighting half of this crazy kingdom. We can't afford to fight angry husbands and wives too!" I put my hand on the crutch and staggered up. "So we're stuck here until I recover from whatever this is?"

"It is the poison of the leeching of love…." The Count of Alchemists smirked. "Otherwise known to dimwitted locals as heartbreaker venom." He gave a chuckling smile. "I assume you've seen the creature that produces it?"

"Oh, yes. And the woman who rides it." I sighed and leaned on the cane, hobbling out of the bed. "What exactly does the poison do, anyway?"

"It consumes you from within, using your passion to burn you up." He gave a cackling grin. "Very nasty! Your friend the Organ Grinder could use some." He gave a wry chuckle. "The creaking of the cart keeps me awake, too."

The Organ Grinder grinned, still rubbing his arm where the Stone Preacher had squeezed it. "Do you have anything for purple bruises, sir?" He winced, glowering at me. "I think the Preacher stunned the monkey."

"Good. I can't stand the hooting sounds of triumph when you rut, either." I glanced at the Count. "So if you know about the creature, do you know anything about its rider?"

"The Weeper in Shadows is the assassin of the King of Feathers," the Count of Alchemists wheezed. "Bear with me, young lady, for I am old and feeble, and may not get all of the details straight. She, if she really is a 'she' and not some horrible beast in a sheath of flesh, carries out the wishes of the King in all matters such as this. You must have made some enemies along the way."

"That sounds uncomfortable. What about the King? What's he like?"

"Very few have ever seen his face, dear child. He wears a leather mask when he goes out in public, but I am certain that you know that already. He doesn't like new appointments. Now that the Queen of Castles has confirmed you, he will be doing his best to kill you until he accepts you."

"This land is brutal!" I snapped. "One would think he would want it pacified." For the first time since I had awakened, I felt the dimming of my passion. Something not quite right pricked at my chest.

"That's the problem with old orders and hereditary systems, dear girl!" He chuckled. "Everyone wants to hold on to what they have. If one gives something, one has to take it away from someone else, probably by force. Although the King is feared, if all the nobles rose up against him, there would be nothing he could do." He grinned. "So unless you can find your true love and marry yourself off, which you should do for no other reason than you want to, I'm afraid you're going to be hunted down like a rabid dog. Set afire, too!"

"That's not very reassuring," I said.

"It's not meant to be," the Squire of Cloaks said. "These gentlemen obey you out of obligation. I must leave these lands before the King of Castles finds me and punishes me."

"Punishes you?"

"For betraying him with the Organ Grinder." The Squire sobbed. "I am so ashamed, but none can resist the tones of the accordion." He buried his head in the quilt near my legs, still weeping.

The Organ Grinder merely leered with pride. The picnic basket growled at him. His monkey peeked out from under the coat and hissed, flicking the knife attached to its tail back and forth, as if threatening the basket.

"You're not winning this argument. If you wish to fulfill your obligations to me, you will have to obey me in this." I glowered at the Organ Grinder, then turned back to the Squire of Cloaks. "Don't worry. We'll get you out," I said sadly.

I felt a strange sense of isolation, and leaned on my crutch. "Let's see what the Count of Alchemists has outside my bedroom." I pulled myself forward, threw open the door, and stepped into a chaotic mess of sounds and objects.

***

I stared with the wonder reserved for museums and old churches. The high, vaulted ceiling kept in a million unusual smells that assaulted me from all directions.

The Count of Alchemists turned to look at me, while I leaned against the doorframe, gaunt and haggard. "Well, then, I see you're mostly up and about!" He gave me the condescending look that grandfathers give to people who are not their grandchildren.

"I just wanted to see it," I said eagerly, looking around the room. We were in a vast wooden longhouse. Tables were laden with smoking beakers. More than a few open flames burned beneath bubbling pots. A faint smell of strange earth smoldered in the room. Some dry hisses and pops came from tubes that decanted odd-colored liquids into bottles. The tables were made of shiny, black wood, reflecting the bottles that danced with the light of flame.

"Well," The Count of Alchemists spread his arms, giving a wide grin. I noticed he had a few teeth missing. "Do you like it?" He bowed, smooth and gracious, as if it came from a lifetime of experience.

"It's..." I had to think of a word as heard the Stone Preacher glide up behind me. The picnic basket rustled against my leg. "...different."

"Not so different." He chuckled. "In the world that you come from, much of this, people don't believe in. But here... here all of these ingredients really do have magical properties."

"So all that eye of newt and wing of bat stuff really works?" There was a funny bubbling sound. A noise erupted from one of the strange tubes.

The Organ Grinder limped up behind me, wincing in pain. "Oh, yes, it does. Do you know the monkey is still unconscious from the beating the Stone Preacher gave me?"

"A fact for which we are all grateful," the Stone Preacher rumbled. The picnic basket gave a wiggling rustle in assent.

"Oh. Your potion is boiling over." I indicated the hissing tube to the Count of Alchemists. He turned and raced for it, grabbing it and getting out a cork and sealing it, quickly dripping some hot wax over it from a nearby pot.

"Was it important?" The Stone Preacher rattled a little bit.

The Squire of Cloaks gazed at the Count. "One would assume so." He murmured. His voice was filled with relief, and his features seemed to be a little brighter.

"What is it?" I asked.

"I was decanting my missing teeth into an elixir with highly explosive properties." He cackled. "One should do something with them after they fall out, after all."

"So you drink it and explode?" I asked. "Isn't that a little bit unproductive?"

"No, no," he said. "It explodes into a giant whirl of teeth, consuming everything in its path for about... about..." He stopped. "I don't know. Anyway, it's not important. The important thing is that it explodes!" He let out a jolly laugh.

The Stone Preacher, the Organ Grinder, and the Squire of Cloaks all looked at each other. Not one of them seemed the slightest bit surprised. They all wore looks of worry as though their days were numbered if we spent too much time here. At my feet, the picnic basket gave a rustle that sounded vaguely like a terrified whimper.

"Oh, how much longer are we going to be here?" I asked. "I do have someplace to get to."

"Well, you should be up and about in less than a day if I can find this heartbleeder root." He said with a smile, rummaging through a table of ingredients and mumbling to himself.

"He doesn't have any," the Squire of Cloaks said. "He told us that two days ago."

The Count of Alchemists scratched his bald head, and idly stroked his tattoo. "Ahh, yes. But I know where some can be picked."

"You can't be serious." I scowled. "You expect these people to just drag me out into whatever misery lies beyond this lab, and go poking through the forest for herbs?"

"There isn't much choice in the matter." The Count of Alchemists sighed. "I'm afraid if you don't go out there and get the root, you'll likely die."

"Can't someone else get it?"

"Heartbleeder root can only be picked by women, and you're the only one here." The Count of Alchemists raised an eyebrow and tapped the tattoo on his forehead again. "It's one of those magical rules I don't fully understand. I only need to know what it does to make the potion. I don't have to care about why it is!"

"What made you people think it was safe to come here?" I turned to the Squire and put my hand on my hip, supporting myself with the crutch.

"He was the only one with the talent within range," the Organ Grinder sighed. "The King of Alchemists is hundreds of miles away, and the Duke of Alchemists, well he's quite insane. His wife was easy to bed."

"Thank you so much for explaining. So where is this root?"

"It lies in a forest clearing, where it is guarded by the Tree of Bleeding Axes," he said with a sigh. "I probably should have told you that first, shouldn't I?"

"It might have been nice." I limped forward to extend a hand, and performed a makeshift curtsey while on the crutch. I let my hand slip around the vial of exploding teeth, and slipped it into my peasant shirt. Firing a bow would be too difficult, but I might be able to throw something that exploded.

"What does a Tree of Bleeding Axes do?" I asked the others, shifting my body so none of them saw that I had stolen the Alchemist's elixir.

"I'm not sure," the Stone Preacher said. "Still, given your remarkable record of survival, I am certain that there will be no trouble in defeating it." He gave a low, creaking bow. The rocks cracked at his torso a little bit, and reformed.

The Organ Grinder chuckled. "Pah! We'll carve it into logs and bring it back for him to make potions out of."

"I could make arrows out of it," I offered. "There is nothing like the arrows you make yourself!"

"Yes, indeed!" The Count of Alchemists laughed. "Now where did I put my gravy?" He rummaged through the table as the Squire of Cloaks nudged us toward the exit.

***

From the outside, the longhouse appeared built into the side of a hill. It was brown, with dried grass and a thin coating of snow and ice on top of it. The forest was thick with trees. I heated my boots to keep myself warm, and limped after the others on my crutch, panting as I walked. "So first we beat up a giant plant, and then I can pick this flower? This sounds really stupid. Like, get ourselves killed stupid." Above us, I could practically feel the moon beating down, echoing my answer with fear.

"If you want to live," the Stone Preacher rumbled. "You should ask fewer questions and stay out of range of the tree."

"You've heard of trees like this?" We descended the hill, the picnic basket making odd trilling noises. We passed a lumpy looking sign that read *Keep Out!* with a skull beneath it. "I see our host is both malicious and friendly. How did you get him to cooperate?"

"Well, magic trees have magic wood, so you should be very excited!" The Organ Grinder grinned, and the monkey hooted. Behind me, the basket shifted left and right, as if looking for threats. If I slowed down too much, it gave a gentle nudge. "We got him to cooperate by threatening to mix all his potions – at once!" Something in the forest whistled, deep, hungry, and alone.

The forest was overgrown and choked with weeds. Wounded black limbs thrust up against the sky, leafless and cold. A sheet of ice covered the ground. As my boots melted white, I pushed across the cracking ground with my crutch, tilting my head. "Wouldn't that have killed us?" I shouted forward to the Organ Grinder.

"Yes!" The Squire of Cloaks smiled. "But it was an effective blackmail tactic."

"Which one of you evil geniuses came up with it?" The picnic basket stuck itself under my foot, enabling me to get over a rough knob of wood merged with the thick grass.

"It was the Squire," the Stone Preacher rumbled grimly. "I fear the Organ Grinder has been... rubbing off on him." He grinned. There was a sound like slate cracking under a hammer. I winced a little bit at the joke.

The picnic basket hopped about, as if burned, and coughed up four large biscuits and a trough of gravy, which spilled into the cold grass. "Oh," I reached down to soothe it. "Sorry." The basket gave off a little clatter, and then rubbed against my leg.

We trudged on through twisted trees, and stepped our way around a murky pond, frozen in winter. I thought I could see faces trapped in the ice. When I stared too long, the Stone Preacher glided back, and pulled me along through the woods.

***

"So what's all this about the Duke of Alchemists?" I asked the Organ Grinder as we made our way through the forest. The picnic basket nudged me constantly for close to a mile. Even with the warmth of the boots, I didn't have much strength left.

"We're here," the Stone Preacher said. "Do not let the tales of the Organ Grinder's exploits seduce you into his heretic's bed." He leveled a scowl at the Organ Grinder. "Look you into the valley there."

The Organ Grinder moved to say something, but his eyes were captured by the massive thing before him. Our gazes followed.

I took a sharp breath. I stared at a knotted, tangled mass of bark and leaves, all brown and covered in sharp strands of blue ice. Dry brown cracks in the thick wood rose up to the sky. The hooked multitude of dry, frozen limbs sprouted downward from the thick, wide trunk. Ice shone at the edges where some of the leaves should have been. When I squinted hard, I could see faint tinges of red through the blue ice, as if something bled there.

I flicked my eyes down to the base of the tree, and saw a little mass of ice-covered blossoms, red and orange, growing through frost with determined fierceness. They were lodged between two roots of the tree. I looked over to the Squire of Cloaks. "That's what we're looking for, isn't it? We have to get right up next to it?"

The Squire nodded, more determined than I had ever seen him. "Indeed, dear girl," he said with a gentle smile.

"Can I ask another question before we go closer?" I looked nervously over at the Stone Preacher, and then back at the massive branches.

The Stone Preacher nodded, his neck making a rocky crack. I continued. "Is it intelligent? Is this going to try and kill us like everything else I've seen here?"

The picnic basket made a hungry growl. Its tongue slithered out for a moment before giving a disappointed whistling noise.

"It probably will," the Organ Grinder responded." "As we have no axes, I shall release my monkey upon it first!" He unbuttoned his coat, and reached in to grab the monkey. It huddled in his pocket and refused to come out. "Out, monkey!" He thundered. "Can you not climb! Are you not the spirit of the Organ Grinder?

Go!" He drew the creature out and hurled it towards the tree. The monkey let out a chittering howl. It grabbed on to the thick wood and skittered up.

There was only silence from the tree. The monkey chittered and cheerfully began swinging from a branch. The tree barely shifted under his weight. "Well," The Squire of Cloaks smiled. "It seems this might be a little easier." He began sauntering down the hill. The Stone Preacher glided along next to him, and put his hand on his shoulder, stepping in front of the massive dark wreck.

"I do not think so," the Stone Preacher rumbled as I brought up the rear, nudged and shoved by the picnic basket.

The Organ Grinder laughed and clapped his hands. "I do believe the tree is merely trying to lure us in!" he said in a joking tone. "Come, monkey! We'll soon put this to rest! Go pick the flower, girl!" He cackled throatily.

There was a faint sound of cracking ice, and a horrible wrenching of wood and bark. The monkey was hurled off into the darkness of the forest, a wild shriek echoing from its lips. Bark writhed and shifted, and the limbs of the tree began to quiver and shake, as eyeballs opened on the ends of the branches. Ice sheared off to reveal sharpened, thick axe blades that swished and writhed. In the center of the tree, a vast, sideways maw loomed, grinding with teeth and boiling red bile.

"Forget everything I said about unlucky transformations!" I shouted. I began limping backwards as the picnic basket charged.

The massive thing let out a horrid whistling noise, baleful and cold, bringing down axe blades towards the Stone Preacher. Powerful, rocky arms reached up to intercept the branches. In the branches, the monkey screeched. The picnic basket dived aside from a thick limb as several axe-tipped branches rose, preparing to fall on us.

Massive branches swung. Axes fell in shades of red, hacking down in the dirt as I limped backwards. As an axe descended, the Squire of Cloaks gracefully vaulted into the air and turned his cape, catching the wet weapon at the end of a branch. The cape moved, seemingly of its own volition, slamming the thick metal wedge into the ground.

The Organ Grinder dived aside as one of the axe blades rammed into the ground, throwing up clods of frozen earth. Wet blood sprayed from the tip of the cleaving branch. "You will pay, tree, for hurling my monkey!" He began racing forward, drawing the heavy revolver out of his greatcoat, and fired into the massive trunk.

There was a wet spray as the tree began pushing the Stone Preacher down into the earth. Red blood spurted from gunshot wounds as it ripped through bark and wood. The Stone Preacher let out a dull, rumbling laugh. "You were once human." He chuckled as the tree roared. "You can be killed." His feet sank into the cracking, frozen earth. He squeezed hard at the axlike branches, driving fingers into thin bark above wooden hafts. The eyes at the ends of the branches bulged, as if under pressure.

"Now!" The Squire of Cloaks shouted as the tree drew the ax back, yanking him skyward as the cloak trailed in ribbon-threads, knitting around the limb.

I charged forward, leading with my feet as the boots of fire roared to life. A powerful howl came from the open mouth of the tree as a long, sideways tongue slithered out of it, wrapping around the Organ Grinder's waist. The Stone Preacher was half-sunk into the earth from the force of heavy branches. Another axe-blade lunged down at me, hacking as I struggled to step aside.

There was a powerful gurgle as the tongue released the Organ Grinder. A gross wooden sound clattered as the ax slipped away from its arc. The Stone Preacher flew upward into the sky from of the creature's strength. The Squire of Cloaks flew into the air above as the might of the tree forced the magical cloak to unwind. He slowly floated groundward, out of the reach of chopping tree-limbs. When I looked down, I saw the picnic basket, digging its teeth deeply into the gunshot wound the Organ Grinder made. Short, stubby legs struggled as one of the large, thick axe-blades hacked downwards towards it.

"Look out!" I shouted. The basket leaped away with a chunk of the tree in its teeth. Wood and human flesh mingled in its mouth as it swallowed and gulped. The axe retracted. I dove for the flowers at the base of the tree, watching as my burning boots smoked in front of the creature. I reached down, and yanked with all my strength at the small blossoms. A few of them came away in my fingers.

The Organ Grinder struggled to his feet, woozy as the tongue retracted. The thing's tongue was around my waist. The muscular, slithering organ crushed me in its grip. The Cloak of Runes barely resisted it. I could hardly even concentrate enough to call an arrow, let alone use the bow.

The Organ Grinder leaped, and began to wrestle with the wet, sticky tongue. His arms gripped it. An axe flashed down towards his back; wood cracking as branches flailed.

The falling Stone Preacher grabbed a branch and snapped it off. Several axe blades hacked around the picnic basket, wicker shivering as it dodged reddish metal wedges. Blood from axes dripped across the basket as it dashed out of range. Wicker gulped down wood and flesh, licking itself clean of blood flecks. It let out a horrid belch that reeked of the marsh and wetlands. If I lived, the food in the morning would be amazing. The Stone Preacher crashed into the ground, face first.

With brutal rage, roots wrenched free of the ground. A horrid crackle of branches and axes breached earth. The thing began to walk, lumbering towards the Organ Grinder. The long tongue drew itself back into the sharp-toothed mouth. Wet blood leaked from the broken branch, the eyeball at the end glassy and dying as the axe blade shuddered there.

The Squire of Cloaks landed near the axe, the blinking, twitching eye still red with blood. He picked it up, as another pair of axes from the massive, branched tree swung down at him. He dodged one, and his cloak gracefully brushed the second aside. He struggled to lift the axe, racing forward in the muddy, blood soaked ground. "You'll not have her! The Queen of Castles commands it, though I love her husband! I shall kill you, ungrateful beast!" He drew back the axe and hacked at the long, fleshy tongue. It burst forth with red gore as the Organ Grinder pulled, jamming his fingers into the wound and tearing from within.

The tongue released me. I crashed to the ground, struggling to get to my feet as the Stone Preacher forced his head out of the mud and muck. The Organ Grinder was drawn towards the gnashing wooden maw, dragged by the huge mass of tongue. I reached for the stolen bottle inside my blouse, dug it out, and hurled it with all my might. The Organ Grinder struggled to crawl away.

The mouth closed around the strange concoction, and there was a dry gulping sound, followed by a confused, deep murmur. The creature lumbered forward, raising a massive wooden foot to crush the Organ Grinder, who dove away. The Stone Preacher leaped under it, lifting up his arms to stave off the massive blow. There was a wet, sucking noise as the foot slammed down. The Stone Preacher was driven deep into the ground below as the Organ Grinder struggled to regain his feet.

Axes whipped towards the Squire of Cloaks.

The Squire threw out his cloak. The weave tattered into a thousand strands as it wrapped around the cluster of axes. The sideways mouth bellowed a helpless, desperate roar as fabric wrapped around it, locking tight. The Squire screamed aloud as he was dragged about by his shoulder epaulets. He slammed into the wooden branches just above the eyes. A spray of red gore burst forth as his body crushed one of the orbs to pulp, the Tree of Bleeding Axes a victim of its own strength.

The creature brought its foot down again on the Stone Preacher, trying to drive it further into the muck. It let out a horrid, dry belching noise. A booming roar came from inside it. Sharp, small teeth blasted outward from the mouth, spraying wood in all directions as a gout of flame burst forth. The splintered maw roared in a dying whimper. The creature tilted back, split in two from the explosive blast. A wretched gout of purplish gore and ichor exposed dull thuds of a massive dying heart in the core of branches and bark.

The immense tree grew silent, broken and shattered in the depths of the forests, dripping its dark core of human flesh.

"Did you get the flower?" The Stone Preacher asked. I raised my arm and showed it to him, clutching it desperately as if it were a part of my hand.

"Good." The Organ Grinder gave a wicked grin. "Monkey! Come out! It is time to celebrate! Soon our lady will be healthy, and once again a fair target for my accordion!"

In the distance there was a whimpering, desperate hoot.

"It seems we made it through and everyone survived!" The Squire of Cloaks grinned. "Let us return to the Count of Alchemists. It seems that our potion for the lady awaits us, and then we can leave the lands of the King of Castles."

"If we can ever find the monkey in this mulch," I said. As we began searching for the monkey, I thought I heard the woods whisper "Jennifer" in the same voice as the tree, on the edge of my hearing range. I pushed some branches out of the way and prayed that I was wrong.

***

It took two hours of searching to find the monkey hanging desperately from a tall oak. Its knife was driven into the wood by the force of our enemy. After the Squire of Cloaks brought him down, the Organ Grinder threw his arms around the diseased creature and joyfully nuzzled it. The Stone Preacher turned his back, and the picnic basket slavered. The Squire of Cloaks and I looked on in horror as we began walking back to the longhouse of the Count of Alchemists.

"I cannot believe I was a slave to that man and his accordion." The Squire of Cloaks sighed to me as we made our way back.

I clutched the flowers desperately. "Don't be sad. He can't do that to you anymore. This place has rules."

"And severe punishments," the Stone Preacher rumbled behind us. The picnic basket bounced around me joyfully. The wonderful smell of baking waffles leaked out below the lid.

"It seems the tree must have been particularly vile." The Stone Preacher rubbed his rocky chin. "The basket seems to have outdone itself, and is particularly excited."

"Well, that waffle smell is making me hungry. I just don't know if I should eat anything until after I drink this cure the Count is supposed to brew." The basket's lid tipped open. The rich malted smell of waffles floated towards my nostrils. They had honey and strawberries, figs and a thick layer of cream, and I reached in and snatched the plate out. I ate slowly as I walked, being careful not to touch the messy parts too much.

"On the other hand," the Squire of Cloaks mentioned, checking to see if there was another waffle for him. "Who cares?" He peered down towards the lid. The basket flipped open, dispensing another waffle much like the first.

There were enough waffles for all of us. When the Stone Preacher took a few measured bites before handing the rest of his to the Organ Grinder, who devoured it without sharing any with his monkey. At the last swallow from the Organ Grinder, a wicked grin of vengeance broke out across the lid of the basket. Its tongue slithered out to taunt the monkey, who huddled in the Organ Grinder's greatcoat, terrified and unfed.

***

We returned to the Longhouse tired. The marshy smell of the fen was mitigated by the warm, sugary taste of waffles, fruit, and cream. All of us were smiling except the monkey, who huddled unseen inside the Organ Grinder's greatcoat.

I banged on the door of the longhouse, concealed in the side of the hill. The Count of Alchemists opened the door, peering out.

"Oh," he said with a relieved look on his face. "It's you." He wore a thick cassock that appeared to be the local equivalent of pajamas, and a funny looking hat on his head, shaped like a diseased mushroom in a radiant yellow. He opened the door with a cheerful grin, making a gesture of allowing us inside. The laboratory looked much as before, with several doorways I hadn't previously paid attention to now standing open, leading deeper into the hill. Behind one of them was a plush poster bed.

"Sorry to wake you," I said as coolly as I could. "But we thought it best to return as soon as possible." I looked at the basket. "You don't have another one of those waffles, do you?"

The Picnic basket turned to me, extending its legs up, and then yawned open. There was a waffle there, fresh cooked and with the same accessories. I reached into the basket nervously, and picked it out, holding it up for him. "If you brew this cure right now, even though you're in your nightclothes, I'll give you this waffle."

"Ahh, the techniques of bargaining." The Organ Grinder let out a low laugh. The Stone Preacher nudged his finger roughly against the Organ Grinder. The Squire of Cloaks stood stiffly next to us, looking a little fearful in the dark.

"It is a worthy bargain." The Count of Alchemists grinned. "I have never seen a waffle like that before. Does it taste as good as it smells?"

"I shall verify that with the smile on my face, the smile that is still as large as those on my companions' faces. Trust me, it's worth it."

The Count tilted his head as we slipped inside, and took the plate with the waffle. "I shall take you at your word. I fear you must wait over there while I finish this. It looks magnificent." He indicated a bench where we could sit. The Stone Preacher stood beside it, while the Organ Grinder sat on one end. The Squire of Cloaks closed the door behind him, and settled on the other end of the bench. I slipped in between them, holding out my arms for the basket. It raced across the room and leaped into my embrace.

The Count moved over to a table and settled the plate onto it, sitting down on a stool. We watched the Count of Alchemists get a fork out of his pocket. He was a slow eater. I felt my chest cramp with bitter cold from time to time as his eyes lit up. He rubbed his bald head a little between bites. "However does your basket make such food?"

I curtsied daintily to him. "It is a magical secret, my lord." I smiled. "A brave innkeeper gave it to me as if it were his finest possession." I kept my face as straight as I could. I didn't want him to know I was lying, or what the basket did.

"Ahh, and what would that magical secret be? A dash of bitter-root perhaps, or some other replicable potion?" He glanced to me hopefully.

The Stone Preacher, the Organ Grinder, and the Squire of Cloaks all sat on the bench, their gazes as impassive as the grey night sky. The basket cuddled up against me, its long tongue hanging out from beneath the lid. "I'm afraid that the only the basket knows." I winked. "And it doesn't talk."

"Well, that's quite terrible, quite terrible. I would love to know the secret firsthand." I didn't tell him what firsthand knowledge usually meant.

When he finished, he patted his stomach as though it was the best meal he ever had, and rose. "Young lady, on the strength of your waffle, I shall attempt to brew the cure for you." He flashed me a winning grin. "May I have the flower?"

I released it into his fingers, and sat back down patiently on the bench. "You have a little waffle on your upper lip."

The Count reached into the pocket of his cassock and wiped his mouth. "Thank you, my dear." He turned to his work, dumping the flower into a vial and pulling out some liquids and herbs I didn't recognize. He poured them into the flask and swirled them around with his hand before stoppering the bottle. He moved over to a different bench and sat down, activated a small fire, then placed the bottle over it on a hook and let it simmer.

"That looks dangerous." I said to the Stone Preacher. "He's setting my potion on fire."

The Stone Preacher chuckled. The rocky crackle vibrated through the bench as the picnic basket huddled in my lap. "I thought they all required fire. It's an essential magical element."

The Organ Grinder laughed, and looked over at the Squire of Cloaks. "If he lectures us, I'll be very disappointed."

"Pah!" The Count of Alchemists sneered. "You are not fit to learn the secrets of alchemy, Organ Grinder! A legend you may be, but you are the vilest sort of legend. Even my dirty-fingered art is beneath your lizard mind." Underneath the Organ Grinder's greatcoat, the monkey made a chittering sound.

The Squire of Cloaks allowed himself a small smirk. "Good sir, if I could prevail upon you to not insult the lady's companions? Otherwise, you too may find yourself under the spell of his accordion." The Squire took a moment to restrain himself, his right fist clenched away from the Organ Grinder.

The Count of Alchemists pulled the corked bottle off the hook, and walked over to me, gingerly holding it in his hands. "This should do it!" He cackled ruthlessly, a child's twisted glee on his features as he handed me the bottle, which still felt horribly warm to the touch. "Drink it down, in one gulp now, or the effect will be lost."

"Thanks." I pulled the cork open and winced at the smell. Like all medicine, it tasted awful. I could feel my nostrils burn as I brought the thing to my lips and guzzled it. There was a brief smell of pleasant flowers. A horrible, rancid taste afflicted my mouth and lips as the liquid burned down my throat. I thought about the man with the green eyes and my eyes widened. I hadn't been thinking about him so much since the poison entered my system.

"Ahh, the power of alchemy." The Count of Alchemists grinned, a sly look on his face. "That poison might have broken your heart forever, and made you live like that poor tree out in the woods that guards the flowers. Did you sneak past it or just kill it?"

"It's dead. I can't believe it was a person, once. I wonder what it fell in love with, but not too much, you know?" I could practically feel the sideways mouth of the tree, breathing on me as the tongue drew me forward.

I saw the Organ Grinder shudder slightly. The Stone Preacher's rocky grin spread wide. "I suppose that we might pray for more such trees once this journey is complete. I am sure the world can live without the Organ Grinder and his dirty monkey."

The Organ Grinder scowled at the Stone Preacher and gently reached inside his greatcoat to comfort the distressed creature. "Oh, surely you cannot mean it," he purred as he inched away from the Stone Preacher, moving closer to me.

"I think he does." I said. "I would encourage more politeness, and less accordion music."

The Count of Alchemists smiled. "I don't know who it fell in love with. I am just pleased to be able to use the flowers without having to avoid it. In my youth, I was spry and sprightly, and could nimbly dodge the beast. In my old age, sadly, I have to gather things more slowly."

Something battered hard at the door, a savage, resonant thump that boomed through the lab. There was another thump, and another. A large, bricklike fist smashed through the door, rocky and cold in the late night.

"I know that hand!" The Squire of Cloaks shrieked. "It is him! It is the King of Castles! His castle-people have found us!"

"And you did not think to tell me this?" the Count of Alchemists thundered, raising his voice as the Stone Preacher glided towards the door, grabbing the thing's wrist and merging it with the stone of the hill. There was a strange, awkward howl, then some spastic flopping.

"Do you have a back door?" I asked the Count of Alchemists. "It would be really nice to run away right about now. He doesn't want you."

The Count of Alchemists pointed to one of the closed wooden doors. From beyond it, we heard a distant, hollow noise. "Do you know what they say about a man's home?" The Squire looked for something to hide behind. "He's the King of Castles. He already knows everything about it."

***

The thought sobered me for half a second as hammering on the door continued. I looked to the Stone Preacher with terror in my voice. "Can you make another exit?"

"Alas, no." The Stone Preacher rumbled. "Our friend the Count of Alchemists has warded his home against such intrusions, has he not?" His eyelids narrowed with a quiet snap.

The Count of Alchemists tapped his bald head for a moment, then defiantly pointed at the Stone Preacher. "Perhaps if you weren't so terrifying, I wouldn't feel the need to guard myself against your entry!"

The Squire of Cloaks looked at all of us, horrified. "Is there nowhere we can run to?"

"No place whatsoever." The Organ Grinder leered. "I would seduce the King of Castles, but I fear the dead are immune to the sound of the accordion."

"That never stopped you beforc," I muttered.

The Count of Alchemists paced back and forth, his hands behind his back like someone he knew was about to give birth. "Aha!" His eyes widened with excitement. "Bar the doors! Block everything! I shall keep him out for a time!" He smiled eagerly as thumping on the doors continued. "I shall ward him off with my ugliness!"

I looked at my companions. "He's kidding, right? I mean, he doesn't look particularly ugly."

The Count of Alchemists chuckled. "I am an old man! What difference does it make if I am handsome or hideous? You will horribly scar me, and I shall drink the potion, lest the King of Castles deprive me of my last few years of life!" He cackled and bent over the table.

The Stone Preacher pushed furniture while the Organ Grinder and the Squire of Cloaks worked together, sliding chairs in front of the door from which sounds came. I floated up towards the ceiling, and called the bow, aiming it at the main door.

Ingredients toppled to the floor as the Count of Alchemists began work. He shouted aloud, making strange incantations in a loud, hollow language as he mixed things and set a whole table on fire. "Burn! We shall brew this Ward of Ugliness and fend off these murderers, though it costs me my lab and my supplies of nightshade! Cook, cook, potion of hideousness! Let it taste of vileness and repulsion, so inglorious it be!"

"Could you stop setting things on fire and start brewing, my lord?" I called out. I summoned an arrow, nocking it to the bow.

The thumping continued as the Count of Alchemists stirred furiously. The door in front of the Stone Preacher crashed down, revealing a thick and lumpy man of brick. The Stone Preacher waved his hand. The castle-man burst apart, wet blood and ancient bones rolling across the dirty floor. I fired an arrow into the press behind. Stony troops struggled forward as the Preacher's fingers pushed back through splintered wood.

The Organ Grinder pressed his back against the door while the picnic basket growled, peering out behind the Stone Preacher's leg. The Squire of Cloaks huddled under a table.

Flames roared around the Count of Alchemists as he let out a wild cackle. "You who try to kill me in my home, I shall lead a damaged life, but you shall pay for these indignities, no matter how many you send to your deaths!" He howled and thrust his hand into the fire, grabbing the clay beaker. "To me, girl! We shall repel these gross corpses!"

I ran to him on boots of fire and reached out for him. He swallowed the liquid, and let out a choking gasp as the Stone Preacher drove a fist through another rocky torso. "Quickly, girl!"

he shouted. "Ruin my face! It is the only way!" He smashed the beaker against the table and handed me what was left.

I had never mutilated anyone before. My fingers took it, and I shook. "Are you crazy?"

"No! I am merely old, and if you do such a thing, you could be ruined, even though it is likely you will be ruined anyway!"

The Stone Preacher stepped forward to block the door. The rear door against which the Organ Grinder pressed buckled under the heavy thud of a massive fist. The Organ Grinder was knocked forward into the room.

I gritted my teeth. I let the bow fall to my side. I sighed, squeezing the grip tightly. "I'm sorry." It was all I could manage.

I took the broken beaker, and hacked at his face until he was ugly enough.

***

The Count of Alchemists bled horribly from a dozen slashes. He grinned as wounds leaked down over his robes. "That's better." He breathed a sigh as he rubbed the wounds with his fingers, covering his hands with blood.

The Stone Preacher grabbed a stony castle man and hurled it into the midst of the others. The rocky crunch echoed inward as the Count stood in the door. "Gather round me!" he shouted. "None may look upon my ruined face and approach! It is powerful magic!"

The Squire of Cloaks scampered for the circle as dull sounds of tumbling rock thundered. I closed my eyes and turned away from the Count of Alchemists, as the Organ Grinder crawled forward. The count's wounds seethed with burning light. My eyes could barely stand the sight of him. I could hear the picnic basket hissing. It recoiled in a corner and then backed up towards me, bumping against me as I reopened my eyes.

"Back up!" the Organ Grinder thundered at the Stone Preacher. "They'll wear us all down!" There was a crashing sound from the rear of the longhouse. The door smashed down. More rocky men poured into the room, shoving aside tables and smashing through benches.

The Squire of Cloaks put his back to the Count of Alchemists as ugliness radiated outward. Maimed features broadcast their repulsive nature. They let out bellows as if they could not see anymore, and began backing up towards exits. The Stone Preacher ground his rocky teeth with a low crackle.

"How many of these things does he have?" My voice dropped. "It never seems to stop."

"I think he has as many as there are people who have ever lived here," the Squire quavered. "It could be as many as a few million."

"A few million people?" I snapped. "I swear, my entire life story for the past month is the story of 'Why didn't you tell us this before?'"

"I didn't think of it!" The Squire whimpered. "The Organ Grinder was plundering my flesh! I swear, I didn't think of it."

There was a dire, rumbling set of thuds. The noise didn't come from the Stone Preacher. It was as if the men of stone and mortar heard him. All their fists had clenched at once, and they let out a howl of fury, making the whole longhouse shake with rage.

The Organ Grinder muttered. "I think that if I were not a prisoner of this magical field, surrounded by rocky hands that could crush me to a pulp, I would be seeking to get as far away from this location as possible."

"This is your own fault. You rutted with him. You had the choice not to play that stupid accordion of yours, and now the angry, dead King of Castles, who is likely still in love with the Squire here, thinks the Squire cheated on him!" I turned and pointed the arrow at one of the rocky humanoids, as it backed up towards the entry. "Bring me your master, and I shall make obeisances appropriately! You are nothing but a dead peasant in a walking coffin! Do it! I command you!"

The Stone Preacher's eyebrow lifted with a cracking sound. The shambling rocky masses backed off, thudding out through shattered doors. "It would seem that you are of high station indeed," he rumbled. "A duchess at least."

The Count of Alchemists shouted, shaking his fist. "Flee, you worm-ridden, brick-covered dead! I spit upon your sanguine taxation, and will collect your hearts for potions! The potion will wear off, but my ugliness will not, and I shall loot your tombs and disturb your rest! Ha! I shall give your descendants pox, and flense your daughters with such rutting that it shall make the Organ Grinder pale!" He laughed maniacally as his wounds flared with sickly light. His blood glowed with a faint green tint.

"Wow." I grinned to the picnic basket. "He really did go to mad scientist school, didn't he?"

There was a rocky rustle as the basket let out another low growl. An impressive, well-built man stepped into the room from where the mortared men retreated. His features were sunken and sallow. Rich, rotting robes hung loosely on his dead frame. The corpse was still handsome, mustache perfectly waxed, the sharpness of his chin unmarred, with perfect hair. He wore a gorgeous leather doublet pierced in the heart by a knife. His features were etched with thin, rocky lines of mortar and brick. "I am the King of Castles." His voice was so low I couldn't help but look down to a view of his boots, cast of blackish metal. "I understand that there is an unnamed noble in my lands, and that your name is Symantha?"

The Squire of Cloaks whimpered a little bit, his voice soft, as he went to one knee. "My lord, my heart—"

"At least Bazelgard did his job," the Stone Preacher rumbled. "I think this just became more complicated."

***

The King of Castles looked at us, standing in the doorway, wincing as he gazed beyond us at the bleeding face of the Count of Alchemists. "Though your magic is powerful, it is not as powerful as my station! Kneel before me, Count of Alchemists. It is a shame you treat your guests so!"

"You dare to try to kill me in my own home?" The Count of Alchemists cackled. "I shall die old, ugly, and alone, but you shall not take me within my longhouse! You dare to ruin my labs and spite my potions! I shall wear my ugliness in response to your assault, and bear it proudly!"

I didn't know where the British accent came from, but out it sprang. "In short, your highness, it is not my magic that compels you out, and you did try to crush us to a pulp," I said reflexively. "One might think it less than sporting."

The Organ Grinder stared at me. "Where did you learn to talk like that?"

"I watched some movies with people that spoke like that. I'm really not from England."

The King of Castles glowered in the doorway. "I shall withdraw my troops if you hand over the Squire of Cloaks to me. Our romantic squabble is not yet ended." He gave a cold, creaking smile. The stony castle-people ground their hands, unable to move forward.

"Not yet ended?" I tilted my head. "Your Majesty, I mean no offense by this, but you are dead as a doornail, and you're likely to stay that way."

The Squire looked to me. "We promised each other we'd be together forever," he said nervously, clutching the Stone Preacher's hand out of reflexive terror. The picnic basket let out a low growl, and I released the arrow slowly, reaching down to grab it by the handle.

"Hold your beast — basket — whatever that thing is!" The King of Castles glowered at me. "Such a ragtag group of common folk and a girl with pretenses to nobility, hiding behind an alchemist whose only defense is his newfound hideousness! It is appalling. Step forward, my beloved. Join me and we shall be together. If you refuse me now, you must make me an offer of equal value."

The Squire of Cloaks thought about that for a moment, and tilted his head. "What could I give you, my love? I have already given you everything."

The King of Castles grinned, a wide creaking smile. "You could take her endorsement. Is that not the bow of the Prince of Archers?" He smiled as I reached down to summon an arrow, but it was too late. The Squire of Cloaks, his eyes lit with the desire to survive, had already wrapped the bow tight in his cape as the picnic basket leaped for him. He dived for the cover of his one true love. The King of Castles snatched up the bow. The Stone Preacher bellowed in rage and gave chase, the Organ Grinder following as the legion of rocky soldiers began to block our path.

I tried to call the bow, but the King of Castles gripped it tightly. "The cold embrace of death prevents the calling." He grinned. The Squire of Cloaks raced forward, running for him as the Stone Preacher began ripping the castle-men apart.

The picnic basket leaped at one, and ripped its arm off, as the Organ Grinder's monkey jumped out from under the coat and stabbed into the open, rotting wound. The gleeful sound of the Count's voice could barely be heard over heavy thuds and crashes of combat. "Retreat now, dead king!" He shrieked as I dove forward, the Stone Preacher clearing a path for me. I heard a funny thunk as the basket swallowed the stony arm. A faint scent of jam and tarts wafted across the room.

In the distance, I could see the Squire of Cloaks and the King of Castles disappearing into a wrathful mess of a thicket, the King's cold visage locked on his lover's eyes. "I'm getting my bow back!" I shouted, and rolled between two of the castle-creatures, the din of battle in the air. My boots flared to life with a roar. I noticed the slightest of approving nods from the Stone Preacher. The Organ Grinder kicked one of the castle creatures in the chest, using the brief moment to draw out his revolver.

The creature's chest shattered in the wake of the gunshot. I could hear keening whines from inside as blood splashed loudly about the room, the consequences of years of brutal toll payments and a castle that absorbed the dead. As I flew out the door after the Squire of Cloaks, the air creaked with the sound of thunder. It began to rain in reddish opalescent drops.

***

I raced towards the retreating King of Castles, in a trail of fire. The picnic basket flounced through the array of castle-men behind, chasing, dodging, and growling as they attacked. The thicket was filled with leaves; the high, thorny stand pierced with uneven holes.

Two of the castle creatures opened their stony mouths and let out hollow gurgles. There was a noise that sounded like stone breathing in. Gouts of wet, burning blood poured out of their mouths. I ran upward, boots alight, to escape it. Flames roared beneath my feet, and blasted downwards towards earth, scorching the ground. Behind me, the basket gave chase, dodging through the legs of the rocky creatures as they breathed upward.

I raced above the thicket, trying to catch the King of Castles and the Squire. The King forced his way through brambles, into a denser mass of trees and heavy roots, clutching the bow as he moved. In the distance, I could hear the crash and boom of fighting, and the occasional report of a gunshot.

The King of Castles turned his head. "Young Symantha," he boomed, "I warned you not to interfere." His hand clenched into a fist, and hurled a thick glob of wet, sticky mortar at me. I tried to slip aside, but it slammed into me, and stuck. It was so heavy that I crashed to earth. Thorns of the thicket stabbed at my cloak of runes and tangled me up. "Give me back the bow. It isn't yours."

The King of Castles chuckled amid the trees as he lumbered forward. I tried to peel the heavy weight of the mortar off my clothes.

I could hear the Squire of Cloaks begging from behind him. "Don't hurt her! She saved me!" In the eyes of the King of Castles, there was no mercy or justice, only the punishment of transgressions. I knew the Squire's begging was useless.

The red rain poured down over my face. "You mean the way the Organ Grinder saved you?" I smiled, still trying to rise as the heavy footsteps of the King of Castles lumbered. "Weeks of being unable to sleep, with you and the Organ Grinder rutting in the bed of that dirty, creaking cart, hard moans pouring out of it as I was awakened, over and over!" The red liquid touched my lips. The taste of alcohol dripped into my mouth.

The King of Castles head turned to look at the Squire of Cloaks. "The Organ Grinder?" His dead eyes flashed with hate. He dropped the bow as if in shock. The mortar seemed to get heavier as the King grew angrier. The bow was only a few feet from me. I stretched out my arms to reach it as the King of Castles, cold and dead, turned toward the lover who had killed him. He waded through the wine-weeping sky, advancing on his beloved.

The Squire of Cloaks began backing away, putting up his hands as the King of Castles lumbered towards him. I tried to crawl towards my bow, but it was too far from my fingers. I struggled to get up, but the mortar pressed me into the cold earth, making me feel so heavy that I could barely move.

There was a keening wail. The picnic basket barged through the thicket, thrusting aside thorns and munching on something that looked like a large rat. It swallowed it down with a hiccup and raced over to the bow, picking it up in the lid, and carrying it the rest of the way. It deposited the bow right in front of my fingers, and leaned down, letting out a strange trill. I wrapped my hands around it, beginning to angle the rune-carved wood into the ground, and began forcing myself up. I reached back, the mortar tugging me down, and summoned an arrow.

"You and the Organ Grinder?" He stared in bitter fury at the Squire of Cloaks, who kept slipping backwards through the thicket. "You murdered me, and then bedded the Organ Grinder!" I lifted myself up as his tone grew harsher, while the Squire retreated from him.

"It's true." I said coldly as I staggered to my feet. "The Organ Grinder rutted with him like a beast, over and over again until that dirty, old cart stank and his horses wanted a turn." I smiled at the Squire of Cloaks. "The truth is lovely, especially when it's what you get for stealing." The Squire shook his head, and I summoned a second arrow, drawing them both back on the bowstring. The arrows leaped forward, and the Squire's cape leaped out to catch one. The arrow slammed backwards into the tree, pinning the cape there with a dull crack. The other arrow slammed into his thigh, pinning it against the dark, thicketed wood.

The Squire let out a squeal of pain, and the King of Castles smiled, reaching back a hand. "You have betrayed me twice." The dead man sobbed. He cried tears of blood and mortar, his fists knotting with a crackle that seemed louder than any noise the Stone Preacher had ever made.

The Squire of Cloaks writhed against the trunk of the tree, lips bleeding and his fingers gaunt. The King of Castles advanced on him. He tried to wrap his cape around the dead king's hand, but the King of Castles grabbed him, still pinned. "No, please," the Squire whimpered. "My love, please. It was the Organ Grinder – I swear! Please, don't do it! Please, it was the accordion – please!" He struggled against arrows, hands wet with blood in the rain.

The mortar pulled me down again, smashing me into the ground with a heavy crash. My face was scratched by thorns and my cloak grew even more tangled. I scrabbled on the ground, watching. I didn't want to stop it even if I could have.

The King of Castles let out a guttural grunt, his dead throat thick with hatred. He drew back a fist and smashed it into the Squire's chest. Blood bubbled up from the lips of the Squire of Cloaks, mixing with red rain in the skies and the red wine on his jacket.

The Squire crumpled to the ground with a whimper, my arrow snapping as the King of Castles smashed his fists into the cape, over and over again. I watched the pummeling helplessly. My cloak of runes steamed as the King of Castles unleashed his murderous rage. Bones cracked under hard, dead hands. The whimpering continued until all that was left was the cloak, covering a paste of human meat.

The King of Castles stared down at the crushed, broken heap that was the Squire, then crashed atop him. His eyes were empty. Drool of blood and mortar leaked out of his open mouth.

And so it was that the Squire of Cloaks died, wet and stained with wine under the bramble-boughs.

***

The rain of wine poured over me, battering my cloak and boots while the mortar weighed me down. I could smell alcohol coating my cloak. It made the mortar heavier as the mashed pulp of the Squire's corpse mixed with the red drops. The wide, dead eyes of the King of Castles stared, his corpse heavy atop his lover's. Thorns were pushed aside by the heavy tread of the Stone Preacher's feet, the Organ Grinder close behind him. The rocky visage stared down at me. "Oh." The Stone Preacher glared disdainfully at the corpses, and yanked the poultice of mortar and blood aside. "Are you hurt at all?" His face was covered with lack of concern as the Organ Grinder made his way up beside him.

"I'm fine." I struggled to my feet, glaring at the Organ Grinder. "It never ceases to amaze me how useful you are, even by accident rather than design."

The monkey hooted triumphantly from inside the Organ Grinder's greatcoat. It hopped up and down, leaping out from between buttons to stand on its master's shoulder, flicking its knife-tail. The Organ Grinder bowed, his greatcoat creaking in the rain of wine. He gave a low smirk that almost passed for a smile. "Think nothing of it. Where is the Squire of Cloaks?"

I looked over to the place where the King of Castles had fallen. My jaw fell a little bit. Rooting around the dead body of the King of Castles was the picnic basket, lapping up pieces of mashed bone and crushed muscle. It was gulping quietly, the lid chewing, fiercely pulling in pulped meat. It swallowed the cloak and gave off a loud, raucous belch. "I think most of him is in the picnic basket. No eating for a day or more, you glutton!" I scowled at the basket. It responded with a keening whine.

The Stone Preacher let out a grinding sigh. "We should return to the longhouse and say our goodbyes. There is nothing more for us to do here, except perhaps bring you closer to the Castle in the Sky." He shook his head.

"We don't even need to stay the night." The Organ Grinder chuckled, his smile spreading. He gazed longingly at the picnic basket, which loped over to me, apparently sated as it rubbed against my leg. "A fine meal awaits us in the morning, although it is probably too classy for my tastes."

"You'll eat it anyway," I said coldly. "How's the Count of Alchemists handling things?"

"Not too well," the Stone Preacher rumbled. "I believe he's staring in a mirror and whimpering to himself."

"Let's get out of here, then." I shuddered. "We should still say goodbye to him. He did save us, and we owe him for that, at least."

"We do indeed." The Organ Grinder chuckled. "You are learning much about the owing of favors. It is the true currency of this land."

We made our way back through the ruined thicket, the longhouse almost invisible against the night sky. When we found our way to the doorway, the Count of Alchemists giggled and clutched his sides, laughing in a pool of his own blood and sweat. "Hideous – I'm absolutely hideous!" The potion had worn off. His ruined face stared back at us, his smile brimming with excitement as blood clotted on his head.

"I suppose that means it's time to say good-bye." I looked down at him. He whimpered in his ugliness. "Could you perhaps give us directions to the Mountains of Existence, in a way that would take us through the lands of the Half-Bone Maiden?"

"Oh, the Half-Bone Maiden!" The Count of Alchemists leapt to his feet. "You have talked to her? She only talks to the most interesting of people! I wonder what makes you interesting, hmm?" He tilted his head toward me, and squinted through slashes and the oozing blood. "You should travel in that direction!" He pointed to the back of the longhouse. "We don't really have North, South, East and West here. But you should pass her tower in a few days' time, if you like those sorts of things." He murmured and leaned in to whisper to me. "She fancies the unusual. It could be any of you." He looked over at the picnic basket. "You might have to give that thing up."

The picnic basket let out a disgruntled hiss, as if to say it wasn't going anywhere. "I don't think it will like that. We'll figure something out. We have so far." I gave the Stone Preacher a bright and cheery smile. He assumed a grim look and said nothing.

The Organ Grinder sighed. "Are you sure this is all worth it to you? You could settle for a few nights with me and roam the land as a discordant spirit." He laughed, and the picnic basket growled at him. The thought filled me with sickness as the handsome face of the man from the woods and his green eyes burned into my chest and filled my mind with delicious dreams.

"Of course it's all worth it to me." I reached down to stroke the lid of the picnic basket. It stretched up to rub against my fingers.

It made a strange rustling noise that seemed like contentment. "I still need to find him."

The Stone Preacher walked over to the Organ Grinder's cart, the horses strangely untouched by the King of Castles' attack. "Are you driving it?" the Stone Preacher's voice rumbled, taunting the Organ Grinder. "If not, we shall leave you here in this place, with only a mad alchemist and his ruined face for company. Somehow I do not think it bothers you either way."

The thought put more sickness into my soul. I made my way up onto the seat. The Organ Grinder sullenly walked over to the cart, hopped up, and lashed the horses cruelly with his whip. I closed my eyes as the cart lurched forward, dreaming of broad shoulders and that slender waist until dark thoughts came.

I prayed I didn't end my days like the Tree of Bleeding Axes.

Chapter Fourteen

The Cheerful Presence of the Half-Bone Maiden

The cart rattled through the night, over moor and thickets, bouncing on bumpy trails I thought I felt before, but never saw. Horses howled in pain under the Organ Grinder's whip.

"Do people betray each other like that often?" I asked the Organ Grinder.

His eyes focused on the road ahead. He gritted his teeth as he pulled a monocle out of his pocket and shoved it into his eye. "Often?" The Organ Grinder smirked. "It's always this way." He lashed the horses hard again as we clattered through the night. "It's almost a game to some of us: Cruelty, lies, and the games of control. We'll never know what the Squire of Cloaks planned. Indeed, it matters not because you are alive, and he and his bastard king are dead." He turned his attention back to the horses, his leer turning fierce.

"Are you saying that because he wouldn't sleep with you or because he tried to kill you?" The picnic basket huddled in my lap, the furious pace of the horses jiggling it about as it rustled a little bit with the bumps in the road.

"Oh, because he tried to kill me." The Organ Grinder chuckled. "I couldn't care less whether the one in my bed is a man, a woman, or a three eyed reptile. There is no jealousy in my life, girl. There are only those who listen to the accordion, and those who don't!" He chortled. The monkey let out a howling shriek, sticking its head out of the greatcoat as the wagon rattled along.

I shook my head while the Stone Preacher grimly glided beside us with a purposeful walk. "So we're going to find this Half-Bone Maiden?"

"I know of her," the Stone Preacher rumbled. "She's usually easy to deal with."

I looked to the Organ Grinder and a smirk burst out on my face. "Does she like accordion music?"

The Organ Grinder's eye behind the monocle widened as he whipped the horses, and his cruel cackle split the night. "Oh, child, you have just made my whole evening, and spared your own ears for quite some time! It simply never occurred to me that you might make such a trade!" He patted me on the shoulder as if I were a daughter.

"As long as it's not me." I shuddered, wrapping my cloak around myself. The picnic basket nuzzled up against me as the wheels clattered on.

The Stone Preacher glared at me. "That's no way to behave. At least have the dignity to find out what she wants first before being wily. If you want to achieve your station, you should at least be polite about it."

I rolled my eyes teasingly. "I suppose you're right. It can't hurt to ask her if she wants us to give up something unimportant. But if it's the basket, she gets the accordion." The picnic basket let out a little rumble of victory.

The Organ Grinder tipped his top hat to the Stone Preacher, as if he had won something. A sigh escaped from the Stone Preacher's mouth.

The monkey joined the basket in a howling duet. I snapped angrily at both. "Quiet." We hit a deep bump, and rattled around in the seats. "You'll attract monsters with all that noise. We don't need anything else to make our lives miserable."

***

For once, monsters did not come. The Organ Grinder's cart crunched around curves in the frozen ice. The horses let out cries of pain with every taste of the lash. I clutched the picnic basket and watched carefully for the monkey creeping out from the Organ Grinder's coat. It was getting harder to resist the desire to throw the monkey to the basket.

It was a little past dawn when we emerged from the thickest part of the forest into a secluded clearing. It looked like some sort of village, echoing with the clanking of chains. "The Organ Grinder chuckled. "Why, this place seems like an open sort of dungeon!" A sinister smile crossed his face.

The Stone Preacher glanced about, his granite neck shifting from left to right as he surveyed the area. The picnic basket let out a low rustle at my side.

I had never seen anything like it. Manacled men and women were savagely yanked along, brutally whipped by people who were better dressed. Several people wore collars, and haggardly dragged things from place to place. Atop a thick metal pole, several frost covered heads were impaled on jagged spikes, their lips frozen open. "Oh," I said. I couldn't tear my gaze away from the mass of impaled heads. Their bulging eyes stared back at me.

Houses seemed plain and ordinary, built into the sides of massive trees or cruelly hacked out of the tallest. A pleasant row of ornate homes nestled among thick boughs. Every so often, the crack of a whip echoed. I looked over to the Organ Grinder. "It seems like your kind of place. Would you like to ask someone if there's a place to stay?"

The Organ Grinder shook his head. "I think I shall adopt the motto of safety. Do not speak unless spoken to. I fear you will have to ask on your own."

"You are a true coward," the Stone Preacher rumbled. "One day, your accordion will no longer protect you. On that day, I pray it is you who are brutally despoiled into your grave."

I motioned to the picnic basket. It leaped off the cart after me as I approached one of the more pleasantly dressed folk. He was brutally whipping a grey-bearded, whimpering man, and drove a foot fiercely into his stomach as I approached.

"Good morning, sir." I gave him a pleasant smile and curtsied. "May I acquire directions to the nearest inn?"

The man's face drew back in a cold scowl as others turned to look. He coiled up the whip and put it on his waist. Thin features and sallow cheeks accented a sneer. Pale blond hair was well appointed. On his head was a boxlike purple hat. It shifted on his head. His blue and red clothes were tightly buttoned in a doublet and hose. On his feet were elegant black shoes that seemed to hide light. His voice was haughty even in deference. "Ah, my lady. You interrupt my disciplining of this slave for such trivial matters."

The groveling man struggled to crawl away. His tormentor slammed a foot down hard on his leg. A cry of pain travelled through the village. "My associates, the Organ Grinder and the Stone Preacher, require lodging." I kept my eyes locked on the man in the hat. "You are not of such high station that you dare refuse me. I assure you, the gout of blood that will fly from your neck when the Stone Preacher rips it from your shoulders will be magnificent to see." The picnic basket slid its tongue out from under the lid.

The Organ Grinder raised an eyebrow. "Do you think she means it?" I was surprised I heard his words.

The Stone Preacher tilted his head, and clasped his hands in prayer, appearing more solemn than usual. He lowered his head with a sound of shifting rocks. "That depends on whether or not she feels the need to have the basket eat something. On the other hand, it had a good meal last night and hasn't produced anything yet."

The slave-owner continued. "Why, it is right over there, around the side of that large tree. What is that thing?"

"It's a picnic basket," I said coyly. "It eats rude people." The basket rubbed against my leg, and coughed up a breakfast roll into my outstretched hand. I took a bite. It was delicious, warm and buttery with just a hint of crunchiness on the outside. "And makes breakfast out of them. Now, stop whipping him unless you want to provide me with lunch." I took another bite out of the roll. "And thank you for your courtesies."

The man scowled at me fiercely, but yanked the slave to his feet and stormed off towards the pleasant row of houses. "What do you think?" I asked the Stone Preacher.

"Eh?" The Stone Preacher responded with a little bit of confusion.

I reached down and stroked the picnic basket. "Buttered rolls for everyone?" I began heading towards the inn. "Not necessarily in the same way."

***

We stepped into the inn. The picnic basket let out a little whiffing noise as we entered. We stood in something that looked almost like a medieval dungeon, with whipping posts, stocks, and an iron maiden elegantly displayed in a corner, open and roped off. The spikes were rusty and slightly stained. Low chandeliers dangled strange hooks. My eyes widened.

Over in one corner, a slave was chained to one of the chandeliers. A chain hung from a hook while attached to a neck collar so there was no escape. He groveled occasionally while a well-dressed lady, seated at the table, ordered him to brush her hair. Two slaves tied to whipping posts felt the taste of the lash from their masters, one slave human, the other some sort of gorilla-like monster, with shovel-like clawed hands and a face with sharp, curved teeth. Smoky incense mixed with the tangy scent of wounds.

The host of the inn approached us, unfazed by his brutal surroundings. "Ah," he purred. "Does the lady have any slaves?" He bowed. "I am the Master of Inns, and this is my demesne, where all who enslave others may find their needs met." His bow was exceptionally low and gracious. His elegant black doublet and leather pants contrasted with the unusual purple beret on his head. His shoes were black and white. They highlighted a somewhat heavyset frame and thick, burly arms. His smile was as graceful as his elegance. Dark brown eyes twinkled with a merry look under slick black hair.

"No slaves, good sir. They are my escorts, and therefore, my bodyguards." I gave him a pleasant smile. "And this is my picnic basket, who you would do well to not offend." The lid of the picnic basket opened. It let out a little yawn. I reached in and passed him a pleasant-looking pastry that smelled vaguely of caramel and cherries. "I think it wants you to have this."

"I think it overate," the Stone Preacher grumbled.

"The Organ Grinder and the Stone Preacher," The Master of Inns laughed. "Impressive bodyguards indeed. Surely two such legends can keep a noblewoman safe and satisfied on her journey to find the thing she desires most." He let a smirking grin cross his features.

The Organ Grinder chuckled. "I suppose this place really isn't that much different indoors than outdoors." The monkey peered out beneath the Organ Grinder's greatcoat, and looked longingly at the picnic basket. The lid slammed shut as quickly as it had opened.

"We will require a room, a key to it, and privacy." I said. "But above all, we will require silence."

"I shall see what I can do." The innkeeper bowed to me. "In the meantime, you should have a seat, and decide if you wish to enslave anyone of relative unimportance. I am certain they won't mind too much. Everyone has a breaking point, after all." A horrid scream leaped from the lips of the ape-thing.

"Is food served here? I would assume, given your nature, that it is prepared by slaves?" I gave him a casual grin.

"Of course, my dear," the Innkeeper said. "I would hate to place the burden of feeding one so noble on her pet basket."

We walked over to a table and sat down, the creaking chandelier sounding as if someone was being tortured while we sat. The Organ Grinder smiled. "Do you think we could purchase just a few people? After all, you won't let me sate my urges while I'm with you anymore."

"Whose fault is that?" I scowled. "You almost got us killed with your urges."

The Stone Preacher settled into a chair that groaned under his weight. "Her point is clear," the Stone Preacher observed without emotion. "Unless she says otherwise, you have to obey her wishes."

"I know," the Organ Grinder grumbled. "However, we can eat what we like as long as we continue to abuse our privileges." He laughed and called for food. Shortly thereafter, there was a large roast sitting in front of us, coated with fine spices and surrounded by thick wedges of something that looked like potato. At my feet, the picnic basket rested, as if relieved that it did not have to give up a meal.

"I don't know whether I should eat this." I said. "Slavery is illegal where I'm from."

"You're not there," the Stone Preacher rumbled. "You're here, and it's getting cold."

I sighed and stared at the roast. "Let's eat."

The food was good, though not as good as Bosquoverde's, or the picnic basket's, but good enough that none of us were disappointed. A well-dressed man approached while the Stone Preacher relaxed in the chair, the cracking of whips sounding in our ears. He was round in the stomach, and wore a wig that rose high above his head, in the manner of a man who had little hair but a lot of money. He wore a thick waistcoat with brass buttons that covered his stomach, and magnificent boots of leather from some kind of reptile. They were buckled with silver, and framed pleasant looking woolen pants. He dragged a slave, attached to by a gold chain tied to a pearl handled cane, and he gave me a pleasant, if slightly gap-toothed, smile. "You must be the noblewoman." He tilted his head and tapped the cane. "I am the Count of Burgomeisters." He idly drummed his fingers on the pearl handle. The head of the cane looked like hungry teeth, trying to swallow the rest. "You may, however, call me Rudolf."

"You have no idea how much of a relief it is, my lord, to not have to address someone by their title in everything I do." I settled back in my chair. "Allow me to introduce my bodyguards, the Stone Preacher and the Organ Grinder."

The slave at Rudolf's feet, a somewhat slender woman with buck teeth and slightly bulging eyes, struggled at her collar. The Count reversed the cane and wickedly thrashed her on the skull. She let out a little mewl in her painfully tight corset, but did not speak.

"You are the Stone Preacher?" The Count peered forward to look at him under the cloak of granite.

The Stone Preacher looked over the Count of Burgomeisters, his eyes narrow. "What god do you serve? I have been lax, perhaps, in befriending this one too much, but what god do you worship, sir, that keeps people in such imprisonment?"

"I worship only money and power," the Count replied. "As my people desire these creature comforts, and the comforts of creatures." He paused for a moment, gazing at the sagging, bleeding ape-man tied to a post. "Who am I to refuse them if I wish to remain in power?" The Count stared with his green eyes at the Organ Grinder. "Perhaps, if you truly are the legendary Organ Grinder, I have some organs I wish you to grind?" He grabbed the slave girl by the throat and choked her. "Not my own, of course."

As the girl gagged, the Organ Grinder let out a little laugh. "A man after my own heart!" He grabbed the man's hand, shaking it as he leaped up from the chair. The monkey shrieked, leaping forward out of the greatcoat. The Count jumped back, releasing the Organ Grinder's hand. Just as suddenly, the Stone Preacher reached out with a single granite hand and grabbed the monkey, dumping it unceremoniously into a coat pocket.

The Organ Grinder apologized. "Please forgive the creature. He does not like people with few redeeming qualities. They have nothing for me to despoil." He offered the Count an elegant bow.

"I see." The Count harrumphed a little bit, turning his gaze back to me, a brutal leer crossing his lips. "They are as unique as their legends. I should always profess to worship nothing, lest the Stone Preacher decide I worship a deity who is false in his eyes. In this case, the truth is often the most potent of weapons." He bowed. "Shall you be spending much time here?"

"I fear I shall be leaving in the morning." I tried to sound haughty and dainty at the same time. "However, your lovely town should consider a less violent method of discipline, if you want more guests."

The Count laughed, a deep, barrel-like laugh that echoed through the room. "Guests? What would we do with all of these people if we had guests? We don't so much have guests as customers." He smirked thoughtfully. "Do you see anything you'd like to purchase?"

I smiled coldly to him. "Not at this time, good sir. We all trade in favors from time to time, and I do not think I am willing to become a slave." The mewling girl let out a little whimper. "I bid you good day, my lord. Should you hear grinding and creaking from the cart, I would suggest you check your bed swiftly, for the Organ Grinder rarely listens to me. Should your wife hear creaking and grinding from the cart, I fear you shall be quite sore."

The Count of Burgomeisters shook his head. "Good day to you, milady." He stormed out of the bar with dull fury on his face, dragging the woman behind him with a relentless series of yanks. There were several patrons laughing at him. It was the first time I had ever seen the Organ Grinder and the Stone Preacher smile at the same time.

***

After we made our way up to our room, I settled into a plush chair and turned to my bodyguards, crossing my legs and settling in. "I really want to do something about this place. It offends the freedom in my gypsy soul."

"If I did not know better, I would swear that you were being sarcastic." The Organ Grinder chuckled. The monkey let out a low screech. "Must we save these horrid wretches? Most of them are brainwashed and drooling."

I reached down instinctively to hold back the picnic basket from attacking.

The Stone Preacher folded his rocky arms in front of him and shook his head. "There is no need to do so. All it will do is leave a wet trail of red. While I despise these perfumed fops and their whimpering servants, showing mercy will only leave a trail of sheep eaten by monsters."

I sighed. "Is this the sort of thing I should do something about later?" I asked brokenly. "I had to watch hours of torture over dinner, and I didn't feel as much as I thought I should. All I want is... him. I know everything will be all right when I find him, even though I know nothing's going to be all right because of how things work here. That's not very comforting."

"Perhaps," the Stone Preacher said coldly. "Or perhaps you will grow to see it as part of the natural order of the way things are here and leave them alone."

"I don't know if that's what we should do," I sighed. "Shouldn't people be free to make their own choices?"

"As much as possible," the Organ Grinder laughed wickedly. "Around here, a lot of the locals rely on this thing called destiny. What if it's their destiny to be beaten roughly over the head by a fat man in a waistcoat?" The monkey hooted assent, and I yanked on the basket, which let out a low growl.

"No eating," I said. "You've eaten too much these past few days without giving us any food."

The picnic basket hiccupped out a plate onto the bed with a collection of turnovers on it, still steaming as if from an oven. It did its best to huddle and look contrite. The Organ Grinder sighed and grabbed a turnover. "Now that's more like it!" he murmured. "If you beat it, it will be more honest."

I sighed and bit into a turnover. "I'm not beating up the picnic basket." I glared between bites. "It's a friend, like it or not, and I swear if you act against it, I'll let it eat you."

The Stone Preacher looked at me as though his rocky jaw had completely unhinged from his mouth, and his eyes made a strange cracking sound as they went wide. "It's a pet. It's not a friend." He shook his head, and his neck cracked. "Curse that Bosquoverde, he's doomed you with this basket."

"I don't think so." I said, and clutched the basket protectively. "He stays. We can leave the town of slaves alone. It just makes my skin crawl."

"You never know," the Organ Grinder chuckled. "You may have thousands of your own someday." He grinned like a cat. The picnic basket growled again. "It seems to dislike what you dislike. It's only a pet. You should stop calling it 'he' in case you have to put it down."

"I refuse. It's 'he' and that's the end of it. But no interfering. That's the deal."

The Stone Preacher nodded approvingly, his eyes savage and cold. "It is a deal," he said firmly. "You are learning quickly. To change the keeping of slaves, you would have to kill a lot of people. So many people, in fact, that you would no longer be welcome in this land, and you have a purpose here." His face cracked into a rocky leer.

I looked at the Stone Preacher and shuddered, choosing an early bedtime without another word. I cuddled up with the picnic basket and dreamed of a day when it would eat the slavers and torturers that lived here. I would serve them up to the slaves as buttered rolls, perhaps with a little ham and cheese on the inside.

***

Morning finally arrived. I threw myself out of bed and slipped into a side chamber to take a bath. The Stone Preacher turned his back as I slipped out of bed. The Organ Grinder snored, a heap on the floor with the monkey sleeping on his back.

There was a thump as the picnic basket leaped off the bed, and tried to get into the bathroom with me. "You'll warp," I said. "Stay outside."

There was a masked slave there, who held out her hands and offered to bathe me. I slipped into the bath, and became lost in soap and warm water. The woman washed my back and hair in her plain black cassock. Fingers teased my scalp and cleaned me off.

"I should leave you money," I said quietly.

"Don't," she said. "If they find out we have money, they cut us and scar us. I have four from when I was a child." She whimpered.

"Why? It's only money."

"Money can be used to buy weapons and armor, and if we are lucky, a gun like the one your friend the Organ Grinder carries."

"Do you have a name?"

"My master calls me twenty six." She sighed softly. Old hands creaked over my fingers. "But I am probably four or five times that old, if I could remember how to count."

"I'm clean enough, I feel dirty anyway." I slipped out of the bath and toweled myself dry, not even waiting for her to hand me the cloth. I struggled back into my clothes and hurried out, shaking the Organ Grinder awake. "Let's get out of here." I said hurriedly, turning to the Stone Preacher. "I can't be here anymore, or I'm going to start killing people."

"That's the spirit." The Organ Grinder yawned, stretching as he sat up. The monkey tumbled to the ground as the picnic basket flounced after me, sniffing me as if I might be good to eat.

"I don't even care if you stink." I hurried for the door. "Let's hope we can find someone to give us directions at this hour." I paused and looked down at the picnic basket. "One day, you'll get to eat some of these idiots." I stormed out the door, not even waiting as I heard the rumble of the Stone Preacher behind me carrying our luggage.

I made my way for the cart, boots thudding as I ran for the door of the inn. We could find directions outside, or on the road. I didn't want to become a slave. Inside the cart, my living dress waited. Better times were ahead, if only I could find my love before the people of this town found an excuse.

There was no one outside to stop us. There was only the smell of fresh-baked bread and a few people walking about in the street, dragging other people by their collars. The icy smell of morning in winter attacked my nostrils. I leaped into the cart without another thought, dragging the picnic basket with me.

The Stone Preacher glided out the door, his gaze turning from left to right, as if he were expecting something. The Organ Grinder moved out close behind, adjusting his top hat on his head as the monkey savagely clutched it.

With a heavy tread, the Count of Burgomeisters lumbered his way towards us, his buck-toothed slave girl in tow, her fingers freezing in the cold as she was dragged along. "Good lady!" he shouted. "Are you leaving us so soon?" He was wearing a thick greatcoat so heavy it looked like it weighed him down. His stomach bulged against it. The dark coat highlighted bags under his eyes. He was clearly eating too much, and sleeping too little.

"As soon as I can." I gave him a sheepish smile, and looked around for whatever might pass for his bodyguards, town watchmen, or assassins.

The Stone Preacher and the Organ Grinder moved to intercept him, the grim stride of the Stone Preacher across the ground throwing up rocks and dirt as the fat Count halted. The Organ Grinder jovially made his way up to the Count, eyeing the slave girl.

"If you have something to say…" I let the morning air carry my coolness for me. "You can say it to these men – unless you can tell me the location of the Half-Bone Maiden's residence."

"Of course, my lady." The Count of Burgomeisters bowed. "She lives in a rocky spire less than half a day from here. She refuses to enter our town. She says she finds our company bothersome, and our antics unseemly. Her primary characteristic seems to be a love of the pleasant, and she finds us very grim… an unusual thing in this world." He bowed in his greatcoat. The buttons threatened to pop.

"When I do, I'll bring buttered rolls for everyone," I said with a sly grin, and reached up as if to tip my hat. I could almost feel the low rustle of the picnic basket against my leg, anticipating my return. "Come, Organ Grinder. Let us leave this place."

I patted the seat beside me. The Stone Preacher turned away from the Count of Burgomeisters. "You are a heretic," he said coldly. "One day, I will return, and compared to the mercies that the Organ Grinder or this young waif might grant you, I swear that I will use every device in this town on you and your filthy kind before you die. There should be no slavery but that of religion. And I assure you, priests are the most accomplished torturers." He gave a cracked smile of granite that sounded like a cliff was about to shear off.

The Organ Grinder's head turned to look at the Stone Preacher as he leapt into the seat and gathered up the reins. The Stone Preacher falling into step with us, the graceful movement of the rocky legs thudding as we headed up the trail. "You, sir, seem to have a very cruel background." He smiled as if he understood something.

"You used to do all that stuff, didn't you?" I asked the Stone Preacher from the cart as we headed out of town.

"I still do." The Stone Preacher shook his head, a little cracking sound coming from his neck as he matched speed with the cart. "However am I to extract conversions before people die?"

The picnic basket made us magnificent wheat cakes for breakfast. No matter how good they tasted, a sourness in the back of my throat lasted until the gray sun crested in the sky and beat down with the smallest of shadows.

***

We drove the cart for a little while after the sun began to set. The wheels creaked as we saw a spire above the trees. There was a strange, slightly shimmering aura to it, shining with dull light as we drew closer. The cart hit roots and bumped against shrubs. We were roughly jostled by the pits in the road.

"This way is not traveled often," the Stone Preacher rumbled. "You are sure it was the Half-Bone Maiden who spoke to you on the branch at Bosquoverde's inn?"

"Owls don't talk," I said firmly. "Either someone is impersonating her and wants us to come here, or I'm invited. Either way, it might be nice to know."

"It could be a trap," the Organ Grinder offered cheerily, as the picnic basket shuddered on my legs. The monkey hooted as it climbed out of his greatcoat and slowly turned its head. It scanned the trees for trouble as it flicked its tail back and forth, the knife whistling as the wind rushed over it.

"I don't think so," I said. "The voice of the owl was nice. I didn't get a creepy feeling, just a cheerful one."

"It is always the happiest who are the most dangerous," the Stone Preacher rumbled as we drove through a copse of trees.

"That would make you the happiest person in the world," I scowled. "So is it true? Are you happy?"

The Stone Preacher tilted his head as if he had to think about it. The cart pulled around the corner into view of the tower as he glided along the ground to catch up. "A sharp tongue will get you no favors." His voice was hollow and cold.

The tower was hungry for the light of the gray sun. Bits of quartz and other reflective stones embedded in its surface. Rough-hewn edges and facets caught the grey light and hurled it about at odd angles, making the whole tower difficult to look at. If there were windows, it was difficult to tell. At the base of the tower, there was a simple basalt tethering post for animals, rarely used. People didn't come here very often.

I squinted as we grew closer, and turned to the Organ Grinder. He furiously lashed the horses while pulling on the reins, as if trying hard to bring them to a stop. He drew the cart up to the tethering post and leaped off, tying the reins off as fiercely as he could. As he finished, the monkey, who fell off when he jumped, leaped from the cart and landed on his shoulder, sliding down into a pocket.

I climbed down from the cart and set the picnic basket on the ground, and I looked to the Stone Preacher. "Does the tower look dangerous? You should be able to tell, right?"

The Stone Preacher scanned the tower for a moment with narrow, creaking eyes. "It seems safe." He indicated a place where there might be stairs. "But I don't know whether that means we should be assured, or more careful."

"I opt for careful," I said, and summoned the bow into my hand, slipping an arrow to the string. "If the Stone Preacher could go in front, I would much appreciate it, sir." I gave him a pleasant smile.

The Organ Grinder let out a laugh and took up a position next to me. "I take it this is mine?" He slid an arm around my rear end.

"You're in front, too." I slipped away. "Grope me again and I'll shove arrows up your butt until you have two of those organs you love so much."

The Organ Grinder's eyes widened, one seemingly larger than the other behind his monocle. "I'm shocked that you would treat me so." He cackled and stepped up, blocking off the rest of the stairway as I followed.

The stairs were made of the same material as the tower. The Stone Preacher glided upwards without a hint of trouble. I ignited my boots and walked on air up the stairs, hanging onto the picnic basket as we inched our way along the outside curve. Creaks of the nails in the Organ Grinder's boots seemed louder against the quartz. We stepped up onto a balcony where the stairs appeared to stop, the blank curve of the tower taunting us. We were level with the treetops.

When we turned, we saw the faintest outlines of a door carved into the rock. Thin hinges were made of the same material. A bone skull, nearly invisible in the blackish basalt, looked oddly like a handle. "I think that's a doorknob," I said. "If one of you could knock?"

The Stone Preacher looked at me quizzically. "If she's going to kill us, it would be fairly easy to shove us off the edge from here." His voice turned crackling and sour.

"Do not worry." The Organ Grinder smiled and reached for the accordion. "We'll be having none of that. Plus, it leaves the business of knocking to my granite associate." The monkey gave a little trill of noise, and the picnic basket hissed at it in response.

The Stone Preacher reached out and banged on the door with a hard, booming fist. A deep thrumming noise shivered through the rock. There was a little creaking noise as he drew back his fist to knock a second time. The doors, silent and slow, opened before he could knock again.

There was a woman standing in the doorway, a pleasant smile on her lips. Half the skull of some unpleasant looking monster adorned the left half of her face. The right half was elegantly framed in blonde hair, well-combed. A single red jewel glared out from the eyesocket of the half helmet, contrasting with the wide green eye on the left side of her face. Her right arm was covered in thick, chitinous plates that covered the same half of her chest. She was wearing a brilliant, swirling gown of gold and silver. The cloth was silky and diaphanous on the right side next to the plates, highlighting a figure that made me jealous of the voluptuous all over again. The last thing I expected was for her to produce a salver from nowhere, with a tray of small chocolates on it.

"Why, hello!" She gave me a delicate curtsey while her bone armor clattered. "I've been waiting for you for some time. Would you like to come in?" Her voice was cheerful, courteous and practiced. For the first time since I had entered the Otherworld, I understood what real power was. The Organ Grinder's hands fell from his accordion. I saw a shivering lump in a pocket as the monkey dived into the greatcoat. I felt a cowering rustle behind my leg, as the picnic basket cowered.

"A pleasure to see you again." The Stone Preacher bowed, an exceptionally low bow that made the basalt echo.

"Why don't you come in?" She said with a soft wink from her green eye. "I promise that none of you are for dinner."

***

We stepped into the room. It was vast and cavernous, with paintings of skulls adorning the walls. The Half-Bone Maiden stopped and daintily took a moment to survey the Stone Preacher. "I know that you do not approve of me, nor do I expect you to, but despite my necromantic appearance, I try to be cheerful in all things. Would any of you like a sweetmeat?" She deftly offered the salver with one for each of us.

"Don't eat it," the Stone Preacher growled. "She breaks all the rules of civility, and is nice to every living thing. We are no different from dogs and mice."

"And this is bad, why?" I asked, reaching out for a chocolate. "May I have a chocolate, ma'am?" My instinct was to be polite. Someone who had no servants and was unafraid to face the three of us alone didn't need them.

"You may." Her voice was soft and gentle. I wondered if that smile ever left the half of her face. She offered me the salver, and I took one. It was like a rush of fresh happiness. I hadn't had any chocolate since I arrived in this place. I realized that I had been here so long, when I returned, I wouldn't have anyplace else to go. I would have to borrow a phone or get a cellphone. I didn't have any money. Missing person reports would be filed. I threw all those thoughts into the back of my mind, and chewed on the candy.

"Thank you." I managed between chews. "How do you make them?" I asked. "It's not an eye of newt and toe of frog thing, is it?"

The Stone Preacher and the Organ Grinder shook their heads as she turned and made her way deeper into the tower. She laughed lightly "I make them by hand, with sugar, milk, and other ingredients. You should all come in. I fear the Organ Grinder is stirring a fire in me, and I will not be warm if you leave the door open." She gave a saucy wink, and the jeweled eye in bone flashed with light.

The Stone Preacher's face twisted in a crackling scowl as he glided in, and the Organ Grinder eyed the Half-Bone Maiden with a leer and a twisted smile. "You're only going to encourage him," I said with a sigh. "I made him promise not to rut on my watch."

The Half-Bone Maiden gave me a soft, sweet smile. "You've met 'him' haven't you? Whoever he is?" She gave me a teasing grin. We walked down a basalt hall filled with portraits, some beautiful, some monstrous, all women dressed in clothing from various ages of history. She gracefully held the salver as if she were the most skilled waitress I had ever seen. The monkey perched on the Organ Grinder's shoulder and stared. The picnic basket bounced around my legs excitedly, as happy as our hostess.

"How did you know that? I mean, it's not a big secret, and he's wonderful, but I don't even know his name. As for the Organ Grinder, it's just that I can't get any sleep when he does those things, and it bothers me a great deal."

"That's usually how it works." The Half-Bone Maiden grinned, the skull mask, if it was a mask, widened with the flexing of her lips. "The ones I can find I offer shelter here, and a chance to be safe for a time. I could have been Queen if I wanted. My true love turned out to be happiness itself, and so as long as I am happy, I am in love, and as long as I am in love, I am happy. So I see to the happiness of others in this wicked world, though it usually doesn't turn out the way that they plan it." She gestured to the walls as we came to a door and snapped her fingers. There was a strange pop. The doors ground open for her.

"That's real magic, isn't it?" I said. "Not the stuff that the rest of us do, but honest magic magic?" My heart leaped into my throat.

"Well, yes," she said with a clever grin, and marched us into what looked like a sitting room. It was opulent, with a thick Turkish carpet and small couches, framed by beautiful oak paneling. It was a sharp contrast to stone corridors laden with paintings. "If you could all have a seat, I'll bring you dinner, and then we can enter into some negotiations."

"Negotiations for what?" I asked as the Stone Preacher tilted his head. The Organ Grinder admired her form. "We accepted your hospitality, so what would we be negotiating?"

"Clever girl," the Organ Grinder muttered, sinking into a chair where he could ogle the Half-Bone Maiden without catching my disapproving glare. "We'll get to the Castle in the Sky yet, and get to the root of all this."

"Oh, my." The Maiden grinned her skull-like grin. "That's where you've decided to go? What makes you think you'll find him there, and not in some dirty old town?" She laughed. "Why it's almost as if the Weeper in Shadows is trying to kill you."

"Well, she is," I said. "She tried to kill me, murder all of us, and break my heart with that frozen knife of hers. I don't get it."

"That means you're in love with someone important, someone the King of Feathers values or has plans for. You should feel privileged, that fate has dealt you such a lucky card." She rose, laying the salver on a small table, and glided for the double doors. "I have to cook, for I am alone here." She slipped through them.

"That was unnerving," the Organ Grinder said. "But I think she's lying. Everyone lies about something. No one can possibly be happy all the time."

The Stone Preacher turned his cold, rocky gaze to the Organ Grinder while I relaxed in my chair and watched them, the picnic basket rustling around. "What makes you think that such a thing is not a curse?" he said with a deep rumble. "Happy to live, happy for happiness, happy all the time, but also happy to die, happy to cause suffering, happy when others are happy, happy when they are unhappy." He tapped a rocky finger to his narrow chin. "Good things aren't always good."

I thought about that for a while. The wonderful smell of baking pie reached our nostrils through the door. The picnic basket sunk low against my leg, as if ashamed that it could not make such a thing.

***

We waited and made small talk while whatever was in the pie baked. I settled back in the chair and crossed my feet, looking over to the Stone Preacher. "Do you think there's any danger here, or is she really as nice as she says?"

The Stone Preacher looked at me with a dry scowl on his features, his rocky face making little cracking noises. "Oh, make no mistake. She's really as nice as she says." He rumbled furiously. "That's the problem. No violence is allowed within these walls, no matter how heinous the offense. No weapon should be raised, no blow be struck, not even in jest."

"What happens, pray tell, if this is broken, old friend?" The Organ Grinder chuckled and relaxed, idly petting the diseased face of his monkey.

"He's not your friend," I said.

The Stone Preacher inhaled reflexively, letting out cold, musty air from his lips.

"She is extremely brutal to people who break this rule," the Stone Preacher rumbled.

"Why?" I asked. "She seems so nice that almost any offense could be forgiven."

"Forgiveness in death is still death. Few want to die for kicking a puppy. Fewer still want to die for vengeance in the house of another."

"She kills people who violate her hospitality rules?" I asked. "How long has this been going on?"

"Since I became who I am, at least." The Stone Preacher rubbed his brow in a rare moment of discomfort. "That's at least a thousand years."

"A thousand years? She's a thousand years old?" I tried to change the subject out of shock. "Does she really have a bone half or is it some sort of armor?"

"I actually don't know," the Stone Preacher said. "But she is the kindest person you are likely to meet here. Why take chances?"

"Pah!" The Organ Grinder smiled. "Half a beautiful woman is beautiful enough. I shall play my accordion and she shall be drawn to me as moths are to my radiant flame." He leered pleasantly at me and idly petted the monkey.

"*No* means *no*." I glowered at the Organ Grinder. "You'll take a bath and sleep alone. I'm sure she's already taken, besides, and you don't want to make someone that powerful mad at us." The picnic basket rustled in agreement at my feet.

"I suppose." The Organ Grinder leaned back in the chair. "The nice ones are never any fun, anyway."

"A wise decision," the Preacher murmured.

The doors swung open, and the Half-Bone Maiden stood there, with a large tray of meat pies, a bowl of root vegetables, and something that smelled like gravy. "Dinner is served." She smiled coyly, giving the Organ Grinder a look reserved for romantics. The Organ Grinder paid it no mind.

She brought each of us a meat pie, and handed us a plate, placing the bowl of root vegetables on a small table in the center of the room. She poured the gravy over each meat pie. The picnic basket settled onto the ground as if ashamed. She looked down at the basket. "Oh, my! Is it yours?" She stared straight at me and kneeled down to embrace it.

The picnic basket leaned up against her and rubbed gently, as if it were an old friend, and let out little rustling noises that echoed in the chamber. "It's mine. I take it you're not fond of the Organ Grinder's monkey."

"I fear disease," she said sweetly, and rubbed along the handle. The picnic basket wiggled as if it were a contented cat.

"That's all I needed to hear," I said. The basket continued to cuddle with the Half-Bone Maiden, and rubbed against her bone leg, making little rustles.

"It's not so terrible." Her eyes flicked over me. "I really did want to meet you. Sometimes, my consciousness just wanders, as I am connected to the world itself."

"Are you really half-dead? It would explain a lot."

"Don't think of me as half dead. Think of me as half-alive. You should eat your meat pie. If the Stone Preacher actually eats anything, you should eat it too. And yours is getting cold." I turned to look at the Organ Grinder and the Stone Preacher. They were eating meat pies as though their lives depended on it. The monkey slithered back into a pocket of the Organ Grinder's greatcoat, a stain of gravy left behind near the opening.

The meat pie turned out to be exceptionally delicious. I stuck a fork into it while the picnic basket glared at me jealously. "Okay. You can have a little." I broke off a piece of gravy and meat pie and fed it to the open lid-mouth. The long tongue slithered out and licked the gravy. There was a rustle that I assumed was happiness. The basket resettled at my feet.

"This is a very nice pie," I said. "So what's all of this really about? I assume you're going to offer me some form of aid?"

"Oh, indeed." She smiled, her bony half clattered slightly as she turned. She sat demurely and faced me. Her smooth and perfect hand linked with her bone one between the fingers. "But, of course, as are the rules with such things, there is always a price."

"Well, what are you offering? I assume the meat pie is just a courtesy?"

"I would never think of not providing for my guests." She idly leaned to one side in her chair. "I will aid you in your journey by giving you a token, that shows that you have my favor. It means little to many, but there is enough fear there to keep the ambitious at bay."

"And in exchange for this token, what do you want?" I finished the last few bites of the meat pie. The Stone Preacher glared at me, even though he was finishing his own portion/ The Organ Grinder relaxed with satisfaction, eying the Half-Bone Maiden. She returned his gaze with a dainty tilt of her head, and turned to face me.

"I want your bow and arrows." She said with a magnificent smile on the fleshy half of her face. "Nothing less will do."

***

"Can I think about it overnight?" I kept my fingers folded delicately in my lap. "If you are willing to endure us as guests." I glared at the Stone Preacher. He had a worried glance on his face, though his eyes were still alight with satisfaction at the taste of the meat pie.

The Half-Bone Maiden grinned as she raised her human eyebrow, and daintily crossed her flesh leg over her bone one. "I see no reason why I cannot have guests. I am terribly lonely here. After you depart, the tower will move anyway." She gave me a bright grin, the bony edge of her lip shivering.

"What if I need to find you again?" Everything was becoming curiouser. "You seem to be a cheerful sort who bargains in good faith, and that's rare here."

"The tower moves so I am neither bored nor looking at the same thing every day. I've been here for about sixteen of your years. I've been waiting for you. I will find you again and I will talk to you. That's just how these things work. You are one of those people with whom I share a special bond. I do not understand why or how, it is just how the magic of this world speaks to me." She waved her bony hand. A pretty little flower grew in it.

"And you want my bow and arrows?" I asked. "Is there any particular reason?"

"I think if you don't have them, you'll be happier. You still might die, but I'm only trying to help." She got up from her chair and gently patted my hand, the fingers of her human hand warm and comforting.

"I think it would be better if I kept them. But I'll talk it over with my companions. All of your cheer could be a sinister trick to get us to lower our guard and murder us in our sleep. I really don't think so, but you could be doing that, too."

"You're wise and clever. Not often enough". She gently patted my cheek and returned to her seat, relaxing there and running her flesh fingers over her bone hand. I was almost sure the bone half wasn't a helmet, but some sort of carapace affixed to her skin. "I assure you, the King of Feathers himself has no hold over me, and has to obey all my rules. When he visits my tower, he treats me as a great lady without laying a hand on me, even though his wicked heart drives him to kill all who threaten this emaciated social order, dying on the vine." She gave me a pleasant wink.

"So he has to obey the same rules of hospitality as everyone else? That's somewhat reassuring. It means he can't just kill me outright if I get to his house. I have to give offense."

"You should probably still sneak in." The Half-Bone Maiden smiled. "Would anyone like a peach custard? After that, I'll show you to your room."

"That sounds lovely. You're a great cook. You should get out more. All of these nobles would fight to have you, but I guess there's something to be said for having real magic."

"Well, that's why I don't." She smiled. "Magic can be harnessed or forced. I will not become a tool of eager madmen, jockeying for power in bloodthirsty dances all over this world." She handed me the flower, and stood, heading for the door.

***

She led us down a corridor, the curved angle under our feet rising slightly as we followed. "This is one of my four guest rooms," she said. "It took a great deal of time to finish them. I personally arranged all of the furniture. I find myself doing petty things as an immortal sorceress." Her smile spread across her face again, the bone half warping slightly.

"It must be beautiful," I said. "You seem to have a knack for everything else."

"I just practice a lot. My magic is an innate talent, but when you live as long as I do, you learn to do everything else because it's something to do, and an idle mind is a sleeping mind. I really don't want to be 'The Sorceress who Sleeps Forever'."

"I suppose I can see that." She was getting past my emotional defenses. She was so friendly it almost hurt.

The Organ Grinder chuckled, and stared lewdly at the Half-Bone Maiden while the picnic basket flounced behind us. "Why would you need the right man to wake you up when you could have my caresses?" The monkey hooted agreement, from somewhere deep in the greatcoat.

The Stone Preacher turned to the Organ Grinder. "I beg of you silence on your lecherousness."

"And what will you do if I do not?" the Organ Grinder sneered.

"I will rip open your greatcoat and crush your monkey, and then beat you to death." The Stone Preacher grinned, the rock of his face making a little crackle.

"As you wish, sir." The Organ Grinder bowed. "But there shall come a day when you will bend to the will of my accordion."

The Half-Bone Maiden merely giggled as she opened the door to our room. "Here you are." She daintily pointed inside.

The room was simple, yet somehow magnificent, as if all its designs had been plotted over the course of a century. A simple bed of unusual reddish wood settled in one corner. A writing desk rested next to it. A small cuckoo clock sat on the wall above the desk. Two loveseats framed a plain table made out of the same black basalt as the tower. The walls were not painted. A glowing yellow light radiated from some sort of dish on the table, illuminating the room. "It's lovely." I said.

"There is only one bed." The Organ Grinder protested, and then leered at me. "Are we to share?"

I shot him a cold glance. "You can take one of the loveseats or the floor. You're not staying in other rooms, no matter how safe the Stone Preacher thinks we are."

"I shall be about after you make yourselves comfortable." The Half-Bone Maiden slipped away down the hall, the rattle of bone echoing as footsteps faded.

The Stone Preacher glowered as he moved over and closed the door. "Well," he murmured, a little clatter in his voice. "What are we to do? It seems she wants your item of power."

"Well," I said. "I have limited ideas here. If she's as powerful as you say she is, our options are few."

"I could play my accordion for her." The Organ Grinder grinned. "Perhaps make her open to the possibility of renegotiation?"

"That is a dreadful idea." The Stone Preacher scowled. "I am certain that it will only end in tragedy, and it is we who will pay for it."

"No one else has been able to resist the lure of the accordion," I said. "Why should she be any different?"

The Organ Grinder's face wrapped up in a malicious grin. "We could start now." He offered, and the monkey crowed with little hoots, sticking its diseased face out of the greatcoat to climb up the Organ Grinder's shoulder.

"I see no reason why not," I said. "Lure her out to the cart and let the rest of us get some sleep."

"You cannot be serious!" the Stone Preacher thundered. "What if she takes offense and turns us all into sofas? Where do you think this furniture comes from?"

"Well, as long as he's playing outside, he's not breaking any of her rules, is he?" I shot back.

The Organ Grinder laughed out loud. "I believe, sir, that you are defeated. Come, monkey! Let us prepare a warm welcome for our lady friend!" He chuckled and slipped out the door, his heavy boots thudding on the ground.

"I don't like it." the Stone Preacher scowled. "They say if she becomes unhappy, the world ends."

"It's just sex, not love." I said. "There's some kind of weird distinction there. And if you really love someone, the sex doesn't have to be magical every time."

The Stone Preacher grumbled. "I will strive to protect you from her if this effort fails. But I am most disappointed in your solution to this problem."

"You're not the only one," I grumbled. "I just couldn't think of anything else."

Sleep came slowly. The echoes of the accordion wafted up through the halls of the tower. When I finally slept, I had nightmares of the bone half of the head of our hostess, her mouth crushed between the Organ Grinder's legs. She spat and choked in fury as she took his pleasure from him, then turned him into a rickety wooden chair for vengeance, one body part at a time, while he screamed and begged for mercy from the pain of his transformation.

***

Morning clawed into my consciousness with the Stone Preacher standing over me. "It's almost noon," he said coldly. "We weren't even served breakfast."

"Is that good or bad?" I struggled to get the heavy sheets off and let out a yawn.

"I do not know. It could be good or bad. I do not eat, nor do my rocky parts require energy."

"It means that something happened, that's for certain. We should get dressed and go down to the sitting room." I dressed quickly and called my bow to me, throwing the cloak of runes over my shoulders and drawing the hood up.

The Stone Preacher gestured, and the rocky door opened. We crept out into the corridor and down the stairs toward the sitting room. I prayed the Half-Bone Maiden wasn't dead.

I pushed open the door to find the Half-Bone Maiden laughing gently in her chair, brushing her hair and idly crossing her bone leg over her flesh one. She gave me a cheery look that was somehow tinged with bitterness. "Oh!" She said in the most pleasant of tones. "You've returned. You've very cleverly found a way around my rules, though I must confess that were I not resolved to remain pleasant, I would turn you into a divan." She gave me a green-eyed wink.

The Stone Preacher rumbled "May I sit?" He cast me a look that spoke of how awful my idea was.

The Half Bone Maiden gestured with her brush, a fine platinum thing that was covered with the hairs of some monstrous creature. "Of course you may. And you, oh lady in training, will sit, too."

I sat obediently. I didn't want to spend the rest of my life as a piece of furniture. "Thank you." The Stone Preacher sat next to me. "May I ask where the Organ Grinder is?"

"Oh." She giggled. "He is in my bedchamber. I know he does not love me, but he is terribly fun, and I should hope that one day I see him again."

"You and every other woman in the Otherworld," the Stone Preacher rumbled. "I apologize, on behalf of my young friend."

"There is no need!" A cheery smile appeared on her face. "I am certain that one day he will see the wisdom of staying."

"And if he doesn't?" I asked.

"Then he will spend the rest of his life as an ordinary wooden footstool, far from other furniture," she boldly declared. "And I will burn his monkey into ash. Are you not pleased, Stone Preacher? At last the Organ Grinder has made a dreadful mistake!" She flashed him a pleasant smile.

"That is true." I flicked my gaze to the Stone Preacher. "He didn't have to listen to me. So, will you give me the token you offered in exchange for not interfering in anything that occurs between you and the Organ Grinder?"

"It would seem a fair trade instead of your magic bow," she mused, idly producing a tray as if from nowhere. "Would you like a custard crumpet?"

"No thank you. If you could prepare the Organ Grinder for departure?"

"I fear I've quite worn him out." The Half-Bone Maiden smiled. "But I will see what I can do."

"So how long does he have before you turn him into a footstool?" My voice quavered slightly. I didn't want anything like this to happen.

"Ten years. If I do not possess the joys of his heart in ten years, I shall find him and work my magic, and destroy him and his accordion." She gave a polite giggle.

The Stone Preacher let out a low rattle, almost like laughter. "Are you celebrating victory?" I said. "After all, you live a long time."

"Actually," the Stone Preacher responded. "I wish them much happiness, if the Organ Grinder survives." His glee was impossible to hide.

There was a dull thumping at the door of the tower, a metallic fury of clanging chains and spikes that battered against the stone. "Oh, dear," The Half-Bone Maiden smiled. "It seems we have more guests. Shall we go down to greet them?"

"Why not?" I smiled. "Surely things can't get any worse than they are right now."

The pounding continued as the Half-Bone Maiden rose and bade us follow, making her way down the long flight of stairs as we followed her. "I suppose the Organ Grinder will miss all the fun." She let out a little light laugh, and threw open the door.

"Sorceress!" The voice was cold and familiar. "The King of all these lands demands our entry." From across the threshold, I stared into the iron face of the Weeper in Shadows, a phalanx of Chain Hook Guards and Spiked Wrath Men behind her.

***

The Half-Bone Maiden brought her hands up to her chest in surprise, an image of demure politeness, and the chains of the hook guards rattled behind the Weeper in Shadows. "You do not have permission to enter my home." For the first time her voice was firm and stern. "These people are my guests. You know what I can do, and what will happen to you if you persist."

"It is not my will." The Weeper in Shadows clenched one of her gauntlets, and her knife of ice leaped into it. "It is the will of the King of Feathers, his demands wreathed in platinum and gold." Her iron mask moved with beautiful features, and smiled its mirrored smile.

The Stone Preacher folded his arms and gritted his teeth. The loud cracking sounded like a shelf of rock breaking. "If you want to go outside, you are no longer in my demesne, and you may fight them all by yourself." The Half-Bone Maiden sighed. "Not even the mighty Stone Preacher can beat thirty of them and the royal assassin. You might wish to relax. Your fury betrays you."

The Weeper in Shadows kept her metal glare on the Half-Bone Maiden, who responded with a pretty curtsey. "You know the rules. There is to be no violence in my home for any reason." She smiled. "And of course, then there is the rule of masks." She curtsied even lower. "While I am bound by obligation not to simply dismiss you out of hand, servant of the King, the rules of magic that apply within my home state that no one is ever to wear a mask but me." Her green eye winked.

"That is the most outrageous thing I have ever heard." The Weeper in Shadows snapped. "You know I cannot remove my mask in front of others! It is who I am. Without it, I am something else, a wretched, forgettable thing!"

The Half-Bone Maiden laughed. "Or someone else," she cooed politely, as dainty as the most elegant of high class matrons might. "I only have the rule because I am not wearing a mask, and people tend to make mistakes, you see."

"Silence, witch, or I shall have my chain guards yank you out the door and butcher you, bone by bone, the tear of muscle and flesh echoing in the mist." The Weeper in Shadows smiled, giving a deep bow. Her iron lips curled subtly, as if appreciating the moment.

"If your chain crosses my door, I regret to inform you that I will be forced to do violence." The Half-Bone Maiden smiled, the bone half leering along with dainty, perfect white teeth. "You do remember what happened the last time I became violent? The Forest of Screams, I believe they call it?"

"A curse upon you and all you defend." The Weeper in Shadows scowled, and turned. "We will leave this place. But I will see your charges again, when they are not under such protection." She turned and sheathed the ice knife. Her armored guards gathered behind her as she walked through them, a tiny ripple in a sea of massive thugs. "The air shall whistle with your blood, and the angry moon you dare not see shall taste the delicious poison of your days."

At my knee, the picnic basket growled. I bent down to yank its handle so that it didn't give chase. The lid flipped open. A gourd-like cheese popped out, rolling around on the floor.

The Half-Bone Maiden smiled and closed the door as the heavy treads echoed down the stairs. In a few moments, I could hear the massive wings of her strange flying snake beating. The Chain Hook Guards and Spiked Wrath Men marched into the distance. "The King of Feathers holds no power over me," she said fiercely, as the Organ Grinder shambled into view, wearing nothing but a rumpled blue bathrobe and smelling of sex and perfume.

"Perhaps, do I?" he managed, with a greasy leer.

"Indeed." The Half-Bone Maiden said. "If you do not give your heart to me within ten years, I will take it, and I will be far less kind. Your wandering days are over." She gave him a fierce look, as if that was all there was to say.

"Ten years?" The Organ Grinder blinked. "But that is a mere slip of time that I have left to obey my nature." Then he stopped. "You, girl! You tricked me!" From underneath the bathrobe, I heard the monkey's familiar hiss of hatred.

"I did no such thing." I smirked. "I merely said I wouldn't interfere. Let's hope it doesn't take ten years to get to where we're going. I would hate for your still-beating heart to be ripped from your chest by a vengeful lover. If I were you, I'd find her a nice wedding gift before she turns you into a sofa." I winked at the Half-Bone Maiden with the look that all women give each other when they conspire. Her jeweled eye flashed.

"A footstool," the Half-Bone Maiden corrected. "You have given me a possible husband, to share my lonely life with, although he is not what I expected, he is magnificent between the sheets. I suppose that does count for something, however infuriating." She gave me a look that might have been angry, but which was suffused with happiness. "We should go and prepare your token. Come, my love." She smiled to the Organ Grinder, who stood there in pale-faced horror as the rest of us walked by, up the stairs and beyond the guest rooms, the picnic basket flouncing in our wake.

***

The Half-Bone Maiden pushed open the doors of what looked like a magnificent laboratory, filled with stone pots, glass beakers, and a few closets that smelled of unusual things. The tables were all made of the same basalt as the tower, and a pot bubbled slowly with a strange scent of cinnamon and spices. "Here we are," she said softly.

"Are you making your lunch in the magic lab?" I was curious but probably shouldn't have been.

"Absolutely not." She tittered like a schoolgirl. "It is a three-hundred year potion." She moved over to it and stirred it for a minute.

"What?" Confusion crossed the Preacher's face. "Why would you make a three hundred year potion? Surely that is beyond the bounds of madness?"

"Ask me in another hundred and sixty-seven years." The Half-Bone Maiden responded, opening one of the cabinets to dig through the contents, tossing about brooches, rings, and tiaras. "We'll know then."

"You don't know what it's going to do?" My eyes widened. "How can you brew a potion that you don't know what it does?"

"It's one of those magic things," the Half-Bone Maiden said. "It could be important then, or totally worthless." She gave me a grin as she yanked an old tarnished silver coin out of the depths of the cabinet. "Here it is!" She gave a little cheer as the Organ Grinder peered around the corner, the monkey giving a little unusual trill.

The Stone Preacher let out a gravelly sigh. "That cheap coin is going to gain us entry to the home of the Duchess of Candles?"

I looked to the Stone Preacher. "Why does everyone already know these people?"

"They're legends," the Half-Bone Maiden said. "You're not." She idly rubbed the coin on the side of my cheek as she turned and stood. "Well, not yet, anyway." Her grin warmed.

"What's all this about?" The Organ Grinder was already struggling into his greatcoat, his pants half-pulled on. He reeked of a musty cologne that was overpowering and thick, and I watched the monkey slither into a greatcoat pocket as he buttoned his pants.

"She's enchanting me a token." I gave him a smile. "A token that will begin ten years of horror." I let out a little laugh and stepped aside. The Half-Bone Maiden moved to a table with colored liquids in jars and a mortar and pestle. She tossed the token into the center.

"Ten years of horror?" the Stone Preacher said.

"Yes." I looked at the Organ Grinder peering in through the doorway. "Ten years of fear of commitment, slowly driving his hips to break in half."

The Half-Bone Maiden gave a little giggle as she began chanting words in a strange language, which rippled in our ears. It was as if a strange scent wafted across our nostrils, pungent and powerful. The monkey screeched and the picnic basket gave a wobbling rustle.

"Magic has a smell?" I asked as she turned to me, flipping the token into my outstretched hand.

The Organ Grinder paused for a moment, staring at me with bitter fury as he slipped his hand into the other pocket, yanking out the gourdlike cheese and breaking open the rind. He chewed on it. His mouth puckered. "Ugh. It is highly sour. How delightful!"

A grin at the staleness of his food came over him, and I turned to the picnic basket. "You're still full! How could you make such a nasty cheese?" There was a little rumble from it and it coughed up a wedge of delicious-smelling chocolate, wrapped in wax paper.

"I hope you'll take this in exchange for the token." I said as I picked up the wedge of chocolate and handed it to the Half-Bone Maiden. "It isn't much, but everything the basket makes is very good."

"Oh." She dropped her gaze and took it with the same radiant smile she did everything else with. "Thank you so very much. I shall savor it, and your wisdom. You will be a legend indeed. The only question is a legend of what." She gave a loving smile to the Organ Grinder. "I will see you in ten years, my love, if you have not already returned. I would encourage you to make good use of your journeys, and procure for me a belated wedding gift." She idly indicated a footstool in the corner of the room.

"Wedding gift?" the Organ Grinder thundered. "But it is only sex!"

"Not so for sorceresses." The Half Bone Maiden waved daintily. "We are married, by all the laws of the land. It gives me great pleasure to know that either you will be civilized and become a proper gentleman, or that my spell of rapture will rip out your heart that I might consume it while your flesh burns to ash." She gave me a naughty wink. "After all, even horrible monsters such as I need to be loved."

The Organ Grinder's jaw fell.

"I think we should be departing before we have to put his teeth back in his mouth." I smiled to the Stone Preacher. The granite man guided the Organ Grinder toward the door, the monkey whimpering in his pocket.

"Safe travels to you." The Half-Bone Maiden smiled the most beautiful smile she could manage. "Give the Duchess of Candles my regards. Tell her that I am terribly sorry for the disastrous cake I prepared for her as a gift. The honor of housing you should be repayment enough! If you travel along the furthest fork, you should make the road to Cliffedge by nightfall."

We made our way out of the room, the Half-Bone Maiden turning to clean up the mess of ornaments she pulled from the closet. "Take care of my new beloved! And by the gray sun, cut his hair and trim his beard!"

***

"You should take better care of your bodyguards!" The Organ Grinder thundered as we walked down the basalt stairs outside. "Married! To the Half-Bone Maiden at that! Have you gone mad?"

"I would hate to bring up the point where you volunteered for that mission," I said coolly. "But you did. And you forgot the haircut part. "

The Stone Preacher nodded, a grim smile on his face. "You have at last been defeated by your lusts, Organ Grinder. She will either make an honest man of you, or a footstool." His rocky chuckle echoed down the stairs as we made it to the cart.

"In ten years," the Organ Grinder sneered. "In the meantime, I am free to plunder the flesh of others as I will, and who knows what will happen in time, with the sting of my accordion in her soul?" He let out a choking sob. "And a haircut, too."

"The Forest of Screams," I said. "That's what will happen again if you're not careful. What is that, anyway?"

The Stone Preacher rumbled. "The Duke of Bonnets was rude to the Half Bone Maiden at one of the King of Feathers' parties. He said she was a penny-pinching, money-grubbing harlot who found joy in too many things and smiled only because she was so powerful that no one could dare to oppose her. Yet she would not seize the throne and rule with an iron fist." The Stone Preacher rumbled. "The story is legend. The Half-Bone Maiden smiled, gave him a delicate curtsy, begged him for an apology and wept. The Duke of Bonnets refused."

The Organ Grinder chuckled. "I always love to hear this story. I never liked that pompous swine. And his wife, while not pretty, has a delectable and skilled mouth."

The Stone Preacher sighed like wind between mountain fissures. "The Duke of Bonnets returned to his forest castle, only to discover that the trees themselves howled his name, crying for vengeance and demanding his apology. They plucked his clothes from him, and savaged his flesh, and finally consumed everything but half of his shadow. They say it still wails in terror in the forest."

"What about the trees?" I asked.

"The Forest of Screams is the only place in the world where the Stone Preacher and I do not cover our heads in public. No one does, if they want to live." The Organ Grinder grinned and stroked the monkey, while the picnic basket shuddered against my leg.

We reached the cart and unhooked the horses. The Organ Grinder crawled into the saddle, looking up at the tower. As if taunting and loving him at the same time, the Half-Bone Maiden gave a joyous wave from an upstairs window that appeared by magic. She daintily fluttered her kerchief in the breeze, pressing her lips to it before slipping back inside.

The Organ Grinder gave a halfhearted wave. He guided the horses away from the tethering post, his head hung low while the monkey gave a distant whimper. The cheerful rustle of the basket shivered in my lap. The Stone Preacher moved alongside the cart, a subtle, crackling smile on his face.

The wan horses thudded along the road. The Organ Grinder resolutely whipped them, occasionally glaring at me with unmitigated rage.

Chapter Fifteen

The Duchess of Candles Entertains

The road wound, serpent-like, stretching over the landscape of rocky hills. The Organ Grinder hadn't spoken for several hours. His teeth gritted as he brutally lashed the horses. Blood dripped from their flank. His knuckles were white with hatred.

"You can't stay mad forever," I said. "You did it to yourself."

"Bah." The Organ Grinder scowled. "I still have ten years of freedom. It is sufficient time to leave enough bastards that the world will sing of me. I shall sire a legion of progeny and fill the world with Organ Grinders."

"You don't like her, do you?" I sighed. "But you're afraid of her."

"Perhaps, before she eats my heart, I will take you to the Forest of Screams. I could not disobey her in any way. She might butcher me, or turn me into a footstool."

"If you don't marry her, you will be a footstool," I said. "Quite frankly, I think that's tame compared to some of the things you do."

"She will make me bathe often," the Organ Grinder grumbled. "And the joys of rutting will be gone. She will keep me on a leash, and treat me as dogs do."

"How can you be mean to her? Didn't you listen to the Stone Preacher? She only gets mad when you do awful things to her. It's like kicking a puppy, only to discover that there's a rattlesnake on the inside."

"I would kick a thousand puppies to be free of her. How did I allow you to talk me into such a thing?" The Organ Grinder shook his head.

"You'll get to like her. In the meantime, it's a good thing you can't become a thousand footstools."

The Organ Grinder thought that over for a moment, and tucked the lash under his arm. He reached into a pocket of his greatcoat, producing a marshy-smelling pipe and a bag of some sort of ground leaves. He stuffed the dirty weeds into the pipe, then lit it by striking a match on the boot of his heel. The cart lurched. Rancid smoke wafted through the air. He grabbed the reins more tightly and whipped one of the horses so hard that he cut their flesh open. "You are as cruel as this world!"

He smirked as the Stone Preacher stared at him in silence.

"But make no mistake, that cruelty will turn upon you a thousandfold before it is over." He blew a cloud of the smoke in my face, and coughed. Then he laughed for miles, blowing out misshapen, unpleasant-smelling smoke rings with the pipe clenched between his teeth. In the pocket of his leather greatcoat, I could hear the monkey coughing. I wasn't the only one who didn't like it.

***

We drove up to a lumpy, misshapen longhouse at a crossroads. Ugly-looking shapes, crudely fashioned, bulged from the edges of the building. It looked like a wasp's nest fallen on its side.

I was as far from the Organ Grinder as possible and still sit. His head was wreathed in plumes of foul-smelling pipeweed. The Stone Preacher's glares of disgust grew onerous as the day wore on. As soon as the Organ Grinder drew his bleeding horses up to the tether amid the others, I leaped off. The picnic basket followed, flumping into my arms and letting out a little cough. "He's really angry." I said to the Stone Preacher, as the Organ Grinder began tending to the horses. There was a keening grunt from one of them as I turned. The horse bucked hard as the Organ Grinder's hand clenched on the reins, covered in white powder.

"Oh, yes, indeed," the Stone Preacher rumbled with a pleasant smile. "I thought that was only a rumor, but it seems that it is not. Rubbing salt in the wounds of his own pets – very amusing."

"Should I apologize?" Screams and sounds of combat echoed from inside the grotesque longhouse.

"And make him more vengeful?" The Stone Preacher's throat crackled. "Absolutely not. You can never afford to show compassion to anyone. Hold your counsel in private. Never show that you care for your bodyguards, lest someone take it the wrong way and try to use them against you." He moved to the door of the inn. "I think you like us more than you want to admit. You need to learn to conceal it."

He held open the creaky wooden door, and the two of us stepped into a scene of rowdy madness, the Organ Grinder's heavy tread plodding behind us.

***

We stepped into a bar fight of relentless brutality. A chair was being broken over someone's head. There was a wailing scream from a man somewhere in the press: He was clutching a bloody stump. On the straw covered floor nearby, the severed hand clutched at the air, spasming in a welter of red.

"Should we wait for it to end?" I asked. "We're all tired from the road, I would like to get a room and some rest."

"It would seem that this is the Organ Grinder's sort of place," the Stone Preacher rumbled as the footsteps stopped behind us. There was a podium next to us, a thick crossbow bolt sticking out of it, with no one behind.

"We could just sign in." I said, slipping to the other side of it and applying the Organ Grinder's name to the guestbook. "It isn't as if it's unbelievable. You said it was his kind of place." I saw the unpleasant smile on the face of the Organ Grinder widen, and he stuffed his hand into his pocket to restrain the monkey. A pair of men struggled on top of a nearby table, strangling each other and driving knees into each other's bodies.

"Find us a table." I grinned to the Organ Grinder and stood back as the Organ Grinder cruelly doffed his top hat. He walked over to the two men fighting on the tabletop and shoved them off, driving his boot into the nose of one of them. Blood sprayed. We heard facial bones snap. The Organ Grinder drove a heavy, booted heel into the throat of the other man. He gestured idly to the seats as he brutally shoved the bodies out of the way with his boot.

The Stone Preacher turned to me as the melee began winding down and sighed. "Did you do that just to release his anger?"

"No. I did it because there weren't any tables." The three of us sat at the table as the picnic basket flounced up to the two crawling, bleeding men. I didn't look. Some of the moaning stopped. There was an ugly gulping sound. The Stone Preacher came to look as the picnic basket came trotting over amid the gore and the violence.

One of the heads of the two men who had been fighting at our table was missing. Gore and ichor leaked from the bloody stump as the brawl swirled around us. People slowly returned to their tables or fled out the door. The picnic basket let out a satisfied belch, and moved over to settle at my feet.

"Well, at least we don't have to worry about feeding it." I sighed. "No doubt some local housewife will be infuriated and outraged that my basket has murdered her spouse and seek revenge."

The Stone Preacher let out a gravelly rumble. "Or, she might thank you and reward you."

The Organ Grinder laughed. "I would thank you if you had your pet attack my new wife. It seems to like her." The monkey hooted.

"You will like her," I said. "How could you possibly turn your back on someone so nice? Surely she will not turn her back on you, and she did give you ten years of freedom."

"Like a yoke, it hangs around my neck," the Organ Grinder sighed. The monkey keened with it. Sensing a moment of dejection, the picnic basket lurched forward, but I grabbed it by the handle before the lid could close.

"It's been less than a day," the Stone Preacher rumbled. "Surely your feelings will one day change, or she will transform you into furniture."

"Like all the rest of them?" The Organ Grinder scowled. "I am certain that every one of those chairs, seats, and tables is one of her former lovers. She was too specific."

"Then one should be careful to avoid their fate," I said, as a woman dressed in plain peasant garb came to offer us drinks. She deftly dodged the headless corpse on the floor as it was dragged to the exit and hurled out. She was not particularly attractive. The Organ Grinder leered at her anyway.

"Can I get you drinks and food?" She smiled to us as she noticed the Organ Grinder and the Preacher. "The Stone Preacher and the Organ Grinder! Who is your charge?" She curtsied graciously. "I will bring you food and drink, and it shall be free. To have such magnificent legends together in our establishment!" She raced for the door to the kitchen, the bloody sounds of combat slowly giving way to moans of pain.

The Organ Grinder smiled, his hands settled on the table. "This seems a wonderful antidote to my troubles."

The Stone Preacher let out a dim rumble. "A temporary one at best, and certainly one that could produce more trouble for us."

"He has a point," I said. "Do you really think the Half-Bone Maiden will tolerate that much infidelity so soon? Maybe if she were to become bored of you, but I somehow have a feeling there will be no such feeling. And think of the horrors you'll create if she catches you." I gave a wicked smile.

The Organ Grinder sighed. "You take all the fun out of it," he said gloomily. "I've been married for less than two days, and already, you torture me with it."

"You torture yourself," the Stone Preacher rumbled. "You are behaving like a foolish child. Do you know how many people would murder their mother to be married to the most powerful woman in the world? Because she is the most powerful woman in the world." He gave a rocky grin. "It is amazing how people always receive something they do not desire when they do something they want to do immediately."

"He's completely right," I added. "The reason it's so fun to tease you about it is because you mope so much about it." I crossed my legs. "You will enjoy being married, or you can just be furniture. The question is which one it's going to be."

The Organ Grinder sighed. "I prefer to keep my own skin, if you please."

"I thought that would be the answer." I grinned as the barmaid returned, carrying three big mugs of fizzing liquid.

"Is this beer?" I asked. "Or is it something else?"

"A wise question," the Stone Preacher rumbled. "When in a strange place, one should ask what you're drinking." He reached out for the glass and took a sip of it. "It's ale, only more brutal." He let out a little rattle from his throat.

The Organ Grinder downed his in one gulp. Foam trickled around his mustache and goatee as he leaned back in his chair. "Ah, truly, this is the finest swill I have ever tasted."

I looked at the mug, sighed, and took it, gulping some down. It was absolutely awful. Bitter notes and sour fruit assailed my tongue and making my teeth ache. My face screwed up and I coughed a little bit. "What is this?"

"Well, it's ale." The Organ Grinder gave a crude smile. "It's just not ale as you know it."

"I'd rather I'd never known it at all."

"Well, you have to finish it now," the Stone Preacher added. "Because I wouldn't let the Organ Grinder touch any cup I drank from."

I sighed and drank the rest of it as quickly as I could. The horrible taste coated my mouth as pots of stew were brought by the barmaid. "Such legendary company deserves a legendary stew." She grinned and set the bowls down. I needed something to settle my stomach after the awful beer, so I spooned some into my mouth as quickly as I could. It was thick and fatty, with a greasy taste to it. Somehow, it merged with the beer and made my mouth feel better. The Organ Grinder finished his whole bowl by the time I had eaten three bites. Grease dripped from his mustache as the Stone Preacher shook his head.

"It's lovely," the Organ Grinder patted his stomach. "It reminds me of the time I was forced to eat cow testicles in a graveyard."

I sighed. "You take all the fun out of mediocre meals." I turned to the Stone Preacher and got out of my seat. "I'm going to get us a room, then we can all turn in early. I'm sleeping on the floor. The Organ Grinder can have the bed. Married people deserve a little solitude." I winked and slipped away, over to the podium.

On my way to the lectern, I noticed the picnic basket creeping over to the severed hand and sneaking the equivalent of an after-dinner mint into its mouth before crawling back. I idly tapped the lid when it skulked up to me. "Hey," I said. "No more freebies, okay?"

***

The room we were given was plain, with a mattress filled with straw and a crude cup filled with water on a splintered table. Through the window, on the grounds behind an inn, I could see a large sawed off barrel that passed for a bath, with a crude wooden outhouse assembled not far from it. "This is a pit," I said as I stepped inside.

"It's perfect for the Organ Grinder," the Stone Preacher murmured as his rocky hand pushed the door open

"Indeed," the Organ Grinder thundered, and the monkey hooted as he stepped into the room. "Will you be requiring the bed, my lady?"

"Your lady is the Half-Bone Maiden now, like it or not, and you can have the roach infested piece of straw. I'll take the floor. The bugs will crawl over me less." I grinned.

The picnic basket got up on its hind legs and offered up a sugary pastry that seemed covered with mangoes and papayas, and I snatched it up before anyone else could get to it. "This might

ease my stomach." I ruffled the lid as it closed and received a
happy rustle in response. I bit into the sugary pastry and was
rewarded with the taste of better food. My stomach settled almost
at once.

The Organ Grinder smoothed out the crackling mattress as the
picnic basket made a little trilling noise, and the Stone Preacher
looked him over. "Feeling more signs of dejection?" He rumbled.
"You're not the only one in the world with a marriage you didn't
choose." His smile cracked wider.

"Well, that's hardly a comfort," the Organ Grinder grumbled. "I
never expected to be married at all, least of all to someone who
could turn me into furniture."

I spread out my cloak of runes on the floor while the Organ
Grinder prepared the bed, and the Stone Preacher turned to me
with a smirk on his face. "As I already am furniture, I decline
comment."

"You're more of a church ornament," I said. "But I'll settle."

The Organ Grinder sighed and fell into the bed. "One might
expect we would be attacked by muggers or assassins in this
hellhole. I do not intend to sleep. Plus, I might dream of her, and
that giggling, heaving half-smile."

"She's a sweetheart," I said. "She'll grow on you like a weed."

"More like a pox!" The Organ Grinder thundered. "I am the
Organ Grinder! I cannot be tied down to some woman whose
vengeance is legendary! No one dares tame my manhood!"

"Footstool," I said, as the stew and pastry thickened in my
stomach. "Or maybe the Forest of Screams if you're really
unlucky."

The Stone Preacher's face cracked in a gravelly smile as he
looked at the Organ Grinder. "On the bright side, no more vengeful
husbands."

"Bah!" The Organ Grinder scowled. "I despise having to defend
the honor of anyone beyond my necessary obligations."

"How does that work, exactly?" I hadn't meant to ask. I
snuggled up against my cloak and looked up at the Stone Preacher.

"It is a principle you should know well, gypsy," the Stone
Preacher rumbled. "No one is willing to be the only dupe. So those
of us who find newcomers strive to educate them in the ways of the
world, in order to help them survive the ordeal."

"So it isn't out of any sense of nobility?" I asked. "Just a kind of
bitter camaraderie as you enjoy people suffering a miserable fate?"

"Did you really think there was some sort of 'ever after' here? The Stone Preacher and I have done this with hundreds of others. You're the only one who even tried to trick their way around the initial bargain. All things considered, you've been alive for over a month. You haven't been tortured more than once, been imprisoned no more than a few times, and you've even won some battles without cowering. I know you find me repulsive, and cling to the Stone Preacher and his bloodthirsty fists like a desperate child, but once your journey is over, we are no longer your friends. Indeed, we may oppose or try to destroy you later." The Organ Grinder sneered. "I long for the day when I shall be released from my leash, as the Half-Bone Maiden will certainly not allow me any freedom. Then I shall play my accordion for you, and I shall reap the benefits of my long overdue reward. If you are lucky, a little Organ Grinder will be in your pouch!" He cackled and pulled his hat down over his head.

"Why couldn't I be the Queen of Deafness?" I muttered. "Then I wouldn't have to hear you or your accordion anymore."

The Stone Preacher let out a low rumble, and the Organ Grinder joined him, cackling with laughter. I didn't think it was funny at all.

I slept poorly, tossing and turning on the creaky floor. I heard the dirty rustle of straw shuddering in the bed. I dreamed of the Organ Grinder, civilized by the Half-Bone Maiden, her feet up on his shoulders as if he were nothing more than a piece of furniture. It didn't give me any comfort. I wanted it to.

***

In the morning, I was awakened by the yawning grunt of the Organ Grinder, who reached up for his hat and grabbed a cockroach off the top. He handed it to the monkey, which stuffed it into its mouth. The picnic basket, vigilant, was chewing on something also.

"It seems the place is infested with bugs," the Stone Preacher rumbled. "We should leave as quickly as possible, and perhaps save breakfast for the road."

The picnic basket let out a rustling sigh. "You don't want to feed everyone this morning, do you?" The basket shook. "Too bad. You had an extra head and hand last night, and that should be more than enough for everyone." The basket backed up and let out a whimper. "No whining," I said. "You eat too much."

The monkey hissed at the picnic basket, which turned and leaped at it. The Stone Preacher reached out with a lightning-fast grab, and yanked it by the handle, returning it to the floor. "Everyone should get ready to go."

I gathered my cloak, and we hurried for the door. "I'd like to take a bath before I leave." I stalked out to the bath with the picnic basket following me. The half-open barrel swirled with leaves, and it took me almost an hour to pump water into buckets and fill the barrel. The picnic basket shied away while I lit the fire, and didn't come any closer while I bathed.

When I was finally clean, I didn't really feel any cleaner than I did before. I dressed as carefully as I could, and gathered my bow to me just in case violence waited in front of the inn.

When I moved around the front, the Organ Grinder chuckled while the Stone Preacher stood there grimly. Flies buzzed around the headless corpse from the previous night. The Organ Grinder joked with passers-by as they came to get their horses. The Stone Preacher's head ground from left to right. I did my best to avoid the corpse as the Organ Grinder untethered the horses.

"Well, at least he's in no shape to be well cared for!" the Organ Grinder thundered. "And the lack of vengefulness seems to suggest that he is not missed."

I shook my head. "He paid a price, and that's the end of it. There's no need to be so cheerful about it." I sighed and began climbing up onto the cart.

The Stone Preacher rumbled. "Your callousness is showing. You're becoming more like us." I picked up the picnic basket, which wiggled in my grasp, and settled up on the seat.

"Come on," I said to the Organ Grinder. "Let's get going."

The Organ Grinder gave a wistful look at the corpse in front of the inn, as if there was something he had yet to say to it. He walked over to the hitching post, untied the emaciated horses, and climbed up into his seat. He drew the whip out of his greatcoat. "Come!" he thundered. "We shall reach Cliffedge, that notorious hive of murderous swine, and beat our path to the door of the Duchess of Candles!"

"We have news of her relative," I said. "That might get us in the door."

"Good thinking," the Stone Preacher mused, a lilt of wind brushing across sand in his tone.

"Oh, by the way, the next time we're traveling to an unpleasant place, could I at least be warned the night before? It might be helpful in being prepared."

"Nothing you do will prepare you for Cliffedge," the Organ Grinder gave a low cackle. "It's my kind of city, all the way through. Bribable guards, a seedy underworld, and cruel, unforgiving people. There is not a single inch of Cliffedge that is not filled with moral turpitude, except, of course, for the home of your miserable new friend, the Duchess of Candles."

"I would not call her miserable," the Stone Preacher rumbled. "Her estate is perfectly safe."

"When she hears what you did to the Seneschal, it won't be safe at all." The Organ Grinder chuckled. "How do we propose to get around that?" He lashed the horses with fury as we took off down the road.

The question of whether or not lying would invalidate the Half-Bone Maiden's token clawed at my mind for several hours, until the sky grew bleak and the weather grew colder. We drew the wagon to a stop at the side of the road. I huddled near a small fire. The Organ Grinder spent the night in his cart alone while the Stone Preacher stood watch. I knew he was suffering over his sudden attachment. I was filled with secret glee.

***

The Stone Preacher ground his way over to me by the campfire. "You are enjoying his suffering. Perhaps you are enjoying it too much."

"Those are big words from someone who regularly kills people and never seems to feel any remorse." I said. "You're very old. How many people have you killed in these journeys?"

"Many. Their deaths are unimportant because, in the end, importance is only for the living. It may seem callous, but when one deals with my cold god, whose name I dare not speak, one does not argue."

"So you can't speak your god's name? That must get difficult during services." I laughed.

"It is not necessary to invoke the name during prayers," the Stone Preacher rumbled. "However, among the faithful, and only when they are alone, it may be spoken."

"What happens if someone speaks the name around people who aren't of the faith?" I asked. "It seems almost like a cult."

"I kill them," the Stone Preacher said flatly. "No rituals, no complicated sacrifices, I simply locate the heretic and kill them. Faith is a commitment untainted by forgiveness. It is enlightening in its beauty and searing in its brutality."

"You'll excuse me for not joining your religion," I said. "It seems unfriendly."

"You are not required to." The Stone Preacher let out a throaty chuckle. "Just as I am not required to have compassion. Though, you are exceptional. The Organ Grinder mentioned it."

"I have a plan for getting us through the Duchess of Candles' home, but you have to not admit to killing the Seneschal of Votaries, if there is some sort of weird mystical link."

"It can happen," the Stone Preacher admitted. "I did not think we would have to visit another person of a similar affinity, but if not now, when?"

"You're looking forward to this. Don't kill her, too. It's poor etiquette to kill someone who is helping you out."

"While she is, no doubt, responsible for my imprisonment in some unusual or obligatory fashion, I'm certain that we can come to an agreement. She likes to obey the rules."

"I think we should lie. I think that we should construct a heroic story of how he died defending the temple from bandits or the like. She'll never know."

"If she finds out that you lied, she'll be a powerful enemy."

"And if we tell the truth, I'll have to spend days finding a way to unchain you again," I said. "This time, with malice aforethought, and more killing that makes being social very difficult."

"When she finds out you lied, you might have to do that anyway," the Stone Preacher rumbled. From the cart, the snoring of the Organ Grinder rattled through the wooden slats. In the fading light, I could barely see images of animals on the wall of the cart, and made out a word that seemed like *Circus* in the fading paint. It was the first time I noticed it. I hadn't been paying attention.

"Was the Organ Grinder ever in a circus?" I asked. "The cart looks like it might have been."

"I don't know. You could ask him, but as you have seen, we are notoriously silent about our pasts, lest they be used against us."

"That sounds uncomfortable," I said. "You mean people actually blackmail people about their former lives?"

"Not exactly," the Stone Preacher said. "The past can be a weapon for people like the Half-Bone Maiden. Charms can be constructed. Sorceries and magics can be performed. A history can become a means of destroying one's enemy or taking advantage of someone."

"Wouldn't that make a new enemy?" I asked.

"Certainly," the Stone Preacher rumbled. "But dead people rarely get a second chance."

I huddled for the rest of the night in silence, and I didn't sleep at all.

***

When the Organ Grinder woke up in the morning, he glanced over to my bleary eyes. I huddled near the smoking remains of a fire. I was idly stroking the handle of the picnic basket, eating something that looked like a gravy and doughnut sandwich. It had a lot of sugar in it. The basket made little wiggling rustles as the monkey peered out from under the Organ Grinder's coat. "Pining for the desire of me?" the Organ Grinder cackled.

I mumbled something angry. I don't even remember what it was. I was only grateful that my mouth was full. "What was that?" His voice carried across the roadside.

"I would rather desire being eaten by the picnic basket." I reached into the Basket, which happily rustled. I felt a tongue slide over my hand. I fumbled around inside it and reached the edge of a warm plate. "You should eat the biscuits and gravy. They're even topped with chicken." I grinned as I pulled out the plate. "No more lewdness for the day, or I'll put it back inside him."

The Stone Preacher turned, glowering. "Eat," he said. "Today's journey will be long, and I have no desire to hear hunger complaints."

The Organ Grinder scowled and stalked over, taking the plate. He stared. There was even a fork at the side. He glared down at the picnic basket. "What is this thing?" He said as he glowered downward. The picnic basket slunk behind me a little bit.

"It's a fork," I said. "You use it to eat with." There was a creaking smirk from the mouth of the Stone Preacher.

The Organ Grinder actually chuckled and settled down on the rock. "I see the sharpness of your wit has not declined." He began to nibble on the biscuits and chicken gravy. "This is quite fine. Not quite coarse enough for my tastes, but sufficiently fatty and greasy. My thanks."

The monkey let out a little cackle and swished the knife on its tail about after crawling up onto the Organ Grinder's shoulder.

"Is there any reason you're placating him this morning?" The Stone Preacher asked.

"I'm tired of watching him whip the horses in anger. He doesn't do it as much when he's stuffed to the gills, so the picnic basket and I had a talk."

The Organ Grinder and the Stone Preacher just stared. "It talks?" The Preacher's rocky eyes cracked open. The Organ Grinder shoveled food into his mouth faster, as if to keep himself from saying something he might regret.

"Well, I can sort of tell it what to make. It really doesn't talk. But it does communicate." I ruffled the lid of the Basket and it rolled over on its side, kicking short wicker legs in the air.

"That doesn't make me feel particularly comfortable," The Organ Grinder mumbled. "I wonder who it ate to make this."

"Probably the head and the hand from the other day," I said. "It still seems pretty heavy though. It's probably working on something really big." I ruffled the basket's underside, and it gave a happy little wiggle, and righted itself.

"Does that bother you at all?" the Organ Grinder asked. "It seems you're adapting particularly well."

"It only bothers me a little. I've kind of gotten used to what it does. I just have to be mindful not to let it eat anyone too important."

"That's the spirit," the Stone Preacher rumbled. "It is true that allowing it to eat a few influential people could make you unpopular."

"Well, it ate the Duke of Bells," I said.

"Yes." The Organ Grinder chuckled. "But no one liked him. If it eats people nobody likes, then you're a hero. If it eats popular folk, then you're a monster. I'll always be a monster. I'll not let that calcified wench civilize me." He shoved the last few crumbs from the plate into his mouth and hurled the plate aside, shattering it against a rock. He wiped his mouth on his leather sleeve.

"That calcified wench won't civilize you," the Stone Preacher said. "She'll do something terrible and awful to you. And it is like kicking a puppy."

"He already beats horses for no reason." I got up and made my way to the cart. "What makes you think he doesn't like kicking puppies?"

The journey for the next few hours was quiet and sullen. None of us had very much to say to one another as the cart wobbled down the road. There was only the occasional rustle in my lap from the picnic basket, and a quiet whistle of the monkey slashing the knife-tail in the air.

***

The road ratcheted under the cart as the air gathered around our ears and stung them. I huddled in my cloak and the Organ Grinder slunk into his greatcoat. The Stone Preacher just shook his head and laughed as we moved along the road. The picnic basket whistled loudly in the wind, and the monkey shivered in the pocket of the greatcoat.

To our left, the bleak grass gave way to a massive cliff, where the wind ripped and roared. Somewhere below it, we could hear the roar and clench of the tide's fingers, trying to crush rocks with force and noise. "We're almost there, aren't we?" I shouted to the Organ Grinder.

"Oh, aye," the Organ Grinder grinned, the cold moving his goatee about. "When we get there, we'll no doubt have to stay in a horrid inn full of filthy scum." He grinned to me with a wild laugh on his face. "I fully intend to take advantage of my ten years of freedom."

The Stone Preacher gave a rattling smirk, his movement somehow heard over the roaring wind as we made our way along the trail. In the distance lights flickered, and something was coming into view. "I will watch you carefully, sir, to thwart you if I can."

The Organ Grinder laughed. "Your attempts have proven fruitless so far."

"The beast is most complacent when he is in his homeland." The Stone Preacher rumbled as we came around a turn in the road. I stared at the wrecked mass of stone that was the city of Cliffedge.

It towered up into the sky at confused, darkened angles. Black stone masonry pitted and mismatched along uneven walls. Guards patrolled walls with a gloomy, indifferent pace, all of them either too fat or too thin, as if bloated or starving. The drawbridge settled along a half-moat, and beyond it loomed a murderous mouth of a portcullis filled with sharp, uneven teeth. There were misshapen guards at the gate, as if some were lurking creatures rather than people.

On the side of the cliff, some objects that looked like boats floated, settling there in midair, half shrouded in darkness and concealed by the massive walls.

"Stand aside!" the Organ Grinder bellowed. "It is I, the Organ Grinder! Stand aside!" The lathered horses lurched forward, thumping onto the drawbridge as six creatures that were more monsters than men closed ranks. Fishlike eyes bulged inside their swollen faces, their angled heads sprouting seemingly random tufts of fur and hair. They wore strange piecemeal armor that hid their limbs and torsos. Odd looking helmets bristled with randomly placed spikes. Every one of them carried a polearm, a twisted mass of hooks and edges. They pointed them at the horses, as the Organ Grinder drew the cart to a stop.

"Taxes," one of them hissed. "Pay the tax of flesh!"

"What's the tax of flesh?" I asked the Organ Grinder.

"I can't pay it," the Stone Preacher rumbled matter-of-factly. "I don't have any flesh to pay with."

"Pay in flesh," the creature hissed. "Down there." He looked over the edge. In the half-moat rested dozens of dead bodies, and body parts. Some were impaled on spikes. Entrails hung from rocky protrusions. There were arms, and hands, and a few feet spread out amidst the bodies, and as I looked down, I finally became aware of the horrible smell that my mind had been blocking out. There was no water in the moat at all.

The Organ Grinder turned to the two of us and shrugged. "I don't know what this is." A look of confusion crossed his features. "This is new."

"That's not terribly civil," I said to one of the creatures. "Which one of you is in charge here? I am a noble, and these are my escorts, and you oppose us at your peril."

"No creature is immune to taxes," the voice of the largest hissed. "Pay! Pay! The Duchess of Candles demands this tax!" He took a few steps forward, his grin wide on his lips.

The picnic basket growled in my lap, and the monkey hooted. "I have a token here." I said. "It allows us passage into the home of the Duchess of Candles. Stand aside." I summoned the bow into my hand, letting the smooth black wood shiver in my fingers. I would have to compensate for the wind.

The squad leader peered cruelly at the token, and backed away as he saw the bow manifest. "Rune summoner," he murmured. "Noble indeed."

"So you're not a noble?" I scowled. "Answer!" I motioned the Stone Preacher forward.

"No." His buggy eyes fell. "Please do not do anything! I have a wife, despite my foul appearance."

"Then the Organ Grinder will not be lonely." I turned to the Stone Preacher. "Pay our taxes with this idiot."

It happened in a second, so fast I could barely see it. The Stone Preacher leaped forward, grabbed the monster by the throat and hurled him into the spiked moat of rotting flesh and corpses. There was an agonizing scream, and a sucking thump of flesh against stone. "Your taxes are paid, my lady." The Stone Preacher's face cracked into a rocky grin.

The Organ Grinder chuckled. "We forgot to find out his name." He laughed as the others began backing away from us, allowing us passage into the city. "I thought you were intent on denying me all such pleasures."

No one even moved to raise an alarm as we rode forward.

"I am. I like the Half-Bone Maiden. But that doesn't mean I can't lie to a hairy beast."

The Organ Grinder laughed, and drove the horses forward. The satisfied smile on the Stone Preacher's face told me everything I needed to know. It took everything I had to keep the picnic basket from leaping into the moat, struggling with the handle as we thundered inside.

***

At night, the city was bleak and cold. Wind whipped off the cliffs, blasting us as the Organ Grinder drove his cart through narrow streets. There were almost no people on them.

"Do you remember how to get there?" I asked the Organ Grinder. "I doubt any guardsmen will give us directions after our little taxpaying stunt."

"I was never there. The last thing I wanted was to be subject to the whims of the Duchess of Candles."

"Would she not love your accordion, as all the others do?" I said in mocking tones. "After all, you were able to lure even the Half-Bone Maiden into your wicked cart, and now you are joined in matrimony."

"I do not believe that the Duchess of Candles would fall prey to my accordion." The Organ Grinder sighed, his monocle shifting a little bit as he turned to look at me. "The Duchess of Candles likes girls."

"Oh. So it can't overcome preferences?" There was something curious about the powers and rules, but apparently everything had its own laws.

"Perhaps if I had thought about it when I had the accordion made, but I fear that I was not nearly so wise in my choices." He smirked. "We all have little things that we regret. Fortunately, I am not really missing anything by not being able to bed the Duchess." He cackled as the Stone Preacher walked alongside us.

"I suppose now you'll suggest that I should go to bed with her." I said. "You know, borrow your accordion, play a few bars, lure her in and rut."

"That would be a magnificent idea! Then I could join in!" The Organ Grinder chuckled. To my left, as we headed through the streets, I could see the Stone Preacher burying his face in his hands. The monkey hooted viciously, sticking its head out from the Organ Grinder's coat pocket.

"I take it you aren't enjoying the conversation?" I looked down at the Preacher from the seat. "I'm not really enjoying it either." I ruffled the picnic basket. "It's okay. You'll have something to eat again, soon."

The Stone Preacher looked up at me and gave a rocky crackle that might have been a sigh. "I am simply tired of hearing him. I require respite from his loathsome practices."

"It's only nine years and three hundred and sixty two days to civilization or furniture," I teased. "I'm sure the way you measure time, that's less than an eyeblink."

The Stone Preacher's lips cracked into a granite smirk. "You do have a point." He smiled up at the Organ Grinder. It was as if I could feel his imagination roam to the future.

The Organ Grinder stared at the Stone Preacher, his eyes sullen as his free hand moved to pet the diseased face of his pet. "If you would not remind me, it would be appreciated."

We lurched past a small group of night watchmen, patrolling with polearms and fishlike faces. The Organ Grinder stopped the cart, his leer returning. "Gentlemen, if you could, perhaps, direct this noble lady and her cart to the Estate of the Duchess of Candles?" He stood up in the cart, and bowed very low to them, tipping his hat.

The sergeant spoke up, his voice a dry, thick drone. "Go down four blocks, past the lantern sign, and make a left towards the Wind Docks." He pointed his polearm and let out a yawning hiss.

"What's a wind dock?" I asked.

"A wind dock is for flying ships," the Stone Preacher rumbled. "I thought I would save that little fact for morning, when the sun was out and they looked impressive."

"That's cheating," I looked out towards the edge of the cliff, imagining what the ships looked like in the daylight.

"How are you supposed to get to the Castle in the Sky without some means of flight?" the Stone Preacher rumbled. "Yes, you could run up there alone, but if the King of Feathers wants to kill you, it is likely you would be cut down. We must arrive stylishly and invoke the laws of royal hospitality."

"That's an even better kind of cheating." I grinned.

The Organ Grinder laughed as he drove the cart forward, and I shouted "My thanks, good sir!" in as pompous an attitude as I could. I had to spend a little time working myself up to be haughty so the Duchess wouldn't comment on my peasant qualities. I could feel the intelligent dress slithering over my legs, and oozing up over my body. I didn't even know where it had been hiding itself.

***

We wove through streets and followed directions. Narrowness almost squeezed the cart. The Stone Preacher was forced to walk behind us. The cart emerged onto a large boulevard, well lit and empty. A few prostitutes and beggars crawled about the shadows of alleys as more of fish eyed guards patrolled. "What do these guards call themselves?" I asked the Organ Grinder. "All of the other guard types seem to have unusual names."

"I don't know," the Organ Grinder said. "They didn't look like that the last time they were here. They were merely the Watchers of the Cliff." He shrugged. "Things change. Curses happen. Do you really want to investigate it?"

"No," I said. "But it may find us anyway."

The Stone Preacher grimaced. "We do not have time to investigate this," he rumbled. "We need to stay at the Duchess of Candles' home tonight and fly off first thing in the morning. The Weeper in Shadows will have many allies and contacts here, and we do not."

"You could have told me that part," I said to the Organ Grinder.

"I didn't think I needed to." The Organ Grinder grinned as the horses, whinnying with the pain of the lash, thundered down the cobbles, passing the occasionally lit window. "There don't seem to be a lot of people out. I don't like the look of it."

"It could be a holiday," I said. "Royalty does randomly declare them."

"I don't think so," the Stone Preacher murmured, as the picnic basket echoed with a weary rustle. "A trap seems much more likely."

"We could try not being paranoid, but I think you would both look at me with eyes like the fish guards." I smiled. "Alertness is the better part of valor."

A gate between thick stone walls waited in front of us, dark mist rising up as we moved closer to the wind dock and the sea below.

"I don't like fog." I shuddered. "That was how I got here."

A few guards moved about the walls of the estate. Thick black armor creaked in the darkness. Unlike the watch, the helmeted figures carried huge curved swords. Each of them must have been seven feet tall. On their backs, they had quivers full of javelins. I couldn't see their faces. The helmets looked unpleasant, with yellow lights burning from within. "Are they all made of wax?" I asked the Stone Preacher.

"It is likely," he replied. "You're very observant. Is your vision improving?"

"It has, a little." I admitted. When I squinted, even in the dark, I could see the guards on the other side of the gate, hidden in the bushes that led up to a squat, palatial manor of stone. "You there, at the gate!" I shouted. I had to start getting used to being in charge. "I bear a token from the Half-Bone Maiden! I demand entry for myself and my servants!"

"Oho, it's servants now, is it?" The Organ Grinder laughed roughly. The monkey chittered. I gripped the handle of the picnic basket tight, as it lurched forward towards the Organ Grinder's pocket.

The Stone Preacher's lips cracked in a rocky snapping noise. "Why not? It is true for the moment." His features shifted under the hood, as if he were trying to remain unnoticed.

The guards hiding in the bushes slipped out. One of them gave a little hiss before speaking, as if gathering air through waxy lips. "Show us." The voice was hollow and almost toneless, an emanation rather than a noise.

I reached into my cloak and pulled out the token, showing it to the guard. With a dull, thunderous clank, the gate began to roll aside. The two guards watched our wagon as the Organ Grinder whipped the horses towards the manor.

***

The door to the grim stone manor was already open by the time we made our way up the walk. Thick columns supported a heavy set of stone crenellations. More crossbowmen stood on the rooftop, their eyes focused on us as we padded up the gravel path. I could see strange flowers on either side of the walk, huddled under hedges that seemed to wander up to the walls of the courtyard in darkness. I could almost hear flowers make whispering noises. The picnic basket slavered as I reached down to grab the handle.

"The hedges are alive," I said to the Stone Preacher, lifting the basket off the ground as its legs churned in gravel.

"That's not a surprise, girl," the Organ Grinder interrupted. "They're plants. Of course plants are alive."

"I don't mean in that way. I mean in an 'it's intelligent' kind of way." We walked a little further as the picnic basket struggled, legs wiggling in the air. "The basket wants to eat them."

The Stone Preacher and the Organ Grinder peered, and the Stone Preacher's eyes widened. "I know them," he murmured oddly. "The flowers look like some people I used to know. However, I fear it is too late to turn back."

The Organ Grinder let out a laugh. "That is the first time I have ever seen him show fear. No wonder I never came here. It seems she has some means of placing enemies within her hedges. That is ominous indeed."

At the door, a well-dressed servant stood, an opulent hat with a candle sitting in the center of it on top of his head. He was slender and wore a black doublet above grey hose and a pair of polished black boots.

"Fashion here is a mishmash." I said as I looked at him.

"When people live for hundreds of years, their traditions are thrown into a mixing bowl and coughed back up." The Organ Grinder chuckled. "This is why many of the punishments for crimes seem odd, and feudalism still reigns."

"It's certainly helped you," I said with a smirk. "In a democracy, where divorce doesn't come at the end of a sword, your abilities wouldn't be nearly so feared."

"Bah," the Stone Preacher rumbled. "Only theocracies truly serve the people. Otherwise their minds are cluttered with things of the earthen world. I stand here a symbol of that corrupt transformation." He scowled as we made our way up the steps. The servant bowed to us.

"I am the servant of the Duchess of Candles." The servant smiled and produced a burning taper from under his doublet. He lit the candle on top of his hat. It blazed before settling down to a flicker. "If you will please come inside, I will take your bags. I understand her good friend the Half-Bone Maiden has given you a token?"

I showed the token again, and he gave me a clever grin. "Wise you are indeed to not let me handle it, young woman." He gestured graciously to usher us through the open door. We walked inside. "I must take your bags to your quarters. While I am doing that, the Duchess will receive you." He smiled as though his wit had increased after he lit the candle. He did not seem waxy like the rest of her guards, what little I'd seen of them, anyway.

The foyer was a magnificent affair of marble and tile, gloriously polished to a perfect shine while twin staircases led up to an ornately crafted overhang. Enameled in black wood, the overhang reflected dark light off multiple portraits of candlesticks in various positions, adorning the walls. Two arches rested on either side of the walls. At the back of the foyer a stood a large pair of double doors engraved with candlesticks.

"You take the bags," I said to the Stone Preacher. "It is a valuable and important thing to make sure my room is safe." I curtsied as gracefully to him as I could.

The Stone Preacher smiled. "Your penchant for guarded courtesy knows no bounds." He returned to the cart to gather our things.

The servant waited patiently while I held the slavering, struggling picnic basket in my arms. The Organ Grinder chuckled, idly stroking the diseased monkey in his pocket. "You do have a way of defusing situations."

"I want to keep my head on my shoulders." I glowered at the Organ Grinder as we waited patiently.

When the doors opened, my stomach crawled. I began to slip into the curtsy I had been practicing, in the hope of currying favor.

***

The first thing I saw of the Duchess of Candles was her shoes: Elegant, smooth, and crystalline, with little circular hoops at the backs of the bases. They were almost translucent, shining in the light reflected off the banisters. I gazed upward, my vision travelling over silky folds of maroon in her dress to jewel-covered bangles on her wrists. Her arms were mostly bare, but her shoulders were covered in large puffs of gold fabric that highlighted her mountain of dark hair and smooth, pale skin. Her deep brown eyes gazed down at me from behind an oddly cute nose and wide mouth. On her head was a crushed velvet cap, supporting a maroon candle reeking of fresh tallow.

"So you are the unnamed one who is causing all the ruckus?" She smiled. "I understand your bodyguards have created quite a stir among the nobility."

"It is not my choice, my lady. They are who they are."

"You are too polite. Rise, we shall talk as equals."

I stood and the dress wiggled to dust itself off. "Thank you," I said. "As it is your home, I shall defer to you on the topic of conversation."

"I see you are practiced at the art of etiquette." She gave me a pleasant wink. "Have they been teaching you?"

"I fear the answer to that is no. I was always this way," I lied.

"Excellent. I understand that you came here by means of the dark forest. You have not, perhaps, heard news of my cousin, the Seneschal of Votaries?"

"Nothing that befits a lady of your station. He was courteous and polite, and it was altogether boring." I decided to omit the part about the Stone Preacher killing him.

"Of course." She gave me a cheerful smile. "So tell me of your travels."

I blushed. The Organ Grinder moved to open his mouth as I heard the picnic basket growl. "I would appreciate silence." I whispered to the Organ Grinder, his hands sliding slowly towards the grips of his accordion. The monkey whimpered from underneath the greatcoat.

"I see you control the Organ Grinder well." She gave me a slight laugh as the Organ Grinder glowered at her, his eyes taking in her smooth skin and female shape.

The Organ Grinder's mouth opened, but I raised a finger. "Bite your tongue," I said to the Organ Grinder. "You're a married man now." I allowed myself a little pleasure on the inside.

"Oh, really?" The Duchess of Candles teased. "And who is the lucky lady who has captured the heart of the Organ Grinder?" The Organ Grinder gritted his teeth, and his fists clenched together.

"The Organ Grinder made the mistake of assuming that his charms worked the same way on the Half-Bone Maiden as they do on others. He regrets it every day, but she's not someone you say no to."

"Congratulations!" The Duchess curtsied to the Organ Grinder. "I shall send your new wife a wedding present. But no furniture. I fear that will be your fate if you hurt her feelings."

The Organ Grinder let out a low growl from his throat, and the picnic basket growled back at him. "Stop it," I said fiercely. "You're embarrassing me."

"We shall talk later," the Organ Grinder murmured

"Do you always allow him to do such things?" The Duchess asked.

"I do, from time to time. It keeps me amused."

She nodded slightly. "Any friend of the Half-Bone Maiden and her new husband, is a friend of mine. I shall have to throw a celebration in honor of your arrival and the Organ Grinder's good fortune."

"It is nothing, Madame." The Organ Grinder grinned, bowing gently to the Duchess. "I am sure my wife and I will find time to visit you soon."

"I shall repair to my chambers. I'm sure your quarters will be easy to locate. I gave the servant instructions to stand outside until you arrived."

I curtsied in return, and the Organ Grinder rose from his bow. "We'll try to make certain that your celebration tomorrow is of the highest quality." I kept an eye on the Organ Grinder's eyes as we turned and she exited through the same pair of black double doors.

"How could you do that?" The Organ Grinder scowled to me as we began ascending the stairs. "She is lush and attractive, with a firm bosom and, no doubt, smooth, long legs."

"She could also be made of wax. Do you really want to bed a piece of tallow?"

The Organ Grinder sighed, and the monkey chittered. The picnic basket leaped up and I caught it by the handle, stroking the lid. "I hadn't thought of that," he said a little wistfully. We travelled along the second floor towards our room, where the servant dutifully stood.

***

I stepped into the room with the Organ Grinder behind me. The Stone Preacher was already arranging our belongings into three distinct and neat piles. "I take it you survived?" He raised a granite eyebrow and stared at the Organ Grinder. "You seem a little out of sorts."

"The Duchess congratulated him on his marriage," I said cheerfully. "He didn't take it well." The picnic basket rustled and I gave the lid a little rub.

The Organ Grinder scowled. "It is like a yoke around my neck. Am I an ox, to breed with a sorceress for your amusement?" The monkey chittered assent. I yanked on the basket, who tried to seize an opportunity.

The Stone Preacher chuckled as he finished arranging the bags, and motioned to the servant to shut the door. There was a click and we were inside a room lit by thick green candles in heavyweight wooden sconces.

The room was thickly carpeted in red. Bulky black curtains obscured the windows, filtering the light from outside into a dreadful haze. The bed was a four-postered affair crammed up with thick sheets and thicker quilts of crushed, ornate velvet. The furniture in the room was equally ornate, and seemed just as heavy. Massive chairs and a chest of drawers sat in weighty repose on the carpeted floor.

"It seems that the Duchess of Candles likes to melt her guests." I said, looking over the quilts as if they would crush me. The dress slithered about on my shoulders. I sighed and summoned the bow and arrow, peering under the massive bed.

"What are you doing?" The Organ Grinder stared. The picnic basket dug its claws into the carpet, opened its lid, and growled under the bed in the direction I was pointing.

"Looking for monsters," I said. "If ever there was a bed that looked like it could have monsters under it, it's this one."

"Sometimes the best monster is the one who shares the bed with you," the Organ Grinder leered. "After all, I have a little less than ten years before I am a doomed man. The least you could do is accommodate your poor, lonely bodyguard since you have convinced me that bedding the Duchess is like bedding a lump of wax."

"I merely made the suggestion. You did all the convincing yourself." I flashed him a winning smile. Even though I wasn't looking at him, I thought I could hear the Stone Preacher's lips crack into a smirk.

There was nothing under the bed at all, just air and dust motes. "Ha," the Organ Grinder chuckled. "It seems that complacency, for once, is its own reward."

"So were you in the circus?" I asked the Organ Grinder. "I saw a faded outline on your cart a few nights ago."

"I was, indeed."

"He is a walking circus," the Stone Preacher rumbled.

The Organ Grinder's monkey took a moment to peer out from the greatcoat and chitter at the Stone Preacher. It reached back underneath its knife-tail with a tiny hand. The Organ Grinder stuffed it downward. "Never do that," he scolded. "Do your business elsewhere."

I failed to suppress a chuckle.

The Organ Grinder guffawed. "That is a place where even I, craving rumpledness and the stains of used sheets, draw the line," he said fiercely. "Indeed, I was in a circus for many years, a fabulous carnival, at which I was the star attraction. Needless to say, many of the local women found me irresistible." He smiled. "Somehow, you seem to be able to resist my charms. Your desire for your true love must be powerful indeed."

The merest mention of my desire made me think of those emerald eyes, and I was nudged by the picnic basket before I could sigh. "It relieves me."

"In any case, I bedded the wives of the town council in a single evening, and chased by the folk of that town – whose name I do not even remember, some filthy little Balkan province – I found myself here. They did injure me severely, and there was the little matter of several local women who found themselves so enamored of me that they committed suicide."

He leered a little bit. "Wounded when I arrived, I was found by a kindly old man, whose face I do not even recall. When I first awoke, in a haze from strange medicines I did not know, I thought him one of the townswomen come to rescue me. I seized him, rutting with his dirty old flesh as though he were a young farmgirl." He let out a little laugh. "I was surprised but felt no remorse. Much to my surprise, I discovered that my accordion had magical effects, and all the poxes I had acquired had somehow transferred themselves to my monkey. The incident where a knife was tied to his tail had nothing to do with it. Now I wander the Otherworld, in search of beautiful women and handsome men, taking my pleasure where I can find it."

The Stone Preacher scowled roughly. "That explains a great deal."

"Let me guess," I said. "You were the old man, who, embittered by lasciviousness, sought solace in the woods as a hermit, only to rescue someone you didn't recognize, who was badly wounded and wearing a top hat. You nursed him back to health, repaired his cart for him, and when he awakened, you found yourself very sore and unable to stop him."

The Organ Grinder guffawed and the Stone Preacher rumbled. "No, I'm hundreds of years older than that."

"It was still magnificent." The Organ Grinder cackled. "It almost makes me wish it was true."

"Sorry," I said to the Stone Preacher, whose teeth gritted with frustration. "I had to say it. It doesn't matter how impolitic it is. You simply refuse to talk about yourself."

The Stone Preacher scowled. "It is but a simple thing that I endure in the name of my cold god," he said with a hallow voice. "Will you require me at the party tomorrow evening?"

"I think so. Be on your best behavior. I don't think the Duchess wants her party disrupted by violence. I told her a story about the Seneschal. You don't have to be wary."

The Organ Grinder laughed. "See, she even lies for you! But she will not protect me at all! You should be so lucky. Perhaps you will discover that she is your one true love, and be liberated from your rocky shell by the power of rutting!" He almost sputtered with laughter.

"It's not a shell," I said. "He's made of stone all the way through."

"Well, you'll never lack for something hard to get you through the night." The Organ Grinder chuckled while the Stone Preacher scowled.

"Be silent, or I shall forget her command not to kill you." The Stone Preacher's fist clenched.

"Both of you stop." I sighed. "We need to decide how to present ourselves tomorrow. This has to be a paragon of elegance with no embarrassments."

"Well," the Organ Grinder smiled. "I could indispose the Duchess even if she does have a body of wax."

"That won't be necessary." I gestured to both of them. "The Stone Preacher will be on my right, and The Organ Grinder will be on my left. The pets stay upstairs."

Violent chittering from the monkey echoed from the greatcoat pocket, and the picnic basket tried to jump from my arms to get at the beast. "Don't eat it while we're out." I said icily to the picnic basket. "Or I'll set you on fire."

The basket shivered a little bit in my grip and made a desperate trilling noise. "But if you're good, and don't eat the monkey, I'll let you eat something eventually, ok?" The basket calmed as I gently rubbed the handle.

We practiced our entrance for at least an hour as the smell of scented candles wafted through the room. When our rehearsal was done, I crawled into bed as my dress slithered off me, hanging and fluffing itself on a nearby rack. When I slept, I dreamed of green eyes and kisses touching my eyes and my ears. Even when I dreamed he was inside me and we rutted like beasts, I never felt once that he was anything like the Organ Grinder.

***

The clattering of a rolling serving cart echoed in my ears. I awoke to the thunder of the Organ Grinder snoring in a chair. The Stone Preacher was standing to one side of the door, holding it open with an irritated look on his face. The servant had returned with a wheeled cart, topped with trays that filled the air with wonderful smells. Half-crushed by covers, I instinctively reached for the handle of the picnic basket and squeezed as the boy hurried out. I was rewarded with a hiss of jealousy from under the lid, and some struggling in the direction of the door the servant. "Quiet," I said. "You'll wake the Organ Grinder, and his snoring is preferable to his conversation."

The basket settled down. Across the room, the Stone Preacher's face was quirked in a clever smirk. "I didn't hear anything." He rattled a little bit. "Let's see if what's under the lids is safe." He bent down and lifted one of the covers. "It looks like eggs. And a full rasher of bacon." He glared suspiciously at the Organ Grinder. "You'd do well to save him some. He'll be furious if he doesn't get any grease or lard into his gut."

I ruffled the picnic basket, which had settled itself in the quilts, making a depression in them. I struggled out of bed and took one of the plates, and allowed myself one slice of bacon. The yolks were blue in color, and the outer ring of the eggs was black. "What are these things? They don't smell like wax."

"I don't know." The Stone Preacher muttered. "I've never seen eggs like these before. No doubt, you'll find out later if it's important."

"I was more thinking of whether or not they're poisonous."

The monkey whuffled as the Organ Grinder awoke, and toppled off the hat with a screech as the Organ Grinder reached for it. "What's this I hear about poison?" he thundered. His voice grew excited, as if the invocation of disgraceful behavior had summoned his consciousness.

"You should look at breakfast." I said as I waved a piece of yolk and egg at him. "Have you ever seen eggs like this before?"

"No," he said. "But I don't think they're unsafe." I responded by taking a bite. They tasted vaguely smoky, with a hint of something spicy that I couldn't place. "They don't come from chickens. But they're all right."

"I find that reassuring." The Organ Grinder got up from the chair, lurching over to the trays to unfold one, and took some eggs and the rest of the bacon. "Truly, you are a kind noblewoman, to allow me all this bacon for myself." He laughed raucously as he settled back into the chair to gorge himself.

I was happy to see him eat the bacon. The thought crossed my mind that the Organ Grinder might be useful for keeping my figure. While he stuffed his mouth with bacon, I nibbled on the egg on my plate. The flavor of the spices was growing on me.

The picnic basket whined at my feet. "You don't like it when I eat from other places?" The basket rustled, and bumped my leg.

"She talks to it too much," the Organ Grinder mumbled between mouthfuls of bacon. The Monkey grabbed a few pieces of bacon and shoved them in its own mouth.

"I agree." The Stone Preacher's voice crackled a little bit. "On the other hand, you taught a largely plant-eating animal to eat meat, so I hardly think your suspicion is unwarranted."

The Organ Grinder laughed. I just shook my head as I finished my breakfast. "The only problem is having the dress and not being able to go shopping in this town." I said. "I just wish I had something new to wear."

There was a rattling from the stand where the dress had hung itself, and a shuffling sound. The fibers of the dress shredded and tore themselves apart. There was a faint sound like the clacking of looms, and a shuddering slither of threads. As one, we turned to look at the dress. Several strands of fabric had reached down to merge with the carpet and tear its fibers apart, writhing and chewing amongst them.

Bit by bit, the dress began weaving itself into something else. "Maybe this really is a fairy tale of some kind. A one piece wardrobe is every girl's dream. All that extra closet space can be for shoes."

"I would not get your hopes up," the Stone Preacher rumbled. "The carpet seems to be suffering for your desire."

The rattling from the dress increased, as the fabric shimmered and changed, becoming more full bodied, wider, and more pinched at the waist. When the shuddering was done, a high-backed, ruffled collar with large, puffy expanded shoulders dominated it. The entire dress was a deep silvery red, as if it had fed on the colors of the carpet. Heavy petticoats ballooned outward from the hips. There were lace ruffles at the wrists. Ornate patterns danced around the silvery red hem.

It was one of the most beautiful things I had ever seen – and one of the most frightening. "What else does it do?' I asked.

"I don't know," the Organ Grinder responded. "But it will be a pleasure to peel it off you."

"Don't invoke things with double meanings," I said. The Stone Preacher seemed surprised. It seemed he had been about to say exactly the same thing.

***

We decided to arrive fashionably late for our own affair, and hold off recruiting a boat until later. After spending most of the day in our room discussing points along our route that we were going to avoid, we heard sounds of carriages arriving and loud noises from downstairs.

The Organ Grinder reached into his waistcoat for a dirty old pocket watch, and flipped it open. "We should probably wait another few minutes. Things won't get really exciting until the alcohol starts flowing."

"By the time we get down the stairs, all the alcohol will be gone," I said "Of course, that might not be so bad for you." I smirked at him.

The Stone Preacher's scowl turned into a grin with a sound of shearing rock. It seemed that lately all I had to do make him smile was abuse the Organ Grinder. "Positions."

The Organ Grinder took the monkey out of his pocket and put it on the chair.

I turned to the picnic basket. "If the monkey isn't here when we get back, I assure you that you'll spend the rest of your short life on fire." The basket whimpered and huddled in a corner, slavering at the monkey as the beast taunted it and chittered in the chair.

"Tell it not to fling any you know what," I said, as the Organ Grinder formed up on my right and the Stone Preacher formed up on my left.

The Organ Grinder sighed. "Sully not the room, monkey." We moved towards the door. The stairs had been lined with silk. I walked on them with a surprised shift in my step. Behind me, the Organ Grinder and the Stone Preacher crushed the delicate fabric under their weight, making little creaking noises, even on the stone.

We moved down towards the large black doors, now flanked by servants and thrust open. In the foyer, more servants carrying platters and dressed in livery of the Duchess of Candles approached us, offering hors d'oeuvres and drinks I didn't recognize. Everything was opulent. I waved the servants off, catching a look of disappointment from the Organ Grinder.

We entered into a mass of luxury and chaos. Conversations swirled about people in arrogantly appointed dresses and smoothly arranged doublets. Hairstyles looked as though they had stepped out of a medieval painting. Several people wore powdered wigs. Amid white-frosted heads were faces I thought I recognized. In the mass of people, I soon lost track of them.

As we entered, an attendant motioned for me to hold up, and lifted a small trumpet to his lips. Then he blew on it, sounding through the rumble of guests. Some didn't even look up from their conversations. "The Lady Symantha, in search of a name!" he bellowed. His voice carried well. I couldn't tell if anyone noticed. The attendant sighed and wiped his sweaty face. I moved with my bodyguards into the maze of partygoers.

A leering face I didn't recognize, attached to a beige and blue doublet, sauntered up to me, craning his neck. He slid himself into a bow that almost mocked me. "Good lady," he purred. "I am the Count of Sieves. If you would allow me the luxury of greeting you?"

"Of course, but no more, there are many people I must speak with." I tried to wander through the crowd. The Stone Preacher and the Organ Grinder moved in such a way that people graciously chose to step aside. More than a few women gave the Organ Grinder sly, almost imperceptible smiles. I shook hands and memorized names that I would forget in only a few minutes.

"Dreadful day to you." A familiar voice came from behind me. "What an awful party." The handsome face dipped to me in a seemly bow, and I offered my hand as though I had always wanted to. "I really wish I could find somewhere else to be."

I smiled at the supplications of the Knight of Lies. "How is it that wherever I go, you somehow manage to arrive? It's almost as if you're courting me."

"I never court anyone." The Knight of Lies smiled back at me. There was no spark in my heart and I regretted the question. He released my hand. "Are you, perhaps, feeling a little tired?"

"I have only just arrived. I am trying to make sense of this swirl of madness and society, and I'm mostly just watching my back."

"Your bodyguards don't seem to be doing a very good job." The Knight of Lies murmured in a complimentary tone. Others who tried to get too close to our conversation were ushered away. "You hate private conversations?"

"Absolutely." I responded with a wicked grin. "You will forgive me, I must have no more private conversations at all."

The Knight of Lies blended back into a small sea of young women, whose eyes were all focused on the Organ Grinder.

***

As I made my way through the party, the Duchess of Candles spotted me from amid a group of sycophants. She hurried over in a glorious yellow dress, replete with a feathery hat and high, delicate shoes. She did her best to walk daintily amid frills and petticoats, but her smile was ruthless as she approached, keeping a careful eye on the Organ Grinder. "Ah, there you are." She smiled as she reached out to take my hand.

I gently clasped her palm in both my hands. It was a little dry.

"I would like to introduce you to some of my friends." She gave me a cheerful smile that seemed wider than it should have been. She neatly curtsied, and gestured with her hand, "May I introduce the Count of Lemons, the Countess of Cheese, the Duchess of Verdigris, and the Viscount of Bowls." She spoke each of their names as if they were very important.

I looked at the little group of nobles with as much decorum as I could manage. Each of them looked as though he or she had stepped out of a caricature of the court of the French or Spanish kings. The Count of Lemons had a thin pinched face, and smelled as though he had recently been cleaned in a dishwasher. He had an ornate gold cane that was topped with a brass lemon, and he wore a doublet in a variety of greens that seemed to stipple and seep in the light.

Vaguely cowlike and portly, the Countess of Cheese was stuffed into a reddish-orange dress that was two sizes too small. The middle-aged, gray-haired beast of a woman looked like the aunt that nobody wants to meet. Her gaze filled me with dreadful discomfort. She gave me a sickening smile as if she were going to hug me. I prayed she wouldn't.

The Duchess of Verdigris and the Viscount of Bowls were engaged in a conversation when my hostess introduced us, and they looked up at me with strange faces as she gestured. The Duchess, in late middle age had a faint greenish tint to her narrow features. She was wearing a bronze colored dress that almost appeared to be slightly stained.

In the light of the bronze color, the bowl-shaped white hat on the head of the Viscount looked ridiculous. He was dressed in a doublet of deep blue and a cape of a lighter, sky color. His face was almost as round as the moon, with flat features and wide eyes.

I curtsied to the four of them and smiled. "I'm pleased to meet you all." They turned to look at me with grim acknowledgement, and returned to their conversations.

"Don't worry." The Duchess of Candles smiled at me. "Your journeys will reveal your true love in time. Mine, alas, melted away in my arms, but I make do in this city of vice and iniquity." She tugged me over to a corner, as if conspiring. "So, tell me: What has it been like on your journey?"

"It's been interesting," I murmured. "I made some friends and enemies, but a lady does have to have her secrets." I gave her a knowing wink, shuddering under her smothering nature.

"I'm sure you'll find your place," she whispered, casting a glance at the little crowd of women surrounding the Organ Grinder, who laughed among them and idly doffed his hat. The Stone Preacher lurked nearby. He rebuffed everyone who came near him, and several times, at the edge of my ears, I could hear his fists clench. "So shall I rescue your friend?"

"I don't look at it as rescuing him from them. I look at it quite the other way around." I smiled. "He is the notorious lothario, the Organ Grinder, after all. I suppose those beastly horses in the drive did give it away."

She gave me a light laugh. "You are quite right," she murmured. "But it is the prerogative of the lady of the house to decide what to do with her guests."

"I forbade him to do that anymore while he's my bodyguard," I sighed. "I have not sampled his greasy pleasures, and I have no desire to."

"Truly, love is blind," the Duchess sighed. "One day, when your ardor is cooled, you may appreciate the touch of one such as he. I beg of you your indulgence and allow me my little gift. My bed is cold and empty, and I huddle under the covers and whimper." She gave me a matronly, yet petulant look.

There was a thump from the door as it was practically kicked open. I turned to watch a man yank the trumpet from the hands of the servant near the door.

Chapter Sixteen

The Captain of Clouds Announces Himself

There was a loud blare of noises as the man blew the trumpet, leaving a look of shock on the face of its previous owner. He idly tossed it back to the servant, covering the man's mouth as he thundered to the room. "Announcing the Captain of Clouds! Let no man's trumpet or lips speak for me but my own!" His voice was loud as thunder, and he gave a delicate, yet elegant bow to everyone, dipping low as the light reflected off his mustache.

He was tall and slender. His blue hat had a cloud-white feather in it. His leather jerkin with shining studs on it seemed well cared for. His boots were so finely oiled that I could see the vague images of wings tooled into the ancient leather.

"My apologies to your servant," he murmured, idly tapping the cutlass at his waist. Then he glided forward into the room, as if nothing had happened and he had offended no one. Several of the women surrounding the Organ Grinder politely excused themselves and daintily fluttered their way towards him.

I stepped forward for a moment to approach him, but the Duchess of Candles, as if her eyes had never left me, slid her arm gently into mine, and coolly guided me away. "The Captain of Clouds," she sighed. "How depressing that such a rude vagabond has come."

"You shouldn't be so bitter." I looked over as the Organ Grinder found himself with half as many women as before.

"Well," the Stone Preacher rumbled from behind me. "He's saved half of them, at least. Do you know anything of this Captain of Clouds, Duchess?"

"Oh, he is all the rage among the younger girls." She stared at the Captain, surrounded by the women who had left the Organ Grinder. "He is a crass miscreant who stole a noble title from someone in a duel, killed him, and thus acquired the title of

Captain of Clouds. He commands the *Aegis of the Skies*, a warship that formerly belonged to the King of Feathers, but due to the terms of the duel, the King of Feathers can do nothing. There is a duel I would very much like to see, with the Captain's throat ripped out in a wet gobbet."

My stomach turned. There might be more to the Duchess than I wanted to know. "I can't believe he's really so awful. Besides, he has a flying boat, and I do need to present myself to the King of Feathers without getting killed." I smiled. "This really is kind of like a magnificent game of sorts, isn't it?"

"That's why we don't involve ourselves, as the favor we curried for a nameless one would be slight."

"What happens in cases like that?"

The Duchess shrugged. "People take sides. Wars happen. People die. When enough people die, the King usually decrees that the new noble can have the property of one of those who died." She tittered lightly. "My favorite was the Duchess of Trees living on the edge of a volcano."

I chuckled. "That sounds lovely. How did she take it?"

"Not well. She still lives there, in constant fear of being consumed by lava." She laughed. "She spends a lot of time traveling, and her castle is almost empty of possessions. Nonetheless, her husband, the Duke of Trees, is a most impressive figure, who spends his time finding ways to make new trees that will prevent lava flow in case the volcano should erupt." She smiled again. "One day, I hope, the miserable witch will suffer the sting of the accordion." Her mouth turned into a wicked leer as she gazed at the Organ Grinder.

"You will forgive me. But I cannot take a hostess away from her guests, and I very much do want to meet this Captain of Clouds." I put on my most pompous air, and daintily curtsied to the Duchess, then slipped off towards the Captain, who began barging his way through the girls to meet me, as though they were nothing but air.

***

"Get away from me, you sycophants!" the Captain of Clouds roared, his light green eyes flashing towards me, a bright grin appearing between his elegantly trimmed mustache and goatee. The sand colored hair set off his tanned skin, and he bowed before me. "A pleasure to meet you. I understood that there was someone new, and I simply had to meet her as soon as the word spread. The Duchess is notoriously mouthy among her servants." He gestured to a nearby table, a hearty swagger in his walk. "Come. Tell me of yourself."

I turned to the Stone Preacher and smiled for a moment. "If you can stand the attentions of my two bodyguards, I would be happy to speak with you for a time." I gave him a curtsy.

"Fa!" he said dully. "No need to put on airs with me, lass, and you are. You don't need to impress me in the same way that you impress the Duchess." He gave me a sarcastic wink and headed off towards a chair. I followed.

The Stone Preacher murmured from behind me "This man has something we want, and you should be wary of him. It is all too convenient."

"I think I can handle him."

The Captain of Clouds chuckled as he turned. "Did you, perhaps, not hear me announcing myself? I am not the Captain of Clowns, after all."

"That would be more interesting to see," I smiled wider. "But not nearly so capable."

The Captain of Clouds laughed as he moved over to a table near the wall and kicked out a chair, settling neatly into it. He deftly settled his boots up onto the table and reached over to toss a chair my way. "Sit," he said. "Few would dare to call me the Captain of Clowns."

"Oh, forgive me," I mocked. "When surely it has come from your own lips."

The Captain of Clouds laughed out loud. "It is good to see that you are not an idiot." Behind me I heard the rattling crackle of the Stone Preacher's lips. "Your wit, sir, is palpable." He let out a dry chuckle that sounded like the rasp of wind on stalagmites.

I turned to the Stone Preacher. "Fetch the Organ Grinder," I said. "I require his presence, even if it removes him from the pleasure of grinding his organ." I smirked to the Captain of Clouds.

The Captain of Clouds laughed as the Stone Preacher headed off. "Is that the Stone Preacher?" he asked. "He's usually not given to being commanded."

"It's not about being given commands," I grinned. "If it ruins the Organ Grinder's party, the Stone Preacher would obey his worst enemies." I winked. "So while the Preacher is ruining the Organ Grinder's fun, how exactly did you hear about me?"

"From one of the Duchess's servants, who I happened to be speaking to..." He murmured. "She was most attentive, after all." He gave me a sly grin.

"You're not so much different from the Organ Grinder, are you?" I asked him as the Stone Preacher began guiding the Organ Grinder away from his cluster of women.

"I prefer to think of myself as a gentleman caller," the Captain of Clouds smiled. "And, of course, I do not interfere in those sorts of matters of the heart." He tilted his head slightly. "After all, where a woman will not be bent, she will kick you over the rail, and as I have a flying boat, and no wings, it will not be long before I strike the ground, eh?" He seemed to find this raucously funny and laughed at his own joke until the Stone Preacher and the Organ Grinder arrived.

"What's he laughing at?" the Organ Grinder asked, adjusting his monocle. "It can't possibly be that funny."

"It can," the Stone Preacher rumbled. "He was saying he doesn't need an accordion to get women into bed."

"Ah," the Organ Grinder sneered. "But he has to be choosy."

"Both of you be quiet." I grumbled to the Captain of Clouds. "So I understand you have a flying boat?"

"Indeed!" the Captain of Clouds chuckled. "For noble am I in the eyes of the King of Feathers, who did choose to grant me the station of one of his generals after I slaughtered him in a duel." He cackled. "It wasn't much of a duel, really. I got him drunk, provoked his ire, and ran him through, but it took a few more stabs to really get the job done. Nonetheless, I am now ennobled, and worthy of speaking to such a magnificent troublemaker as yourself."

"I'm a troublemaker?" I asked. "No more so than any other new arrival, apparently."

"Well, the sorts of people I know say that you are trouble. You've survived four encounters or more with the Weeper in Shadows, a lady who bears me no small amount of ill will. I didn't know who she was at that party, and she'd had quite a bit to drink herself. Furious with me, she was." He cackled.

"You slept with the Weeper in Shadows?" The Organ Grinder's eyes opened wide, and his lips let out a horrible laugh. "Why, so have I! Was she as much of a bedwrecker as I remember?" He let his eye fall into a brutal wink.

The Captain of Clouds was about to reply when I sighed.
"Could we please talk about the boat? I really would like to see it,
and see if it's sea — well — airworthy."

"Ahh!" The Captain of Clouds chuckled. "A sailor of the skies at
heart! Few have the stomach for such a journey. Come by the boat
tomorrow. We shall make arrangements!" He called for wine. "I
shall see you in the morning. Make preparations to stow your cart
somewhere here. I am sure there will be rats and other animals
rutting within its confines when you return."

"Thank you, good sir." I rose and curtsied. "I shall see you at
the docks come morning."

"Good luck to you, young lady." He gave me a pleasant wink.
"And if you should ever give up on your quest, there is always a
home in the romantic life of the Captain of Clouds!" He rose and
bowed, deftly snatching a glass of wine off a tray as he returned to
his seat.

I melted into the crowd, slipping among the echoes of
unimportant things. I had just found a place to relax when the
Lady of Masks gave me a subtle grin from behind a garish visage.

***

I halted the Organ Grinder and the Stone Preacher as the Lady
of Masks approached, and I gave her my best curtsey, tilting my
head a little bit.

"I understand that you have had some trouble traveling?" I
could tell that under the mask she was smiling. She was wearing a
dull gray dress, and her mask was that of a bland silk wrap,
wrapped around her lips hurriedly as a bandit might.

"I understand you may have crashed the party?" I smiled. "Or
decided to come at the last minute?" I liked the Lady of Masks far
more than I should have.

Under the mask, her visage fell, "You have me at a
disadvantage." Purring gently, she daintily curtsied to me. "I had
to make a mask out of a kerchief. A terrible thing to be sure. I
simply had nothing appropriate." She leaned in toward me, and
whispered. "This really is not my kind of party, but I am certain
that something deceptive has happened to you, and I do not know
what it is. I hoped that I would catch you before your boat ride."

"How did you know I was going to take a boat ride?"

"This is the closest city with a wind dock. The next one is over
six hundred miles to the... I think it is the left. Compasses really

don't work here. And here you are." She gave a delicate grin as the Viscount of Bowls waddled by and bumped into us, heading for the exit.

I staggered aside as the Lady of Masks was pushed, and the Viscount of Bowls made a wet, blubbering noise and grabbed the nearest cloth, his face rounder than usual as his lungs heaved and his portly belly shifted. Then he began to vomit up blood, mucus, and something that looked vaguely like meat and wine. He collapsed to the floor in a wet heap, and there was a brief silence as the Lady of Masks looked on.

"Poison," she said with a sigh. "It looks like one of his enemies found him." She shrugged as servants came over, trying to rouse him. People stared in horror momentarily, and the Captain of Clouds shook his head while surrounded by women.

The two of us stood back, and the Organ Grinder chuckled. "It would seem that the Viscountess is free this evening, and for the foreseeable future." He gave a hearty laugh.

The Stone Preacher's fist was already brutally buried in the Organ Grinder's stomach, and he was clutching it with a red face. "Don't do it again," I said. "His corpse isn't even cold yet. Twenty four hours, at least, please!"

The Stone Preacher didn't say a word, but gave me a satisfied smile.

The Lady of Masks let out a little giggle. Suddenly, everyone was laughing with us as the servants dragged the Viscount of Bowls away. I refused to laugh with them. The raucous howls lasted a few minutes as the dead body was pulled through the doors and they slammed shut.

"This is why I like it here," The Lady of Masks smiled. "It is proof of how our world works."

I offered a gentle hand on her shoulder. "What do you mean by that?"

The Lady of Masks tilted my chin up. "Do you believe in fairy tales?"

"How could I not?" I offered.

"Perhaps you shouldn't." Her voice chilled.

"Don't worry, everyone!" The Duchess of Candles smiled as the laughter died down. "A food taster will be around for the rest of you! Make certain no one touches his plate."

"I'm sure no one else will die this evening," the Lady of Masks murmured. "It takes hundreds of years to set one of these poisonings up. Enjoy the rest of the party. A good poisoning is always a treat." She daintily curtsied and headed over to the Duchess of Candles.

"Are things always like this here?" I did my best not to shudder. "I've never been so grateful for a carnivorous picnic basket in all my life."

"That's how things are here." The Organ Grinder chuckled, pulling a little black book out of a pocket in his greatcoat. "I see that the Lady Viscount of Bowls has moved to my list, and I have a little less than ten years to succeed." He gave me a sly wink as he scribbled the name in the book.

"Footstool," I said.

The Stone Preacher's nascent scowl turned into a firm granite smile.

***

The party ended with quiet gossip and whispers about who had done in the Viscount of Bowls. Murmurs continued for most of the night, with the Knight of Lies being the traditional favorite, though others were mentioned. Several people felt the need to defend their honor. When the Knight of Lies drew out a glove and slapped someone across the face with it, I slipped back to my room, leaving the Organ Grinder and Stone Preacher behind.

I stepped inside and found the picnic basket settled quietly on the carpet, while the monkey was perched on top of the four poster bed, far from the teeth of the basket lid. The little beast snored as I crept up to the basket, scooping it up by the lid. It trilled as it slept. I made my way over to one of the candleholders, lighting it so that I could see what was inside.

It was empty. I blew the light out, creeping up to the bed and crawling into it, leaving the basket beside me. There was a low noise as the basket made the wicker equivalent of snores. With an empty stomach, I watched the basket warily, as though it might awake and eat me at any moment. I hadn't fed it anything for a while. Whatever it was, I didn't want to antagonize it.

***

I tossed and turned for most of the evening, finally falling asleep as sounds of departing carriages filled my ears. The basket and the monkey slept through everything. The green eyes of my lover bored into me, making me wish for his presence, close and infinitely comforting.

My tossing and turning was finally interrupted by the snoring of the Organ Grinder. The odd gliding sounds of the Stone Preacher closing the door to the room. I forced myself to wake up, the fog in my mind making me feel weak in the dark.

"Return to your slumber," the Preacher murmured. "They all wondered where you were."

"That was the point," I mumbled "I didn't feel like eating, and the picnic basket didn't feel like giving me food." There was a sound like a hiccup from the basket, who coughed up a loaf of warm, hot bread and some cheese.

"Wicked girl," the Stone Preacher murmured. "Manipulating your own pet like that."

I broke off a few lumps of cheese and some bread. Before I knew it, I had eaten everything while the Stone Preacher watched in silence.

***

A brief, more contented sleep followed my snack. I was awakened by the savage light of morning hammering on my eyelids. "Arise, girl." The thunderous noise of the Organ Grinder's voice roared in my ears as the filthy monkey jumped up and down on my stomach. I slapped it aside before it could slash me with the knife-tail. The Organ Grinder grabbed it protectively.

I instinctively reached for the handle of the picnic basket. It growled at the monkey as the Organ Grinder slipped the creature into one of his many pockets. "Stop!" I pulled at the basket until the monkey disappeared from sight, and it settled down. "What's going on? You've been bothered since we got here."

The picnic basket rustled a little bit and spit up two plates of ham and eggs. They smelled delicious and I grabbed one of the forks and ate desperately. "Are you sick?" I didn't expect much of an answer.

"It's disappointed," the Stone Preacher rumbled. "I'm sure the Viscount of Bowls has already been buried. It was probably starving."

I sighed. "Is that it?" I ruffled the basket near the edge of the handle. "Are you ok?"

The Organ Grinder shook his head in disgust, but grabbed a plate and began to eat.

The picnic basket rustled from side to side, as if to indicate that all was well.

"I need a bath." I crawled out of bed and slunk into the washroom, where I filled a small tub and started a fire under it with available charcoal.

I bathed quickly, and threw my clothes back on, slipping back out as the Organ Grinder made ready to leave. "Take a bath," I told him. "You smell like dead fish."

The Organ Grinder sighed and stalked into the bathroom, slamming the door shut. I watched my dress slither into my luggage and fold itself up. "We need to leave quietly, through a side entrance," I said to the Preacher. "I don't want to be surrounded by people who might impede our progress, and there's a poisoner about."

"That's good thinking." The Stone Preacher walked over to the bathroom door and hammered on it. "Do not pretend!" he thundered. "Uncleanliness is the worst sin." The sounds of splashing water followed.

I gave the Stone Preacher a slight smirk. "It's like you've known him for ages."

The Stone Preacher turned to me with a sour look on his granite face. "Just because I am made of rock doesn't mean I have no sense of smell."

We waited for the Organ Grinder to come out and hurriedly gathered our things, slipping down the stairs and out a side door. We went around the side of the building to the hedges and the courtyard, almost invisible without the pomp and circumstance of the evening before.

As we walked out through the courtyard, I saw the Knight of Lies and another man I didn't recognize draw close together, fighting a duel with swords. There was a brief shove and the Knight of Lies forced himself forward, locking the other man's sword arm as he drove the sword fiercely into his opponent's stomach. Then he took the sword in both hands and heaved upward, splitting the man open. As we passed through the gates, I turned to look as the Knight raised his sword, proclaiming his own defeat.

***

During the day, Cliffedge was a madhouse of scum and despicable behavior. Slavers offered up people in cages as the

Organ Grinder drove his cart through the streets. More than one alchemist offered the Stone Preacher thousands of gold half-lunas for a single finger joint. The trade in human flesh and the flesh of monsters was brisk. The call of barkers for unsettling things sounded off the tight, rocky streets. Crowds were thick. The Stone Preacher had to ask nicely before shoving people out of the way. Many refused to move until they were forced aside, unwilling to lose a spot in line over a choice slave.

"Ah," the Organ Grinder chuckled as he lashed the horses along the cobbles. "The sweet sounds of the slave market. Perhaps you would like a few of them?" He gave me a pleasant nudge. "They are always compliant and meet your basic needs."

I scritched the picnic basket, still settled on my lap, and looked the Organ Grinder over, dreams of green eyes and slim handsomeness filling my thoughts for a moment. "That doesn't meet my basic needs."

The Stone Preacher forced his way through the tight crowds. He kicked two people, who were struggling with knives, out of the way. Our cart moved forward as the men moved. Cheap leathers and dirty knives suggested the brawl was of minimal importance.

Ahead of us, a few blocks away, the wind docks loomed. "Perhaps the Captain of Clouds can do it for you." The Organ Grinder smiled. "You seem to like him a great deal more than me."

"He's fun to talk to, but I'm not in love with him."

"All loves grow tired," the Organ Grinder laughed. "And then it is to me, the Captain of Clouds, or some other provider of lusts to whom you will turn."

The Stone Preacher let out a little rumbling sound as we cleared the latest cluster of people. The streets narrowed even more as we headed towards the docks, struggling between men, slaves, and their animals, some of which were unusual and unfamiliar.

***

We pulled out onto the wind docks with a rattle of wagon wheels. We heard the shouts of sailors amid tall boats held against the docks with ropes. The strange whistle of the wind echoed up from between the boats and rock. Beyond the boats was only open air.

Loud shouts and strange songs I didn't recognize assaulted my ears as people moved over boats like insects, each giant schooner festooned with flags and heraldry. Most of the flags were covered with depictions of monsters I didn't recognize. Crowds of rough men and women paid us no mind as we drew up the cart. They were all dressed like pirates.

"We need to find out which boat is his. Should one of us ask one of the locals?" In my hands, the picnic basket shivered, and coughed up a small loaf-like cake.

"We could offer them food," the Organ Grinder suggested. "Compared to what you usually get on ships, that might be a blessing."

"Can you do it without rutting with any sailors?" I scowled, handing him the loaf and reaching into the picnic basket. A warm cupcake appeared in my hand.

"It is not a problem." The Organ Grinder gave a lascivious grin. "But I shall demand a kiss one day for this." His voice dropped in a momentary pause. "Is that a cupcake?"

"You shall not receive it – the kiss or the cupcake," I said, adopting the tone of the nobility and drawing the cupcake up into my hand. It was a rosy, white frosted cake of reddish chocolate, and it smelled of the oven and lots of buttercream.

The Organ Grinder headed off to speak to the sailors playing cards, while I savored the cupcake, the warm, sweet cake and frosting trickling down my throat. "Good... basket." I managed between bites, not really knowing what else to call it. I really didn't want to give it a name. That might be going too far.

The Stone Preacher gave a rocky chuckle. "Usually, a creature like this wants someone else to eat by now. Perhaps it just isn't through with its last meal?"

"If you could taste what this cupcake was like – and you're not going to–" I grinned. "You wouldn't care how many people it ate."

The Organ Grinder moved over to the small group of sailors playing cards and tipped his hat with a low bow. "Good day." He gave a smiling leer at a chunky woman with an eyepatch and reddish-brown hair. "I am the notorious Organ Grinder, on a journey of obligation. I was wondering if you might help me find the boat of the Captain of Clouds." He gave a smirking chuckle and offered them the loaf.

One of the men grabbed it with a laugh. "So you're the Organ Grinder!" He cackled roughly. "You're taller and thinner than I thought you'd be!" He grabbed a mug and drank something down. "Fresh bread, lads! It's over there!" He pointed four docks down.

"Easy, woman." He patted her on the shoulder and broke off a piece of the loaf. "We wouldn't want you to spend any time in that cart when yer fer us." He gave the Organ Grinder a raucous laugh.

The Organ Grinder returned it with a laugh of his own, and clapped the man on the shoulder. "Do I know you or your wife?" He roared with a full grin.

"No! But you might if I die or she dies!" He seemed to find this immensely funny, laughing with a gap-toothed smile, and slapped the Organ Grinder on the back.

The Organ Grinder returned to us after a moment's more laughter, and climbed back up into the cart. The monkey hooted and stuck its head out of the Organ Grinder's pocket. He began to lash the horses bloody as we moved toward the boat of the Captain of Clouds.

***

The schooner of the Captain of Clouds was one of the most beautiful things I had ever seen. The cold gray sun beat down on us and the sailors on board cleaned with a desperate fury. The warship towered over the dock, accessible by only a slender gangplank. It seemed to be made of smooth, reddish-black wood that whispered between gusts of wind. Towering masts clawed their way into the sky, eager to unfurl the sails.

On the front of the schooner was a massive figurehead of a slender, masked figure with wings, spreading out over the ground far below, black with simulated armor and green jewels for eyes. "What's that?" I asked the Stone Preacher, pointing at the figurehead while the Organ Grinder pulled the cart to a stop and dismounted.

"That's the King of Feathers." The Stone Preacher rumbled. "The Captain of Clouds acquired his flagship in a duel, and the King had to build a new one."

"I suppose they don't like each other very much. He seems very graceful. Though he could use a little less severity in his appearance."

"A duel is a duel." The Organ Grinder laughed. "There was nothing he could do about it except build a larger and grander one to replace it." He held out a hand for me to step down. I ignored it and leaped to the ground without help. "I see you would rather die than be seen in public holding the hand of the Organ Grinder?"

"She isn't the only one," the Stone Preacher rumbled as we walked up to the gangplank. As we made our way up the smooth, beautiful wood, I thought I saw one of the horses glare balefully at the Organ Grinder, as if it wished to have the ability to tear him to pieces.

"So, did he finish the replacement boat?" I asked as the Captain of Clouds began striding from amid his crew to meet us.

"Not yet, I'm afraid. He has to wait another eighty seven years. The special tree has to finish growing."

"That's a joke, I hope."

"I'm afraid not," the Organ Grinder chuckled. "Special boats require special magic."

"From a special tree that only grows once every how many years?"

The Captain of Clouds laughed deeply as he approached us, greeting us with a bow as he watched the Stone Preacher glide up the gangplank behind me. "A hundred and four," he said. "It takes a hundred and four years to grow a tree capable of being a fleet flagship." He gave me a slow smile. "My lady seems to have questions that most people do not care about the answers to. It is a little unseemly for a noblewoman to be fascinated by boats."

"Who are you to tell me that, without truly knowing my station?" I answered with a smile.

"It seems your tongue is sharp." The Captain of Clouds smiled as he gestured up to the crow's nest of the boat, turning his gaze skyward. "Do you like it? I am a magnificent sailor as well as a master swordsman. If you require passage, there is no finer vessel."

The Stone Preacher looked at the Organ Grinder for a moment, then turned to me. "He is asking you to make a bargain with him," he rumbled.

"Aye." The Organ Grinder chuckled. "You could certainly make a bargain with him that I would approve of."

I shot the Organ Grinder a cold look, and turned back to the Captain of Clouds. "What bargain can I make that will not compromise my virtue, sir? As you know, I am a woman in love." The merest thought made my heart shudder. I didn't know who he was, but I wanted him just the same.

"There is no virtue here." The Captain of Clouds laughed. "There are only better and worse bargains, and if you get the worse of one, I am certain you shall find yourself all bargained out with no one but the Organ Grinder or myself to see." He deftly tipped his hat.

"I shall vouch for you at court with the King of Feathers when my influence is great," I said. "In so doing, I shall hope to gain you a portion of forgiveness for your ventures, and gain you a portion of your apology."

"Well done, indeed," the Organ Grinder murmured. "Risky, but well done indeed." The monkey hooted under the Organ Grinder's coat. I grabbed at the picnic basket to settle it.

"Your bargain," the Captain of Clouds paused, "…is accepted. If you should die, you must swear that you will return from the grave to fulfill it."

"Can't I just write a last will and testament?" I asked. "It's less painful. I've seen what returning from the grave is like."

"Wills can be burned." The Captain of Clouds chuckled roughly, and he looked firmly at the Stone Preacher, as if reminding him of something. "Only an oath is forever here."

"Then I swear," I said. "But if I do not die, and the price of this should be my life, then it is you who I will seek out and punish. This I also swear."

"Clever enough," the Captain of Clouds nodded. "I suggest you find a place to sequester the Organ Grinder's cart. Where am I to take you?"

"The Castle in the Sky," I softened my voice. "I assure you that you will not have to wait long for me to fulfill my side of the bargain."

The Captain of Clouds swallowed hard, and turned to his crew. As if defeated already, he began shouting orders to them. We walked back down the docks to get our things.

***

I unloaded bags from the cart while the Organ Grinder sat in the seat. The Stone Preacher stood ominously, glaring, his head tilted toward me. "I don't understand why you want to do this yourself. There's no need. We are here to aid you."

"Because I don't want everyone around me to know I'm Miss Green-eyed Amazing," I sighed. "It's easier if I drag them onboard, and then you two put them below. That is the right term, below?"

"I can see you've never been on a boat before." The Organ Grinder laughed, and scratched the Monkey idly in a pocket.

"Nor a flying one. None of this would be a problem if anyone had a real airplane." The picnic basket rustled up against me, trying to agree. "Don't be silly," I said to it, running my fingers over the lid. "You don't even know what one is."

The picnic basket ruffled against my leg again, and settled there, waiting. I pulled the last of the bags from the cart. "Where are we going to put the cart?"

"I suppose we could ask the Duchess of Candles to stable it." The Organ Grinder laughed. "But that would require you to offer her a favor or for me to play my accordion." He chuckled, his lips spreading out wide, and he adjusted his monocle.

"Your horses will, no doubt, be better treated under someone else's care," I said with a scowl. "Or is it just in your nature to mistreat animals?"

"I consider it a privilege to mistreat animals. After all, you have a basket that mistreats people." He chortled to himself.

The picnic basket let out a growling rustle and hiss. "It's not mistreatment if they attack me first, or try to kill me, or are just rotting carrion by the side of the road," I said.

"Well, then," the Organ Grinder chuckled. "I'm going to show you a trick, though the effects might not be immediately obvious."

The Stone Preacher looked askance at the Organ Grinder, and his fingers knotted with a rocky crack. His lips twisted into a grimace as the Organ Grinder drew out his revolver, and brutally fired a shot into the head of each horse.

"Why?" I snapped. "Why did you do that?" I lifted my hand and pointed at the dead horses. Stains of red seeped across the stone.

The picnic basket leaped forward as I turned. The mouth and tongue slid out. Crunching sounds of teeth chewing on bone and flesh filled the dock. People pointed and began to stare. The Organ Grinder's laughter rose as sailors began shouting. Even the Captain of Clouds came to the edge of his boat at the sound of gunshots. "Eat up!" The Organ Grinder's laugh came deep and bellowing as the picnic basket feasted. "That's how you treat an animal that no longer has any use!"

Raucous laughter of sailors came as the picnic basket savored lumps of horsemeat and organs. Floundering animal twitched as their dead bodies responded to the cracking of bone. The Organ Grinder reached into another pocket and lit a pipe, tossing it onto the rickety cart, spreading hot ash everywhere. The flimsy wood began to catch and burn.

The picnic basket recoiled, growling in fury as the meal was interrupted. The half-eaten bodies began attracting flies even as the cart burned. The basket huddled behind me as the cart burned. The monkey screeched eagerly in concert with its master.

The Stone Preacher turned to look at me and shook his head. "You'll learn." He said firmly. "This isn't what it looks like."

"Oh, no," the Organ Grinder laughed as the burning cart began to blaze hotter. "This is exactly what it looks like." He gathered a pair of bags and walked toward the boat, shouldering them as he walked up the gangplank.

I watched as the Stone Preacher picked up the rest of my things, and followed him.

The Captain of Clouds giving me an elegant bow as I came aboard. "My lady?" he said as the picnic basket trotted up. "I see that your unusual pet is somewhat discomfited."

"I fear he's not the only one." I adopted a more haughty tone of speech, looking back at the burning cart. Even as I stared, sailors armed with knives came forward, racing to cut off the best horsemeat to roast in the ashes of the burning wood.

***

"Oh, dear," the Captain of Clouds muttered as the sailors roasted the Organ Grinder's horses, smirking a little bit. "I wonder if it will have an effect on his legend."

"I doubt it," the Stone Preacher rumbled. "He will find other places to rut."

I turned to look at the Organ Grinder, who had settled over the railing, grinning as he watched the burning cart and the groups of sailors, cooking the remnants of half his life.

"You don't look troubled at all," I said with a concerned glare on my face. "You caused a riot, and those people are eating horsemeat."

"Why not?" The Organ Grinder responded with a chuckle. "Your picnic basket does too. I'll wager my monkey would have had the joy of jumping up and down on its wicker remains when it burned."

"I'll thank you not to threaten my basket again. What are we going to eat if you set it on fire?" I took a moment to hold up my hand as the growl of the picnic basket began below me. "Don't bite his leg."

The four of us looked down as the picnic basket's mouth was open, wide around the Organ Grinder's leg as if about to close. It backed up a few steps and the lid closed.

"No," I picked it up by the handle, stroking the lid. "Behave. You just ate."

The basket sagged against my hip. The Captain of Clouds nodded. "You seem to have the thing well under control. I don't know if it's a thing or a beast."

"I don't either," I said. "An innkeeper named Bosquoverde gave it to me. I liked him. He was pleasant, and he told great stories. At least, that's what they say."

The Captain of Clouds laughed. "That's an obscure corner of the world, all right." He laughed. "There isn't even anyplace to park a ship like this one."

"I'm sure you'd be welcome. Say hello to the fencepost out back when you go. It's lonely."

The Stone Preacher's lips spread as his teeth made little grinding sounds. "That was terribly polite of you," he muttered.

The Organ Grinder seemed to be suppressing laughter, his hand covering his mouth as he chortled slightly. "Oh, indeed."

"Oh, that's right," I said to the Captain of Clouds. "You don't have competition anymore. The Organ Grinder is married." I smiled to the Organ Grinder and daintily stroked the picnic basket. It rustled a bit in my arms.

The Captain of Clouds extended a hand to the Organ Grinder and gave a courteous bow. "Congratulations, sir, who is the lucky lady to have the hand of such a — gentleman?" He seemed to be smirking. It was difficult to tell with his head lowered.

The Organ Grinder sighed and walked away. The monkey hissed and stuck its head out of the pocket. The diseased, chittering face shrieking louder as heavy boots thudded to the mainsail.

"The Half-Bone Maiden," the Stone Preacher chuckled, rocks whistling as if falling down a pit in his voice.

The Captain of Clouds gazed in wonder at the two of us. "No wonder he is so miserable." He smiled. "Even though he is not of my station, I feel I must console a fellow lothario. One will never be far from her, and he shall find himself romantic, or underfoot." As he made his way towards the Organ Grinder, he thundered. "Make ready to cast off! We sail for the Castle in the Sky! The King of Feathers awaits! And it is the week of his masquerade! No one will challenge us with masks on! It is magnificent!" He clapped the Organ Grinder on the shoulder and began talking in low tones. The sails unfurled and the massive boat caught wind, slowly moving out over the edge of the cliff.

I felt my stomach lurch. The Organ Grinder and Captain of Clouds suddenly laughed together as the ship began moving away from the dock, the sails full of air. My gaze still locked on the ground below. "You didn't tell me he was having a masquerade ball," I said. "This is going to be a lot easier than I thought. All I have to do is lock eyes, right?"

"After you lock eyes with him, neither of you will care." The Stone Preacher said. "Look down there, on the docks. You will see exactly what I mean. They will find him. They always do."

As I looked down towards the ground, I could swear I saw the ash from the cart struggle to move together, as if the Organ Grinder's cart was trying to rebuild itself before my eyes.

***

The Captain of Clouds allowed me his stateroom, which was little more than a plain wood cube with a desk, writing tools, an angled bookcase with air charts and maps, and a hammock. A few portholes barely large enough to see out of brought light to the desk to read and write. I piled my things neatly in a corner and tied them down with some netting, then tested out the hammock to see if I was too light for it. Happily, it didn't wrap around me or smother me.

Afterwards, I stepped out onto the deck in the morning sun, which beat down us with cold gray light, and wrapped myself in my cloak. The Stone Preacher stood near the bowsprit, and the Organ Grinder had settled sullenly on some boxes. The picnic basket bounced about the crew, making itself popular by offering apples and cheese. I beckoned it. "Are you feeding everyone already?" I said as the Captain of Clouds walked over to me.

"They all think you're very generous." He smiled as the picnic basket loped up, rubbing against my leg.

"I'm a little worried it might eat them later." I said. "It's like an evil pelican sometimes."

The Captain of Clouds laughed a little bit. "So do you like it? I can see you're getting your 'air legs.'"

"Well, in my world they have these funny metal tubes that fly around, they're called airplanes. They use a complex mixture of burning gases to fly. This is much better."

"I'm glad you think so." He laughed and pointed to the crow's nest. "From up there, you can see for a hundred miles on a clear day, as blue-gray as it will let us see. There hasn't been a blue sky in the Otherworld for four hundred years."

"What happened?" I asked. "Surely someone knows the answer."

"No one really does. Perhaps one day someone will bring back the blue skies of my youth, and we will sail into yellow and gold and all sorts of shades of rose." He gave me a subtle smile. "One of the reasons people obey their obligations is that small hope." He gently kissed my hand, and I felt a thrill, but it was not the thrill of love.

"You were born here?"

"Many are." He sighed. "But few live forever. Everyone forgets about the little people. To become a noble is to live forever, but most of these folk are simple peasants who toil for their masters and die. I do not offer a truly better life, but I offer a free one and a chance to sail the skies, and that is better than most receive. I am a rare creature indeed. Most of the rulers of this land came from outside and were transformed." He shot me a sly smirk. "I have no doubt that one day you will exceed me."

"That's not terribly reassuring," I said with a laugh. "I'm driving you into the lion's den for nothing, really."

"Why is that? Freedom is built on taking these kinds of chances. I would not give up a chance at the masquerade ball for anything. We will have to select masks, of course. Hopefully the Weeper in Shadows will not make an appearance. That one kills parties as fast as she kills people."

"And I presume your charms have no effect on her – which seems odd, they seem to work on everyone else."

He smiled. "The Weeper in Shadows is the King of Feathers' assassin. She does nothing without his say-so. If she is breaking his rules, it is because she is in love with him herself. It could explain why she despises newcomers from the outside so much."

"Do you think the King of Feathers could really be my one and only? That sounds like a fairy tale ending." I laughed. "Even if it is true, it sounds exceptionally lethal. She did say 'may the best woman win.'"

"You've survived longer than most, and I can't think of a reason why," the Captain of Clouds said. "You do have exceptional talents, but you can't fight her hand to hand. I can give you a few lessons, but she is far too experienced to fall for simple tricks."

The next six hours were spent in combat with eighteen inch knives, darting for each other's eyes and pulling back at the last second, hard kicks and punches delivered with fury. I got in a few good blows, but he was bigger and stronger. I wound up on the deck flat on my back more often than not.

"That's enough," he said. "We'll try this again later. You have to get inside my guard. We'll try it with wooden knives tomorrow. Nothing will prepare you for the pain of taking that first knife thrust. But you can take it in a place where it won't kill you."

Nearby the Stone Preacher watched with a cruel fascination. The Organ Grinder kept an eye on me as the monkey hooted and shrieked, satisfied every time I got hit or kicked. The picnic basket finally came over to me and opened, offering a bottle of crystalline, greenish liquid. When I drank it, my eyes grew heavy, and I yawned a little bit, the heady scent of the alcohol slamming into my nose. "I think I need sleep," I said as the Captain of Clouds escorted me back to the door of the cabin.

"You do," he said. "It seems your basket is a loyal companion." He dutifully opened the door and let me slip inside, closing the door behind me. I took a few steps forward, closed my eyes and settled into my hammock, dreaming of green eyes loving me from a clear blue sky.

***

The next few days were punctuated by more painful lessons and shipboard concerns. The Captain of Clouds put the Organ Grinder to work among the sailors. The Stone Preacher was told to minister to the needs of the crew. When he prayed for them, he always prayed in silence, and I was grateful that he didn't throw anyone overboard during his prayers.

The Organ Grinder found his time with the other sailors to be pleasant, and kept them entertained with crass jokes and stories of his many escapades. We were fortunate that none of them involved anyone who was already on board.

I spent much of my time with the Captain of Clouds, fighting with knives and swords and fists, kicking out towards his form while he blocked me casually and brutalized me with hard punches. "You have to learn how to endure pain," he said. "You've been very lucky so far, and if you do not train harder, you will die."

The nights were more gray than dark as the boat climbed through cloudy skies. Occasional shouts and hailing of other vessels were a welcome interruption from the daily routine of fighting practice and staring over the railing. After several days, the wind grew harder. Mountains loomed before us, with peaks covered in brutal black ice.

"We have to go up!" the Captain of Clouds shouted. "Preacher, move to the back, lend your weight to angle us!"

The Stone Preacher glided across the wooden planks with a heavy tread, hurrying for the area behind the helm.

The Captain of Clouds raced to man the helm himself. "Stand aside!" he bellowed. The helmsman backed off. The Captain grabbed the wheel, turning it hard as the Stone Preacher's heavy weight made it to the back of the ship.

The Organ Grinder laughed and clutched the ropes as crewmen turned sails and pulled at yardarms, trying to take advantage of the wind. For the first time, I wondered how the ship sailed through the sky, and hoped that it didn't pay a cost in blood. The trip had been magnificent.

The ship angled sharply. I grabbed the ropes as quickly as I could, the picnic basket slung around my arm let out a rustle of surprise as the ship flew upward towards the black peaks. Shrieking sounds mixed with the howl of strained timbers as the boat struggled up. The shout of sailors filled with joy as black ice fell away below us, with only grey horizon in front. With a triumphant slurp, the basket leaped off my arm and wiggled on the deck.

The dull gurgle from the crow's nest cut our celebration short. A spray of red trickled away as the lookout's body slumped into the wooden cup around the mainmast. The muscular thump of wings was everywhere. As Chain Hook Guards and Spiked Wrath Men hit the deck all around us, we heard the bellow of familiar poison-tailed beasts above.

I took a deep breath and looked up, calling my bow into my hands, and gazed forward past the central sail. A poison tailed worm hissed as I aimed. Our boat was flying straight into the eyes of the Weeper in Shadows.

***

She vaulted towards me at once, leaving her mount behind; batting aside the arrow as though it were too easy. She kicked me hard across the deck as she rolled into a combat stance. In a single moment, I slipped sideways and fired again. She leaped forward and hurling the knife of ice. It slammed into the wall near my head. It was close enough to be suddenly cold.

From behind her, I saw the picnic basket leap onto one of the chain guards, biting and gnawing on its hand. Teeth crunched through armor and the guard wailed as it struggled. The Stone Preacher grabbed the tail of one of the flying beasts and was twisting it, as if to wrench the tail off. Everywhere, there was chaos as the boat lurched and battle flowed.

There was a muscular thud from the side of the boat. A lashing tail of a stinger flipped over it. Two chain hook guards landed on the deck as they swung up over the lip. The massive bulk of their riding worm smashed into the boat, tilting it sideways and dumping two crewmen towards the black ice below. In the thunder of battle, the boat pitched and yawed.

The Weeper raced for me, launching a kick. I rolled aside, firing another arrow. She tumbled beneath the shot, yanked the knife free from the wall and stabbed. I deflected the blade with my bow, driving my knee upward towards her stomach. She was surprised enough to weave aside.

I fired another arrow as she doubled back over and sliced it apart with the knife, flipping back up. She leaped for me, her whole body lean and taut with a corkscrew motion, reducing the profile of the target. I nocked another arrow and breathed deep, pulling back the bowstring.

The Captain of Clouds and his crew fought hard. Several of the men were eaten during the initial assault by flying worms, but they slowly retreated, giving as little ground as possible. The Captain scrambled among the ropes and leaped onto the back of a flying beast, hurling the armored figure towards the ground below. "Fight on!" he shouted. "This ship is not to be taken!"

Amid the chaos, the Organ Grinder battled, surrounded by crewmen and armored creatures. There was a keening shriek as the monkey stabbed at something's eyes. Nearby, the wet crash of a corpse struck the deck. The picnic basket howled and leaped at the nearest monster, jaws locking on it and tearing. Blood leaked out from the stump that once held the guard's arm.

There was a sickening crack and a strange howl as the Stone Preacher stabbed the worm with its own stinger. The creature floundered. Purple venom leaked around the wound as it teetered over the edge and fell. The Stone Preacher took the helm and held it steady as the boat spun, heading downward for the peaks of black ice. Wood shrieked as crewmen fell out of the boat. The Weeper's soldiers hurtled with them.

I grabbed a piece of the rigging and slid my boot through it to anchor myself. The Weeper did the same. When the boat righted, I saw the Captain of Clouds flying one of the worms about and battling with her soldiers. The monkey hooted from the crow's nest, stabbing at a chain hook guard who had lashed his chain around the mast. Blood coated the decks. Several bodies lay pinned amidst the carnage.

I tried to move out of the rigging. My leg was twisted tight between the coils of rope. I looked up at the Weeper and the grinning face of flesh-like iron.

"Trapped in the ropes like a spider, your blood will soon coat my lips," the Weeper whispered as she gracefully disentangled herself, hanging there as the ropes swayed.

I took a deep breath and ignited the boots, trying to burn the ropes away as the Weeper leaped. There was a crackle of fire and a few strands snapped, enough to fly free. She caught the ropes and regained her footing, flipping acrobatically to stand on the rigging. The boat held steady as the Stone Preacher gripped the wheel. From the mess of bodies, the Organ Grinder crawled, kicking one of our enemies in the face with a boot. I couldn't see the basket anywhere.

The Weeper in Shadows hissed at me and licked the edge of the ice knife, frost spilling across her lips as she hurled it at me end over end. I launched myself skyward as the knife flew past. "Good aim!" I teased as I rose. Then the knife curved back towards me. She laughed and called out to her worm. It descended to flank me, wings beating furiously. I flew out of the way of the knife a second time. She caught it, as if she had practiced the maneuver a thousand times, vaulting into the saddle as several of her guards tore at the masts. I fired an arrow as she turned the worm skyward.

This time she wasn't fast enough. The arrow sank into her leg, pinning her to the mount, and she let out a wailing howl. "Foul witch who turns my desires to ashes, I shall pluck out thy heart and string your muscles up, to wallow in despair and bile." One hand guided the mount upward, her other hand squeezing her leg. She held her fingers tight around the arrow, framing a widening circle of red.

I barely had the time to look as her beast tilted and sagged, and she sank from sight, a black shadow lost in black ice.

***

It would only take one more arrow. If I pursued, almost everyone on board would die. The masts were shuddering. Even the Stone Preacher's weight and strength couldn't keep the boat's nose up as he tugged at the helm. I turned my attention to soldiers attacking the masts.

Around the helm, the Stone Preacher barely fended off four more soldiers. I raced on fiery trails beneath the sail, and launched a pair of arrows in a single shot, spreading them to catch the two leftmost. He kicked one aside as the boat lurched. The guard tumbled over the edge. The second met with a brutal punch that smashed into the creature's throat armor. The thing crumpled. The Preacher returned to holding the wheel.

Amid the press, the Organ Grinder lashed out with a hook he had found somewhere on board and drove it into the gap between two pieces of chest armor. He pulled, and there was a keening bellow as the creature pulled back, lashing a chain. Before the Organ Grinder released his hand, the monkey leaped to the thing's chest and drove the knife-tail into the gap, letting out howls. It withdrew the knife, most of its tail wet with blood; the thing sank to the deck.

Even as it crumpled, three more moved forward, tossing aside crewmen and breaking limbs. I fired arrows at them, racing along with footsteps of flame. The masts had been abandoned for the pleasure of violence. The Organ Grinder put his shoulder into a heavy tackle, and brought one of the creatures down. Like madmen, the crewmen descended, hacking with knives and swords while the monkey jumped to eyeholes, stabbing them. Bellows of pain came from the helmet as yellow liquid poured from it.

Above me, the Captain of Clouds wove a magnificent dance on his riding worm, keeping several of the soldiers in the air. His saber defended the ship in grey light as he drew his mount about, thrusting and stabbing. He bled slightly and pushed the metal aside when the chain guards tried to engulf him. After a few passes, he drove the saber into the neck of one of the worm creatures, and it plummeted towards the ground, leaving only a few scattered beasts and their riders fleeing the scene in his wake.

The boat began to lose altitude as the crew struggled to their feet. I put arrows into the last of the soldiers, ending my burning flight to land on deck amid the carnage. The Stone Preacher shouted, "I require assistance! My ability to steer is far from magnificent!"

The Captain of Clouds glided downward, leaping off his mount to land near the helm. The beast followed its fleeing comrades, turning away from the ship.

"Did we win?" I looked around as the masts creaked, the ship badly damaged by the attack.

"We have defeated our enemies." The Captain of Clouds gazed at the dots in the distance, a touch of admiration on his lips. "The Weeper in Shadows never ceases to amaze me. We almost never see her at court. And you wounded her! Even if you don't survive, this story will live forever." He clapped me on the back.

"Twice," I said.

The Organ Grinder struggled up, petting the blood-soaked monkey, which swiftly disappeared into a pocket before he could clean it off. The Captain raced to the helm, relieving the Stone Preacher, who tended to people he could save, mercifully ending the lives of those he couldn't.

As if a sign that the battle was finally over, the picnic basket crawled out from the hold and shook itself with an eerie rustle. It wandered over to the nearest enemy corpse, feasting on flesh, marrow and armor.

"Does it always do that?" The Captain of Clouds asked.

"You want to eat well tomorrow, don't you?" Slurps and crunches vibrated as the boat sank downward, down towards the ice and the few trees we could see. "How do we fix the boat?"

"We'll do what we can." The Captain sighed. "I have some supplies." As if in answer, a dull wrenching noise sounded, as the boat skidded to a stop on the black ice. "Let's hope they don't return to finish us off."

"Why would they need to?" the Stone Preacher said grimly. "Just because you have food doesn't mean the cold won't win."

The Organ Grinder glared at the Stone Preacher, a sullen noise coming from out of his bloodstained pocket.

"He's right," I said. "We have to get back in the air as fast as we can, or we'll all freeze to death."

"The coldest part of the season is coming," the Captain of Clouds said. "That's why the King of Feathers throws the party now. It ensures the fewest guests and the most vacancies."

"Does he try to kill everyone who tries to crash his parties?" I asked as the surviving crewmen lowered the gangplank to forage for supplies.

"Only the pretty ones," the Captain of Clouds assured me with a grin under his mustache. I felt warmer already.

***

The men wandered off into the black ice to look for trees to help repair the boat. The Organ Grinder and the Stone Preacher busied themselves with repairing damage to the masts and the hull wherever they could.

"So how does it fly, exactly?" I asked the Captain of Clouds, while he shouted orders and I threw my cloak back, flying about in the rigging to help where needed.

"It's magic wood," the Captain of Clouds responded. "Once the boat is built, a few boards here and there simply absorb the properties when you repair it. I don't understand it."

"Lovely," I called down, tying off a rope. "So you really don't know how it works?"

"Absolutely not," the Captain laughed. "If someone were to find a way to undo the magic of the boat, we would be in terrible trouble."

"Don't you mean falling to our doom? I take it you've noticed I'm not exactly the most upper class of ladies."

"Well," the Captain of Clouds laughed. "I was trying to be a little less pessimistic. You move around those ropes as if you were raised in a circus."

"Dead is dead!" The Organ Grinder bellowed, helping the Stone Preacher reset the mainmast as he interrupted. "Whether your guts spill out on the ground, or you're crushed to death when a boat smashes around you, it's all the same!"

The Stone Preacher scowled at the Organ Grinder. "The earth may come to claim us all. But some deaths are more painful to watch than others. If I crush the life from your disgusting monkey, even the vile Organ Grinder will weep, because it is the only thing that you truly love."

The Organ Grinder pushed his bulk against the mast, putting his rage into work instead of responding.

The picnic basket gave a heady rustle. He had eaten almost all of the bodies, and the lid opened, the tongue slithering out. A brackish belch echoed through the mountain skies. "Are you full?" I called over to it.

The picnic basket slumped, as though it finished. It still eyed the Organ Grinder's pocket with the desire for the taste of monkey.

"It's all right," I said. "I suppose I owe you, Captain, for the crewmen it ate?"

"Whatever for?" The Captain of Clouds tipped his hat. "If worst came to worst, and we didn't have any food, we would have eaten them anyway. Not everything about sailing the skies is romantic, and if there's no wind, it's easy to starve."

Sobered, I returned to work as the Captain of Clouds directed me. When the men began to return with what little wood and supplies they were able to scrounge, the work went faster until the sun went down.

"We'll take off in the morning," the Captain of Clouds said when it was over. "Tonight, we'll feast on what your picnic basket provides."

We gathered in the hold that evening as the picnic basket disgorged a twelve-course meal of fruits, vegetables, sweetmeats, and several dainty plates of foods that the sailors weren't used to. I wasn't even sure what some of the meats were. The Captain of Clouds assured me that they were served in the most unusual and exotic of kitchens.

"I'll keep the dishes," he said. "These table settings are excellent, though I do not know what I shall do with the leftovers."

"Salt them," I said. "It isn't as if all of them will taste bad when you do."

"I was thinking to eat them first thing in the morning." He said. "The cold outside should keep them. We need only warm them over a fire."

The night was bitterly icy. I gathered my cloak around me while I slept in the Captain's hammock. I could hear the Organ Grinder playing his accordion deep in the hold, and the hooting of the monkey as he told lewd stories of his conquests. When I slept, there were only hazy dreams of the Half-Bone Maiden, her face laced with bitter tears of betrayal.

***

Morning forced us awake with the smell of roasting goose livers and leftover meats. The cakes and pastries the basket made had all been consumed the previous evening, leaving us with roasted meats that were a little too cooked and breads that were a little too toasted. It was still better than they were expecting.

I came out to eat with them, and sat on a barrel, slowly defrosting the meat and vegetables that had frozen during the night. No one said a word when I reached for a piece of frozen cake and nibbled on it slowly. A few of the sailors even stared at me with admiration.

"You seem to have their eye," the Organ Grinder rumbled as he stuffed something that looked like it might be a goose liver into his mouth. "Ah, the delicious taste of fat and lard."

The picnic basket rubbed against my leg, as if struggling to keep me warm. The heat of the small cook-fire warmed the leftovers from last night's dinner, and began to cook them. "Where's the Stone Preacher?" I asked.

"Up on the stern," the Captain of Clouds responded, sticking his knife into something that looked like a roasted haunch of recently warmed meat. "I need him there for when we take off, which will be shortly after breakfast."

"So what is he doing now?"

"Praying. He's talking to the mountain to see if he can get it to crumble a bit below the ice and make it easier to take off."

"Does that work?" I asked. "I didn't even know he could talk to rocks."

The Organ Grinder laughed. "You should ask more questions of your bodyguards," he said, and stuffed another piece of meat into his mouth. "There is a reason why I fear the Stone Preacher, though one day, I assure you, he shall be at my mercy and on his knees."

"If the picnic basket doesn't eat you." I smiled to him. "After all, it would be a shame if I had to consume you as a steak, or a pie, instead of the way you would prefer according to your natural inclination." I let my tone drop low and icy. "I'll bite it off if you ever touch anyone other than your wife."

"Wife?" a shocked male sailor sputtered. "You're married?" His jaw dropped and he leaped to punch the Organ Grinder, who deftly dodged and kicked the man in the face with a steel toed boot. He collapsed in a heavy lump. The other sailors laughed.

"Well, better to have your enemies on your plate than at your feet," the Organ Grinder laughed raucously. "I can certainly think of better places for them, but it is breakfast time." He clapped a sailor on the back, who poured something from a flask down the Organ Grinder's throat.

The picnic basket slipped away from me and moved over to the frozen bodies that remained. Slowly, with heavy crunching sounds, it began to gnaw through them with a rough snap of its teeth. As it pulled and tugged, the dead flesh came apart under the ice and disappeared under the lid.

The Captain of Clouds raised an eyebrow. "Food for the coming journey," he murmured. "If only the food didn't taste so good, milady." He looked over at the picnic basket with hatred and a little terror.

The ice roared with a shuddering crack, and the Captain of Clouds leaped up. "The Preacher is successful, men! Positions! Positions! Get you to the ropes, stoke those sails, and catch the wind! We're taking off!" He raced to the helm, where the Stone Preacher's arms finally lowered in triumph, fists against the deck. The boat lurched and the wind whipped up. Ice shuddered around us as the picnic basket fled to a corner to hide between some buckets.

I grabbed the edge of the boat, and it leaped away from the mountain. The ice gave way beneath us as the sailors worked and the Captain of Clouds yanked hard on the helm. My stomach lurched. I felt my breath go slack as we plummeted into the rocky pit. Ice receded in the distance. Then the ship caught wind and rose into the air as I struggled to not slide downward towards the stern.

"Free and clear!" the Captain of Clouds shouted.

The Stone Preacher turned to rise, and solemnly walked towards me. The mountains receded far below us. The sailors cheered their captain, nodding with reverence for the Stone Preacher.

The picnic basket wandered to me after the boat leveled off, and stood up on its hind legs, opening the lid to show me a candied apple. I stared into the horizon and ate it slowly, scratching the basket's lid while the mountains rolled on.

When the grim dot on the horizon came into view, my stomach knotted up. I knew that I was nearing the end of my journey. Somewhere in that castle was the person to whom I belonged, and who belonged to me. I carved rune arrows all day in the hold, knowing I would need them no matter how much I told myself I wouldn't.

***

The sailors began making ready to moor against the massive, floating castle. The Captain of Clouds shouted "Raise the flag to the highest mast! Let him know we're coming! I'll spit on his disdain and laugh, for the King of Feathers has a new lady to approve!"

I almost smiled but kept myself ready in case the King of Feathers decided to send our boat crashing to black ice below. One experience of almost freezing to death was enough. The Stone Preacher stayed at the rear of the boat, his grim eyes focused on the Captain of Clouds, who shouted orders as we came into view of the floating fortress.

It was magnificent and sinister at once. Eight towers, fluted and twisted, rose up out of the rocky mass. Savage angles met graceful contours as they reached for the sky above. Crenellations were subtle dips placed between sharp barbs. The whole floating structure was made of charcoal granite that rippled in light, hiding arrow slits and angles that might be windows, looking out onto the cold peaks below.

The portcullis was open, wide stairs led down through the craggy rock to a series of docks, some of which had boats of various sorts, ornate and plain, tied up. A few dockworkers hurried about. I couldn't even tell if they were humans as we approached, but they seemed to come into view for me earlier than the lookout. I could see farther than other people. Something was happening to me.

The Captain of Clouds slowed the boat, guiding it towards the docks. It settled into a berth. The men tossed out ropes while the Organ Grinder and Stone Preacher moved up to stand in front of me.

"Go nowhere where we do not precede you." The Stone Preacher rumbled. "Occasionally, force may be required."

The Organ Grinder leered. "Occasionally, some playing of the accordion may be required." He stroked the monkey idly, a muted shriek of pleasure wafting from the leather greatcoat.

I obligingly stayed behind them as the crewmen lowered the gangplank, and we walked down. Sullen faces of black robed servants in hoods greeted us. None of them met our eyes as they tied off ropes. One of them stepped forward with a dull, listless gesture. He pointed to the stairs, which shimmered a little, pushing the light of the sun away. The picnic basket rested on my arm. I didn't want it to be far from me.

As we moved up the stairs, they seemed to get steeper and more angular. By the time we reached the top, I could see Chain Hook Guards and Spiked Wrath Men roaming the walls, keeping an eye below. I wrapped my cloak around myself to hide. We stepped onto the threshold of the wide area beneath the portcullis.

All the while, reflected light made it seem as though the whole castle would swallow me up.

Chapter Seventeen

The Castle in the Sky

We stepped into the court amid the bustle of arrivals. Porters carried bags and others hurried about, some openly wearing ostentatious clothing while some covered their heads in cloaks and hoods. The Organ Grinder raised an eyebrow as arrivals handled their baggage. A few of the women winked or leered at him. "The celebration is fuller this year," he muttered. "Something is different, as if there was something people wanted to see."

"Well, what usually happens at this party?" I asked. "We're not really crashing, as all who are appropriately associated are invited." Behind me, I could see the Captain of Clouds chatting with some porters.

"Well, the King of Feathers is trying to kill you," the Stone Preacher murmured in a gravelly whisper. "You should probably invoke the laws of hospitality as soon as the porter greets you, lest someone see something."

"Is he trying to kill anyone else?"

"Who knows?" the Organ Grinder muttered, giving a polite grin to a passing noblewoman when her husband looked away. "You could try and prolong it to see what happens, but I'm currently obliged to assure that you not wind up dead. Besides, I'm looking forward to getting your other shoe." He smirked.

"He's correct." The Stone Preacher drew himself up fiercely in front of me as the porter approached. He was a strange-looking man with an unusual wooden hat and wrists wrapped in rope. He shuffled a little bit as he walked, as if ropes controlled him, moving his hands like a puppet's. His nose was long and sharp. Tufts of hair pushed out from under the wooden hat, thick and curly. Long muscular arms were a little too big for his torso. He was wearing a brown uniform. Work boots on his feet clicked as though they had gears of some sort in them.

The porter bowed to me. "Good evening, milady, if I may use the term. I am the Hetman of Pulleys, a minor servant, I assure you, assigned only to carry your luggage and that of your associates." His eyes widened as he stared up at the towering Stone Preacher in front of him. His voice turned to a wretched stammer. "The Stone Preacher? The Organ Grinder? You are to be a prestigious one indeed." He blathered and stumbled over the words as he gathered up the bags, his movements quick, strong, and mechanical.

"Perhaps, sir, I am just lucky in my journeys." I smiled to him. "If you would take us to our quarters, I would appreciate it."

"This way." The Hetman of Pulleys lurched forward, leaving the Captain of Clouds and his crew behind. We moved into black depths, past another gaping portcullis with slight shimmers in the gray rock. As I squinted, I could see that they were holes, designed to pour oil or worse things from the Otherworld down on people who tried to breach the castle and take it by force. I wondered how the King of Feathers defended against attacks from above. I didn't see anything obvious.

When we turned the corner, there was a large man in reddish black metal standing there. He slumped under the weight of thick plates, as if they pulled his visor down. He was completely enclosed. Fists and shoulders were covered with wicked spikes, the whole appearance made seem wider. "Ah," the man intoned more than he spoke. When he bowed, the armor made a wicked clank. "Milady, I am the Viscount of Chains." He gathered his belt. It was designed to detach. "I am the Captain of the Guard here. I see your bodyguards are the Organ Grinder and the Stone Preacher. Very impressive."

"By the laws of your King and your land, I invoke the rules of hospitality." I curtsied to him. "I thank you for the compliment. They are both unique in their own ways." The Stone Preacher remained steadfastly in front of me, while the Organ Grinder smiled pleasantly to the Viscount.

"Word of your marriage is spreading, Organ Grinder." He let out a low chuckle. "I fear your reputation could well quell itself in a paroxysm of needless furniture."

"I see you have a sense of humor despite wanting to kill me," I smiled to him. The Organ Grinder scowled, but struggled to give no offense. I restrained the picnic basket on my arm while it growled. The monkey made a low shriek from the Organ Grinder's pocket.

"Make no mistake. I am the leader of the Spiked Wrath Men and Chain Hook Guards. I make them from the defiant and those who the King of Feathers strips of their titles. I have no desire to kill you personally, but even if I did, now I cannot. I shall inform my lord that you have arrived." The Viscount raised a metal hand and gave some sort of signal with two fingers. I could hear the rattling sounds of armor dispersing in the distance. "Your bodyguards do you credit," he said icily. "I'm sure I'll see you about the castle. I look forward to the end of this, whatever it is." He turned and clanked away, his fist clenched slightly in frustration.

As we moved down the hall, led by the Hetman of Pulloya, we heard agonizing screams and the sounds of heavy blades chopping flesh. Someone else had done something inappropriate, or forgotten the rules of hospitality.

***

The Hetman guided us through narrow corridors in one of the spires, just within the outermost walls. Cold winds gusted through apertures as we moved. I held onto the picnic basket tightly as wind whipped through it. Eerie rustles rattled against its contents. I thought I heard it grimace and whimper.

The Organ Grinder and Stone Preacher stayed in front of me the whole way. The Hetman lurched forward, pulling himself along. Ropes on his wrists writhed. "So how long have you served the King of Feathers?" I asked.

"A fair question!" he shouted over the wind. "Five hundred and sixty three years!"

"That's a long time. Do you do anything other than escort people?"

"I have chores," he said sullenly. "And I get to eat, every so often."

"Stop," I said. "We can sit here for a moment." I reached into the picnic basket and pulled out a hot steaming sandwich, rich with a layer of gravy, and handed it to him. "Eat. I don't know how you're supposed to carry my belongings without eating."

The Hetman protested for a moment, as if I were trying to trick him, but I placed the sandwich into his hand. "Compassion is weakness."

"Dead on the stairs is still dead," I responded. "Eat the sandwich. If you cannot carry anything, you cannot take me where I need to go."

The Hetman sighed and took the sandwich, chewing on the thick slices of meat and licking gravy from his lips as he slowly savored it. The Organ Grinder turned to me, his eyes filled with longing. "Perhaps there is one for me in there?"

"If you don't share it with the monkey, maybe." I turned to the Stone Preacher. "They do have the rivalry that pets have when they don't like each other."

"I don't think it's a rivalry so much as a hatred and a craving," the Stone Preacher rumbled. "Still, such things are good for the spirit, having a pet, even a malicious beast that eats the dead and makes meals out of them."

"Do you understand how it works?" I asked, as the Hetman of Pulleys made his way through the sandwich.

"No," The Stone Preacher said. "When I pray to my god of granite, it is not one of the things I wish to know. And when I do not pray, it is also one of those things that I do not wish to know. If I did know, no doubt you would find yourself without a picnic basket, and, since that would cause you harm until the conclusion of your journeys, I choose not to think on it." He gave me a gravelly smile as the Organ Grinder tried to open the lid of the basket. The basket struggled to stay closed.

"Oh, give him a sandwich," I said. "Don't you see it's cold up here?" As if in response, the wind howled a little more, and blasted us through the open arches. The basket relented, opening the lid to give the Organ Grinder a similar sandwich, though this one was blasted through with heat and seemed warmer, the bread cracked from coming out of a hot oven. Thick gravy seeped between the gaps. The Organ Grinder seized his prize and thrust it into his mouth, chewing fiercely as his teeth ground bread and his throat gulped meat. Little droplets of gravy appeared at the edges of his mustache and beard. He took the time to wipe his lips with the sleeve of his greatcoat.

"That was fast." I idly petted the lid of the picnic basket, looking over to the Hetman of Pulleys, who savored each bite as though it were his last.

I thought everything would be fine as the Hetman wiped his lips and returned to his burden, lifting our luggage and staggering forward in his broken, shifting walk. We made it up only a few more steps before the Squire of Sages and the Cowl of Serpents came around the corner, the rough sound of a cudgel impacting the snake creature's head.

***

There was a disgruntled hiss and a scream of pain from the Cowl of Serpents as he clutched his head, whimpering as his master brought the wood down on his scaled head.

"Oh, my!" The Squire bowed to us, his eyes wide. "You've certainly changed a great deal."

I curtsied in return, the wind catching my cloak and making it rustle.

The picnic basket huddled behind me. Its lid opened as it studied the Cowl of Serpents, trying to determine whether or not the creature was edible. I grabbed the handle and squeezed tightly to prevent the creature from launching itself and eating a possible ally. "I have. How did you get here?"

"Well, I came on a flying boat, like you, of course." The Squire chuckled. "Everyone's talking about you, especially that horrible incident with the Duke of Bells and that mess with the Brotherhood of Doors. You're a folk hero, which has made you popular with many of the lesser nobles. Normally there would be squabbling over the Duchess of Bells' territory, but no one really wants to live in a wretched swamp castle with a bunch of toads. Perhaps you could marry her yourself?" He cackled. "No matter! It cannot be that important."

"I should hope she does marry her, if I am allowed to watch or participate." The Organ Grinder leered as the Hetman of Pulleys put the luggage down.

"You're married to the most powerful sorceress in the world," I said. "Someone should hire the proclaimers to let all the world know just what sort of bastard you are.'

"That's a fine way to treat your bodyguard," the Organ Grinder scowled.

"Why not?" The Squire of Sages suggested. "You're of a lower social class, and you spend all your time rutting with people above your station, which they adore, and many of the ones who resist are curious." He gave a sly cackle. "I suppose the Half-Bone Maiden does not have your heart, but make no mistake. Betray her, and she will rip it out. You have been very lucky so far, Organ Grinder. But I look forward to the day when your organ is ground."

The Stone Preacher remained silent, his rocky face cracking in a smile while the Organ Grinder locked gazes with the Squire of

Sages. The Cowl of Serpents hissed at him. The picnic basket jumped at the creature, while I yanked on its handle.

"Don't eat him," I said. I curtsied as daintily as possible while the basket's legs pinwheeled in the air. "Good Squire, I would beg of you to stop tenderizing your servant in front of my pet."

The Squire of Sages sighed. "He does require a great deal of discipline, but it shall be as you wish." He looked a little nervously at the slavering basket. Its tongue slithered out of its lid while legs gyrated.

"Calm down." I ruffled the lid. "If you could tell me a little about this place? It's my first time here."

"It is a magnificent maze of dark corridors and secret passages." The Squire of Sages chuckled. "No one has ever been able to catalog them all. When the King of Feathers took the throne from the last ruler of our lands, he erased that worthy's name from history, and none of us are allowed to speak it, on pain of death. It keeps issues of authority to a minimum."

I looked to the Stone Preacher. "Do you know where all of them are?" I asked. "The secret passages, I mean."

"That is an interesting thought," the Stone Preacher responded. "In truth, I never tried to discover them." He let out a rocky laugh. "It seems I owe you an unusual favor, of sorts."

The Organ Grinder chuckled throatily. "It could be of much use to me, here among the many noblewomen whose husbands are either not about, or occupied elsewhere."

"Your marriage?" I countered icily. "Your prospects with other women now include the prospect of small, wooden foot supports."

The Organ Grinder scowled. "Fie on your orders," he grumbled. "If only I had not been given your shoe."

"I do not have any shoes," the Cowl of Serpents whined. "Master takes them away." He looked pleadingly to the Squire of Sages, who shot him a dirty look.

"Go hide under your hood," the Squire of Sages snapped. "I own your thousand-times cracked skull, and I'll crack it some more!"

"Did he actually do anything to deserve this treatment?" I asked the Squire.

"Probably not," the Organ Grinder muttered to himself. "It's just another case of forced subjugation, no doubt."

The Squire of Sages laughed. "I do not care. He is my servant. I treat him as I choose." He chortled gleefully. "You'll understand more of this in time, my dear. I must be off, as I require sustenance." He dragged the Cowl of Serpents down the stairs past us.

The Hetman of Pulleys turned. "He's a bastard, that one." He grumbled and lifted the luggage. "But he did give me a rest inadvertently."

"I'm never giving him anything out of the picnic basket," I said. "Those disgusting teeth alone make me think it's sullying the food."

The Hetman led us up around the tower to a high room with a view of both the courtyard and the skies around us. Beautiful skies were patrolled by savage winged worms, mounted by guards armed with their lashing chains. For every word that said that we were guests, there was an unspeakable sign that we were all prisoners.

***

The Hetman forced the door open with a strength I thought he couldn't possibly have, and deposited all of our luggage right inside the door. Everything was magnificently arranged in the position that he had picked it up in. "Blow the whistle if you need anything." He scuttled off, leaving us in a large bedchamber.

The bars on the windows said everything.

The Organ Grinder stepped in and closed the door as I marveled at the room's opulent furnishings. The carpet was so thick I felt I was walking on the sky. The four-poster bed was made of marble. Walls were paneled in thick black wood. Strange purple mushrooms in jars gave off a brilliant white light, illuminating the room from claw-shaped sconces. They produced a faint smell of earth and incense. I couldn't tell whether it was from a perfume or the mushrooms themselves.

On the bed was a wrapped black box, covered in a thick spool of ribbon. It almost begged to be opened, and I gestured to the Stone Preacher. "Open it," I said. "I don't want it to kill me."

"Your paranoia does you credit," the Organ Grinder chuckled as the Stone Preacher yanked the ribbon off and flipped the lid up.

"It appears to be safe," he said. "It's your mask for the ball."

It was a beautiful thing of etched porcelain, half white, half black, the left depicting a beautiful woman's face not unlike my own, the right a mass of shimmering, beautiful stars that seemed to glisten and shine in the lacquer. The eyeholes shone as if to hide the color of the wearer's eyes. A silvery strap slid around the back of it, calling attention to the hand-written note at the bottom of the box. "From a lady who knows the most about masks to the one who needs one more than any other." There was no signature at the bottom, just a flourish of insignias that didn't make any sense to me.

There were four dressers, each with a mirror on top, made of a strange reddish wood carved with the faces of monsters. There was an adjacent room for bathing, from which a little steam pushed out in a brief cloud.

"Your bath is drawn, it seems," the Stone Preacher rumbled.

"So who else has made it this far?" I asked. "You've been notoriously reticent to talk about it."

"Not all journeys lead here." The Organ Grinder grinned. "Most end before they begin – with terror, screaming, or a beast with a mouth larger than most people."

"What about the ones that did?" I asked, nervously looking at the bars. "Can one of you remove them? They make me nervous."

"I think that you should wait until the time comes. When one is a prisoner, however gilded the cage, one should never alert the cage owner that you feel it is time to leave," the Stone Preacher rumbled. "Unless you are one of those honorable folk who insist on dying stupidly."

"Well, I think I've done pretty awful so far, except for the driving off the Weeper in Shadows for a few days. That was an achievement worth writing songs about."

"It was a magnificent shot," the Organ Grinder responded. "So why did you save us instead of finishing her? I am curious. You should have let us all die. That would have made you worthy, indeed." The monkey squeaked eagerly from his pocket, agreeing.

I looked down at the picnic basket. It wasn't disagreeing. "Don't you go eating everyone," I said. "You have to save a few of them."

"It is a terrible thing, to be saved for later," the Stone Preacher rumbled. "At least if you are my associate of the moment." His eyes creaked over to the Organ Grinder.

"So you would mind being saved for later yourself?" The Organ Grinder raised the eyebrow behind his monocle. "It would seem that you would take pleasure in my demise."

I gathered my things and headed into the bath, letting steam suffuse me before I disrobed and slipped into the warm water. "He's not alone in that assessment," I called to the other room. "When some people die, there is a grim funeral where sadness afflicts those who mourn the departed. But think, without the Half-Bone Maiden, you will likely die alone. There's a sobering thought for you. Dead or with your wife's feet resting on you for eternity."

"Why not?" the Organ Grinder growled. "Her feet rest on me now. My time of freedom slowly slips away."

"You didn't have to play the accordion. You like her. You just don't know it. And she's very nice."

"Too nice," the Organ Grinder thundered. "That is not a recommendation!"

"All that power, all that pleasantness, and all of it at your disposal, and you still won't commit." I teased/ I reached for the azure lump that looked like scented soap. "You are a beast."

"I am indeed!" the Organ Grinder cheered.

The Stone Preacher moved over to the window with the bars.

"Do not hurl me down, sir." The Organ Grinder backed up towards the door.

"Not you," the Stone Preacher responded. "Your monkey."

Even in the bath, where luxury and relaxation nearly consumed me, and into the bed, Dreams of the Organ Grinder and Stone Preacher locked in battle with each other assaulted me. Prison bars on the window clawed at my mind.

***

I awoke in a dreamy haze, the violent struggles I imagined between my bodyguards behind me. I felt around for the picnic basket as if it were my only friend. It rubbed its lid underneath my hand and shoved hard a little bit, as if it were trying to wake me. I hoped it didn't need to eat. I could hear the gruff snores of the Organ Grinder.

The Stone Preacher turned to face me, arms folded. "A gentleman came to the door when you are sleeping. He is still there."

"Is it the Captain of Clouds?" I asked, hoping it was someone I knew. The picnic basket hopped up and down on the bed excitedly. "No," I stroked the picnic basket. "Don't eat the Captain. He's our transportation out of here if things go bad."

"Alas, no," the Stone Preacher rumbled. "It's some ridiculous idiot in a turban who calls himself the Vizier of Pestles. He says that he needs some information about you for your testing ceremony."

"A testing ceremony? I wasn't aware that there was one." I sat up. "Is everyone who makes it here without vouchsafes tested?"

"Well, you do have letters and promises, but in the end, they could mean nothing."

The monkey crawled out of the Organ Grinder's pocket, and clambered up to his head, lazily waving the knife-tail as spittle drooled from its lip.

"I, for one, would expect to be betrayed." The Stone Preacher glared at the monkey disdainfully.

"Tell the Vizier I do not exist at his convenience, and I will be ready in a few minutes." I smiled wickedly to the Stone Preacher. "That's an hour and a half in girl time."

The Stone Preacher's rocky lips cracked in a smirk, a slight echo of pebbles clattering in the wake of his lips moving. "I shall." He turned and moved toward the door.

I slipped into the bath, unable to hear the quiet tones while I relaxed in the warm, scented water and sang crass melodies to the sound of the Organ Grinder's snoring.

When I got out of the bath, I let the dress slither over me. It changed into something elegant and red, with a tight, hiked bosom and wide, puffy skirt that traveled down to my ankles. I took another thirty minutes to finish doing my hair, just to be sure that frustration and relief would be on the Vizier's face.

The Stone Preacher glared to me as I came out. "He's knocked on the door twice since you were in there," he grumbled.

"Kick the Organ Grinder awake," I grinned. "But not too hard."

The Stone Preacher moved over to the Organ Grinder with a savage, quick glide, and, grabbing the neck of his greatcoat, tossed him onto the floor. The Organ Grinder thudded and shook his head in mid snore, and struggled to wakefulness as the monkey screeched and howled. The Organ Grinder picked himself up. "Why did you throw me?" He glowered up at the Stone Preacher as he rose.

"She asked me to." The Stone Preacher's voice was flat and unwavering. "It was only a couple of feet."

Knocking sounded at the door again. The Organ Grinder rose to his feet, and lumbered over to the door to answer it. He pulled it open, and stepped aside. "Gentlemen, the lady is prepared." He rumbled, and gave a low bow to the man in front of the door.

The monkey leaped from the sconce onto the Organ Grinder's hat, and bowed too, flicking the tail-knife over its diseased head.

The Vizier entered the room with measured care, his round face, thick mustache and beard framing a bulging nose and wide, fearful eyes of green. "Greetings." He bowed low, speaking with a nasal voice. "You still seek your name, and yet you have made it this far. Impressive." He was wearing a thick brocade robe that his belly forced outward. Slim legs were clad in luxurious silk pants. His feet wore far more modern shoes in black. The turban he wore seemed to crush his face and widen his cheeks.

"Not nearly as impressive as your achievements, my lord." I curtsied. "I fear that I cannot recite a list of them, but I am sure that one as storied as yourself must be very impressive." The picnic basket scampered over to my leg from where it hid, and opened its lid, letting out a low growl. I yanked the handle sharply to make it stop.

"I am the adviser to the King of Feathers. I assume that you will be available for testing later in the day, around the time evening falls?"

"Of course." I smiled to him. "Will I recognize you, or will you be wearing a mask?"

"Witty," he murmured as he rose from his bow. "I will send an escort to bring you to the testing chambers at eight."

"My bodyguards are coming with me," I said sweetly. "And I'm not going anywhere without my picnic basket. I periodically have these terrible bouts of hunger."

The Vizier's smile was wide in his cheery face. "It shall be as you wish. Do not be late. The ball will already be in progress. The announcement of new arrivals is always put off until later, for dramatic purposes, you understand."

"What kind of test is this?"

"To see if your eyes are fake," the Vizier cackled. "All of these nobility games are magnificent. Many try to gain entry to such an affair only to be forced out."

"Am I allowed to explore the grounds?" I was eager to be out of a room that came with bars on it. "I don't mean to impose, but it seems kind of awful to be cooped up all day."

"You may. You may not enter any of the forbidden areas, however. And you must wear your mask. The rules of this world are very strange. Eye contact is not enough. You must gaze upon your true love's naked face to discover him – or her – or sometimes it–" He shuddered a little bit. "It–" He quivered again. For the briefest of moments, I thought I saw the turban move.

"What happens to those who are forced out?" I asked. "Or those whom the King of Feathers simply doesn't like?"

"We throw them down the hole in the center of the ceremony room." The Vizier smiled. "But your skills have preceded you. It shouldn't be any trouble." He didn't so much walk as slither out the door, leaving my throat in discomfort behind him.

"That didn't go well at all," I said.

"It went better than expected," the Stone Preacher said. "He told you something important, something I did not even know."

"The whole face?" I shuddered. "At a masquerade ball? That could be complicated."

"It usually is." The Organ Grinder smiled. "Have any of your charges ever made it to the Castle?"

"I'm afraid not. This is all alien to me. There is a possibility, but I don't wish to speak it."

"Why not?" I demanded.

"It will destroy you," the Stone Preacher said firmly. "And if it does, I'm afraid I don't wish to be the one responsible. You're the first person I've liked in over four hundred years. I don't want to see you changed because of my arrogant assumption and no evidence."

"How nice of you," I muttered. "I know better than to try and get you to change your mind." I stormed over to the couch and sat, pulling on my boots. "Subdued," I said to the dress. "Preferably black, and without much fanfare."

The dress obeyed my request, and slithered about me into subtlety, removing hoops and restitching itself into a weave of blandness. I tugged on my cloak and pulled my hood up, dragging my boots on afterwards.

"Are you sure you want to go out?" the Stone Preacher said. "You'll be going alone. This castle resists my entreaties. No doubt the King of Feathers foresaw a day when I might try to kill him."

"Do you have a history with him?" I asked. "That would certainly explain the room with bars."

"Alas, no." The Stone Preacher muttered. "The truth is I lack flight, and he can fly whenever he wants. I have never encountered him. He lives here in his floating fortress, and wanders the land in secret, gathering information on the land and its subjects. Political advantage here is always complex."

"That doesn't reassure me," I said. I slipped out the door. "I should be back in a few hours." The picnic basket ran up to the door after me. "Stay. I said. You're my favorite pet, but you're too distinctive to drag around."

The basket let out a low whine, but the Stone Preacher grabbed it. I closed the door to the room, free to skulk about the castle in the gray day.

***

I was back on the windy stairwell where cold air blasted my face, even with my hood drawn. I gathered myself in my cloak, and activated my boots, leaping over the edge in a brief blaze, floating downward against the basalt, trying to remain hidden from flying patrols. When the worms came close, I leaped back onto the spiral, huddling until the rotation passed.

It took me almost an hour to get to the bottom between waiting and skulking, but I did it without being detected. I stood at the entrance to the main courtyard as if I had just walked down. There were still guards walking about the compound, carrying torches that flickered with the same strange mushroom-light as the ones in my room.

The torches made hiding in shadows easier. I waited for a patrol to pass. As two Chain Hook Guards made their way into the castle, I shadowed them, keeping a close eye on their movements as they slipped into the building through massive doors. Most of the windows were barred, except for several large sections of stained glass near the top of the central building. Every one of them was beautiful, depicting scenes of broken romances and doomed lovers, a series of tragedies wrought in melted sand.

I crept amid shadows and floated above them. When they opened the doors, I scuttled up underneath the top of the frame and flattened against the wall, peering into the foyer. Twin staircases curved around the walls, leading up to a landing with a massive set of unguarded double doors. Below, four doors led off into various parts of the castle.

I followed the guards through one of the openings, keeping my eyes focused as the strange torches lit the way. Their clanking sounds covered my movements as I huddled near the ceiling. There was a faint sound of howling that grew louder as we descended.

The cries grew louder as the guards reached the bottom of the stairs. Older, dimmer torches flickered with the sounds of screams as the guards clanked off. I tried to listen for where they were coming from. I wasn't sure I wanted to rescue them. Curiosity still overcame me. I crept towards moans of pain, gliding between shadows in the tunnels below.

I could hear the hissing of forges amid screams. I headed for the noise. Ahead of me was a vaulted archway that led into a large room that blistered with heat. Hammers rang on metal as chains were forged.

I settled against the wall and looked in, staring at helpless people writhing in iron maidens and tied to racks. Their eyes were glassy; their bodies wracked with scars from whips. I turned my eyes away for a moment, unable to cry for any of them. Beyond them were three massive forges, where Spiked Wrath Men sat, hammering at anvils where they shaped pieces of armor and other metal things.

The screaming continued with occasional whimpers as I studied the guards and the prisoners. I didn't recognize any of them. I craned my neck to try and see more. There was too much outside of my range of sight. My stomach felt all curled up. I would have to force fear aside.

I slipped into the torture chamber, where I saw the massive form of the Viscount of Chains, hunched over a screaming man chained to a basalt table. He was cutting out his victim's heart and replacing it with a knobby ball of metal and spikes. The odd slurp of the man's heart being ripped out and quickly replaced by a ball of metal grated on me.

The body on the table struggled up, popping its bonds and making a strange hissing noise, as it pointed to me, its finger extended in my direction as the pulsing, writhing metal ball began to seal the wound in its chest.

The Viscount turned his helmeted head toward me and extended a hand, raising the helmet slightly with a cruel smile on his face. "An adventurous supplicant." He rose and bowed. "I see you are blessed with some curiosity." He turned to the spiked wrath men. "Equip him." He murmured as the creatures rose from their seats. "I will entertain our guest."

"I'm certain this will be a pleasure." I curtsied daintily, letting my boots settle to the floor under the robe. "It is a pleasure to see you again." The lie came as easily to my lips as many others had. It didn't even matter if the Viscount saw through it. There were proprieties to be observed.

***

The Viscount let out a low chuckle as the Spiked Wrath Men brought armor and implements for their new associate. He tilted his head, savoring the agonizing screams behind him while he extended a hand to me as if he were a perfect gentleman. He acted as if what was behind him was perfectly ordinary, and he could easily pay it no mind. "I will escort you outside this chamber, if you should wish it."

"I do appreciate the gesture." I offered my arm. The massive black armored arm slid into the crook of mine, and we stepped out of the forge, the screaming of the Viscount's victim left behind as the hot armor and weapons fused themselves to his flesh and bone.

We slipped out into the hall as the screaming stopped, and the Viscount disengaged his arm from mine. "You're not supposed to be down here," he said firmly, his fingers closing about the chain on his belt.

"I wanted to see what this was all about. It isn't every day that someone like me manages to get to a masquerade of this magnitude. Your forge is impressive, Sir Viscount, but not nearly as impressive as your manners."

"We do try to keep things in order." He chuckled. "Now for the excellent explanation of why you want to see what everything is all about?" His dark gaze focused on my fingers.

"I know that things here aren't what they seem, and if things went sour, I wanted to be sure I knew where everything was." It wasn't a lie, but it was admitting that I had been sneaking around.

"A good answer." The Viscount of Chains laughed.

"Isn't there some other way to get good guards?" I asked. "Don't you think ripping their hearts out and putting weird balls of metal in their chests is a little inefficient?"

"The King of Feathers is not interested in efficiency. He is interested in the consolidation of his power. As long as his power is consolidated, so is mine." I could almost feel the lizardlike smile under his helmet.

"So he just terrifies his subjects? Or is there more to it than that?"

"A terrified population is easier to subdue." The Viscount raised a finger, as if he were lecturing. "You, too, will learn this when you find the one you are looking for. Your lands will be rife with rebellious peasants and people who supported your predecessors. They will remember the so-called good old days when someone else's guts were about to be put on a spike in front of them, and it was someone they disliked."

"So if I require assistance in keeping the people under my yoke, I presume I can call upon your aid in exchange for a favor?" I smiled. "After all, that does seem to be the real trade currency of the land, no matter how many gold half-lunas there are."

"Yes." The Viscount chuckled. "From what I understand, the price on your head is phenomenally high. However, the rules are specific in that once you're here, until after the ball, no one may collect it. You seem well versed in the currency of favor trading, for one who has only been here a little while." He tilted his head. "Perhaps there is something you require now?"

"Other than knowing who my love is, a fact that nobody seems to actually know, I wouldn't really require much of anything." I offered a dainty curtsey.

"I would not refuse such a request had I anything to offer, but sadly, I do not," the Viscount rattled. I thought I detected a trace of deceit, but it wasn't important enough to press when I was surrounded by his men and my bodyguards weren't nearby.

"I think that concludes our conversation." I smiled a little bit. "I should return to areas that are not restricted."

"But I am so proud of my creations." The Viscount of Chains protested. "Allow me to show them to you and explain how they are made."

"I don't know that it would be such a good idea." Visions of my heart being ripped out and replaced with a spiky ball dominated my consciousness.

There was a loud clattering noise and some clanking sounds. Shards of metal dropped to the floor, as the open mouthed face of the Hetman of Pulleys stared at us, reaching down to pick up his burden. "An intruder!" he shouted. "Viscount, raise the alarm!"

"Our conversation, madam, appears to be ending. I have no choice." He lashed out with his chain as my bow came into my hands, and I rolled under it. The Hetman of Pulleys picked up two metal spikes and bashed them together as loudly as he could.

"I think you did. He's only a peasant." I retorted as I retreated up the corridor. The Hetman grabbed the two spikes in his hands and lashed at me. I was barely able to escape the stabbing as the Viscount reeled in his long, sharp chain and came at me again. I was going to die here, deep in the belly of the Castle in the Sky, and I had told my protectors to stay away.

**

I drew the bow back as I rolled under the Hetman of Pulleys and tripped him forward. Two spikes grated along the stone as I began flying back down the corridor. I couldn't go at full speed. There would be more of them on me in seconds. I fired an arrow as best I could, and it bounced off the lashing chain the Viscount whipped down the corridor at me. He withdrew it and prepared to lash again as I made for the stairs. The Hetman of Pulleys righted himself and charged after me.

The Viscount ran forward, lashing out with his chain as I fired again. The arrow was easily deflected as the Hetman came on, stabbing with iron spikes. I made my way back upstairs, toward the grey shine that passed for light. Spikes scraped along the wall, making angry shrieks like sharp fingernails. I could hear clanking sounds of the Viscount's guardsmen.

The Hetman closed in, his long arms like ropes, whipping around me as I flipped, turned, and dodged in the cramped quarters. I couldn't fire the bow. The walls were too close. I kicked out with a burning foot and drove it against his chest. There was a thumping sound and the whine of clockwork. The force of my kick pushed me further back towards the stairs as the Hetman shrugged off the blow. I only needed to cover another twenty or thirty feet.

The Viscount clanked forward. His chain slithered toward me, low along the ground as the Hetman jumped over it. I rolled away, but the chain caught my leg. I slammed hard into the stony wall. I could feel it rake my skin. The Hetman came down, leaping forward to stab again with both spikes. I tumbled to the ground, the clanking of the Viscount's armor heavy in my ears as the Hetman stabbed.

There was a wet thud. The Hetman of Pulleys gurgled, clutching at his throat. A long, narrow shaft protruded from it. He rolled and flopped on the ground as the Viscount drew his chain back and held it at the ready, spinning it over his head. I struggled to my feet and looked behind me. I stared at the elegant boots of the Captain of Clouds, who was grinning and held a crossbow on the Viscount. Several Spiked Wrath Men suddenly came to an abrupt halt, their master at a disadvantage.

"Now it's two against one," he said cheerily, stepping up and keeping the crossbow pointed firmly at the Viscount. "I suggest we resolve this without bloodshed, now that there aren't any living peasants to make noise about it."

The Viscount put his chain away while I struggled to my feet. "Well spoken, sir. I was only doing my duty, you understand. Now that there is no need for an alarm to be raised, I'm certain that the young lady may proceed unimpeded. I suggest you escort her. We wouldn't want any improprieties spoken of in dark corners." He let out a raspy laugh.

"How did you find me?" I managed to the Captain of Clouds.

"It wasn't that hard," the Captain responded. "I supposed that in the manner of all curious people, the first place you would find would be the dungeon. And if it wasn't, all I had to do was wait until you got here."

The Viscount of Chains barely suppressed a chuckle. "Well played, sir. Now, go. I must return to my duties."

The Captain of Clouds slid his hand under my arm. "I fear it's back to your room, lass." He gave me a wry chuckle. "Not every ploy is successful, and I'm sure a little minor rescuing won't cut into your journey any."

"Thank you. I suppose there's no harm in it."

He doused my lips with a little rum to deter suspicion and helped me stagger up the stairs. When the Organ Grinder opened the door to stare at us, I was actually grateful to look at his monocle and thick mustache. The Stone Preacher's grim stare cracked into a rocky smile. When the picnic basket raced up to rub against my legs, it almost felt like I had come home to something special.

The Captain of Clouds bowed before the door and gave us a clever smile. "It's been entertaining," he said it as he doffed his cap. "I believe the lady needs some rest."

I staggered over to the bed and fell into it. Just as I thought I was going to fall asleep, I saw the picnic basket's lid open wide to the Captain of Clouds, and offer him a magnificent smelling smoked turkey.

It was all that I dreamed about until I woke up.

***

When I awoke, it was to the smell of roasting squash, rich maple-soaked beans, and buttered bread. "You have to stop it," the Organ Grinder growled. "Your basket's been running about and coughing up food for at least an hour."

There was almost no room to move. The room was filled with strange smells and delicious pastries. As fast as the Stone Preacher could move the dishes towards the door and the line of eager nobles desiring unusual meals, the picnic basket was coughing up more.

"I'll try," I said, staring at the procession of courses that had been pumped out of the picnic basket. "Stop it!" I grabbed at the handle. "You've got to save some for later."

The picnic basket hiccupped and stopped, leaving a few crisp apples rolling across the floor. "It must have eaten someone who didn't agree with it," the Stone Preacher muttered, continuing to hand plates, bags, and baskets of food out the door. "On the other hand, there appears to be something for everyone." He reached down and handed a platter with a roast, simmering in gravy, to a grateful-looking noble with a wig.

"If you wish to be popular, you have succeeded." The Organ Grinder laughed. He was sitting on a couch, patting his belly. "I ate three meals in the time you slept."

The picnic basket let out a little whine as I grabbed it. "No more barfing," I said fiercely. "You've made enough." I kept the lid closed as the Organ Grinder lurched towards the door, scooping up a platter of cold meats and cheeses and handing it off to the next person in line.

"I can't believe you two have turned my room into a soup kitchen!" I said angrily. "And it's a soup kitchen for people who don't even need it."

"How else would you suggest we get rid of it?" The Stone Preacher scowled. "Most of these things can't fit through the bars on the windows."

I sighed and looked over at the barred window. "Is there going to be anything left now that we've pawned off our meals for the next hundred days?"

"I suspect, yes." The Organ Grinder chuckled as the last of the line trickled away. "There's still four turkeys, three plates of roasted squash, and several dozen vegetables." He glanced carefully over at the pile of desserts resting against one corner of the room. "Oh, and twenty-two cakes." He rolled his eyes. "I have no idea how you never put on any weight."

"I beg your pardon?" A man stuck his head in. He was wearing a prodigious wig and an impressive waistcoat. "What exactly is 'barfing'?"

"It's when you cough up too much food," I smiled, telling a half-truth. I didn't want anyone to take offense at what they were eating. Apparently most of the eating was going on right outside my room, on the heavily guarded stairs.

"You haven't let any of them see me, have you?" I sat up from the bed and scampered into the bath. "It would be a lot easier to be presentable for guests if you would wake me." I gently placed the picnic basket on the bed, where it seemed to visibly settle for a moment, as if some great weight had been discharged.

"We didn't see a need," the Stone Preacher responded. "Where could you have gone in this clutter of foodstuffs? It would have looked undignified no matter what."

"I suppose I should get dressed," I said. "This testing business is in a few hours." I slipped into the bath and quietly called for my dress, which scuttled in along the floor and reoriented itself into a deep-cut black affair with a tight corset and smooth, sweeping hiplines. "Are you sure?" I asked it.

The dress didn't even wiggle. It knew what it wanted. The Stone Preacher looked over and scowled. "That is, perhaps, too undignified."

The Organ Grinder peered at the dress, and squinted through the monocle. "It could show a little more skin," he said gently, as though he were putting on a façade of sophistication.

"Well, I'm keeping it, then," I said. The dress didn't say a word, but there was a strange rustling whine from the picnic basket, as it leaned over the edge of the bed to see into the bathroom. Then it leaped off the bed and ran in, hopping about the dress as it struggled and twisted, avoiding the nipping of the picnic basket. "Stop!" I snapped. "You're incorrigible." I grabbed the basket by the handle from the bath and gave it a little shake.

The picnic basket relented, and settled in next to the dress. "You think I'm going to lock you up in the room again, don't you." It wiggled excitedly and jumped up and down a little bit. "All right. I promise you can come with me. But no arm sitting and no eating people without permission, ok?"

The picnic basket sunk a little bit, but then opened the lid and offered me a peach. I reached in and took it, and the basket capered about while I ate.

"You're communicating with it," the Stone Preacher rumbled. "That's either a good sign, or a sign that we're all doomed."

"I think it's a good sign." The Organ Grinder chuckled. "Soon she'll take her place among us. Then the games will really begin." He shot me an evil leer and fingered his accordion while I reclined in the bathwater.

***

Bathing took a little while. I pulled the cloak of runes on over it and struggled into my boots while the Stone Preacher prevented the Organ Grinder from looking. I put on the mask that the Lady of Masks had given me. It felt cool and supple on my face, almost a shield against the world. I felt safer, as though there was a measure of safety in anonymity. A thick-faced servant who asked no questions about the fate of his predecessor escorted us down through the vaults and caverns of the Castle to the testing chamber.

It was a massive vaulted room, with high fluted columns supporting a basalt statue of black wings spread out from a sphere. The sphere was carved with leering faces that glared down on us. A strange golden illumination radiated outward from the eyes. A circular pit rustled with cold air at the center, its edges covered with strange runes in a language I didn't understand. There were eight stone basins filled with burning coals. The smell of something acrid and roasting came out of them, similar to fire on bone.

Four huge arches leading to stairways settled heavily in the corners, as if they were giant mouths filled with teeth. On either side of each archway, there was a massive stone statue of a heavyset man, fat and bloated, a long flail dragging on the ground in one hand while a shield rested in the other.

Standing near the center of the room was the Vizier of Pestles, along with the Viscount of Chains and thirty armed soldiers. We had entered last, and already, there were six other excited men and women like me, dressed in various forms of unusual garments, some like mine, others more advanced, and others more primitive.

"Ah, the last of you has arrived!" The Vizier of Pestles smiled, wide and false, as he looked at the others. "We will now test your nobility to see that each of you is true." He chuckled to himself as he stared at the other six, four men and two women. "Please get in line."

I moved into the line, and took a moment to take in the scene of masked people and bodyguards. One young girl looked as if she was going to chew off her own lip, while the man first in line stood confidently, his eyes bright green and his smile wide.

"Now that you are arranged," the Vizier of Pestles chuckled. "I regret to inform you that one of you is an impostor."

The Viscount of Chains walked forward.

"There is only one punishment, and we don't stand on ceremony with it." He stared at me with a deep bow, his grim eyes locking on mine before he turned to the lead man in line. "You've come quite far for a liar, but I'm afraid you are going to die." He lashed out with the chain and before the man's bodyguards – a stunning girl with whips made of vines, and a heavyset barrel of a man wearing only a loincloth – could protest, the smiling young man was hurled into the pit in the center of the room, screaming desperate cries before his screams faded.

The Vizier of Pestles chuckled as the Viscount of Chains folded his arms. "We apologize for the King of Feathers not arriving for the testing ceremony. However, he is disappointed that someone has tried to deceive him." If anything, his smile grew even wider. "Sister of Jungles, I apologize for this farce that you have been involved in, and to you, Sir Thickness of Girth, I apologize for the fact that you have been deceived. You may depart without incident."

"How does such a thing happen?" rumbled the Stone Preacher to me under his breath.

"He couldn't fly," the Organ Grinder whispered sarcastically.

"Contact lenses," I hissed back. "I'll explain later."

The woman with vines and the heavy man sighed to each other and made their way up the stairs, the silence falling over the other bleak faces and surprised bodyguards. "You're – just going to let them leave?" One of the men stammered the words out, as though his lips were barriers.

"Of course." The Vizier licked his lips, as if he were savoring a moment yet to come. "Now that the unpleasantness is over, please approach in order of the line. All the riches of desire shall be yours if you can find your true love. And if they are not here, your journeys will continue, but the seal of my approval shall travel with you."

The line proceeded while I waited at the back. Each of the applicants stood near the Viscount of Chains as the Vizier peered at him or her. Every so often the turban would shift the slightest bit. Once, I thought I saw a tail, like that of a rattlesnake, slither out between the folds of fabric.

One by one, the Vizier merely nodded at them, and allowed the people in front of me to pass, elegantly gliding up between the arches as the Vizier of Chains stood aside for them. "And now, we come to you, my dear," the Vizier crooned, eyeing my bodyguards as I stood at the edge of the chasm. "Oh, you are indeed real, though I wish it was not so. The Captain of Clouds managed to save you before. All of this unpleasantness could have been avoided had the Viscount not been such a gentleman, and true to his station."

The Viscount of Chains took a step back, and bowed deeply. "Once again, I apologize for any unpleasantness that this may cause. It is not in my nature to be unruly to guests."

The Vizier doffed his turban. A slithering worm burst out, hissing and spitting poison as I rolled to one side. "Kill her!" he shouted. "She must not reach the grand ballroom!"

***

The Stone Preacher moved faster than I did. He stepped in front of me, his hand whipping out to grab the worm and rip it in two. As the circle of guards moved forward, the Viscount of Chains lashed at me. The Preacher's other arm let the chain wrap around it.

"Surround the Stone Preacher!" the Vizier wheezed. "Pick him to death with your spikes!"

The Viscount pulled, but the Stone Preacher's arm did not move. "I've been looking forward to killing as many of you as I can." His face cracked in a grim smile, sounding like shearing rock. "I do not care how mighty you think you are." The circle of guards began to close around the Stone Preacher as the Viscount's chain returned to his hand, filling the air with rocky powder.

I rolled to my feet and summoned my bow. The Organ Grinder moved forward, yanking the Vizier of Pestles by the shirt and tearing the turban from his head. He ripped the fabric apart. Blood leaked from the strands of cloth, and the Vizier howled, diving on the shards of his true love. His fingers spattered with leaking gore as strange entrails poured out of it. "Well..." the Organ Grinder chuckled. "That takes care of that." He drove a foot into the whimpering man's belly, and shoved him into the hole.

The sobs of the Vizier of Pestles lasted in the chamber longer than the scream of the man he had hurled down only moments before. "Get to the ballroom!" The Stone Preacher shouted. "We have powerful enemies indeed. Get away from the hole, girl!"

I rose into the air as the Organ Grinder charged the press of attackers. The Stone Preacher followed. He sank into the ground, leaving the Spiked Wrath Men with nothing to grasp at but the Organ Grinder. There was a shriek as the monkey leaped, and jabbed its tail into the eye socket of one the armored men, howling and stabbing as others bent down to grab it.

I fired my first arrow then, straight at the Viscount of Chains. His armor proved to be lighter than I thought. He batted aside the arrow and leaped back toward the stairs. The swirling mass of guards gathered around the Organ Grinder. His leather-booted foot kicked a hand away from the monkey, who bounced to another looming monster as though its only pleasure was killing.

The picnic basket charged into the fray near the Organ Grinder. Sharp teeth under the lid clamped down hard on the leg of one of the creatures and tore it off as the monster bellowed. It punched down. The basket nimbly dodged and swallowed, letting out a belch as the creature teetered.

There were too many of them. I couldn't chase the Viscount while the creatures swarmed the Organ Grinder. The Stone Preacher was nowhere to be seen. I fired sharp arrows into the joints of those closest to the Organ Grinder. The explosive eruptions from within at the tip were impressive. As bodies twisted and died, I silently thanked the Jack of Forests for his gift.

The Organ Grinder was hurled back by the force of the blasts, out over the yawning hole in the center. I dived, firing more arrows into the troops to knock them down. The picnic basket and the monkey leaped away in opposite directions. As the basket and the monkey landed, I leaped out to grab the Organ Grinder by the boot. "That's two you owe me." I tugged him up over the edge of the lip.

The ground of the chamber burst upward in a massive explosion of rocky spikes. The monkey vaulted upward to perch atop one, making keening shrieks and desperate howls. Sharp points slammed through armored soldiers, already disoriented from the explosive bursts. The picnic basket struggled, its handle caught on the tip of a rising spike.

In the midst of the sudden carnage, the Stone Preacher erupted, flinging his arms forward. As he gestured, the spikes moved, impaling the horde of disoriented guards.

The wails of pain from the guards were the last thing I heard before the Stone Preacher drew his hands down. Spikes grew knobs, pulling the small army of enemies into the granite. The picnic basket, released from the spike by the Organ Grinder, hopped back and forth on short legs, testing to make sure that it was still in one piece. The Stone Preacher grinned. The floor made a terrible noise: a muffled sound of mashing flesh and twisting metal.

***

There was an uncomfortable silence as we stared at the cold light of pleasure in the Stone Preacher's granite eyes. "Come, heretics," he whispered. "This cold ground is yours now. Who dares to steal a mountain and disconnect it from the world?"

"We need to get upstairs," I said. "There'll be more guards coming."

The Organ Grinder grinned and petted the monkey as the floor gave another shuddering crunch, and the Stone Preacher raced for one of the stairways. "This one," he said. "I know the shortest route."

The picnic basket flounced after him. I ran into the air, my feet licking flames, while the Organ Grinder charged behind, reaching for his accordion. "This is a special occasion!" he thundered. "All we have to do is get in the door!" Low, morbid tones whined from the accordion behind me. We began to ascend the stairs, a grim affair laden with bas-reliefs and metal statues with mouths gaping in shock, horror, and rage.

The staircase began to whisper, a babbling noise crawling out of the mouths of the statues and faces, cooing against the tones of the accordion. "How did you know?" the Stone Preacher thundered as I raced after him, his unearthly glide rising up the stairs.

"I didn't."

The Organ Grinder laughed raucously.

Slithering tormented bodies burst forth from the stone, stabbing at us with knives from horrified mouths and slashing at us with their weapons.

"They fear the King of Feathers, so they come—" The Organ Grinder began to dance his way up the stairs.

The Stone Preacher gestured and shattered the bas-relief faces of stone, hurling shards about as the statues attacked. The picnic basket leaped and cavorted, opening its mouth as it gulped down a few shards and dodged between sharp objects. The monkey hooted in time with the accordion, gleeful and savage.

Graceful music throbbed and clawed at us, burning between my legs with desperate heat born from lust inspired by the Organ Grinder's accordion. The picnic basket skipped and danced while the monkey hooted. I knew the statues felt it, too.

The statues grabbed each other, kissing and grinding, as though their stone were flesh. They clutched each other and rutted in the tight confines of the stairs as we dodged and rolled between them. The Organ Grinder laughed as he capered up the steps. The picnic basket leaped and flounced at my burning heels as we raced after the Stone Preacher.

The Stone Preacher turned from the top of the stairs. He glowered down at us as we raced forward. "Hurry!" he snapped. "I'm not amused by your solution, Organ Grinder!"

I turned to the Organ Grinder and smirked as the metal and stone creaked below us. "I am," I said.

As I reached the top of the stairs, the picnic basket skidded to a stop next to me, just out of reach of the flickering flames on my boots. I looked up at the inner courtyard and the fluted columns, the guarded doors to the ballroom beyond. From every high window, guardsmen stared down. A thick press of more Spiked Wrath Men and Chain Hook Guards arrayed themselves in a semicircle in front of us.

The Viscount of Chains stood at the fluted arch filled with holes, just before the ballroom doors. His helmet didn't move a fraction as he stared at the four of us. "Well played," he said, offering a cursory bow. "But I think it's time for the two of you to just give up the girl." He raised his hand. More flying worms and their riders circled overhead.

"You know the rules that I live by." The Stone Preacher's eyes were cold. "To rescue the servant of my god is to rescue my god himself. The answer is no."

The Organ Grinder fiddled with his monocle and stretched his arms up. Then he yawned, cracked his knuckles, and adjusted his greatcoat, sliding a hand up under the back, where he scratched an itch. "What will you give me?" The Organ Grinder had a lewd grin on his face. He took cautionary steps forward, his boots heavy along with my heart.

***

"You can't be serious!" I snapped, drawing an arrow to my bow and nocking it, holding it on the Organ Grinder. "You're going to betray me? Now?"

The Organ Grinder sighed. "Some things are not worth doing anymore." He bowed and began walking toward the Viscount of Chains, half shoving me out of the way. "Let us talk, sir, about making a deal, a deal where I, the Organ Grinder, am accorded some virtues of respect and power."

The Stone Preacher gently put his hand on my shoulder. "Let him do this." He grinned with a cracking, rocky smile on his face. "If I die, I swear to you, I will crush the life from him before I depart."

I lowered the bow and sighed. There was an odd shiver under my cloak, and a hairy shudder. The monkey slipped its tail into my hand.

The Organ Grinder reached the Viscount of Chains as the small army of monsters and guards parted for him. "Fetch a table!" he thundered. "We shall discuss terms! It is difficult to break a contract of this sort. You should reward me well for it."

I raised my hand a little bit. "Stop." I hissed the word. "If we're going to discuss surrender, Organ Grinder, I'll do it. I don't want my lackeys to negotiate bad terms." I scowled at the Organ Grinder and moved forward.

"You're going to let them kill you?" The Stone Preacher's jaw dropped open, a vague sound like a cliff face shearing off rustling at the edge of my ears.

"Not if this goes the way I want it to," I said icily. "I didn't ask to fall in love with some stranger, and as much as I want it, I'm not sure it's worth it." Against my back, the monkey nuzzled silently as I took a few more steps forward. Its heart beat against my back. I held the tail tightly. It was eager to kill. I didn't have much time to negotiate anything.

The Viscount tilted his head and smiled. "Stand aside, Organ Grinder..." He laughed and walked up to me. "You will let us rip out your heart?"

I wilted. "Only if they get to walk away," I said. I felt a crushing pounding in my chest, as if my body were about to give up everything. It was hard to think about giving up the most important feeling I had ever possessed. It clawed at my insides. I had to struggle to get the words out. I was so close, so very close.

The Viscount of Chains laughed as the soldiers closed in. "You've killed too many," he said. "You are a potent threat indeed, little girl. But you are no match for my soldiers, and the Captain of

Clouds is not here to save you." He indicated the Organ Grinder. "Again, sir, I must ask you to stand aside if your betrayal is sincere."

The Organ Grinder let out a laugh and stepped away, and he gave me a sly smirk. "Had you but given yourself to me, this might never have happened. Instead, I fear that your journey has come to an end."

"Bastard," I said as I turned to the Viscount. I ignited my boots, yanking the monkey out from under my cloak and driving the knife-tail into the eyeslit of the Viscount's armor. There was a shocking suck and then a howl of pain as the monkey wiggled, driving the knife in deeper. The Viscount's armor rattled as his metal hand launched towards his helmet to rip the creature away. The monkey giggled and hooted, thrusting its hips against the eyesocket as the tail drove in and out. Savage shrieks filled the air, a tinny resonance off the Viscount's metal shell.

I summoned my bow and fired into the air, launching shot after shot at the flying worms that ringed the courtyard. As the arrows slammed into the hissing, winged tubes, they burst forth in shattering thuds of fire, ice, and noise, raining pieces of massive bodies downward into the courtyard. Soldiers dived out of the way, clattering about with shrieks of metal on stone. Many didn't come out from under bleeding worm corpses that peppered the yard. Crushed arms and broken legs were barely visible underneath.

As I fired, the Organ Grinder moved, yanking the monkey off the face of the Viscount and tucking it gently into one of his huge hands. "There, there," he crooned like a father comforting his child. "That one's not yours." He turned and leaped into the press of charging guards, hurling the monkey at them as he went.

As the arrows flew and the Organ Grinder leaped, the Stone Preacher laughed and brought his fist down hard on the stone of the courtyard, making flagstones erupt and mortar splinter. Guards in their spiked armor shot upward to crash into dead worms and thud against the massive towers, some embedded in the walls. "This is your punishment." The Stone Preacher's voice was cold and somber, as if he were intoning rites of passage into the next world.

I backed off from the Viscount of Chains as he pulled his gauntlet away from the bloody eye. He launched the chain at me as I leaped upwards, flames licking from my boots. The spiked lash yanked around my burning feet. He pulled hard, slowing my flight.

In the background, I heard the Organ Grinder and his monkey savagely fighting the hordes. The Stone Preacher slaughtered his way through just as many on his own.

The Viscount pulled harder. I pumped my legs, trying to back away as I fired another arrow. It awkwardly bounced off his armored chest, sailing into the wall of one of the towers. It detonated with a booming noise, throwing guards to their knees and hurling chunks of dead worm about the courtyard.

"I fear your struggles will soon be at an end." The Viscount of Chains tilted his head as the Stone Preacher waded into the press of guardsmen, ripping off limbs and hurling bodies about. Keening screams came as spikes drove towards the Preacher. Dust clouds erupted from his arm, leaking into the air as he kicked back at them.

I writhed as the Viscount pulled me forward, my gaze momentarily distracted by the Stone Preacher's powdery bleeding. I crashed hard into the arch before hitting the ground. I could feel blood trickle down my lip. My head rang as the sounds of battle swirled around me. I could hear the picnic basket leaping about and biting off things, chewing fiercely and making gulping noises. Then all I felt was the dragging of the chain, pulling me forward as the Viscount's throat rumbled. Barbs struggled against the cloak to cut my flesh. The fabric strained against it to resist.

"You put out my eye," the Viscount said. "Do you know how difficult it is to get a new one?"

"Probably only as far as the nearest victim—" The Viscount's metal boot slammed hard into my stomach. I doubled over, blind with pain as the chain tugged, launching me backwards into the air. I crashed against the tower wall and my vision blurred. He was going to kill me.

There was a rustling noise, the picnic basket racing forward as it sensed my fear and pain. I heard the sound of the Viscount's boot slamming into it. The basket collided with the stone of a nearby tower with a horrible crunching noise. I clawed myself halfway up, but the Viscount pulled harder, and the dragging began again, slower and more purposeful. "You should not fight so hard." The Viscount of Chains let out a dull laugh. "I enjoy it when you struggle like this." The chain barbs dug deep into my leg. The dress slithered about until it made a keening snap. Blood leaked from the dress and mingled with my own, burning my skin with a cool agony as the fabric dribbled onto the stone.

I tried to get to my feet, igniting the boots to fly, but the Viscount tugged harder on the chain, swinging me around. The Stone Preacher abandoned the guards he was fighting, powdered rock bursting from his cassock. The Organ Grinder leaped into the breach. Guards began clawing at his limbs, pulling him down.

The Stone Preacher glided forward. I gathered my strength as he headed for the chain. "A hole..." I managed. "I need a hole! In... in the archway!"

The Stone Preacher tilted his head and concentrated as the Organ Grinder was kicked hard in the spine, blood spewing from his mouth. The shrieking monkey leaped at the kicking guard, eager to murder whatever it could.

The Stone Preacher gestured, and the archway buckled above the top, stone peeling away and crumbling. Bricks flew out of the arch; some burst out in puffs of rocky dust, while others melted like liquid, dripping about in pools of watery rock. The Stone Preacher staggered and leaned against the rock as I pushed off the tower edge. I flew at the Viscount as he yanked the chain, and tumbled around his neck, spinning the chain to catch him around the throat. He grabbed at it and tried to pull it away. I raced towards the hole the Stone Preacher made. I flew as fast as I could, leaving a trail of fire behind. There was a horrid, struggling jerk as the chain ground over the rock of the arch. The Viscount of Chains gurgled, his arm wrapped against his chest while the barbed chain scraped his gorget. His feet lifted off the ground as I braced my leg around the other end of the chain, panting hard while the remaining guards stared.

I was on the ground as the Viscount's heavy body gurgled, my flaming boots planted against the edge of the arch as I summoned the bow to my fingers. I lifted the bow to fire from my leveraged position, the Viscount howling in agony as I choked him and drove the barbs against the thick gorget. "I surrender!" he thundered. "Please, spare me! I will give you the best of my lands!"

I didn't say anything. I fired arrow after arrow into his body as though he were the sole enemy I had in life. The arrows rang loudly when they pierced the armor, jerking and booming as the guards about the courtyard let go of the Organ Grinder and put their hands on their heads. The Viscount swayed until his gurgling form died.

The Organ Grinder staggered over as the Viscount's body went limp, and the picnic basket came up to me, licking at my face with its long tongue. With an eerie squish, the chain shuddered and melted. The Viscount of Chains crashed to earth, his soldiers staring in shock at the body filled with arrows.

I struggled to my feet, bruised and with chain marks across my feet, the dress bleeding out life across my knees. "Your commander is dead." I swayed a little bit, dreaming of green eyes. I focused on the door as the bloody dress shivered against my legs. My mask felt cold against my face. I panted, the bruises and wounds on my legs making them ache. "Go back to your holes."

It was more desperation than command. The soldiers began to back up. The Stone Preacher clenched his fist and concentrated. His rocky cassock was studded with holes, and he leaked small puffs of powder. "Don't." I said. "It's not about taking your vengeance. It's about saving energy."

"It will only take a minute." He panted, his eyes narrow as he drew the cobbles up into himself. There was a rattling crackle echoing as the wounds in his body closed. "It takes something out of me, but I need to be able to move my arms."

The Organ Grinder chuckled. "So you do have weaknesses. Ahh, the sweetness of the day when your rigidity shall be punctured forever." He gave a gloating grin and rubbed his hands together.

"Footstool," I said with a smirk, just to watch the Organ Grinder's face fall. As I watched his eyes narrow, I heard some sharp crunching noises of tearing flesh and ripping metal. The monkey peered out from the Organ Grinder's pocket, staring down near my feet.

The picnic basket was already eating the corpse of the Viscount of Chains.

I gathered myself up with as much dignity as possible, and staggered a little bit as the Organ Grinder and Stone Preacher moved in front of me. "Just like we practiced." I panted and took a deep breath. I could feel my legs shudder, and I sent the bow away, using the cloak of runes to hide the bloodstains on my leg from the dying dress.

"As we were." The Organ Grinder gave a sneer. "I hope you are ready to be disappointed, perhaps with a dirty old man or a fat sow." He gave a smile, wide enough to show his teeth, and took up a position next to the Stone Preacher, who scowled at him.

"It could be a rare moment of happiness," the Stone Preacher rumbled. "But no matter what happens, you'll always be one of the lucky ones for making it this far." His jaw set in a rocky crack as we moved forward in perfect step, each of them standing aside. My throat shivered a little bit, and I reached out, lightly tapping on the door as if nothing were amiss.

There was a heavy clack, and a series of noises that sounded like knobs and gears turning all around us. It went on for what seemed like ages while the beat of my heart quickened. "Five million gold half-lunas." I said. "I want every single one of them."

It was one of the few times I ever heard the Stone Preacher and the Organ Grinder laugh together.

When the doors gently swung open to elegant music of brass instruments and formal arrival, the crunching slurps of the basket's teeth gobbling up the Viscount weren't heard at all.

***

The attendant next to the door stood only four and a half feet tall, but his hat seemed twice that size. His beady eyes, set in his shallow, square features were square, as if he had a terrible encounter with a hot, flat object as a child. "Oh," he managed. "You must be one of the fashionably late." His eyes glared, and I immediately felt the sense of being unwelcome.

"I'm the one who survived the welcoming committee," I said in as dignified a manner as possible. I held my head high and looked around the room, the Organ Grinder and the Stone Preacher standing in front of me. There were a number of stares, as if the entire celebration had been interrupted, and some soft murmurs. As I glanced about, I thought I saw the Lady of Masks, but she was obscured by two other women who were complimenting her on her dress.

The attendant scowled up at me as the first blare of trumpets subsided, and whispered, "Your name, girl! I need it. You weren't expected." He glowered down at the picnic basket, who was shuffling near my leg, gulping down the Viscount's boot.

"Lady Symantha." I scowled back at him. "Your manners are deplorable."

The attendant turned. "Lady Symantha!" he thundered. "Another nameless wretch waiting for the one who is her heart's desire! Let your eyes fall on her, and hers on you!" The trumpets blared with excessive pomp, as the Stone Preacher reached for the throat of the man.

"Don't." I said softly, turning to the attendant. "You owe me." My lips quirked into a smirk and I moved into the swirl of colors, to meet the man who would change my life forever, and make my heart soar.

***

I stepped through the crowd, curtsying and making my way toward the Lady of Masks, who almost seemed to sense me coming and blended into the crowd, socializing her way away from me. A rotund man and his equally round wife, garbed in resplendent matching waistcoats of bright red and wearing large baker's hats, introduced themselves as the Duke and Duchess of Cake. I gave them a polite smile and shied away, shuffling through the crowd in the hushed moment.

Everyone was staring at me, as if they knew what I had somehow survived. I could hear faint whispers under the mumble of cheerful music as quiet conversations became even more hushed. I slipped up against a fine lady and her gentleman, swathed in togas. They gave me amused and contemptuous smiles. I daintily curtsied to them, even though they did not speak to me.

In a corner of the room, I could see two noblemen having a sour conversation as a small cloth purse changed hands. As I stared, a familiar voice purred from behind me. "It's lovely to have your fellow nobles bet on your survival, isn't it?"

I turned and stared into the masked face of the Duchess of Bells, her polearm slung over her back.

"You made it here?" I stared. "Am I really worth that much money?" She was wearing a mask that looked like an elegant eight-legged tiger, carved in bronze and studded with little jewels. Her body was covered in light fluted armor that seemed almost flimsy, and she was wearing a pair of heavy dark riding boots. Someone else, it seemed, had her own adventures getting here.

"Where else was there for me to go?" she asked. "You'll understand that feeling soon. You must come with me. We should talk." She gave me an elegant curtsy and sauntered off with me through the crowd, a smile on her face. The mask obscured almost everything but her lips, and she drew me into an alcove while the people chuckled and swirled, their whispers muffled by music and money changing hands.

"Are they all betting on my survival?" I asked. "That seems like highly irregular behavior." I craned my neck. Out of the corner of my eye, I could see the Organ Grinder and the Stone Preacher, their eyes trying to stare through the mass of brightly colored guests. "Unless it happens all the time."

"Wagers are wagers," the Duchess of Bells said. "I will call you Symantha if you call me Amalinda. That, I think, is a much better start, if you agree." There was a shoving rustle as the picnic basket made its way into the alcove with us, hopping up and down and rubbing against Amalinda's leg.

"You're remarkably forgiving for someone whom I graciously allowed to be ensorcelled by the Organ Grinder," I smirked. "What's the reason for it, Amalinda? And my basket wants food, because it recognizes you and you fed it."

"You need to leave," she said. "Five million gold half-lunas is a lot of money." She reached down and scratched the lid of the picnic basket. It gave off a satisfied rustle.

"Everyone is trying to kill me?" I asked. "Are times so hard? I should snap my own neck and collect the money."

"Almost everyone." She grinned. "I won't. You need to get out of here. Run far. Run fast on those burning boots of yours, child. I can only help you so much."

"You can't help me?" I stared angrily. "And all I can do is run? This is ridiculous. I come all this way and you try to shoo me off like a crazy butterfly?" My face drifted into a scowl. "What are you trying to do?"

"I am trying to save your life," she snapped. "If you don't run in the next few seconds, there will be nowhere for you to go." Her eyes narrowed as the words turned colder.

There was a blare of trumpets, powerful and strong, amid the mass of forms in the ballroom. The doors burst open from every wall. Chain Hook Guards and Spiked Wrath Men thundered into the hall in perfect formation, and stood in a cross shape, dividing the room into quarters, two by two. The center of the dome opened wide, a series of spikes coming from a circular door in the ceiling. Everyone's eyes turned skyward as black wings burst forth from the back of a falling man, red with blood fresh hewn from his torn shoulders.

He was a grim figure, blind with his lack of mercy. Wet wingtips shuddered as his slim body floated downward, each beat fluttered across the room as nobles retreated away from the guards. He made strange clicking sounds with his teeth behind an elegantly crafted mask of a forged golden face. His whole body was clad in perfectly toned leather of similar darkness. Studs forged of metal blacker than basalt shimmered, reflecting light from the hanging chandeliers. His boots were thick and shod with iron.

I stared into the leather mask, a mask without eyes.

"His Majesty, the King of Feathers!"

His audience politely clapped, and I joined them.

The King of Feathers dipped his head towards the guards below, and he clapped his hands together, leather on leather. His voice should have been muffled by the mask, but it wasn't. "Find the girl who just came in." His voice was cold behind the eyeless mask, so cold that the shadow of the alcove froze my words in my throat. "Kill her, and kill the Organ Grinder and the Stone Preacher, too."

The Duchess of Bells wept, and drew her polearm off her back, the wicked glaive shimmering in the alcove. "I warned you," she said softly. "Now something terrible is going to happen, no matter what."

***

They found the Stone Preacher first, the granite of the ballroom resisting his entreaties as the King of Feathers flew down towards him. "So long you have waited," he purred through his mask, making strange clicking noises. "I am not disappointed in your resolve." He rocketed upward, wings beating as red blood dripped across the floor.

The iron soldiers clustered around the Stone Preacher, who drew a fist back and grabbed one by the neck, snapping it. The battle was joined.

The Organ Grinder leaped into the press as the King of Feathers swooped down. Long sharp talons extended from his boots and pierced the Organ Grinder's greatcoat. Flying upward, he hurled the Organ Grinder across the room.

I leaped into the air, my footsteps leaving acrid smoke behind. I barely caught the Organ Grinder before he crashed into the Spiked Wrath Men battling the Stone Preacher. "Amalinda!" I shouted. "I call upon the favor you owe me!"

From the alcove, I heard the Duchess of Bells say something unladylike. "You learn too well," she admonished, and stepped out, spinning her polearm and stabbing one of the guardsmen. "You make me a traitoress and a harlot, too, and battle against my king! You are a magnificent monster, indeed!" She giggled as the thrashing arms of the Chain Hook Guard spasmed, and twisted the polearm inside the thing's chest, driving for the metal ball in the center.

The monkey leaped down, stabbing the eye of one of the guards, and shrieking as it toppled. As the spikes hammered toward the monkey, the scuttling picnic basket leaped forward and closed its jaws on the thing's head, wrenching it and snapping it off with a belch.

The King of Feathers swooped down at me without restraint, talons extended. I leaped away and fired, dancing in the sky with him as if he were my desire itself. Long, taloned fingers reached out for the arrow and caught it as he sprang to a statue head mounted on the wall. I hurried away across the granite. Polite clapping came from the nobles below. He spread his wings and launched black feathers, tipped with blood, at me.

I fired a second arrow into the feathery mass. There was a terrible roar as runes met the King's blood, feathers erupting in fire as I leaped away. Hungry talons stretched for me as I flipped up over him, leaving fire in my wake. He rolled across and below me. Feathers cut my cloak as I tumbled. Below me, the Organ Grinder and the Stone Preacher stood back to back as the Duchess of Bells fought her way towards them.

The pile of bodies grew around the Stone Preacher and the Organ Grinder, amid shrieks of excitement from the monkey, the knife-tail stabbing about. Stony powder erupted from the Preacher as blows rained down on him. The Duchess of Bells closed in, hacking about her with the long weapon.

There was a horrid bellow as one of the Chain Hook Guards jumped up and down for a moment, and then disappeared into the cluster of bodies, with both of his legs missing. I knew the basket would be overstuffed again in no time.

The King of Feathers dived at me again. His claws raked along my stomach, drawing blood. He kicked me harder than I had ever been hit. I slammed into the stone with a loud crack. I could feel my blood sticking to the soles of his leather boots, and my lip twitched, a trickle of red leaking out. He flexed his wings and slashed, but I wasn't there anymore. The butt end of Amalinda's polearm doubled me over and shoved me out of reach. I gripped the thrown weapon reflexively and skidded along the black walls, flipping like a circus acrobat. As she focused on me, the Duchess of Bells didn't dodge the nearest guard. He grabbed her by the throat, the spikes digging into her gorget as she began to choke.

I threw the polearm toward her waiting hand, then ran as fast as I could, leaving fire behind. The King of Feathers turned and gave chase. The Duchess of Bells let out a low ringing hum from her lips. Several of the guards grabbed their ears. As the hand left her throat, she caught the polearm and stabbed about her.

I tumbled away, drawing an arrow to fire as the King of Feathers came on. Another volley of feathery blood-darts whistled in my direction were met by a wet burst of acidic slime erupting from the arrow. The filthy smell of burning blood filled the air. Feathers shattered from the explosive burst. He was too fast and too strong. All I could do was keep him away while others battled on the ground below.

Whirling and dodging, the Duchess of Bells made it to the center of the room and put her back to the Stone Preacher's, a triangle against the horde. "You kill like you were born to it!" The Stone Preacher laughed as the Duchess slipped beneath the clumsy grip of one of the thick fisted guards. Spiked knuckles closed on empty air.

"I like to think that it is a matter of simple desperation," the Duchess murmured haughtily. The massive polearm deflected a blow past the Stone Preacher's shoulder.

The Stone Preacher casually reached out for the hand and snapped it off, spraying purplish blood. Nobles dived behind cover as the soldiers swarmed. I could hear the faint clinking of money exchanging hands.

The Organ Grinder reached for his accordion and laughed. Hairy fingers clutched the keys as he began to play. The Organ Grinder capered, dancing and dodging amidst the blows of the guards. The moans of the accordion blasted through the ballroom. Soldiers and nobles alike tore at their armor and tore at their clothes. The Spiked Wrath Men and Chain Hook Guards began ripping themselves to shreds while nobles disrobed, straining at their codpieces and their corsets. Amid the chaos, the Captain of Clouds struggled, at first heading towards the battle until ladies tearing at his jerkin and shoving their hands into his pants pulled him down.

Almost everyone was affected. Shrieks and moans of lust echoed in the grand hall, mixing with the creatures' howls of pain. Those who couldn't resist pawed at each other, kissing and sucking their partner's flesh with fury and abandon. The wet sounds of beastly rutting mingled with shrieks of pain, raw desire mixing with battle.

I made the King of Feathers chase me. I quickly changed direction as he sped forward, dodging as he caught up. Dartlike feathers slammed into the wall and exploded in bursts of blood. I stepped aside and tumbled amid lustful nobles, using them as shields while he pursued. I nocked another arrow and fired, his quickness unimaginable. If I wanted to beat him, I would have to cheat.

The Stone Preacher laughed as the battle continued, punching his fist through one of the guards as sounds of metal on flesh and skin on skin merged. "Fools!" he thundered. "Rut yourselves to death! Vengeance is nigh for all you heretics!" He let out a deep, rumbling cackle, making the floor and walls shake. Tiny cracks appeared in the stained-glass ceiling.

The Organ Grinder dived between guards, his teeth gritted while his fingers played. The moaning continued as the Duchess of Bells stabbed at the guards, now trying to pin her to sate her desire. Her low, keening hum kept her mind free from the Organ Grinder's enchantments.

The picnic basket leaped at the heads of rutting guards, biting them off and chewing as fountains of gore erupted from neck stumps. As the Organ Grinder danced, his monkey hooted with satisfaction as it bathed in blood fountains of the dying.

The Stone Preacher was unfazed. He matched the tone of his fervor to the hum of the Duchess, using it to ignore the Organ Grinder's accordion music. Everything had descended into chaos, orgy, and butchery all at once.

My ribs hurt so much that I was having trouble breathing. I still hadn't found my heart's desire. All I had to do was kill the King of Feathers, as the prophecy said. I lashed out with a burning boot, and pedaled my fiery heels against his wings as he threw them in front of him to block. There was an agonizing shriek of pain as his wings began to burn.

I took my only chance, calling for an arrow, trying to time it so it would strike just as he spread his wings to steady himself. I knew then that I was going to die. I felt a single moment of emptiness as I drew back the string as far as I could manage.

The arrow leaped from the bow, hungry for life, and hurtled across the room into the chest of the masked king. The wicked shaft split him and ripped ornate leather as it punched out the back. He stared and clutched at the fletching as his mouth fell open. The King staggered against the stone, the beautiful golden mask falling from his face. The guards stopped moving, and they turned to look at the fallen lord while the nobles gasped in horror and pleasure.

I stared into the abyss of desire and my heart broke. I could not stop my sobs, and the palace echoed with them. I stared into the beautiful eyes, as green as my whole journey, and his lips formed a jagged smile. "I love you," he whispered. Blood trickled out of his mouth in a slithering line. "I should have known better, and so should you."

The King of Feathers was my one true love.

He sagged to the ground. I ran to him in the air with my boots of fire, across the tables and through the silence of nobles' wicked prosperity. Some giggles echoed through the crowd, while others simply smirked. I held him. His blood trickled across my hands while I tried to seal the wound. A few voices laughed out loud. I could hear the picnic basket galloping behind me on stubby legs, not even stopping at any of the corpses.

"Don't die!" I begged. I felt my throat clench up.

He slid a leather-clad hand against my cheek, a wicked smile on his face, and kissed me, with sweet blood on his mouth. I couldn't help myself. I pressed my tongue against his lips, desperate for his warmth as his body grew cold. His hands circled my face and tousled my dark hair. With my breath on his, his throat rattled.

Then his fingers slackened in my grip, and his body went limp. The whole room heard only my sobbing.

"Magnificent!" the Squire of Sages shouted from somewhere near the back. "Such artistry cannot be denied." I heard him club the Cowl of Serpents again. There was a horrid hiss. There was nothing I could do. Several nobles began to clap, pulling their skirts and pants up, some satisfied, some shocked at the nature of their partners.

I barely managed to pull the picnic basket aside before it started to eat.

"A regicide!" someone shouted. "Brilliant! A tour de force!" The excited tone rang through the ballroom, but I couldn't make out who said it.

"We must choose a new King or Queen!" a voice rang from the back. "But first, we must decide her fate!" From under a worn leather greatcoat, a monkey chittered. I had to get out of there.

I leaped from the body of my beloved on my boots of fire, and soared up towards the ceiling, more furious than all the chariots that ever flew across the sun. I hurtled my way towards windows, painted with the scenes of broken romances and shattered dreams, and forced my way through them in multicolored shards. The picnic basket howled as we burst out into the open air, leaving my bodyguards and the audience behind.

Shrieks of rage came from the room below. I raced across the sky, pursued by no one. I flew across the parapets and leaped into the open abyss. Mountains racing by as I blazed across the sky. I stopped for nothing and no one until I couldn't see the Castle in the Sky anymore. I barely realized that I landed.

I had run so far that the snow on the mountains wasn't black anymore. I dug my fingers in and punched hard ice underneath until my fingers bled. Tears froze on my face. They burned my soul the same way that acid burns flesh. I couldn't even cry. It wasn't fair.

I would be empty forever, hollow until the day I died. I stared up at the pale, bleached sun, and stared at the space between my legs, shaped into a 'v' by the snow. Silently, the picnic basket settled next to me and nudged me, as though it was trying to force me to move.

I crawled down the mountain, so tired that I thought the ice would collect me. I was almost disappointed that the boots of fire kept me warm. I had no choice but to go home. The Weeper in Shadows would come for me. I knew she would.

Chapter Eighteen

Return to the Carnival of Monsters

When morning came, I rose up from under my cloak. I gathered up the picnic basket in my arms and scanned the mountain for signs of pursuit. The skies were cold and empty. There was a little creak as the basket opened. Inside was what looked like a warm bowl of oatmeal seasoned with fresh fruit. The scent of maple slipped up against my nostrils, and I reached into the basket with a spoon to eat.

After breakfast, I walked down the mountain, burying the bowl and my mask in the ice before making my way across the cold landscape. I didn't know where I was, or where to go, except to navigate by cold stars of the gray sky at night, and pick a direction. When we reached more even ground, I looked down to the picnic basket and sighed a little bit. "Do you think they'll come for me? I couldn't stay there."

My heart filled with empty space. I murdered the one I wanted most, battled him while he was blind and kissed his bloody, dying lips. I wept for hours as I walked across the plains, searching for signs of civilization, followed by the picnic basket. It offered me a hot sandwich for lunch and a dipping sauce made of things I couldn't recognize. It was delicious anyway.

I don't know how long I traveled, or how far, but I knew where I had to go. I had to get out of the Otherworld and go back to the forest where I first got lost. Maybe I could find my way home if I was lucky.

The first day turned into night, and the second soon after. The picnic basket trailed behind me on short and stubby legs, offering me snacks as I walked, along with the occasional malt beverage or a bottle of wine. I could feel my broken heart beat in my chest as I walked. I dreamed of the King of Feathers, majestic and blind in his descent, before we fought. I relived the moment over and over, sighing with pleasure and sadness in my sleep, tasting his blood in our last kiss before he died.

There were many places I could have stopped. I didn't stop at any of them. The Organ Grinder and the Stone Preacher would be looking for me. The Weeper in Shadows would be able to find me easily as long as they were with me.

I cradled the picnic basket in my arms on most nights, and hid in the hollows of trees, hoping the Weeper in Shadows would not spot me in my hiding places. *May the best woman win.* I understood it now. She loved him too. She would not rest until her knife of ice was breaking my frozen heart. She was both my test and my punishment.

I stopped counting days and ate only when the picnic basket nudged me. When I finally stopped to rest by a pool, brackish and nearly frozen among the wintry grasslands, I looked in to see my face. My eyes were sunken, and my face was narrow. I could feel mirrored water of the pool as it trickled over my fingers. I stared into my own broken eyes. I wished that the pool could weep for me, and carry away my sadness.

When I woke up in the morning, the picnic basket was shoving me aside to drink from the pool, gulping down water as it hiccupped. It was the first time I had ever seen it drink. No water leaped out of its sides. Nothing dribbled. The cold gathered around us, and I picked the basket up. "Are you ready to fly?" I asked.

The Basket gave a little rustle and settled in against my arm. "We need to hurry," I said. "The others will be looking for us. We're going to see Bosquoverde, all right? He'll treat us well and give us directions."

Filled with new purpose, I launched us into the air on my boots of fire and ran, leaving crackling trails in the air behind me until the gray sun sank down below the hills. More than anything, I hoped that the Organ Grinder and the Stone Preacher couldn't move as fast on the ground as I could in the air.

***

I walked across the hills below the mountains for a very long time without seeing anyone. As the picnic basket followed me, my heart grew emptier and emptier, but still, it snuggled up against me at night, warm from the food cooking in whatever space resided inside it. I didn't understand how the creature did what it did, but since I couldn't hunt or fish, I was becoming dependent on it.

After several days of walking, I found a road, desolate in the wintertime. A single set of wagon tracks headed off in the snow, into the gray world. The picnic basket trundled behind me, leaving squat penetrations in the snow and whiffing to keep up.

When I finally saw a roadside inn, I struggled towards it as the wind whipped up. Snow blasted into my face as I grabbed the picnic basket, holding it under my cloak as we made for the door. There was a ramshackle cart there that looked like it didn't belong to the Organ Grinder. Loud sounds of boisterous laughter came from within.

I pushed the door open and slipped inside, taking in the scene of crude tables and benches. An ill-crafted wooden bar loomed with a few bottles behind it. A loathsome-looking bartender stood behind the bar, his face and bare arms covered with hair as his open shirt revealed a fat, white gut under a mound of black curls. "Hah!" he thundered as I looked at him. "Step lively, girl! You and yer basket can come in and have a little grog." There was a pot hanging over the fire in the fireplace, and something hot and thick bubbled in it.

The picnic basket shuddered, and shivered against my chest as I slipped in and sat quietly at one of the wooden tables. The chair creaked oppressively under what little weight I had, while surly travelers looked at me, eyeing me and the picnic basket. "Grog is fine." I said. "What are you serving?"

"It's a stew, I think." The hairy man rubbed his beard and shuffled over to the open fire, stirring it a little bit. "Would you like some?"

I turned and focused on him eye to eye.

"At once, my lady." The few inhabitants quietly stared, looking at me and whispering to each other. He pulled out a plain wooden bowl and spooned some of the slop into it, carrying it over to me and hurriedly running back to get a spoon. "My apologies. It's the best I can do."

It was hot, and looked wonderful, thick chewy chunks of meat and vegetables simmered for long hours over a fire were like nothing else in the world. The picnic basket rubbed against my leg, as if jealous. "Don't be silly," I said. "I just need a little contrast. Every meal can't be gourmet quality." I hid my fear from it. I didn't want it to eat anyone for a while.

The innkeeper returned with a spoon. "I have but one private room, and it is occupied, though not by someone of your station."

He smiled, as if his prestige would rise just from my presence. I looked down at the picnic basket and thought for a few moments, as if the implications of my journey were somehow clearer.

I took a bite and thought for a moment, glaring around the room to see which of the people in the room with me looked the richest. "Throw him out of it." I said. "It's my room now."

***

It took a while for the innkeeper to remove the room's occupant while I waited at my table, and a little while longer for him to come down the stairs, holding a body over one shoulder. A rolling pin covered with hair and matted blood sat in his other hand.

After the room's occupant was rudely hurled out the door into the ice and snow, and the innkeeper had remade the beds and cleaned the room, I slipped upstairs while other customers trembled with fear, the picnic basket flouncing in my wake.

The room was plain and simple, the main attraction being a stone fireplace against one wall with a fire in it, and a lumpy looking bed across from it. There was a plain low bucket for bathing, and a small desk for writing. A candle on the desk struggled to maintain the light.

I settled into the bed, exhausted. I didn't even remember how many days I had been moving. All I wanted to do was rest, even if it was in a lumpy bed of straw, it. I crawled under the covers, not even taking off my clothes. The picnic basket jumped up onto the bed with me, rustling against me to cuddle its wicker against my skin.

There was a rustle from the lock, but the door did not open. I called my bow and aimed, pointing it fiercely as the Half-Bone Maiden, tinier than a finger, stepped through the keyhole and grew to full size in the shadow of the door.

"You've certainly created a stir." She smiled. "I can't say anything so impressive has happened in the Otherworld in ages. Do you have news of my husband?"

"I left him behind." I replied. "I couldn't be sure that he wouldn't betray me because he's the Organ Grinder, so I grabbed the picnic basket and escaped. I killed my one true love." I hung my head and wrapped it around my knees. "Now I'm going home."

She walked over to the bed and reached out a hand, gently patting her fingers on my shoulder. "There, there," she said. "You don't have to go home if you don't want to."

"But I do. There's nothing for me here. Just monsters, politics, and your husband trying to seduce me."

"He hasn't succeeded yet." The Half-Bone Maiden snapped her skeletal fingers. "And if he does, he'll pay for it. The King of Feathers is gone, and the land will be a better place."

"What do I do about the Weeper in Shadows?" I asked. "She's just going to keep coming after me until I die."

"You defend yourself. I always knew the King of Feathers was your one true love. I could see it in your demeanor, and smell his scent on your hair."

"Why didn't you tell me?" I snapped. "How could you possibly have not? You knew what I needed?" I let out little choking sobs. "I needed him and now he's gone."

"He may have needed you," the Half-Bone Maiden sighed. "But he knew that you were a weakness. Once you were removed, all threats to his rule were secure. I'm sorry you lost what you thought was most precious. But you used me and gave me to the Organ Grinder!" She let out a little sob that matched mine. "My Organ Grinder." She let out a soft whisper. "So think about who you trampled to get to where you are! You even fled from your naming ceremony! I'm sure they told you nothing about that either." She gave me a hurt look. "More terrible things will happen in your life, and most of them will never be made right. It's an unjust life we live here, and you'll learn to live with it when you return."

"When I return?" I scowled. "I never want to come back to this forsaken place! Everyone is evil except you!"

She gave me a little smile and stuck a finger out, wiping a tear from my eye as it began to fall. "You will come back. When you return, you'll feel tiny and small. The Otherworld will pull at your heart, and tug at it, and you'll have to come back. The power of your legend is a like a drug. If you take too much of it, it will destroy you, but if you do not take any of it and use it, you will be consumed by your own emptiness and bitter should-haves." The bony half of her mouth quirked into a smile. "So you killed him. You can still have sex with anyone you want, as long as you're discreet." She rose from her seat, and embraced me. "Thank you."

"For what?" I asked. "You seem fairly angry about the Organ Grinder."

"It was bound to happen sooner or later," she said with a sigh. "Who else could control him?"

"Why did you give him ten years? You have to know he'll rut with every animal, man, woman, piece of furniture and plant between this inn room and the Castle in the Sky."

"Because when he comes back to me, I can put him through some tests, and if I don't like the answers, he shall become whatever piece of furniture I choose." She winked. "Fare you well, Queen of Lost Love. That's what they want to call you. And something else, but I can't remember it right now."

"That's ridiculous!" I snapped. "They chose me? I killed him! They should want to hang me or set me on fire or something!"

"Don't be silly." Her voice was soft and soothing. "You had a dark and terrible journey, overcame many obstacles, traveled to a castle in the sky, and became a Queen. You should be thrilled. Isn't it what every girl wants?" She bent down and kissed me on my forehead, as Madame Zhalla used to do when I was younger.

I pulled the dry, raspy covers up over myself, and huddled there. "Every girl wants her handsome prince," I said. "That's what it's supposed to be all about with these things, isn't it? I killed mine! I kissed his bloody, dying lips! Do you have any idea what that's like?"

"No," she said quietly. "But I have a feeling that one day I will. You made sure of that. So you already have your revenge. Being in love with the Organ Grinder is a gift. I treasure it, even though I shouldn't."

"Revenge?" I sighed. "It's so important to everyone around here. What does it matter if it's preemptive? I just did what I had to so I could get what I needed."

The Half-Bone Maiden tilted her head, her white bony eye staring at me as if it were cold porcelain. Her lips curved in a fabulous smile "Every day you live is a gift, O Queen." She delicately curtsied. "Do not lose sight of that."

She turned her back to me gaily, and with a rattle of bone and a rustle of her gown, she shrank as she stepped forward and slipped through the keyhole, leaving only her giggle behind.

***

The Queen of Lost Love – I hated it from the moment I heard it. I tossed and turned all night with my tears. When I finally awoke in the morning, my fingers fumbled around in the picnic basket and dragged out a crisp rice cake, laden with fresh fruit and with a little cream in the center. I ate it desperately as my stomach growled, and wiped my eyes from exhausted sleep. I gathered up my things around me, and slipped outside to roll in the snow for a moment, naked, before getting back into my clothes in the pre-dawn light.

My boots warmed me at once/ I slipped around to the front of the inn, eager to leave. In the cold, a frozen corpse rested. The thick, icy clot of matted blood from his head shone in the rising sun.

I stepped over the corpse and moved away down the road. Day after day passed with quiet unrest in my stomach, until I ran in the air up the side of a cliff and made my way along a familiar looking road that I thought might be in the lands of the Jack of Forests, newly liberated from the King of Feathers.

The high trees beckoned, shifting in the cold wind. I slipped into them while the picnic basket scuttled behind me through the trees and branches. I looked for signs of human passage in the underbrush, but there was nothing. It was as if the Jack of Forests had covered everything up, and moved to a far off place where no one would speak of him.

When I reached the site of the battle where I had been poisoned, there was only thick snow, and a few lumps of Chain Hook Guards and Spiked Wrath Men that I found by brushing powder aside. The tents and campfire were gone, their marks long since covered with new snow and ice.

I wandered through the trees to the special place where the Jack of Forests had taught me how to use my bow. I moved snow aside to see where the marks of the arrows and signs of battle were. In between two branches was a new hollow, carved to be perfectly circular.

I floated up on my boots while the picnic basket wiggled below me, and reached into the hollow, pushing aside a squirrel and some acorns. The squirrel raced out onto the snowy bough and chittered at me through leafless trees. My hand closed around a smooth case of leather. I yanked it out to discover a top sealed with a burned sigil of a bow and arrow. Shivering in the cold, I unscrewed the top and looked inside.

There was only a single sheet of paper, rustling as wind touched it. I pulled it out and read it, floating in the air, forgetting the rules about reading strange papers written by unknown hands. The letter was written in a perfect, meticulous hand, without error or misspelling, and almost seemed as if it were speaking to me as I read.

Dear Symantha,

If you are reading this, you are certainly alive, and have made it here despite the villainy of many. I congratulate you as if you were my daughter, and you may very well be, with what I have taught you. Do not look for me. If we meet each other again, we may be able to test the truth of such a claim, if you are dutiful and I am honest. But such things are very difficult in these lands, and I must leave to escape the wrath of the King of Feathers. Be brave and strong, and ruthless too, and you shall live a long life while others fade. I wish that, perhaps, our teaching had not been interrupted. What was taken from me cannot be regained, nor what I gave away. I shall have a new bow when I see you again, and may well be the Prince of Archers once more.

I raise a glass to a friendly contest between us,

Jack

I folded up the note and slipped it into my pocket, smiling. His survival meant something to me. If by some chance he were my father, I might not have minded it. I walked out of the forest on foot, crunching in the ice and snow, the picnic basket following behind. The basket sniffed the frozen corpses of the spiked wrath men, and then raised its front half up as if it was turning up its nose. I shook my head, patted my arm, and it leaped up to settle there.

Together, we walked out of the forest, trying to find where I began so I could go home.

***

I ran on boots of fire for days, past the crossroads of the Queen of Castles, past the cruel domain of the Count of Locks, and the dreadful toad lands of the Duchess of Bells. I stopped only to rest in hidden places. I knew people would be looking for me, to seek revenge or drag me back, and I knew the Weeper in Shadows would not be far behind.

In the distance, the massive stone tower of the Priest of Gears beckoned/ I roared down to the ground to land, all too conscious that my safety was dependent on not being found with the Organ Grinder. The picnic basket shivered a little bit as I let it off my arm.

"Come on," I said. "The Sisterhood's not going to fight over the Organ Grinder while we're here without him." The picnic basket gave a rustling whine, as if it didn't want to go back in the building. "We'll find you something to eat, I promise – but no people. You'll have to settle for animals. And I know a place we're going where there's lots of ragamoffyns." The picnic basket hopped up and down excitedly. A queasy feeling crept into my stomach as I stepped up to the large basalt door.

The Sisterhood of Symmetry opened the door at once, their uniforms clean and new as they daintily curtsied as one. "We have been anticipating your return." They smiled. "Do you require refreshment?"

"It might be nice. I've traveled a long way."

"Where is our Organ Grinder?" one of them begged.

"Yes, our Organ Grinder!" the other pleaded.

"I bring sad news." I gave them my best consoling look. "He is to be married to the Half-Bone Maiden some ten years hence."

The sisters looked at each other and let out synchronous little sobs. "It is so unfair," they chimed. "Surely he could spare some time for us."

"I fear that if he does that, he will enjoy his new role as a piece of furniture under the feet of his new wife." I sighed. "Such is the way of this place we live in." I refused to pity them, even for an instant.

The sisterhood collectively sighed. "Let us show you to a room." They glided down the corridor and up the halls to a lavish, opulent room, with a mammoth bed, a bubbling hot bath, and a fabulous mechanical wet bar operated by a measuring machine I didn't understand the workings of. It was so thickly carpeted the picnic basket had to plow through it as it walked. The two women petted it as it rolled over and flopped. It deposited a small round cheese on the floor covered in thick black rind.

"Isn't this a bit much?" I asked.

"It is a room fit for a queen!" They bowed and spoke in unison, gears clicking under their skirts. "We are most pleased with your ascension."

"I don't want to ascend!" I sighed. "It isn't worth it. I killed the person who would have made it worth it."

The two women smiled, as people who were going to eat a lovely meal might. "That is what makes it all so fabulous," one of them began.

"No one has ever wanted to not be king or queen before," her sister finished.

"Why not?" I said. "Doesn't the real world teach you about those things? We hardly have them anymore."

"You mustn't be afraid." They both spoke together as one fluffed the bed and the other patted the pillows. The picnic basket was all too eager to hop up into the bed and roll around on it. It making crackling noises as the handle flopped down. "You are already famous. You will be a magnificent queen, ruthless and beautiful. You will reward us for treating you well, yes?" They leaned in towards me with desperate, petulant looks on their faces.

"I shall." I smiled to them. "Does your master, the Priest of Gears, know I am here?"

The two looked at each other with a sad expression on their faces. "No. He is out looking for rocks that fall from the sky. He has heard of one in the eastern lands, where the dog people live."

"Then you must thank him for his hospitality when he returns. Don't worry about bringing me anything to eat. If you like, you may keep the cheese for yourselves." The picnic basket rolled over and spit up a loaf of bread. "That, too," I said. "I think it likes you."

One sister grabbed the loaf while the other bent down to pick up the cheese, still in its rind. "Thank you," their voices chimed. "We shall always remember your gratitude." They curtsied with a metallic clanking sound, and glided out, ethereal and beautiful, half-mechanical in their gait and smiles on their faces.

I ate a pleasant meal of stewed fruit and chicken in a sweet sauce, with some yams steamed in a bowl of gravy. I didn't ask what kind of gravy it was. In the morning, just as before, I slipped away before the Sisterhood could find us, the picnic basket skulking on my arm. We found a window and flew away, burning across the morning sky.

***

When we reached Bosquoverde's, it was almost nightfall. The town nestled in the giant trees was filled with few souls. Smoke rose from the inn's chimney, smelling of something that was roasted and had far too much blood in it. The doors to the inn creaked open with a gentle shove. People looked up from their drinks as I walked inside, the picnic basket at my heels.

I couldn't see Bosquoverde, so I waited, settling in at an empty table as a few gathered in the evening, their faces dark and surly.

Several of them looked up at me, but turned their heads, as if afraid to look at me for too long. The picnic basket eyed several of them hungrily. "Stop it," I said. "You've eaten so much that you'll feed people for a thousand years. Greedy thing," I ruffled the lid as if I were petting a dog, and it settled down.

When Bosquoverde finally sat down at my table, he sat down next to me, turning a chair around and leaning on it as he stared at my sullen face. "You're going home, aren't you?" he asked me, a rumbling grin on his face. "We'll see you again eventually."

"Thank you for the picnic basket." I said with a smile. "It's turned out to be a wonderful friend." I petted it again, and it wiggled back and forth under my hand.

"It's a hard thing to give up your picnic basket," he said with a rough smile. "But at least it seems to like you. Can I fetch you something to eat?"

"Oh, please!" I said with an eagerness I hadn't felt since the last time I had been in the inn. It seemed as if all the most wonderful food was here, all of the time.

Bosquoverde laughed. "The roast beef will be out in a little while, lass. You should tell me how things went. Even a sad story that is new is better than no stories at all." He patted me on the shoulder. "You don't look like you got everything you wanted."

"No one ever does here. Wasn't it you who warned me about that?"

"In a roundabout way, I suppose." His laughter carried through the inn. The picnic basket tried to match his tone. I gave the lid a sharp yank.

"He's feisty," I said. "But reining him in is a challenge."

"So, are they dead?" He raised an eyebrow. "Because if they're not, they'll come looking for you."

"No. And I'm expecting them – the Weeper in Shadows, too." I sighed. "I killed him, and she loved him too. Do those things happen?"

"They do in the real world." Bosquoverde smiled sadly. "Why not here?" He paused briefly. "I'll get you something warm. Just because that cape of yours keeps you warm doesn't mean that you don't need a hot drink now and then." He rose from the chair and headed for the kitchen, returning with something that smelled of apples and alcohol. When I reached for the mug, it was heavier than I expected.

"Just hold it for a little bit." He chuckled. "If you've never understood that feeling before, you will now. Besides, it tastes better with your meal, young heroine." He moved back into the kitchen, singing some sort of cooking song while I stared at the kitchen doors.

"I don't feel like one at all." I sighed, and reached down for the picnic basket. It hopped up into my lap, and settled there, making comfortable rustling noises. The creature soothed me for a little bit until Bosquoverde returned, bearing a plate with a thick cut of roast beef slices in gravy, adorned with roasted potatoes and thick root vegetables I didn't recognize.

"I trust the basket's been keeping you fed?" He smiled at the rustling creature, settled in my lap as I leaned forward a little bit to eat. It hopped off, plopping onto the hardwood floor.

"I have a question to ask." I shivered. "Is it cannibalism? And where do the things it eats go? Where does the food it makes come from?" I took a sip from the cup. It was cider so thick and creamy that I thought my tongue would melt under it.

"I haven't the foggiest." Bosquoverde laughed and leaned back in the chair, deep and raucous as I looked at him oddly. "You should eat your roast beef, my queen. And I am certainly happier to follow you than your predecessor."

"Why is everyone calling me that?" I snapped at him. "I didn't earn it! I didn't go on any great quests, or prove my love to anyone!" Tears leaked from my eyes. "All I did was fight, and fight. I didn't think that all I had to do was find a way to get his mask off." I huddled in my cloak and stuffed a piece of potato in my mouth. It was rich and delicious enough in the gravy to stop my tears for a moment.

"Like it or not, it is your job now." He smiled warmly. "Remember that this is a land based on fear and power. You killed the only thing they were afraid of. Now they are afraid of you." He patted my hand as I ate slowly, cutting the tender pieces of meat with a fork.

"Will you come and cook for me?" I asked. "Perhaps you can regain your storytelling powers, the ones that everyone talks about."

"I don't think so." Bosquoverde laughed. "It is enough trouble to have an inn here and take care of naughty girls who don't want to be queen."

"But it's crazy. I don't know the first thing about ruling a kingdom. My only qualifying characteristic is that I killed the man I should love more than any other. And I get the impression that no one comes back to life here."

Bosquoverde scratched the back of his head as I took a few small bites and another sip of the thick cider. "Not in a positive way," he said solidly. "Your journeys are your own now. You don't need advice from an old man like me on how to do things." He chuckled. "But that doesn't mean you can't come back and see me whenever you'd like. You are a queen, after all." He rose, and made his way back to the kitchen, as if the weight of better stories he never told held him down.

I finished my meal, and found myself exhausted from my journey. I crawled upstairs to sleep off the meal, wrapped in pillows and wishing the Half-Bone Maiden's owl would come to the window and explain things.

***

The Knight of Lies was waiting outside for me in the morning, polishing his helmet next to his tethered horse. Bosquoverde made a magnificent breakfast of oatcakes and maple syrup, topped by unusual looking berries I had never seen before. The picnic basket raced out just before I closed the door, shaking itself from left to right. It gave me a narrow-eyed look from under the lid, as if I tried to trick it.

The Knight of Lies bowed courteously to me. "Greetings, lowest of peasants," he said as nobly as he offered. "May I perhaps walk away from you on your pleasant journey?"

"I accept your generous offer." I smiled. "You should move as far from me as possible, then, and travel in the opposite direction."

"You flatter me with your beastliness," he responded. "You should hide behind me."

I was beginning to understand the Knight of Lies and how he worked.

The Knight walked over to his horse, untethered it, and vaulted into the saddle. He rode ahead of me, measuring the steps of his horse's gait to stay close to me while remaining in front. "I shall flee in terror from all foes!" he proclaimed boldly, making his way towards the forest from which I had come, and from which I hoped to return to the real world.

"Flee like a coward," I teased.

The Knight of Lies flipped up his helmet and stared down at me. His face was etched in a broad smile, yet he seemed to be crying, a few tears trickling down his cheek. "You are my worst enemy." His voice was soft as he slammed his visor down, and urged his horse forward while the picnic basket trotted at my heels.

We journeyed for the entire day, and when it came time to rest, I walked right past the chapel where we had freed the Stone Preacher, and the Nun Who Leaves No Stains now held sway. The building was exceptionally clean. Even the corpses outside trying to get in seemed fresher. When they saw us, and tried to follow, the picnic basket turned towards them, hoping for a meal. Then it turned up its lid indignantly as it bent slightly in the middle.

"You're refusing to eat?" I said. "Do they smell that bad?"

I received a wobble that resembled a nod for an answer, and there was subtle rustle from the basket as it hurried along in the early evening. "Your basket is highly unimpressive." The Knight glanced down at it. "And it is disloyal filth with an undiscerning palate."

"You don't mind that it eats people?" I asked.

"Not at all." The Knight smiled down at me. "But it is my place to judge you, lowly peasant. And I shall." He quickened his pace as the People Who Pretended to Die began shambling towards us. They were easily outdistanced.

"I don't think I'm going to ask how you became the Knight of Lies," I said. "Really, you could tell me anything, and I know it would be a lie."

The Knight of Lies shook his head and laughed. "That isn't true at all! You are completely wrong, lowly peasant." He grinned at me, and I grinned back.

"We could move a little faster if I was on your horse instead of walking." I said, looking up at him into his radiant smile.

"I don't think so. But I shall sully myself with the burden of it." The Knight of Lies reached down and pulled me up onto his horse. The picnic basket trotted behind us. We slowly drifted out of sight until we had to camp under the sunless sky.

***

Silence greeted us in the morning, a noiseless moment without even the normal sounds of animals. It gave me the feeling of being stalked. The Knight of Lies was settled near the campfire, cooking something over a stove. The picnic basket was sitting there next to him, dispensing meat cubes and coughing up a jar of gravy, which took a little bit of effort. "It is dinner," he declared. "The largest meal should be eaten at the beginning of the day."

The basket wiggled as I rose, and I moved over to sniff the food. It wasn't particularly wonderful, but the smell after a cold night wafted towards my nostrils, and the Knight of Lies offered me a spoon. "You can't have any," he said, pouring some into a bowl he produced from his saddlebags, and offering it to me.

I took the stew and chewed thoughtfully. It wasn't bad. The picnic basket wandered over to me, whuffling against my leg. "You had better not be hungry," I said to it. "You ate all those people, and then you ate even more people again and again."

The picnic basket slurped its tongue along the lid with satisfaction. The Knight of Lies stared at it, as if a little disturbed, but poured himself a bowl of the meat and liquid and sipped it with his own spoon. "It is more than palatable," he declared as he settled back next to the campfire. "Your basket is ordinary. And it obviously doesn't eat people at all."

I looked down at the picnic basket and watched it sit on its haunches while I ate. I leaped up behind the Knight on his horse as we rode towards the forest. By the time we reached the woods, it was almost dark. I resolved to wait until what passed for morning before moving on. It began to snow.

***

The snow was already thick around our camp when I said "Hello" to the Knight of Lies, before he began preparing breakfast.

"I will never serve you!" he boldly declared. "Let me always meet defeat in your name."

"I shall not." I smiled. "You shall not be my champion, Knight of Lies." His face spread in a handsome, beautiful grin, and he turned, walking toward his horse, his armor shining.

"I shall always betray you!" he said with great pleasure, and mounted into the saddle, raising his sword on high. "When I next see you, I shall not defend you at all!"

I watched as he spurred the horse forward, the hooves thundering down the road as he deftly slammed his sword into the scabbard. "Do you think he'll be all right?" I asked the picnic basket.

The picnic basket rustled a little bit and ran its tongue over the lid. "Come on," I said. "There's a place in this forest where you can eat all the ragamoffyns you want." I slipped into the woods, the picnic basket hopping after me, leaping over roots and stumbling past branches.

When I heard the sounds of sobbing water, I knew I was close to a place I had to visit. I made my way through the trees, pushing branches aside, to stare at the Weeping of Lost Children's pool. "Come out," I whispered. "I'm not going to hurt you."

The liquid mass formed into a woman's shape as she stared at me, the picnic basket behind me, my hood covering my face. "You've returned." She murmured, her eyes dripping watery tears. "I fear that there is not much I can offer you."

"There is not much I can offer you," I said, "and I will not give you my picnic basket, either." The picnic basket let out a low growl. "All I have are my failures and my tears."

"Will you give me some of yours?" she asked. "So many people are happy after what you've done that I fear I may dry up."

I waded into the pool and threw my arms around her wet form. My cloak floated back and forth on the surface of the water as I embraced her and she dripped about me. I cried then, wet against wet, until I heard a pleasurable sigh from between her watery lips.

"Thank you," she whispered. "That should give me a few more years, at least."

The picnic basket frolicked back and forth on its hind legs while I was in the pool, sniffing the air as it sat. Its tongue hung out as if it were getting tired.

I stepped out of the pool and dripped across the grass, moving over to touch the spot where I made love to him. I bent down and kissed each spot where he stood, wishing I was back in that moment, with his hips pushing between my thighs, filling me with desperate desire. I turned and looked at the Weeping for Lost Children, and my eyes turned hard.

"You owe me a favor," I said.

"You aren't lost anymore," she smiled a bit amidst her wet tears. "But even if you go home, you'll always come back."

I wandered into the forest, the darkness gathering thick and cold as the gray sun rose, illuminating the mist before dawn. I heard the tapping of the picnic basket's feet behind me, relentless as it followed me through the woods. It was only a few moments before I heard the clank of armor and the clatter of chains and spikes.

She was there. The Weeper in Shadows had found me.

***

I flattened against a tree, the wind whispering as the picnic basket began to rush forward. I grabbed it by the handle and put a finger to my lips. "Shh, we're outnumbered." My feet were sunk deep in the snow, and the heavy crunches of the Chain Hook Guards thudded in my ears.

There were eight soldiers and her, a thick bandage tied around her leg where my arrow had pierced her. Underneath I could sense new armor had been placed over the old. I could see her in the center of a clearing amid the woods, the eight Chain Hook Guards beginning to lurch forward to encircle me. "As bait for a beast, I shall find you wanting in life," she purred. "But without your pretty broken heart, I shall find you more sympathetic," She motioned with her fingers, and the guards split into two groups.

I couldn't risk flying. They would close to where I was and pull us down. I drew the bow, breathed and waited. Turning to catch the first of them in my sight, I released the shaft. It sank into the head of the creature.

There was a thunderous explosion. The head came away from the body, the guard teetering back and forth as I raced through the trees. I drew another arrow and fired it into the three guards near it as they turned.

The picnic basket rocketed forward. "Eat everything!" I shouted as I released the arrow. Another explosion rocked the forest and blasted trees apart, sending them into the sky and crashing about. I rolled to the left and right. The three guards were hurled apart while the last closed in. There was a ripping sound and a gulp as one of them landed too close to the basket.

I heard a satisfied trill from my pet as the other guards circled. I fired another arrow into the wrecked forest, sending it into the trees before I could see them. The explosion burst high in the trees, making wood chips rain down around us from the leafy tops. As the snow and branches tumbled through the trees, I only hoped that it would catch them. I could hear the sounds of the picnic basket feasting on the guards that struggled to their feet behind me. I glanced from my position to where the Weeper in Shadows stood in the center of the clearing.

She hadn't moved at all. This wasn't a fight. This was a hunt, her metal dogs with chains sent to wear me down before she finished me. "In the cold, you have no hope," she whispered. Her breath puffed out through her mask of iron. "But you will come anyway."

The Chain Hook Guards hurled the fallen wood and clusters of snow aside as they moved forward. Their feet kicked up thick clots of dirt and powder. I drew an arrow back while they closed. They moved faster than I expected, while the Weeper in Shadows purred in poetic litanies. I shot another arrow into their midst and it exploded. One of them fell to the ground while the others came on.

The three guards raced for me, chains whipping. I rolled and ducked, igniting the boots to distract and make steam. I fired an arrow at close range. The blast ripped open the chest of one of the guards as he sagged, crashing to earth. I rolled to my feet, struggling to stay out of their reach. Chains hacked about, tearing away bark and throwing splinters into the air. I raced up into the nearest tree and perched there, out of range of their chains. In the background, I could hear the picnic basket feasting as other guards were sucked beyond the lid.

There were two left. Already tired from journeying and hiding, I was losing strength. The chains of the iron-clad guards wrapped around my tree trunk and pulled. Wood shuddered, struggled, and ripped apart. I leaped from the tree as it fell, rolling in an agile twirl as I reached back and drew two arrows, launching them at the creatures.

One of the shots went wide. My last arrow slammed into the one on the left, piercing armor and driving him to the ground. The second creature's long chain wrapped around my throat and pulled me in. The iron gauntlet drew back and punched me hard in the face, and I slammed into the ground. The creature drew back a heavy armored leg and kicked me in the stomach.

I doubled over and scrabbled with the bow, trying to hook it around the creature's leg as the next kick came in. I pulled and he fell to earth, the iron shod foot slamming into my head. Although my cloak protected me from the worst of it, I could barely think. I struggled to my feet as the guardsman pulled on the chain to yank me forward and hit me again. I couldn't dodge. My limbs felt like lead as I tried to pull back. The heavy metal fist closed in.

There was a howl, then a rustling and a tearing. The picnic basket appeared atop the creature's chest. The lid gnawed and chewed through the guard's arm as it choked me.

"All kinds of beasts we use to hunt." The Weeper in Shadows purred, my ears ringing with pain as my breath began to falter. "I shall burn yours with pleasure as you beg, sobbing in the cold world we share."

There was a horrible wet snap and the creature's arm came away. The picnic basket growled as my cloak was coated with thick, purple gouts of blood.

I struggled free of the chain and got to my feet, panting and gasping. The chain lashed at me. I couldn't clear my head completely, even in the cold. I clenched my fist, grabbing the bow to lean on it. Blood trickled from my nostrils and over my lip, the taste of copper on my tongue as I stared at the Weeper in Shadows. There was a wet snap as the picnic basket ripped through the gorget of the last guard, his tortured head disappearing into the yawning gullet.

"Stay back," I said to the picnic basket. "She'll burn you with my boots if she kills me. Run now." The picnic basket trilled and backed off, gnawing on the remains, chewing through metal and flesh alike.

The Weeper in Shadows purred in her iron mask, the smile creaking. "Broken with no defense, your lost love and mine bleeds in the beyond. Your heart is broken, and as I freeze it, I shall add it to my collection, the last of my collection. A certain mark upon your tears brings you to a soft and bitter conclusion, and I shall have it."

I held my bow in both hands, as the Jack of Forests had taught me, and walked toward her. "I don't blame you for wanting to settle up," I said, the cold air pulling at my lungs. I felt them burn between breaths. "It's the way of things around here."

I charged forward, and so did she, long blonde hair flying behind her as I swung the bow upwards to block the thrust of her frozen knife. The bow crashed against the hilt.

She drove her knee into my stomach as I spun the knife aside and drove my elbow forward. She rolled into a backflip and I stepped back, the sharp iron edge of her boot nicking my face and making a small cut. "One lucky shot makes not an easy victory, child."

She was fresh, and I was wounded and tired. Her cruel iron smile came at me as she spun the knife in her hand, weaving a trail of frost in the air as I backed up. Then she pounced like a cat, leaping high in a graceful arc to launch another kick at my head. I rolled under her in the snow and the dirt, throwing up leaves and powder. I swung the bow at her wounded leg. There was a loud crack as the wood crashed into the leather and spun her sideways, but she rolled. The knife came back across, cutting the bowstring and bouncing off unharmed wood near my fingers.

The snap rung in the air as she came down in a catlike stance, gritting her teeth from the pain as she landed. "You fight like the torturers of old, to cause pain before a kill." She flipped up to her feet by pushing off a fallen branch, tumbling in a low arc as I scrambled to my feet. I couldn't exchange blows forever. I was going to die here, in the forest where everyone never came back from. "I wish to have your pain for mine own."

Her low tumble took me by surprise. She kicked the bow from my hands as she rolled upward with the knife. I desperately crossed my hands to block her thrust, my forearms out as I ducked under and pushed up, clutching her wrists as she drove the frozen knife forward, the iron mask grim and cold except for the metal smile. I knew she shared it.

We struggled, there, the weight of her tall body pushing at mine as I heard a rustle from behind. The picnic basket leaped, and she rolled to one side, taking one hand away from the knife to punch the creature as it rolled away. The basket coughed up a hot, steaming pastry, which melted snow around it on the ground, and lay momentarily still. I twisted my body hard and drove my knee into the bloody bandage around her leg.

She screamed in pain, already off balance as I wrested the knife of ice from her grip. Her eyes narrowed in anger as I took what could only be her most precious thing. Her roar of rage carried through the forest, the cry of a cheated animal. I stabbed forward just as she stepped inside my guard, driving an elbow into my jaw. Her arm twisted against my wrist, holding it there as I struggled to bring the knife to bear. Her lips began to smile as I realized the simple truth that she was bigger and stronger.

She drove a fist into my stomach. I almost left the ground, but struggled to bring two hands up to the knife and push, driving it down towards her face. She slid a leg back and pushed against my wrists, forcing me downward. She drove a powerful kick in at me and I took it. Hard iron making me cry out. I wouldn't let go of the knife, not for anything. I drove my foot forward towards her wounded leg. She used my weak kick to vault upward, swinging forward in an eerie twist to roll onto my chest and crush me to the ground with her weight.

I drew the knife of ice back with all my strength and slashed upward as she came down, hacking at the mask of iron as it quirked up in her one moment of disadvantage. Black iron shards flew everywhere in frozen, tiny droplets as she landed. We pushed away from each other as I finished the spin and struck the ground. I looked up at her in her coldness and her slim beauty, eye meeting eye. She was cool and beautiful and blonde and slender, and I looked into my own green eyes, the same slim shape of my face, the smoothness of my skin. The last mask had been torn away.

"Damn you! Damn you a thousand times! I cannot kill my daughter and look upon her with a naked face!" There were no lies there. How I wished there were.

"I freed you! This is crazy! You can love who you choose!" The feeling of rage at her bitter competition washed through my skin, my fingers freezing in the cold ground.

"What does it matter if you can't have what you want?" Her eyes were furious and possessive. The iron mask had erased her compassion as surely as the mask of the King of Feathers had erased his sight.

"You could have had him!" I shouted back. "I would have let you!" I reached for her hand, begging as all children beg for their mothers to come to them when they have never met them before. In the back of my throat, I felt a little twinge of the Weeping of Lost Children's pain.

"He chose who I was to marry, like all of us before him!" She wept and leaped for the knife, and clutched my wrist. I punched her as hard as I could in the face. A red trail leapt from her lip, maiming her beautiful smile.

"And then my husband rebelled when he knew I would have a daughter! I didn't care! I loved the King of Feathers anyway!" She locked my arm and threw me over her shoulder. We rolled in the snow and the ice, skin raw from our wounds and leaving red trails behind. "It just wasn't as pure and true as yours." She bled heavily from her lip, and I could feel my broken ribs ache. She was too well trained. I didn't have enough experience.

"Why didn't you come for me?" I cried then. I drove my knee into her stomach, and didn't feel anything give.

"Once I gave you up, you weren't mine anymore." She punched me so hard I thought my jaw would crack, and I stumbled back, struggling to rise. "But you came back anyway. Now we both have nothing!" The ice knife sank into the snow. Close as it was, it seemed too far away to reach.

"We could be mother and daughter!" I shrieked as the Weeper in Shadows stood, breathing almost as hard as I did. "It doesn't have to be like this."

"Yes, it does." She hung her head and stalked across the ice. "You won. I can't look at you and kill you. I can't do this anymore." She reached down and picked up the knife of ice. "I don't think I can afford to give this up. There are a lot of hearts left to break." She gave me a bloody smile, and tossed her beautiful, ice blonde hair. "I couldn't have asked for better, really."

Then she began walking away. "Go home," she said softly. "When they come for you, you'll understand. Then you'll come back here."

"Will we fight?" I shouted, but her footsteps were already crunching through the ice, and her glimmering, slim figure was lost in the trees. "Is the Jack of Forests my father?" The picnic basket flipped up onto its feet, ran forward, and rustled against me as I struggled to rise, as if to help me up. After the most brutal fight of my life, all I wanted was for her to return.

I clutched the picnic basket in my arms and sobbed. There was nothing else to do.

***

When I could finally stand, I crept among the trees and fired arrows. Ragamoffyns were driven from their perches, forcing them low to the ground while the picnic basket ate. After they were driven into the shadows, the picnic basket rolled over against a tree and let out a satisfied belch. "They're not people," I said. "But a little revenge and feeding your picnic basket at the same time? That's just the way of the world around here."

I scooped up the picnic basket, making my way past a dusty pit that filled with dead bodies I didn't recognize. In the distance, I could hear the faint sound of carnival music from ferris wheels and merry go rounds. I was almost home. I stroked the picnic basket gently across the lid, and put it down on the ground. I stared at it like I was going to cry.

"Go." I smiled a little bit to the Picnic basket. "I think there's a Duchess of Bells who might need a little help. You'll see me again sometime."

The picnic basket let out a crying little whine, and trundled over to me with an unhappy rustle. It opened its lid and made a sorrowful noise, rubbing against my hand, and it made little sniveling noises. I reached down and petted it. It gave a mournful howl, refusing to leave my side. "Oh, okay." I sighed. I didn't even know why I said it. "But no eating people, and you have to stay hidden. I'll find things for you to eat, all right?"

The basket made a happy little trill, and it shuffled alongside me, sad with my sadness. We walked out of the dark woods into the cold, cruel evening. It was still winter. The snow melted on my face. I patted my arm, and the basket leaped up onto it, hanging by the handle.

The best thing about it was that somehow, the picnic basket didn't seem to mind.

***

They caught up to me when it was over, there on the edge of the forest, with the lights of the big top dancing and the sounds of the carnival in the distance. I knew their voices even when they were behind me.

"You've led us on a merry chase, girl," the Stone Preacher rumbled.

The Organ Grinder chuckled. "Alas, we must obey our responsibilities."

I turned around. There were only two of them, the Stone Preacher and the Organ Grinder. There wasn't anyone else with them.

"You have something that belongs to us," the Organ Grinder said, avoiding formalities.

The Stone Preacher bowed, and his gravelly voice rumbled. "You did outsmart one of us. We can only take half."

"I don't suppose you'd take one of my boots now?" I offered to the Stone Preacher. He grimly shook his head without saying a word.

I watched as the Organ Grinder pulled out his stone knife, colored like the night sky, and plunged it into my right eye. There was no pain. Instead, my lips grew wet. My fingers twisted in knots and he drew the dagger out. A few bright white twists of light danced on the end of the tip. I giggled a little bit and smiled, even as I could feel a distant half of myself separated. The moon was bright, and it was delicious.

"You will come here again, when the sky is dark and the moon is full," the Stone Preacher smiled, and shifted his rocky robe.

"Can I stay in the real world?" I whispered. I pulled up my hood with my right hand. The flesh was black and starry like the night, gaping into a beautiful void. When I moved my fingers, I thought I saw fog on my wrist.

"When you are in the real world, you will be ordinary," the Organ Grinder said. "But having half a soul is a power all its own. You will never die. Your wicked half of murder balances your innocence. You are marked forever. Now your story is cruel, as I told you it would be."

"You've cursed me." I cried from my left eye. From my right eye, I could feel something hungry that wasn't tears.

"Look, child," the Organ Grinder whispered. He got out a bowl, and filled it with water, to show me my reflection. The cackling monkey at his feet hooted.

I looked. The right half of my face was black as misty night, split by a horrid burning eye. It shimmered like the stars, hammered from obsidian. I could feel it in my skin. I screamed. Half of me sickened. My fingers flexed with joy, the right half of my mouth exultant. I could feel the picnic basket behind me, huddling in stark terror, a rickety rustle echoing in my ear.

"Now we will give you your name," the Stone Preacher rumbled.

"You are beautiful," the Organ Grinder said. "You have made love to a king, and his blood taints your fingers and haunts your lips. You are more than a simple girl. You are a thing of legend: a bastard murderess tasting royal blood in a bastard world. Your mother is so proud of you." He bowed, and swirled his cape around himself, dipping his top hat. "And like your mother, you are now what you are meant to be. You were always meant to be divided." He put the stone knife back on his belt, and the monkey huddled underneath his coat. "You are Hellbow Rune, the Queen of Lost Love. This is your name among our kind."

"This is the end of my journeys with you." The Stone Preacher smiled. He ground himself into his cape of granite, and held out his hand. "But you will see me again, I think." He smiled and sank into the earth, a dim growl of rocks falling as I stared through my unseelie eye. "When you call upon your dark soul, your powers will return. And of course, as is the way of such things, you can come back any time you want." There was a rocky clatter, then nothing.

When I turned to look at the Organ Grinder, Only the faint sound of accordion music marked his passing. I could still cry only from my left eye. I had lost everything. In the distance, I thought I heard the monkey's victorious shriek.

The picnic basket rubbed against my leg, as if to remind me that it was there.

I crept out of the forest in my cloak. The black bow crackled with blue light in my hand. I skulked, low to the ground in my boots of fire, leaving the burning footprints behind. The lights of the big top beckoned, and the carnival played on. Behind me, the picnic basket followed, its dry rustle keeping me careful, watching for other things in the dark.

When I returned to the circus, Madame Zhalla was gone. I never saw her again. My black bow faded into the ether. I don't know how I get there. But I know how just the same. Now I put on my rubber mask, and I tell fortunes in the Carnival of Monsters. But really, I'm the only monster here.

And that is the story of how I journeyed through the lands of the King of Feathers, killed my one true love, and gave up half my soul to return to a world of feeling small. I haven't aged a day since. When the nights grow lonely, and my skin grows cold, I huddle in my trailer where no one can see. I look into the mirror, and my right eye burns bright like an evil star. Then I carve the runes on my arrows and make my peace with the dark half that claws out when I travel.

So let me tell you your fortune, when the night grows dark, and the lights in the fortune-teller's tent grow dim. Behind my rubber mask, my wicked heart burns, and I smile my secret monster's smile. But if you wish to hear more than your fortune, and the tales of my return to the Otherworld, I shall tell you of it another time. You may believe it all...

Or you may not believe a word of it.

END?

Also from Michael...

Foxbat for President

The Mighty Foxbat is a loony supervillain, who never really hurts anyone in his strange plans. Now, he's gotten enough signatures to allow him to run for the highest office in the land, still in his mask. While honored, the opportunity comes as a surprise to him. But then, who's *really* behind it, and *why*?

Imaginary Friends

An imaginary friend is killing other imaginary friends and dumping the bodies in the real world. What a place to start an investigation! An entertaining array of sinister and unique characters engage in tests of combat and the mind unlike anything you've seen before.

King of the Mountain

In every century, there is a special person. A mythical king who is the symbol of the time in which he lived.

Now, an evil sorcerer is going to bring the King of the twentieth century back to life. And rule the world through his millions of fans.

Every century has its heroes.
Every century has its king!

at www.blackwyrm.com

Pretty Hate Machines

Beauty is only skin deep, but ugly goes straight to the bone...

Mr. Hideous is the ugliest man in the world. He has come to the city to make everyone as ugly as he is. Getting beat with that Ugly Stick is gonna hurt. Only your heroes stand in his way.

Things are about to get *ugly*!

Unkindness

An evil man in a bird costume is on a crime spree throughout the city. Can your superheroes put an end to his rampage before he begins kidnapping children?

War of Worldcraft

Robots attack a sales event for the hottest online superhero roleplaying game. Now players are falling unconscious at their computers. Your superheroes must find a supervillain *inside* a computer game, fighting their way past numerous virtual threats to free the minds of thousands of trapped players.

at www.blackwyrm.com

About the Author

Michael Satran has been gaming since 1979, and running his Legacies *Champions* campaign since 1987. A graduate of Rutgers University, with a master's degree in English from the University of Rhode Island.

His gaming universe currently contains more than one hundred superheroes, untold numbers of supervillians, and a backstory that starts before World War II and threatens the peace and security of Earth into the future. Mr. Satran's game store of choice is The Gamer's Gambit in Fair Lawn, NJ.

This picture was taken at Mr. Satran's home, owned by his two cats, who charge him rent.

www.ingramcontent.com/pod-product-compliance
Lightning Source LLC
Chambersburg PA
CBHW070540030726
47505CB00001B/100